Marshal Shawn Felton and the Wild Bunch

Copyright © 2014 Terry Larkin
All rights reserved.

ISBN: 1505372313
ISBN 13: 9781505372311
Library of Congress Control Number: 2014921775
CreateSpace Independent Publishing Platform
North Charleston, South Carolina

KEEP YOUR RECIEPT !
WHY ?

Because I did not write this book alone! I had been remodeling a 1912 block house in Circleville Utah for four years, and I was totaling burnt out. I had so many hind sight's that I had to go back and re-do, they were to numerous to count.

One day when running around town in my power chair I was expressing my frustrations to the Lord and just how I felt and would he Please give me something fun to do.

About two weeks later I went up and bought a pad of paper and started figuring out some of what might happen till my daughter could get me a type writer for Christmas.

I honestly have to tell you the next year and a half of my life was the most fun, relaxing, and enjoyable time of my life.

I'm sorry if I offend anyone who doe's read this book…But then I pretty much slam my family and friends. So if you can not take a BULLSHIT SLAM (joke) then please do not read this book.

These are just a few of the reason's why I will warranty the ride for six month from time of perchance. So if you can Honestly tell me you Did Not Enjoy The Ride…Then Me and All Of Heaven will Graciously buy it back from you.

I will reimburse amount shown on sales receipt for this publication. However, the book must be in good condition. No torn, folded, or written on pages.

Send to

Terry L. Larkin

P.O. Box 48

Circleville, UT. 84723.

Marshal Shawn Felton and the Wild Bunch
Witten By Terry Larkin

Marshal Shawn Felton in widely known for bringing the outlaw's in over the saddle as opposed to setting up. HIM, Being Judge, Jury, and Executioner, you might say. Followed by the fact that this time there wasn't any body's to bring back to be bury, because everyone and everything had been blown all to hell and back, outside Prineville, Or

The head outlaw Brad Moen just happens to have a set of Identical Twin's cousin's, in Baker City, Or. Larry and Gary Larkin who think that Old Marshal Felton needs to be held accountable for his action's. Why did he do what he did...was there any other way he could have brought them in alive!

The twin's figure they will go up to Sumpter and get their brother Randy to go with them to Prineville to question the Marshal.

Riding over the Elk Horn Mountain range from Baker Valley to the Sumpter valley where the dredges are mining up the entire Sumpter valley from bottom to top in that order. Pulling out more gold than anyone could imagine.

Riding into town the twin's are telling Luis it used to be a nice hundred town logging community. Now's there's over eight thousand hopeful starving miner's.

Don't ask me how Butch Cassidy and the Sundance Kid sat down at the table at the " Elkhorn Saloon, Brothel, and Eatery" while the twin's and Luis were playing poker with CHIP'S, Not Money, but when they did it was no longer the " The Marshal's Last Ride "

So then I had to go back and write chapter one, and get the Marshal on the trail. Where a young Indian buck by the name of Wapiti come's to the Marshal and asks him to teach him to be a lawman, so the Indian's will have the law on their side to.

In agreeing to take young Wapiti on Marshal Felton outfit's him with a sawed off double barrel TEN gauge shotgun, to made most men think twice before starting anything stupid.

iv

How ever, when I brought the Marshal and Wapiti back into the story, I found out that they only loaded the real gold one day a week in Sumpter. So I came up with a high dollar poker tournament in John Day, Oregon where Wapiti get's tested as a Wanna Be Indian Lawman in the 1892 west.

Where even Marshal Felton get's to Crow, but in the end... he EAT'S crow.

First I have two group's I have to write morning, noon, and night for. Then after the robbery I have four groups which I have to bring all back together to one group, then No groups.

I knew how I hoped it would end... but it ends even better than I could have hoped for.

If you enjoy the RIDE even half as much as I enjoyed the WRITE, then set back and get ready for a fun filled Western comedy that will keep you laughing from beginning to end.

Thank you for your time
Terry Larkin

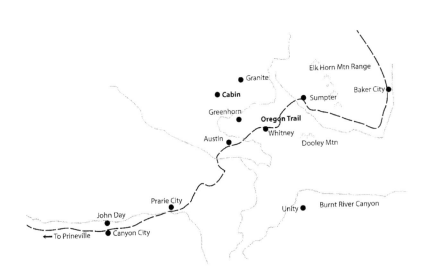

Marshal Shawn Felton and the Wild Bunch

Terry Larkin

CHAPTER ONE

Marshal Shawn Felton awoke with the fresh smell of coffee filling the room. This meant Carmen was up early as usual, it was barely dusk outside. Sitting up and stretching Shawn rolled out of bed and walked over to the coffeepot, filling up his cup. He grabbed the pot and the hot plate and walked outside to a rocking chair that sat in front of his one room cabin that he rented from a young Mexican Senora, Maria Carmen. She also owed the main building that faced Main Street, she had a restaurant downstairs and her and her two children lived upstairs.

Shawn really liked the arrangement, because his meals came with the rent while he was in town. Not to mention, she was a very beautiful young lady. If any man could ever win her heart, he would be a very lucky man, he thought to himself. Her parents had sold her to a rich rancher down in Mexico when she was just sixteen. After living with the man for a couple years, she had had all of him she could handle. So in the middle of the night, she grabbed her two small children and ran away. Carrying those two babies over hundred's of miles across the desert of Mexico coming to America, hoping for a better life. Every time he saw her, it made him wish he was twenty years younger. Those two children, a boy Jose eight, and a girl Griselda nine were so smart; they could speak both English and Spanish, fluently.

Sitting there, Shawn started daydreaming about what Judge Monson had said to him yesterday in court, about the outlaws he tried to arrest a few days earlier. It had been his intention to bring them

1

in alive. That shale rock slid under his foot just as he pulled the trigger, causing his bullet to hit the wagon load of nitro instead of just wounding the driver like he intended, there was 50 cases of nitro, each case had 24 12 oz bottles. Each bottle was equivalent to 1 case or more of dynamite. 24x50…that was one hell of an explosion. Causing the percussion blast from the explosion to blown him a good 10 feet backwards before he rolled down to the river edge himself. Starting to chuckle just a little, he hadn't seen an explosion that big since the war when they had to blow up a Yankee naval ammo dump on the coast outside Yorktown VA.

Judge Monson had threatened to take his badge, yet again. Judge said, "Counting these seven or eight men, God only knows for sure just how many men there really is out there in that pile of crow bait… But counting them that makes over a hundred men you've killed in the twenty plus years since you've been a U.S. Deputy Marshal." Waving his gavel around, said, "It was his job to determine whether a man should die for his crimes, NOT No Marshal."

I reminded him that it was one man against eight men, and I did try to bring them in alive. Hell, that's why I followed them men for three days and night looking for and waiting for the right place at the right time, so I could get them in a situation where they had no choice but to give up. That river was the perfect spot. Sure, I wish that shale rock wouldn't have slipped out under my feet just as I stood up and pulled the trigger.

He sure wished Judge Monson had to go out on the trail, spending all those cold nights out there trying to find them outlaws. THEN, try to get them to give themselves up peacefully. Everyone he had killed started shooting first; he couldn't help it if he was a better shot.

He wasn't sure just how long he had been daydreaming before little Jose was tapping him on the shoulder, "Marshal, there's a hombre here to see you."

Looking up at the man, Shawn could see it was a young buck Indian.

"Excuse me, Marshal," the Young man said. "I wonder if I might have a little of your time?"

Chapter One

"You got it," Shawn said, waving his hand towards another chair. "What's on your mind, son?"

"I'd like you to teach me how to be a law man," the Young man replied sitting down in the chair.

"WHAT," Shawn shouted out. "Have you lost your mind Young man?"

"No Sir," he answered, in an excited, but stern voice. "I was talking with Running Bear, Chief Joseph's son... He told me, that you had told him last year if he wanted to be a lawman you would be glad to teach him..."

"That I did," Shawn answered, filling an extra cup up that sat on the table. "But he's too young now."

"I'm not, Marshal, I'm 19 almost 20," the Young man said, "and I would like to be a lawman."

With a smirk on his face, Shawn glared into the Young man's eyes, "You want to loose your scalp, son? Why every white eye we come across will want a piece of your hide...Give me just one good reason why you want to be a lawman."

"To protect all the Indians rights too," Wapiti answered, sternly.

"All right, fair enough," Shawn said. "But every cow town or city we came to you're going to have to fight your way through."

"I'm not worried about what a man can do to me with his hands and feet," the Young man answered.

"You'll be damn lucky if you ever find an outlaw that will want to fight hand to hand," Shawn answered. "You have to know how to use a gun... and use it well." He stated firmly, glaring straight into the young man's face.

"I know Marshal, that's where you come in. Like I said, and I'm sure you've been in enough Indian villages to see some of the wrestling competitions. Not to brag, but no one has beaten me since I was 12, not even the braves six to eight years older than me. My Dad taught me to fight, and my Grandfather taught me to track... Been doing both for as long as I can remember.... Not to brag, again, but there's nothing I can't track. When the time comes not to be seen or heard, you won't even know I'm around. That is why when I became a man my Grandfather named me, "Wapiti."

3

"And just what the hell does Wapiti stand for?" Shawn asked.

"Ghost of the forest. You white eyes call them Elk…they can sound like a mighty herd of buffalo going through the timber, or be as quite as a mouse, moving through timber and brush that you and I can barely walk through, and you won't even know he's there."

Shawn had been looking the Young man over as he talked. He figures he stood at least five foot ten, maybe eleven inches tall and went a good 180 plus, with that wiry muscular build of some of the other young braves he had seen. The Young man was right, he had been in a lot on Indian villages and had had the pleasure of seeing some of those wrestling matches. He was also glad that none of them wanted him to join in; instead they just wanted to show off to the white eye lawman. Even though he had had to fight hand to hand with a few of them in his life. When he was younger, and his ass was on the line. He could also remember being glad he had his pistol with himself more than once. If it wasn't for that gun he might not be here today.

Ya, I bet that Young man could stand his ground, but with a gun…. That was a different story all together. The boy needed to know how to handle a gun. Not only with a pistol from his hip, but also with a rifle… He was going to have to be able to draw, shoot and aim all at the same time. Some times he's going to have to know how to shoot at sounds. He didn't figure he would push him in too deep, too fast. He was thinking of just where they might go for a while and let him get his feet wet, slowly.

Wapiti was also right about the elusive bull elk. Why you could be standing ten feet away from one and not even know he was there. How they went through the brush and timber with those big horns without being seen or heard, he could never figure out.

"That still leaves the gun play, if you go and get yourself killed, Chief Joseph would be all over me like stink on shit." Shawn answered.

"No Sir, Marshal," Wapiti answered. "Fact, he told me that if I really wanted to be a lawman, that there is no better man to teach me. Said you would make sure I would know how to use a gun and when to use it, most of all, you were honorable, and would make sure I'd have a fair chance."

Chapter One

"He said that, did he?" Shawn said, with a smile on his face, leaning back in his chair. "There's more to learning how and when to use a gun than I could teach you in just a couple of hours. It takes months, hell, it takes years to get good with a gun and you had better know how to use one if you put that badge on."

"I know you're right, Marshal," Wapiti answered. "I can shoot a rifle; it's a pistol I need help with. Those are only used close up, and you'll be there then."

"Well... I suppose we could give it a try. But if you want people to take you serious, you're going to have to get a hair cut." Shawn told Wapiti.

"No sir Marshal, I won't do that. My hair is worn long for pride and spiritual strength in my people's beliefs. It makes our spirit and strength stronger." Wapiti answered, holding his head high.

"Well you keep it long like that and you'll definitely have to show these cowboys and loggers your strength." Shawn said, chuckling.

"I would like to see anyone try and cut my hair Marshal!" Wapiti said

"Well, all right then Wapiti, but I think you'd be better off. You'll see, one night a drunken cowboy is going to try and get himself a long lock of Indian hair... Don't be crying to me if you loose...mind ya, I will watch your back for any gun play." Shawn said, assuredly.

"You just let them come and try Marshal," Wapiti told Shawn with pride in his voice. "I'll show you and them all, I can stand my own ground."

"Well, I guess it won't hurt anyone...except you and them." Shawn replied with a big smile on his face. "It would be nice to have someone along on the trail to talk to."

"You mean it Marshal? You'll teach me?" Wapiti asked with even more excitement in his voice.

"Alright Wapiti... why don't you go down to the court house, pick up any wanted posters they have, then take your horse and gear over to the livery stable. Tell Gordy to have my horse, mule and all my gear ready to pull out at sun up. Tell him we'll need supplies for a two week trip."

"Sure Marshal, right away. I'll be back as soon as I can Marshal." Wapiti answered. He jumped up, and started walking back towards the restaurant.

Shawn stood up, looking briefly at young Wapiti, smiling. He walked back over to his bunk and laid back down.

He would have to get some gun practice in soon, you will never know when or where he might have to use it. He would have to learn to use his pistols, like they were an extension of his hand. He'd have to be able to pull, aim, and shoot without thinking about it, and his shot had better be true. If not, he wouldn't be around very long, and Shawn didn't even want to try and explain to Chief Joseph how and why Wapiti didn't make it. These cowboys, loggers, and other white people wouldn't take too well to an Indian telling them what to do, he was thinking to himself as he fell asleep.

Wapiti walked across the yard, and between the buildings, grinning and standing just a little taller, thinking of just what may lay ahead for him. It sure was going to be different. He was sure some of it was going to be fun and then again, some of it not so fun.

Wapiti walked up to untie his horse, he felt like every eye in town was on him. He started leading his horse across the street toward the stable. Walking slowly and looking around, he could see he was right. Just about everyone was looking at him and talking quietly amongst themselves. A couple groups of cowboys, made him feel real uncomfortable. He was glad the stable was so close. That way he got out of sight from all the people quick.

Walking into the stable, he slowly looked around. Not seeing anyone right off hand, he yelled out, "ANYONE HERE?"

"Be right with you," a voice said, coming from the back.

Wapiti started walking in the direction of the voice. "The Marshal said to tell you to get his horses and gear ready for tomorrow, sir."

Just then a little, short stocky man, about five eight to nine inches' tall, easy one ninety plus pounds, but it wasn't fat, his face was covered with a big black beard came walking out of one of the stalls. Looking over he saw Wapiti for the first time, an Indian in his stable, instantly he blew up, "YOU GET THE HELL OUT OF MY STABLE BOY, I

Chapter One

DON"T WANT ANY DAMN INDIAN IN MY BUSINESS" Waving his cigar toward the door. "NOW YOU JUST GET THE HELL OUT OF HERE!"

"But sir," Wapiti started to say.

"DON"T BUT SIR ME, YOU HEARD ME!" the man said yelling at him.

"BUT SIR, Please...The Marshal sent me over." Wapiti answered, walking backwards.

"YOU... What the hell is he doing sending you in here for?" Gordy said putting his cigar back in his mouth.

"He asked me to tell you to get his horses and mule ready for tomorrow," Wapiti started to explain... "He said to tell you to get them ready for a two week trip."

"That still don't explain why he sent you, and not Little Jose or Griselda." Gordy said, still talking loud.

"He asked me to have you look over my horse also, make sure he was ready for the trip ... cause I'm going with him," Wapiti said.

"What the hell is the Marshal doing taking an Indian with him on one of his hunt'en trips, as he likes to call them?" Gordy asked.

"He's going to teach me how to be a lawman," Wapiti answered.

"WHAT?" Gordy hollered out, "An Indian lawman...Are you crazy boy?"

"No sir, I want to be a U.S. Deputy Marshal someday." Wapiti answered

"What? Are you joking with me boy? You think for one minute they're going to let an Indian be a U.S. Marshal? That is plum crazy." Gordy continued, waving his cigar around. "Hell, the next thing you know, they'll let a black man run for President of the United States... That'll teach those damned Yankees... Well all right then." Gordy said as he stuck out his hand. "Gordy Miller's my name. Guess I'm going to have to get used to an Indian being around here."

"Thanks" Wapiti said shaking Gordy's hand.

Gordy took the reins from Wapiti. He quickly glanced over the horse. "I have a better animal I'll lend ya for the trip. But I said I'd LEND him to you."

"Thank you Sir; I'll take good care of him" Wapiti answered.

"You damned straight you will boy," Gordy stated putting his cigar back in his mouth. "If you prove to me you can take care of him, I'll think about letting you keep him."

"Yes sir, anything you say. But now could you tell me how to get to the court house?" Wapiti asked.

"Ya, ya, down the street two more blocks. You can't miss it." Gordy said pointing.

"Thanks," Wapiti answered. He turned and walked back to the door, and outside. Stopping for a minute, he looked up and down the street. He had never seen this many white people in one place before, and they were all staring at him. He could tell they didn't care much for an Indian being in their town…

Slowly he turned and started walking up the street towards the Court house. He was glad to see that both the saloons were on the other side of the street. That way he didn't have to walk up close to all those cowboys that were hanging around outside. He couldn't help but notice that as he walked by people, they all stepped back. Looking at him like he had some kind of disease or something like that. Never the less, he sure was happy when he got to the Courthouse.

Wapiti couldn't ever remember feeling this nervous before. However it didn't change when he got inside either. Everyone seemed to step aside and stared at him. Fact, it was all he could do not to laugh, walking by a lady, she pulled her son up next to her, like he was going to take him or something like that as he walked by. He looked at her and smiled, thinking to himself, maybe I should tell them I don't take scalps… But then thought better of it when he saw the Judge. Walking up to the man, "Excuse me sir, Could you please tell me where the wanted poster's are?"

The Judge looked Wapiti over, "They're right over there on the wall," he answered pointing.

"Thank you sir," Wapiti answered. Turning, he walked over to the wall, looking up at all the posters.

The Judge walked up beside him. "Is there something I can help you with Young man?"

Chapter One

"No sir," Wapiti answered, taking a couple posters off the wall.

"Well then, what are you doing here son?" Judge Monson asked.

Wapiti looked at the Judge. "The Marshal told one of the young braves, Running Bear, that if he ever wanted to be a law man he'd be happy to teach him. So I came to see if he'd take me on instead, and he agreed."

"HE'D DO WHAT?" The Judge yelled in an angry voice.

"He'd teach me to be a lawman, if it was what I really wanted," Wapiti answered, still looking up at the Judge.

"Are you crazy Young man? An Indian lawman, why not too many white folks would listen to ya… Why that old fool. That would be like putting a fox in the hen house." The Judge shouted out.

"HUH, what do you mean sir?" Wapiti asked.

"You don't worry about it Young man, you JUST tell the Marshal, I'll be by tonight, after dinner." The Judge said turning and walking away, talking to himself. "That old fool." He'd have to put a stop to this.

"Yes sir, Judge, I'll be sure and tell him just as soon as I get back." Wapiti answered, looking back to the wall, taking down about ten different posters. Then he turned and walked back out the door.

Wapiti could hear some of the men over at the bar laughing and inviting him over for a drink on them. OH YA, he thought. I'd be lucky to get in alive, let alone, get back out again. He headed back up the street toward Carmen's restaurant, he sure would be glad when he got there. Walking up the street, he could see that everyone was still staring at him. All wondering, "What the hell is an Indian doing in town?" Some of them started making comments to him. "Let's scalp him!" one hollered. Another one hollered, "Hell lets get a rope and string him up."

Wapiti didn't say a thing. He just walked up the street, holding his head high. It really only took him maybe five minutes at the most, to walk back to restaurant and back safe with the Marshal. But it was the longest five minutes he could remember walking.

Wapiti opened the door and walked in the restaurant, looking over at Carmen. "They sure let you know when they don't want you in their town, don't they?"

Carmen just shook her head in agreement.

"Where's the Marshal?" Wapiti asks. "I've got some good posters here on different outlaws, even on Butch Cassidy and Sundance kid. They're worth twenty-five hundred dollars each, they've been seen in the area recently."

"He's out back sleeping," Carmen answered. "Please don't wake him up, cause if you do then he'll be in here and in my way. He thinks he's helping me out while I'm getting everything together for one of his hunt'en trips. I've been getting his supplies together for the last six years, I know more about what he needs than he does."

"Ok" Wapiti answered, "So what can I do to help you out?"

"Like I just said, I don't need the help," Carmen patted him on the back. "You'll just be in my way too. Why don't you go take a nap as well?"

"All right," Wapiti answered, walking towards the door. "What are all these biscuits here for?"

"Corn biscuits with extra salt, for the hunting trip. You need lots of salt on hot days. You'll see… Now you go, so I can work." Carmen answered.

"Heck Carmen, I can't sleep. Let me help you, I'm too excited to sleep." Wapiti pleaded.

"No, No." Carmen answered, giving him a small push. "You go to other room with the kids," She said pointing to the back room.

"Alright," Wapiti answered, turning and walking into the back room.

He was so happy that the Marshal had agreed to take him on as a Deputy. He was taking him on one of his so-called hunting trips. He slowly walked over to a cot and laid down. He laid there day dreaming, he knew the Marshal would teach him how to use a gun, that was one thing he wasn't looking forward to. He wished he could do the job without having to use a gun. But he also knew that just wasn't possible. He was still thinking about the guns, and what the next few weeks would bring. When somehow he fell asleep.

Wapiti wasn't quite sure just how long he had been asleep, when the Marshal was shaking his foot and waking him up.

Chapter One

"Well, come o-+n son," Shawn said. "Don't just lay there and sleep all day. We have things to do, and supplies to get before we leave." He said, pouring himself a cup of coffee. "You want a cup of this?"

"Sure, Thanks Marshal." Wapiti answered rubbing his eyes. "What time is it?"

"You don't worry about what time it is," Shawn said, handing Wapiti the cup of coffee. "You just wake up and we'll go down to the mercantile for extra supplies."

"Yes sir," Wapiti answered, reaching for the cup of coffee. Then he reached for his moccasins, and started putting them on. The two didn't say much, as they sat there drinking their coffee and waking up. Reaching over, picking up the coffeepot, Wapiti started refilling their cups. "Do I really need to go with you Marshal? Those people out there don't like me to much."

"Aw heck, Wapiti. They're just fun'en with ya is all. If you're going to be a lawman, you had better get used to it." The two just sat there finishing their coffee. After about five minutes, the Marshal stood up. "Well, lets get going."

"At least this time I'll be walking with you. I'll feel a little safer," Wapiti said, standing up and shaking his legs out and followed behind the Marshal

Shawn started chuckling as they headed towards the door. Hollering back over his shoulder, "Carmen we're going to need extra corn biscuits for this trip."

"OK, OK," Carmen answered "I'll get them... You just get out, so I can get everything done."

"Alright, Alright." Shawn answered as he and Wapiti walked out the door and headed in the direction of the saloons. This made Wapiti feel very uncomfortable inside. They were going to have to walk right past all those drunken cowboys and loggers cause the mercantile store was in between the two saloons.

The two walked in silence, Wapiti could not only feel every eye in town on him, he could also see that everyone was still staring at him. Walking up to the store he noticed the loading docks on the back-side of the store with wagons backed up and loading supplies, while

11

others waited close by for their turn. Looking up at the sign he read it Kennedy's Eastside Mercantile, Logging, Ranching, Mining, Lumber, Plumbing, Clothing, Food, Guns and Ammo. If we don't have it ~ you don't need it. That thought made Wapiti chuckle. He was probably right, eight stores in one... that was one smart white eye. Taking one more quick look around town he followed Marshal Felton into the store, a crowded store. There had to be 30 or 40 customers. Thinking to himself he had never seen this many people in one store. There was at least a dozen kids between 6 and 16 helping costumers and restocking shelves, with 4 ladies running the cash registers, 2 of which were pregnant. Everyone stopped what they were doing, and started staring at him. Wondering just what it was he wanted, and what's an Indian doing with the Marshal.

"What can I help you with today Marshal?" Wapiti heard a voice say, turning in that directions, seeing a half-bald, middle aged man walking towards them.

"Yes you can Roger," Shawn said holding out his hand. "First, I'd like you to meet my new Deputy, Wapiti," shaking Roger hand, and pointing his other hand at Wapiti. Wapiti, this is Mr. Roger Kennedy, he's the curator of this fine establishment.

"Your WHAT?" Roger said, extending his hand towards Wapiti. "Have you gone off your rocker Marshal? An Indian for a lawman?" then turning back to Wapiti, "You got a death wish son?"

"No sir," Wapiti answered as the three started walking across the room towards the guns.

"We need to outfit Wapiti here with some fire power." Shawn said.

"WHAT?? You want me to sell guns to an Indian?" Roger shouted out, "Won't I get arrested for that?"

"Hell no," Shawn said, lighting a cigar. If he's going to be lawman; he needs to carry a gun." While he was talking, he was looking down at all the pistols. "Fact hand me that forty-four there and a holster for starters."

"Now you just wait one minute, I don't need any trouble with the law..." Roger said poignantly. "I'm going to need you to sign a piece of paper saying you made me sell him a gun."

Chapter One

"I told you not to worry about it." Now then, looking up at the rifles, slowly looking at all of them. "We'll take that forty-four- forty as well…" Shawn said pointing.

Still looking at the guns, Roger handed Shawn the pistol. "You give it to the lad Marshal… I'm not taking the chance that it's not against the law. This way, they'll have to arrest you, not me"

Chuckling Shawn took the pistol and handed it to Wapiti. "Here son, strap this on. Make sure you tie the holster down to your leg, that way if you have to pull it, your holster won't pull up and cause you to be slow and dead on the draw before you get it out." Looking back up at the guns. "Give us that double barrel ten gauge as well. I'll have you take it with the rest of our supplies over to Gordy; tell him to cut it down to pistol size. Speaking of which, do you have a holster that might fit it?"

"Ya," Roger answered, "I have one for a twelve gauge, it'll stretch out. Why do you want Gordy to cut it down?"

"Cause Wapiti has a lot to learn when it comes to handling that rifle, yet alone learning how to use a pistol. He will need to be able to use that pistol as if it were an extension of his hand. In the mean time, when we go into a town, I'll have him put that on. Then he just has to shoot in the general area. If he should miss, it won't be by much. Either way, it will make everyone take a second look, before they try something stupid."

Looking back over at Wapiti, Roger shook his head. "Well Young man. If you want these white folks to take you serious, you had better get your hair cut."

"Nope," said Shawn sternly and proudly, puffing his chest up. "Says his people believe that their hair gives them extra wisdom and strength."

"Well, I sure hope it gives him a whole lot of strength, cause the first place you come to, I'll guarantee someone is going to try and take a big lock of that hair as a trophy," Roger said, smiling and re-shaking Wapiti's hand again. "Good Luck Young man, you're going to need it."

"Wapiti looked back and forth between the two of them." So long as it's only three or four at a time I'll be alright," Wapiti said with a small smile on his face, then looking the revolver over in his hand. I think I can handle that many by hand... The Marshal will be there to make sure no one shoots me in the back."

"Now that's being just a little cocky," Shawn said with a big smile on his face. "Reminds me of me when I was his age. Thought I was unbeatable. Boy I tell ya, there's nothing like a good fistfight. But now days everyone wants to use these damn guns." Looking back at the counter, "We're also going to need five cases of forty-four shells; we'll take one with us tonight." Throw in three cases of rifle shells, just one case of shot gun shells."

"You go'en on a hunt'en trip Marshal?" Roger asked.

"Yes we are, figure I'd take young Wapiti here, and go over towards Sumpter. That way he'll get to see a boomtown. I tell ya Roger, that town went from maybe a hundred loggers and a few miners to a town of maybe eight to ten thousand people over night. All looking for that yellow rock...Roger, I remember one time when I went looking for some of that when I was younger. Damn near starved to death." Looking back over at the shelf, "you better give me three more boxes of forty-four-forty shells for tonight."

"With all this ammunition you look like you're ready for a war... You expecting trouble Marshal? Roger asked.

"No, No, nothing like that. Young Wapiti here has a lot of target practicing to do. He not only needs to learn how to shoot from his feet, but he also needs to be able to shoot off his horse as well. Fact, I've had to shoot quite a few men from my horse... I'll also need my usual supplies for a two-week trip, maybe a little longer. You know, flour, beans, bacon... Oh ya, throw in another bed role. Can't have my new Deputy freezing to death on me." Starting to chuckle, Shawn picked up the ammo and headed towards the door. Then he stopped, turned and looked back at Roger. "Say did my cigars come in yet? I'm getting a little low on them."

"There in, I'll put them in with everything else." Roger answered.

"Thanks Roger." Shawn said, heading for the door.

"Don't worry Marshal; I'll make sure you have everything you need. I've been doing it for what, ten years now?"

Chapter One

The two walked out the door; Wapiti pulled on Marshal Felton vest making him stop. Curiously, Wapiti looked over at the Marshal, "What do I need all these guns for?"

"Well, that shot gun is for real close shooting, the pistol for medium range, and the rifle for your long range shots. I have a shoot'en range set up back behind the store."

Just then Roger came running out of the store," Marshal, how are you going to pay for this?"

"The usual way, send the bill to the Judge; I need it to do my job." Shawn answered.

"Why don't you pay me for it, then you get the money back from him yourself? Roger asked with his hand held out. "You know it takes me forever to get my money out of him. He always finds something that he won't pay for, and I know he's going to argue over all this ammo."

"Tell him it's for training purposes," Shawn said with a big smile on his face.

"Well, will you at least pay me for the cigars?" Roger asked

"Ya I will. Fact I'll send one of the kids down with the money. Just how much money do I need to send with them?" Shawn asked.

"With all three cases, it comes to Thirty dollars," Roger replied.

"WHAT?" hollered Shawn. "Thirty dollars, have you gone crazy?"

"Now Marshal, you know I order those cigars special just for you." Roger explained.

"Alright, alright." Shawn yelled back, just as they started walking past the saloon. This time everyone was still staring at him, but word had gotten out from some of the customers at the Merc, that the Marshal was hiring that young buck Indian as a Deputy. A few of them had asked him in the past for that very same job... But that old fart told them, quote. "I don't think you have the right stuff to make a lawman." Just what the hell did that young buck have that they didn't? Wapiti didn't have to look at them to know they were all glaring at him. He could feel their stares, fact it was making the small hairs on the back of his neck stand up.

Looking over at the Marshal walking down the street. "Marshal why does Roger have all those kids working for him? Isn't it illegal to have children that young working in a business?" Wapiti asked.

"Not when they're your children" Marshal Felton stated,

"Oh come on Marshal there is no way one woman could have that many children" "YOU'RE RIGHT, one didn't…. He's a polygamist," Shawn answered with a big smile on his face.

"What's a polygamist?" Wapiti asked.

"It's a Mormon. That's some new fangled religion that started back east awhile back. They believe in having multiple wives. Not to mention a new brood of children every year."

"You're pulling my leg, Marshal, that's against the law isn't it, having more than one wife I mean, isn't it?" Wapiti asked.

"Now it is," Shawn answered. "So when the government went in to arrest them, a whole lot of them left the country. Left Utah where they were from, and went all over the west here. Trying to avoid being arrested. Some came to Oregon, others to Montana, Idaho, Wyoming, and just about anywhere else they thought no one would bother them."

"Why don't you arrest him then, Marshal? Wapiti asked.

"Oh hell, he doesn't hurt anyone." Shawn answered, "Fact is, he's a real nice man, and all his wives and children are very polite and pleasant to be around… I just don't know how he can put up with all them women and children all day long."

"So how many wives does he have?" Wapiti asked.

"Not exactly sure," Shawn answered chuckling a little. "Three I know for sure…but last year he went back down to Utah and came back with another young lady, about eighteen. First I thought maybe she was a niece, but she's due to have a baby just about any time now. So I think she might be a forth wife."

"Maybe she's for one of his sons to marry." Wapiti said, wondering.

"His oldest boys only fourteen, maybe fifteen." Wapiti heard a voice say from behind them. As they both stopped, turned and looked at the man standing behind them.

Chapter One

"Well hello TWICK, I Mean Sheriff." Shawn said, reaching out and grabbing hold of the badge pinned to his shirt. "I see they went against my opinion and hired you for the job after all."

"Ya well, somebody had to take it, but back to what I was saying, "Wapiti… is it? That young lady is eighteen and Rogers's eldest son might be fifteen at the most. He works with Gordy and me over at the livery sometimes. Good kid, hard worker…."

"Wapiti I'd like you to meet the towns new Sheriff, Twick Shaver," the two shook hands. They both started eyeing each other over.

"It's a pleasure to meet you… Twick…is it?" Wapiti asked, "What kind of name is that?" Wapiti asked, looking him over. Twick was a good four-inch's shorter than him, Wapiti thought. But with all those muscles, I mean damn! How does a man get arms and a chest that big? His forearms had to be bigger in diameter than my biceps flexed up. Shoot I bet he weighs as much as me. Those arms looked like they could squeeze a man in two, and then tear him into still even smaller pieces.

"My dad had a friend growing up, guess you could say Dad thought of him as a Grandfather figure." Twick said smiling. "He had a real long name…Davis…was his last name, but he had a real long name, four names all together. So when he came in on the train from back East, and moved over to Ion, where my dad lived. The town people couldn't remember all the names, so they ask him where he got off the train at … he told them Twicking Ham Oregon. So they said they'd just call him Twick… So there you go."

"His name was William Peter Parky Davis," Shawn stated firmly, "He was in the war against the States, too. Only he was a Yankee… still not holding that against him. He was a good man…Honorable man."

"So where and how did you get all those muscle Twick?" Wapiti asked looking at Twick with a smile on his face.

"I work over at the Livery stable and Black Smith yard," Twick answered, flexing his arm. "Replacing those log truck trailer wheel's," pointing down the street. "Some are six foot high and some are eight foot high, and all heavy as hell."

Still continuing to flex his muscles, his arms and chest up at the same time. Wapiti thought his T-shirt was going to tear right off. He also KNEW he didn't want to pick a fight against him…There was power in those arms and legs. He had fought some Indian kids built like him; they were unusually wiry and never gave up in a fight, no matter how many times you hit them.

Twick turned back to the Marshal, "So you really didn't recommend me for the job Marshal? Mind if I ask why?"

"You're too hot headed Young man," Shawn answered, puffing his chest out. "You get to drinking and you like to fight. It's not fair to the other guy. Not only will he get the shit beat out of himself… but then he gets arrested for assaulting a peace officer." Starting to chuckle, "No, I think you should go back to your black smith job. Then when something or someone pisses you off, you can take it out on something at the livery stable, like before."

"Oh, I'll still do that job too Marshal," Twick answered with a big smile on his face. "You know they don't pay much for wearing this badge… I promise I won't arrest them if I start it, only if they do and after I finish with them… I hear tale you're hiring this buck as a Deputy?" Twick said sizing Wapiti up.

Marshal was right Twick thought. I do like to fight. Fact the best fights I've been in were with Indians. Give one of them half a chance and he'll out wrestle ya. Have you in position to break your back faster than most men could throw a punch. Let you know he could finish you off right now. They're wiry as hell, yet fun as hell to have a wrestling match with. Trying not to smile to big, he knew Wapiti was a good four inches taller at least…he might out weigh me, but I bet I could still beat him one on one.

"Yes I am." Shawn said, still puffing his chest out. "You have a problem with that, SSHHEERRIIFFFF?"

"Nope, none at all, was just kinda hoping you might take me on instead. We've all heard about your hunt'en trips." Twick said looking up at him smiling.

"Told ya Young man, you're too hot tempered. You fly off the handle too quickly if you've been drinking. But if you ever see me in

Chapter One

need of help in a fist fight… I'd appreciate it if you'd felt free to join in," Shawn answered, chuckling. "We're fix'en to go have some target practice, Twick. How are you at handling that side arm there?" He asked, pointing at his pistol, "Fact, why don't you just come on and join us? We'll see just how long you'll keep that badge in a gun fight."

"Thanks, I would like some pointers on that Marshal," Twick said still smiling. "So now that I'm a lawman, does that mean I can call you Shawn now?"

"NOPE!!" Shawn said with a stern look on his face. "Only my friends call me that. Lets go back between the building here Wapiti. That's what's nice about being on the edge of town; I have me a nice target range." The three walked between the buildings, then down to Carmen's restaurant. Walking over to a wood box, Shawn opened it up, taking out a hand full of paper with targets on them. "Alright, now you men go put one of these on every bag of straw you see hanging up out there."

The two each took some, turned back around and started looking for all the target locations as they walked. The targets started at about twenty feet, and went as far as three, four hundred yards. Those were the rifle targets of course. Some of the targets were in trees, beside or inside heavy brush. The Marshal didn't have a standard flat range. There were even some targets over and under a gully, even up on the hillside. Had to be at least thirty plus different targets. When the two finished and got back, the Marshal had all the ammo laid out on the table. He was loading up a couple extra pistols he kept inside the box, Just in case someone came though the front door and he had to go out the back fast. Fact it had proved to be useful more than once in the past twenty plus years he'd been a Marshal.

"Now then… First thing, just practice pulling your pistol out of the holster and bringing it up level on the target. Don't worry about how fast you can draw. Right now you concentrate on hitting your target. Slowly your draw will get faster, right now you think about your shot and your target… You don't always get a second shot, so your first one had better count." Then he reached back down into the wood box and pulled out a bottle of whiskey. Taking a big pull off the bottle, Shawn

19

turned and looked at the two. "WELL, get shooten, you two." Then looking over at Jose who was running towards them. "Jose, would you please go get my rifle?"

"Yes Sir," Jose answered. "Can I get my twenty-two pistol you got me too Marshal?" Jose asked, with excitement in his voice.

"Sure you can son," Shawn answered. Watching him run towards the one-room shed he lived in.

"How about you hand that bottle over this way?" Twick said with a smile on his face.

"No sir, Sheriff I don't believe I will. It's still fairly early yet, and this evening you have your Sheriff duties to perform. I ever catch you drunk on the job and I will personally take great pleasure in kicking your ass up between your shoulder blades... Then you'll have to take off your shirt to shit... DO I MAKE myself clear, Twick?".... Shawn said very sternly, Now both you make sure those holsters are tied down to your legs. "Like I said earlier to Wapiti, Twick, you don't want that holster pulling up while you're trying to pull out your pistol. Those few seconds could mean your life or death... While we're out on the trail Twick, if you want to come over here and practice, you're more than welcome. Just bring your own ammo and whiskey. I come home and this bottle isn't here, I'll have to a stomp a mud hole in you."

"Shoot Marshal," Twick said chucking, reloading his pistol. "You want to stomp a mud hole in me for just about anything I might do wrong. What'd I ever do to piss you off at me like that for?"

"You put that badge on Young man. If you ever do have to pull that or any other gun, you had better make damned sure it's your last resort... and that you're right! You had better be dead right, cause one of you will be... dead!"

Just then Jose returned, and Shawn loaded up the twenty-two for him, and loaded his rifle at the same time. Having both men pick up their rifle's as well.

Right off they both noticed that the Marshal's rifle had a much bigger than usual lever. Twick was the first one to ask him why was it so much bigger, and who made it.

Chapter One

"Gordy made it," Shawn answered, holding the rifle in one hand, and holding his other hand up. "You see men; my hands are bigger than most men, so the standard lever is too small for my hands. So I had Gordy make this for me." Looking the rifle over. "But it also allows me to re-cock it with just one hand. Like this," he said, as he showed them how to do it. Being able to cock on the run like this has saved my bacon more than once," Shawn said, with a big smile on his face.

Both young men tried to do it with their rifles. But they weighed too much and it was too awkward to do. They both figured they'd work on it later. The two kept firing at the targets, Shawn was telling them little things they were doing wrong, and suggesting a different or better way, or even an easier way to do it. With time and practice they would get faster and better. "Don't aim that pistol, point it, just like you was pointing your finger. That pistol has to become an extension OF your hand… A part of your hand you might say." Then he walked up to the line, while he was still looking at them and talking, he pulled his pistol, turned, fired all six shots, hit six different targets, hitting each one almost dead center.

Then little Jose stepped up to the line, "Watch me guys," he said. Pulling his little twenty-two pistols out that the Marshal had special ordered for him. Firing all six rounds as fast as he could pull the trigger into the same target at about thirty yards. Ever bullet was inside the two-inch diameter bull's eye. Both men were impressed, and said as much to him.

The four had been practicing for a couple hours, when Carmen came out. "Dinner is ready," she hollered.

"Alright," Shawn yelled back. "We'll be in, in a few minutes."

"NO, Not later, NOW! You come now before it gets cold, or then you won't want to eat it. Then I'll have to throw it out," Carmen shouted back.

"Alright, alright, we're coming. Just let us clean up real quick," Shawn said, looking over at the other two. "Damn woman, it's either get out of my way, or get in here right now." Shaking his head, picking up the empty cartridges and putting them in the bucket, so he might reload them later to use for target practice again. "But she's a better cook than I am, and the rents fair, so we had better hurry up. Twick, you want to join us?"

"No sir Marshal. I have to get over to my girl friends house, or she'll be mad at me," Twick answered chuckling. "She might think I've been out with another woman.

They all quickly picked everything up, and everyone shook hands while saying Good bye." Wapiti and Shawn went and washed up. "Make sure you wash good," Shawn said, with a big smile on his face. "She won't let you eat, if you're not clean. She's picky that way… Hell I don't care if I have blood on my hands…When I get hungry, I eat… But not with Carmen."

Wapiti didn't care just how picky Carmen was, the last time he had really eaten anything was back at camp this morning, it had taken him two days of hard riding to get here from Wallowa Lake. Well, not counting that piece of jerked meat he had at the Merc earlier, and he was hungry then too.

Neither one said much of anything while they ate. Except Shawn when he asked Carmen to get him a beer. Then looking over at Wapiti, who was shoveling down his food, "Slow down son, there's plenty of food, you're not going to starve. The way you're shoveling that down, you would think you hadn't eat'en in days."

"Sorry Marshal, I haven't eaten anything since this morning and I'm hungry." Wapiti said in between bites.

"Understood, but you keep shoveling it in that fast and you're going to get sick," Shawn answered.

Then they both sat in silence till they finished. After Shawn finished his he sat the plate down on the floor. "Here ya go Jake," he said, as a little Chihuahua came running over to lick the plate clean. Then picking up a saucer, he filled it with beer and sat it on the floor. "There, now you have something to wash it down with."

"You get him drunk again, and he pees on my floor I'm coming out and waking you up to clean it up," Carmen said, in a serious voice, picking up the dishes.

Looking over the table, holding up his empty beer glass, Griselda darl'en, could you get me another beer please?"

Chapter One

"Would you like one too Wapiti?" Griselda asked.

"No thanks," Wapiti answered.

"Are you going on another hunt'en trip Marshal?" Jose asked with excitement in his voice. Looking over at Wapiti, "He blew a gang of outlaws up last week…That must have been cool to see, KA-BOOM." He said throwing his hands up in the air. "I sure will be glad when I'm old enough to go on a hunt'en trip."

Just then someone knocked on the door that leads down to the restaurant, and Jose took off running and opened it." Hello Judge," he said. "Are you here to yell at the Marshal again?"

"Something like that son," the Judge answered, rubbing him on the head, as he walked into the room.

"WWEELLLL HHEELLLL," Shawn said, pulling out a cigar and lighting it. Looking up at the judge, "And just what do we owe such a prestigious moment of your time to? YOU'RE HIGH-N-ASS… Griselda darl'en, grab the Judge a beer too, please. Wapiti, I'd like you to meet your new boss, Judge Ralph Monson." Waving his hand back and forth between the two.

Instantly Wapiti jumped to his feet, and held out his hand. "It's a pleasure to meet you again, sir."

Shaking Wapiti's hand, the Judge sat down, "I'll high-n-ass you Marshal. Just what the hell you doing telling this young Indian lad here that he could be a lawman?" The Judge said speaking in a loud, semi-angry voice. "Have you lost your mind? Oh, thank you Griselda," he said, reaching for his beer.

"If you're going to yell at the Marshal again, can we stay in the room this time? Griselda asked, smiling. "We can still hear you from our room anyway, but it's more fun to watch your face turn red trying to make him listen to you."

"Now your honor, the Young man wants to be a lawman, and I happen to think he'd be a good one, given the chance." Shawn answered, leaning back in his chair.

"I'll agree to hire you a new Deputy, but, an Indian? Come on." Judge Monson started in. "There's a whole bunch of young men who put in for that Sheriff's job. Why don't you pick one of them for a Deputy?"

"I didn't recommend a single one of them for that Sheriffs job. Why the hell would I want one of those bone heads for a Deputy?" Shawn said leaning back over the table, glaring straight into the Judge's face.

"I got the bill from Roger for your next hunt'en trip. You take this kid out there and get him killed, we'll have us one hell of an Indian up rising on our hands, and I don't think even Chief Joseph could stop it." Judge Monson said, leaning over to get face to face with Shawn.

"No sir your honor," Wapiti said "Chief Joseph and I talked about it; he knows I've always wanted to be a lawman. He said if I was set on it... he trusted no other man to teach me, only the Marshal."

"You have a death wish boy?" Judge Monson asked, looking Wapiti over. He was quite stocky, five feet maybe ten, eleven inches tall, MMM... One hundred seventy, maybe, one eighty. Like most Indians, he had a big knife on his side. He knew just by looking at him, that he knew how to use it. Them Indian kids grow up wrestling too... makes them better fighters. He could no doubt defend himself hand to hand. Then looking back over at Shawn, "I'll give it to ya by the looks of him; he could defend himself in a hand to hand fight, but what about when guns get involved? You know Indians can't have guns?"

"Well now Your Honor, we're working on that." Shawn said, smiling and leaning back.

"Ya, I know. Everyone in town heard you," the Judge said taking a drink off his beer. "You telling me maybe two hours of practice is all the lad needs?"

"Hell no!" Shawn snapped back. "That's why I'm taking so much ammo. So he can practice."

"What about when you pull into a cow town? You think them young men are going to listen to an Indian?" The Judge said pointing over at Wapiti. "Every drunk cowboy will want to get him to draw his gun, just so they could say they killed a Deputy U.S. Marshal, he'll be dead before he even gets wet behind the ears."

"That's what that double barrel ten gauge is for your honor." Shawn said with a big smile on his face. "When we ride into town, those boys

Chapter One

see that sawed off ten gauge on his side and each and everyone will think twice. I will guarantee you that."

Starting to chuckle, with a big smile on his face, "I was wondering what that was for…" The Judge said. "I'll buy it for ya… But still, him being an Indian, not to many white men will respect him."

"Not at first they won't," Shawn said smiling. "But after he busts a few heads, word will get out about him real quick. They'll all know who he is before we arrive into any town in a couple months."

"Excuse me, your Honor." Wapiti cut in. "Are you one of those hanging Judge's?"

With that comment Shawn busted up laughing. The Judge gave him a stern look. "Only when the law tells me I have to Young man. That's when I get to judge them… instead of a Marshal judging them himself with the death penalty first."

"Now, your honor," Shawn spat out waving his cigar in one hand and his beer in the other. "Every man I've shot was shoot'en at me first. I can't help it if they can't hit what they're shoot'en at and I can."

"Why don't you just wing them and then bring them to me?" The Judge asked. "That's what I will expect from you lad."

"He does and he'll be dead," Shawn snapped back at the Judge." I've tried that twice, and both times they still tried to kill me… No SIR, you pull that gun, you had better intend to use it, or you'll be the one ending up dead."

"So just when do you expect to go on your next hunt'en trip, and where are you going?" Judge Monson asked, still having a skeptical look on his face.

"Well, I figured we'd go over to Sumpter, I hear those new dredges are pulling out gold hand over fist. Figure Wapiti could cut his teeth on a few drunken, hope'n to get rich quick miner or two." Shawn answered

Standing up and pulling out the posters with excitement in his voice, Wapiti was looking through them till he came to Butch Cassidy and Sundance kid. "They said that these two robbed a place over in Haines yesterday."

Looking over at the posters Shawn smiled. "It sure would be nice to catch the Wild Bunch… but not likely. They'll be clear out of the

25

country by the time we get there. But then if they were planning a big job, like the gold train, that could take a while to plan."

"You really think taking this young lad to a town filled with a bunch of drunken miners and loggers is a good thing to do?" Judge Monson asked.

"The lad has to cut his teeth somewhere, why not there? It's just as good a place as any." Shawn answered, proudly

"Well I guess if he gets a hair cut." Judge Monson started to say.

"Nope, he's not cutting his hair!" Shawn said sternly.

"WHAT? He needs to at least get his hair cut." Judge Monson demanded.

"Nope, he don't have to. His people believe there's great spiritual strength in their hair. I don't know it to be true, and I don't know it isn't. But I do know that sometimes you need an edge… That little something that gives you that little extra strength? That little bit can be the difference between life and death." Shawn stated.

"I know you're right about that," Judge Monson answered. "Could you at least keep it tied in the back?" Then turning back to Shawn, "You go and get this kid killed and I'll have your badge for good this time!

"Now, I don't expect to get into no gun battles." Shawn said chuckling.

"You never do Marshal." Judge Monson stated firmly, taking his last swallow of beer, "Yet you always seem to find them don't you?"

"Ya, you're right about that you're Honor, but like I said, I only shoot those that are shoot'en at me first." Shawn answered, braggingly.

"Well then," Judge Monson said, standing up. "I guess there's only one thing left to do, and that is to swear you in Wapiti. Being a real Deputy might stop a few others from trying anything. So stand up here and let me swear you in."

"YES SIR," Wapiti answered, jumping up with a big smile on his face. "Thank you very much your Honor, I won't let you down."

"Don't be thanking me just yet son," Judge Monson said. "You haven't seen all that comes with the job." Then he pulled out his bible and swore him in. Then he shook both men's hands and headed

Chapter One

towards the door. "I'll see ya when you get back." Then he walked out the door.

Shawn stood up from the table, stretching his big arms out. Looking over at Wapiti who had a big smile on his face. "Well that's one job over with. Now then I want to get an early start, so let's turn in Wapiti, I mean Deputy."

"Sure thing Marshal." Wapiti answered, walking towards the back door and down the stairs to the Marshal's shack. Looking at that shiny new badge the Judge had just pinned on his chest the entire way. Lying down on the extra cot, he was so excited he didn't know how or when he fell asleep.

The next thing Wapiti remembered was waking up because the Marshal was shaking his foot, and handing him a cup of coffee. "Thanks," Wapiti said, sitting up and wiped the burning out of his eyes. Wapiti reached for the cup of coffee. It was still pitch black outside, he couldn't see a thing, but he could smell Carmen's perfume still lingering in the air. It must have been her who brought in the coffee. The Marshal didn't say much as they ate, he was in a big hurry to get down to the stable to make sure everything was in order. Even though he knew it would be. Hell Gordy had been getten his gear together for years. But there was always one little thing he might forget, and the Marshal didn't like forgetting anything. Fact he kept saying so. Wapiti figured they hadn't even been up for thirty minutes when the Marshal stood up, wiped his mouth and looked down at him. "Let's go, Deputy."

"Yes sir," Wapiti answered, taking one last bite of food. Then picking up his coffee cup he ran after the Marshal. Catching up with him quickly, the two walked down the street towards the livery stables. It was still pitch black outside. There wasn't a light on anywhere in town except at the livery. It didn't take them but a couple minutes to walk the two blocks down the street and into the livery.

"Gordy, you up?" Shawn shouted out as they walked in.

"Back here Marshal," Gordy hollered back. "Just getting one last thing ready for the trip." Then he walked out of the stall leading a big black and white Medicine Hat gelding; he stood all of seventeen hands tall, maybe a little more. Wapiti's heart hit the floor. Only the Great War chief's and Medicine men rode medicine hats, if they could catch one. Most of them were usually red and white. It was said they had special powers, they could out last most horses in distance and endurance. "I thought the lad might like this horse, I think you'll find he's better in the backcountry."

"OH YES SIR," Wapiti answered, walking over and took hold of the reins.

Shawn just stood there and watched all the going ons, fact he was enjoying it. Just the look on Wapiti face, when he saw that horse. With a big smile on his face lighting a cigar, he looked over at Gordy. "You do have a soft spot in you, don't you? That's a strong looking animal… So did you cut down my toy that I had Roger bring over?"

"Sure did Marshal," Gordy answer's, handing it over to him in its holster. "I soaped that holster to; it should stretch out some and fit better."

Shawn pulled it in and out a couple times. Then he looked over at Wapiti. "Here son, put this on your left side. We'll work on you pulling it as well as your pistol." Starting to chuckle, "We don't have to worry about you hitting your target with it. Just anywhere in the general area will do." Then he looked back at Gordy, "Well, is everything else ready for us to leave?"

"You know it is ya ole fart." Gordy said sternly. "Have I ever let you down yet? By the way, why you taking so much ammo with you? You expecting to run into trouble this trip?"

"Well I hope not." Shawn answered reaching for the reins and lead rope for his horse and mule. "Hope we just need it for target practice for Wapiti." Then he turned and headed towards the door.

"Let's go, Wapiti." Looking back at Gordy, "Figure we should be back in about three weeks at the most. So you take care of yourself."

"ME," Gordy shouts, "you two take care". While the two climbed aboard their horses. "You're the ones who might be getting shot at, not me."

Chapter One

"Do me a favor will ya Gordy? Make sure Twick uses that target range of mine. Fact, you go with him and give him some pointers." Shawn said, turning his horse and mule and headed down the street.

Wapiti looked up at the sky. It was still dark outside, fact the light was just starting to come up over the mountaintops as they rode out of town.

CHAPTER TWO

It was still early in the evening, fact the party'en had really just started. The Saloon began to wake up you might say, when a middle age ranch hand walked into Cattleman's Saloon and Brothel. He started looking around the room for the twin Larkin brothers. There they were, he said to himself, walking towards them. Gary and Larry Larkin and their Mexican friend Luis Nevarez were sitting at a table on the other side of the saloon. Larry already had a little Betty on his lap as usual. Gary was leaning up against the wall. The three were starting to unwind after a day of breaking horses out at the Boyer ranch. He was looking them over as if for the first time. They were only five feet seven maybe eight inches tall, and weighed about one sixty. He knew Larry didn't carry a gun. Claimed he liked to party and drink too much. Figured if he carried a gun he'd get shot. But those who knew him, KNEW he carried four knives on his body somewhere, and could pull and throw one before most men could draw a pistol. Usually taking their hats right off with the first one, just to get their attention.

Gary, he did carry a pistol; Fact that was how you knew which one was which. Those two were identical twins. Hell, out at the ranch when neither one was wearing a gun, you would have no way of knowing which one was which. Ever since they were kids, they called each other Bub. All's you had to do was yell out "Bub" and one would come running. Gary was the level headed one of the two. He did carry a pistol, definitely knew how to use it and wasn't the least bit afraid to either.

Chapter Two

He preferred using his fist over a gun, but then who didn't. He also had won the long range shooting competition for the last three years.

Luis on the other hand, the Mex, he was another story all together. He wore two pistols and two ammo belts across his chest, thought it made him look cool. He played the hard ass, he could back it up if he had to. But for the most part they all were just a bunch of jokers. BUT YOU DID NOT WANT TO BE THE ONE TO HAVE TO WAKE ONE OF THEM LARKIN BOYS UP FROM A NAP. They'll wake up right now, mad as hell, ready to hit the first one or thing they see. If you're lucky they would just bite your head off, instead of taking your head off.

Walking up to the table the old ranch hand looked at both of the twins, "Boys I'm afraid I have bad news for ya." Still glancing his eyes off both them as much as possible. "Seems Marshal Shawn Felton killed your cousin Brad Moen and his band of outlaws the other day."

"WHAT," shouted Larry, jumping up, throwing the young lady off his lap. "When and where did this happen?"

"Two maybe three days ago over by Prineville. Seems they had stolen a wagonload of nitro from one of the big mines over there. According to Marshal Felton he was all-alone, so he waited till they started across the river to get them all out in the open and him still in the brush. Claims he was just firing a warning shot, just wanted to wound the driver, but he slipped just as he pulled the trigger causing the bullet to hit the load of nitro instead." Starting to chuckle, "They claim there was 50 case's of 24-12 ounce bottle's on that wagon, it blew the wagon, all the horses and the men to hell and back." Trying not to bust up laughing, the man continued, "They said you couldn't tell where the horse flesh ended and the human flesh began. All's that was left was crows bait and a real nice new swimming hole for the kids. Either way they won't be having any funerals, cause there is nothing left to bury."

"Now that's bullshit," Larry shouted. "Just who the hell does he think he is? The big and bad Marshal Shawn Felton…Hell, shooting into that wagonload of nitro, he didn't even give those men a chance to defend themselves. Why that's plum chicken shit."

"Larry just settle down," Gary demanded of his twin brother. "You know as well as I do that Brad had robbed a few banks now and then." Looking back over at the man. "So what really happened?"

"Told ya," the man answered.

"It obvious what happened," Larry shouted. "Ole Marshal Felton decided to be Judge, Jury, and Executioner at the same time. You know he brings almost everyone back in over the saddle, instead of sett'en up."

"Hell Gary, Aunt Ethel can't even have a funeral. We need to go check it out. It'll only take four, five days at most to ride over there. Hell, we can go out to the ranch, get some supplies and be in Sumpter by tomorrow night."

"So where's the Marshal suppose to be now?" Gary asked the man.

"They say he hired a young Buck Indian for a Deputy, said they were heading towards John Day, then on to Sumpter. Said he wanted to show that young buck what he would be up against if he really wants to a lawman."

Gary walked over, leaned down and put his fist down on the table. "Alright Larry we'll go but I don't want anyone knowing which way we went." Looking around. "We'll go up over the Elkhorn Mountains. See if Randy might want to come along."

"Let's get going then." Larry said reaching for the bottle of whiskey. He put the cork back in it, and then put it in his pocket.

"Don't forget me," Luis said standing up, turning, he grabbed his two rifles. "That Marshal Felton killed my pa and brother two years ago. I'm not missing out on this one."

The three each took one more drink off their beers, and then headed towards the door. As Larry walked down the bar he grabbed another full bottle of whiskey. "Thanks boys," he says with a big smile on his face. "I'll be needing this more than you to keep me warm tonight."

"Wait just one minute," a man hollered at him. "We just bought that bottle.

"Remind me next time you see me and I'll buy you another one." Larry said laughing. Then he turned and walked out the door.

Chapter Two

"Come on Larry," Gary shouted back, as he and Luis climbed up into their saddles and headed out of town "Wait just a minute will ya?" Larry shouted back, climbing in the saddle, kicking his horse to catch up. "Why don't we go up over Marble Creek Pass?"

"First we have to get our gear from the bunk house," Gary shouted back.

Luis looked over at Gary, as Larry rode up to them. "Sure am going to miss Mrs. Boyer's cooking."

"Ya, me too." Gary said. "But, if old man Bill Boyer won't hold our jobs for us, we can always find some work over in or around John Day or Prairie City, after we finish with this."

"What about my idea of going up over Marble Creek Pass?" Larry said, taking a pull off the whiskey bottle and handing it to Luis.

"Too many people that way," Gary shouted, pointing at the whiskey bottle. "That's another thing; I'm not going to have you getting drunk and stupid on me. So that had better be your only bottle till we get over to Sumpter. Understood?"

"Ya, ya, fine," Larry snapped back.

"I figure we'll go up through Pine Valley, then over the top down to Twin Lakes, drop down to Deer creek, then on to Sumpter," Gary said.

"That back side is straight up and down, almost a shear cliff," Luis answered. "With a whole lot of shale rock to send you and your horse head over heels. If you get my meaning."

"I damn sure do," Larry said, "this old nag I'm riding wouldn't be worth a shit in country like that Gary and you know it."

"He'll be alright." Gary said, "Just make sure you hold on tight, but not too tight. You're going to want to be able to jump off quick if you need to."

"I don't think it's a bit funny, Gary, you know damned good and well you wouldn't take this horse into that country," Larry shouted back. "He's too green, born and raised in the valley. Hell, I haven't even had the need to take him into the timber, let alone take him into the high country."

"Well Amigo, why don't you just trade him to old man Boyer for one of those mustangs we brought in last week? Luis said. You know

33

Bill won't mind. Even the worst one of them is more sure footed than that nag your riding," Gary started chuckling, and reaching for the bottle.

"Ya, but only a couple of them will even let you on their backs yet, forget trying to ride him anywhere." Larry said taking his bottle of whiskey back.

"Ask Grandpa Dude" Gary said. "You know he'll pick you a good horse."

"Ya Hombre, you know Dude will pick you a good horse for the trip," Luis said.

"Ya, one that he's still training, with my luck," Larry said, as the three turned off the main road and headed up Griffith Gulch. The Boyer's main ranch house was just a couple miles up the little valley. "Dude will tell me, "Well hell Larry I can ride him.""

"There's not too many horses that man can't ride." Luis said chuckling.

Before they knew it they were riding into the barnyard. Both Mr. and Mrs. Boyer were standing on the front porch.

"Boys," Bill hollered at them. "Got a minute to talk?"

"Yes sir," they all answered, turning their horses and riding up to the house.

"Boys I heard about what happened to you cousin, and I know you were close. I just hope you aren't thinking of trying to get revenge for him on Marshal Felton. That man don't play around," Bill stated firmly.

"Somebody has to find out why he blew them to hell and back," Gary said. "I need to know what went down…Why he did what he did Bill."

"If you boys ride out tonight, don't bother coming back," Bill said in a very stern voice. "Your jobs won't be here."

"Oh, come on Bill, just give us two weeks to get over and back," Larry asked.

"If you boys go up against Marshal Felton… You had better make damned sure you're in the right," Bill answered turning around and headed towards the door.

34

Chapter Two

"Mr. Boyer?" Larry asked. "Do you think I could trade this valley horse for one of those mustangs we brought in last week?"

"Go ahead," Bill answered. "Ask Dude to pick you one out... I just wish you boys wouldn't do this, somehow, someone always ends up getting hurt."

"Sorry Bill," Gary answered, "but we need to know the truth about what happened out there. I'm not going in with guns a blazing, but I do want to know why he did what he did."

"LOOK, Brad was a bank robber and you boys all know it as well as I do!" Bill snapped back.

"Ya, I know, but blood IS thicker than water... He's family, he'd do the same if it was one of us," Gary answered.

"You boys come back by the house on your way out. I'll have some grub for you for your trip," Violet Boyer told them.

"Thank you ma'am," Gary answered, tipping his hat. He turned and headed his horse towards the bunkhouse with the others following him. Riding up to the bunkhouse, they all dismounted and walked inside. Gary had only gone in a couple feet, when he stopped and looked around the room. There were maybe ten men inside the room, some lying down in their bunks; four were playing poker for payday money. How stupid was that?" Gary thought chuckling. Playing with money they don't even have yet. Hell at least two of them will be broke five minutes after they get paid. As soon as they walked in, everyone stopped talking and started looking at them.

"Alright boys, lets get our gear and get the hell out of here," Gary ordered walking to his bunk. Rolling up his bedroll, picking up his sharps, then pulled out a box from under the bed. This is where he had a couple more boxes of shells and an extra pistol and holster.

Slowly the conversations started back up. Then one of the cowboys hollered out, "You boys really so stupid as to want to try and go up against Marshal Shawn Felton? Hell, you sure you're only half Polish?" Everyone started laughing at that comment.

"Well, now just where the hell else do you think we'd be going?" Larry shouted out. Looking over towards Gary, making sure he wasn't looking, Larry stuffed a couple more bottles of whiskey in his saddlebags.

Marshal Shawn Felton and the Wild Bunch

"Well then, you better make it look fair and just, or every lawman and bounty hunter in the country will be out looking for you men," Dude warned the boys.

"Oh, it'll be fair." Gary said, holding his sharps up.

Larry still watching Gary stuffed a shirt between the bottles so they wouldn't make too much noise, and hopefully not break either. Tying everything down, he picked up his rifle and pistol. "Sure hope we don't need these. But I would rather not need them and have them, than need them and not have them. If you know what I mean." He threw everything over his shoulder and headed towards the door, with the other two right behind him. Stopping. "Oh ya Grandpa Dude, Bill said I could change my horse in for a better trail wise one. Said to ask you to pick me one out, do you have anything to recommend?"

"Well, if it was me I'd take that big Roan I got from the Colonel at the fort a couple weeks ago. He's still on the awnrey side, but I'd say best of the lot, still a little green."

"GREEN, I TOLD YA GARY, ANOTHER DAMN GREEN BROKE HORSE! Just how many times you been on him old man?" Larry shouted back at him.

"Old man, I'll show you old man, you little smartass," Dude said. "But to answer your question, I've been on him a dozen times at least in the last few weeks. I was training him for myself, so I've only been able to work with him on my own time. He's starting to come around."

"Ya thanks Gramps," Larry answered, walking out the door, over to his own horse, which Gary had already unsaddled.

"Well, what did he say?" Gary asked.

Picking up his saddle, throwing it over his shoulder, "Green broke. I wonder just how much fun this is going to be?" Larry mumbled Turning and walking toward the barn. Still mumbling under his breath, "Green broke!" "Thanks Dude," Larry shouted out walking into the barn while everyone else was coming out of the bunkhouse.

"Yo Larry, just cowboy up." Luis shouted, laughing.

"Ah hell, he can't be too bad. Dude rides him." Gary said smiling and looking around at everyone.

36

Chapter Two

"Ya, but that crazy old man likes riding bucking horses," Luis said.

Then they all three walked into the barn; There he was, in the last stall. That BIG Roan, Dude had told Larry to take. Hell he was just about the biggest horse they had seen, he wasn't a draft horse, but he was just as tall. Hell, he stood every bit of eighteen plus hands, and a good thirteen hundred pounds of muscle, maybe more. Gary looked over at Larry. Still laughing and looking at the Roan. "Sure am glad it's you needing a new horse and not me."

"Thanks smartass," Larry answered, grabbing a lead rope and headed back to the stall. Opening the gate, he slowly started walking in, talking to the big Roan the entire time. "Easy big boy, I'm not going to hurt you."

"NO," hollered Gary, "but he sure as hell is going to hurt you!"

"SHUT UP," Larry snapped back, as he reluctantly attached the rope to the halter, and led him out of the barn. "Well that part was scarier than it really was." Then reaching for his saddle, he stopped, tied the Roan to the hitching post. Then he threw his saddle up on his back. Shit, he thought, tightening his cinch strap. He's so damn big I almost couldn't get that saddle up that high. Looking around, he could see that everyone had come out to watch him mount this monster of a horse, and he could see Dude was taking bets on him.

"Make sure that cinch is tight, Hombre," Luis hollered. "Hate to see both you and your saddle go flying through the air."

"Piss on you, all of you." Larry shouted out, looking around at everyone. "Any of you want to try him first?"

"Oh hell no, No thanks!" they all answered at the same time, waving their hands and backing up.

"Well at least he leads well," Gary said, still chuckling. "I'd like to get out of here real soon, Larry. So don't play around with him."

"Why the hell don't you guys leave me alone?" Larry snapped back, taking an extra pull on the cinch. "This horse looks scary enough; I don't need to hear it from you too." He tied his bed role down to the saddle; he almost couldn't reach that high. He tried to stretch his leg up to the stirrup but couldn't quite reach. With a small jump up, his foot landed in the stirrup and he pulled himself up in the saddle, waiting for all hell to break loose. "SSHHEEWW, guess all that worry was for nothing." Larry said looking around at everyone standing there watching. "Well, come on you two, let's get going." Larry turned the Roan towards the front gate. After just two steps, all hell broke loose. The Roan took to the sky, sending Larry flying up into the darkness and out of sight from everyone.

The dust flew from where he came crashing back to the ground. Everyone busted into laughter and shouting. Dude ran over and grabbed the reins. "Here you go son." Dude said, leading the big Roan back over to Larry, who was slowly getting up, wiping the dust off himself. "Damn that ground is hard." Looking over at Dude taking hold of the reins, "Is this horse even ride able?" Larry asked, climbing back in the saddle. This time the Roan didn't wait. Larry hadn't even got settled in the saddle as the big horse went to town bucking. Everyone was cheering, some for Larry, and some for the Roan.

"Looks like you got him beat," Luis hollered out, just as Larry went flying through the air again.

"Oh shit," Gary scrunches up, "That looks like it's going to hurt like hell!" as Larry came crashing back to earth.

Dude hollered over to Larry lying on the ground, "How many times I have to tell you, reach for the ground, son?" Some of the other ranch hands were egging him on.

Rolling over in the dust, laughing, he stood up. "This is not any fun," Larry said. "Any time any of you heroes want to try him, you just let me know, I'll be glad to let you try." Looking around at everyone, then he started chuckling a little bit.

"Well, you two saddle up and get ready to ride. I think I have him figured out." Walking around the Roan, Larry tightened the cinch back up. "He's going to take off and I don't know which direction. I just hope it's the right one, cause there won't be no stopping him," Larry said pointing a crossed the barnyard. He picked up the reins, patted the big horse on the head. "I hope you're through playing, cause you ain't throwing me again." Pointing down at his spurs, "See these big fella…? You're going to get to see what they feel like." Then he looked around at everyone and climbed up into the saddle.

Chapter Two

This time it was just like the first. The big Roan just stood there. After a minute or so, Larry put his spurs into his side to start him, and the Roan took to flight. Larry could see everyone waving their arms and hats. He couldn't hear a thing they were saying; he had other things on his mind. He wasn't about to let this Roan beat him again. After a good six, maybe eight real good bucks, clearing the ground six feet or better with each jump, also twisting and turning his body in every which direction. Larry and the others had seen bulls twist and turn like that, but never a horse. That Roan flat didn't like anyone on him. Then all of a sudden he took off at a full run across the barnyard and down the road. "Come on guys, let's get going," Larry shouted back

"We're coming," still laughing both Gary and Luis climbed aboard their horses and started out. Gary looked back over at Luis, "Maybe we'll catch him in a couple miles, cause I want to go the other way. Over Elk creek and out thru Washington Gulch."

Riding by the main ranch house Violet came over to them, handing Gary a bag of food. "It isn't much boys, but it will help out a little bit."

"Thank you Mrs. Boyer," both men said at the same time.

"Don't do this, Gary," Violet pleaded. "You know he was always in trouble with the law, you know that as well as everyone here knows it." She pointed at everyone still standing around.

Just then Dude came walking up behind them. "Gary, you know Larry can get a little hot under the collar, if you boys use those guns… you had better make damned sure you're in the right. You know Violet's right, that boy robbed his first bank when he was only fifteen, and you know it."

"Ya grandpa, I know you're right, still… Marshal Felton blew them all to hell and back," Gary said tying the food down. "That's not right and you know it. I just want to know if he had any other choice. And if there was, why didn't he choose it? Don't worry about Larry and his guns, you know he don't wear those inside saloons, only his knives. But if we should need to shoot it out with whomever, Larry's good with both pistol and rifle, Hell you know that Dude. You not only taught us how to ride these wild things," patting his big Sorrel. "You also taught

39

us to shoot. Don't worry; I'll make sure there's no gun play, if I can prevent it."

"I'll talk to Bill for you, I think I can get you your jobs back as long as your not wanted men." Dude says. "You know Bill won't hire a wanted man."

"Yes sir, I know that. We'll see ya in a couple weeks if everything goes well." Then Gary turned his horse, kicked him in the side and headed out of the barnyard with Luis right behind him.

Larry had the Roan held up just a half mile down the road, waiting for them. As the two rode up, Larry was still chuckling. "Bet neither one of you could have stayed on him, fact if it was you Luis, we'd still be waiting for you to cover him."

As Gary and Luis got closer the roan jumped into a full rare. "Ready to go? Easy, big boy." Larry said, trying to talk the big horse down. "I wasn't sure how you wanted to go, Gary."

"Well I thought we'd go over Elk Creek to Washington Gulch for tonight," as the three started riding together, Larry trying with everything he had in him just to hold the big Roan back.

"Damn," Larry said "I need to let him burn off some steam, or he just might start bucking again. I'll catch up to you guys later." He kicked the Roan in the side. Boy, was that the wrong thing to do. That Roan drove his head down between his front legs and went to bucking again. Larry did good to stay on for about four and a half, five jumps if he was lucky, before he went flying hard to the ground. The big Roan stopped, walked over to Larry, and lowered his head nudging Larry a little, as if to say, "You ok?"

The other two started laughing. "He like's you anyway Amigo," Luis said chuckling. "Look, he's giving you a kiss."

"Go to hell, both of you," Larry said, still setting on the ground looking up at them, and then looking up at the Roan. Picking up his reins, he stood up. Knocked some more dust off and climbed back aboard, waiting for the Roan to make up his mind about just what it was he was going to do. Just as Larry tried to turn him, the Roan started bucking, but only half hearted. It was only a couple good size

Chapter Two

crow hops, and then he took off into a full out run. Hollering back, Larry said, "I'll see you somewhere around Washington Gulch." Then the two were out of sight into the black darkness of the night.

Gary and Luis were still laughing, trying not to fall off their own horses. Gary pulled out a bottle of whiskey and held it up. "Stole this out of his coat sleeve before we left the ranch." Opening it up and taking a drink before he passed it to Luis. "I tell ya Luis, he has a bottle hid in every pocket." The two rode in the general direction of Washington Gulch, they talked about Larry and the Roan and what else lay ahead of them.

"Sure hope that Roan doesn't kill Larry out there tonight by taking his head off on a low branch or two." Luis said still laughing about it.

The two rode and talked a little longer. Gary put the bottle back in his saddlebag. He looked up at the sky; don't look like we're going to have much moonlight tonight. But we need to kick these two as well, if we hurry we can make it there before midnight. "Just watch your own head." Gary said, slapping his reins to his big Sorrel. Dude sure had picked him a good horse when he gave this one to him last year. He was as big and as strong as the Roan, just never really been as mean as the Roan. He'd heard those Calvary boys had caught him almost two years ago for that "Mister know it all Colonel."

Gary couldn't stand the Colonel. He was from back East somewhere. You could tell his dad didn't take him out behind the barn enough. Gary started to smile just thinking about it. Not like Dude had done us boys growing up. Hell, if we hadn't gotten our daily spanking, it wasn't bedtime yet.

After we had our little trips behind the barn Dude would tell us to go tell Mom why he spanked us. Like hell we would, that little Pollock would do a whole lot more harm. Make what Dude did, seem just a pat on the ass in comparison. We're only half Polish, not stupid.

The two rode in silence, Gary was thinking to himself, wondering just how this thing was going to play out. What was that old Marshal really like? Was he quick to draw? Did he really give every man a fair fight? Deep inside he knew he did. But still, there wasn't nothing left to even bury. WHY!

They had been riding for almost two hours at a real good clip when they heard Larry and the Roan coming up the valley at them. Larry pulled up beside them, they could hear the Roan was breathing heavily, they couldn't see the sweat on him, but they damned sure could smell it. "Looks like you've been having some fun." Gary said Chuckling.

"Hell yes," Larry said, pulling out another bottle of whiskey. "He'll be thinking twice before he tries to buck me off again. There's a new ranch house being built just at the mouth of the canyon. But I found a place to camp just up ahead."

"Good Larry, I'm just about worn out," Luis answered.

"You," Larry shouted. "Hell me and this Roan have been running all over the country side."

The three rode for about fifteen maybe twenty minutes, when they came to a spot next to the creek that Larry had picked out. They dismounted and unsaddled, then tied up their horses. Gary looked over at the others and around the area. "There'll be no fires tonight. Larry, give me that bottle you took from the bar."

Pulling the bottle out Larry handed it over to Gary. "Well, are you at least going to let me have a cigarette?" Larry said with a smartass attitude. As he started rolling one up.

"Well ya, fact throw me that pouch," Gary said.

"You wouldn't have anything to drink or smoke tonight if it wasn't for me now would ya? Here take it," Larry said, tossing the pouch. "And give me that bottle back". He demanded, taking the bottle back and taking a big pull off it.

"Hey, slow down Hombre," Luis said reaching over and grabbing the bottle. "Share that with the rest of us."

"I just want a couple more swallows; there will still be some left for you." Larry said.

"Like Hell," Gary said, taking the bottle. "Give me one last pull, then you two can have it, cause I'm going to get some rest. Which I

Chapter Two

suggest you do as well. I want to get us an early start." Taking one last drink, he handed Luis back the bottle. Took his bedroll over, found him a flat spot, laid down and went to sleep. It would have been easier if those two weren't being so loud. But he was too tired to argue with anyone

CHAPTER THREE

It was barely dusk when Gary woke up. Rubbing his eyes a little, he looked over at the other two. Who both obviously had too much to drink last night? Not one of them had a blanket over them and it was a little chilly out. He couldn't help but chuckle at both of them as he stood up and looked at them lying stretched out over the ground. It looked like they fell asleep in the same spot they had been drinking at.

Looking around camp, he found enough wood to build a small fire, just big enough for one pot of coffee. They would have to eat jerky and whatever else Violet put in the bag of food. Putting some coffee grounds in the pot of water he couldn't help but smile. Luis was right; he sure was going to miss her cooking. Leaning over he picked up a couple rocks. He figured he'd just toss them at the two to wake them up. Tossing the first one at Larry, it bounced off his forehead, making Larry wake up, jump up and start hollering.

"What the hell is your problem?" Larry shouted rubbed his forehead. Looking over at Luis, who was stirring from all the noise. Leaning over Larry picked up a rock of his own and threw it at Gary, who was laughing and trying to apologize at the same time. "Damn you, my head hurt's bad enough already." Stumbling a little as he tried to stand up. "Damn Luis, why'd you let me drink so much for? I think I'm still half drunk."

"You probably are," Gary said angrily. "You never let anyone tell you enough. Hell if they do, you just drink more."

44

Chapter Three

"Don't holler. Do you at least have a cup of coffee made?" Larry asked, looking over at Luis, who was still trying to stand himself. Larry couldn't help but chuckle a little, walking over to Gary.

"Well ya, I'm not a total a-hole," Gary said. "I wouldn't wake you up till it was ready." Pouring each of them a cup, and handing it to them.

"Hope its strong Amigo," Luis said. Holding his head too, "Why the hell did you get us up so early for?" He asked, walking over to Gary, taking his cup of coffee.

"How come your limping this morning, Larry?" Gary asked, with a big smile on his face.

"I'd like to see either one of you try to get on that Roan first this morning ahead of me." Larry answered, bending over and opening his saddlebags, pulling out another bottle of whiskey. Pulling the cork, he poured a little in his cup. "A little bit of the hair of the dog you might say." He spats out, with a big smile on his face. "Might say, it cures what ails ya.

"Damn you Larry," Gary shouted, standing up, walking over to Larry, yanking the bottle out of his hand. "How much more of this do you have and what the hell you doing drinking before noon?" As he started looking through Larry's bedroll and pulled out two more bottles of whiskey. "Damn Larry, we'll be in Sumpter tomorrow."

Starting to chuckle. "Ah hell Gary, don't get your tit in a ringer," Larry said. "What's the big deal? I don't have a whole lot of money on me, figured this would last till…."

"Till when, noon today Larry?" Gary said, smashing one bottle against a tree. "Is that all you ever think of? Where you going to get your next drink of whiskey or beer at?" Then he stood up and headed for his gear. "Damn you piss me off with all your drinking," smashing another bottle against a rock.

"Yo Gary," Luis said, "I agree he likes to drink too much, but don't break that last bottle just yet. It's going to be cold up on that mountain tonight."

Looking at the last bottle of whiskey in his hand, "Alright, but I'm the one hanging on to it. Now let's get saddled up and get the hell out of here." He kicked the small fire apart, picked up his gear he headed over to the horses. Still talking under his breath.

"Well la-t-da," Larry said, pouring him and Luis one more cup of coffee. "He always makes a big deal out of nothing. We'd better get saddled up or he won't quit hollering, and my head hurts bad enough already from last night."

"Mine too, Amigo," Luis agrees with him. "But he's right. You do drink a lot, kinda like my dad used to down in Mexico, only he would get real mean. You just get stupid and funny both at the same time. Hell, that's how I tell you two apart." Starting to chuckle and picking up his saddle. "You always smell like whiskey or beer, usually whiskey, cause you can hide a fifth in each coat sleeve."

"Ah hell," Larry said, as the two head toward the horses. "He always takes things to serious anyhow."

"Well, somebody has to, if it wasn't for me and Randy, your ass would've been in jail a long time ago." Gary stated firmly, pulling his cinch strap tight.

"So which one of you wants to climb aboard this big fella first this morning?" Larry asked, pulling the cinch just a little more before he tied it down.

I thought you said you rode it all out of him last night." Luis answered, climbing up in his saddle. "Look at that face; he's watching every move you make, as if he's daring you to climb aboard."

"Well come on," Gary said, as he and Luis both start chuckling.

Larry grabbed hold of the reins in one hand and reluctantly puts his foot in the stirrup. In one swift move he threw his leg up over the top, just barely getting his other foot in the stirrup as the Roan went flying sky high, pulling his rein up high. Larry had been ready for this, but he thought he might at least get set first, he was wrong. The Roan went up on his second jump with such force and twisting in every other direction at the same time, sending Larry flying into a grove of young fir tree's. The trees actually broke his fall. Larry had no longer left his back and the Roan stopped bucking, looking around for his rider.

Looking over at Larry lying in the trees, then slowly he started climbing out Gary started laughing harder. "I remember when those

Chapter Three

Calvary boy caught him a couple years ago, fact every week he was breaking the bones of anyone who tried to ride him. I couldn't believe it when Dude brought him out to the ranch. Said that Colonel was ready to kill him, because no-one could break him"

"I'm about ready to," Larry said, climbing out of the trees. Then he walked back over to the Roan, grabbing hold of the reins again; he pulled the Roan right up to his face.

"Alright big fella, we can do this the easy way or the hard way, either way I'm going to ride you... so get used to it." Walking around the side he put his foot in the stirrup.

"You'll ride him only when he says you can," Gary said, still laughing.

"You have to stay on him first." Luis added between laughs.

They both watch Larry swing back up into the saddle. Just like the first time, Larry had barely got in the saddle when the Roan left the ground, farting and snorting with every jump. They couldn't believe Larry was staying right with him. Fact that made the Roan even madder. It looked like the Roan was going to win. But Larry was putting his spurs into his front shoulder's with every mighty buck. When all of a sudden that Roan switched direction three different times all in the same jump, sending Larry flying again.

"DAMN, I thought I had him that time," Larry said, standing back up, he started knocking some dust off. "I thought I had him that time." He kept repeating, while walking back over to the big Roan.

"That's just it, Larry, you thought." Gary said. "Now this time stay on him so we can get going."

"Well now, Superman," Larry said tightening the cinch again. "Anytime you want to trade horses, you just let me know and I'll be glad to oblige you." He looked back over at the Roan, who was still watching every move he was making. As if to say to him, "Come on big boy, just climb right back on." and that's exactly what Larry did. This time the Roan just stood still. "I'm wearing him out," Larry started saying. But no sooner did he try to turn the Roan in the direction they wanted to go, and that Roan went sky high again.

47

"You're tiring him out all right, Hombre," Luis shouted as the Roan was still flat getting with it, and Larry wasn't giving him an inch either. Fact if they were in the rodeo Larry would definitely win it all. That Roan kept it up for an good ten hard, highflying, twisting jumps. All of a sudden he took off at a dead run, with Larry waving his hat and hollering back. "We'll catch back up with you around Pine Creek, if not sooner."

"Did you see that ride?" Gary said with a big smile on his face. "I'm sure glad that was him and not me. That horse has more power and heart in every jump than any horse I've ever seen, and trust me growing up with Grandpa Dude, hell we always had at least eight to ten horses in the barn he was breaking."

"I know that's right, about the Roan I mean," Luis said. "I've only been around you guys… what, three years? I've never seen a horse go even half that high, and I've never seen any horse go in so many directions at the same time. Hell, usually a horse bucks straight out; a bull make moves like that … but never a horse."

"I hear ya." The two kick their horses into a good gallop. "Least he's heading in the right direction probably be awhile before we catch up with them." They rode the next few hours mostly in silence, staying just inside the timberline. So as not to be easily seen by passer's by on the main road just a few hundred yards away.

Baker Valley was a huge valley. There were a few houses out this far. Mostly this land was owned by the big ranchers still. They used this land and up onto the mountains for summer grazing. Which was still a few weeks off. They didn't bring them up here till the first of June and that was ten days away from now at least. Heck, some of them cattle ranchers were still having one or two late calves.

The fences haven't made it this far out yet either. This was still mostly open, where as down in the valley the smaller ranchers were putting up wire around their places. Hell, down there you needed to carry a pair of fencing pliers so you could cross from one small ranch to another. Cut the fence, go through, and then splice it behind you. Piss's them off, but what the hell, sometimes there's just no other way out of trouble in the middle of the night. That's when you make your

Chapter Three

escape from the law, or in Larry's case a husband. The two had been riding for a couple hours, they knew they were coming up on Pine Creek, cause they could hear the flow from the river. When Larry and the Roan came running up along side them.

"Gary, I've been doing some thinking while I've been running some of this orneriness out of this Roan."

"Oh shit! Just what kind of lame brain idea have you come up with this time?" Gary asked sarcastically.

"Now, just hear me out. The train leaves Sumpter early in the morning, if we get over the mountain tonight, then tomorrow we get up early, ride down to the gorge were the train goes into the canyon."

"What, you want to try and rob the train?" Gary snapped out with a discussed look on his face.

"Will Ya just listen," Larry says pulling back on the reins. "Shit, I ran the hell out of him for the last two hours and he still wants to go, just look at him. Any ways back to the train, we stop it at the gorge, take the gold and be in Sumpter and past before they get down to Baker City and report it. Hell, by then we could be half way to Granite."

"Larry, you know they don't ship that gold everyday, and when they do, shit, there are more guns on that train than what the three of us are carrying."

"Not if we disconnect the box car loaded with gold." Larry continues telling them his plan, "The train is moving down hill, and the breaks on the box car automatically come on when the trailers become disconnected, which will bring the box car to a stop while the rest of the train keeps going. Shoot by the time they get stopped and back up to the box car, we'll be gone … what do ya think?"

"Just like I said before you started. It's a lame brain idea," Gary answered. "Like I said, they don't ship that gold but one day a week. All the other times it's just for show, to make people think they are. Hell, that gold you see them load is nothing more than painted rocks. No one really knows just how or when they load the real stuff. Hell, we'd

49

end up going to prison for attempting to rob the train, and wouldn't get one ounce of gold for our time."

"What do you think Luis?" Larry asks with excitement in his voice.

"I have to agree with Gary. I think we would end up going to prison for nothing. Besides, I wouldn't do anything like that unless your brother Randy had checked it out first. He's the one with the brains to not get caught, or a way out of trouble before it happens."

The three turned and headed up the mountain pretty much following Pine Creek as they went. The rest of today the terrain would be some rough country. Especially over the top with all the rock cliffs and the loose shall rock facings. Why if your horse took one wrong step ... you would slide all the way to hell before you got stopped. There would also be snow on top still. Larry was thinking to himself. Least he still had two bottles in his saddlebags that Gary didn't find. It is going to be cold up there tonight; Gary will be glad I have more. Least if you drink enough, you won't think you're as cold as you really are. "Well then, let's rob the passengers; we'd get some money that way."

"Larry, the only people on that train is broke miners and loggers." Gary said. "Hell, even if that train was totally full of people. I bet you would be lucky to get fifty dollars, if we were real lucky, we might get a hundred."

"You know he's right Larry." Luis said. "That is just about the dumbest idea I think you've come up with yet."

Even though they were heading up the steep mountain terrain, and through the thick timber, that Roan still wanted to go. It was all Larry could do to still hold him back. He could hardly believe it; he had run him pretty hard before catching back up with Gary and Luis. He soon found out that if he stayed up in front of the others, the Roan was a little easier to handle. But he still didn't like this slow pace. Every now and then he would just say hell with holding him back and take off running up and around the mountain just trying to tire him out. Which was easier said than done. After about thirty or so minutes he'd catch back up with the others, who couldn't believe just how ornery and full of fire that Roan was.

Chapter Three

It was mid afternoon when they rode into lower end of Pine Valley. "There's a real nice lake up here," Gary said looking over at Luis. "You still carry that fishing line Larry?"

"Well ya, I never go on a trip without it." Larry answered.

Looking back at Larry, Gary couldn't help but chuckle, cause it was all he could do to keep that big Roan under control. "Well when you get tired of playing around with that horse, let me know and I'll find a camp site."

"Well anytime one of you wants to trade horses you just let me know. This big fella only knows two speeds, fast and faster and you never know when he's going to start bucking again, just to see if you're paying attention to him. He caught me off guard a few times already today, and I'm here to tell you that ground is not soft."

"Hey guys, look at that herd of elk over there." Luis said, pulling up on the reins, stopping to get a better look.

Gary pulled up on his reins as he came along side him. "I wonder if there's any bull in with them?" Then they heard a rifle firing; they both turned just in time to see Larry go flying one way, and his rifle the other. The Roan once again went sky high.

Both of them busted up laughing at Larry, as they seen Larry come crashing back to the ground. "What the hell you doing?" Gary asked.

Rolling over, smiling, Larry started to stand back up, knocking dust out of his face and his cloths. "Guess Dude hasn't shot a gun off him yet." Larry said smiling and looking around. "Did either of you see where my rifle went?"

"Guess you're right," Gary answered pointed to Larry's rifle. "It's right there, but just what the hell were you shooting at?"

"Shoot'en at hell, I got him." Larry said, picking up his rifle and walking towards the Roan.

"Got what?" Gary asked again, still looking around.

"That bull elk over there," Larry answered, pointing toward the herd.

"Over where? And just what the hell you doing killing an elk for?" Gary shouted at him.

"The one laying right on the other side of that log." Larry answered grabbing the Roan's reins, and started leading him over towards the dead elk. But as soon as he smelt that blood, he started fighting. He didn't know what that smell was, but he didn't like it. Pulling on the reins with a firm grip, and talking to him, slowly Larry got him over to the elk. Tying the Roan off to a tree, Larry walked the rest of the way to the elk. "Dinner, I don't want trout. I want elk steak." Leaning over he started cutting the back straps out.

"That's wasting a lot of good meat," Gary said.

"AH hell, the wolves, lions and the bears have to eat too." Larry answered, grabbing up a hand full of blood and rubbed it in the Roan's face. Who instantly rears back away from it. Larry just grabbed some more and repeated the process. Only one way to get him used to the smell of blood, so he not so finicky. "I don't think he liked me firing that rifle off him either, did he?"

"Noooo, I don't think so Hombre, I think when we get down in the valley tomorrow, maybe you should start shooting more off him." Luis said.

"Ya think?" Larry picked up the meat, handing it to Gary. "Here you take this so I can get back aboard. Then we'll find us a good place to camp."

"Well alright, but we're not waiting around to see if that Roan is going to let you ride or fly. Whichever it is, you come and find us. I might have this cooked by the time you catch back up to us, Young man."

"Young man, my ass, I'll remind you I was born an hour before you. So you're the Young man here." Larry stated, climbing back aboard the Roan, then turning him up the mountain he kicked the big horse and took off leaving the others behind. After about thirty minute's he was back at the dam for the lake.

It sure was a beautiful area; every now and then you could see a fish jump up out of the water after a fly. Heading the Roan over to the edge so he could get a drink, Larry pulled the bottle out of his saddlebag. Looking around, he could see Gary had worked his way to the back side of the lake, taking a pull off the bottle, putting the

Chapter Three

cork back in the bottle, he quickly put it back before Gary could see it. He started to turn the Roan away from the water and on to camp. But he wasn't through drinking yet, and to let Larry know he started bucking again, not real hard. But Larry wasn't paying attention, so of course he went flying into the lake. Which was colder than hell! Heck, up where Gary had picked for camp the lake was still covered in snow and ice. Looking up at the Roan with a disgusted look on his face, he could swear the Roan was smiling at him, not to mention he could hear Gary and Luis laughing. He stood up; soaking wet and looked down at the bottle in his coat sleeve, he hadn't even spilt a drop. Walking over he grabbed the reins and led the Roan around the lake over to camp.

Gary already had a fire going, and he and Luis were lying back against a log relaxing. When Larry came leading the Roan into camp, "Alright now a-hole, get that bottle out that you took this morning." Larry said, unsaddling the Roan and tying hobbles around his front legs. Most people hobble their back legs too, but up here in the high country; there was a whole lot of lions and bears. This way he has both back legs free to defend himself as well as his front legs. Larry walked up to the fire to warm up, with Gary and Luis still laughing at him.

"Looks like that horse still don't want you, or anyone else for that manner on his back." Luis said.

"Ah, you guys just shut up and Gary you get that bottle that you have in your saddle bags. I'm cold and I'm thirsty."

"You're not that thirsty, Larry," Gary said with a growl in his voice. "I smelt it on you when we got together at the bottom. So, you've been drinking all day."

"No Sir," Larry was smiling, "That's from last night. I hadn't washed up yet."

Starting to chuckle, "Well you sure have now, haven't you." Gary said tossing Larry the bottle.

Pulling the cork, Larry looked over at the other two. "I tell ya, that damned horse threw me at least six to eight times today. So, if either one of you wants to switch with me. I'll be more than glad to oblige you tomorrow. There ain't a bone one on me that don't hurt."

"No thanks, I'm having fun watching you fly threw the air, and might I add, not with the greatest of ease either." Gary said still chuckling.

"That caballo is just flat out ornery," Luis said, reaching for the bottle. "I think he like's bucking."

"Well, the day you start staying on him will be the day he stops bucking." Gary said, turning the elk back strap over,

"I've said it once and I'll say it again. ANY TIME either one of you want to switch, just ask." Larry pulled his saddle around for a pillow and laid down next to the fire.

"You're the one who picked him, little brother." Gary answered, "You didn't have to take him."

"No sir, Dude did… and how many times I have to remind you, I was born an hour earlier than you, so you're the little brother"

"He told you he was green." Gary said. You could have picked another one.

"I know, but I didn't think he'd give me a horse that would try and kill me. Hell I'm his grandson for cry'en out loud. I'd like to see any one else try and ride him…I bet you no one else will ever ride him, either. Hey Luis, will you help me off with my boots?"

"WAA, WAA, I wouldn't help him." Gary called out, taking the bottle back from Larry.

"Na, I'll help the poor cripple." Luis answered, reaching over and grabbed Larry's boot, "but I'm not moving any further than I have to."

The three just set there passing the bottle around till dinner was ready. Larry had been right, Gary thought to himself. This elk was better than any trout; still he wasted a lot of good meat.

"Hey Gary, how are we going to find where Randy's logging at?" Larry asked.

"OH NO, he ain't coming along is he," Luis asked. "That little dude is plum crazy."

"No more than me and Gary," Larry said smiling, pulling out another bottle from his saddlebag.

"I knew you had another bottle." Gary shouted out, smashing the near empty bottle in the fire.

Chapter Three

"The Hell he ain't crazier than the two of you, that little man likes to fight and hurt people." Luis answered in a serious voice and even more serious look on his face.

"Ya, but they usually start it, by making fun of his stuttering," Gary answered. "You think they'd learn to leave him alone."

"Hell, that guy makes men two or three times his size look like mince meat when he finishes with them," Luis said. "Which comes from the Irish side of him, I think."

"You Larry, you got most of the Pollock side of the marriage... Gary, an equal amount of both, Irish and Polish, cause you lose your temper easily too."

"Ah, what the hell would a Mexican know about someone being crazy?" Gary said reaching for the bottle. "I knew you had to have at least one more bottle somewhere."

"We Mexicans know loco when we see it, and I'm here to tell you, that little man don't know when to stop. Hell when and if you do get him stopped, the other guy needs a doctor... BAD!" Luis shouted, remembering the last time he seen Randy fight.

"I know, but he does it all with his hands. Hell, I don't even know if he remembers how to use a gun anymore. Does he Larry?" Gary asked

"Sure, he's pretty good with a rifle," Larry answered. "But I don't think he could hit the broad side of a barn with a pistol anymore. Beside Luis, he'd be on our side if anything did go wrong."

"I don't care if he looses it and gets into a fight, I just hope he don't put us right in the middle of it." Luis said, throwing a couple pieces of wood on the fire.

"Who cares? He won't need no help, unless there's more than five. Any less than that... shoot, just set back and enjoy the fight." Gary answered.

"Well, I'm decent in a fist fight, don't get me wrong... I can hold my own, but it still usually hurts the next day," Luis said still complaining.

"Hell, there's nothing like a good fist fight. Even in a bad gun fight, someone ends up dead," Gary said, trying to reassure Luis.

"Well, alright. But you hombres keep that temper of his under control," Luis demanded.

"Ya, Ya. Now how about we get some sleep? It's going to be a hard ride over the top tomorrow. I'd like to make it to Sumpter tomorrow night," Gary reached for his blanket.

Taking the last drink out of the bottle, then holding it up side down. Larry looked over at the others. "Well, we better, cause we're out of whiskey."

"Larry you lush, that's all you think of. When and where your next drink is coming from." Gary shouted out.

"Ah, leave him alone Amigo, we all have our problems," Luis snapped back.

"Even Me?" Gary asked.

"Yes, even you're an a-hole at times," Larry answered.

"Fine, let's talk about it in the morning, besides we don't even know if we can find out which logging camp Randy's working out of. Besides, he never did like Brad and you know it Larry." Gary said, in an irritated voice because of Larry's drinking.

"I know, I know, but he was still family. Family sticks together through thick and thin." Larry replied.

"OK, OK," Gary answered, pulling his blanket over himself. "Let's get some sleep."

"We know, you want to get an early start," Larry answered, making a pillow in his saddle out of his horse blanket. "So since you're the one in such a hurry, you can throw a couple more logs on the fire so we don't get too cold." Pulling his blanket over himself, and closing his eyes.

"What's wrong Larry, you don't have enough FIREWATER in you?" Gary smirked; doing just what Larry had mentioned and put a couple more pieces of wood on the fire. "Besides you probably still have a bottle hid somewhere on ya."

"No I don't, but if you hadn't thrown and broke the other two, I would have," Larry shouted back.

"Why don't you two stop bickering like a couple old ladies and just shut up and go to sleep?" Luis stated, rolling over to sleep himself.

"Stay out of this Luis," both the twins said at the same time. Looking at each other, they both started chuckling. Then they all lay back down and went to sleep.

CHAPTER FOUR

"Marshal, when are we going to take a break in a town?" Wapiti asked. "We've been running around in circles for the last three and a half days. Tracking and untracking. Trying to shoot every branch, pine cones, or best of all, those corn biscuits, plus you can't cook for shit."

"Well, if you think you can cook better, why haven't you offered?" Shawn said, looking over at him. "There will come a time when we will need to move and move fast. We're going to be out of a town for weeks at a time. But we'll stop tonight in a little cow town over here named Dayville... Not much there, a one in all store, bar, small restaurant and a couple rooms upstairs. I was through this way once or twice before... Damnedest thing, most towns have nicknames for their school sports teams. These people call themselves the Dayville Devil's. I guess they figure there can't be a worse place than there, not even Hell itself could be as bad."

"Some ranchers this far out take whatever outlaws or in-law that comes along as ranch hands. You might just have papers on some of them. Why don't you pull out those papers and let's take one last good look at them?" Shawn said, pulling up on his reins.

Pulling up along side him, Wapiti stopped and pulled out the posters. He had been looking at the ones with Butch Cassidy and Sundance Kid's pictures since they left. With excitement in his voice, pulling their poster out first. "Do you think we might find these two hiding out there?"

57

"OH NO, NO, if those boys are still in the area, they'd be up around Baker City or Sumpter trying to rob one of those gold trains. I doubt very much if they've ever been in this part of the country… Naw, we'll be lucky to find some young wanna be outlaw," Shawn stated, thumbing through them. "Someone who did something stupid and got caught." Holding up four posters, "Like these four here, they've been holding up stage coaches."

The sun was just setting behind the mountains as they came riding into town from the west. Wapiti could see the Marshal was right. There wasn't much here. Just the store he talked about, which had six, eight horses tied up in front, along with a couple wagons. A Livery Stable, maybe two dozen houses that all had grass yards. There was a small school on the very top of the little mountain in town. But something was missing, though. The two rode up to the Livery; Wapiti was still looking around, what was it that was missing? Wapiti also notice the Marshal was looking around the Livery Stable. "What's up Marshal?"

"Something just don't feel right, is all." Shawn said, walking into the livery stable. "I guess we have to put everything up ourselves." He said, starting to unsaddle his horse. "Leave your pistol here with the rest of our gear and put that hog leg on. Just in case we run into trouble tonight."

Quickly they unloaded, grained, fed, and watered the horse's. The Marshal kept looking around, as if he was expecting someone to come out of nowhere and want to try something. There were three other horses in the Livery that were covered in sweat, which meant they had been rode hard. The two walked out of the livery and they both looked up and down the street. "Mark my words Wapiti; watch your back in there. You never know what some young wanna be famous outlaw will try and do. Getting him the first ever Indian wanna be lawman would look real nice on his belt. Fact, I don't think any jury from here would hang him either."

"That's it!" Wapiti blurted out.

"That's what?" Shawn asked, stepping up on the boardwalk.

"There's no church in town." Wapiti said, still looking around the town.

Chapter Four

"Told ya, they call themselves The Dayville Devil's." Taking one more quick look around town, they opened the door and the two walked over to the bar with the Marshal leading the way, licking his lips as he walked up and leaned over the bar. "Bar keep, we'll take two shots of whiskey and two beers, please."

"Now you just wait a minute mister. I ain't serving no damn Indian in here." The man demanded, pointing at Wapiti.

Shawn leaned back, pulling open his coat. "It's alright, I'm U.S. Deputy Marshal Shawn Felton. You'll either pour us those drinks or I'll throw you out that window and help myself."

"I I I'm sorry Marshal. I didn't know who you were." The man stuttered, reaching for a bottle and glasses.

"Well, now you do, so start pouring." Shawn ordered, pointing his finger into the bar top.

"Isn't it against the law to sell alcohol to Indians?" The man asked, shyly, pouring a beer slowly. Wondering, just why the hell would any lawman, even the big, bad Marshal Shawn Felton himself; bring an Indian into any bar? He had to know that was just trouble waiting to happen."

Leaning over, Wapiti spoke in a low voice. "Marshal, I've never had any whiskey or beer before. Why if my dad found out, he'd kick me in the behind. He says no good comes from drinking."

"Well now, Wapiti. First, your dad ain't here. Second, moderation son, you drink in moderation. Don't see how much you can drink, just enjoy your drink." Picking up both shots Shawn handed one to Wapiti. "Now, this will warm you up inside out, so you take it all in one swallow." Shawn said, swallowing it down. "Drink up son." Picking up his beer, and then you wash it down with this.

Wapiti picked the glass up, took a deep breath then drank it down. "WOW!" He shouted as the fire hit his stomach. "I see how it warms you up from the inside." Then he grabbed his beer to wash it down with. .

"Just what the hell is this?" A man shouted out standing up from one of the tables and walked up between Shawn and Wapiti. Pushing Shawn back just a little. He didn't hear the Marshal say just who he was.

59

"This buck Indian thinks he can just walk in here and drink our beer and whiskey?" The man put his hand on Wapiti's shoulder and spun him around. "This is what we do to Indian's around here." The man already had his fist drawn back and ready to throw.

When just from anticipation Shawn throws a big smashing right back hand into the mans face sending him flying across the room, over a chair and crashing to the floor. "Sorry Wapiti. I know I should have let you handle him. I just couldn't help myself." Turning towards the tables so everyone could hear him. "Now, I'm U.S. Marshal Shawn Felton, and this is my Deputy Wapiti."

One of the other cowboys hollered out, "Who the hell would make an Indian a lawman?"

Pulling his coat back with one hand, showing his badge, and reaching for his pistol with the other. "I SAID… I'M SHAWN FELTON, U.S.MARSHAL, I made him a lawman. Now if any more of you want to end up on the floor like your hero friend there," Shawn says, pointing at the man who was rubbing his jaw and still setting on the floor.

"Not me," the man answered, standing back up. "I just wish you would have told me earlier." The rest of the people were agreeing with the Marshal. They all had heard story's of Marshal Felton…How he brings them in over the saddle. "That's more like it." Shawn said, putting his pistol away, and watched the bartender with shaky hands, fill both shot glasses again.

"This ones on the house Marshall. If you promise not to tear my place up tonight?" The man asked cautiously.

"Well now sir, that's going to cost you two hot baths as well, then I would have to say it's up to them." Shawn said, waving his hand around the room…

"No problem, Marshal. Go right through those doors. Mary Jo get two hot baths ready for the Marshal and his Deputy, the man ordered out."

Picking up his beer, Shawn looked around the room. "Come on Wapiti, this is going to be a fun night yet. I promise."

"Yes sir Marshal, I'm right behind you. I don't think these people like Indian's around here." Wapiti said looking around the room.

Chapter Four

"I don't think they would have hurt you to bad." Shawn said smiling and looking around the room one more time himself, before they walked into the bathing room. Which had two tubs sitting in the open. Mary Jo was filling them up with hot water.

"That's easy for you to say, Marshal; it's not your scalp they want." Wapiti said looking at the tubs. "What? Don't they have separate rooms?"

"What's wrong?" Shawn shouted throwing his chest up and out. "What's wrong? You don't want to see this magnificent body?"

"No, not really." Wapiti answered with a smirk on his face.

"I'll tell ya son, when I was your age, women use to stand in line for a glance of this big magnificent body of mine." Shawn said making a muscle with his arm.

"Well, I think you're full of shit, Marshal. Besides I'm not a woman!" Wapiti answered, smiling a little.

"Ah, don't worry about it, Wapiti; they have a blanket they pull between the tubs." Shawn said chuckling

They started getting undressed; Wapiti looked over at the Marshal. "So what time do you figure we'll get out of here in the morning?"

"What are you in such a hurry for?" Shawn shouted out. "Heck, a few hours ago you couldn't wait to get to a town? Now you can't wait to leave. Hell son, make up your mind."

"That was before I found out these people didn't like Indian's." Wapiti stated, climbing into the tub and the hot water. "Boy, did it sure feel good."

"Don't let them boys bother you too much son." Shawn said, asking the young lady to bring him another beer. "Besides I'd like to see just how well you can fight with your fists."

"I'll be glad to show you anytime, but not eight at a time," Wapiti answered.

"Oh now Wapiti, I don't think they all would have joined in," Shawn chuckled. "I wouldn't have let more than four try ya before I'd have jumped in and helped out."

"GEE, Thanks Marshal." Wapiti answered. "That would have been nice of you."

"You bet son, anytime. I'll always have your back covered, and I expect you to do the same for me. That's if there's more than three or four at a time." Shawn said braggingly.

The two finished their baths and returned back to the bar area. They sat down at a table and ordered dinner. Wapiti was slowly looking around the room. Just about every set of eyes was on him. "Ya know, Marshal, maybe we should get our food and go to our rooms."

"Now Wapiti, why would you want to do that?" Shawn held up his empty beer glass.

"Because, the way they're all looking at me. You'd think it was me that scalped their families." He didn't have to keep looking at them to know they were still checking him out. He could feel their eyes on him. It made the hair on the back of his neck stand up. He couldn't help but scratch it.

Shawn couldn't help but chuckle. "Well, I suppose I could hurry a little. I would like to get an early start in the morning. We'll pick up supplies in John Day tomorrow."

The two sat in mostly silence. The food sure was good, Wapiti thought to himself. He just wished he was eating around a less hostile group of people. He couldn't remember ever feeling so out of place. He was happy when the Marshal finally finished his meal and the two headed up stairs. Wapiti could still feel every eye in the place on him and it was eerily quiet. It was if someone had just got shot or was about to. Nobody was saying a word.

"Lock your door and bolt your window, son," Shawn said smiling, walking into his room.

"Gee thanks, Marshal." Wapiti answered, walking in his room and looking around. Then doing exactly what the Marshal had suggested.

He took the top blanket, one pillow from the bed, made the bed look like he was sleeping in it. Then Wapiti went and laid down on the backside of the room. If anyone tried to come through the window or door would think he was in bed and they would get both barrels from the ten gauge. He'd have the drop on anyone.

It was to quiet downstairs. Wapiti didn't know just how long he had been laying there when he finally fell asleep. The next thing he

Chapter Four

remembers was the Marshal knocking on his door, telling him it was time to get up and get going. He'd meet him downstairs.

He was going to go make a pot of coffee for them. It didn't take Wapiti long at all to gather up his things and head downstairs. He didn't know what it was that gave him the creeps just being in this town. Kinda like visiting an old Indian burial ground. He'd never been in any town that didn't have a church in it; maybe it had something to do with them calling themselves, "The Dayville Devil's." He didn't know what it was, but he sure would be glad when they got the hell out of this town. The Marshal was just putting the pot of water on the stove as Wapiti walked in.

Speaking in a low voice, well low for him anyway, "Guess these people don't get up too early," Shawn said. "Shoot, I had to go out and split my own wood for the fire. If they think I'm leaving a tip, why they had better think again."

"Coffee does sound good Marshal, but it won't be daylight for at least thirty minutes. So how about I go start loading up so we can get out even sooner." Turning, he headed toward the door, placing his hand on the butt of the sawed off ten gauge. Just then it hit him, he couldn't remember if he had reloaded after his last target practice or not.

"What wrong son, you look a little pale." Shawn said, with a smirk on his face,

"I'm fine," Wapiti answered, turning, he quickly crossed the street and into the livery. Lighting a lamp so he could see what and where he was going. First thing, he checked to make sure no one else was in there, then he checked to see if the gun was loaded, it was. He started loading up the pack mule first, that would take the longest. It seemed like it was taking forever. Where was the Marshal? Why was it taking him so long? Hell, he's usually first up and out before anyone else. He had the mule almost loaded when the Marshal finally came in the livery.

"I left them a note, told them they could find their coffeepot over here." Shawn said, holding up the pot and started pouring each of them a cup.

63

It didn't take them much longer to get loaded and ready to head out. First they each drank one more cup of coffee. Then mounting up, they headed out of town. Looking back, Wapiti still felt uneasy. If he could, he would avoid this town next time... There was some bad spirits in that town, uneasy spirits.

They weren't on the trail ten minutes and the Marshal was talking about last night. There hadn't been any trouble in that place all night and it was all because of who was upstairs. According to him at least, because Marshal Shawn Felton was upstairs sleeping and none of them wanted to be the one to wake him up. His reputation of being in bar room brawls was legendary. He didn't use his guns if he didn't have to. He had hurt a lot of men real bad. Sent them to the doctor, and he enjoyed every bit of it.

They weren't thirty minutes out, when he pulled out his first bottle. Then being a Lawman for over thirty year's, the story telling and bragging started flying about some of the outlaws, in-laws, and every kind of character he had come across over the years.

The Marshal had said they'd make John Day before nightfall if everything went as planned. Wapiti knew even before noon, that wasn't going to happen cause he was well on his way of getting drunk.

Reaching in his saddle bags, Shawn pulled out a couple corn biscuits, "You have your pistol on son?"

"Yes sir Marshal." Wapiti answered, with excitement in his voice.

"Good," Shawn hollered "PULL," and threw two corn biscuits in the air. Wapiti drew and fired as best he could. He hit one, but not the other. The Marshal kept telling him, "learn to draw and shoot straight first, speed will only come with time."

Shawn tried reaching into his saddlebag again, but lost his balance and fell to the ground. Blaming it on his horse, "I think we need to take a little break, son. Get you some more practice in. We'll camp right here tonight." Pointing his finger into the ground, and then leaning backwards with his arms holding himself up.

"Sure thing, Marshal," Wapiti answered, starting to climb off his horse.

Chapter Four

"Oh no! You just stay right on top of that horse. You need to know you can shoot and shoot straight from a horse on the run." Shawn yelled out, throwing another biscuit in the air hollering pull, trying to catch Wapiti off guard. But it didn't work, from half off his horse Wapiti pulled his pistol and blew it out of the sky…"Lucky shot," Shawn yelled taking another pull off his whiskey bottle.

"I'll show you "Wapiti said, reloading his pistol. "This is going to be fun."

"Fun? Fun? Why this just might save your life one day. It has mine, fact, more than a couple of times." Shawn yelled, "PULL," throwing a biscuit and two sticks up in the air.

CHAPTER FIVE

As usual Gary was the first one up. Looking around, he could see that someone had put more wood on the fire during the night. Most likely within the last couple hours. Stretching out, he stood up, picked up the coffeepot and walked down the lakeshore, he glanced around. Man was it peaceful and quiet up here. The daylight was just starting to come up over the horizon. The surface of the lake looked alive as the fish were jumping for breakfast.

Just down the bank about a hundred and fifty yards was a small herd of cow elk and their calves drinking and eating. Filling the pot up, he stood up, shaking his head. Sure was a shame Larry had killed that bull and wasted all that meat. He was right; the other animals had to eat, too. Like Larry said last night, elk was better than trout for dinner anytime. Starting to smile, it was also better for breakfast, too. He thought walking back and put the coffee on. They had only eaten one of the two big back straps and he had buried the other in the snow pack.

Gary walked over and started digging it up. The trouble was he couldn't quite remember where he buried the other back strap. By luck he found it. Walking back to the camp, he was still looking around at all the peace and quiet, which would all be gone when he would have to wake Larry up. What a waste he thought. For once he didn't want to wake him; he started chuckling, as the coffee started to boil.

He was just sitting there in peace and quiet enjoying his cup of coffee and truly enjoying the morning up high in the mountains like

Chapter Five

this. It's too bad you couldn't live up here all year, but for at least five months out of the year your cabin would be under snow.

About ten minutes later that elk meat started smelling real good. Larry and Luis started to stir. "Well hell, there goes the neighborhood." Gary said, pouring each one of them a cup of coffee.

"What the hell you talken about?" Larry said rolling over, and trying to stand up, reaching for his cup. Taking a drink, and stretching out and looking around at the same time. "Sure is beautiful up here isn't it guys?"

"Was peaceful too, till you woke up." Gary said sarcastically.

"Oh, piss off. I sure hope that Roan settles down some today, going over that back side." Larry said, pointing up on the mountain. "In that big bowl there is where the shadow of the Indian face is."

"Now, I now you're full of shit, a shadow of an Indian ... When and where?" Luis asked.

Larry turned and looked at Luis, pointing his hand and arm towards the top of the mountain. "Right up there in that big bowl," Larry said, bragging.

"No, it's not bullshit," Gary said. "Remind me about it next winter and I'll show it to you."

"Why wait till next winter?" Luis asked with a strange look on his face.

"You need the snow pack up there for the shadow. When we get back I'll show you the Chief, Squaw and baby lying down." Gary said pointing around at different mountaintops... "They follow the ridge tops in the morning and evening, just as the sun is rising or setting and you can make out all three. The squaw is real easy to find."

"This I definitely want to see." Luis said, reaching over and tearing some steak off.

Gary stood up and looked at the other two, "Well let's get saddled up."

"What? You aren't even going to let us eat first?" Larry asked, climbing back out of his bed role.

"We can do that while we're loading up." Gary said, walking over to the horses. "I said I wanted to make Sumpter tonight, and like you said Larry, going over that back side can be tricky. For once you might have the best animal to be on."

"Glad you feel that way, you can ride him today." Larry shouted out.

"I don't think so, that big ornery fella's all yours." Gary answered, with a big smile on his face, looking at Luis.

"Gee thanks," Larry said, twisting around, trying to stretch out his sore muscles. "I just hope he settles down soon... Luis, you want to take the first couple hours on him this morning? Maybe try to settle him down a little for me?"

"Hell no, Hombre. I wouldn't get on that caballo for a months wages, yet alone, just so you only get bucked off one or two times less. Just how long you want me to try before he settles down? What two, maybe three times? Just wear him down for you... Forget you, Hombre." He continued saying, as they all were saddling up.

Larry was talking real softly to the big Roan while he saddled him. Which made Gary started chuckling. "Like that's really going to help you."

"SSHH," Larry said, holding his finger over his mouth, and whispering. "Don't get him excited." He gave the cinch an extra pull, before tucking it away.

"I think he already knows Larry," Gary and Luis both said, busting up laughing.

"Ya Amigo, did you see his eyes light up with that last pull?" Luis said pointing into the Roan's eye.

"Sure did," hollered Gary.

Looking around the area, "Well at least it's flat around here." Larry says, putting his foot in the stirrup and swung up into the saddle, anticipating the Roan's first move. Which he didn't make. So Larry turned him and started walking. Looking back at the others, he started chuckling. "He knoooowwws." Just then the Roan hit the sky and sent Larry flying through the lower branches of fir trees and crashing back to the ground. "DAMN, I thought he was going to be good today."

"Guess you were wrong, AGAIN." Gary shouted, as he and Luis climbed aboard their horses. "Well, let's get going." They turned the horses toward the timber. "You can catch up to us when he does settle

68

Chapter Five

down." Still chuckling Gary looked down at Larry still sitting on the ground.

Standing up and knocking the mud off himself, Larry was cursing them as they rode away. Walking over to the Roan, he picked up the reins again. Then looked him face to face, Larry pointed down to his spurs, "You try that again, and you'll feel steel ... Understand?" He walked around and climbed back in the saddle. But this time the Roan didn't hesitate before he went flying in the air. Larry fighting him all the way, yet staying right with his every move. He'd been down this road before; if he could only last a couple more jumps he'll settle down, he thought to himself.

Each buck seemed like a lifetime. After eight plus hard bucks he took off at a dead run through the timber causing Larry to get many of the low branches in the face. He'd try to duck from one but got hit by another. It didn't take them long to catch up with and pass the other's. "I'll catch up with you boys on top." That Roan was on an all out run straight up the mountain.

Both Luis and Gary were starting to laugh; they had heard all the commotion behind them as Larry tried to calm that big horse down. Then in no time at all, that Roan not only caught up to them, but passed them, then disappeared into the timber ahead of them.

"Hell, by the way it sounds up there, he'll be lucky if he gets him stopped at the top." Gary said pointing

"I don't think that caballo will ever like anyone on his back." Luis said, taking a drink off his canteen. "Maybe we can talk Larry into putting him in the Haines stampede this summer."

"I'm not sure Larry will still be riding him then. Hell a couple more days like yesterday and he'll shoot that Roan." Gary said.

"Really Hombre, you think Larry would really shoot him?" Luis asked seriously.

"NO, I was just joking," Gary said. "We get over by John Day and he might buy a different horse and turn that Roan back to the wild where he belongs. You never know."

It was proving to be a hard climb up the mountain. Fact some areas were so steep, they had to get off their horses and walk. Hanging on to their horse's tails, and being pulled up the mountain. They could see that Larry and the Roan had come this way. The trail they were leaving, a blind man could read. Larry wasn't leading that Roan, that Roan was flat gett'en with it.

Gary was impressed. By the size of the strides he wasn't slowing down much. Larry was a lucky man, it was all him and Luis could do just to hang on, as they climbed and crawled up the mountain. Sure they rode when they could, but there sure wasn't enough of that. Hell, it took them a good two and a half to three hours before they finally made it to the top. Looking around for Larry, wondering just where he might be.

Luis and Gary couldn't believe the view. You could see the large Baker Valley behind them and the Sumpter Valley down in front of them. They could also see them gold dredges working their way back and forth across the Sumpter Valley.

"Damn," Gary said. "You know how many times I fished that Powder River down there? If I had only picked me up a gold pan… Hell, I could be rich enough to buy all Baker Valley back there." Pointing at the trail that lay ahead of them. "I figure we work our way down this shell rock till we get to Twin Lakes. We can stop there and take a quick bath, … cold … but we'll be clean when we get in to Sumpter. While everyone there is waiting in line for a luke warm bath. We'll already have all the good-looking women for ourselves. While everyone else is waiting in line for a bath"

Luis pointed on down the trail, just ahead of them. "Here comes Larry now. Looks like maybe he found a way down off here."

Larry couldn't help but laugh as he came riding up. Looking over at the two, who were both, covered with mud and dirt from climbing up the side of the mountain. "What's wrong with you two? Couldn't your horses handle the trail up? Hell, me and this big boy have been up here for almost an hour waiting for you."

"Well, just what the hell have you been doing? You wouldn't happen to have a bottle on ya? Would ya?" Gary asked, "We're half frozen."

Reaching down into his saddlebag, Larry pulled out a three quarter full bottle and tossed it to him. 'Here, just don't drink it all, IT IS my last one."

Chapter Five

"Thanks." Gary said, pulling the cork and took a swallow then handed it to Luis. "I knew you still had a bottle stashed somewhere. So mister high and mighty, did your big strong Roan find us a way off this mountain yet?"

"Sure did," Larry pointed back behind him. "There's a real nice trail about quarter mile back, looks like an old cow trail. It'll drop us out just above Twin Lakes. Then hell, you know as well as I do, from Twin Lakes to Sumpter is just maybe a three to four to hour ride."

"Good," Gary said, climbing aboard his horse. Taking the bottle back from Luis. "I'll hang on to this, so we'll have enough to help us warm up after we take our baths in that ice cold lake."

"You joking? Taking a bath in those lakes? Hell, the upper lake is still mostly under snow pack. We'll freeze our asses off. Why not wait till we get to Sumpter and get a nice hot bath?" Larry yelled out.

Turning his horse down the ridge and looking back. "We'll be hours waiting in line for a hot bath," Gary said. "You know that, and I want to unwind a little."

"Well at least give me my bottle back," Larry said. "I'm thirsty."

"What the hell you carry that canteen for?" Gary said pointing. "Just for looks?"

"No, I usually fill it up too. I drank it the first night out while me and this fine horse here were running around in the dark wearing him out." Larry reached out his hand for the bottle.

"Hell no," Gary said. "I told you, I want it to help warm us up after we jump into that cold water."

It didn't take long and the Roan was back fighting with Larry, He was still trying to see who the boss really was. It was all Larry could do to keep him under control. Looking around, the only thing Larry could see was just how far down the side of the mountain it was before the timberline started. Where you might come to a stop if you got thrown. If he didn't get out from behind of everyone before they took the cow trail down. Get this Roan in front where he wants to be, if not, he just might end up down there. Turning him up hill, Larry gave him a small kick in the side. That damned horse jumped straight up the hillside. It was lucky he was ready for it or he would be picking himself up off the ground again. It was only a couple jumps later and he had past everyone and heading down the mountain, at a speed that was even a little to fast for Larry. He knew the Roan was as sure-footed as a mountain goat, or he better be. He thought, looking down the side of the mountain again. Then looking back at the others. "You can't miss the trail down. We'll see you at the lower lake." Then turning, he let the Roan have the rein to go.

Gary and Luis both were glad their horses didn't even want to try and keep up with Larry. They both couldn't help but look over the edge. "Damn, it's a long way down if that horse misses a step." Gary stated, pointing down.

"I hear ya Amigo; I meant it when I said you couldn't give me a year's wages to ride that caballo." Luis said worriedly, looking down the side of the mountain.

They both started chuckling, as they followed Larry's trail. Which again was real easy. That Roan was flat tearing up the ground, literally. They each trusted the footing of their horses but not at that speed and not in this country. It was well known to everyone that Larry was more than a little crazy, so that horse fit him just fine.

The two talked all the way down. Larry was right, the trail down was easy to find and follow. However it was only about two feet wide at it's widest point and steep as hell, one wrong move and it would all be over. They were glad when they finally reached the bottom of the shale rock, and back into the timber to a flatter and much easier ride to the lower lake.

They rode up to where Larry was already taking a bath and noticed he already had a fire going. "Why the fire?" Gary asked as he and Luis climbed off their horses and started unsaddling them.

"Cause this water is cold as hell, and when I get out I want to get warmed up as soon as possible…You'll see when you get in here." Larry said, walking out of the water and back up to the fire. "Now give me my bottle back."

Walking down to the lake and taking his cloths off, "You'll just have to wait till we get out." Gary shouted, diving into the lake. Coming up from under the water and screaming. "DAMN, this water is cold."

Chapter Five

Luis walked up to the edge and stuck his foot in, then instantly pulled it out. "DAMN, you sure we can't wait till Sumpter?"

"There's only one way in, that is all at once," Gary demanded. "If you try and walk in, we'll be here all day. So just jump in and get it over with."

"Alright," Luis answered, taking off his clothes and reluctantly jumping into the lake.

Neither he nor Gary either one wasted any time getting washed up and out of the water. Then they both ran up to the fire. Looking around, Gary could see Larry had already been going through his gear looking for that bottle. Walking over to where the horses were tied up at he reached into a bush where he retrieved the bottle. Then returning to the fire, taking a drink before passing it over to Luis. "Now hurry up and get dressed. I want to get out of here as soon as possible."

"Hurry, hurry, hurry, that's all you know. You need to take time to smell the flowers." Larry said, waving his hand around. "Besides I'm already dressed and ready to go, so you're not waiting on me."

"Is that all you two ever do?" Luis asked. "Fight? I mean hell you can't even talk to each other in a normal voice. You have to holler at each other all the time like a couple old ladys!"

"That's the only way to get him to listen," Gary said pulling his pants on.

"ME," Larry hollered. "YOU"RE THE one who won't listen to anything."

"If you ever had anything to say that didn't get us into trouble, I might listen. Here Luis, throw me that bottle," Gary ordered. "I'd like at least one more drink before its empty."

"Piss off, a-hole," Larry said, grabbing his gear and walking over to the Roan. "Just keep it; I'll get another when we get to Sumpter."

"What? You don't have another one hid someplace in all your gear?" Gary shouted at Larry, watching him saddle up.

"Even if I did, I damned sure wouldn't tell you." Larry said, tightening up the cinch. "I'll see you two down the trail." He climbed up into the saddle, and damned if that Roan wasn't scared from all the yelling and he took to the air, again, almost loosing Larry. But Larry grabbed the saddle horn pulled himself back down and put his spurs into the Roan. Which was even a bigger mistake. That Roan's body went in ten different directions at the same time, sending Larry flying back into that ice-cold lake. Standing up and shaking himself off a little, he hollered at Gary, "Damn, if that just don't piss me off. If it's not you…" shaking the water off, "If it's not you pissing me off, then it's this damned horse that Dude told me to take." Larry said, walking up out of the water. Everyone was trying not laugh at him, but what made it even worse was when that Roan held its head high in the air and started whining at him, as if he was joining in on the joke.

"That'll cool ya off?" Gary shouted, doing his best not to bust up into total laughter.

Larry started talking to himself walking up to the Roan, "Piss off, I don't care anymore." Reaching out Larry grabbed the Roan's reins. "You want to play? Then let's play." Putting his foot in the stirrup, he climbed aboard, waiting for the Roan. After about ten maybe fifteen seconds, the Roan once again whinnied holding up his head. Then turning, he started walking down the trail.

Pissing Larry off even a little more, then again maybe the Roan was going to settle down. Starting to laugh at himself and everything that had just happened he looked back at the other two, who were just climbing on their horses. "Hey guys, is there at least one swallow left in that bottle?"

Gary pulled it up and looked. "Ya, there's just one good shot left and you deserve it." He kicked his horse and pulled up along side Larry. "Sorry Bro, but I wish you didn't drink so damned much."

"Don't worry about it," Larry answered smiling. "But from now on, NO ONE, and I mean NO ONE takes the lead away from the Roan. I'm tired of trying to hold him back. As long as you stay behind him, maybe he'll settle down some."

"Alright," Gary answered, slapping Larry across the back, and then falling back in line, it was easy riding following the creek down the hill for just over a mile before it flowed into Deer creek. From there they turned and cut off through the timber. It took them about an hour before they came out of the timber and into the big grass valley.

Chapter Five

Gary figured they where just about in the middle of Sumpter Valley. From there they figured it to be maybe an hour plus ride into Sumpter. "Looks like we'll get in just before dark." Gary said to the others.

"So you figure about an hour then?" Luis asked.

"Forty-five minute's anyway," Gary said, chuckling and pointing up at Larry. "I think he's still a little pissed off."

"Ah hell, he'll dry off before we get to town." Luis hollered loud enough for Larry to hear, just to see what kind of reaction he'd get, if any. Which he didn't.

The three rode down the trail in silence. It only took them twenty minute's to catch back up to the main road, where the train tracks ran along side it. From now on the trail would be easy going, just had to watch out for some crazy miner saying they were on his claim. The three kicked their horses in the side and took off at a good gallop. Every now and then they would jump a couple deer or a small flock of birds. Larry couldn't help but notice the Roan was enjoying himself. When the others had to go around a log or brush pile, the Roan just flew over the top of them. Larry was enjoying this run as well. It was actually the first time he could see where they were going, not going straight up or down a mountain.

Looking back Larry could see the others were falling back, he chuckled a little. "Come on guys," he hollered back. Then kicked the Roan again and really took off across the valley.

In no time at all they could hear the sound of one of the dredges digging up the ground. They pulled up on their reins and stood and watched the dredge for a couple minutes. It really was a beautiful grass valley that went on for a long distance. It was at least a mile wide and fifteen plus miles long. That dredge was leaving nothing but piles of rock behind it, from one side of the valley to the other, slowly working its way towards Sumpter, which was on the top end of the valley.

Turning their horses, they headed up the main road. It wouldn't be long now and they'd be in town with plenty of beer, whiskey, women, song, and lots of party'en. They could smell the smoke from all the chimneys and open fires as they rode up to the edge of town.

They couldn't believe how many people had moved up here. This used to be a nice small logging community, maybe a hundred people. Now look at it, more people than down in Baker City. Hell, at least half the log yard was covered with tents. Now there was hundreds of tents everywhere there was room to put one up. People had clotheslines running from one tent to another. While some people were taking baths in that ice cold Cracker Creek before it poured into the Powder River. There still weren't too many new buildings in town yet, but what was new was a whole lot of Saloons and Brothels, they were going up everywhere. The three figured there was at least eight thousand people, maybe more. It was like this all over the west, whenever someone struck it rich on gold, every idiot from hundreds, hell thousands of miles away came running. Hoping they to might strike it rich. Nothing but a bunch of idiots, they all thought. Chasing after a dream like that. Hell the only ones that were getting rich was the ones who were lucky enough to get a job on one of them dredges or as a carpenter building these Saloons and Brothels.

"How'd you like to live like that?" Larry asked pointing around.

"No thanks," answered Gary as the three rode up to the livery stable. "I'd rather live in a logging camp any day. Least there you know you're going to eat at the end of the day."

"I hear ya," Luis cut in as they rode up to the livery. "You also have firewood to keep you warm at night. Why you taking off your guns for Hombre?" He asked Larry.

"You joking? With all those drunken idiots around here? Anyone of them might want to start a gunfight. Hell, I don't mind a fist fight… but you never know who might be just a little faster and shoot a little straighter than you. No sir, I have my knives if I need them." He looked at some of the drunkards falling down in the streets, not realizing he was thinking out loud, "Hell that could be me in a few hours."

"What do you mean could be? Hell I know it will be," Gary shouted out. "But how about this time you don't make too big a fool of yourself?"

"Ah, take a chill pill will ya; I just want to have a little fun is all. Larry said. "Why do you think I suggested we take our baths back

Chapter Five

there at Twin Lakes? We're already cleaned up and I hear they just brought in a new shipment of young ladies in over at the Elkhorn Saloon and Brothel and I haven't had a nice lady in quite a while."

"That's cause you have to pay them just to get near you, Hombre." Luis said

"Oh Bullshit," Larry answered, taking a receipt for their horses and gear.

The three started walking across the street, and up one block. "Hell they can't keep their hands off me." Larry said, tucking his shirt in, chuckling. "Shit they don't even charge me, after I finish with them. Why hell, they all want to get married."

The three walked up to the door; they all took one more look around town. "That gold strike sure has brought a whole lot of people to what once was a peaceful town." They turned and walked into the saloon, which was full of hopeful miners and some loggers. That beer sure was going to taste good; they had had all the whiskey they could handle for awhile.

"There's a table," Larry pointed toward the back. No sooner than they got sat down when a young lady came up to the table, putting her arm around Larry's shoulder. "What can I get you boys?"

"Told ya, Luis." Larry said putting his arm around her slinder waist. "Out of the three of us, who did she put her arm around first?" starting to chuckle. "Ya darling, we'll take a bottle and three no, make that four beers. One for you as well if you're not busy. We'll see what else I might need a little later if you know what I mean?"

"Alright, Sweetie," She answered leaning over and gave him a kiss on the cheek. "I'll be right back."

"Hey darling," Larry hollered at her. "Could you get us a box of chips, too?"

"Sure thing sweetie," She yelled back.

"Told ya, Luis, She's already calling me sweetie." Larry looked back towards her, "I sure hope she gets back soon. I'm thirsty." He says, adjusting his hat and licking his lips.

"Hell Larry, you're always thirsty," Gary said. "You got your cards Luis?"

"Ya, I do. So how much are the chips going to be worth?" Luis asked, taking the cards out of his vest pocket.

"Nothing," Larry said. "I'm saving my money for beer and women."

"Shit Larry, why don't you just take her upstairs and get it over with? Instead of spending all that extra money on drinks?" Gary stated.

"Ah hell Gary, you got to get to know them first." Larry said, still looking for her to see if she was coming back yet.

"Come on, you two," Luis butted in, "let's play some cards."

"Fine." Larry turned back to the table. "But like I said, I'm not playing for money. Hell, I never win any how."

Just then the young lady returned to the table, sitting down four glasses of beer, one bottle of whiskey, and four shot glasses. "So you did say you was going to buy me a drink too?" She asked, setting down on Larry's lap.

"Hell, I already said I would. What the hell else you want?" Larry said jokingly.

"Well, now then, what else can I get?" she asked, kissing him on the cheek.

"We'll just have to wait and see darling. For right now, how about you count out these chips. That way it will look like we're playing for real money, and make these two happy. Second thought how about you go get us another pitcher of beer so we don't run out."

Watching her walk away, Larry took a good second look at her. She was maybe five feet two inches, "MMM," maybe one hundred ten-pound, beautiful long black hair and big brown eyes. Reaching over and slapping her on the ass, "hurry back darling, I've been all alone for too long."

She looked back at him smiling. "Well, stop sending me away for things and maybe we'd get to know each other better."

"Ya, Ya," Larry said, turning back to the others. "Hell, just how well do I have to know her to get what I want? I mean hell; I don't want to get married." Larry started, piling up his chips.

"What the hell would give her an idea like that? You... getting married?" Gary asked

Chapter Five

"HELL NO! I ain't even going there, no way- no how. I'm not like you, Gary. I'm not a one woman man." Larry shouted out.

"What's wrong with wanting just one lady to share your life with?" Gary asked, shuffling the cards.

"Nothing, if that's what you want. I want to play with as many as I can, while I can. Right Luis?" Larry said chuckling; filling everyone's shot glass.

"You know it Amigo," Luis shouted, toasting a shot of whiskey with Larry. "Now how about you two stop arguing and let's play some cards?"

"Fine," Larry answered, still looking across the saloon to see if that young lady was returning yet. "Here give me that bottle so I can get the night started off right."

"Here you go, Amigo." Luis asked, "You know what I'd like to know Gary?"

"No, what's that, Luis?" Gary asked, dealing the cards.

"Why is it that Larry always has to have the whiskey bottle in his hand?" Luis said.

"I just like to know where it is whenever I need a drink is all," Larry answered, filling his and Luis glasses back up.

Just then the young lady returned and put the pitcher of beer down. She sat back down on Larry's lap. The four had grown to five as another young lady came over and joined them. Sitting on Luis lap. Gary was being real picky as usual.

As it started getting later, more and more people were coming into the saloon. All talking about how their day had gone. No one had stuck it rich yet. Most of them wanted to join in on their game, but quickly changed their minds when they found out no money was involved. The five had been playing, joking and having a lot of fun for a couple hours. When two men came walking up to the table, dressed up as cowboys. Right off everyone knew the only cowboy'en those two had done was in between bank job's, if any real cowboy'en at all.

"You boys mind if we set down?" the shorter, stockier one asked.

"Nope, not at all." Gary said, pushing a chair out with his foot.

"So you men from around these parts?" The shorter man asked, setting down.

"You could say that. Gary answered, dealing a new hand of cards. "We've either logged or ranched most of this country before the gold strike. There isn't much about this country we don't know."

"So which one do you do, log or ranch?" The taller of the two asked.

"Well it depends on which one pays better, or what time of the year it is." Gary answered.

"Ya, you can make better money logging," Larry said. "But it's a whole lot warmer going down to Baker Valley in the winter. That's when you get a ranching job."

Then one of the cowboys stuck out his hand towards Larry. "I'm Leroy Parker and this is Harry Longbaugh." As they all shook hands and everyone introduced themselves.

"Well hell," Larry shouted, in a loud, but low voice. "Why we're sitting here with royalty."

"What the hell you talking about?" Gary asked.

"WHAT, you trying to tell me you don't know who these men really are?" Larry asked

"Ya, that one is Leroy, and that one's Harry." Gary answered, pointing at each one.

"You dumb shits," Larry answered leaning over the table, speaking in a low voice and pointing. "That's Butch Cassidy, and that's The Sundance Kid."

"Well now, I know you're plum loco," Luis said laughing. "What the hell would big famous banditos like them be doing up here?"

"Well how the hell would I know?" Larry said, leaning back in his chair, and waving his hand. "Why don't you ask them yourself?"

Luis looked back over to the two men. "He is plum loco right...? You're not really who he say's you are, are you?"

"Ya, we've been known by those names now and then. Leroy or Butch answered. "But we try not to let it out when we're scoping out a job."

"Scoping a job?" Gary picked up his new hand of cards. "Just what kind of job would you be planning up here?"

Chapter Five

"What the hell you think they're hoping to rob?" Larry answered. "Hell, they think they're going after that train."

"Well, you boys interested in making some extra money?" Harry asked, picking up his cards, and leaning back.

"Nooo, not that way." Larry said. "Hell, Dude would kick our asses. Maybe we could help out in other ways. For a small fee."

"Who's Dude?" Sundance asked.

"He's our Grandpa, when we were little our Dad was killed in a logging accident. He helped our mom raise us." Gary answered

"So which one of you is it that's from Utah?" Larry asked. "I can't remember."

"I am," Butch said, throwing two cards back towards the dealer. "Why you ask?"

"Just going to say, I know why the hell you left there." Larry said

"Cause, I drove a herd of cattle from Denver through Salt Lake City, isn't it? Larry asked.

"Ya, that's the name of it, why?" Butch asked back.

Looking over at the others. "Cause that country is plum messed up. You can't even get a beer there." Larry shouted out, picking up his beer and taking a drink.

"Oh Bullshit, Larry," Gary said. "There you go again with one of your stories"

'No, he's right," Butch said, with a smile on his face. Their religion don't allow them to drink."

"That must have been pure hell for you, Larry," Luis shouted out, laughing.

"Worse than that, those guys have three, four or more wives, too," Larry said with excitement in his voice, taking another nice long drink off his beer.

"Now, I know you're full of shit Larry." Gary said, downing the last of his beer.

Again, Butch looked over at Gary, "Nope, he's right, again."

Gary leaned back in his chair, "You're crazy, ain't that against the law."

"Not down there it's not," Larry shouted, discarding three cards. "Hell, I couldn't believe it either till I saw it first hand."

"Ah hell," Gary said with a small smile on his face. "You're both just pulling our legs."

"No, really," Butch said. "Fact my dad has five wives and his dad had nine."

"Now, I know you're full of shit," Gary shouted out. "How the hell could you put all them women and kids in one house?"

"Oh, that's the best part; each wife has her own house," Butch answered. "So you get tired of one, just go over to one of the other houses."

"So, what you're saying is…" Gary started, looking around the table. "If one won't give it up, then you just go over to one of the others?" he was laughing so hard he could hardly sit in his chair.

"Yep, and that's just what most of them do." Butch answered, as everyone started laughing.

So how many wives do you have, Hombre?" Luis asked.

"Me…? None… I'm not real welcome back there you might say." Butch answered, with a smile on his face.

"Well, gee whiz. I wonder why?" Gary stated. "I mean hell, you're only wanted in half the country for robbing banks and trains."

"Give us a little longer and we'll be wanted in the other half too." Sundance said.

"Well, I guess not all of your stories are all bullshit, Larry," Gary admitted. "Some of them are actually true."

"Ah, piss off Gary," Larry answered. "I know what I'm talking about… Well sometimes I do."

Butch leaned over towards Gary, "I'm not quite sure just which one you are, Gary or Larry. But you seem to be the one with the brain between you two."

"Hey," Larry shouted. "Watch what you're saying there bud."

Butch looked back and forth between the two again. "Well, like I was starting to say, if you were thinking of trying to take that train. Where would you stop it? Then, how would you get out of here afterwards? That's if you've ever thought about it."

"Hell, who hasn't thought of it? Gary answered chuckling, Hell, I think everyone around these parts has day dreamed about that… But

Chapter Five

I'd take it just at the start of the canyon; it narrows down real tight right there. They have to slow down because of the cliffs and turns next to the river."

"After the robbery, I'd send half the guys back this way. Have them go through Whitney and out through John Day. The others should go down over Dooley Mountain, to the other side. Once you get to the valley and river on the other side of the mountain, follow the river east; through Blacks Canyon till you come to a little cow town of Durkey. There's a stage stop there, they have good food, so stop and get a meal. Then keep following the river through the Burnt River gorge. That will bring you to the Snake River. Take the road to Ontario, cross over to Idaho, then your free to go wherever. If you ride fast enough, you can make it in a couple days."

"Ya, then you can head back to that good for nothing country of Utah where your from." Larry say's, pouring everyone another round of whiskey.

"You better watch out what you say, Larry," "Gary said. " These men don't know you and might take offence of you cutting down their homeland. I know I would."

"Ah hell, you boys can take a joke, can't you?" Larry asked with a questionable look on his face.

"Well I can," Sundance said smiling. "But Butch does get a little touchy at times."

"Ah, come on guys, Larry shouts out, I'm just having a little fun. Besides, you said yourself you didn't like it down there."

"Don't worry about it," Butch said. I'm just fun-nun with ya is all. BUT, I didn't say I didn't like it. I said I wasn't too welcome back there. But I can see why you don't carry a gun."

"Why's that?" Larry asked.

"Cause, your mouth could get you into trouble real quick." Sundance answered

"Ya, Ma always told us, and I quote, "Don't let your ass over run your mouth "in other words, think before you speak. But you can see he doesn't listen to well." Gary told Butch.

83

"Well, I suppose we all need to be able to take a little joking." Butch answered

"Thanks," Larry said, as his face turned a bright red from embarrassment; with a small smile on his face.

"I can see how you could piss someone off and start a fight," Sundance added.

"Oh hell, it wouldn't be my first fight, and I doubt like hell it will be my last." Larry say's, starting to chuckle. I'm not afraid to finish what I start, when I have to.

"Ya, but its no fun watching you get the shit kicked out of yourself." Luis said. "Fun is watching your brother Randy, now that's fun."

"Why's that?" Sundance asks.

"Cause, you can't hurt him." Gary say's

"Ya," hollered Larry. "He likes to get them big men, the bigger the better. Then he literally kicks the shit out of them."

"Really," Sundance answered, as he was finding this hard to believe, because neither one of them was five feet seven, maybe eight at the most, and only, maybe, one hundred fifty plus pounds.

"When he finishes with them, they need a doctor." Luis say's, with a serious look on his face. REAL BAD to Dude!

"He's that good uh." Butch asks

"He has this temper. Gary say's, looking both men in the eyes. I swear his eyes turn deep red. Blood red! When he's done with them, there's blood all over the place."

"Ya... Their's," Larry hollered, "Then they go over to visit Doc Bones."

"Doc Bones... who's Doc Bones?" Butch asks

"Oh, that's not his real name. Gary answers, starting to smile. It's just that's what Larry started calling him a couple years ago when we all three came up here to log... and well, it stuck."

"Why you call him Doc Bones?" Sundance asked, looking at the three strangely.

"Cause," Larry said, filling his beer up. "Cause when Randy finishes with them, that's what he has to do... Fix their bones, usually a whole bunch of them."

Chapter Five

"Just how big is this brother of yours? What six foot, three hundred pounds?" Butch asks, throwing a blue chip on the table. "I'll raise fifty dollars."

"What the hell you talking about raising fifty bucks? Gary shout's out. That ain't worth fifty cents."

"What the hell you talking about?" Sundance said, looking a little confused. "That ain't even worth fifty cents?"

"Just what I said. Gary repeated, "that ain't worth fifty cents." If we were playing for money, we'd have money on the table, not chips." Gary slowly looked around the table, taking a drink off his beer.

"Now you just wait a minute there," Butch said. "I don't know just what you two look alike twins are up to, but the young lady that was setting on his lap earlier when we set down sold us five thousand dollars worth of chips."

"WHAT?"... Larry kicked his legs up in the air and busted up laughing. "I wondered why she took off after you guys got here. But hell, I just figured she didn't like you... Didn't know she ripped you off. Damn and I thought I was going to get lucky tonight too."

"You did." Butch said, looking around the table. "She ripped us off, not you."

"Your right, Mr. Cassidy," Larry answered, leaning back in his chair with the bottle of whiskey. "Cause none of us have even half that much between us to loose."

"Well, I have to admit, we did just talk to her before we set down, while she was on one of your beer runs. So any way, lets get back to this brother of yours, hell neither one of you are very big. So just how big is this... Randy?" Sundance asked

Gary looked over at them, "that's just it, he's only five feet, five inches tall, and maybe one seventy five."

"No he's not," Larry shouted out. "He's five, five and a HALF inch's tall.... He always says it's that extra half inch that they don't expect that gets them every time."

"So what makes him so mean? Does he drink like this one?" Sundance asked, pointing at Larry.

"Nope... not at all," Gary answered. "Fact, he hardly drinks at all, but he stutters sometimes when he gets excited. People start laughing at him, and he just looses it."

"What's he do for work...?" This monster of a man." Butch asked, starting to- chuckle.

"He runs a team of horses, skidding logs, six of them... all Clydesdales." Gary answered

"Six," Butch shouted. "I've seen them use two or three, but six? Just how many logs does he get with each drag? Better yet, how the hell does a man that small control that many horses at once?"

"Told ya... he's half crazy," Gary answered, reaching for his new hand of cards. "Fact, he flat lets each and everyone of those monsters know who's in charge to."

"Who trains them to pull as a team?" Sundance asked.

"The same man that trains eighty percent of the horses in this part of the country." Larry stated firmly, raising two blue chips.

"Who's that? And just how much are those two blue chips going to cost me?" Butch asked.

"Well, it's going to cost you two blue chips. How many times do we have to tell you we're not playing for money?" Gary said, throwing in two white chips. "They're all worth the same and the horse trainer is Dude... Our grandpa."

"So just how mean and crazy is he? I mean hell, you boys had to learn how to bullshit from someone," Sundance said.

"Ya think?" Larry said. "Actually, I think it's a family trait, tell ya the truth. I think we're born with it. The ability to tell a good bullshit story I mean."

"Well, one thing he did teach us, was never bite off more than you can chew and stand up for what's right." Gary added.

"You boys sure you don't want in on this job? It would be real nice to have someone along that knows the country." Sundance asked again, throwing three cards over. "That way we could get out of this country quicker."

"Done told ya how," Larry said, pointing in the direction of the road. "Ride down river till you see the bald ridge, go through the saddle

86

Chapter Five

between it and the mountain just west of it. When you get over the top and reach the valley below, you'll come up on Burnt River. Just follow it through Black's canyon. Then follow that river to the Snake River, then onto Idaho. Make sure you stop and eat in Durkey. That lady puts a nice spread out. From there I figure you can find your way back to Utah."

"We can find our way from Ontario," Butch answered. "But with your knowledge of the area, hell you boys could save us half days traveling time. Besides, it sounds like you boys could use the money."

"We already have something we have to do," Gary said. "And that kind of money we don't need." He stated, leaning back in his chair.

"You just ain't a whistling Dixie," Larry shouted out. "Dude would kick our asses from here to tim-buck-too and back.

"Then he'd kick my ass for letting you get in on the job." Luis added, "And that's one man," looking around the table, "I WOULD not want mad at me." Raising one red chip.

"How much is that chip worth?" Sundance asked, reaching for a red chip. "And what's this job you have to do?"

"How many times we have to tell you? Gary say's firmly. "That chip don't cost you anything, but one more red chip, and as to your other question." Marshal Felton killed our cousin earlier this week, and we're going to find out why."

"Hell he didn't just kill him," Larry shouted out. "He blew his ass from here to hell and back, They said there was at least fifty large cases of nitro in that wagon. Hell our Aunt couldn't even have a funeral. They said you couldn't tell were the horse flesh ended and the human flesh began."

"You guys are planning to go up against the great Marshal Shawn Felton himself? Butch asked, with a smirk on his face. Hell, you boys Polish or something?"

"As a matter of fact we are. The other half is Irish. Gary say's proudly, setting full up in his chair. We get mad and do something stupid, or we do something stupid and get mad. Either way somebody will be hurt'en in the morning."

87

"Still, going up against Felton takes guts." Sundance say's

"Well, he's known for bringing them in over the saddle. HIM... Being Judge, Jury, and Executioner! We want to know what the circumstances were. Why he had to kill them that way." Larry stated

"Well good luck to ya, Sundance say's. But let me get something straight here, these chips aren't worth a damn thing? He asks, holding one up and looking at it. Just how the hell do you know who the winner is at the end of the night?"

"Whoever has the most chips at the end of the night is the winner." Luis say's

"Winner of what?" Butch asks.

"Winner of the poker game. This way the only money you spent was on drinks. Which speaking of, I do believe it's your turn to buy the next round. Isn't it? Hell you boys should be thankful we let you into our high dollar game. It's the least you can do." Larry said. "Still, I am sorry that little Betty ran off with all that money of yours. Fact I've been keeping my eyes open for her, just in case she's still around."

"How about you boys help us out a little on this job and we'll call it even?" Butch say's, paying the waitress. "We pretty much figure that the gold they load everyday really isn't the real stuff."

"Your right about that, Gary say's with a big smile on his face. That's just for show. They really only take it down once a week. But I'm here to tell, they get fifty plus bags a week, and each bag weighs fifty pounds."

"They really pull that much gold out of the ground around here?" Butch asks, with amazement in his eyes.

"What the hell you think those big dredges are for?" Larry asked. "Just look at how much of that valley they've already mined. Shit, I don't think they've even been up here a year yet. That ground is chucked plum full. Some of the men off one dredge said they had one piece that was at least four foot in diameter go completely a crossed the top deck and back into the ground before they could get shut down."

"I see what you mean, when you say he's full of shit." Butch say's, starting to chuckle, and looking at the others.

Chapter Five

"No, I can't believe it myself, Gary speaks up, but he's right again. I know the man who told him the story. The entire top deck crew on the dredge all verified the same story. But they just can't stop fast enough, or turn them around in the dredge path, so they had to leave it. Hell the smallest screen in those things is one inch, so everything one inch and smaller is going right back into the ground. Ya know guys; I have to say I'm sorry that young lady ripped you off all that money".

"Ah hell Gary, we've lost more than that gambling before, Sundance say's. Besides, it's been a lot of fun playing cards and bullshitting with you men tonight. Who knows, we just might talk you into helping us after all."

"Five thousand is a hell of a lot of money to us, Gary answers. We'll be glad to help plan it, and I might know some good men you can trust to help you, but like I said, we're not interested in joining you."

"Well hell, if everything works out we'll end up with a hell of a lot more than that five thousand in a couple days. That's if we can find out how and when they load the real gold." Then looking back over at Sundance, "ya know Sundance I can't tell which one of them is uglier... shit, I've seen twins before, but there's always something that tells you which one is which. But these two... I can't tell."

"Now you just wait one minute," Larry hollers, "we're both good looking. Its just I'm better looking."

"Now let's don't be getting personnel," Gary said, "You two don't look all that good to me either. Fact is, not only are you ugly, but you don't have the right equipment for me." He said.

"Ya know Butch, I think that one is the smart one of the two," Sundance said, pointing to Gary.

"Maybe your right Sundance, but that one can sure put the liquor away," Butch said, pointing to Larry.

"That's me!" Larry held up the bottle. "This is what we call ANTI-FREEZE up here. For those cold nights like tonight when you have to sleep outside. Even that hay loft above the Livery is going to be cold tonight."

"Anti- freeze?" Butch busted up laughing. "I've heard it called a lot of things, but never anti-freeze."

Taking a big pull off the bottle, Larry looked back at the two out-laws. "You drink enough of it, and you don't realize just how cold it is outside. Least not till you wake up and see the fires gone out."

"Ya, Hombre," Luis said, reaching for the bottle. "We don't have five thousand dollars to loose, let alone pay fifty dollars for a room for the night. Fact most folks around these parts don't have that kind of money."

"Hell, sometimes they even charge more than that for a room." Gary said.

"Well hell, you men are alright, Sundance say's, smiling. So why don't you just tell that fat lady at the bottom of the stairs to put your rooms on our bill tonight."

"Thanks," Larry said leaning back in his chair and putting his feet up on the table. "Does a little Betty come with that room, or is it just going to be a warm lonely night?"

"Don't complain, Larry," Gary said. "It beats sleeping out in that cold hay loft".

"Ya, but sure would be a hell of a lot warmer if you had a little Betty in bed with ya, don't you think? Larry say's, looking around the room, like either one of those two over there, he say's pointing.

"Well shit," Sundance answers, chuckling, "you want us to pay for everything? Next thing you know, you'll need us to show you what to do with that little Betty as well."

"Oh no… I can handle that part just fine, Larry snap's back, chuckling. So if you all will excuse me, I'm going to go get me a bed warmer." Standing up from his chair, looked around the room, picked up the bottle, turned and walked towards the two young ladies'.

"Your brother is quite a character." Butch said, chuckling a little.

"Ya, that he is, Gary answered. I wouldn't want anyone else with me if I was to run into trouble,"

"So what happens if he does something stupid? Don't people sometimes think it was you?" Sundance asked

"NOO… Not at all, anyway not those that knows us," Gary said. They know which one is always getting into trouble, sometime with just with his mouth."

Chapter Five

"Ya Amigos," Luis added, "take Gary there," pointing at Larry walking away. "His mouth is always getting him in trouble."

"WOW, just wait one minute, I'm Gary." Gary yelled back.

"Oh hell, I know that Hombre, Luis answered. I'm just trying to mess with their heads is all."

"Well," said Gary, standing up stretching out his arms. "Think I'll take you up on that room."

"What? No little Betty for you? Butch asked.

"No, Amigo," Luis say's, picking up the cards and put them in his pocket. "No, he has a lady down in the valley. Why someone who is not married, won't pick up on a woman when he's out of town, is beyond me." Standing up. "But if that offer for one of those little Betty's extends to me...? I'll be glad to take you up on it."

Butch looked over at Luis, "it does, so go find ya one." Looking back at Gary. "No woman is that special. Hell, you have to have some fun once and awhile."

"Especially when someone else is paying for that little Betty." Sundance said with a big smile on his face.

"Naw, I think this one is worth it," Gary said, reaching out his hand. "It's been a pleasure meeting you men. If you're in town tomorrow evening we might be back, but if not, then you men DON"T get caught. If we're not here and our brother Randy is, talk with him. He'll know how to pull that job off... Fact he's already said as much, said it would be like taking candy from a baby."

"What do you mean by "don't get caught"?" Sundance said, acting surprised.

"Well, I'd tell you to stay out of trouble, Gary said, smiling. But obviously you're not going to stay out of trouble... so just don't get caught."

"You sure you won't at least lead us over the mountain and out to Idaho?" Butch asked. "We'd more than make it worth your time."

"I appreciate the offer, but we're going to pass." Gary said. "Don't worry... your plan won't be told by any of us, till and only after your gone. I hope you understand."

"Ya, we do, Butch answered. Just thought I'd ask one more time. Just in case we don't see each other again, I have to tell you, I don't think we've ever seen so much bullshit flying around a table before.""

"You won't ever see it again, either!" Luis said, shaking their hands. "You men are welcome at my fire anytime." Then he turned and walked away, and Gary headed up the stairs.

CHAPTER FIVE

It was almost seven thirty in the morning when Gary rolled out of bed. Walking over to the table that had a wash bowl and pitcher of water setting on it, he dumped some over his head and looked in the mirror. Rubbing his face and chuckling. He couldn't remember when he had had so much fun and drank that much whiskey and beer. Not to mention sleeping this late. Pouring some more water in the bowl, he began to wash his face. It had been a night to remember. Now things had to get back to being serious.

They were fixing to go up against Marshal Felton. He'd have to watch Larry and his drinking close when they do meet up with him. Getting dressed, he walked out the door, opening the door to the room next to him. He knew Larry was in there because he heard him most the night. Sounded like he was trying to knock the walls down.

Sticking his head in the door, he looked around. "Sorry ma'am. Larry get up and let's get out here. You find Luis and I'll order breakfast and get the horses saddled, and I'll meet you two out front. First I'll go by the Sheriffs office and find out where Miles is logging at... Larry do you hear me?"

"Ya, ya, I hear ya... Just give me a couple minutes will ya?" Larry answered. Pulling his pillow over his head, Dam if my head don't hurt. Every sound anyone made seemed to echo louder than it really was.

93

"Thirty minutes, Larry. Then your ass had better be downstairs ready to go... Understand?"... Gary yelled out, slamming the door behind him and then he walked downstairs.

The next time the three met was outside the saloon. Gary was setting atop his horse with his leg wrapped around the horn of his saddle, drinking a cup of coffee when the other two came outside. "I don't know why the hell we had to get up so early for." Larry said, putting a couple bottles of whiskey in his coat and saddlebag's he had just bought. "Need to get these out of sight before Gary sees them or he'll raise hell".

"Too late! Gary shouted out. What the hell you bringing that along for? Hell, we'll be back tonight... You know that."

"Ah, shut up. Let's get the hell out of here." Larry said reaching for the reins to the Roan, picking up the stirrup, he re-checked the cinch. "Did you at least find out were he's logging at?"

"Well ya, what the hell you think I've been doing?" Gary said, with a smile on his face. "They're just up Cracker Creek a couple miles. So let's get out of here."

"Ya, Ya," Larry said as he and Luis climbed aboard their horses. No sooner had Larry set down in the saddle and that Roan raised up in a full rare. Taking two mighty crow hopes straight up in the air, just clearing the heads of a couple people who just happened to be in the wrong place, at the wrong time, some falling over others so as not to get ran over or kicked. Then that Roan took off like a bullet shot out of a gun, straight down the street and out of town at a full run.

With a big laugh and chuckle, Gary shouts, "Well at least he's heading in the right direction."

"Come on Luis, maybe we can catch up to him in a couple miles," Gary said, turning his horse and starting up the street. No sooner had he finished and Larry and the Roan came running back into town at a full run.

"Well, you coming or not? Larry shouted, pulling on the reins with everything he had. Talk about High-Ho Silver. "He holler's, still trying to get the Roan under control." I've said it once, and I'll say it again. ANYTIME you want to switch mounts you guys let me know. Now

Chapter Five

let's get out of here." Then he turned the Roan up the street and out of town.

Gary and Luis turned their horses and fell in behind Larry, still laughing. "That's not the kind of horse I'd like to start out my morning with." Luis said.

"I hear ya Bro, Gary say's chuckling. But it looks like he's finally starting to settle down a little bit, least he didn't buck this morning."

The three rode out of town in silence, looking around the area.... All up and down the river, every couple hundred yards or so there were tents. People already up working their slue boxes or panning for gold. All hoping on hitting it big. The three continued riding up the river, joking and laughing at all those idiots digging in the ground. Hoping to find that big jackpot of gold. Some of the lucky ones had a tent to sleep in, but there were a lot of lean-tos as well. They were all just about two maybe three hundred feet apart, on both sides of the river.

With them all nursing massive headaches from last night, it hurt to laugh. But sometimes it was hard not to, for once Larry was bringing up the rear. The Roan didn't seem to mind being in back of the others. Every once in awhile when Larry thought Gary couldn't see him, he would take a pull off one of the bottles. It sure curses what ails ya, Larry thought to himself with a small chuckle, sliding the bottle back up his coat sleeve.

As they rode up Cracker Creek they couldn't help but laugh at all the hopeful miners. Some of who were still in their long johns drinking their morning coffee. Some even trying to catch a fish for breakfast.

They had been riding about forty-five minutes when they came up on a camp. Gary hollered back to Larry, "check it out," pointing at a man, who was working his slue box, while his wife, naked as a jaybird was taking a bath in the river. She was almost as wide as she was tall, going at least two hundred plus pounds.

"Maybe he hopes some horny miner or logger will come by and pay him for her," Luis said.

"Well, there you go Luis," Larry said. "You always said any naked woman, any time."

95

"No way, Amigo, not even, she's too fat and too ugly for me." Luis say's

"Ya, maybe so," Gary added, "but I'll just bet you he makes more on her in a day than he does by mining."

"You're probably right." Larry answered; taking another pull off the bottle thinking Gary couldn't see him.

"LARRY, Damn you, put that bottle away or I'll break the damn thing." Gary shouted

"Oh, you just don't worry about it Little Brother, Larry snarls back. It'll be alright. By the way, how much longer till we get to the logging camp?"

"Shouldn't be too much longer, Gary answered. The Sheriff said they were just about an hour, maybe two at most up the river here."

Just then, from out of nowhere they heard a man holler, "T-I-M-B-E-R," as a massive Douglas Fir tree at least two hundred feet high and seven feet through at the butt, came crashing to earth, scaring everyone's horse. The others just reared up and fought back just a little, they'd been around logging before. But the Roan hadn't, and he came unwound, pulling his head and the reins down between his front legs and he went to town.

All the loggers and miners were yelling with great cheer. That Roan went sky high. At least eight plus, mile high jumps. There was Larry, staying right with him, jump for jump, putting his spurs into him. "Come on you son of a gun, you want to buck? You're going to feel my iron," Larry shouted out. Which make the Roan even madder. Then finally after a couple more half as high bucks the big Roan started settling down with only a couple half hearted crow hops, then raring full up, making Larry have to stand almost straight up himself and grabbing a hand full of main, or he would have fallen off. It was as if that big horse was saying he was still the boss

"Sorry," one of the fellers hollered at Larry.

"Ah hell, it's alright," Larry hollered back, chuckling and pulling out his bottle of whiskey and started to holler over everyone's cheers, "He's going to have to get used to it sooner or later, just as well be now." Larry took a big pull off the bottle, then bragging, and shouting out, "This isn't my first time with him." All the people were talking;

Chapter Five

they couldn't believe just how high that horse could fly or even better, "How the hell did that man stay with him?" None of them had any interest in trying that Roan.

Quickly Gary and Luis came riding up, Larry took his hat off, wiping the sweat off his head. "I was hoping that if I had to make a dismount, it would have been in that river there." He say's pointing and chuckling. While the Roan set all bright eyed and still checking his surrounding nervously.

"Hey Hombre, you're getting good at that." Luis said.

"How many times do I have to say it? Larry shouts out, "Anytime you want to change critters, you just say the word."

"No, No… Amigo, Luis say's, I like my horse just fine. Besides, didn't Dude say he still needed a little work? Hell, you keep this up and you'll have him broke before we get back."

"I'm here to tell you he can stop with all this shit just anytime." Larry could see everyone still laughing and carrying on. "You a-holes can all go back to work. The show's over." "Now, let's get going," he said, turning the Roan and heading up river.

"Go where?" Gary asked. "We're there! Hell Randy's setting right over there. He's been watching your show as well." Turning his horse, he rode over to Randy, who was setting on top of a big log; his team of Clydesdales was tied next to him.

"Hey Larry," Randy hollered out. "Why don't you do that again? We haven't had that much excitement around here in a long time, and the Doss's have another tree ready to fall"

Taking another pull off his bottle, Larry looked over at him. "No thanks, twice in one day is enough for me."

"Just where the hell did you get that big ass horse anyway? Randy asked. You look like a kid on a Welch pony." Randy could hardly talk, cause he was laughing too hard and starting to stutter.

"Well, anytime you want to try him, you just come climb aboard Big Boy," Larry answered.

"Naw," Randy answered, taking a big bite off his plug tobacco, then looking over at Gary, "Just where the hell did he get that big Roan anyway?"

"He told Dude he needed a good mountain horse, Gary said, smiling. You see which one he told Larry to take. Watching him try to ride that animal has been a whole lot of fun."

"Did he say he was broke? Randy asked

"No, he said he was still green." Gary answered. That's what makes it so dam funny

"Hell, even I'm smart enough to know if that old man says he's still green, I'm not getting on him." Randy said, looking back at the others, "So what brings you boys up this way?"

"Brad got himself killed over outside Prineville last week," Gary started to say but Randy cut him off, "Hell; we all knew it was going to happen sooner or later."

"Ya, I know but it's the way he got killed." Gary said sincerely

"What happened? He get caught in some woman's bed?" Randy asked

"Noo…Marshal Felton blew him and his friends up in the middle of the Rouge River. They say there was over 50 large cases of nitro, and each case had 24-12ounce bottle's. " Gary said

"WHAT?" Randy shouted. "Blew them up with that much nitro…? Was there anything left?"

"Nope, fact they can't even have any funerals." Gary answered.

"So why'd you come up here?" Randy asked, looking back and forth between the three.

"Well," Gary said, "we were kinda hoping you'd go with us. That's if you're not too busy."

"Not to busy? What the hell you think I do up here all day? PLAY…? Just what are you going to do?" Randy asked

"Well, we figured we'd take us a ride over and ask Marshal Felton a few questions, find out what really happened." Gary answered

"What? You going to go up against Felton?" Randy say's, hell that sounds like some lamebrain idea Larry would come up with.

"Hell Randy, It all depends on what went down…," Gary said sternly,

You know he's known for being Judge, Jury, and Executioner. He brings them back lying over the saddle, NOT setting up."

Chapter Five

"Hell, I don't even have a saddle horse," Randy said. "All I have is my draft team here." Taking another big bite off his plug chewing tobacco.

"Just ride your stallion like you always do," Larry said. Just make up your mind…. You coming or not?" Larry was getting very anxious to go after Marshal Felton.

"Let me take care of those last two drags over there. Then we'll go back into town tonight and talk about it." Randy answered

"Talk about it? Either you are or you aren't. Larry yells at him. What's there to talk about?"

"Well, for one thing, you usually go off all half cocked without thinking it over." Randy snaps back.

"Alright," Gary held his hands up. "Now let's don't be getting mad at each other… Larry, let's just do what Randy suggested. Let him finish up his days work, and then we'll go back into town and talk it over."

"FINE," Larry hollered. "Let's just forget we've already lost our jobs."

"NO WE DIDN"T," Gary shouted back. "You know damn good and well old man Boyer will give us our jobs back."

"FINE, I'm going to go lay over there while you two figure it out." Larry said turning the Roan around and headed for an area where there was a nice grassy area in the shade. Loosening his cinch strap just a little, then he put a pair of hobbles around the Roan's front legs. Turning around, he looked at everyone, "Any of you want to try and steal him… you just go right on ahead and try him out, see how fare you get." Starting to chuckle, laying down at the same time. "NOW… You all just leave me alone, so I can get some rest."

Gary looked at Randy and Luis; "Well he does have a good idea… I haven't partied that much in a long time. Besides, Randy you said you still have work to finish."

"I was going to say you looked hung over and that's usually not like you, Randy said. What happened in town last night?"

"I'll tell you about it later, on the ride back into town… Trust me, you won't believe it, Gary said. So right now, I'm going over and join

99

Larry." Gary led his horse in the same direction. "Wake us when you finish."

"I'd get done a lot faster if I had someone set my chokers for me." Randy said pointing over at the trees.

"Sorry Amigo," "Luis said. Heading in the same direction as Gary. "Like Gary said, you're not going to believe it... And my head still hurts like hell... all the pounding. Why don't you ask those fellers if they could fall those trees a little quieter...? Tell them there's people sleeping over here."

CHAPTER SIX

It was barely dusk out when Shawn woke up. Looking around camp he could see Wapiti was sleeping like a log. There were still some nice coals burning in the fire. Standing up, he walked over and picked up the coffeepot and dipped it in the river to fill it. Putting the coffeepot next to the fire, he added some wood to get it cooking. Shawn stretched out his arms. He sure had a good nights sleep last night, he thought to himself. Pulling out the frying pan and started cooking breakfast. The bacon hadn't been in the frying pan for even a minute, as the smell woke Wapiti up. Rubbing his eyes a little with his hands he slowly got up and walked over to the fire. "How long till the coffees ready, Marshal?"

"Give it time to cook son, Shawn answered. You can see I'm working as fast as I can."

"What's wrong with the fish I caught last night?" Wapiti asked, walking toward the river.

"Why nothing," Shawn said, looking at Wapiti. "I didn't know you had caught any."

"What else was I supposed to do? You fell a sleep around five." Wapiti answered, picking the string of trout out of the river, already cleaned and ready to cook. "I damned sure wasn't going to practice any shooting alone... I really didn't want to get anyone's attention, what with you being pasted out and all."

101

"Hell, I'd have heard if someone came along." Shawn said, reaching for the bag of corn biscuits. "How many of these you want for breakfast?"

"None thank you, Wapiti said. And like hell you would have woke up. Hell, I don't even think a case of dynamite could have woke you up last night."

"Oh now, I wasn't THAT drunk." Shawn answered, pouring each of them a cup of coffee, and handed one to Wapiti. "What happened to all my corn biscuits?" He asked, looking back in the bag.

"Best thing that could have happened with them, Wapiti answered. Target practice on the way here."

"Speaking of here, just how far from John Day are we?" Shawn asked

"I don't think we even made it half way," Wapiti said. "Fact the sign on the road over there says Widow's Gulch… So you think we'll make Sumpter today?"

"NOOO…Shawn said, we'll stop off in John Day, get supplies and maybe if we push it, we can make a cabin I know of. It's over where Granite Creek pours into the John Day River. Then on to Sumpter tomorrow."

The two set and ate breakfast; Wapiti really enjoyed that first morning cup of coffee. That was just about the only drink the white man brought with them that he liked. He could hear the Marshal talking; he was trying to pay attention. But he had other things on his mind. He was hoping for a hot bath in John Day…That's if he could talk the Marshal into it.

"You paying attention Wapiti," Shawn spoke up, pouring what was left of the coffee into their cups.

"What…? Oh, yes sir Marshal. It's just you have so many stories, it's hard to tell just how much of them are real." Wapiti says, starting to chuckle.

"I'm here to tell ya young Wapiti that all my stories are the truthful and you had better pay attention. One of them just might save your life one of these days. "Shawn said waving his hands around." Now, let's get packed up and get out of here, we're burning daylight."

Chapter Six

"Yes sir," Wapiti answered, picking up and cleaning up. "Just funn'en with ya is all, you old fart."

"OLD FART, why... why you little shit." Shawn chuckled and kicked Wapiti in the ass, before he got out of range. "I'll kick a mud hole in you. I'll show you just what this OLD FART can still do."

"No thanks, Marshal," Wapiti answered still laughing, loading up the packhorse.

"You sure are full of yourself this morning. Shawn said, puffing his chest up. You put that double barrel ten gauge on your left side today, no tell'en just what kind of men we will run into from here on in to John Day."

"Yes sir, Marshal." Wapiti said, as they both started saddling up. "It's just... Well, your so easy to get you riled up... it's actually fun."

"I'll show you fun." Shawn said, grabbing the lead rope to the pack mule and climbed up in his saddle, "Let's get out of here. Maybe we can get to John Day early enough that I can find a restaurant to make some more corn biscuits." Shaking his head, "I can't believe we went through that many... That's why I was using these pine cones."

"Don't worry Marshal, target practice is all those things are good for any ways, Wapiti said. Those thing's are to daw gone salty to eat."

"That's what is good about them," Shawn said pointing up in the sky. "That sun when it gets hot..... It takes a lot of salt out of the body... you lose too much salt you'll pass out. Second, it don't take too many of them to fill you up when you get hunger. That way you don't have to hunt for food, and the outlaws do. That gunshot can be heard for miles in all directions...might say they'll lead you right to them. Also, you don't have to pack as much grub and you can pack more ammo... Now then, put your pistol back on and we'll do some more target practicing... But if any men come riding at us, you get that hog leg back in your hands. I want to be ready for any little surprises."

"Alright Marshal." Wapiti answered, putting his pistol on and tying it down to his leg. "You just throw those corn biscuits in the air... I'll show you what I think there good for." He started smiling, sliding the pistol in and out; you can start throwing them when you're ready.

From then on the ride was fun and enjoyable. Well, at least for Wapiti it was. The Marshal was telling him stories about the country they were going to be going through after John Day. Every now and then the Marshal would holler "PULL" and throw up one or two corn biscuits for Wapiti to shoot at. Wapiti was feeling pretty sure of himself, cause he was hitting most of them. Then all of a sudden he threw one right into the sun, so it blinded him and he didn't get a shot off.

"Your DEAD," yelled Shawn. "Don't every let anyone get the sun in your eyes. You're not only blind and can't see where he is... but you can bet your life he can see you and... you're dead."

"Yes sir, Marshal." Wapiti was thinking to himself, "could he really do it...? Kill a man that is...? What would it feel like...? When and where would be the first? A fistfight he wasn't afraid of... Fact fighting a man hand to hand is fun; he'd like to show all these white eyes how Indians fight. That would be fun... But a gun...? The Marshal said if you hesitate for even a half second your dead."

Wapiti wasn't real sure how long he had been thinking to himself, when all of a sudden they came riding up on the lumber mill at the edge of town.

"Alright, Wapiti, you get that hog leg back on, Shawn ordered. We'll stop in up here at the jailhouse and see who's in the area... Any big outlaws you might say."

"Yes sir, Marshal." Wapiti answered, quickly doing as he was asked to do. Looking at the people walking the streets. Noticing that they all were looking straight at him, sending a small shiver up his back. "WWOOO," he thought to himself as he shook it off.

"Will you just look at all them logs over there, Wapiti?" Shawn said pointing and looking at them men doing the work. Lighting a cigar. "Them men work real hard for their money. When they go to the Saloons to unwind, they like to fight... You might say, they like to see who the big kid on the block is."

"Lots of gun fights, Marshal?" Wapiti asked, still looking around at everyone.

104

Chapter Six

"NOOO… Loggers like to fight with their hands." Shawn boasted it usually starts when someone looses an arm wrestling match and wants to show just what he's made of.

"GOOD!" Wapiti answered.

"Don't worry about it son." Shawn said, pulling up to the Sheriffs office. "They only come out to fight at night… and I'm hoping to get our supplies and be out of here just after we eat a early lunch." Pulling out his watch and looked at it. It was just barely ten o-clock "We shouldn't be too long in here Wapiti. If we're going to make that cabin before it gets too dark. So we can't lolly-gag around." Tying their horses up, Shawn was looking the jailhouse over as they walked through the door. "I haven't seen a wood jail house in a long time." On one side of the room, the Sheriff was at his desk. On the other side were two cells. In one cell a Young man was laying on the cot smoking a cigarette.

"What kind of Jail is this? " Shawn asked, waving his hands around. "I mean now days at least the jail cells are usually bricked in… Hell, any outlaw with a couple good horses could pull this place apart."

The Sheriff stood up from behind the desk, held his hand out, and chuckled, "Sheriff Beyer, Dennis Beyer, and Marshal. It's a pleasure to meet you."

"Felton," Shawn said puffing his chest up. "U. S. Marshal Shawn Felton and this is my Deputy Wapiti." He said, pointing in Wapiti's direction and sizing the Sheriff up. He figured the Sheriff went at least six-foot, maybe two hundred pound. Shacking hands, Shawn noticed he had a good firm hand shake, which he liked. This Young man looked like he could handle himself in a fistfight. Which Shawn knew he had already been put to the test if he'd been on the job very long. He looked to be in his early twenties, maybe mid twenties. "So who died and made you Sheriff?" Shawn asked.

Chuckling a little himself at the comment. "Well, you might say the gold rush made me Sheriff," Dennis said. "Our Sheriff's brother struck gold just outside of Whitney about three months ago. One thing lead to another and well, the town council asked me if I wanted the job." Dennis looked over at Wapiti, sticking his hand out. "It's nice to meet

105

you… Wapiti, is it?"… Then looking back over to the Marshal. "What are you trying to do, get this kid killed Marshal?"

"I wouldn't worry about him too much, Shawn said. I wouldn't call this place much of a jail though."

"Well Marshal, we have a county lock-up just up the road two miles in Canyon City." Dennis said, walking over towards the coffee pot's. One filled with coffee and one filled with hot water for tea. "If I get any real outlaws, I take them up there. Can I get you men a cup of coffee or tea?"

"Thanks', so what did this scoundrel do to end up in here?" Shawn said, pointing to the jail cell behind them.

"BULLSHIT CHARGES!" the man hollered out, jumping up and walking over to the cell bars. "BULLSHIT CHARGES! I'm telling ya Marshal, they're all Bullshit charges." The man said, still hollering.

Reaching for the cup of coffee Shawn started chuckling. "Haven't met a criminal yet that wasn't innocent according to himself."

"Settle down, Floyd," Dennis said with a big smile on his face. "Well Marshal, this time I think Floyd might be right." Handing Wapiti a cup of coffee.

Setting down in a chair, Shawn put his feet up on the desk. "So just what was it he did wrong?"

"Well, he got caught with the judge's daughter." Dennis said, trying not to laugh.

"Hell Marshal, she was almost eighteen years old," Floyd said, still speaking in a loud voice. "Hell, she is eighteen now."

"Almost eighteen!" Shawn shouted out. "Hell, most young ladies I know are married by the time they're sixteen, maybe seventeen at the latest."

"Well Marshal, like I said… She was the JUDGE'S. YOUNGEST daughter, and in these parts, if you're a Larkin, your guilty until proven innocent, Dennis said. I felt sorry for him, so I talked to the judge and got him put into my care. Told the judge I could use help around here to clean up."

"Just how much time did he give him?" Shawn asked

Chapter Six

"He gave me a year," Floyd hollered back. "But I'll get out of here WAY before then."

"Ya right," Dennis hollered back. "The only time your out of that cell is if I'm here, and I keep the keys over here in my desk... So what you going to do... Make yourself a key?"

"You never know Sheriff. So how about it Marshal, you want to talk to the judge for me and tell him to let me out?" Floyd asked

"OH NO! Not only NO, but HELL NO. I'm not talking to no judge for you or for anyone else. Hell, if I did that... he might just put me in there with you... No sir, Shawn yelled out. You made your bed, now sleep in it." Standing up, Shawn walked over to the coffee, "So what's up with this, being a Larkin, in these parts?"

"Well, Floyd here comes from a large family something like ten, twelve kids." Dennis start's to say, when Floyd jumped in.

"Fourteen," Floyd hollered out.

"Ya, whatever Floyd," Dennis said. "They're not a bad bunch mind ya, it's just they get caught at everything they do. He's got some cousins over in the Sumpter area logging. If your head'en that way, you'll run into them...Twin's... Identical...But I'll tell ya Marshal, if I ever needed some one to back me up... I'll take any Larkin any time... Those men can shoot...But they do seem to always find trouble."

"NO, trouble finds us, Marshal," Floyd yelled out.

"Well Mister Larkin, it sounds to me like YOU got caught with the wrong person at the wrong time again," Shawn said chuckling. Looking back towards the Sheriff. "So have you heard of any big outlaws in these parts lately?"

"Well, they say Butch Cassidy and the Sundance kid were seen over around Haines, four maybe five days ago." Dennis answered, putting his hand over his coffee cup. "No thanks Marshal, I only drink herbal tea, and I've had all that I can handle right know. So where you two headed anyhow?"

"Well, I figured I'd take young Wapiti here up to the Sumpter area and show him what a real boomtown looks like." Shawn said

"Boomtown, you got that right Marshal, Dennis shouted out. I logged over there a couple years ago, before they discovered gold in that valley… Now everyone and his brother is heading that way hoping to strike it rich. Hell" you might get lucky and find Butch and Sundance up there somewhere."

"Oh, I doubt that. Those boys are probably out of the country by now, Shawn said. But if they were planning to do a job, it would take them at least a week maybe two to plan it out."

"You really think it would take them that long to plan the robbery?" Dennis asked.

"Think… Hell, I'm counting on it," Shawn answered. "Those boys will have to figure out how and when they transfer the gold, then they have to figure out the best place to jump the train, then they have to figure out how to get out of the country."

"You think they'll get much gold, Marshal?" Wapiti asked, with excitement in his voice.

"Son, they're using those new dredge's over their, Shawn said. I hear tell they're pulling it up in bucket loads."

You sure your not just exaggerated a little Marshal, Floyd asked.

"Which way do you figure they will go after they rob the train?" Wapiti asked.

"Well, that Butch Cassidy is from Utah, and Sundance is from New York or New Jersey I think, Shawn said. You ever been down in that Utah Country, Sheriff?"

"No sir, Marshal. Dennis answered. My parents came out here from Michigan when I was three. So you might say Eastern Oregon is the only area I know."

"Well, I'm here to tell you you're not missing much, Shawn said, waving his arm around. They have the Great Salt Lake down there. Some days when the wind blows right, it blows the worst stench you ever smelled off that lake. And those salt flats go on forever. Nothing but white land as far as you can see. No drinkable water anywhere. They have their own religion down there, too. They call themselves Mormons… They have multiple wives. I hear some have up to ten or more."

"Not anymore they don't " Dennis said with a discussed look on his face

Chapter Six

"The hell they don't, Shawn said, glaring straight at him. Fact I hear tell one of their Governors had over fifty wives and at least one hundred children."

"The government outlawed that practice quite a few years ago" Dennis said

"I don't care if they did, Shawn said seriously. Why, back home I have a real good friend Roger Kennedy…he has four wives and a whole brood of children, to many to count. But I was just thinking that from here back to Utah is a long hard ride across the desert through Idaho. If I were them I'd either head south to California, or to get there even faster, I'd come through here. Follow the John Day River till I got to the Columbia, down around Arlington; get on one of those barges down to Portland then another one down to California."

"What if you're wrong and they do head out across Idaho?" Dennis asked.

"Well, if the Lords willing…we'll be right on their trail, Shawn said, pointing. Can't help but notice your gun rack on the wall Sheriff. Most Sheriffs are happy with 30-30-"s."

Dennis turned around and looked at the gun rack which had ten 44-40"s and his holster and pistol. "Ya, I like to know I can reach out and touch someone if I ever need to."

"What's that pistol doing hanging up there when it should be on your side Young man?" Shawn asked.

'We don't have too many gunslingers in this town, Dennis said. Usually just a drunk logger and a young cow hand in fist fights." Rubbing his right fist into to his left hand. "They can be fun to break up sometime, if you get my meaning."

"I sure do. Shawn answered, as he to started rubbing his fist in his hand and puffs his chest up. I'll take a good fistfight over a bad gunfight every time. Still I wouldn't be caught out of bed with out mine." He say's, slapping his pistol. "Fact sometimes I wouldn't even be caught in bed without it either." Starting to chuckle a little. "If you're going to be a lawman you had better keep it on you… It's better to have it and not need it… than it is to need it and not have it… then you're a dead

109

lawman… that's a good notch in a young wanna be outlaws gun… A Sheriff…Who thought he could do his job without a gun?"

"Speaking of guns, I can handle one fair mind ya, Dennis said. Just how big of a hurry are you in to get to Sumpter?"

"Why, what's up Sheriff?" Shawn wanted to know.

"We have a high dollar poker tournament in town this weekend. It sure would be nice to have a couple other lawmen around to help out. I've tried to hire a couple Deputy's, but no ones biting. It would be real nice to have you Marshal… Hell, your reputation alone will stop ninety percent of any trouble before it even gets started." Dennis offers, hoping the Marshal will stick around, and help out.

"Well now, just how big a tournament we talkin'?" Shawn asked.

"Fifty Thousand Dollars'," Dennis said, with a serious look on his face.

"Fifty thousand? Shawn yelled out. Where the hell did anyone around here get that kind of money?"

"Its a thousand dollar buy in, Dennis said…There'll be a few players from around these parts, but most of them won't be from here. Hell Marshal, every motel room from Mt Vernon to Prairie City… they're all booked up. Corky Bukowiec over at the Silver Dollar Saloon has been advertising in Portland and Seattle for over six months. I hear tell people as far away as San Francisco are coming. I believe he has confirmed 85 to 90 participants."

"Hell, those boys just might be coming over here instead, Shawn said. Those men don't know when they will be shipping that gold, but they will damn sure know where fifty thousand dollars plus will be."

"You really think they would come here Marshal?" Dennis asked.

"Never can tell Young man, never can tell. Shawn said, walking back over to the coffeepot. Maybe we can get this Corky fella to pay us a little extra for security? With that many players, why hell he's making out like a thief himself. He's going to make more than the winner is before it's all said and done. Like you said, my reputation alone will discourage most of them scoundrels from trying anything"… Looking over at Wapiti… "Hey Wapiti, you still have those wanted posters? If

110

Chapter Six

I remember right, you had a picture of Cassidy and Sundance in that pile."

"I sure do, Marshal," Wapiti spoke up with excitement in his voice. Opening his saddlebags, and digging for the wanted posters.

Shawn reached into his vest pocket and pulled out a flask of whiskey. Pouring a little in his coffee "Helps me think sometimes,"

"Really," Dennis answered. "I find it makes me forget things." Looking around the room at Wapiti.

"Don't look at me, Wapiti said, holding his hands up. My Father said firewater makes men stupid, and makes them do stupid things... From what I've seen I have to agree with him."

"Moderation gentlemen, moderation." Shawn said, with a smile on his face taking a sip of his coffee. "Well, Wapiti why don't you take the horses over to the Livery stable? Me and the Sheriff will go to the Silver Dollar Saloon and talk to this Mr. Bukowiec fella about paying us to help watch over the festivities." Turning his attention back to the Sheriff, "so tell me Sheriff, just where is this Saloon?"

"It's down by the mill, just across the street from the train station, Dennis answered, pointing in the general area. That's one place I DON"T go with out my pistol. You never can tell just what or who you're going to run into down there. Had the pleasure of breaking up a fight in there the other night. It is a classy place, don't get me wrong. Cork usually sits above the bar with a double barrel shotgun, only his is a twelve gauge. It's not cut down like that hog leg there." He say's, pointing toward Wapiti shot gun, "I haven't seen too many ten gauges... Never seen one cut down."

Wapiti kinda smiled. "I'm not real good with a pistol yet, so the Marshal figured I couldn't miss with this if someone started something."

"I hope not! Dennis yelled out, smiling, Hell, even I couldn't miss with that."

"Wapiti, why don't you get going up to the Livery, and me and Dennis will head on over to the Silver Dollar?" Shawn ordered, trying to get Wapiti moving.

"I don't think that would be a good idea Marshal," Dennis said, looking Wapiti over... "You look like you can handle yourself, but these boys around here see an Indian wearing a badge… Well quite frankly, I know someone is going to try him… Least till they get to know him. There'll be a young boy outside here some place playing, if you give him two bits he'll not only grain and feed your horses, but he'll brush them down too."

Taking a big pull off his coffee, Shawn looked Wapiti over. "You know Sheriff; you just might be right about that."

"I sure hope you can handle yourself Wapiti, Dennis said, with a serious look on his face. Cause you know before the weekend is out, someone is going to try you. Not with a gun, I don't think, but they will invite you to show them what you're made of."

"As long as there's no more than four at once, I think I will be all right." Wapiti answered with a big smile on his face. Putting the pictures of the two outlaws on the table. "Fact, I'm looking forward to it."

"Now you're sounding just a little cocking there, Wapiti," Shawn said, picking up his saddlebags.

"I know you got my back Marshal, Wapiti said, bragging. I think I can handle what's in front of me… up to four that is, after that I might need a little help." He continued with a big smile on his face.

"Well we'll just have to wait and find out won't we Marshal?" Dennis said chuckling. Putting his pistol and holster on. "Told ya, that's one place I won't go without this." He patted his gun, then turned and walked towards the door.

The three men had just gotten outside, the Sheriff was right, fact there were two young lads playing just outside. Shawn gave each one a quarter, which the two were more than glad to earn.

The three headed for the saloon. Shawn was in the middle, Dennis and Wapiti on either side of him. Everyone was staring at them. Who was that big man with the Sheriff, his pistol tied down, and a rifle in his hand? One thing for sure they all knew this man meant business.

The women all pulled their kids back as they walked by. Shawn did what he always did in a new town… Look it over. It seemed to be like most small growing cities. It had its hardware stores; dry goods and mining supply stores. Shawn noticed there was more saloons, brothels,

Chapter Six

and eateries, than anything else. Still there were a few other restaurants, too. Fact over there was a Mexican restaurant; he could get him some more corn biscuits before they pulled out.

He couldn't help but notice the blacksmith shop. All those big draft horses and wooden wagons to bring the logs out of the mountains and down to the mill. "That man earns every penny he makes," Shawn told Wapiti. "Not only that but it takes lots of muscle to pick those big wheel up to replace the ones that break. A good black smith can make a good living, but it takes a lot of years training to be good. Guess it's like that with every job though. You learn a lot of what to do and what not to do on the job. You also will find ways to make it easier with every situation you come across."

They had walked about two blocks when Shawn got his first look at the Silver Dollar Saloon. It was a nice three-story place, with two complete wrap around decks on the top two stories. It was painted light blue with all the trim done in white. There were some of the young ladies that worked there as entertainment sitting out on the decks. They were flirting with all the men down below as they walked or rode by. Shawn could see what the Sheriff meant by there being a lot of fights in that place. Loggers, ranchers, gamblers, women and alcohol don't mix, and that place had everything a man needed to get drunk and stupid.

"Boy, I've had me lots of fun in these establishments in my time," Shawn said, stepping up on the boardwalk.

"Which one, Marshal?" Dennis asked. "Was it alcohol, women, or bust'en heads?"

"Well now, when I was younger it was all three. Shawn answered, with a big smile on his face. Now it's just the alcohol and bust'en heads... Don't get me wrong mind ya, I do miss the woman, so I make do with just bust'en more heads." Looking down at his pocket watch, "Looks like we're going to be talking over a early dinner." Then they walked into the Saloon. Stopping and taking in a big breath of air into his lungs then came a big smile. The smell alone was like a homecoming. Wapiti would be able to get some good experience at handling a rowdy crowd.

113

Looking around the room he could see the room was filled with excitement over the poker tournament. Men and even a couple ladies were in line to put their money down and get their thousand dollars in chips. That had to be Corky setting up in what looked like a fancy shoe shine chair, above the bar, he was setting up high enough for him to over see the entire Saloon. At the base of his chair, set the table where everyone was paying their money. That had to be Corky Bukowiec setting up there with the double barrel twelve-gauge shotgun in one hand and a beer in the other.

The three worked their way through the crowd, there were a few men Shawn noticed that as soon as they saw the badge on that old man, they knew right away is was the ONE and ONLY Marshal Shawn Felton. Some turned and walked in the other direction, as if hoping he wouldn't see them. Like maybe there was paper on them, but if there was he didn't recollect seeing any poster on them. Which meant they were just outlaw wanta –be's. Shawn started chuckling at the thought. Either way they had no problem getting through. Everyone was apologizing or excusing themselves. Anything to get out of his way. Some were even pulling their buddies aside that weren't smart enough to move on their own.

They were only half way across the room before everyone had heard that Marshal Shawn Felton was in the room. The room became strangely quiet and everyone moved back out of his way. They all were wondering what HE was doing here. They all walked up to front of the bar where Corky had his throne set up, least that's what Shawn thought it looked like.

This was his place and he was THE KING, Things would be run his way inside. Shawn sized this Mr. Bukowiec up. He figured he wasn't much more than five and a half feet tall, weighed maybe one fifty, if he was lucky… But wirery… Not for a second would he hesitate to use that shotgun if someone got out of line. Looking up at the roof above him, Shawn noticed a big hole about eighteen inches in diameter. It was from the times he had pulled that first trigger. God only remembers where the other barrel went if it was fired. He sure wouldn't want

Chapter Six

to be in that room above him if Corky fired that thing. Hell you just might get hit by some buckshot.

Dennis was trying to make the introduction of everyone, but Corky cut him off.

"What the hell is this?" Hollered Cork. "Get that damned Indian out of my establishment and I mean NOW, RIGHT NOW!" He stepped down from his chair.

Pointing the barrel of his rifle into the chest of Corky, Shawn stopped him in his tracks. "NOW YOU just wait one minute there Young man and EVERYONE ELSE IN HERE... I AM U.S. MARSHAL Shawn Felton AND This Indian here is my Deputy, Wapiti, IF anyone, and I do mean ANYONE has a problem with that lets get it out and done with right now!"

All of a sudden the room started humming with the sound of everyone talking about an Indian Deputy, why they had never even thought of such a ridiculous idea. Some of them didn't have a problem saying so. They weren't going to listen to no damned Indian.

"The hell you won't," Shawn spoke out. "Unless you want to take it up with me." He turned his head back to Cork, "Am I going to have any trouble out of you?"

"NO SIR, no sir, Cork answered. But I would like to have a talk with you Marshal. If you've got the time?"

"I heard what you have going on here, Shawn said, ordering a beer. Thought maybe you might want a little help with your security?"

"They say great minds always think the alike, Cork answered, slapping Shawn on the back. Charley, take over the shotgun. Any trouble... USE IT. Me and the Marshal are going to have a talk."

"Over dinner, I hope" Shawn said, as they all started walking toward the dining room.

Corky looked up at the Marshal as they walked through the crowd. Corky couldn't believe it. The people were packed in that saloon like sardines in a can, yet everyone stepped aside and gave them all the room they needed. "You were just joking about that Indian being a Deputy weren't you, Marshal?" Corky asked

"No, I wasn't." Walking over to a table and sat down. Still noticing that everyone else in the room was asking each other the very same question about that young buck Indian. No I wasn't, Shawn said in a loud enough voice so everyone could hear him.

Right off Cork ordered two pitchers of beer and three glasses. Which made Shawn real happy. Then he ordered T-bone steaks around the table for everyone. Which made him even happier. "Now let's get down to business, Mr. Bukowiec. I hear tell you have a little poker game about to start."

"Yes sir Marshal, I do and it just got bigger. Bigger than even I could have hoped for." Cork answered

"I heard that." As the beer finally arrived, Shawn picked up a mug and took a big pull. Now that was good beer he thought to himself. "I heard it's a fifty thousand dollar purse."

"Well with six months of advertising in Portland, Seattle and every other port of call coming in from Alaska, I figured I might get lucky and get maybe sixty players, Cork said smiling. Figured I'd make out pretty good on the deal at a thousand-dollar buy in. What, with me keeping the money for all the players over the first fifty, then figure in food, beer, entertainment? But hell, the games are suppose to start at six o-clock tomorrow night, I bet I end up with a least one hundred or more contestants."

"That's a lot of money to have in one spot, what, with Butch Cassidy and Sundance kid being seen over in Haines just a couple days ago." Shawn bragged up as he filled up his beer, again.

"I thought about that too." Corky said.

The waitress set everyone's plate down in front of them. She was a beautiful young lady, Shawn thought. Five feet, maybe two, couldn't weigh much more than a hundred pounds short dark brown hair, dark brown eyes, and a real nice, different, yet one of the prettiest smiles he'd ever seen. Shawn could see Wapiti was taking notice of her, too. He also thought she might just be looking at Wapiti. Fact, now that he took a second look at Wapiti he could see that his face was getting redder. Boy wouldn't that bring the house down. Not only was he an

Chapter Six

Indian Deputy U.S. Marshal, but him and a white girl...? Shawn chuckled at the thought.

"So just how much you willing to pay me and my Deputy for added security? Shawn asked, puffing his chest up. Hell my reputation alone is going to stop most, hell maybe even ninety percent of the trouble before it starts."

"First off, Marshal, I want you to know I won't take any responsibility for this Indian here," Corky stated firmly. "You know as well as I do, that someone will try him." And I'll be dammed if I'm going to let my place get tore up.

"You just let me and Wapiti worry about that, Shawn said. Now let's talk money here. Cause we're not putting our asses on the line for nothing."

"That's no problem Marshal, you name your price. I'll throw in rooms and all your food and drinks."

"Well now, I like your attitude, Young man. Shawn answered. How about two hundred a day, room and board. We have a deal?"

"No problem Marshal, Corky answered. I was willing to go up to a thousand each... but if two hundred each is what you want, then two each is what you'll get, plus room and board."

The three shook hands, Corky once again making it clear about his feelings of an Indian Deputy.

"Ya know, Mr. Bukowiec, everyone is out there in the mountains digging for gold... You just hit a hell of a strike right here," Shawn said starting to chuckle. "So just when do you intend to transfer all that money to the bank?"

"I'm not. Cork said quietly. It's all staying right here under my lock and key. You see Marshal; banks get robbed, so I don't trust them."

"You think keeping it here is going to be safer?" Shawn asked

"They'll have to go through me and both of you two." Corky answered, filling up his and Shawn's beer.

"Well then, if you want this to start by six o-clock tomorrow night we have a lot of work to do. Rules need to be made." Shawn stood up with his beer in hand. "Well, let's get to it."

They walked back into the Saloon side, again. Shawn took him in another big breath of air. He could smell the smoke from the cigars and cigarettes. The smell of that stick water some of them young lady were wearing now days. Heck, he could even smell the beer and whiskey. This was going to be a good place to spend a couple nights, and Wapiti can get a good idea of just what lies ahead of him, if he wants the white eye's to take him serious. He's not only going to have prove he can handle what they might do to him. While earning their respect at the same time.

Looking around the place he could see there were quite a few elk and deer horns on the wall, along with a bear hide, and couple mountain lions. Had at least a half dozen nice chandlers hanging down. On the other side of the room was a piano and a small stage for the young ladies to dance. He figured there was at least twenty tables on the Saloon side, not to count those in the restaurant. They would most likely have all the tables they would need.

"We'll have to move that piano, put it up on the stage, Shawn said pointing. You just tell them young ladies to watch their step...I don't want any of them falling off there."

"I was thinking, if we have extra tables, we can put them out on the board walk," Corky said. "That way we can have a little extra room between the tables in here."

"I think if we rope this area here off, only the contestants and waitresses will be allowed inside this area, with the exception of myself and Wapiti, of course." Shawn said, continuing to point.

"Marshal, before we go any further, we should get a couple things out in the open right now. First my name is Cork, not Mr. Bukowiec. Second, if I want any shit off you, I'll ask you for it, Cork said, ya old fart."

"OLD FART," Shawn yelled back and puffed his chest up. "You call me an old fart again, and this old fart will stomp a mud hole in you." Starting to chuckle, "I see we're going to understand each other just fine...but I can see how that mouth of yours could get you into trouble real fast."

Chapter Six

"That's another part of your job Marshal, Cork say's, smiling. You have to make sure no one comes after me."

"Now, we just might have to double our prices, if that's part of the job, Shawn said, chuckling…Cause I can tell that alone would be a twenty four hour, seven day a week job."

"Well, just remember if I get hurt, I can't pay you." Cork said.

"Well now CORK, I think Wapiti and I will go up to our rooms, get a bath, and wash some of this trail dust off. So if you'll have your bar tender pour me a pitcher of beer and give me two more glasses, we'll say good night to you sir."

"Well I wish you would take a bath, Cork said, holding his nose. Cause you flat out stink Marshal."

Picking up his shirt, Shawn took a big sniff. "Hell we shouldn't be too bad; we took a bath the other night in Dayville."

"Here ya go Marshal," Charley said, handing him a pitcher of beer and two glasses.

Then the two headed up the stairs. Wapiti could still feel all those eyes on him even though he wasn't looking at them.

CHAPTER SEVEN

Randy walked over and saw the three laying in the shade taking a nap. Their horses were hobbled and grazing near by. He knew waking them up meant they would be going into Sumpter tonight. Which Randy didn't do too often.

It would be nice to take a break from logging and relax and unwind a little, he thought. But someone would always try to pick a fight. Not that that didn't help him unwind a little too, because it did.

He started to smile looking back over towards the Roan. It was hard for him to believe Dude had picked this horse for Larry to take on the trip. He sure was big. Shoot he was easily as tall as my Clydesdales. Not as big, only maybe three quarter's their weight, but he was big. With just one look you could tell he had all the muscle he needed, and was at least eighteen plus hands tall.

Gary had told him about some of the times he knew of that the Roan had thrown Larry. Hell his stallion wasn't no piece of cake to break for riding. He remembered what kind of trip this Roan had taken Larry on after that tree came down earlier.

He turned and walked over to him. Picking up the stir-up, he tightening up the cinch, Randy figured he'd give him a little try himself. Hell, if Larry could ride him, shoot, he was a better bronc buster than Larry, any day. "Easy big boy," Randy was trying to assure him it was all right. Then leaning down, he untied the hobbles. Very slowly he put his foot in the stirrup and climbed aboard.

Chapter Seven

The Roan knowing it wasn't Larry so he took to flight. Straight up in the air at least ten feet, hitting the ground he did a one eighty and went even higher, on the second jump. Still twisting and turning every direction all at the same time, sending Randy even higher, into the bows of the near by fir tree's, which broke his fall. The Roan bucked about three or four more times, before running in circles. In the meanwhile, Randy came crashing back to the ground.

Larry slowly raised his hat up, with a big smile on his face. "You just had to try him, didn't ya Randy. So ya want to try him again?" Laughing so hard he could hardly stand up.

Still setting on the ground and looking towards the Roan, "NOPE, don't believe I do." Randy answered, starting to stand up. "That horse has more power bucking than any of my team, but I figured if you could ride him… I could to."

"Guess you figured wrong, didn't ya." Larry looked around, "Anyone else want to try him? Well now since no one else wants to try, what do ya say we get the hell out of here? I'm getting thirsty."

"Larry you're always thirsty," Randy yelled out. "I know you didn't leave town without at least one bottle in your saddle bags."

"When that tree came down, me and the Roan went one way and that bottle went another." "Larry said, waving his arm around trying to show how everything flew.

"What you only brought one? Hell that's not like you, Larry. You usually have two or three on you at least." Randy said

"What happened to that bottle you were drinking on after your ride," Randy asked.

"It only had a little bit left in it," Larry answered. "The full bottle was up my coat sleeve."

Turning around Gary kicked Luis in the side, "Come on, we need to get going."

"Ya, Ya," Luis said. "How about you give a guy a chance to wake up?"

They all started tightening their saddles down. When Randy's boss Kenny Miles came over, shaking everyone's hands. They all had logged for him from time to time, "Randy, if you're not back in the morning, can I have someone else run the other five? I figure with you taking the stallion, most men can handle the others."

"How you figure on running them? Randy asked. And WHO did you have in mind to run them?"

"If I get Goof and Toad off the felling crew, one could run two and the other could run three." Kenny said.

"Alright, I'll allow Goof and Toad only… I DON"T want any of these other ya-who's anywhere near them." He said, pointing around the logging camp, "Or there will be hell to pay when I get back."

"I have no problem with that Randy." Kenny answered, shaking Randy's hand again. "I know how you feel about your team. Hell, if I had that much money tied up in them, I'd be picky too."

"I WANT TONAGE," Randy demanded. "You aren't paying me by the piece. Most of those other teams are just a bunch of saddle horses and mule's and you know it… My five will out skid ten of them any day of the week, and you know that to."

"AGREED, I'll have them skid your logs on a separate deck." Kenny said

The four men climbed aboard their saddles, except Randy. He couldn't get a regular saddle on that big Clydesdale stallion. So he just had a rope with stirrups braided into it, then it was tied around the stallion's waist. They turned their horses and headed back down the river towards Sumpter.

The four headed down the river trail. The same trail the three had ridden up just a few hours earlier. It didn't take them long to get to the camp where the fat lady had been taking a bath when they came up.

"There ya go, Randy," Larry hollered at him. "We know she's clean, cause we seen her bathing earlier when we rode up."

"He makes more off her than he does his mining claim," Randy said.

"So how much does she charge, Amigo?" Luis asked.

'I hear she starts at five dollars and goes up, Randy answered. Depends on what the old man thinks you can afford. Why, you interested Luis?'

122

Chapter Seven

'NO, I figured if you knew how much, then you must have come down here a time or two.' Luis said chuckling.

'N-N-not L-LIKELY. If I need a woman, I-I j-just climbs aboard this b-big fella and head to t-t-town. Randy say's, he knows his way home, so I can sleep.'

"Settle down, Randy," Gary said. "Don't be getting all excited; Luis is just joking with ya, is all."

Everyone knew Randy had a temper. When he got excited he started stuttering. Which meant if anyone made fun of him, he would loose his temper. That meant someone was going to go visit Doc Bones.

"I can't believe you ride that monster of a horse," Luis said. "You have to be half crazy."

"Why do you think he climbed aboard that Roan for?" Gary said. "He's more than half crazy."

"I figured if Larry could ride him, then I could, too." Randy answered

"Guess you were wrong, weren't ya?" Larry said shouting.

"You know, when I was breaking this boy to ride, I figured there wasn't any horse that could throw me higher than he did... I enjoy a good spirited horse," Randy said. " But I was wrong. Hell, I know that Roan threw me higher than the moon."

"You did go flying didn't ya BUTTWHEAT?" Larry was waving his hands around in the air, imitating Randy flying off the Roan.

"You three Hombre's are all crazy," Luis said. "You like riding them bucking horses?"

"I'd rather be breaking horses, than riding fence line or herding those dusty cattle any day." Gary answered Luis.

"I hear ya, Bro," Larry said. "There's nothing like it."

'I don't think, I know all you Larkin boys are crazy, Luis said. But you sure can ride them wild horses.'

'Hell, we should be able to. Dude had us on green broke horses more than he had us on full broke ones.'

"Shit, that's all we had." Gary said. "We always had ten to fifteen plus horses in the barn that he was training. We had to feed and water

123

them everyday. If we wanted to go hunting or to town, he made us choose which one we wanted to try and ride."

Larry chimed in, 'I'd always pick one that had been around awhile, you could at least ride them, and they would only crow hop a few times at most.'

"I knew which one not to take, Randy said. The one you couldn't put a saddle on yet,"

Larry reached into his saddlebags and pulled out about a half full fifth of whiskey. 'That old fart wouldn't tell us if they were broke or not…He'd always say, TAKE YOUR PICK AND HAVE SOME FUN!'

'Ya, but if he chose one for you, you knew you were in for a fun ride. Cause those were usually the ones you couldn't get the saddle on. Gary said.

They all three started laughing about it more, each one remembering different horses that Grandpa Dude had put them on over the years.

"REACH FOR THE GROUND, he'd say," Randy said. "It's a lot closer and you're going to end up there any way. If you reach for the sky…that's the long way to the ground, and your going to end up there anyway."

'Hey Randy, not to change the subject, But why do they say your either an Irish- Polish man or you're a Polish – Irishman?' This had always confused Luis.

'It's because he either doe's something stupid and gets mad, or he gets mad and do something stupid, Gary shouted out. Either way there's a fight involved some how.'

Larry cut in, "You just hope it don't hurt to bad the next day." Then he handed Randy the bottle of whiskey.

'No tha…I THOUGHT you said you only had one bottle on you, Randy stated. But no thanks I don't want any. I can wait till we get to town.'

'How the hell do you drink so much, and still walk, HELL ride a horse? Luis shout' out. I've never seen you really get drunk. Where the hell you put it all?' This was something else that confused Luis.

124

Chapter Seven

"Hollow legs" Larry answered, picking his legs up in the air.

"Hey, do you think we might run back into Butch Cassidy and the Sundance Kid?" Larry asked in a loud voice.

"WHAT?" yelled Randy. "Just how much did you drink last night?"

"NO, really Randy," Gary said, "Remember, I said I had something to tell you about last night in the Elkhorn Saloon and Brothel?"

"Ya, like I'm really going to fall for that," Randy answered.

"You don't want to believe us…We'll just have to prove it to you when we get to town," Larry said. "You'll see!"

"You're really not pulling my leg?" Randy asked, looking seriously over at Gary.

"No Bullshit," Gary answered, smiling. "We'll introduce you to them later."

Riding the rest of the way down the river to Sumpter, they talked about all the miners packing buckets of dirt, or pushing wheel barrel loads of dirt from a small tunnel down to the river's edge to run it threw there sloughs boxes. All hoping to be that one in ten, no twenty thousand to find a decent vain of gold, even less odds of finding the next mother load, Just look at how poor some of them look, some looked like they hadn't eaten much lately. That was no kind of life for any of them. Hell they would at least buy a twenty- two rifle so they could shoot a rabbit or a deer. They damned sure wouldn't go without food.

They rode into town and couldn't believe it. The streets were packed with people; there were people going in every possible direction. They rode straight up to the Livery stable, trying not to run anyone over. "Well, I'll meet you guys over at the Elkhorn in a little while," Randy said.

"Alright, see you there," Gary answered, as they pulled into the Livery. Randy continued on down the street to the old smokehouse. It set all alone in an open area next to the river. There was a train track running right beside it, a spur track really. It was just used to put a few empty cars out of the way, but still close by when needed.

It didn't take the twin's and Luis very long to put their horses up and head for the Elkhorn Saloon. The place was just starting to fill up with

125

people. The twins spotted Butch and Sundance up at the bar right away. They worked their way through the crowd; Gary was wanting a beer.

They had barely started talking, when all of a sudden the Saloon went totally quiet. When the swinging door's opened up and Randy walked in, looking around.

Butch and Sundance were wondering what was going on. They started to look around the room. A man next to them told his buddy in a low voice, "That's Randy Larkin."

"So what's so special about him?" the other man asked.

"Just look at everyone staring at him. You've heard the stories about him... You just watch, everyone of those men knows someone will be going to visit Doc Bones before the nights over."

"Doc Bones, What the hell kind of name is that?" The second man asked. While both men were still speaking in low voices.

"OH, that's not his real name. It's become his nickname ever since Randy came up here a couple years ago. They say, it's because when he finishes with ya...that's what he has to do, fix a whole lot of your bones.'

Butch and Sundance both looked at each other, then back at Randy. "He's going to be sitting at our table...hope he's as likable as these two are."

Randy worked his way through the people. Which was real easy, cause everyone was stepping back out of his way. Randy had a big smile on his face walking up to the others, "I don't know what they're so scared of."

The low mummers slowly started getting louder, but everyone's eyes were still on Randy.

"Alright, A-hole," Larry said in a low voice, "Come here." Grabbing Randy he pulled him over. "I'd like you to meet Butch Cassidy and the Sundance Kid."

"He's full of shit, ISN'T he?" Randy asked, with a little smile on his face.

"No, he's not," Butch said while holding his right hand out. "It's a pleasure to meet you, sir. We've heard a lot about you. Look's like everyone else has to," he says pointing around the room.

Chapter Seven

"Oh hell, guy's, don't believe everything you hear," Randy said. "I'm not as bad as they say. I just like to have a little fun... if someone gets in my way, I just push them aside."

"Does more than push them," one of the working girls said. "We're just glad he don't believe in hitting women... Can I get you a beer, Randy?" She asked.

"Yes, please," Randy answered checking her out. She was actually a nice looking lady. 'How about you bring enough for everyone? We'll be over there someplace,' he said pointing towards the back tables.

'Yes sir, Randy,' She answered, walking away.

"Let's go get us a table in the back," Sundance suggested. They all walked over to a place where a single gentleman was sitting by himself at one table, playing solitaire. Pulling an empty table over so they could accommodate all seven men, then they all sat down. Hope you don't mind if we borrow your table sir," Gary said, in a voice that told the man, it didn't matter even if he did...They were taking over his table either way.

"Larry, Gary, whichever is which, I don't know yet, Luis, this is a friend of ours Harry Logan," Butch said.

They all reached across the table to shake hands. "Aren't you the one they call Kid Curry?" Larry asked.

Curry looked over at Butch; he wasn't quite sure what to say.

"Ya, they do call him that, sometimes," Butch said looking at Curry. "It's alright... these are the guys we met last night. Don't worry about them, fact I'm still hoping they will change their minds and join in on this job we're looking at."

Sundance hadn't taken his eyes off Randy since they set down. He was looking him over thinking to himself. He seemed to have a quiet demeanor, if it didn't need to be said, he didn't say it. Unlike Larry and Gary who turned everything into a good bullshit story...especially Larry, he added extra character voices. But this Young man was only five feet five AND A HALF inches tall. Shit he bet Randy went a good one seventy plus in weight. Just look at those arms and chest. Those forearms alone were bigger than his calf muscle on his leg ... Right off,

127

he was quite sure you did not want them arms getting a hold on you… those arms could hurt you. He just knew there was power inside those arms. He had seen little men like him before; men who made short order work out of men twice their size.

If Randy had even half the temper they had been warned about, he bet Randy could take men even three times his size or bigger. The look in those eyes, they may be laughing now, but they've seen every move anyone and everyone in the general area had made. That quiet demeanor he had. That was a sure sign of a man to watch out for… Quiet but deadly. At least he wasn't packing a gun.

The young lady returned to the table with enough beer and glasses for everyone. She even brought a few extra ladies with her.

"Thanks," Larry said. Reaching for the pitcher of beer and a glass. "Now that's what I call a good lady, not only does she bring the beer, but she also brings a few friends along to make the party more lively."

All the young ladies first walked over to Randy, each hoping he'd pick her over the others. "Why don't you young ladies join the others tonight?" Randy said. "I'm saving my money. I would love to play a little cards, though."

"You must come in here quite often," Butch said.

"Not really, they just don't forget me," Randy answered. "I'm that good."

"You're dreaming," Luis said to Randy. "They just figure that if they can get into your party group…then their paycheck for the night won't end up over at Doc's place."

"Hey Larry," Sundance started to say. "We heard about that famous ride that Roan took you on up on the mountain this morning."

"That wasn't as much fun as you think. I'd sure like to see one of you clowns try and ride him," Larry said, reaching for the bottle of whiskey.

"No thanks," Curry said, chuckling "I like the tame ones."

"So you think it's funny do ya? I bet if we made a bucking chute in the corral next to the stable's, put a flank strap on him…I'd bet no one could ride him for the required eight seconds," Larry shouted out.

Chapter Seven

"Now Larry," Gary said, "just because Dude had that black mustang stallion when we were kids, that he said ten men couldn't ride, doesn't mean that no one can ride your Roan."

"You remember that horse?" Randy cut in. "He would ride him into the bucking shoot, put that flank strap on him, if anyone rode him they got the money."

"I remember it well," Gary said. "He got to keep the money every time, fact we always got a new pair of cowboy boots afterwards."

"How much did each man have to pay for a chance?" Butch asked.

"It was like... ten dollars each, wasn't it" Gary asked.

"I'd sure want to charge them a whole hell of a lot more than that." Larry said, firmly.

"You're greedy," Randy said chuckling a little.

"Maybe so, but these people can afford a whole lot more up here now they could back then," Larry shouted.

"That is a big horse," Curry said. "I couldn't help but notice him as I rode in this morning. Butch and Sundance are both fair with an ornery horse."

"That horse isn't just ornery," Larry said, refilling his beer. "He flat don't want anyone on his back, not even me."

"No horse is that good!" Sundance said, discarding two cards.

"Well, if you think you can ride him hero, put your money where your mouth is," Larry shouted out.

"Well, just how much you boys have between you?" Butch asked. "I'll match dollar for dollar that someone can ride him."

The four all looked at each other with smiles on their faces. "Well, I suppose we could come up with thousand to fifteen hundred." Gary answered.

"Like hell," Randy said. "I got paid yesterday... I have three thousand that says not one in ten men can ride that horse."

"You said ten men right?" Butch asked looking at them.

"That's right," Larry said, looking at the three outlaws. "Ten men!"

"Who gets to choose the ten men?" Sundance wanted to know.

"Whoever wants to," Gary answered. "Just as long as they can come up with the entry money and they are crazy enough to try. But they'd think twice if they saw how high Randy went this afternoon."

"So five hundred dollars entry fee for each rider?" Curry said.

"You're talking about a five thousand dollar pay out," Gary said. Looking around at his two brothers. "We don't have that much money."

"We do," Butch said. "Besides that's just about what you boys owe us from last night."

"Now just wait a minute, just because that little Betty ripped you off last night. You know we didn't have anything to do with that," Larry said, starting to get a little hot under the collar.

"Oh heck guys, we know that. I was just funn'en with ya is all," Butch answered, shuffling the cards. "But if that horse is as good as you all say he is…I was thinking we could get that five thousand back we lost last night and then some… Fact, I might want to try him myself, just for shits and giggles."

"Well, there's one fool," Larry said. "Now we just need nine more."

"Oh hell, just look around the room, it's full of idiots as you say," Randy said, pointing around the room.

"It's my horse and you guys are putting up the money…So, just what do I get out of this?" Larry asked.

"We'll split the winnings with you," Butch told Larry. "But I want a shot at that Roan myself. They used to have a couple rodeos back home when I was a kid, I entered a few times…never won anything, but like Larry said earlier…it's a rush, just you and that horse. After all, like you said, we're putting the money up."

"Alright, but they have to be sober," Larry said. "I don't want anyone getting killed out there."

"Hell, if he's that good," Curry said. "Why don't we get fifteen or twenty riders?"

"Nope," Gary said shaking his head. "Dude always said, a good horse might go through six or seven men, a great horse could take ten, but if you try to go past ten, nine times out of ten…that eleventh rider will take your horse's hard earned money more often than not."

130

Chapter Seven

"Alright, ten it is,' Butch said pushing his hat down on his head. "This could be a lot of fun. Might hurt for a little while, but it will be fun to get on a good bronc.'

"What hurts the worst is that intentional sudden stop when you hit the ground," Gary said.

"You have bigger cahonas than I do, hombre," Luis said. "I've seen the trips he and Larry have been on the last couple days...And I'm here to tell you my moneys on that horse all the way."

"Well, Randy, Gary, you want in on this?" Larry asked.

"Wait just one minute," Sundance said to Larry. "We all heard that you guys grew up riding bucking horses, and you still break broncs for a living. We're not going to put the money up just for one of you to win."

"Darn," Randy said picking up his cards. "I sure would have liked another try on that Roan...That money would have given me the extra incentive that I would have needed. But I'm going to tell you one thing that horse has a wild spirit, and if he don't want anyone on him...you ain't staying on him Butch! I know that much."

"So we hear tell you run a team of horses skidding logs," Sundance stated. "Being from New Jersey, I've never seen a real logging operation." Sundance wanted to find out more.

"No, NO!" Randy said. "A team is two..." Taking a drink off his beer. "A team of two is for green horns and beginners, I run six... Clydesdales."

"What the hell you do when those logs start rolling down hill, towards you?" Butch asked

"MOVE FAST!" Larry shouts and starts chuckling and moving his feet.

"Sure can tell you don't know anything about logging," Randy answered. "That's why you always stay on the up hill side of them big logs."

"So how many logs can you pull at one time?" Sundance asked.

"That depends on their size," Randy say's. "They're usually six to eight foot at the butt cut, then they cut them in half every thirty-three feet. I usually start at the back and pull forwards, picking up each length as I come out. I can usually pull three, maybe four logs each pull, never more than two butt cuts at once. Most other teams only get one butt or two from the middle of the tree at a time. By the way, are these chips worth anything tonight?"

"Well, your brothers don't like playing for money, least that's what they told us last night." Butch answered.

"I told you, I've got better thing to spend my money on." Gary said. "Especially with all these card sharks up here." He says. Pointing around the room picking out a couple of them. "Guys dressed in expensive suits, playing like they're business men from out of town and have never played poker before. But since they are up here, and their wives won't find out, why not try a couple hands. Still there were some who were good, also a lot of cheaters, with an ace up his sleeve… no thank you."

"Just look around, these idiots work all week digging it up, then cash it in over there, then spends it all in a couple hours." Randy said pointing.

"Ya look at the one at that table, you know he can't afford to loose what he has," Gary said. "That can turn a friendly game of cards into a deadly game."

"I've seen that happen to many times," Sundance says. "Someone getting shot, cause he got caught double-dealing."

"Hell, I bet we could make the entry fee one thousand each,' Butch said. "Still only pay out five thousand. Hell, they won't care what they're betting on, only that they have a chance to win big." They could tell Butch was trying to find a way to make some extra money.

The men had been playing poker and still talking about the possible bucking competition for about an hour. They were playing with those worthless chips. Randy leaned back in his chair. He could see the hand of cards of the miner right behind him. He was holding a king high straight flush, all hearts. Just one away from being a royal flush. "HOLY SHIT," Randy shouted. "If I had that hand, I'D BET THE HOUSE."

"WHY YOU NO GOOD"…the man started saying. Throwing his cards on the table, standing up, turned and reached for his pistol all

Chapter Seven

at the same time. When all of a sudden, from out of no where a knife came flying through the air taking the mans hat off and sticking it to the wall just behind him. Bringing the man to a sudden stop.

"Now, that knife has three sisters mister," Larry said. Everyone knows he's not packing a gun. "Either you can set back down, or take that gun off, and fight like a man. Either way it will be over soon."

One of the men at his table pulled on his sleeve…"You know who that is…?' the man whispered.

Butch and Sundance looked at each other, then around for Curry not realizing he had gone to the restroom a few minute's earlier. The two outlaws looked at this man. He was every bit of six and a half feet tall; two hundred fifty pounds, if he weighed one. Randy was just sitting there laughing at him. Which made the big man even madder.

"I DON'T CARE who he thinks he is," the big man said, unbuckling his holster, then slamming it down on the table. "I'M GOING TO TEACH THIS A-HLOE A LESSON IN KEEPING HIS BIG MOUTH SHUT." He lunged at Randy, throwing his right fist with everything he had. Randy flew out of his chair; coming up under the big mans arms. Throwing his own right into the big mans kidney. Picking him up at least eighteen inches off the floor. Taking most of the air out of his lungs. Then Randy threw his left into his rib cage, breaking a couple of them. Making it hard for the big man to catch his breath as he found himself kneeling on the floor, He looked over at Randy, coughing up a little blood. Hell, he was almost as tall kneeling down as this little man was tall. No way was he being beat by this little man. As fast as he could, he lunged up at Randy again; who just stuck his foot out. This sent the man crashing face first into one of the tables. Randy reached down and grabbed the big man by his shirt, spun him around and picked him up like he was just a rag doll. He started smashing his own powerful fists into the man's face. THREE, FOUR, FIVE. Hell no one could count them all. Sending teeth and blood splattering over everyone and anyone close by.

As soon as the fight started everyone moved back. Still setting in his chair, Gary looked over at the outlaws, "Did you see his attack… Kinda reminds you of a mountain lion stocking his pray. Every blow

133

precise and deadly." Larry and Gary both started laughing. Seeing Randy had done more than enough damage, Gary reached out and grabbed his wrist with both hands. "RANDY... RANDY, he's had enough, now it's over with."

"YA, MISTER...P-P-PLEASE... L-L-Listen to him...j-just let me go... I promise I'll leave, Hell, I-I will even leave my gun here." The big man started begging.

"Look Randy, you've got him stuttering just like you do when you get excited," Larry said.

The outlaws could not believe the power in Randy's arms, they knew there wasn't a bone one not broke in that mans face.

"Come on Randy," Gary repeated. "It's over."

"Please mister... I just want to get to a doctor." Randy had that big man pleading.

"He's right across the street," Luis told him pointing and chuckling. "Second building, top of the steps...You're lucky, he still has his light on."

Randy let go of the man. The big man hit the floor with a heavy thud. Slowly he started crawling across the floor, working his way away from Randy. Two of his buddies helped him up and out the door.

Randy turned back around, still smiling; "Hell they usually last longer than that...I didn't even work up a sweat."

The two outlaws were looking at each other, and then back at Randy; each one had heard every punch land. "Did you see the power in those blows?" Sundance asked holding his nose.

"YAA," said Butch. "I couldn't see his arm move, just kept hearing bones breaking and seeing more blood flying every where."

"Look, he's not even mad," Sundance said, whispering to Butch, still looking at Randy.

"Remind me NOT to piss HIM off!" Butch said, rubbing his cheek bone's..."just watching that, HURT'S."

"I'm glad he don't carry a gun," Sundance said.

"He don't need one," Butch answered, leaning back in his chair. "I'm glad he's on our side."

Chapter Seven

"I hear ya," Sundance said, starting to shuffle the cards. "I've Never, and I Mean NEVER have I seen a man that size go down so fast...Hell, he never laid a hand on Randy."

"Hell, I only hit him a couple times," Randy said, sitting back down. "ANY ONE else want to try me?" Everyone was saying, "No SIR," and slowly backed away from him, slowly but quickly.

"Did anyone see where that knife came from?" Sundance asked.

"Came from Larry," Butch said. "But no, I didn't see where it came from."

"Hell, he pulled, threw, and hit his target before most men could draw a gun," Sundance said.

"What do you mean could?" Butch said. "He did...and he said that knife has three sisters. I wonder where he keeps them all."

Looking over at Gary. "Sure wish you boy's would join in with us on that other job we're looking at," Sundance said to him. "You guys aren't gun happy...which is just the kind of men we like to work with."

"Men who aren't in a hurry to pull and use a gun," Butch cut in. "But still have some what a level head on their shoulders."

"You know, there's not much between here and Utah," Curry said setting back down. "So instead of going that way, what do you think about going out through Portland instead?"

"Why the hell would you want to go out through Portland for?" Sundance asked.

"Cause, then we could catch a steamer down to San Francisco," Curry answered.

"FRISCO! What the hell would you want to go there for?" Sundance asked. Looking around the table. "Those guys down there give me the creeps...Hell, the last time we were down there... I felt like the guys were checking ME out, not the women." As a cold chill goes up his back, making him shiver at the thought.

"Alright then, we'll stay on the steamer till we get to Los Angles or San Diego. HELL, I don't care which one; I just don't want to go back out across that desert." Curry said

135

By now everyone is listening to the three talking. "You've never been through Butch's home town of Circleville, have you Curry?" Sundance asked.

"Nope, and I can't say as I care to. The only part I went through was bad enough… hell none of them women there just want to have sex and fool around a little. They all want to get married first."

"Well, what I was getting at is the river that runs through there runs due north." Sundance said.

"Now who's full of shit," the twin's and Randy said at the same time. "Just how the hell does a river run north?"

"He's right," Butch answered, discarding a few cards. "It's called the Sevier River. They say it's the one of the longest north flowing river in America."

"Well now, just how does it get to the ocean?" Randy asked.

"It don't, it flows out into the desert and just disappears…and that ain't no bullshit story." Butch answered

Just then two of the young ladies returned to the table with a couple pitchers of beer and a couple more bottles of whiskey.

"Thank you ladies," Butch said, looking them over. "How about all you young ladies let us talk for a little while, and then we'll call you back over when we're finished?"

"Well you boys don't take too long," one of them said. "We get thirsty too."

Butch reached into his pocket; pulled out two fifty dollar bills and handed them to her. "You ladies get what you need to keep yourselves happy. Then be ready to come back when we finish talking."

"In other words," Sundance added. "Find yourselves an empty table. We won't be much more than an hour…you can wait that long." He said, watching them walk away, then looking back over at the twins. "So you men thought about what we talked about last night?"

"What 'job' are you guys talking about?" Randy wanted to know looking around the table at everyone waiting for an answer.

"They want to rob the train," Gary said. Picking up his new hand of cards.

Chapter Seven

"The Baker City -Sumpter Rail Road?" Randy said with a chuckle. "That would be the one you're talking about, wouldn't it?"

"That's the one," Butch said.

"Hell, I've know how to pull that job off for a long time," Randy said smiling…"I've just been waiting for the right fools to come along so I could show them how! It took awhile… but you finally came around."

"That gold is heavy shit," Randy said. "Fact, you'd want pack mules, not horses. They can carry more weight, and there's a lot of gold on that train."

"How would you know that?" Butch asked.

"I've seen them load it more that once," Randy answered

"So just where do they load it at?" Butch asked with an anxious look in his eyes.

"Right down there at the old smoke house," Randy answered. Pulling out a pipe, loaded a little peyote in it then took a big pull off it. He tried handing it around. "Anyone else want any?"

"No thanks," they all answered at the same time. "Damn that stuff sticks," the three outlaws all said at the same time. Sundance looked over at him. "I've been down to that old smoke house myself. Hell, the only thing left of that place is half the floor, run down walls and an old wood stove… It looks like someone stables a horse in there every once in a while."

"Hell they don't want just anyone knowing where, when, and how they load all that gold." Randy said.

"You still haven't answered my question," Sundance asked the question again, "Just how do you know that's where they load it?"

"Cause, I'm the one who stables my horse down there. They used to load it every Thursday night, but about two months ago they changed it to Sunday nights."

"If they load it in secret, then why do they let you know when, where, and how?" Butch asked, filling up everyone's beer.

"No thanks," Randy said covering his beer mug. "I've had enough." Then he continued, "They dug a tunnel from the bank, under the town that comes up in the smoke house. I've been stabling my stallion

137

down there long before they struck gold around here...They've never bothered me or my stallion, it's like they're afraid of both of us or something."

"We've seen why they're afraid of you," Sundance said. "But why do you stable your horse down there?"

"No where else in town will let me stable him in their stable's anymore," Randy answered

"Why's that?" Curry asked.

"Well, if there's a mare in there and she's in season, no lead rope, hell, not even a logging chain is going to stop that big fella from breaking loose and getting to her," Randy said. "Heaven for bid someone should bring in another stallion... That big stallion of mine is going to let him KNOW just who the big kid in the house is. Either way, he tears the place up. Not to mention, hurting the mare."

"Hurting the mare, just how does he hurt the mare?" Curry asked.

"Like he said," Larry shouted out. "He's a BIG Horse, and those mares are too small for him, if you get my meaning. Then he hurts her again eleven months later when she tries to give birth to that foal." With that comment everyone started laughing.

"Back to the gold," Randy said. "There was a rumor going around these parts last week, that you boys were heading this direction after you robbed that bank in Haine's. They were afraid to ship last week. So they will have even twice as much to ship this week."

"Sunday night?" Butchs' eyes growing to twice their normal size. "You're saying they ship on Sunday's...as in, this Sunday?"

"Yep," Randy discarded. "They ship them in fifty pound bags."

"If it was me, I'd get me a couple big draft horses like Randy has." Larry said. "They're not as stubborn as those damned mules can be."

"That's not a bad idea. So how about it Randy, would you sell use a couple of your Clydesdales?" Butch asked.

"I don't know. You have any idea just how much money I'd be out?" Randy answered.

"Alright, how about we just rent them from you then?" Sundance said.

Chapter Seven

"Still, thinking about it," Randy said. "You're going to have them for at least a couple months…I'll be out quite a bit of money in that time."

"We'll make it worth your time," Curry said. "Hell just one of your horses could carry twice as much than any pack mule could carry."

Butch wanted to know just how much Randy thought his horses were worth.

"Hell, I'd be out at least eight to ten thousand dollars. That's if you had them back to me in just two months." Randy said, "that's a lot of money to loose."

"You drive a damn hard bargain," Butch said. "We'll pay you ten thousand for each. That's if you're willing?"

Taking out a piece of plug tobacco, Randy took a big bite. "Well, I suppose I could lend you my two gelding's."

"Thanks," Sundance answered, "there's a spit-ton right behind you."

"What the hell would I need one of them for?" Randy answered, swallowing the tobacco juice.

"You swallow that shit?" Sundance asked, rubbing his stomach. Just the thought of that made everyone's stomach churn.

"Dude always told us, if we were going to chew it, he didn't want to see us spitting all over the place," Randy said. "Said it made it look dirty, spitting all over the place."

"You are a strange one, Randy," Curry said, "you swallow that shit, and you smoke that peyote shit."

"Hey don't knock it till you try it," Randy said, with a big smile on his face. "You take one hit of that peyote and it relaxes you… The Indian's say if you take a couple big puffs of it, the great spirit will show you visions of what's to come." Moving his hands and fingers up, wiggling them in the air. "I don't know if that's true, but if you smoke too much of it, you just fall asleep. You drink too much of that shit and you start praying to GOD, hoping to stop throwing up." He chucked a little.

"Swallowing that shit would make me sick," Butch said, "and I know when I've had enough of this." Holding up his beer…"although,

139

I will tell ya, last night I thought I could keep up with that one," Pointing to Larry. "But I found out this morning I couldn't, and I'm not even going to try tonight."

"Hell, sometimes at work, I get real hungry…my lunch box is on the top of the mountain and I'm on the bottom, or vice versa," Randy say's. "I've eaten a whole plug before I realize it, tastes kinda like black licorice…"

"Now we know you're crazy." Butch said to Randy.

"An old Indian told me a story once, He told me…'Man made Booze, God made Peyote.' WHO DO YOU TRUST?" Randy said. "Besides, there's no better high. Except maybe for riding a good bucking horse…Now that is flat out fun…Just you and that twelve to fifteen hundred pound animal. Him trying to throw you, and you staying right with him, setting tall in the saddle…Now that's got to be the best high of all highs.'

"Let's get back to more important matters here," Butch said. "Just how many bags of gold do they get? We hear those dredges are pulling out a lot of it."

"I hope to shout," Randy said. "Every time I've seen them load it, they've loaded at least fifty to sixty bags."

"Hell, maybe we should get us some more animals. So we can pack even more gold." Curry said.

"Damn you're greedy," Gary said.

"Do you really think that Roan can best ten men?" Butch asked.

"Wouldn't say he could if I didn't think he could," Larry answered, bragging.

"Good," Butch said. "We can use the bucking competition as a diversion…get everyone good and drunk Sunday afternoon."

"Now just wait one minute there," Larry said. "Just how much money am I going to get for using my horse as your diversion?"

"Well, just how much more do you want?" Butch asked. "I mean hell; we're already willing to give you half if nobody rides him."

"Hell, I'll take whatever else I can get." Larry say's, taking a drink off his beer and gave Butch a big smile.

"You Larkin boys are greedy." Sundance said to the brother's.

140

Chapter Seven

"It's called supply and demand," Gary said, looking over at Sundance. "We have the supply and you have the demand for our horses. Supply and Demand gentlemen!"

"I'm afraid he's got us there guys," Butch replied, "but how much you going to let us put on one horse?"

"Five hundred pounds, but, gold is weighed in troy ounce's.12 ounce's to the pound, so you'll be able to put two more bag, making it twelve bags per hourse." Randy said smiling. "That should keep you from robbing banks awhile…Take it or leave it."

CHAPTER EIGHT

It was early in the morning when Shawn woke up. He slowly got up and walked over to the wash basin, poured in some water and washed the sleep out of his eyes. Glancing out the widow, Shawn could see there was already quite a few people up and about. He could tell by their demeanor that they were loggers heading to the mountains to work.

The window was cracked open just enough for him to smell coffee. Opening it up, he looking out, he could see a whole lot of people coming and going from the restaurant below. That was where the smell was coming from. Reaching over he quickly got dressed and headed out of the room.

On the way down Shawn was thinking to himself, 'Corky has a real nice place here. Right across the street from the mill and just across the street from the train station.' He chuckled a little, why hell, he gets them coming and going. A Saloon, Brothel, Motel, and restaurant all in one. The room he had last night was real nice. He'd been in fancy rooms like that when he had been in fancy motels in big cities. It really was a classy place for a Saloon and brothel.

Shawn stopped at the door that went into the café side of the Saloon. Slowly looking around the room he was surprised to see that at least half the tables were full. He noticed young Sheriff Beyer setting at a table by himself. Shawn walked over, stuck out his hand, sitting down. "Good morning, Sheriff," he said. He picked up his coffee cup

142

Chapter Eight

and started looking around the room. "So what does a man have to do to get a cup of coffee around here?" Not realizing the waitress had walked up between them.

"Well Marshal, if you'll turn back around here and give me your cup, I'll be glad to fill it for you," the young lady said.

Turning back around and feeling just a little embarrass, "I'm sorry young lady." Shawn said, right off he could see it was the same young lady that had served them their dinner yesterday.

"The Sheriff said you'd be wanting a cup before you sat down...I almost made it," she said with a big smile. "My name is Cathey Larkin, Marshal." She introduced herself, while she filled his coffee. "You and your Deputy need anything you just let me know, and I'll make sure you get it first."

"Well, thank you, Cathey," Shawn said, looking at that unique smile she had. It made her whole face light up. Making his heart feel happy just by looking at her. "So what's for breakfast?"

"You name it Marshal, we got it. Eggs, bacon, sausage, potatoes or anything else." Cathey answered.

"How about a little of all that?" Shawn answered. "I'm hunger this morning."

"Yes sir," Cathey answered, "And how would you like your eggs, Marshal?"

"Hard, just like my women. If I was only forty years younger, I'd sure chase after you young lady." Shawn said, starting to joke with her.

"You're not that old Marshal," Cathey answered, "but as far as chasing after me...you'd have a hard time catching me." Pointing around the room, "All these bums keep me on my guard enough."

"You sure are sure of yourself, young lady." Shawn said, smiling. "But then now days you have to watch out for yourself. You just remember one thing young lady; these young men only have one thing on their minds." Holding his cup up, "How about a fill up before you leave?"

"Sure thing Marshal." Cathey said, filling his cup. "I'll be right back with a hot plate and a fresh pot of coffee." Then filling up the Sheriff's cup, she turned and walked back to the kitchen.

143

"She sure is a sweet young lady," Shawn said. Continuing to drinking his coffee, it sure was a good cup. The two started talking about just what lay ahead of them over the next three days. "I'm going to ask Corky to pay you a little extra as well Sheriff, you're going to be just as busy out there keeping the peace, as we are in here."

"Thanks Marshal," Dennis said, "but like I said, it's already part of my job. I'm just glad you and Wapiti came along when you did."

"That's quite alright Sheriff," Shawn said. "This'll give Wapiti a chance at get used to a rowdy crowd, and cut his teeth a little, if you get my mean'en.

"You do know Marshal, most these men around here aren't going to like an Indian lawman, fact I bet someone will try him before noon." Dennis said, with a serious look on his face and looking around the room.

"I figured it will be before then, but I'm not too worried about Wapiti," Shawn said, with a big smile on his face. Reaching into his pocket and pulled out a ten-dollar bill. "I'll put that on Wapiti, say…up to…MMM…three men, hand to hand of course."

"Three men at the same time?" Dennis asked, reaching in his pocket for his wallet. "I'll take that bet."

The two were just finishing up breakfast when Wapiti came walking into the restaurant. Seeing where the Marshal was seated, he walked over, looked around the room at everyone staring at him and no one was talking. "Why didn't you get me up Marshal?" Wapiti asked, sitting down.

"Well, I figured you needed your rest," Shawn said. "You're going to need it tonight."

Wapiti couldn't help but to keep looking around the room, slowly everyone started talking again. But Wapiti knew the conversations were mostly about him. All staring at the badge on his chest, and that hog leg on his side.

Just then three men sat down at the table next to them. He could tell right off that they were loggers by the way they were dressed. The taller one looked over at Wapiti, laughing. "Who does this Indian think he is…A law man…Does he think anyone is going to take him serious?" the man said jokingly.

144

Chapter Eight

Wapiti wasn't sure how long the waitress had been standing there, when she started talking to him. "Don't worry Wapiti, those two are just Jack and Sam Seebart, the other guy is new, but I think his name is Lavern. They just like to talk big."

Wapiti couldn't help but notice it was the same young lady that had served them dinner. That short dark brown hair, those big beautiful brown eyes, and that smile...that smile made his heart thump louder and faster. "Thanks," he said, ordering his breakfast.

Then the Marshal looked over at Dennis. "Well Sheriff, shall we go see where we're going to put everything and everyone?"

Wapiti looked over at the two as they stood up. "Marshal, you're not going to leave me here alone, are you?" He asked in a loud whisper.

"Oh hell Wapiti...Nobody's going to bother you." Shawn said, throwing a silver dollar on the table. Then he and Dennis headed for the door. But no sooner were they out of the room and the three started talking more shit at Wapiti.

The biggest of the three looked over at Wapiti. "I think the lad needs a hair cut? Don't you, Sam?" Jack asked

"Sure do, Jack," Sam said. "He wants a white man's job, I think he needs a white mans hair cut."

"Ya, only half scalp him, you might say." Jack replied, standing up, looking around the room. "What do you all think?" Sam stood up, and he and Jack both walked over towards Wapiti. Everyone started getting excited and anxious to see this wannabe Indian lawman put in his place. Not knowing that the Marshal was just outside the door watching.

"So just what do you think? Wanna be Deputy," Sam said "Do you think you need a hair cut?"

"No sir, I don't believe I do." Wapiti answered, looking up at the two. He knew something was going to happen. He didn't like it, but no one was going to give him a hair cut.

Both men walked over to him, one on each side of Wapiti. Jack reached his big arm and hand across the back to the other side of Wapiti's chair. With all his strength, he started to spin the chair around. Thinking quickly, Wapiti hooked his leg out, tripping Sam and sending him to the floor. When the chair came to a stop; Wapiti came up with all the force and power he had in his legs. Bringing his right fist up at the same time, catching Jack under the jaw and sending him flying backwards, crashing down on top of the table behind him. Seeing Sam starting to rise out of the corner of his eye, Wapiti did a full spin. As Sam was about two thirds of the way up, Wapiti's foot caught him in the side of his head, sending Sam flying over one table and crashing to the floor on the other side. "Why You No Good InJun," Wapiti heard a voice from behind him. Hearing a chair move across the floor at the same time. Reaching for and pulling the ten gauge, he spun back around to Lavern. "YOU WANT IN ON THIS MISTER?" Wapiti demanded.

Bringing Lavern to a dead stop, he stared into those two HUGE barrels. Hell, that wasn't a double barrel twelve gauge that was a DOUBLE BARREL TEN GAUGE. Just one barrel would put a hole big enough in you to read the Sunday paper through, Lavern thought to himself. "N-N-No SIR...I DON'T," Lavern said. Reaching for his chair behind him, but it wasn't there, causing him to fall down backwards on the floor. He was just trying to get away from THAT gun.

Wapiti looked at the other two men, who were slowly picking themselves up off the floor. Then looking around the room. "NOW, if I took scalps, I would have myself three right now. I'm going to be here all weekend; you tell your friends...Next time, I might just really lift me a scalp. NOW you three get the hell out of here."

"Yes sir, Deputy," they all three answered, working their way towards the door. Just then, out of the corner of his eye, Wapiti saw the Marshal and Sheriff come walking back in. The Marshal was taking money from the Sheriff hand and laughing.

"I guess he doesn't need our help after all," Shawn said looking around the room and waving his hand. "Any of the rest of you want to try and give him a hair cut?"

"NO, NO sir, don't think so!" Everyone was saying at the same time. They all started looking around the room at each other, wondering if there were any takers.

Chapter Eight

"Well Deputy, why don't you just go right on ahead and finish your breakfast?" Shawn said, lighting a cigar. "I'm sure no one will bother you for a while,"

Shawn turned around, "Well it sounds like you know who those three men are Sheriff. They started it, so you make sure they pay for the damage." Then he headed back out the door and into the Saloon.

Shawn could see people were already starting to get in line to pay their money to make sure they got in on the poker game. Cork was already up on his thrown, with that double barrel twelve gauge in one hand and a beer in the other. Pulling out his pocket watch Shawn walked up to Corky. "Hell Cork, Even I don't start drinking till noon."

Holding up his beer, and taking a big drink. "Hell Shawn, its noon somewhere," Cork answered. "Besides, it's my place and I'll drink whenever I want to. If I get too drunk, I don't have very far to go to find a bed."

"You're right about that," Shawn answered. "Well I guess it's time we start getting everything in order." Walking to the center of the room, He started giving out orders. "We'll rope this area here off, around these tables. Only ones allowed in will be the players and the waitresses. The people watching can have the area over there, the bar area there, the stairs and balcony up there." Pointing while he's talking. "I'd like to see us start this shin-dig by four o-clock this afternoon."

"Now you just wait one minute Shawn," Cork shouted out. "What if everyone who wants to play ain't here by then?"

"Alright, your flyer say's six o-clock, so we'll start at four, but if anyone comes in later we'll still let them in. Also, I'd like you to pay the Sheriff a bonus as well. He's going to be just as busy out there as we are in here, Hell maybe even more."

"Thanks Marshal," Dennis said. "But like I told you earlier, it's already part of my job. I'm just glad you came along. Hell your reputation alone is going to detour most of the idiots from trying anything, and after seeing Wapiti in action this morning...That will make a few others think twice before they try anything. If you have everyone check their guns at the door, then things won't get out of hand."

"That's a good idea Sheriff." Shawn said. "You're right, we'll make everyone check their guns at the door, and that way I won't have to shoot anyone this week-end."

Soon the gaming tables were all roped off, and the line was growing with people wanting to get in the games. Each hoping he or she would be the big winner. When one man yelled out, "I'm not playing poker with any women." "Me either," a couple other guys started shouting.

"It looks like you're not playing in this game then," Shawn said in a stern voice. "Their money is just as good as yours. So if they want to play, I'm not going to stop them. So you just better get used to it, or get out yourselves."

It didn't take very long for everyone to accept the conditions and live with the women being in the tournament. With all the excitement and commotion going on time flew by. Before they knew it, it was time for the games to start. Shawn stood up on top of the bar. "Now then, let's get a few rules out in the open. FIRST, you go into the gaming area packing a gun, you pull it, I promise you will hit the floor dead before you ever have enough time to pull the trigger. Second, if you're caught cheating…you're out of the game and all your chips go into the middle of the table for the next hand. DO I MAKE MYSELF CLEAR?"

"Yes sir Marshal," they all started saying, as everyone started looking at all the other player's faces more closely. They all hoped there wouldn't be any gunplay as well. That's not what they had come here for.

"Now one more thing Ladies and Gentlemen" Shawn shouted. "You're each going to cough up an extra twenty dollars to be divided up by the young ladies waiting on you for your drinks or anything else you might need."

It didn't take long and all you could hear were cards being shuffled and people talking to each other. Wapiti slowly started walking around the tables, looking down at everyone. Charley had the pleasure of setting atop the thrown, while Shawn and Cork set up at the bar drinking beer and talking, but still facing the gaming area in case something might start. Wapiti noticed that each and every table he came to,

Chapter Eight

everyone shut up and look up at him, and then down at that double barrel ten gauge. Just by looking at them, Wapiti could tell most of them didn't like the idea of an Indian DEPUTY U.S. Marshal. But with Marshal Shawn Felton in the room, no one was about to say or do anything about it now.

The Marshal was well known for being quick to react, and none of them wanted to be on the receiving end if he did pull his pistol, or on the receiving end of one of his fists. They had all heard about what that young buck Indian did to the Seebart brothers this morning. Fact to remind them, all they had to do was look a couple table over. Sam's entire right side of his face was bruised from top to bottom. They wondered with all that swelling if he could even see out his right eye, and Jack, shoot his entire lower jaw was one big bruise. It was a wonder it wasn't broke. They also knew, he wouldn't be eating much solid foods for a while. Wapiti made sure to say good evening to each of them as he walked up to their table, stopping and looking over at them. "I don't mean to sound bossy Sam, Jack," he stuck out his hand to them, "but did you gentlemen get the word to pay for the damages in the café?"

"MM UUHH," they both sounded, nodding their heads up and down, while shaking Wapiti's hand. Neither one could say too much, cause it just flat hurt like hell. "We'll take care of it first thing in the morning," Jack said with only his lips moving his jaw was held tight so it couldn't move. He hadn't been able to eat all day.

Wapiti continued around the rest of the tables. He wasn't sure how long the games had been going on but he knew he hadn't eaten much since breakfast. He was getting hungry, so he was happy when the Marshal came to relieve him.

"Like how you handled those two," Shawn said with a big smile on his face. "So is there anything I should know about?"

"Well, every things going fine, As you can see," Wapiti answered. "There's at least four men that I've seen packing pistols, and one derringer. That I've seen, but I'm sure there's more."

"Alright son," Shawn said. "I think I can find the rest. Just go straight back to the kitchen for your dinner. I had Cathey fix you something, that way you won't have to wait."

149

"Thanks Marshal, I am hungry. Is there anything I can get you before I leave?"

"As a matter a fact there is, have Cathey cut me a big slice of apple pie, and set it aside.. It sure will hit the spot just before bedtime."

"Alright Marshal," Wapiti answered, then he turned and walked out of the roped off area. He was having a lot of fun. He had shown those white eyes he could take care of himself. But he also knew he had gotten lucky the way things worked out in his favor. He was happy the Marshal had brought him along on one of his hunt'en trip. He just hoped he wouldn't let the Marshal down when it really counted.

Shawn slowly walked around the tables, looking down at each player. He could see right off Wapiti was right about the men packing, only he'd counted more than eight after only going around half the tables. All of a sudden Shawn reached down and pulled up the gambler with the derringer in his vest pocket, picking him straight up out of his chair. The mans feet were a good six to eight inches off the floor, scaring the man half to death. He knew the Marshal saw his gun. Slamming the man out flat across the table. He reached over and pulled the derringer out of the man's vest pocket, throwing it on the table…"NOW, that was rule number one…no guns in the playing area and I know there's plenty more of you packing." He purposely reached down, picked the Young man up by his vest, and then Shawn threw the Young man back down into his seat. "ANY one and everyone who has a gun or knife on him has one minute to put it on the table in front of you. IF YOU don't put that gun on the table right now, and I notice one of you still packing; I will personally take great pleasure in punishing you before I throw you out that door. DO I make myself crystal clear gentlemen, and ladies?"

Within seconds he could hear pistols landing on tops of the tables, slowly looking around the room. Then over at one of the waitresses, "Young lady, will you please pick those up for me? Just put them up by Cork."

"Yes sir, Marshal," the young lady answered, doing as he had asked.

"Alright, now let's get back to the games," Shawn said. "We don't have but a couple hours left tonight, and I can see some of

Chapter Eight

you don't even have that long. Now all of you who owns one of those guns up there, I will expect to see you after we finish up here tonight."

Shawn started walking around the room again, looking at the people and some of their cards. He couldn't help but chuckle a little. What kind of idiot would spend that much money gambling on a deck of cards? Just hoping he or she might get lucky and win it all. He walked up to the table that the Seebart brothers were sitting at. They appeared to be doing well, at least as far as the cards game was going they both were up in chips.

"Good evening, gentlemen," he said looking down at them. "Damn son, that looks like it hurts," grabbing Sam's jawbone and turning his face side to side. "Kinda hard to see out that eye isn't it?"

"Yes sir, Marshal," Sam answered looking up at him.

"I don't see the other Young man who was with you two this morning." Shawn said, looking around the room.

"No sir, Marshal," Jack said, still only moving his lips. "He's not a gambler."

"Sounds like he's the only smart one in the bunch," Shawn said.

"By the way, have you stopped by and paid the damage bill in the restaurant yet?"

"No sir," they both said. "But we told Deputy Wapiti we'd take care of it first thing in the morning. ...If that's aright with you to Marshal?" Sam asked.

"I suppose that will do, but you make sure you take care of it FIRST thing. That means before the games start tomorrow...CLEAR?" Shawn said glaring directly into the eye's of each man.

"Yes sir, Marshal," they both answered again. They looked around the room, noticing everyone had stopped playing, and was watching them. "First thing, I promise Marshal." Jack said.

Just then, Wapiti came walking back into the room, looking around at everyone as he walked through the crowd, working his way to the Marshal. Some men did step aside for him. But there were some that did it reluctantly, not for any damned Indian. He walked up to the Marshal, "Well Marshal, what would you like me to do now?"

151

"Well son, why don't you go ahead and call it a night. I'll finish up here," Shawn said. "Then tomorrow I'll sleep in, and you can get things started…I'll have the cook get you up early, so you can eat before most everyone else. You keep every thing under control till I get up."

"Yes sir, Marshal," Wapiti answered. "But you sure you don't need me a little longer? I'm really not that tired."

"That's alright, Wapiti, I'll finish up here tonight…Take a couple beers up to your room, they'll help you relax and let you fall asleep easier." Shawn said.

"Alright." Wapiti turned and walked over to the bar grabbed a small pitcher of beer and a mug, then headed up stairs to his room. Some of the cowboys and loggers that were on the stairs and balconies were making different accusations to and about him. "Like, I'd like to see him try that shit with me, I'd like to teach him a real good lesson, or, if he'd take that gun off, I know I could kick his ass." While other commented on him being an Indian, and there wasn't any way they would ever let an Indian tell them what to do… Wapiti tried not to even listen to them, he wasn't going to let any of them know if they were getting to him or not. He knew he was in for more trouble before the weekend was over. He just hoped it wouldn't be tonight. He would like to just relax tonight.

Meanwhile, Shawn was still making his rounds, but working his way back to Corky. Walking up and pulled out his pocket watch. "Well we don't have too much time left tonight, so I'll take one of those beers myself, please Charley."

"Sure thing, Marshal," Charley answered, filling a mug, and handing it to him.

"Cork, does that office of yours have a door leading outside?" Shawn asked.

"Yes it does, but I keep it bolted shut," Cork answered, "Why?"

"Well I don't think it will hurt to unlock it for a little while," Shawn said, with a big smile on his face. "I would like to use it for a while if you don't mind."

"I suppose, Marshal, but you mind if I ask what you need it for?" Cork asked.

152

Chapter Eight

"Well, I need a place I can return those pistols back to their right full owners, after I told them not to bring them into the game." Shawn said taking a big gulp out of his beer. "Now that hits the spot. So do you mind if I borrow your office?"

"Mind if I ask what you intend to do to them?" Cork asked.

"You'll just have to wait and find out like everyone else in the morning." Shawn answered, smiling. Then he turned and walked back into the playing area. He noticed a few empty seats around some of the tables, including the two that were throwing their last hand of cards into the middle of the table cursing a little as they walked out. Shawn just stood there looking at them shaking his head, 'poor fools' he thought. Pulling out his watch and looking at it again; hell it was close enough to midnight to call it. So he did.

"Alright, Listen up. This is your last hand of the night… when you finish, take your bags of chips back up to the bar. Make sure you get your name or your mark on your bag. This way no one can steal from anyone, and no one will be able to add a few extra chips so they can stay in a little longer. Those of you who own one of these pistols, lets see here," starting to count them. 'Thirteen, You thirteen men can meet me in the office right over here after you turn in your chips. The rest of you, I'll see you in the morning. NOW MY DEPUTY Wapiti will be in charge till I get up. If I hear any fussing over it, WELL, I'll be right down, and whoever is the cause, lets just say there will be hell to pay…Understood?"

"Yes sir, No problem Marshal." All the players were saying, picking up their chips and heading towards the bar to turn them in.

"Charley could you get me another beer? And a full bottle with two shot glasses and bring them into the office for me?" Shawn asked. Picking up all the pistols, he walked into the office, just ahead of Charley.

"Thanks Charley," Shawn said. "Just go ahead and leave the door open, I'll close it later." Then he walked over and unlocked the back door, turned around just in time to see the first man come walking through the door.

"Well, come on in and close that door behind you Young man," Shawn said, filling both shot glasses. Then pointing down at the pile of pistols. "So which one is yours?" he asked handing the man a shot of whiskey.

Looking through them, the man pointed to his pistol and taking the shot of whiskey at the same time. "This one right here, Marshal." He said, pointing to it.

Shawn picked it up, looked it over, and started to hand it to the man, who already had his hand out. Then with his right fist he drilled the man dead center of his face, blooding his nose and blackening both eyes at the same time, sending him crashing to the floor. Looking down at the man. "Now when I say NO guns mister, I mean NO guns, do I make myself clear?" Shawn growled out.

"Yes sir, Marshal," the man answered, standing back up.

"Now, you leave through that back door," Shawn said with a smirk on his face. "Cause you go back out the way you come in, then everyone else will see what's going to happen to them, and I don't want any of them missing out on their punishment. Understand? And one more thing, you bring that gun back, and you're out of the game. Clear?"

"Yes sir, Marshal," the man answered. Picking up his pistol and he used his handkerchief to cover his nose to stop the bleeding. Then he turned and walked out the back door. Cursing under his breath when he thought the Marshal couldn't hear.

No sooner had the first man left and next victim was knocking at the door, putting a big smile on Shawn's face. This night was going to be fun after all. "Please come in," Shawn called out, smiling. He poured two more shots and handed one to the next victim. He went through the next twelve just like the first, each time a new person came in, After seven or eight victims Shawn was beginning to feel a little warmer inside. Course the whiskey helped out just a little. When he finished, he locked the door and staggered back out to the bar with a big smile on his face. "Alright Charley, you can put those bags of chips away now." Then he staggered up to the bar. "So Cork, just how many players did we weed out tonight?"

"Twenty two Marshal," Cork answered. "Seventy eight to go. What was all that commotion we heard going on in there?"

Chapter Eight

"Nothing much, just me having a little fun is all." Shawn answered, sitting down at the bar. "Those boys won't be bringing them guns back tomorrow… I guarantee it."

The two had been sitting and talking about the night for a good hour when one of the young ladies came up and sat down on Shawn's lap.

"Is there anything I CAN do for you, Marshal?" She asked with a big smile on her face. "Fact for you, I'd be happy to give it to you on the house…if you know what I mean."

Shawn looked her over, putting his arm around her; he gave her a small kiss on the cheek. "Darlin' you'd kill me if we went up stairs together."

Still looking at him with that big smile, "Well Marshal, if the good Lord say's your times up, can you think of a better way to go?"

"No…No young lady I can't. But then who'd watch over the rest of the games?" Shawn answered.

"Well if you're sure Marshal, but I'd show you a real good time," the young lady said, giving him a kiss on the cheek.

"I'm sure you would young lady," Shawn answered, slapping her on the bottom. "But why don't you go find one of them other young men over there? You stick around here much longer and you're going to give me a heart attack, just thinking about it."

"Alright Marshal," she answered, then turned and walked away. Stopping and turning around. "It's your loss Marshal, cause I'm REAL good," she said, shaking her hips back and forth.

Shawn turned back to the others with a smile on his face. "I just bet she could teach a man a few things, but I'm going to call it a night"… Standing up, he picked up his beer. "Well gentlemen, I'll see you in the morning." Then he headed up the steps to bed.

155

CHAPTER NINE

"So Randy, if that stallion of yours keeps tearing things up, why don't you ride one of your other horses?" Sundance asked.

"Cause, at the end of the night that big boy knows where his three mares are." Randy answered. "With him I can just lay down over that big neck and go to sleep, then if I don't fall off first, when I wake up I'm back at camp."

Just then a tall, slinder black man, who at first glance they all figured him to be a hopeful, wanna get rich quick miner came walking up to the table." Excuse me," the man said, "but I was just over at the bar and someone said you bet five thousand dollar's that no-one could ride that Roan in the corral over at the livery... is that true? Or were you just running off with your mouth?"

"No, No it's no bull shit," Butch said. "Fact, it was that man right there who said so, pointing at Larry. But it will cost you a thousand to try him."

"I can get the money," the man said looking around the table.

Randy just happened to look down at the man's belt buckle It was from the Calgary Stampede in Calgary Canada. That was one of the Grandfather of all rodeo's. It was seven horse's in seven day's.

"You can see by my belt buckle that I've been on a few bucking horse's," the man said.

"You expect us to believe that buckle is real!" Larry said chuckling. "If your that good then what are you doing up here. Beside's, if that

156

Chapter Nine

buckle was real, it would be worth a few hundred dollar's by itself.... Aren't you afraid someone might mug you for it."

"It's real," the man said dumping his saddle bags out on the table and five more buckle's fell out on the table." My name is Charley Hall, but my friend's call me C.R."

The Larkin brother's started looking the buckle's over more closely. Then looking at each other. Two of them were the previous two year's to the one he was wearing. The other three were from the National Final Rodeo held in Denver Colorado. That rodeo was ten horses in ten day's. Not only did they have the man's name ingraved into them, but they also had his total score, out of a thousand point's total, the lowest score was 841, and the highest was 874.

"This man's good!" Randy said extending his hand. Introducing himself and every one else at the table. Introducing the three out laws by Smith, Jones, and Young.

"Now just wait a minute, C.R. is it?" Larry spoke up. "If your this good, then you get first ride only, Understand!"

"I don't care...but you afraid if my name is draw further down the line that he'll be tiring out and I'll cover him." C.R. answered looking down at Larry, smiling. "I just arrived in the area a couple day's ago, and all everyone who know's you three can say is how crazy you are. I've heard about your grandpa Dude Larkin. Fact, I've had the pleasure of riding some of the stock he has sold to various rodeo stock contractor's... What, did he break the Roan in."

"You could say he started," Larry answered smiling.

"YA, and Larry's been trying ever since," Luis said laughing. "And he still hasn't got it done."

"Some of those men said your grandpa had a black stallion he did this stunt with?" C.R. asked

"I've got a question," Butch said looking around the table." Just how the hell is it that all these miner's and logger's up here know so much about you Larkin men?"

"Dude, our grandpa is the clown and bull fighter at the Haines stampede.

157

His names is Willy Blue then," Larry blurted out." It's the biggest rodeo in this part of the country. Three day's long, with two night's of slack riders for everyone to buck out."

"What's a slack rider?" Curry asked

"That's when there's too many riders," Gary started explaining," When you enter you draw a animal and a time. You get entered late, then your number his higher. They can only buck so many during the main show which gets over around six o-clock. Then most of the patron's go over to the Grange Hall for a feast and big dance. All those lonely young farm girls just looking for a good time… But if you're a slack rider, then your rodeo has just begun. Your still playing for the big bucks, just there's very few people to watch you at your hard earned effort."

"What happens if two or even three people tie?" Curry asked

"Everybody competes the first two day's. But only the top twenty in each event compete on Sunday". Gary answered

"Funny you mentioned Haine's again," Butch said. "We had lunch there just last week. We borrowed money from the towns bank to help pay for it when we left."

"If I remember right," Sundance said, "we didn't even get enough to pay for our lunch."

"So Larry, you willing to go all the way and ride him out of the arena, like Dude did?" Randy asked looking over at him.

"Sure, but I'm taking the flank strap off too. Just like he did," Larry answered. "I just hope that Roan won't hold it against me, and still try to buck me off, cause by then I might be to drunk to be able to cover him."

"If you're lucky amigo, he'll be too tired of bucking by then." Luis said.

"I'm never that lucky!" Larry say's, as everyone started laughing.

"Ya know we could have a log pulling contest earlier in the day." Randy suggested. "We could start it about eleven or twelve. It shouldn't take more than a couple hours to complete. That would get more people party'en even sooner. We could only charge, say, a fifty dollar entry fee."

"Just what kind of competition is that?" Curry asked.

Chapter Nine

"Tonnage," Randy answered. "Tonnage. You see which team can pull the most weight in logs, from one point to another point. That way I'll have a chance to win me some extra money."

"Talk about being greedy," Sundance said. "Hell, just look at all the money we're going to pay you boys already."

"So what, that just means more people drinking and calling it an early night. If you get my drift." Randy said, sternly

"Sure do," Butch said. "We'll need a couple days to get everything ready. It's Friday night or Saturday morning now…I figure we should be good to go by Sunday afternoon. Do you think that will give you enough time to get enough teams for the log pull contest, Randy?"

"Hell yes," Randy answered standing up and hollered out. "LOG PULL, SUNDAY AT NOON."

Just then about a third of the crowd started shouting, "Alright, Great." Some of them started walking towards the door.

"Where they going?" Sundance asked.

"They're heading back to where ever it is they're logging. They need to get their teams of horses, and they'll let everyone else they run into know about it, too. So don't worry, they'll be back to lose all their hard earned money." Randy said.

"I think we can finish the details in the morning," Butch said stretching his arms out.

"You're right," Gary agreed. "I'm tired, too. It won't take very long to get enough fools who want in one way or another."

"I suppose you boys want us to pay for your rooms again tonight?" Sundance asked the Larkin boys, standing up.

"Why sure," Gary said, "That's if you don't mind. We'll pay you back Sunday afternoon after we win all that money…When we won't be so poor."

'Oh I doubt very much you're all that poor, Gary, but we already reserved enough rooms for everyone, including you Randy.' Sundance said

"Why spend our money if we don't have to," Larry chuckled, picking up a bottle of whiskey. "So does one of those little Betty's over there come with that room again, or do we have to pay for that part?"

159

Butch raised his hand in the direction of the ladies that were patiently waiting. "Ya, they're covered tonight as well."

"What about you, Randy," Sundance asked. "Which one of these little Betty's do you want?"

"Hell no, I don't want one of them," Randy answered. "The young lady I want is standing right over there." Pointing across the room. "She costs more than the rest of the ladies put together. But she's worth every cent."

"What makes her so special?" Curry asked. Looking over at her, and at that long thick brown hair. He could only see her from the backside.

"She's not like most these ladies," Randy said smiling. "She may be almost as flat chested as a two by four, but she sure knows how to use what she has…I tell ya gentlemen, that lady can flat keep you up all night and make you enjoy every minute of it."

"What if I was to say I'd like to find out for myself how good she is?" Sundance asked.

"Better not," Gary said in a low voice. "Everyone in here knows Randy and her get together when ever he comes to town. So when he comes to town, even those that can afford her, stay away from her…Remember that unfortunate man this evening that had to go visit Doc Bones. All's I'm saying is do you want to follow in his foot step?"

"They're easy to find, he left a real good blood trail," Larry said, pointing at the blood on the floor.

The three outlaws looked at each other, "Not really," they all answered, shaking their heads. "Nope, can't say as I would want to meet Doc Bones." Sundance said, then looking over at Randy. "You go right on ahead Young man; don't let any of us try to stop you."

"Not that we could," Butch said. "Nor would I even try."

"I really don't want to meet this infamous Doc. Bones, across the street," Curry said. "So why don't you point her out one more time, so I know which one to stay away from?"

"Don't worry, Kid," Randy said, shaking all three men's hands. "I wouldn't hurt you too bad. Hell, I like you guys."

160

Chapter Nine

"Thanks for everything Amigo's," Luis said, with a big smile on his face and a young lady under his arm. "I'll see you all in the morning." Then he turned and headed upstairs to bed. As the rest all followed behind, each was going to their own rooms.

It was about nine-thirty in the morning when Randy and Gary came down to the restaurant for breakfast. They had just set down when Sundance came in and joined them. He stuck out his hand, to shake their hands as he set down, looking at the two. "You're Gary, right, I mean you're not Larry?"

"Ya, I'm Gary." He answered

"I thought so. I think I'm finally figuring out just which is which. Larry's a little wilder than you are. You're more level headed." Sundance answered.

"I'm better looking, too," Gary answered, chuckling.

Just then a young cowboy came walking up to the table. "You the men that say you have a horse that no one can ride for eight seconds? Or were you just blowing smoke last night?" He asked, looking around the table.

"We weren't blowing any smoke," Randy said, "but it will cost you a thousand dollars for the chance to see if you can or not."

"I can come up with the money" He kept looking at all three men. "So just how much does the rider get that rides this Caballo?'

"Five thousand," Sundance answered the man. "Why, you think you got the sand in you to ride him?"

"YA...I do. So just where is this big mean horse? I'd like to get a look at him.' The man said, seeming to be real sure of himself.

"Sumpter Livery corral," Gary answered, taking a drink of coffee. "He's out in that corral all alone. They won't let him back inside, said he tore the stable up night before last. Pissed the workers off. Said they weren't going to let any of us Larkin boys stable our horses inside any more."

"So how many men get a chance at him?" the man asked, looking around the room at everyone. The crowd had grown quite big. Everyone wanted to know the rules.

"Ten men," Gary answered.

161

"What happens if you come up with more than ten men?" the man asked.

"Everyone who pays, their name will go in a hat," Randy said with a big smile on his face. "Then we draw ten names, those that get drawn, get the chance."

By now there was a low mummer as the crowd slowly started talking about what was going on. Some wanted a chance at that horse and all that money. Hell, with that money they could get a nice new start somewhere. While others wanted to bet on just who might ride him, or was he really as good as these men were saying, and NO one would cover him.

By now Larry and Luis had worked their way into the restaurant, listening to all the commotion as everyone was talking.

"So you all talk'en about my horse?" Larry said, as the two set down at the table.

"Sure are," Randy said. "We have some brave or stupid men here that think they can ride him. I just haven't figured out yet just which they are. Brave, or stupid!"

"You'd have to be a little of both," one man yelled out. "Brave, to want and try him, but then a little stupid for wanting to get on a bucking horse. As for me, I like the tame ones. But I'll bet someone will cover that horse."

"Well then, put your money where your mouth is," Larry said

"Where do we sign up at?" another man yelled out. "I'd like a chance at him. Me too," yelled out another man.

"I guess maybe we should set up a table over at the Sumpter Livery stable," Gary suggested. That way everyone can get a good look at the Roan, then those that think they can ride him can put their money down. Everyone else can look at those men and decide on just who they want to bet on."

"I want to know just who it is I'm putting my money on," one man yelled out. "Me too" yelled out another.

"You'll get to," Gary said after their names are drawn. "You can talk to each one yourself. Hell, we're not trying to rip you off. But when you sign up, you have to have your entry money. We'll give everyone

Chapter Nine

till five o-clock this afternoon to enter, then we'll draw names, and those that get drawn will have their chance in the order their name was pulled. From the first, to the tenth."

"And I'll count the money! " Luis said rubbing his hands together.

"You can't do that," Randy said chuckling. "Hell you have to take your pant's off just to count to twenty-one. How the hell you going to count to one thousand?"

"Twenty one at a time," Luis said. "Just keep adding twenty one, till I get to one thousand."

Soon the entire room was buzzing with excitement. Those who wanted a chance and those who wanted to bet SOMEONE would ride that Roan.

"What happens if someone rides him before I get my chance?" someone yelled out.

Standing up and looking down at Larry, Sundance hollered out, "If that should happen, and it better not, but if it does, then those who didn't get their chance will get their money back."

Slowly the crowd started working its way out of the Saloon and over to the Sumpter Livery stable. They wanted to see for themselves just what this big Roan looked like.

"What about the team pulls?" Randy asked. "When you want to start them? We'll have to talk to the mill yard foreman, so we can get the logs laid out."

"Alright," said Sundance, "we can start out tomorrow...Sunday ...around noon with the pulling competition, then follow up with the bucking competition, that should make it last till early evening." Starting to smile, "by then we'll own the town."

Butch and Curry had been stuck in the middle of the crowd listening to what was being said. Everyone was crowding in trying to listen. Holding up his arms, Butch hollered out, "Wait just one minute. I'm the one putting up the five thousand so that if by chance someone rides him before ten riders...I'm not drawing...I AM the first rider... Then you can draw for the other nine."

Butch and Curry pushed their way through the crowd, and over to the table where their friends were sitting. Looking over at Randy,

163

"Didn't you say the object of your competition is to see whose team of horses could pull the most weight?"

"Yep," Randy said. "We call it tonnage, which team of no more than four horses or mules can pull the most weight, the fastest for a pre-set distance."

"Now that's what I'm talk'en about," an old man shouted. "I'll put my team up against anybody's team, any time."

"You must be new to the area?" Randy said. "I'm not one to brag… So I'll let my team do that for me…" Standing up, "so if you guys will take over here, I'll get back up to camp and get the rest of my team and still be back in time to enjoy another exciting night of bullshitting."

"Alright," Gary said. "We'll take care of everything we can, but you get back here and let us know what you've figured out. Besides I'm not only expecting to make money on that Roan, I'm going to make even more betting on your team."

"YA, YA," Randy said, turning towards the door. "M-ME T-T-TOO, I-I want to make some extra M-Money." He started stuttering a little.

However NO one was even going to say one word about his stuttering. Most of the men knew him, and those that didn't had heard all about him. Fact a few more got to see what he could do last night. Come to think of it, they still hadn't seen that man around town yet this morning.

Curry looked over at Gary as Randy walked out the door, "What's up with him and that Sharon lady…is he in love?"

"I don't think in the way your thinking," Gary said, "but even if he was…he wouldn't say so."

"Why not?" Curry asked. "Why don't he ask her to marry him? Take her away from all this? Especially if he's that crazy over her."

"I think he did once, back when he was in fifth grade and she was in third grade." Gary said, smiling

"Grade school?" Butch said. "They've known each other that long?"

"Yep, we have. She told him then, flat out, she was never, and she meant NEVER getting married. Not to anyone, anywhere, anytime,

Chapter Nine

ever...and I believe her. So since then, he's never said anything about it. Fact, I don't think he's ever kissed her." Gary said.

"WHAT!" Sundance yelled out. "After all that money we spent on her last night, and you're sitting here telling us he's never even kissed her?"

"That's what I'm telling ya, but if you'll look, I'm not sitting, I'm standing," Gary said, with a small chuckle.

"How about we all head on over to the corral?" Larry said, "And see just how many are chomping at the bit to sign up and try to ride MY horse."

They all started laughing, standing up; they walked out the door. Curry looked back at a table of ladies just sitting down. He couldn't help but notice Sharon. She was about five feet two inches tall, one hundred ten pounds. He may have been twenty feet from her, but he couldn't help looking into those big brown eyes and seeing that long, thick brown hair. Randy was right; she was a semi- flat chested lady. Yet, she was by far the prettiest and sexiest looking of all the ladies, as well. He bet she would flat tear a man up, in or out of bed. He didn't realize just how long he'd been staring at her, till she looked back at him with a look that sent a chill up his spine. Instantly he knew that young lady could and would hurt any man who went to far.

Curry turned and followed the others outside, it was barely noon and the streets were filling up fast. You couldn't see the Roan down in the corral because of all the people climbing up on the railings to get a better look him. Curry wanted to get a better look at the Roan, too.

"So how does Randy really feel about Sharon?" Curry asked Luis.

"Who knows? Those Larkin boys don't speak much about that. They keep that inside themselves," Luis said sternly.

They all walked over to the corral, so they to could get their first real look at the Roan for themselves. "He sure is a big horse," Butch said looking at Larry.

"Eighteen plus hands high, at least thirteen hundred pounds of pure hell," Larry stated firmly, pulling a bottle of whiskey out of his coat pocket.

"So you guys really think he can best ten men?" Butch asked.

165

"Not only can…But he will." Gary answered. "I'll bet everything I own he will. If you could have seen just one of the trips he's taken Larry on the last couple days, you wouldn't doubt it either."

"Listen to him," Randy said rubbing his behind. "We all grew up riding, or trying to ride horses our grandpa Dude was breaking. Fact," he said, starting to chuckle, "We spent more time on green broke horses, than we ever spent on ones you could ride. I tried him yesterday after work, just for the heck of it. I'm here to tell you," Pointing in the direction of the Roan, "that horse has a Wild Spirit…he can flat get with it, and he DON'T want ANYONE on him."

"What are you still doing in town Randy?" Sundance asked. "I thought you left over an hour ago?"

Randy was standing there holding the reins on his big Clydesdale stallion. "Aw, this shit for brains broke loose last night and went about two miles down the road. Broke a fence down and got into a herd of registered Quarter horse mares…You might say their owners are going to have a couple foals that won't be registered. Shit." Randy answered, standing there with a big smile on his face.

"Now that's a horse!" Curry said. "Why don't we try and buck him out?"

"What, this old boy?" Randy said, patting his horse on the head. "He'd just walk out of the chute. I don't think he'd hurt a baby."

"You're right about one thing," Gary said, "that big stallion loves babies, but he would kill any man but you that even gets to close to him, and you know it Randy."

"Just look at both the Roan and that Clydesdale," Butch said. "That Clydesdale is bigger boned and body, but there isn't a whole lot a difference in height."

Randy led the stallion over to the corral, and started climbing up the fence.

"What are you doing?" Sundance asked. "Why are you climbing up on the corral for? Can't you see the Roan good enough from here?"

"Well YAA!" Randy jumped onto the back of the stallion. "It's easier to get aboard when I'm tired. As you can see I don't have a saddle, and these stirrups are too high for a short man like me." Then

Chapter Nine

he turned the stallion and headed up the street. "You boys have fun, and I'll help cover all the bets you get…We can use all the money we can get our hands on."

"I hear ya, Bro," Larry said waving the bottle of whiskey, then taking a big pull off it.

"DAMN LARRY," Randy yelled, "I bet by the time I get back you won't even be able to stand up."

"Don't you just worry about it. It's me drinking, not the Roan… And he's the one that has to do all the work tomorrow, not me." Larry shouted back.

Randy kicked the stallion in the side and headed out of town, he couldn't help but listen to the people talking as he rode past them.

"That Roan don't look like he's all that mean. I mean hell, just look at him, those little boys and girls are petting him."

"That man said he couldn't ride him," another said pointing at Randy riding by on that big Clydesdale stallion.

Then another man, "I've seen a lot of horse flesh in my time, just look in his eyes. Tomorrow is going to be fun, fun watching all those idiots fly with the eagles. If you get my drift." That one made Randy chuckled. Then one man hollered out, "What's that big 55 brand on his right hip for?"

"Sure can tell you aren't from around here," Gary said. "When they round up a heard of mustangs, they brand a number on them to count them as they move through the counting shut. That way there's no mistakes. Then the Calvary buys the best out of the lot first…Fact, the Colonel at the fort down in Baker City, had him for almost two years, till two weeks ago." Starting to chuckle, "Only problem he had was, he couldn't get anyone to break him. That Roan broke more legs and arms than I care to count."

"How'd you men end up with him?" one man shouted out.

"Our Grandpa was taking a new string of broke horses out to the fort. Said that Colonel was ready to shoot him. So, Grandpa offered to take him off his hands. Then Larry needed a good mountain horse, so he suggested Larry take him. The rest is history."

"So, how come he can ride him and no one else can?" another man yelled out.

"He can't," hollered Luis, "he's still trying to though."

The crowd was slowly growing larger and louder. "There ain't any horse I can't ride," a man shouted out.

"Put your money where your mouth is, hero," Gary shouted back, "let's see what you're made of."

Pulling a table out of the stables, Butch set it up on the side of the corral. "All those who want a chance to try and ride him, bring your thousand dollars and sign up right here. Make sure you get a tag for your money. If you loose it, and your name don't get drawn, you won't get your money back. And I can use all the extra money I can get."

Looking at his watch, Butch looked over at everyone. "How about we leave Larry and Luis here to take names and money and the rest of us go get some lunch? It's almost two o-clock, and me and Curry didn't get breakfast."

"Now just wait one minute," Larry shouted, "We're hungry too."

Reaching over and taking the bottle of whiskey, Gary looked at the two, "Well, you did say it was your horse Larry. This way you can get a good look at those who are entering, and you can let us know if there's anyone we should worry about."

"Give me that bottle back, then." Larry said, reaching out for the bottle. "We're going to get thirsty out here, and send us some food too."

"We'll send out food and beer," Gary told Larry. "I don't want you getting too drunk too early. When you have fifteen names you can come in."

The crowd was growing louder and more boisterous. Some of the men who wanted a chance were all talking with their friends or who-ever else might help them get enough money to enter.

"Alright," said Larry, "but you better send out a couple pitchers of beer. Who knows how long it's going to take."

"I've noticed that about you, Larry," Sundance said. "You're always thirsty."

Gary and the three outlaws started working their way through the crowd of people which took them a good five minutes to do before

Chapter Nine

they finally worked their way back over to the Elkhorn Saloon and Brothel. According to Gary, they also had the best food in town.

"So you are starting to figure out which one of us is which?" Gary asked Sundance.

"It's getting easier. Larry usually always has a drink in his hand, and it's usually alcohol of some sort," Sundance answered

"I'm always on him about his drinking," Gary say's, looking over at him. "But he is my brother and I love him. Besides, he's good to have around if you ever get in a bind."

"I notice that last night," Butch added. "Who taught him to throw those knives?"

"Grandpa Dude did, fact he taught all of us," Gary said. They were finally standing on the boardwalk. "He taught all us five boys, its just Larry prefers them over a pistol. He can use a pistol just as fast, mind ya. No one expects him to be carrying any weapons at all, till that first knife takes their hat off, Every time…just like last night. He stops them dead in their tracks. Besides there's nothing like a good fist fight."

"I agree," Sundance said, "and nobody ends up dead in the end."

"That right," Gary said. They all sat down at the table.

Just then Sharon came walking up to the table, leaning over she gave Gary a kiss on the cheek. "How you doing, little brother?" she asked, looking over the other three. "Gentleman, how are you?" She didn't know just who they really were, but with just one quick glance she knew the law was definitely on their trail.

"Just fine young lady," Sundance said, checked her out. Randy was right, she was a little flat chested, but beyond a doubt she was the prettiest lady and sexiest lady he'd ever had the pleasure to meet. That long thick dark brown hair, those big brown eyes, and that sexy body under that short tight skirt and blouse. He could also tell by her demeanor, this young lady didn't take no shit off any man!

Sharon looked back down at Gary, "So sweetie is Randy coming back, or is he through for the weekend?"

"No Sis, he'll be back, he just went up to get the rest of his team for the log pull tomorrow," Gary answered, putting his arm around her narrow waist.

"Alright, but tell me just what is it you men are really up to?" Sharon asked looking around the table. "You're planning something besides a bucking competition, I can smell it."

"No ma'am," Curry said. "We're just going to have a little fun this weekend. If we're as lucky as these Larkin men think we will be, why hell, we could make some real good money."

"Oh BULLSHIT," Sharon raised her voice. "I've known these three since we were kids. I know when something's up."

"AWW, don't worry about it, Sharon," Gary told her. "We're just going to have a little fun is all. Hey, before I forget, could you get one of the ladies to take Larry and Luis something to eat and drink? But NO whiskey, we need him to use his brain today."

"That's two things I didn't think existed. Larry having even half a brain and any time of day Larry don't have anything to drink…I doubt he's empty. But ya, I'll send one of the ladies out." She waved to one of the young ladies to come over, and asked her to do just that. Then she looked back at the other three men. "I don't care what you say, I'm not falling for this Mr. Smith, Mr. Jones," she said pointing at Curry and Sundance… "And what are you saying your name is again?" She asked Looking down at Butch.

"Young ma'am, Brigham Young from Utah," Butch said, smiling.

"I remember a couple years ago Larry help bring a herd of cattle from Denver through there, Utah that is." Starting to smile, Sharon continued, "he had a bullshit story he tried to get us to believe. Said you guys had your own religion down there. That you had four, five or more wives'."

"That's no bullshit," Butch said, "fact right now I only have twenty five, I'm hoping to have at least one hundred someday…You interested in becoming number twenty six? I'd like to have a wife as full of fire like you obviously are."

"Honey, if you have that many wives, you could never keep me satisfied." Sharon said smiling.

"Ya know Butch, I was thinking," Sundance said, "Who we are we going to have build the bucking chute? Hell, there are already grand stands there, from the previous log pulling competitions. That way we

Chapter Nine

can charge people to sit and watch…Then we can make even more money."

"Now who's getting greedy?" Gary said looking at them.

"Well, I'll let you boys plan out your games." Then Sharon looked down at Gary; "I do expect you to tell me who these men really are SOONER, not later." Turning, she walked away.

"She's quite a lady," Sundance said.

"You'd better watch yourself," Gary warned. "She has sent more men than Randy to visit Doc Bones. They just don't need quite as much repair…But she takes no shit off anyone, and never will!"

The four men had been sitting in the saloon talking about how the betting scale should go. When Curry suggested they pay five to one for the first man, then drop it a half percent after each rider. That way if the sixth or seventh rider does ride him, we're not paying out as much.

"WHAT?" Gary shouted. "You don't have much faith in that Roan. I'll bet you right here and now, just between us. Five to one, NO ONE will ride that horse."

"I know Butch won't ride him," Sundance said, "I've seen him ride."

"Well, why don't YOU enter?" Butch suggested. "We'll see which one of us stays on him longer."

"No thanks, I'll set this one out." Sundance answered, smiling.

"AH hell, it only hurts for a little while." Gary said. "It's that initial sudden stop that hurts the worst. But then you had better keep your head down so he don't kick it off. Trust me, that's something I know too well. Our grandpa Dude had us on horses he was still training when we were kids. He had a leather strap around the shoulders of the saddle. When, not if, but when he started bucking, you laid the reins down over the saddle horn, grab that strap and put your spurs to him…Then when we got bucked off he'd always say, 'don't worry son, I'll bring him right back for ya.' Tough loves is what he called it.

"Is that what's wrong with you Larkin boys, landing too many times on your head?" Curry asked, chuckling.

171

"Who you trying to kid?" Butch said. "I'm sure you didn't have it all that bad. Try growing up in an area where you're related to half the county. Hell, my first girl friend was my second cousin on my mom's side."

"COUSIN?" Gary laughed. "You guys really are in-bred down there in Utah, aren't you?"

CHAPTER TEN

The morning light was just coming up over the town, when Wapiti woke up. Stretching out a little, he walked over to the wash basin. Looking in the mirror at himself, he wondered just what kind of day today would be. Bending over he splashed water in his face, and then he looked back into the mirror. The Marshal wouldn't be down for a couple hours. Maybe it would have been better if he had gotten his hair cut. But his long hair was strong medicine to his people. Looking around the table, he saw a piece of cloth. Tearing off a piece, he tied his hair back. Turned back, he walked over to the bed and started getting dressed. He was just pulling his boots on, when there was a knock on the door.

"Come in," he said, placing his hand on the ten gauge. "It's open."

The door opened, and Cathey walked in. She was holding a tray in her hands, "the Marshal thought you might want a cup of coffee up here first," she walked over and sat it down on the table.

"Thanks," Wapiti told her.

She poured him a cup and handed it to him. "You really a law man Wapiti?" Cathey asked him.

"Yes ma'am," Wapiti answered, reaching for the coffee. "Well, I'm just starting out...But the Marshal is teaching me."

"You know don't you Wapiti, that there's still some people around here think the only good Indian is a dead Indian?" Cathey said, with real concern in her voice.

"Trust me, I know," Wapiti answered. "But the Marshal says in time the people will grow to respect me." He turned, picked up the shotgun and strapped it on.

"Well, I don't know how long that will take," Cathey said smiling. "But as long as you have that on," pointing to the gun, "I don't think too many men will bother you."

"The Marshal thought it would be best if I used this for a while," Wapiti answered, tying the holster down. "Least till I can handle a pistol better. Well hell, I guess I had better get this over with and get down there, I'll let you go first, then I'll follow behind you."

Walking up to Wapiti, Cathey leaned over and gave him a small kiss on the cheek. "Don't worry too much Wapiti, Sam's already down there eating breakfast. All's they have to do is take one look at him... they'll think twice."

"Thanks for the vote of confidence," Wapiti said, opening the door. "Well, you better get going." Watching her walk down the hallway, then turn and go down the stairs. Waiting just about two minute's, he took in a deep breath, stepped out in the hall and started down the stairs. Everyone in the place went totally quiet as he walked down the stairs; they all stared at him. It really wasn't that far to the restaurant, but this morning it felt like the longest walk he had ever taken. He sure was glad when he got to the door to the restaurant. Looking around the room, he could see everyone was still staring at him and starting to talk in low voices. Walking over to a table next to the wall he sat down. This way he figured no one could get behind him, he thought to himself, as Cathey was pouring him another cup of coffee.

"Well Deputy, what would you like for breakfast?" Cathey asked with that big beautiful smile, which made his heart start beating even harder. He didn't know why she had given him a kiss upstairs, but he sure hoped like hell that she didn't do it down here. That ten gauge only held two shells. "Eggs and bacon sounds good to me, please."

"Sure thing Deputy," Cathey said turning and walking away.

Wapiti couldn't help but look at her. If these white eyes knew what he was thinking...they'd scalp him in a second. Slowly Wapiti started looking around the room. Everyone was still whispering and glaring

Chapter Ten

at him at the same time. Just then, he heard a chair move beside him. Turning and reaching for the hog leg, Wapiti looked up; he could see it was one of the men from yesterday morning. The whole right side of his face was still swollen up and bruised. Wapiti couldn't help but chuckle a little inside. The man stuck his hand out.

"Sam, Sam Seebart, it's a pleasure to meet you Deputy. Mind if I join you?" He asked, sitting down, "I'm sorry for the trouble me and my brother gave you yesterday. We were just joking and having a little fun. UUMMPP," he said, holding his hand up to his side of his head. "It still hurts to smile or laugh, but, well I guess you could say we got what we deserved…Just want you to know there's no hard feelings. Will you accept my apology?"

"Sure," Wapiti answered, shaking hands with Sam.

"So tell me Wapiti, why do you carry that shotgun?" Sam asked.

"The Marshal figured if any trouble started, I couldn't miss with this." Wapiti said, assuredly.

"I hope to shout not. Least not at close range," Sam answered.

The two sat and talked while they ate breakfast, Wapiti was enjoying the company. He knew Sam was a stand up man, and he meant what he said, when he apologized, Wapiti actually felt that if he needed any help, Sam would back his play. The conversation in the café had slowly grown louder. Men talking about Wapiti, an Indian lawman, he didn't mind some of them. But some did get under his skin. Fact he wished he could just go over and smash his fist into a couple mouths. He knew that he couldn't, because it might just make things worse. The two had been talking for over an hour when Wapiti looked over at Sam, "Mr. Seebart, it's been a pleasure meeting you, but I have things I have to get doing, so I'll talk with you later sir."

"It's Sam, Deputy. Please call me Sam…Also, if you need any help, you just let me and Jack know…We owe you." Sam said looking him straight in the eye shaking his hand one more time.

"Thank you," Wapiti said, "Please call me Wapiti." He turned and walked into the Saloon, stopped and looked around the room. Just like yesterday Cork was already sitting on his thrown, with his twelve gauge in one hand, and a beer in the other. Wapiti couldn't help but chuckle

175

at him. Walking across the room over to Cork, he couldn't help but notice at least half the players were there, and the games weren't do to start for a couple hours yet.

"How's everything going this morning, Wapiti?" Corky asked, stepping down from his thrown, and shook his hand.

"Just fine, there's a little tension among the natives," Wapiti said, looking around the room. "If you get my meaning."

"Oh hell, Wapiti don't worry about them. Some of them were here yesterday morning when you took care of those Seebart brothers, and if they weren't…Well hell, all they have to do is look at them. That and that hog leg on your side," Starting to chuckle Cork continues, "That'll make all of them think twice, so you will have a slight advantage."

"Well, I hope you're right Cork." Wapiti answered.

"How about we bring those bags of chips out? We have more than enough players here to start playing, and those that aren't here are in the café finishing up breakfast," Wapiti suggested to Cork.

"Alright," Cork answered, turning and asking Charley and a couple of the waitresses to bring the bags out.

"You sure do have some real nice ladies working here Cork." Wapiti said walking behind the bar and filling up a cup of coffee.

"Thanks Wapiti, but you remember, they're White girls. If you get any ideas about any of them…Well, I don't think even the Marshal could save your hide from these boys," Cork said, turning and going back up to his thrown, and setting down.

Charley and the ladies brought out the chips. Charley looked over at Wapiti, smiling, "You should feel proud, he don't come down off that thing for just anyone."

They both laughed about that comment a little. Wapiti turned to the crowd, "Alright, listen up," He shouted. "You players, who are here already, come up here and get your chips. We'll get started as soon as you have at least three players per table."

It didn't take but a couple seconds and everyone was in line to get his or her chips. "ONE MORE THING…These waitresses worked their tails off for you last night, so just like yesterday, you will put up another twenty dollars to be divided between them for today. When the

Chapter Ten

noon shift comes on, those of you left will put up yet another twenty dollars, and every shift there after, Understand!." Wapiti couldn't help but notice the look in everyone's eyes as they walked by him. They didn't like the idea of any Indian telling them what to do, but Marshal Shawn Felton was sleeping upstairs and they did NOT want to wake him. There's no telling what he would do, they had all heard he had a short fuse, and none of them wanted to be on the receiving end of his guns, or those big fists of his. So nobody said anything, they just went over and sat down at a table, and started playing.

It only took about thirty minutes and they only had seven bags left. Wapiti had been watching over the crowd as they slowly sat down and started playing cards. The waitresses were all pouring coffee, beer, and whiskey. Wapiti couldn't imagine starting to drink that early in the day. He too did enjoy a cold beer. The Marshal was right, one or two beers did relax you and make it easier to fall asleep. That whiskey though, too much of that in a short period of time could turn a man into a total fool, in a very short time. It makes them feel invincible, which usually lead to trouble.

Wapiti looked over at Charley, "Could you make sure these last few bags get to their rightful owners when they arrive? I'm going to go take a walk through Purgatory," he said with a small smile on his face. Then turning, he walked into the roped off playing area. Walking through the tables he couldn't help but notice everyone was still looking at that double barrel ten gauge. He could also see at least a dozen of them were wearing a big black eye, some had two. He couldn't help it; he started chuckling walking by a couple of them. "Looks like the Marshal gave out his punishment for those who brought a gun into the game last night," saying it loud enough for everyone to hear him. Still every table went quiet as he walked up to them; they were all looking at that U.S. Deputy Marshal badge. They all knew, not just anyone could get one of those badges.

Wapiti could also hear some of them making comments about him behind his back. When he walked by one table, he was looking over at another. A man stuck out his foot tripping Wapiti, causing him to fall to the floor. The entire Saloon busted into laughter.

Wapiti wasn't on the floor for a half-second, when he reached back, grabbed the man's chair by the leg, pulling his chair out from under him, sending the man crashing to the floor backwards. Pulling out his knife, Wapiti leaped and grabbed the man by his throat, just laying his razor sharp knife on the man's fore head. Rolling the knife just below the hair line making about an eight inch long cut. The blood started dripping down his face; Wapiti stood up and showed the blood on his knife. "NOW, I could have just taken my fourth scalp, if I wanted it...I may really take the next one." Reaching over he pushed the mans chips into the middle of the table. Looking back down at the man Wapiti yelled, "You're finished...Get the hell out of here while you can still walk."

"NOW YOU just wait one minute," the man shouted. "You ain't throwing me out of these games. I was just having a little fun."

Wapiti reached down and grabbed the man by the throat, helping him the rest of the way up. Bringing the man to a full standing position. The man had both his hands around Wapiti's wrist and forearm. It was all he could do to breathe. "I SAID YOU'RE FINISHED," Wapiti said, throwing the man backwards. Crashing back down to the floor, he was still trying to get his breath back. "NOW...Anyone else want out of the game? Just try this shit again." Looking around at everyone, with a glare in his eye. "I promise the next one WON'T walk out of here. Now, any of you want to try me? Just wait till the Marshal gets up and I'll meet you out in the street, no knives, no guns...just hand to hand...Anytime!" Looking back at the man who was still trying to stand and get his breath back, with the blood running down over his face. "Now you get the hell out of here. I don't even want to see you in the crowd. If I do...That means your back for revenge, and I'll be on you like stink on shit...Understand MISTER!"

"Yes sir," the man said, standing up, "but I had close to four thousand dollars in chips. I want my money back."

"You're out one thousand dollars," Wapiti said, "that was your buy in...And you knew the rules. You cause any trouble and you're out of the game. No questions about it."

Chapter Ten

"You haven't heard the last of this," the man said, wiping the blood from his eyes and face. He didn't realize it was that bad a cut, it didn't hurt too much, but like most head wounds, it bled heavy. Slowly the man walked out of the Saloon, cursing the entire way.

"Now the rest of you get back to playing your games," Wapiti said, starting to walk around the tables again. Slowly working his way back to the bar. It didn't take long and everyone was back to doing just what Wapiti had told them to do, playing cards. "Charley, could I get another cup of coffee please?"

"Yes sir, Deputy," Charley said with a big smile on his face. "I'll be glad to get you anything I can Deputy. Just don't scalp me."

"I liked that final touch," Corky said. "Offering to meet any of them out in the street. That way you won't tear my place up."

"I wasn't joking. I meant it...!" Wapiti said, proudly.

"You sound pretty sure of yourself," Cork said.

"I'm not saying I've never been beat," Wapiti said smiling. "Fact I have, and I'm sure I will again...But I will back up what I say."

"Well, if and when it does happen, I sure would appreciate it if you did take it out side. I have a whole lot of expensive furnishings in here." Cork said, pointing his finger around the room. "But just so you know, you did good...Believe it or not, you did earn a little more respect from them."

"Thanks," Wapiti said. "It looks like the Marshal had a little fun himself last night." He said, pointing around the room at the men with black eyes.

"YAA, he did," Cork answered laughing a little more. "Those are the ones that brought guns into the game. Fact, he said he couldn't remember ever having that much fun, in such a short time before."

Wapiti and Cork had been talking for about twenty minutes when Sheriff Beyer came walking into the Saloon. He had a big smile on his face, holding out his hand out as he walked up to Wapiti. "I see and hear you already had yourself some fun this morning Deputy. Charley, can I get a cup of coffee, please?"

"Sure thing Sheriff," Charley answered, refilling Wapiti's cup too.

"Just someone thought he'd try and be funny," Wapiti answered. "How'd you hear about it already?"

"Not much anything happens in this town I don't hear about," Dennis said. "I just had a man come in my office with a nice cut along his hair line," starting to chuckle. "That was a nice touch, by the way. Fact I think I might just start carrying me a knife and serve up the same punishment. He was pissing and moaning about how things got out of hand and for no reason at all you threw him out of the game, wanted me to get his money back."

"So what did you tell him, Sheriff?" Wapiti asked.

"Told him it was none of my business," Dennis said. "Then he really got mad when I told him to take it up with the Marshal...He also thought I should arrest you for using your knife on him. Said if he hadn't moved, you would have really scalped him."

"What did he mean by if he hadn't moved?" Corky said. "Hell, with the hold Wapiti had on him, he couldn't move. If Wapiti wanted his scalp, it would be hanging on his belt right now, not still on his head."

"I thought real serious about it," Wapiti said. "Besides, I didn't hurt him too bad. Least I let him walk out."

"I just told him he knew what the rules were more than I did," Dennis said, "and there wasn't anything I could or would do about it."

About that time, they all saw the Marshal come walking down the stairs. You could tell he was feeling real sure of himself, just by the way he was walking. Head held high, and his shoulder full up and his chest puffed out.

"What was all the ruckus I heard this morning?" Shawn asked, walking up to the bar. "Anything I need to know about?"

"Nothing really, Marshal," Wapiti answered. "Just some wise guy trying to start trouble."

"You'd have been real proud of him, Marshal," Corky said. "Young Wapiti there took the bull by the horns you might say. Let everyone know who was in charge."

"Well, glad to hear it.' Shawn answered, reaching for a cup of coffee. "That way I can rest a little easier." Taking a drink off his coffee, "now this is just what I need this morning. A good hot cup of coffee."

Chapter Ten

All of a sudden a man yelled out, "CHIEF, IF you're still in charge you better get your ass over here before I beat the shit out of this cheater." As a man stands up, pointing at the man he was accusing.

"What the hell you talking about?" the other man asked, as Wapiti started walking over to them.

'What…What…I'll not only tell you what, I'll show you what." He turned over an ace of clubs. "THAT, come from the dealer," he pointed down… "Where the hell did that one in your hand come from?'

Wapiti walked up to the table; first he looked at both men. "Sir, would you please sit back down? I'm sure we can get to the bottom of this." Looking over at the dealer, "Was that deck checked before the game started?"

"Yes sir," the man said. "Fact we all took a look at that deck," one of the men said. "You think we're stupid boy?" The other said as both of them moved their chairs back from the table.

"NOW, don't anyone be getting bent out of shape. We're going to get to the bottom of this. SO I will ask the questions." Then Wapiti picked up the accusers cards, reached over and picked up the other ace of clubs. Looking it over, he noticed right off not only was there a small tear in the top, but it was also a shade or two lighter, which meant it was older. He could see the accused man was starting to get restless in his seat. Slowly Wapiti looked back over the cards, turning each one over then back again.

Wapiti looked over at the man being accused, "Mister, I'm no gambler…But not only does this card have a small tear in it, but it's also an older card…look at the color. Just how many more cards do you have up your sleeve?"

"WHAT? WHY you no good red skin," the man hollered. Standing up and yelling, "You calling me a cheater?"

"Well sir, the cards don't lie. So, YES, I AM calling you a cheater," Wapiti stated, sternly. "So…Unless you want more trouble, I would advise you to throw all your chips in and get out of here while you're still able to walk."

"Like hell I will," the man shouted back "I'll trade them in for cash money, but you're crazy as hell if you think I'm walking out of here with nothing."

"Yes you will," Wapiti said, glaring into the man's eyes. "You knew the rules when you set down just like everyone else. You get caught cheating, and you forfeit all your chips."

"That's right," half the crowd shouted. "We all knew the rules," one man yelled out. Another yelled out, "I don't think he shouldn't just be able to just walk out of here. I think you should really scalp him Deputy."

"SCALP HIM, SCALP HIM," the crowd started hollering.

Holding up his arms, "Now calm down everyone," Wapiti shouted. "I can't legally do that…But back home on the reservation if you got caught stealing, we have a little thing called the GAUTLET RUN. Everyone in the tribe lines up in two lines and take leather straps, big stick, anything they could hit with. Then the guilty person runs down between the lines while everyone is swinging with all their might, hitting him till the man reaches the end. This type of punishment might make the rest of you think twice before you try cheating." He said, looking the crowd over.

"Now just wait one moment there Chief," the man said. "Marshal, you can't allow them to do that to me."

"Well back home," Wapiti said, "if the man still believes he is innocent, he WALKS through the Gauntlet line, he doesn't run through."

"That sounds like a lot of fun," one man yelled out. "I hear ya," hollered another.

"Marshal, I'll throw my chips in and just leave," the man started pleading.

"Well sir, you played the card and got caught," Shawn said. "I think Deputy Wapiti's punishment fits the crime, and just like he said. IT will make everyone else, who wants to cheat, think twice. Fact, everyone lay your cards on the table, and make two lines through here. Don't worry about your chips, cause I'll be keeping my eye on them, while Wapiti makes sure everyone plays this game according to the rules."

"How many times do we get to hit him?" one man yelled out.

"As many as you can, as long as he's within your reach, you can't move further down the line to get him twice," Wapiti answered.

Chapter Ten

The man slowly started headed towards the door, but no one was about to let him get away. They were all hollering and shouting. "GAUTLET, GAUTLET, GAULET!" Wapiti grabbed the man by the arm, and led him to the beginning of the two lines. It just wasn't the gamblers in line, but even the spectators wanted in. The man tried to pull away one last time, but Wapiti reached up with his other hand and caught a hold of the back of his neck. It stopped the man dead in his tracks; it felt like someone just put his neck in a vice. Wapiti turned him and lead him to the front of the line. Then looking back over at him, "Remember, if you're innocent, walk through the line. But if your guilty, then you…"

That was as far as Wapiti got when the man took off running as fast as he could, hoping to catch some of the men and women off guard. It didn't work however, as everyone started swinging belts, leather straps, hell even a few grabbed a couple pool cues. It wasn't long and the man was going down to his knees, then he was crawling along the floor. No one let up; they just kept hitting him as he slowly made it to the end of the line and out the door. It actually only took maybe two minutes, but it was the longest two minutes of his life. When he finally did get to the end of the line, he slowly stood up. Looking at his torn and bloody clothes and wiping the blood from his eyes, "I know most of you," the man said, "I'll get even with you later. You just remember me, Chief… I'll get even with you, too. You can count on it." The whole room busted up in laughter and cheering.

"I did say earlier this morning, if you want a piece of me, you just say when and where. If the Marshal don't mind taking over for a while, I'll be glad to step outside right now."

"No, hell no. I don't mind taking over for a little while," Shawn answered. "If you're going to do it, then hurry up and get it over with, cause I'm getting hungry."

Slowly, everyone started returning to their seats, and then all of a sudden one of the lady gamblers kicked the man between the legs, bringing the man to his knees. "I knew you were cheating," she said, kicking him in the face, sending him flying backwards, and laying flat out on the floor. "Don't worry," she said looking at the man, "I didn't cheat; I was the last one in line. Now, if I were you, I'd get the hell out of here while you still have a chance."

Everyone was laughing and talking as they returned to their seats. Wapiti had proved yesterday, and again this morning that he could handle himself. The Marshal had had his fun last night with the men who had brought guns into the game. But this time, thanks to an old Indian custom they all had gotten in on giving out the punishment, and it was fun. Maybe this young buck wasn't as bad as they thought.

"Alright," Wapiti hollered. "The fun's over with. Now lets all get back to the games." Then he turned and started walking towards the Marshal and Corky. Everyone could tell he was walking just a little taller in his boots, and he had a smile that went from ear to ear.

Wapiti walked up to the Marshal, as Shawn slapped him on the back. "You handled that just fine. Yes sir, fact, your suggestion of punishment made everyone happy, which isn't easy to do."

"LOOK OUT," someone hollered. The man who had just been kicked out of the game came running back in with his pistol in hand and was trying to aim it. Everyone knew just whom he was planning to shoot. All of a sudden Shawn pushed Wapiti aside with one hand, drew and fired with the other. Half the people were ducking; trying to get out of the way, while the other half didn't even realize what was happening till it was over. Shawn's bullet was true, drilling the man right between the eyes, sending him flying backwards to the floor dead. Slowly Shawn started waving his pistol around the room. "Anyone else want to try and do something stupid like that man there?"

Everyone started looking at the person next to them, then around the room. They were all saying, "NO," at the same time.

"Good then," Shawn said, helping Wapiti up from the floor. Shaking his head, "I sure hate killing a man, but he left me no chose. Now I'm going to go get me some breakfast, and again my Deputy will be in charge…And I don't want to be disturbed. Do I make myself clear? Cork, get someone to bury him," handing him twenty dollars, "I'll pay for this one." Again, everyone was still agreeing with him.

"Sheriff, would you like to join me?" Shawn asked.

Chapter Ten

"Sure Marshal," Dennis answered, smiling. "I'd be glad to join you." He looked over at Wapiti; "I like your game...I might just use it myself next time we have a cheater. I just hope I don't have to shoot anyone in the end."

Shawn looked down at the Sheriff who was not even wearing his pistol. "You won't have to worry about that Sheriff, cause you're not wearing your gun, right now an innocent man would be dead and another waiting for the gallows."

Reaching down at his side, Dennis realized the Marshal was right. He didn't have his gun. All of a sudden he felt sick inside.

"Like I told you yesterday, Sheriff, you never know when, where, or how you're going to need it. SO YOU had better always have it on you as long as you're wearing that badge," Shawn demanded. "I was going to tell you that at breakfast, but I think you had better go get it on while you still have a chance."

"Yes sir Marshal," Dennis said watching Shawn walk towards the café for breakfast. Dennis headed back to his office to get his pistol.

Corky turned to Wapiti, "Young man, you have a good head on your shoulders, letting everyone get in on the punishment, and my place didn't get tore up... That was a lot of fun to watch from up here."

"Thanks Cork," Wapiti replied. "I appreciate your confidence in me."

"Charley, why don't you pour this Young man a beer?" Cork said.

"No thanks Cork," Wapiti answered. "Not while I'm working, and definitely not when guns are around. But this evening when the Marshal takes over, I'll be glad to take you up on your offer."

"Well then, anytime you want anything to drink," Cork said slapping Wapiti on the shoulder. "You just let Charley know, it's on the house."

Shawn had been sitting enjoying his coffee, and just about to enjoy his breakfast, when a short, fat, almost bald headed man walked up to his table. Shawn couldn't help but chuckle a little. Whoever this man was he could tell he hadn't missed a meal in a long while. Fact, Shawn bet he was first at the table every meal.

"Marshal Felton, I suppose?" the man asked.

185

"Yes sir," Shawn answered, pouring a small shot of whiskey from a flask into his coffee. He had been around enough Judges' in his life to know one straight off. From the times when he had done something wrong and got caught, or from all the ones he come across since he was a Sheriff's Deputy, all the way up to a U.S. Deputy Marshal. He knew the shot of whiskey would up set him just a little, or he hoped it would.

The man reached across the table to shake Shawn's hand, setting down, "Judge Earl English, it's nice to meet you Marshal. I've heard a lot about you. Now, you haven't even been in my town for two days and you've already killed a man."

"NOW YOU just wait one minute, Your Honor," Shawn shouted out. "That man pulled his gun first and he was fix'en to back shoot my Deputy," he said, pointing his fork at the Judge.

"I heard..." the judge started to say.

"Well then, what the hell are we talking about this for?" Shawn demanded.

"Let's just say I wanted to meet the great Shawn Felton, Deputy U.S. Marshal," the Judge said in a stern voice. "I've heard you like to bring them in over the saddle as apposed to letting a real Judge pass judgment on him."

Taking a bite of food, Shawn looked over at the Judge, staring right into his face, "Now, your honor, you just hold it right there, I only shoot those who are shooting at me first. I can't help it if they can't hit what there shooting at. Maybe I'm not as fast as I used to be...But my shots are still dead center, that's what counts, hitting your target first shot." Then Shawn started chuckling, looking back over at the Judge, and thinking of poor Floyd, sitting in jail for having sex with this mans daughter. He wondered just how many other men this Judge had sent up the river on trumped up charges.

"Well Marshal, what I really stopped by for was to find out just how much longer we'll be honored with your presence in our fair city?" the Judge asked.

"What's wrong YOUR HONOR, you don't want me in you fair city?" Shawn asked, sitting full up in his chair.

186

Chapter Ten

"NOO...I'm not saying that. Fact, the Sheriff and I both were glad when you rode into town...I'd just like to know what idiot would make an Indian buck a Deputy U.S. Marshal. I mean what was that Judge thinking?...If in fact he was thinking at all." The judge answered, with skepticism in his voice.

"Well now, Your Honor, that would be Judge Ralph Monson back home in Prineville." Shawn said, proudly, returning to his food.

"Well now, I know who, but really Marshal, stop and think about it." the Judge said. "An Indian Lawman? Why I bet that boy don't live a week, two if he's lucky. And just what the hell is he doing with you?"

"NOW, you just wait one minute Your Honor, Shawn said. "That boy came to me and asked me to help him along. I gave him my word that I would, and I will. Fact, I'll put that Young man up against any white man anytime. If you ask me, that Young man has more brains and common sense, and not only that, but Grit. Fact is Your Honor, that lad in there is going to make a dam good Deputy. I'll go one better. That lads going to make a good Marshal, you mark my words."

"Well Marshal, you just don't go and get that boy killed, cause if you do, I'm here to tell you there'll be hell to pay," Judge English demanded. "We've been real fortunate; all the Indians have been stay-ing on their reservation, and have been peaceful. But you go and get that boy killed...Let's just say some of them might retaliate, if you get my meaning."

"Yes sir, I do," Shawn answered waving his fork. "But, if you go in there and see just what kind of side arm he's wearing, you'll see not too many people will be in a big hurry to try him."

"Ya, I heard all about that sawed off ten gauge from a young man who came to me this morning. Had dried blood all over his face," Judge English said. "He claimed your Deputy threw him out of the game for no reason. But no one would back him, because of that gun... That was his side anyway, claimed he was up over forty five hundred dollars."

"Well now Your Honor...Did he also tell you he tried to pick a fight with my Deputy?" Shawn said, puffing his chest up. "Young

Wapiti was just defending himself. Also, he knew the rules; starting trouble is one of them…That's what got him thrown out."

"He claimed he was just sitting there playing poker when the Deputy tripped over his chair," Judge English answered.

"Well of course he did, YOUR HONOR…" Shawn snapped back. "What the hell would you expect him to say? But do you think those seventy plus players, not to mention the hundred or more on lookers, would have allowed Wapiti to throw him out if he was in the right?"

"Well, I guess you're right, Marshal. But then a ten gauge could be a real big deterrent, if you get my meaning," Judge English said taking a drink of coffee.

"Well hell, Your Honor, wouldn't you try and come up with a lie if you had just got kicked out of the biggest game of the year, by trying to make a Deputy Marshal look like a fool? I'm here to tell ya Judge if you'd been here an hour ago you would have been real proud of the way young Wapiti handled that situation. Fact that man had already been kicked out of the building, WHEN HE came back in pointing a pistol."

"That's another thing, Marshal; just what the hell were you thinking firing your pistol through that crowded room? What would have happened if you'd missed and hit someone else?" Judge English snapped at him.

"Well, you see Your Honor," Shawn said with a big smile on his face. "Like I told you earlier…I hit what I'm shooting at. Especially when it's only thirty feet or less from me. I never miss at that range… NEVER…So, if and when you get the time Your Honor, I'd like to introduce you to him. Then I think you'll change your mind about him, just like Judge Monson back home did."

Shawn looked down at his pocket watch, "Oh Shit, Your Honor, I didn't realize we've been talking for over an hour and a half. Wapiti was up with the sun, and it's going on noon. I imagine he's getting pretty hungry by now." Lighting up a cigar, "Fact, why don't you come and meet the Young man right now?"

188

Chapter Ten

Looking down at his own pocket watch, "Well I suppose I could spare ten, fifteen minutes before I need to be back at the court house," Judge English said.

"Well then, come on Your Honor," Shawn said standing up. "Let's go introduce you two."

The two walked out of the restaurant and back into the Saloon. They worked their way through the crowd. Shawn could see Wapiti was walking inside the roped off gaming area. "Wapiti," he called out.

"Yes sir, Marshal," Wapiti answered.

"Meet us up at the bar. There's someone I would like you to meet." Shawn said.

"Yes sir, Marshal," Wapiti answered. "I'll be right there."

Then a man standing outside the roped area yelled out, "SO CHIEF, now that the Marshal's back, does that offer to meet anyone anytime still stand? OR, were you just talking out your ass?"

Looking over in the direction of the Marshal. Holding his hands up and shrugging his shoulders. "Excuse me for a minute, Marshal," Wapiti said, turning back towards the area of the crowd, where the comment had come…"YA, I'll stand behind what I said this morning. But like this morning, NO guns and no knives. Just you and me…hand to hand."

"That sounds fine with me," the man said. "So when is DADDY going to let you out to play?"

"Well earlier, I suggested this evening after I got off work," Wapiti said, "but since the Marshal in already here to relieve me for lunch… if you're in a hurry, I see no reason why we can't do it now. So when you start feeling froggy, you just come a hop'en…It really don't matter to me, I'll leave it up to you to decide where, when, and how."

"Ya right," the man replied. "The Marshal there won't even let you out of his sight. Hell, the first time you start getting your ass kicked he'd jump in and help you out."

"No I won't Young man," Shawn said smiling. "Not as long as it stays a clean fight. NO GUNS, NO KNIVES, just hand to hand… He's all yours." Gesturing with his hand.

Judge English reached over and pulled on the Marshal's sleeve. "Are you sure that this is something you want to let happen? Don't you think you might be sending the wrong message?"

"Oh hell no! This will show all those others just what he's made of, Sand, and lots of it," Shawn answered. "But you just remember one thing Young man, as long as it stays clean, I'll stay out. But the minute he starts kicking your ass and you reach for someone's gun or knife that's near by watching…You'll leave here wearing whichever you pull…Do I make myself clear?"

"Hell, I damned sure don't need anything but my hands to teach this Buck a lesson in being a lawman… Fact, he just might change his mind about being a lawman when I finish with him," the man said.

"Well, when do you want to do this, Wapiti?" Shawn asked.

Wapiti started unbuckling his gun, "Well, I guess we should get this over with now," Wapiti answered, handing both his knife and gun to the Marshal. Then turning back to the man, "You called it, I'll let you lead the way."

The man started looking around the Saloon, the crowd was getting excited and louder. "FIGHT, FIGHT, FIGHT," they were starting to holler. The man didn't know what to do. He had seen what this Buck Indian had done to Jack and Sam yesterday. HELL, HE WAS THERE, and those boys are big. That Indian made very little work of them. The crowd was getting louder, and louder. Now just about everyone was hollering "Fight," as loud as they could. He had heard what Wapiti did to the man this morning, actually cutting the mans head. Said he could already have four scalps if he wanted them. He said next time; he would take a scalp.

That Buck Indian had just called his bluff; slowly he started having an uneasy feeling in his stomach. As he continued to look around the room, he wondered just how long he had been standing there. Hell, every second seemed like a minute, and every minute like an hour. "UH…UH, I-I was just funn'en with ya, Deputy," the man started stuttering, while he tried to talk. He held his hands up, "Really, I was just funn'en…" He slowly started taking a few steps backwards, towards the door, so he could get the hell out of there. He didn't want to be

Chapter Ten

the fifth scalp; he just might really take it this time. The man's forehead started inching, he started scratching it, and feeling the sweat run off his forehead.

The crowd was growing angry with him, hollering, "COWARD! YOU'RE YELLA! YOU CHICKEN SHIT!" That was just a few of the comments he was hearing. By now he had managed to back up three or four feet. But then some of the people started throwing bottles and glasses at him. This caused him to turn and run as those bottles and glasses were smashing into his body. The ones in the head really hurt.

"WWEELLLL SSHHOOTT MARSHAL," Wapiti started speaking up and looking around the room. Making sure he looked right into everyone's eyes. Making them each feel like he was talking straight to them. Sending a shiver up the backs of more than a few of them. "I WAS HOPING ON GETTING SCALP NUMBER FIVE, but I guess it will just have to wait a little while." He walked over to the Marshal and picked up his gun and knife.

"No you didn't get that fifth scalp yet, but the weekend's only half over. I'm sure more than one of these gentlemen here will help you get that fifth or even sixth scalp before we leave," Shawn answered

Wapiti started putting his gun back on, he continued talking loud enough for everyone to hear him, "Shoot Marshal, I was really hoping on working up an appetite. But I am still a little hungry." He stood full up, putting his knife back in his belt. "You think you can handle things without me, Marshal?" Wapiti couldn't help but smile.

"Think I can? Hell, I know I can." Shawn said in a loud voice. "ALRIGHT, now the excitement is over with, so lets get back to what we're doing and start playing poker again." Still speaking in a loud voice, "Well Deputy, why don't you go get some lunch. I'm sure no one will bother you for a while."

Wapiti turned and walked toward the restaurant, he couldn't help but notice how ALL these white eyes were moving way back. Giving him enough room that three or four people could walk through. He set down at a table and Sheriff Beyer came over, stuck his hand out,

191

sitting down, "Sure am glad I got back to see that. You don't mind if I join you, do you Wapiti?"

"Heck no Sheriff," Wapiti said. "Please, have a seat, Sheriff."

'Thanks, and I wish you'd start calling me Dennis. I think they're all starting to respect you now. I've got to say I had my doubts when I first met you, that any one would ever respect you, I mean. I figured you could fight, just not that good. I like the way you've handled different situations, and I've got to tell you, I've grown to respect you as well. Fact, if I ever needed any help…I hope you're there to back my play."

"Thanks Sheriff, I mean Dennis," Wapiti answered. "And I will, if I can…back ya, that is."

Cathey walked up, with that big beautiful smile on her face, pouring them each a cup of coffee. "Sorry it took me so long to get over here, Wapiti, but every one of these guys think they should be served first."

"That's alright," Wapiti said. He could feel his face turning redder than usual. Those big brown eyes, and that smile. Boy he sure wished he was a white man right now. If he made a move on her, every white eye in the place would be on him like stink on shit. He was thinking to himself, him being an Indian would only cause trouble for her. Besides, did she really like him, or was she just setting him up?"

"By the way, Wapiti," Cathey said. "My name is Cathey Larkin. I don't remember if I ever told you."

"I knew your first name. But Larkin? Are you related to the man Dennis here has over in his jail?"

"YES," Cathey answered, chuckling. "Ya, he's one of my uncles, on my dad's side." She looked over at the Sheriff; "It sure was nice what you did for him. Getting him to clean the Sheriff's office as opposed to being out in the county lock up, making big rocks into little one's."

Looking back and forth between the two, Wapiti said, "most Indian girls are married by the time they're sixteen. Didn't I hear the Judges daughter turned eighteen just a couple days later?"

"Ya, she did," Cathey answered. Covering her face, so no one could see she was laughing about her uncle. "Fact me and her grew up

Chapter Ten

together, and NO I'm not married either… But if I'm not married in a couple years, they'll start calling me an old maid."

"Same with my people, too," Wapiti said still looking back and forth at them…"So why's he in jail? My people would have just make them get married."

Laughing hard, and trying not to fall out of his chair, Dennis looked over at Wapiti, "we call those shot gun weddings around here… But she just happened to be the Judge's youngest daughter."

"It also didn't help that he's a Larkin," Cathey said still smiling. "At least when I get married I get to change my last name. But here in Grant county and over in Baker county…If you're a Larkin, you're guilty until proven innocent in a court of law… And you had better have a good attorney, Right Sheriff?"

"Yep, that's just about the way I see it." Dennis answered.

"They all outlaw's?" Wapiti asked, looking up at Cathey.

"NO, NO…nothing like that. They just like to cause a little trouble now and then. To them, they're just having a little fun. Fact, I have five cousin's over in Baker City, they're the worst," Cathey said

"So does anyone get hurt?" Wapiti asked, still looking up at Cathey's smile, it made her look even prettier. She was easy to talk to, not like some white women half as pretty as her. "AH…I'm sorry," Wapiti said. "I was just thinking of something else." He looked back and forth between them. He noticed his hands were starting to sweat. If she gave him a kiss down here he would definitely get scalped. "Anyway, what's up with them? What kind of trouble do they do?"

"You know?" Cathey said. "Getting caught with someone's girl friend or wife, or they don't watch what comes out of their mouths, that sometime leads to a fight. But actually their smart-ass mouth gets them in the most trouble. They don't know when to shut up. Isn't that the way you see it Sheriff?"

"Sure is," Dennis said. He was still chuckling and thinking about Floyd. "Don't tell me how, but those boys get caught at any and every-thing they do."

"Well, I suppose you men are hungry. So I'll go get your food and another pot of coffee." Cathey said, then she turned and walked away.

Wapiti couldn't help it; he had to watch her walk away, in that tight, short skirt. Then he turned back to Dennis real quick. If these white eyes knew what his was thinking…They would definitely scalp him. No sooner had he thought it, and he got a six to seven inch long tingling feeling across his forehead. Making him rub it. "So Dennis, what were we talking about?"

"Don't rightly recall?" Dennis said, "But I think that young lady likes you.

"OOOHHH NNOO," Wapiti said. He could feel his face get at least five times hotter and redder.

"Ah, come on now, Wapiti," Dennis said. With a smile on his face, "I think you like her to…Don't ya, just a little."

"What with me being an Indian?" Wapiti answered in a low, but loud voice. "Just how long do you think these white eyes would let me live?"

"You have her grow that dark brown hair out and those that didn't know her would think she was a half breed." Dennis said, "just a lighter skinned half breed.

"Ya, right," Wapiti said "NO ONE WOULD KNOW…Hell; you just got through telling me how crazy her family is. Sounds like they'd hang me first."

"No, I really don't think so, not with the Larkin bunch," Dennis answered. "Tell ya the truth; they're a good bunch of men to have on your side if you ever need extra help. Every one of them can ride any horse you give them, and they're all dead shots with either rifle or pistol. They're not afraid to use them. But they're not quick to pull them either. Fact, they'd much rather use their hands to settle trouble if they could. But, hell they're meaner than most, being part Irish. " He said. "Not to change the subject, but I feel like I owe you an apology."

"What for?" Wapiti asked

"For this morning…The Marshal was right…If he hadn't been there you'd be dead right now. There wouldn't have been a thing I could have done to stop it… I…I wasn't wearing my gun. I guess the Marshal was right yesterday. You never know when, where, or how you're going to need it. You can always take it off for a fight…But

Chapter Ten

you'll never now when you're going to need it. Like this morning...I couldn't have done anything to stop that man."

"Hell Dennis, I was already heading for the floor. The Marshal just helped me get there faster."

"So why you carry that ten gauge? Wouldn't a twelve gauge do?" Dennis asked.

Wapiti reached down and put his hand on the butt of the ten gauge. "The Marshal wanted me to wear it till I get better with a pistol. Said this ten gauge would make men think twice before they tried anything, which would give me a half second advantage."

"I know it sure would make me think twice," Dennis said smiling. "And I've noticed everyone in that room has looked at that ten gauge more than once. Not a person in that room is going to try too much. But then, just like this morning, you'll always have the guy who will..."

"Problem with this morning and this gun, I would have ended up putting a few bee-bees into the people standing close to him." Wapiti said

"So tell me Wapiti, what's it like being on the trail with the great Marshal Felton?" Dennis asked with excitement in his voice. "Man, do I envy you. I just got this job handed to me after the other Sheriff quit. Then one night a fight broke out in one of the Saloon's, I broke it up, then they offered me the job. Don't pay much; I get three meals a day, and a bed at the jail."

"Sounds like you're in jail yourself, Dennis," Wapiti said smiling back at him. "But to answer your question, it's been a lot of fun so far."

"What do you guys do and talk about out there on the trail?" Dennis asked with the same excitement in his voice.

"He has me practice a lot with my pistol," Wapiti answered. "Then he has me give him an hour or two head start and he tries to hide somewhere and have me see if I can track him. He's good at covering his tracks, but my grandpa taught me to track...Not to brag, but there isn't much I don't see, and my Dad taught me to fight."

"Well, I've seen you fight," Dennis answered. "And if you're even half as good at tracking, I wouldn't want you on my trail."

195

"He's always telling me a different story about the men he's chased, and all the different positions he had to shoot from. He has more stories than anyone I've ever met," Wapiti said smiling. "I know he's been around a long time, but still, some of his stories are hard to believe. Even though you know they're true, or parts of them are anyway. He said he rode with Quantrill's raiders during the War Between the States. Said he wasn't always a lawman. Fact he told me about a couple outposts he robbed a couple times. But according to him it was just a road stake." This caused both men to start laughing.

"I bet he does have a million stories," Dennis said. "It would be nice to have someone teach me how to shoot someone, ya know. I can shoot, don't get me wrong. I practice all the time. HELL, the city buys my shells; Floyd and me go out sometimes. But…How do you know if you have no choice and you better shoot that man, or you're the one who's dead? We don't get too many big outlaws around here, least none I'd need my gun to bring in. Most our troubles get settled with fists," he started rubbing his right fist into his left hand. "So just how much target practice you get riding trail all the time?"

"The Marshal has these corn biscuits, salty and hard as hell," Wapiti said. "Saltiest things you've ever tasted. As we ride along he will holler "PULL", and throw one or two in the air. I have to find it and shoot at it before it hits the ground." Wapiti started to chuckling again. "That's the only thing; I think those things are good for. But that's one thing the Marshal is big on, Heck, when we left Prineville last week we had three thousand rounds of pistol ammo and one thousand rounds for the rifle, and we're almost out. We'll have to get more ammo before we leave. Don't need any more shotgun shells," he says, smiling. "I don't miss much with it."

"I hope not, Hell, even I couldn't miss with that," Dennis said, smiling. "But does he ever give you tips on how to shoot at different targets?"

"Of course he does," Wapiti answered. "Then he'll have me throw a corn biscuit up, and he'll show me what he's talking about. Only he don't miss, even on his horse, pistol or rifle. Fact, he's had me throw three or four at a time, and he uses both, pistol in one hand, his rifle

Chapter Ten

in the other. He gets three out of four more times than I get two out of four."

"Really?" Dennis was surprised, "both his pistol and rifle at the same time…How's he re-cock the rifle?"

"If you look at his rifle, you'll notice he has a bigger lever. Had Gordy, the black smith back home, make it for him. Say's his hands are too big for a regular rifle levers." Wapiti said. "I've tried to do it, but I'm not strong enough in the arms to hold that rifle straight out and cock it like he does. I know there's a technique to it. I think if I start practicing with his rifle, till I can get Gordy to make one for me, I think I will be able to do it someday."

"I can see where that might come in handy," Dennis said. "So where you guys heading when you leave here?"

"A town called Sumpter," Wapiti answered. "The Marshal said it used to be a small logging town, then they struck gold, and it tripled in size overnight."

"That it did, I logged over there a couple times. Can't tell you how many times I fished that Powder River over there. That's the river that runs through there. Shoot, just think if it would have been me that found all that gold. I wouldn't have to do anything I didn't want too ever again." Dennis said.

"Speaking of that yellow rock," Wapiti said. "Just what do they do with it?"

"Don't really know everything they use it for, but they sure do pay a lot for it," Dennis answered. "I tried digging in that ground, packing all that dirt and rock down to the river to run it through your slush box. I tell ya, it's hard cold work…But I hear now, there's over eight thousand people in Sumpter.'

"I wouldn't do it. I like being a lawman. I know I still have a lot to learn. I just wonder what it's going to feel like when I have to shoot my first man…Have you ever had to shoot anyone yet?" Wapiti asked.

"Nope, not yet," Dennis said. "I hope I never have to. I can hit what I shoot at, don't get me wrong. But I'm not that fast out of the holster, you hear about all those gun fighters. I hope I don't have to face one till I get a whole lot better. I hope I never have to draw against anyone. But if I do…I'm aiming dead center of his chest"

"I hear ya," Wapiti answered. "The Marshal keeps telling me, 'practice at hitting your target first, make sure you hit what you're shooting at first, the speed will come later.' Told me, 'you may only get one shot…so don't rush it, you may not have time to get a second shot off.'"

"I know that was true this morning," Dennis said. "He didn't even hesitate. I couldn't believe he shot through all those people and hit his target. All before most people could even duck out of the way, and he didn't give that man a second shot either."

"Marshal told me, he knew a few men that would still be alive today, but they only shot to wound someone," Wapiti said. "Then the other man shot back and killed them." Taking another drink off his coffee. "He also says, 'he who hesitates, even a half second's the dead one.' Well Dennis, I need to get back in there."

"Alright," Dennis said as both men stood up and shook hands again. "Just want you to know I'll never be without my pistol again. Least not as long as I'm a lawman. So next time you need your back covered, you can count on me."

"Thanks, Dennis," Wapiti said, shaking his hand. "I hope you know I'll be there for you anytime I can be, as well."

Wapiti turned and walked back into the Saloon side. The place was crowded with spectators, yet all those white eyes were stepping back from him, giving him all the room he needed. He couldn't help but chuckle just a little. Walking towards the Marshal and Cork, he couldn't help but notice there was at least thirty players who had lost out. He glanced down at a few of the tables as he walked by them; he could see a few more were just about out of the game as well. Walking up to the two, "Marshal, I think I can take over now, if there's anything you need to do."

"Now just wait one minute," Cork said, stepping down from his thrown. "Just before you left last time, you kinda tore my place up." He started smiling. "Fact, we had a lot of glass to clean up."

"I'm sorry, Cork," Wapiti started, "but…"

Chapter Ten

"Now just wait one minute son," Corky said. "You didn't let me finish." He put his arm around Wapiti's shoulder. "You managed to keep the mess all in one area," he started chuckling. "I think more innocent people got hurt than the coward did. Those bottles and mugs were thrown hard. That man used to be a regular customer in here… Now I bet he won't show his face around here for awhile. So your costing me my customers, so just don't scare them ALL off. I do have to admit though; you have a lot of backbone son. The way you called his bluff…That was exciting to watch. So now I owe you two beers, Young man."

"TWO, like hell," Shawn said. "You'll pour him as many as he wants." Looking over at the Judge. "Now, I know you think Indian's shouldn't have alcohol, Your Honor, but whenever MY young Deputy wants a drink, he's earned it."

"I've seen enough drunken Indian's in my time, Marshal. So if he gets drunk and out of hand…It will be on your head, Shawn," the Judge said, waving his finger.

"Wapiti, I'd like you to meet His Honor, Judge Earl English." Introducing the two, "You'll find they're all the same…Judge's that is."

"Well, Young man it's a pleasure to meet you," Judge English said, sticking out his hand.

"Yes sir, Your Honor," Wapiti said shaking the Judges hand. "It's a pleasure to meet you, sir."

"Well, I'll let you two talk," Shawn said. "I'll take a walk around the tables. But ever since Wapiti ran that last YA-WHO out of here…Hell, it's been real quiet."

"Well, Young man, have a seat," the Judge said pointing to a chair. "I'd like to have a talk with you."

"Yes Sir, Your Honor." Wapiti looked over at Cork and Charley. Feeling just a little uncomfortable, he didn't know what it was about the Judge that made him uncomfortable. It was just like with Judge Monson back home. "Charley, could I please get a glass of ice water?"

"Now son, just what kind of fool idea do you have thinking you're going to be a lawman?" Judge English said, picking up his beer. "I mean, you did handle that situation earlier, and both Cork and the

199

Marshal speak pretty highly of you. I've heard and seen the other things you have done over here to. But don't you think you might be biting off just a little more than you can chew?"

"What, are you worried about that man earlier? I've beat'en a lot of Indian's warrior bigger than him…I wasn't worried." Wapiti answered.

"That's not all I'm talking about son. I'm talking about all those criminals you're going to be trying to bring in. I mean hell, Son, if it wasn't for Marshal Shawn Felton…these men would run you up a pole the second you rode into town. You go and get yourself killed then I'll have to hang a white man for killing an Indian. You have any idea what these people would do to me?"

"The Marshal said that once they all hear about me, they'll know who I am as soon as I ride into town. In time they will start to respect me," Wapiti answered, staring straight into the judge's eyes, with pure confidence in his voice.

"What are you going to do when he's no longer around?" Judge English asked. "Which won't be long, his way of bringing them in over the saddle, is on its way out. Only a Judge and jury should say if a man should die for his crimes, not a lawman. We need Peace officers. Men who can bring them in without the use of guns."

"Well Judge, what is a lawman supposed to do when an outlaw is shooting at him? Stand up and say hold it just a minute Sir, let's talk about this?" Wapiti asked, looking over at Cork for help.

"Ya Judge, what's he going to say?" Cork said, smiling. "You boy's put your guns down and come on in peaceably, SURE, the Judge is going to hang you, but please, put your guns down and come with me peacefully."

"Damn you Cork," Judge English snapped back, getting mad. "You know that's not what I meant. But this is almost the twentieth century; times are changing where more people don't even carry guns."

"Your Honor, the Marshal told me, he never shots a man who wasn't shooting at him first." Wapiti said. "Say's it's not his fault he can hit what he's shooting at and they can't."

Chapter Ten

"I know, I seen his handy work this morning," Judge English answered Wapiti.

"Now, wait just one minute, Your Honor," Wapiti said looking straight into the Judge's eyes. "That man was going to shoot me in the back. Would you have liked it better if he had killed me?"

"That's not what I'm saying and you know it." Judge English snapped back at him.

"That's exactly what it sounds like to me Judge," Cork interrupted. "Hell, he's just an Indian, he don't matter much."

"Now Cork, you knock it off," the Judge snapped back. "You know damned good and well that's not what I meant." Then looking back over at Wapiti, "You just make sure that if you do shoot someone, there is no other way out. I'd hate to have to hang a Deputy U.S. Marshal for shooting an innocent man."

"Well Your Honor," Wapiti said, "does that mean if he's shoot'en at me, I Can't Shoot Back?"

"You know what I mean Young man," Judge English said, finishing his beer, slamming the mug down on the bar, then standing up he looked Wapiti in the eyes. "Just so you know…If you're in the right, I'll back you all the way. Good Luck Young man," He said, slapping him on the shoulder with a smile on his face, and welcome aboard. Then he turned and walked out the door.

Shawn could see the judge was a little flustered as he walked out of the Saloon. So he turned and walked back over to Wapiti, "Well son, did you learn anything?"

"YAA, he said if I have to kill someone, he just might hang me. Besides that Marshal, he makes me feel uncomfortable, just to be around him," Wapiti answered.

"I know just what you're saying, Wapiti," Shawn answered. "All them Judge's have a way of making you feel that way, AND, just like him, they all want you to bring them back alive. They don't seem to understand; you can't do that all the time. Hell, they're always threatening to fire you over something."

"Just like last week, those men stole that wagon load of nitro… It was my intention to bring them men in alive. It wasn't my fault that

201

shale rock slid out from under my feet, causing me to miss fire and hit that load of nitro instead of the driver. Like I told the Judge, I followed and waited three days and nights for the right opportunity."

"Those Judge's don't know the half of it. If they knew even half the things we have to go through, they'd think twice. But NNNOOO, they just sit back home in their homes, safe and sound. No one shoot'en at them...Hell, they think it's easy to track a man down. Why, I'd like to see them try it. On the trail for two, three weeks at a time, no home cooked meals, getting shot at...That would change their tune just a little." Shawn pulled out his pocket watch, "Hell, it's just barely after two. You took all the fight out of them Wapiti, which means it's going to be a long night."

"Speaking of long, Marshal," Wapiti asked. "Just how much longer you think we'll be here?"

"Well now," looking around the room, "Looks like we're down to just above half of the players left," Shawn said. "So if everything goes well we'll finish up here tomorrow night, which means we could be out of here by Monday morning. Why, you in a hurry?"

"Not really, but I would like to get over to Sumpter," Wapiti answered. "I was talking to Dennis at lunch, he said he used to log over there, say's he can't believe how many people have moved there hoping to find that yellow rock."

"Now that you mention it I can tell by his size, he has definitely logged a little bit." Shawn said. "That's hard work. It'll let you know what you're made of. Those men earn every penny they make...And a whole lot of them get killed in the process. Too much work for me, I've done it, when I was younger. But the trees back east are only half the diameter of these big firs and pines out here. But out of all the jobs I've had, I like being a lawman. That way I can work at my own pace. Nice and slow when I can...But now that you mention it, we are going to need some supplies. With tomorrow being Sunday, I imagine the stores will be closed. Won't they, Cork?"

"Yes sir, they are," Cork answered. "The church is open though Marshal," Cork said, chuckling. "Don't you think you should stop in there while you're in town?"

202

Chapter Ten

"I'm afraid if I went in one of those, why it would plum scare God to death, and the building would fall down," Shawn answered, starting to chuckle. "I'll let you take back over Wapiti, and I'll go get some more ammo and whatever else we need. You sure did go through a lot of it coming up, but at least now you're starting to hit more than you miss. I'll stop by that Mexican restaurant and see about getting some more corn biscuits."

"Oh joy," Wapiti said looking at the Marshal. "The only thing those things are good for, is target practice."

"What are these corn biscuits?" Cork asked.

"Something he calls food," Wapiti said smiling, pointing at Shawn. "Only thing I think they're good for is target practice, when he runs out of pine cones."

"I'll tell you what they're good for Young man, when you have to go and go quick, you don't have time or room to take a lot of food… That corn bread will fill you up quick, so you can catch up to your prey faster…Just like I told you earlier, those boys are going to have to shoot their meals, and that gun shot can be heard a long way off… Hell, they let you know right where they are, you might say." Then Shawn turned and walked towards the door.

"Here Marshal," Cork shouted, tossing him a bottle of whiskey.

Turning and just barely catching the bottle before it hit him. "No thanks Cork," Shawn said, tossing the bottle back. "I have to work tonight, a couple cold beers is one thing, but too much of that can only lead to trouble." He waved his hand around at the tables. "I just might have to bust a head or two tonight, if I'm lucky, and I want to be sober when I'm doing it… It's more fun…" Smiling, he turned back to the door, stepping outside.

Instantly he had to cover his eyes, because of the brightness of the sun. Looking around letting his eyes adjust, he could see the mill across the tracks and the train station across the street, which made it easy to see what way to go. Looking up the street he could see the Livery stable, so he headed in that direction.

Shawn kept his eyes open for the Mercantile. As far as towns went, this one seemed to be a nice little city. Everyone was saying 'Hi' to him as he walked by, he noticed a few young men crossing the street up in front of him, but he didn't recollect seeing any posters on them. Which meant they were just small wanna be outlaws. But it didn't take much to become a wanted man if you didn't look out. Being in the wrong place at the wrong time. He himself had crossed the line a couple times when he was younger. But he needed a road stake to help him out; no one ever got hurt. He thought to himself. Before he knew it he was standing in front of the Livery stable. Looking around real quick, he could see small groups of men talking business, but as he walked up, their conversations ceased. "Excuse me, Gentlemen," Shawn asked, "which one of you might be the proprietor of this establishment?"

"That would be me," one of the men said, walking over to the Marshal and stuck his hand out, "Roy Larkin, Marshal, it's a pleasure to meet you...So just what can I do for you?"

"Larkin...Larkin, where have I heard that name...? Oh ya, there's a Young man over in the jail house name is Larkin. Wouldn't be any relation would he?" Shawn asked with a big smile on his face.

"Afraid so Marshal," Roy answered smiling. "He's one of my younger brothers. When he was about seventeen, he wanted to see the country, so he joined the Calvary for four years. Spent those four years down in California watching some imaginary line in the sand. Said it was all right for the Americans to cross over into Mexico, but them Mexicans couldn't come over here. Said it was just about the stupidest law he ever had to enforce. Said it was the most worthless land he had ever seen, nothing but desert, no water for miles."

"Why didn't they want them in, the Mexicans I mean?" Shawn asked.

"Said they worked for less than Americas, so there fore they were taking money away from the real Americans," Roy answered.

"Well hell, the way I look at it, if a man wants to work, let him work," Shawn answered.

"Anyway, he got out of the Calvary about four months ago, came home thinking he was some kind of war hero," Roy started chuckling. "He didn't know old man English had become a Judge. Their family and ours don't get along very well...Fact, we still don't. You know the rest of the story, or you wouldn't have mentioned it."

"Ya I do," Shawn said, chuckling a little. "Anyway, what I came over for was to let you know I plan on leaving early Monday morning, and I was wondering if you could make sure all our animals were ready to go?"

"Sure thing Marshal, anything special you need?" Roy asked.

"Check their shoes, Gordy back home usually has them loaded and ready to go by sun-up for me. That way I can get an early start. Of course I'll pay you extra for your time," Shawn said.

"Don't worry about it, Marshal," Roy answered, "I'm up early anyway, and as far as the bill goes, I'll just give it to the county to pay. If it weren't for you being in town, who knows just how out of hand that poker tournament would get. Besides, it brought the entire town more money than anyone expected. If all the business's pitch in a little, it won't cost them too much."

"Well if you're sure, but if they don't, we'll be back through this way in a week or so, then we'll settle up any difference," Shawn said. "Young Wapiti wants to be a lawman, so I figured I take him on one of my hunt'en trips, Might say, let him see what he's going to be getting himself into...I figured Sumpter would be a good place to start."

"Sounds to me like he's finding out a little here as well," Roy said, with a little chuckle. "Fact, when word got around that there was a Indian lawman in town, well, let's just say most everyone started laughing...But I hear he's been holding up his end real well."

"That he has," Shawn said, chuckling. "Fact is, it's been fun watching him."

"I bet," Roy answered. "Sure wish I could have been there yesterday when he took Sam and Jack out...My little sister and Jack have been dating for a couple years now, the bruises that Young man put on those two will make everyone think twice."

"Well, to tell you the truth Roy, that didn't take him very long. Fact, Dennis and me had just gone into the Saloon before it started...Kinda hoped we might have to help out if more jumped in...But he flat laid those young men out…I think the one he pulled that hog leg on just might have pissed his pants."

"He did," Roy said laughing even more. "I seen Jack and Sam last night, I asked them if they intended on getting revenge. They both said they had had all of that young buck they wanted." The two walked back into the Livery; Roy pulled out a pint of whiskey, taking a small pull off the bottle. "Would you like a shot Marshal?"

"Hell, one shot ain't going to hurt," Shawn said. Taking the bottle and taking himself a big pull off the bottle then handed it back. "Well then sir, I'll see you bright and early Monday morning, if not before." He turned and walked back to the door. Then turning around, and looking back, "Oh Ya, I'm going to have the Mercantile bring over more supplies."

"Sure thing, Marshal. Whatever you need you just make sure it's here and I'll make sure you can get to the important things easy, like your ammo," Roy answered.

"Thanks again, Roy," Shawn said, walking out the door, looking around town. He'd need to go over to the train station and wire Judge Monson of their location. Let him know just how young Wapiti was holding up, but first he needed to get all the supplies they would need.

He worked his way around town doing everything he needed to do; he couldn't get over how friendly everyone was. He couldn't ever remember having to say 'Hello or Good afternoon' so many times in one day. He figured he had been gone for about three hours when he returned to the Saloon. Walking in, he slowly looked around the room, it looked like they were down to thirty some players, however there was only one lady left. Shawn couldn't help but take a second glance; she was a nice looking young lady. She had long dark, almost total black hair; he figured she was just over five feet tall, maybe hundred ten pounds. She didn't dress like most young ladies, that was she wasn't wearing a dress and all that paint on her face like most young women now days were wearing. Which could really confuse a man these days, you think you're going to bed with a pretty one, and you'd rather chew your arm off in the morning, hoping she didn't wake up before you could get out of the room.

206

Chapter Ten

Looking back at her, he could tell she wasn't afraid of work. Just by the way she looked he could tell right off she knew her way around the barnyard. Could tell by her demeanor, she could out do most young men today. He noticed she kept looking at one of those Seebart boys, the ones Wapiti had had his little miss understanding with yesterday morning. The one, whose lower jaw was one huge bruise from Wapiti's upper cut, Shawn started to chuckle. That looks like it still hurts like hell. That probably meant that young lady was Roy's younger sister. Roy had said the two had a thing for each other.

Taking a second look around the room, he was glad to see everything was under control, nice and quiet, except for all the people in the balcony and the crowds watching. Some of them were making side bets on who was going to be the ultimate winner. Working his way to the bar he couldn't help but think Wapiti was right. It would be nice to get back on the trail again, he couldn't figure out why people wanted to live so damn close to each other. He seen some houses built so close to each other and the walls so thin, you could hear your neighbor fart. He couldn't help but chuckle at the thought.

'Well,' he thought as he saw Wapiti and Cork up at the bar, guess I'll see if he wants to eat first or if he wants me to. I hope it's me he thought. Wapiti had already eaten since he had, and he was hungry. Taking a quick look around the Saloon he could see the crowd had grown. So he stepped over the roped off area to take a shortcut to the bar, slowly looking around at the different players. "Well Hell," Shawn said in a gruff voice, "looks like we're getting down to finishing these games up, should be tomorrow as planned." He kept talking as he walked through the tables. "These games are going to start at NINE A.M. SHARP. Those of you who are still in the game after tonight, if you're even one minute late you're out. So…if you gentlemen and lady, ma-am," he said nodding his hat to her. "So if you wanna make sure we're all on the same timetable," reaching in his pocket he pulled out his pocket watch, looking down at it, "Right now my watch said its… lets see here…five…eighteen…so I advise you all to sit your timepieces to match mine." Most of them were already doing it and those who weren't did. "Now that means you are in your seat with your chips in

207

front of you, ready to play. If you arrive at nine o' one you're out of the fun," he said. Starting to chuckle just a little bit with the way he had said that line.

Stepping over the rope to the other side of the room, he looked at everyone, "Wapiti, Cork, and Charlie, how's everything going?"

"Fine Marshal," Wapiti answered. "Everyone's been real quiet, not really anything exciting going on."

"Good, good," Shawn said, throwing his chest out. "Well, Wapiti if you don't mind I'd like to get me some dinner, then I'll come and relieve you."

"What about us?" one of the players yelled out. "Ya, what about us?" hollered out another. "We're all getting hungry, too." By now just about everyone in the game was calling out.

"Well," Shawn said looking at everyone while he walked towards the restaurant…"you all can order your food, and I'm sure if you tip these young ladies, why I just bet they would be more than glad to get it for you." When he finished speaking he turned and walked into the restaurant. Looking around he could see a few empty tables. So he walked over and sat down at one of them. Cathey was already pouring him a cup of coffee before he even sat down. "Why, thank you young lady," Shawn said, looking at her. "What do we have for dinner tonight?"

"Well sir," Cathey answered, "the dinner special is Salisbury steak, it's actually real good."

"Alright," Shawn answered. "That sounds real good. But why don't you ask if they could throw a little extra on mine? I'm real hungry."

"Yes sir Marshal, anything you want, you know that," Cathey said smiling down at him. "So Marshal when does Wapiti get off for dinner?"

"Well, one of us has to always be in there, so he doesn't get off till after I eat." He could hear it in her voice; she was kinda sweet on young Wapiti. "So the faster you get me my food, the quicker he can eat." Shawn said, with a big smile on his face.

"Well then," Cathey said with a real big smile on her face, knowing the Marshal was joking with her. "Well then your food will be right

Chapter Ten

out Marshal, fact I'll make sure yours is dished up next before anyone else's." Then she topped off his coffee and walked away

Shawn started looking around the room. At one of the tables right next to him there was three young men, two of whom was sporting himself one of those big black eyes from last night...nodding his hat to them he couldn't help but grin at them at the same time. Which really seemed to upset them. Shawn could see it in their eyes. Before anything started, but no sooner had he thought about it, and one of them stood up.

"WELL, IF IT AIN'T THE GREAT MARSHAL SHAWN FLTON," the Young man was saying in a voice loud enough for everyone to hear. "Why this great Marshal here, he can't even give a man an honest chance, he asked you a question to get your attention on something else, then when you're not looking, he hits you. Just look at me, last night every one of us; he didn't even give us a chance to defend ourselves. Why he's no more than a backstabbing cheat. What's wrong old man? Cat got your tongue? You too old to take a man on in a fair fight...? Come on... don't you have anything to say?"

"Well son," Shawn said, leaning over the table, putting one arm on the table and the other down on his revolver. "Its looks to me like you're running your mouth enough for everyone. NOW, my advice to you is to sit your ass back down before you do something we're both going to regret."

"You think you're pretty good old man, but you can't take all three of us," he said pointing to the others as they both stood up.

"Well son, maybe you're right...maybe I can't get all three of you at once, but I dammed sure can get at least two of you. So which one of you two boys want to be the one who joins him in the cemetery. One small hesitation is all it takes so you better be damn sure you don't hesitate for a fraction of a second. Cause I'm tellin' ya, I DON'T HESISTATE. I'm here to tell ya, you even start to pull that gun and they will be buryin' ya in the mornin'. You can count on that."

The other two started looking back and forth at each other, then over at the Marshal and their friend. Neither one of them wanted to die. Not just yet anyway, but they would like to get even for the black eyes, they did feel like they deserved retribution, and they said as much.

"Well then," Shawn said leaning back in his chair with a big smile on his face. "You boys want retribution...? Well then just take those guns off and put them on that thar table and I'll be more than glad to oblige you."

"We'll take ours off. But then what about you? You get to keep yours? So that when we're kicking your ass you can pull it on us and kill us?" Their fearless leader said.

"Oh hell no...I'll be more than glad to take mine off as well, just as soon as you boys do. But I'll tell you boys right here and now, you will be paying for all the damages to this fine establishment."

The crowd was slowly growing louder and more boisterous at the thought of a fight. They had all heard war stories about the great MARSHARL SHAWN FELTON; sure he could probably give any one man in the place a good fight, one on one. But three and these three men weren't small. All three were at least six feet tall, one eighty, maybe two hundred pounds. This was going to be a good fight, and most of them were putting their money against that old fart, he couldn't take these three at his age, hell he had to be closing in on his mid-fifty's, if not older.

Wapiti slowly worked his way through the crowd making his way to the restaurant and all the commotion. Walking into the room some men were taking bets against who would win. A man next to him offered three to one against the Marshal. "I'll take that bet," Wapiti answered, handing the man a fifty-dollar bill.

"No problem," the three all said to Shawn. They unbuckled their holsters and laid them on the table. 'He might be able to outshoot us, but there was no way he could take all three of us in a fair fight,' they were thinking. "Let's teach this old man a lesson," their fearless leader said, laying his holster on the table.

"Well then," Shawn said, standing up and started walking around the table to get closer to them. He was standing in front of the one with the biggest mouth, their so-called leader. Reaching down with his left hand, he placed his pistol on the table. At the same time he

Chapter Ten

brought his right hand up catching their leader under his jaw with a mighty right hook, sending him flying over the top of the closest table and crashing to the floor. The other two came rushing at Shawn at the same time, dodging away from one of them, he reached over and grabbing the other by the back of his shirt with both hands. He threw him face first into a ten by ten-solid wood beam, which supported the weight of the motel rooms above. Turning back to face the other man, he felt a blow to the side of his head…"Why you no good little shit," Shawn said, blocking the mans next punch and retaliated with his own blow to the mans sternum, taking his breath away.

With his other hand he sent a crushing blow into his mouth, sending two teeth and blood flying across the room as he fell to the floor. The first one was already on his way back for more, breaking a chair over the back of Shawn, causing him to stumble down to one knee. Standing up as quickly as he could, he turned around just in time to catch a punch in the mouth, knocking his head back just a bit. Reaching out with his left hand Shawn grabbed the man by his shirt and pulled him to him. Then Shawn started hitting him as hard as he could with three massive blows to the Young man's face, knocking him out cold. Laying him on the floor he turned back in the direction of the other two, who were both kneeling on the floor and rubbing their aching heads.

"Well now," Shawn said, rubbing his fists. "Is that all you boys have?" About that time Cathey came out with his plate of food. Looking around the room she couldn't help but laugh. "I see you're working up a bigger appetite Marshal," she said, putting his food on the table.

Reaching over, he picked up his pistol, "Well now young lady you just might say that." Walking back around the table and sat down in front of his food. Looking down on the floor next to his feet he saw the big fearless leader lying there. Shawn picked up his cup of cold coffee and dumped it in the man's face. This caused him to begin to stir and wake up.

211

Shawn looked back over at Cathey, "Darlin' can I get a fresh cup of coffee? This one seems to have gotten cold on me." Then placing his foot on the Young man's shoulder and started shaking him back and forth. "Well hero," he said. "Why don't you and your buddies pick yourselves up? I'll keep your pistols till morning, so you don't try anything else stupid tonight. I think it would behoove you to go sleep it off." He continued, cutting his steak up and chuckling…"Playtime's over boys. I'm hungry."

"Yes sir, Marshal," the other two were saying as they picked up their leader. "No problem Sir, we'll just leave our guns right were they are, we can get them in the morning." With their leader between them the three turned and slowly walked out the door.

Pouring him another cup of coffee, Cathey leaned over with her other hand and took a napkin and started wiping some of the blood from the corner of his mouth. "

"You're bleeding, Marshal," she said. "Here let me help you a little bit."

"OOHH, that's all right young lady, it don't hurt none, and besides it adds a little flavor to the food," Shawn said.

Wapiti reached for the money that was in the man's hand and counted out his one hundred and fifty. "It looks like the ROOSTER is going to crow in the Hen House tonight."

"What the hell you talkin' about, boy? I mean Deputy." The man said, taking the rest of his money back. "What ROOSTER? What Hen House?

"THAT ROOSTER," Wapiti said pointing at the Marshal. "And THIS hen house," he said pointing at the floor. It sure had been fun watching the Marshal fight. The look on his face during the whole fight; well he looked as though he was having the time of his life. "Well Marshal," Wapiti said, leaning up against the wall with his arms crossed, "I thought you might need a hand, so I came to help. But I see you can still handle yourself."

Shawn reared back in his chair and threw his chest out. Looking around at the crowd of people. "Hell there was only three of them… I

Chapter Ten

don't like to brag…but just in case any more of you think I'm too old, you just let me finish my meal and I'll be right with you."

Wapiti turned and started walking back over to Cork. He couldn't help it, he felt like he needed to warn him. "You better watch out Cork, cause that old Fart's feeling real cocky right now."

"You're not saying what I think you're saying, are you?" Cork asked.

"Well, lets just say, I WONT be responsible for anything that happens the rest of the night," Wapiti said still smiling.

"How much is he gunna tear my place up?" Cork asked with a worried look on his face.

"I don't think he'll pick any fights mind ya, but he's definitely going to let them know who the boss is, trust me. WE'RE all going to hear those stories about six and seven men at a time, and I mean all of us." Wapiti said waving his arm around the room. "But I wouldn't put it past him to punch someone if they say the wrong thing at the wrong time." Looking back at Cork and Charlie, "Just don't let him start drinking whiskey too early…Well, I'm going to make my rounds and see just how everyone's doing."

Still chuckling, he turned and walked back into the playing area. Walking around the area he could still see that every one was still glancing over at that double barrel ten-gauge shotgun at his side. 'Lord Help the poor man that ever comes up against that buck Indian and that gun. Cause there sure as hell won't be anything left of them.'

While Wapiti walked around the tables he couldn't help but think about Cathey. He wondered if she would still be at work when he finally got to go to dinner. She had brought him his morning coffee, so he doubted she would still be at work. He'd have to wait till morning to see her again, 'AWW heck,' she wouldn't wanna to be with an Indian anyway. A young lady that beautiful, definitely had a boyfriend, but he couldn't help it, he couldn't get her out of his head. He wasn't quite sure how long he had been day dreaming when the Marshal walked up. Putting his hand on his shoulder, actually startling him a little.

"You all right son?" Shawn said, "thought you were gunna jump outta your skin. What are you thinking about?"

213

"OOHH, nothing Marshal, just wondering about something…is all…it's not important," Wapiti answered.

"Well Wapiti, that 'not-so-important thought,' you're thinking of is waiting for you with your dinner," Shawn said, slapping him on the back. "So you better get going."

"W-W-WHO you talk'en about Marshal?" Wapiti asked stuttering a little.

"Cathey, that's who I'm talking about, so get in there and eat," Shawn said, with a big smile on his face.

"Yes sir Marshal, yes sir," Wapiti said with even a bigger smile. He only hoped that it didn't look like he was running to get into the restaurant. He sure did want to see Cathey, but what will all these white men have to say about it? Well whatever was going to happen, was going to start soon he thought sitting down at one of the tables. He couldn't remember being this nervous, and then all of a sudden he could feel a hand lay over his shoulder. Cathey leaned down real close to him and poured his coffee. 'Oh please,' he was thinking to himself, 'please don't kiss me on the check, these white eyes will go crazy.'

"Good evening, Wapiti," Cathey said with a big smile on her face, and then she stood back up without giving him a kiss. He couldn't help it when she looked at him, all of a sudden he couldn't think of anything to say his heart felt like it had stopped beating. That smile, boy…she had a smile that was very unique, he hadn't seen nothing like it before. Those dark brown eyes and her hair wasn't as black as his, but it was still a beautiful dark brown just about shoulder length. She may have only been about five feet two inches tall, and couldn't weigh much more than a hundred pounds. Wapiti could feel himself getting hotter, in fact he could feel his hands starting to sweat, reaching up and grabbing his shirt he pulled it away from his body, "Boy it sure is hot in here tonight."

Cathey still smiling, "It could still get even hotter before the night is over."

Wapiti could feel his face getting hotter, he knew he was blushing something terrible. It hadn't been all that long since Cathey had left but it seemed like forever to him. Finally she returned with a spread of

Chapter Ten

food fit for a great chief. Sitting everything on the table she bent over and gave him a kiss on the cheek.

Looking up at her real quick…"What are you trying to do, get me scalped?" He said to her in a low voice.

"What are you worried about, most of the people are afraid of you anyhow," Cathey said, smiling. "They've all seen and heard about your accomplishments the last few days, and most of them were here earlier when you backed that man down, not only down, but out. His only chance was to run for his life," She still had a big smile on her beautiful face. She started dishing up both plates, looking down at him. "It is ok if I join you for dinner, isn't it?" Cathey asked.

"Yeah, of course it is," Wapiti answered, looking around the room. "You sure everything is going to be all right?" he asked her one more time.

Laughing just a little bit, she finished and sat down. Wapiti was still looking at everyone in the place, wondering just how many of those smiles were real and which ones were just a cover up.

"Believe it or not Wapiti," Cathey said. "Most of these people have a lot of respect for you, most because of the way you've handled your-self in various situations that you've been in…I'm telling ya, ya have nothing to worry about."

Slowly cutting off a piece of roast he took himself a bite, boy this was the most tender, moistest roast. It almost melted in his mouth and the flavor, he didn't ever remember having anything like it before.

"Well," Cathey asked looking at him. "Is everything alright? What I mean is …do you like it?"

"Yes Cathey I do," Wapiti answered. "I've never tasted anything like it, it not only tastes good but it practically melts in your mouth."

The two sat and talked for almost an hour, but to Wapiti it didn't seem that long at all. Fact was he was enjoying being with her so much. It was like there was no one else in the room with them. All of a sudden he heard a bottle break and a man cursing because he had just put everything he had on one bet, thinking he couldn't be beat or he thought he couldn't. When he lost he wanted everybody to hear about it. Which brought Wapiti back down to earth and all of a sudden he could hear everyone again.

215

He slowly looked around the room, seems like most of the people weren't even paying attention to them anymore. He looked back at Cathey, "I sure do want to thank you for dinner, and it was really good. Most of all, I enjoyed the dinner company. That was even better... What would your Dad say if he found out? Which if he don't already know about me, sure won't be very long before he hears about me."

"AWWW Wapiti...don't worry about it, my family don't care what color a man's skin is. They only care if he's a good man or not, and you are...trust me...My dad will joke with you...but as long as I'm happy, he won't say a word. And neither will anybody else in my family...if they did, Grandpa would be real mad at them, considering our Grandma has a lot of Indian in her."

"I hope you're right Cathey...because I sure would like to get to know you better..." Wapiti said. "But right now I really should get back in there. I can hear the Marshal already starting to tell up some of his exploits as he calls them. Actually some of them are pretty good; if you get the time you should come in and listen to some of them. He admits he stretches them out just a little bit, but like he said, you don't have to believe him, however he is still here and all the outlaws he's chased over the years, well... they're not."

Standing up next to him, Cathey again leaned over and gave him a kiss on the cheek. "Let me get this cleaned up, and I'll come in and say goodnight before I leave. I have to get up early; I have a very important patron that I have to make sure he gets his morning coffee."

"Thanks," Wapiti answered. "I mean for everything...it was good and most of all I got to see YOU again." At that moment she gave him a big smile. Wapiti tipped his head and walked back into the bar area, he couldn't help but have a real big grin on his face, and everyone was still getting out of his way. He glanced outside; he could tell the sun was going down, because it was starting to get dark out there. He knew that tomorrow might be the last chance he'd get to see Cathey for a while because he and the Marshal would be pulling out first light Monday morning. He wasn't sure if they would come back this way or not, he sure hoped they would. Glancing around the tables he figured they were down to around twenty players, before

Chapter Ten

he knew it he was standing in front of Marshal and Corky, who both were smiling at him.

"Well son," Shawn called out. "Did you enjoy your dinner...? I know I sure would have, especially with a beautiful young lady like Miss Larkin there. A special dinner with all the works, why we could smell it clean in here," Shawn said. "I was hoping maybe to get me some leftovers if there were any."

"Actually Marshal there is some left, I was talking more than eating," Wapiti said, starting to smile. "She sure is prettier to look at than you are."

"Well, I'd have to agree with you on that Wapiti," Shawn said, patting him on the back. "I definitely have to agree with you on that. Charlie...Why don't you bring a bottle over here with two glasses?"

"None for me Marshal," Wapiti said. "I don't like whiskey."

"Well that's just fine son, cause this is for me and Cork here," Shawn said. "Since you're back, and I'm sure there isn't going to be much more trouble tonight. What trouble might come up," pointing around the room he continues, "Everyone in here KNOWS you can handle it... so if you don't mind, I'm going to unwind a little."

"Marshal, I couldn't stop you if I wanted to...you know that," Wapiti said turning and looking at the tables. They still had three full tables with five players and one with three players at it left

Sam came walking up to the bar, placing both hands on it he ordered two beers. Then turning to Wapiti, "Good evening, Deputy," Sam said, holding out his hand. "I still feel like I owe you an apology. Fact we both do, but Jack is still in the game as you can see..." He turned back and picked up both beers handing one to Wapiti. He continued, "We were just funning with you the other morning. But you could say we got our just rewards," rubbing the right side of his face. It was still swollen and bruised from top to bottom from Wapiti's foot, "I have to tell you, this hurts..." Sam said. He tried to smile but he couldn't, it hurt too much.

"That's alright," Wapiti said taking a drink off the beer. "I knew someone had to try me, I just wasn't sure who, how, or when. I was just glad to get it over with early."

217

"And real fast too, you might say," Sam said trying to smile again. "You know Lavern pissed his pants when you stuck that shotgun in his face? Said those were the two biggest barrels he had ever seen."

At that remark everyone at the bar started laughing. "I bet he did," Shawn said, "I'll just bet he did. That IS the purpose behind that gun; it will get everyone's attention… real quick!"

"It does that, Marshal," Sam said. "Well anyway, you still have work to do, but Jack will come and talk to you himself when he gets through playing, I'm sure."

"That's alright," Wapiti said as they shaked hands one more time, then Sam turned and walked away.

"Well Wapiti, you've only been a Deputy for less than a week and you're already making a name for yourself," Shawn said, taking a shot of whiskey. "You just keep up the good work."

The night seemed to pass by quickly, why before Wapiti even realized it the Marshal was calling for everyone to turn their chips in at the bar. He was really glad, he had been up all day and all night and he just wanted to get upstairs and get some sleep. He had to be up early to make sure that the games got underway by nine o' clock. With that thought he looked over at the Marshal and Cork, "I think you two can finish up here, I'm going to bed, Charley, could I have a small pitcher of beer and one glass please?"

"Sure thing Wapiti," Charley answered. Filling a pitcher and handing it and a glass to him.

"Thanks," Wapiti said, taking them and headed up the stairs to his room.

Most everyone was still stepping aside as Wapiti walked up the stairs, but there were one or two who accidentally on purpose didn't. They still didn't like the idea of an Indian lawman. Not only could he handle himself hand to hand, but he did it in a respectful way, he could even take a joke too. Fact there had been many Indian jokes over the last couple of days, he even laughed at a couple. None of them would admit it, but they were gaining respect for him as a man, and even more importantly, as a lawman.

Chapter Ten

"That's going to be a good lawman," Shawn said. "That's if he gets a chance and nobody back shoots him."

"Someone already tried that this morning Marshal...remember!" Cork said.

"Yeah, I remember," Shawn answered. "Just glad I was there to watch his back...I might not be next time."

After everyone had turned in their chips and they had all been put away, Shawn turned to Cork, "Well young fella, I'm not as young as I used to be. I can't party all night anymore, so I'll say goodnight to ya and see ya in the morning."

"Alright Marshal," Cork answered. "You know we're down to sixteen players?"

"Good," Shawn said, looking back, standing at the bottom of the stairs, "That means we can start with just four tables...Well goodnight folks." Then he turned and headed up the stairs to bed.

CHAPTER ELEVEN

Gary, Butch, and Sundance had been playing cards for almost an hour, still using chips as money. "Gary, why the hell won't you play poker with real money? Why do you always insist on chips?" Sundance asked.

"Cause, I don't throw my money away like that. Someday I hope to have my own spread." Gary answered, raising two red chips.

Butch couldn't help but chuckle, "Let me get this straight, you don't gamble with real money, but you want to put your money into a ranch...? Hell, that's one of the biggest gambles I've ever seen. Not to mention all the headaches and heartaches and all the work involved."

"I've seen too many people lose everything they had trying to be a dirt farmer or rancher, either one," Butch said.

They could see that what they were saying was starting to get to Gary, but they knew that he could take a joke. Just then Larry, Luis and Curry came in the saloon; Larry was hollering for a round of beer, sitting down at the table.

"Well, all together we got 14 suckers, who wanna take a chance to ride my Roan." Larry said, "Oh, I'm sorry Butch, I forgot you...that makes fifteen suckers."

"I'll admit Butch can be a sucker now and then," Sundance said. "But you really think no one can ride that horse?"

"I noticed you backed out of your chance, Sundance," Butch said.

"Well just remember one thing," Larry said. "Butch, when you get bucked off, make sure you reach for the ground."

Chapter Eleven

"What the hell are you talking about Larry?" Butch asked.

"Well," Gary explained. "You go where you reach..." Gary looked around the table.

"Yeah," Randy cut in standing behind Butch. "If you reach for the sky...that's where ya go, but you still end up on the ground, so when ya get bucked off, reach for the ground...It's closer...and don't hurt as bad."

Everyone started laughing, "Butch, Sundance, I'd like you to meet Toad and Goof," Randy said.

"Toad and Goof? What the hell kinda names are those?" Butch asked, smiling. Looking over at Sundance, who was making a gesture about the size of their noses? The two were checking them out. Toad and Goof were tall lanky men, both well over six feet tall.

The taller of the two started talking, "NOOO...I'm Scott and this is my little brother Randy. We've just had these nicknames all our lives. I'm Toad and he's Goof."

"I can see why they call him Goof," Sundance said, starting to chuckle. "You both are goofy looking." They all stuck out their hands and started shaking hands. "It's nice to meet you gentlemen," Butch said. Sitting back in his chair and gave a quick glance around the room.

Goof leaned over and asked in a low voice, "You're really not who Randy says you are, are ya?"

"I don't know," Sundance said, while still smiling and joking about the size of their noses. "Hell, those are some of the biggest and longest noses I've ever seen."

"Aren't they though?" Larry said. "But you should see their brother Hosey...now he's got the nose."

"BIGGER THAN THAT?" Butch said, pointing. "No way!"

"Yes way," said Gary, "Hosey's nose is at least an inch longer, hell maybe even two."

Curry leans over to Butch and Sundance, "You don't know if it's true, what they say about men with big noses...you know their..."

At first they both looked at him with a crazy look, then all of a sudden they knew what he was referring to. "Hell if I know," Butch said shouting, "And I really don't want to know either."

221

"Alright, alright," Toad finally said. "Enough shit about our noses. Are you guys really who Randy here said you are?"

"I don't know who he thinks we are or who we really are. So who did he tell ya we were?" Sundance said discarding three cards.

"Well," Toad said looking all three straight in the eyes, "He tells me you're someone interested in making a little extra money. In a way I've thought about myself a time or two." Starting to smile, "I've just never had the cohunes to try it."

"Well, Randy said he knew some good men to help," Sundance said looking at Butch.

"Well where's this brother Hosey?" Butch asked. Starting to chuckle again. "You say his nose is bigger than yours? I just can't believe that's possible."

"Oh, it's possible," Toad said smiling. "So just how are you boys leaving here when you go?"

"Well," said Butch. "Thought we might go back out through Idaho. Why?"

"Well, if you don't mind, after the jobs done we'd just as soon take our gold up to Seattle to sell," Toad said. "That way people will think just maybe, we hit it big in Alaska and not think twice about us being a part of this at all."

"Hell no, we don't care what way you go," Sundance answered. "We just want someone we can trust to help out is all."

"Trust me, Butch," Gary spoke up. "You can trust these men, we all grew up together."

"Alright, we'll let ya in, but where's your other brother at?" Butch asked.

"We'll have to go over to the Chinese side of town to get him," Toad said.

"Why, he like those China dolls does he?" Sundance asked smiling.

"NOOO," Randy jumped in. "He likes their opium."

"Now just wait one minute there," Butch yelled. "I don't want no strung out opium bum around. Hell, when they're smoking that shit they don't even know where they are."

Chapter Eleven

"Don't worry," Goof said. "I'll go find him early tomorrow morning before he has a chance to start. He'll want in on this, and besides... he's not afraid to use a gun if we need him to."

"Well, let's get one thing straight," Sundance said. "We haven't ever killed ANYONE in ANY of our jobs yet, and we don't need to start now."

"Well, don't look at me and Goof," Toad added. "We don't usually carry a gun. But I am bringing my rifle and pistol along on this trip."

"We're going into that backcountry," Goof said. "You can damn sure bet I'm bringing my gun's too..." Looking around the table, "Don't get me wrong, I don't want to shoot anyone, but if they start, I'm shootin back, and I usually don't miss what I'm shooting at either."

About that time someone in the saloon hollered out, "HEEEEEYYY...when are you going to draw the names?" "YEAH!" Some one else hollered. "I want to see if I get a chance at all that money." Slowly the crowd grew louder and louder.

"Alright, alright," shouted Larry. Picking up the jar full of names and a bottle of whiskey he walked toward the bar. "Settle down; settle down...we'll draw in just a minute. Luis, will you bring those bags of gold and money over here please?"

"Sure hombre," Luis answered. "But I'm going to need some help; all these bags of gold are heavy."

"AWWW, quit your complaining," Curry said smiling. "I'll help ya." The two picked up all the bags of gold and cash, and followed Larry through the crowd of people in the saloon.

Jumping up on the top of the bar Larry started hollering over the top of everyone, "Now listen up. Everyone's name goes into the hat; those that get drawn will get their chance. Their entry money stays here...those who did not get drawn; you bring me that piece of paper you received at signup. You bring that up and I'll give you your money back...No paper...No money...Anyone in here who knows me, knows I could use the extra money. You're bucking order will be

223

where your name is drawn." Holding his hands up in the air…"Now my friend over there, Mr. Brigham Young," he said pointing at Butch, "He gets in automatically as first rider."

"Now just wait a minute," one man yells out. "Why does he get a guaranteed ride?" "Yeah!" Others started shouting. "What makes him so special?"

Holding his hands back up in the air and shaking his head, "NOW, NOW…he's the one putting up the five thousand dollars prize money. Since he's really putting up the most money, then it's only right he should get first flight…CLEAR…Now…Sharon, darlin' how about you get up here and draw the names." Looking back over at the crowd as Sharon climbed up on the bar. "Now if you're lucky enough and ride my horse, well hell…you just might get lucky enough to ride her too…least you'll be able to afford this young lady… that don't mean she'd let ya. But you could afford her price."

"Not likely," Sharon answered smiling. "Cause I'm not cheap." Starting to shake her moneymaker back and forth.

The crowd started laughing and cheering, cause they all wished they had the money to afford her. Just once, just one night with her would no doubt send you to heaven for a week.

Sharon drew the names; you could tell right off who the person was. In some cases, just a single man would shout out, but sometime there would be a small group of people, the ones who pooled their money together on one rider. Sharon would make a comment on each person drawn; "Maybe!" "I'd need more money!" "No way in hell!" Just to name a few.

Larry was just hoping that C.R.'s name would not be drawn. If anyone had a chance it would be him. Larry kept counting six, seven and eight, only two more; it came down to the last pull. Larry was feeling good, there were five names left in the hat, everything was going his way he thought. Then Sharon pulled the last name out, C.R.." she said… Larry dropped to the floor. "SHIT" He hollered. C.R's name didn't only get drawn, but he was the last rider. That meant the Roan would be tiring out.

224

Chapter Eleven

Everybody turned to congratulate the lucky riders and even buying them drinks for good luck. Then everyone returned to the tables and started gambling.

"DAMMIT Gary," Larry said, sitting down, "Wouldn't ya know that the best rider maybe in the country... I mean hell did you get a look at all those belt buckle's." Looking at everyone at the table at the same time, "He gets the last ride."

"So you think this C.R. guy has a chance at covering him for eight seconds?" Butch asked. Sharon sat a couple pitchers of beer and bottles of whiskey on the table. She turned over to Randy and sit down on his leg, facing outward in case she had to move fast. Sundance couldn't help but look at her, that long, thick brown hair, her big brown eyes, even just her demeanor. She was a lady who knew what she did and did not want, and what she would and would not do with anyone. She was Beautiful and Cocky, Sundance thought to himself, she was definitely beautiful and cocky and wouldn't take any shit off any man, woman, or child. He started to smile just a little bit still looking at her.

The normal saloon Betties would cost you about twenty to thirty dollars for just a couple hours, even more for all night. He had heard that her price's started in the high hundreds of dollars just four one hour of her pleasurable time. He'd be willing to pay that, Hell; he'd be willing to pay a thousand if that's what it took. He didn't realize he'd been staring right at her, or for how long he had been staring, but he noticed that Randy was looking straight at him over the top of his beer. He couldn't quite tell just what kind of look it was, good or bad...Thinking he was still just talking to himself, Sundance said out loud, "So little darlin' why don't you leave that boy there alone and come over here to a real man?" Then sitting his glass back on the table he looked at Randy, his eyes went from smiling blue, to hell fire red in less than one second, his face stern and a serious look. Putting both hands on Sharon's hips Randy started to pick her up, "Mr., you have about one second to shut your mouth...or I will shut it for you... PERMANETLY!"

Sundance looked around the table with an 'OH SHIT' look on his face. He had seen Randy literally destroy that man last night and

225

he was twice my size. He hadn't met the infamous Dr. Bones yet. But he heard that man from last night was still in his office with crushed cheekbones from just one blow from Randy's right hand. He could see Sharon was trying to calm him down, but still looking into those fire burning red eyes sent a cold chill up Sundance's spine, making him shiver just a little. Sundance couldn't hear anything going on, anywhere in the saloon, the only thing he had on his mind was how to get the hell away from Randy, and FAST!

Slowly Sundance started to stand up, "Well boys," he said. "I think I'm going to go up to the bar and see how the betting is going." Standing full up he nodded his hat to Sharon and Randy, "See ya later Ma-am." Then quickly he turned around and walked away from the table, it would have been shorter to walk by Randy, but Sundance didn't care, he wasn't getting any closer to that man than he had to.

"Why the hell do you always have to take things the wrong way, Randy?" Gary said sternly.

"A man, I'll show him a man," Randy said, watching Sundance walk away through the crowd of people.

"Now sweetie," Sharon said smiling, kissing him on the cheek. "You know it just came out wrong, he was just funn'en, he didn't mean anything."

"NOBODY say's I'm not a man," Randy said, looking around the table then back in the direction of Sundance. "He's damn lucky he walked away."

"Well hell," Larry said reaching for a pitcher of beer. "Let's forget it and get back to this high dollar poker game. So Butch, how'd you come up with your outlaw name?"

"My name's Robert Leroy, but when I was a kid growing up in Circleville, they started calling me Butch. But an outlaw needs two name's...I was starting to tell Gary about my first girlfriend."

"Right, your cousin," Gary said chuckling.

"Second cousin," Butch said. "Anyway, she is about five two, weighed about one fifteen pounds, long blonde hair, and big blue eyes. I'm here to tell you that young lady taught me a whole lot...and I was a gooood student."

Chapter Eleven

"That still didn't answer my question," Larry said. "How'd you get your name?"

"Her name is Cassidy. She's married now, but we still meet out behind the church when I go home. Fullmer's store their winter hay just a crossed the street" Butch said, with a big smile on his face.

"So just how many children does she have? And how many of them are yours?" Gary asked filling up his beer.

"Three, and to answer your other question...I don't know," Butch said shuffling the cards. "I've never ask her."

"Why didn't ya stick around and marry her?" Larry asked.

"Cause, when they're sixteen the church elders get first chose," Butch answered.

"WHAT?" everyone shouted. "You're joking right?" Gary asked.

"Nope, and like you Sharon, I don't think she gets it enough either. Her husband has six wives," Butch said smiling. "That's one of the reasons why I want to go back through Circleville. She always has a whole lot of frustration built up, if you get my meaning...So out of my first love I chose her name, Cassidy...Hence, Butch Cassidy."

"So you saying these chips are worth real money tonight?" Butch asked smiling.

"Hell No," Larry yelled. "Let's just get Randy's mind on something else, besides Sundance."

Sundance slowly fought his way through the crowd and up to the bar. Ordering a beer and slowly looking the crowd over, and listening to what most everyone was talking about. Which most of the talk was about that Roan. There was no way that horse could best ten men, they all were figuring six to eight at the most. IF he was lucky, he'd best eight men.

Sundance had only been standing there for about five minutes when the town Sheriff came walking up to him. He was maybe in his mid forties, Sundance thought to himself, looking him over. He was well over six-foot, might have been a bigger and stronger man in his younger years, but now all that muscle had settled in around his fat belly.

"Don't I know you?" The Sheriff asked, sticking his hand out. "Sheriff Ray Hendricksen."

"No sir, I don't believe so Sheriff, Harry Jones, it's a pleasure to meet you," Sundance said, shaking his hand.

"You sure?" the Sheriff asked. "I've been a law man most all my life."

Looking the Sheriff over, Sundance started smiling. "Oh hell, I've been told I look like one of those famous outlaws…What the hell is his name again?"

"I don't know," the Sheriff answered, with a semi-serious look on his face. "Why don't you tell me which one?"

"It's one of those guys with kid in his name…you know…like Billy the Kid, that ain't it though." Sundance said, taking a drink off his beer. "OH YA, Sundance, that's who it is, The Sundance kid…Sure the hell wish I was him. Hell, I'd turn myself in for the reward money; it sure would beat digging in the cold ground."

"Well, I guess you're probably right," the Sheriff answered. "I have been wrong once or twice in my life."

Sundance started chuckling, "Well Sheriff, I've been out of town for too long…so if you will excuse me, I think I will grab me a bottle and one of these young ladies and go upstairs and have a private party, if you get my drift."

"Yes sir I do," The Sheriff answered. "Being Sheriff around here, you might say I get a lot of those private parties free."

"Ya lucky old fart," Sundance said. "How the hell you pull that off…threaten to throw them in jail if they don't give it up, or what?"

"Something like that," The Sheriff answered. "Some of these miners don't have much, but then, some of them have nice looking wives and daughters, once you wash them up."

Sundance picked up a bottle of whiskey, "Well Sheriff, you have yourself a good night." Then he turned and walked into the crowd of people, again taking the long way around the Saloon and back to the table. Hoping that fat ass Sheriff had bought his story. If he didn't, then maybe he would loose sight of him in the crowd. Slowly he walked up behind Butch, acting like he wasn't paying him any attention, speaking in a low voice, "Mr. Young, that fat old Sheriff over there might have made me, so I'm grabbing me a little Betty and head'en to my room, I'll see ya in the morning." Then he turned, grabbed a young lady by the arm, "Come on sweetheart, let's go have ourselves a private party."

"Wait just one minute Mr.," she answered pulling her arm back. "You mind telling me why I should go with you? Why not one of the other girls?"

"Well darl'en," Sundance said. "I've walked all around this Saloon twice, and quite frankly, next to Sharon there, you're the next prettiest lady in here."

"Well, since you put it that way Mr. Jones," winking at him. She said, taking him by the hand and leading him towards the stairs, "I'm going to treat you extra special."

Sundance had not even been gone for two minutes and the Sheriff came pushing his way through the crowd to get to the table. Walking up to the table, a waitress walked by with a tray of beer, reaching up he grabbed one and sat down at the table.

"Evening gentlemen," he said looking straight at Butch. "I'm Sheriff Ray Hendricksen...Ya know Young man, I've been a lawman for quite some time now. I just met your friend Mr. Jones there," he said pointing up the stairs. "I know all these hombres here," he said pointing at the Doss's and the Larkin brothers. "Now for the most part they're pretty good people, but I think the right person just might lead them astray."

"What the hell you getting at Sheriff?" Butch asked in a stern voice.

"Well now, Mr. Young ...or should I say...Mr. Parker or Butch Cassidy," the Sheriff spouts back. "Now I wasn't born yesterday and I've seen you boys around the last couple of days. Now I got to do'en some thinking."

"THAT MUST HAVE HURT LIKE HELL?" Gary shouted, and laughing at the Sheriff. "I just bet that's something you haven't done in quite a while Sheriff."

"Oh shut up, you little smart ass," The Sheriff replied as the entire table busted up into laughter.

"Well now there Sheriff," Butch said, trying to stop laughing. Cause just looking at him he could bet Gary was right. "Well then Sir, just what is it you're getting at?"

"Weelll," the Sheriff leaned over and started talking in a low voice. "I figure you boys are planning something…and if it's what I think it is, you boys think you are going to make yourselves some extra money." Looking around the room to make sure no one else was listening in, the Sheriff continued. "Like I said, I don't know what, or where, or even how…but say for…MMMM…two…three thousand dollars I'll slow the posse up for a couple hours so as you boys can get a little further away."

"Now just why in the hell would I except an offer like that for?" Butch said smiling. "Just what makes you think we're up here to do anything? Can't we just have some fun and party with ouir new friends here?" Pointing around the table. "Besides you are right we are planning to make a little money…" starting to chuckle a little. "Just who do you think is putting up the money for this bucking competition?"

"Oh come on," the Sheriff said leaning back in his chair. "I know this log pulling and bucking competition are to cover up the real job…Now like I said, I don't know when, where, or how…but I know you boys have a plan. You either cut me in for three thousand dollars or I'll make damn sure that the next shipment on the train has one hundred guns on board before she pulls out. Do I make myself clear?"

"Well, how about I just yard dart your ass up and make you spend a couple nights over at Doc's place?" Randy said in an eager voice. "That way we won't have to worry about your fat ass at all."

"Now you just wait there one minute, Mr. Larkin. You come up out of that chair and I'm pulling my gun," the Sheriff said, placing his hand on the but of his pistol.

"Now just settle down there Sheriff and don't get your tit in a ringer," Butch said…"So just how much time is this three thousand going to buy us if and when we do a job? That is, if there even is a job in the planning."

Chapter Eleven

"Weelll, depending on just how far down river you hit the train, I could slow things up here say, three hours most. Anything too much longer than that and they might start to get suspicious. If you get my understanding?" the Sheriff said.

"Well, how the hell do you know what way we're going?" Curry asked.

"WELL I kinda figure you've been talking with these young men here for the layout of the land since you boys come from back east. Well if it was me I'd go back across Idaho especially since you're going to be part way down the Powder River canyon already," said the sheriff.

"Well hell," Luis said. "You guys didn't need to talk to us at all. You only had to go to the local law dog for help." chuckling, he looked around the table and then back to Butch and the Sheriff.

"So what's it going to be, Young man?" The Sheriff asked.

"Okay, say we agree to pay you," Butch said looking straight into the Sheriff's eyes. "I'll tell you right now Sheriff, I've never killed any-one yet…But you double cross us and you'll be my first. DO I make myself clear?"

"Crystal," the Sheriff answered. "So why don't you just give me my money now so that way you don't have to worry about it later?"

Butch reached into his coat pocket and pulled out a wad of money. He slowly counted out two thousand dollars. Reaching over to the Sheriff, he stuffed the money in his shirt pocket. "I'll give you the other thousand after the bucking competition. Now get the hell out of here." Slowly looking around the table at everyone else then back to the Sheriff, "Now like I said, you get out of here and I don't want to see you again CLEAR?"

"Yes sir," the Sheriff said, getting up and patted his pocket. Then headed back towards the bar.

"Well guys," Butch said stretching out his arms. "I'm getting kinda tired, so if you gentlemen and ladies will excuse me I think I'm going to call it a night."

"Yeah me too," some of the others started saying.

231

Randy, still sitting down in his chair looked over at everyone, then looked straight at Butch and Curry, then asked, "Either one of you boys know anything about dynamite?"

"Yeah," Butch answered. "Why?"

"I don't trust that Sheriff as far as I could throw his fat ass. So why don't you and me go make you a back door?" Randy said smiling.

"Back door? What the hell is a back door?" Curry asked, looking back and forth between Randy and Gary.

"Back door," Gary said chuckling. "Randy always has a back door...How the hell do you think we've managed to stay out of jail? It damned sure hasn't always been by luck."

"Well Butch," Randy said. "Let's go out through the back door, that way hopefully no one will see us. You guys all cover for us and we'll see ya in the morning," Randy said

The two turned and slowly worked their way out the back door. "This way," Randy said, pointing down the alley between the two buildings. "The mining supply store is just right over here." Quickly they made their way through the shadows and up the side of the buildings. Then turning, they walked between the two buildings. Pointing at the one next to them Randy whispered, "This here is the mining supply store," they walked up to the side door. Randy looked around. Using his elbow, he broke out one of the small pane of glass, then reaching inside he opened the door. Still speaking in a low voice, "Come on, Butch." The two walked inside. "They keep everything back here." Heading for the back room, "Here, back here," Randy bent over and picked up three large cases of nitro and handed it to Butch. Then picking up two large rolls of fuse and three more cases of nitro for himself. They hurried out of the building, back into the alley and the darkness. "This way," Randy said. Heading down the alley towards the smokehouse where his horses were tied up.

"Damn this stuff is heavy," Butch complained.

"Oh you've been living the easy life too long," Randy said. "This isn't all that heavy. Hell, my harness sets weigh a hell of a lot more than this does. Now, when we get to the end of these buildings, we have at

Chapter Eleven

least a hundred yards of open ground we have to cover to make the smokehouse. So make sure you can cover it fast, and make damn sure you don't fall, we don't need to draw anyone's attention."

When they got to the last building, Randy stopped and looked up and down the street. There were some people still up and moving around, however most of them were heading out of town. Looking back at Butch Randy said, "Alright, let's go. Try to stay over here in the shadows of these trees." Quickly the two covered the ground to the smokehouse. Getting inside they sat everything down; Randy picked up one of his backpacks for the horses. "We're going to have to ride bareback, they don't make saddles big enough for these big boy's," Randy said. Then grabbing the pack, he threw it on top of one of the two big gildings, and then quickly he tightened the straps down. Then the two loaded up the horse, "Here," Randy handed Butch a lead rope. "You take this one here. Trust me; you don't even want to try this stallion. If you're even just a little bit afraid of him he'll sense it and send you to hell in a quick hurry."

Before Butch knew it Randy was already aboard with the lead rope in his hand and ready to leave. Butch was sizing the big Clydesdale up and down. Looking over at Randy he was wondering how the hell Randy got on that big thing. Leading his horse over to one of the stalls Butch climbed up and jumped over onto the back of the big horse. The two headed out. Following the river edge by the log yard, they tried to stay as close to the timber and the shadows as they could, so not to be seen. In no time at all they were on the road that leads out of town and down a crossed Sumpter valley. The road followed the timber line most of the way.

"So why the hell do you want to go out thought Idaho and across that desert?" Randy asked.

"It'll take me back by my families' ranch in Utah. I haven't seen them in quite a while. Besides Larry and Gary told us how to get out over Dooley Mountain and through Blacks Canyon."

"Shoot, it would be just as fast, even faster if you went over through Whitney, then over to Unity. That way you can get to Idaho a lot faster."

233

"Well, if that's the best way out, then why do we need to blow the canyon?" Butch asked.

"Well," Randy answered. "We're only going to make it look like a back door, but it's going to be a fake back door."

"What the hell do you mean? A fake back door?" Butch asked, with a funny look on his face as the two rode at a good steady pace down the road.

"They're going to think you guys went this way. Why the hell else would you have blown the canyon except in the hope of slowing them down?" Randy answered.

"Well, if we're not coming this way, then how are we going to blow it up?" Butch asked.

"That's where I come back into play," Randy said. "When you all get loaded up and ready to leave, fire your pistol in the air three times. That will be my signal to head out of town and blow the backdoor. Trust me they will all hear the blast and think you came this way. But you don't tell anyone about your change in direction. That will be between just you and me."

"How the hell do we get to Whitney and out to Unity?" Butch asked.

"You know that main road that came off this road a ways back?" Randy pointed over his shoulder.

"Yeah, I remember seeing a road, but I didn't pay it much attention" Butch said.

"You take that road for about twenty miles. You'll come to Whitney valley. Just make sure you stay in the timber by riding around the valley going west. When you come to the other end of the valley you'll run into the river. Follow it till you come out on the other side of the mountains, you'll see the lights of a small town off in the distance. At that point if you change your mind and decide to go out through Portland, take the main road over the Blues and down into John Day and out to the Columbia. If you're still set on going out across that desert you can, just remember one thing, you try sell'en that gold this side of Denver and they're going to know where it came from."

234

Chapter Eleven

"So how long would it take to go out through Portland?" Butch asked.

"Maybe, four days to Portland. It's about three hundred miles." Randy answered. "You should be only a few hours behind Curry and the Doss brothers. That way if they should get caught you could work your way around town easier because they'll think they already have everyone."

"That's not a bad idea Randy, fact is if they do get caught, we just might be able to help them out." Butch answered.

'You might just be able to. If you do go that way, when you come out over by Unity you can turn and take the road over to Austin Junction which will put you about twenty miles closer to John Day." Starting to chuckle a little. "Ya know how they always say women get prettier at closing time?"

"Yeah, sure do," Butch said. "It's because you're usually drunk by then."

"Well," Randy said. "Those fat Indian squaws that they have in Austin…lets just say I couldn't drink enough, I'd pass out first. But there are some real nice young ladies in Unity if you're in need of some soft comfortable sleeping partners and rest."

"Thanks for the advice," Butch said. "But what about the posse's?"

"Hell, that fat dumb ass Sheriff will think you did head out over Dooley and down through Blacks Canyon on your way to Ontario. He'll be two days before he realizes you didn't go that way at all. By then you guys should very easily be to Arlington and on a barge for Portland."

Butch couldn't help it till now but noticed how peaceful and beautiful the night was. The moon was almost full, and the stars filled the skies. There wasn't a cloud anywhere to be seen. The road and the train tracks ran almost side by side going around the edge of the valley. That was because the gold drudges were mining the entire valley up from one side to the other, and it was a mile wide if not wider, and a good fifteen plus miles long. They could see one of the dredges all lit up and operating out in the middle of the valley, it sure did make a

235

lot of noise. Of course as they rode Butch asked Randy just how they worked those big dredging machines.

Randy looked over at Butch, 'What the hell makes you think I know anything about them? I'm a logger. I run six of these Clydesdales in a team skidding logs. I can skid twenty five to thirty logs a day. Most other team's of four are lucky to skid half that in a day. This is as close as I've been to that operation, and I don't care to get any closer.'

"So they take a lot of gold out of the ground do they?" Butch asked.

"Well, I hear between all of the dredges, they're pulling out an average of fifty plus, fifty pound bags of gold every week," Randy answered. You're real lucky you met up with my brothers. No one else but me and a very few others know where, and how that tunnel opens," Randy said. "That's where they load the gold."

"How did you get to know where they load the gold?" Butch asked.

"Well, I keep my horses there in the smokehouse, as you well know," Randy said. "That's where the tunnel comes out at and they load the train on the spur track. They don't pay me no never mind." He started chuckling. "One of the deputies that load the gold got too close to this big stallion here and he sent him flying across the room, broke two ribs and a leg."

"So what you're saying is," Butch started saying. "You and your horse both send people to meet Doc Bones, huh?"

"Yep," Randy answered. "In fact that Roan is going to make you have to go see Doc Bones tomorrow Butch."

"You think that Roan is going to throw me that far do ya? Butch said smiling. "I've been on one or two ornery horses in my younger days."

"OKAY," Randy said, pulling his horse to a stop. "Well, there's the spot, the narrows," Randy said, pointing.

With all the moonlight, they could see the canyon walls going straight up, a good three hundred feet on both sides of the river. They could hear the rapids of the river, if you fell in the river here you'd be gone before you even had a chance to holler for help.

Chapter Eleven

"Butch," Randy said, pointing up on the cliff face. "You go just below that big overhang there, you make sure you hide that yellow fuse, there's a lot of traffic on this road during the daylight. I'm going back up river a little ways and cross over when I finish. I'll meet ya back here." Then Randy turned and rode away.

Butch was glad to see that Randy was the one crossing that river and not him, it was too high and flowing too fast. Still where Randy wanted him to put these three cases of nitro wasn't going to be an easy job. It would take a couple trips to get all the nitro up there. Working as fast as he could, it had only taken him just over an hour to have everything set up. He was hiding the fuse under some brush as he came down for the last time.

Walking over Butch untied the Clydesdale, looking him over again. Just how the hell was he going to get on this big thing? He felt like a little kid as he led the big horse over to the rocks so he could climb up on his back. Turning around he could see Randy sitting on his horse and laughing at him.

"Come on, we can run them going back home," Randy said. They turned their horses in the direction of Sumpter, "I don't know about you but I'm tired."

"I hear ya," Butch said. Looking down at the ground. "Damn, that was a long way down." He wasn't in a saddle. "Just how fast do you want to run?" Butch asked kicking his horse in the side. He jumped into a full run to catch up with his two buddies. Butch reached and grabbed a handful of mane just in time, digging his legs into the side of the horse as hard as he could, he damn sure didn't want to fall off this big horse.

"Come on Cowboy," Randy said looking back over the horse he was leading. Kicking his horse in the side, "Come on, let's go…just dig your legs in and hang on, you'll get used to the rhythm in a little while."

"How much longer till daylight?" Butch asked, pulling up alongside Randy.

"Well, by looking at the moon where it is now and where it was when we started…I'd say we might have two hours, and we need to be in bed before people start getting up."

237

"I hear ya," Butch said. Kicking the big gelding in the side, and hung on. He knew they needed to ride hard and fast to make it back.

Randy figured it was right at an hour back to Sumpter, maybe a little closer. Neither one said very much the rest of the way back. This made Butch happy. This horse was the roughest riding horse he had been on, fact his back was starting to hurt from all the hard pounding of each and every step the horse took. He wondered to himself just what it was going to be like to try that big Roan, how many seconds could he stay on, or better yet, how many jumps.

It didn't take long and they came to the edge of the timber and the mill yard. "Stay in the river bed," Randy said. "That way the shadows and smokehouse will hide us." They slowly and quietly worked their way to the smokehouse; they could see that there were a couple people up and walking around town.

As soon as they got into the smokehouse and tied the horses back up, Randy grained them. "Don't worry about wiping them down, we don't have time." Looking over at the other two already tied up. "These animals mean a whole lot to me, Mr. Parker," Randy said. His voice went from joking to serious real quick. Butch didn't need to see his face to tell. "You had better pick someone you can trust to bring them back. Cause if they're not in this good a shape when I get them back, There won't be NO place you can hide. I don't know where this Circleville is, but I will find it. Do I make myself clear?"

"YES sir you do," Butch answered. "Crystal Clear."

"Good then, now let's get the hell out of here." The two men ran across the large open area as fast as they could to get to the alleyway in the back of the stores. The Elkhorn was just about half way down the alleyway.

"We're lucky," Butch said, opening the back door to the Elkhorn. "They forgot to lock the door."

"No, they didn't", Randy said. The two quickly and quietly crossed the room to the stairs. "Gary made sure it would be unlocked, I guarantee it." They could see there were already a couple people in the restaurant ordering breakfast, but they weren't paying them any mind

Chapter Eleven

as they quietly ran up the stairs. Stopping outside their rooms, they shook hands and said good night.

It was just a little before eight o' clock in the morning as both Sundance and Gary came out of their rooms. Looking over to Sundance, Gary held his finger over his mouth, "SHSSSH, Randy and Butch didn't get in till just a couple hours ago and one thing you do not want to do is wake Randy up. You think he can be an a-hole when he's up, just try waking him up…" silently closing his door, Gary continued, "You wake him up and we'll both be going to see Doc Bones."

"Really?" Sundance said closing his door real quiet, whispering.

"Hell yes," Gary said. Turning, the two of them started down the hallway. "Yes sir…and after the way he's feeling about you from last night, before you got smart and got the hell away from him…Why more people don't do that, I'll never know. But you can be damn sure he hasn't forgot what you said last night…" starting to chucle a little, Gary continues, "Lets just say if you woke him up, you'd be spending more than just a couple of days over at Doc Bones healing up."

"Speaking of which," Sundance started, "I've never seen a man's eyes turn to fiery red like his did. I've heard about people like that… but until last night, I've never seen it. You claim to be half-Irish and half-Polish? I'll tell ya Gary; I don't remember anyone ever sending a chill up my spine like that before. I could just tell I was only seconds away from being packed out of the saloon last night. I couldn't get it out of my mind the way Randy threw that big man around like a rag doll the night before. I've never seen him throw one punch into that mans face; it seemed like his arm was always cocked, waiting to go again. His fist flew to fast to see. But the blood and teeth flew everywhere with each punch. The power that little man has in those arms is incredible."

The two walked into the restaurant side of the saloon, looking around they could see the place was over half full. Walking over to a table the two sat down. The young waitress was pouring their coffee. Before they even had a chance to say thank you to her, she took their breakfast order and left. Sundance looked out the window in the direction of the livery stable and the coral next to it, where the Roan was on display for everyone to see. Chuckling a little, Sundance looked over at Gary, "Look, there are already a dozen or more men standing at the corral."

Gary turned his head in that direction, "We do this right," Gary said smiling. "We can make a lot of money on that horse today. By the way, you were right last night … Sheriff Hendricksen did make you and Butch, said he wasn't quite sure who Curry was, but he knew he'd seen paper on him."

Looking back at Gary with a shit-eating grin on his face, Sundance said, "Well, since we're not all in jail, I take it he's not on the up and up."

"You're right about that," Gary answered. "That fat ass… I tell ya that guy needs an ass whooping if anyone I know needs one. He's one that deserves to go meet Doc Bones up close and personal."

Busting up laughing, Sundance looked at Gary, "Well hell, what would you say if he accidentally on purpose got pushed into Randy sometime?"

"I don't know if Randy would," Gary answered. "He pretty much respects law men. He'll see that badge and settle right down…but I think we just might figure some other way to get him."

"So how much did he ask for? For not hauling us in?" Sundance asked.

"Three thousand, but I figure we can get that back off him today, from the Roan." Gary said.

"You still think no ones going to cover him don't ya?" Sundance asked, with a doubtful look on his face.

"Wouldn't say he could, if I didn't believe it." Gary answered, with a big smile. "You just wait and see. Sure wish C.R. was up sooner, but by the looks of at least five or six of those who are riding…I wouldn't give them one or two jumps at most."

Just then Larry, Luis and Curry came up to the table and sat down. Larry looked over at Gary smiling, "So did you tell him about the local law yet, Gary?"

"YA," Gary said. "We just started talking about him."

Sundance jumps in the middle of the conversation, "Ya Gary said he needed to go meet Doc Bones up close and personal."

Chapter Eleven

Larry started to chuckle, "But Randy don't hit lawmen…damn it anyway."

"What do you mean he don't hit lawmen?" Curry asked. "How does he know just who is and who isn't with his eyes turn that red? Just from the view I seen, I was looking for a place to hide."

"He sees that little Silver Star," Gary said. "And for some reason he calms right down."

"By the way, where did Randy and Butch go to last night?" Sundance asked, looking around at everyone then back to Larry.

"They went to make you a back door," Larry said.

"What kind of back door?" Sundance asked.

"Not real sure, but he wanted dynamite, and if I know Randy," Larry started to chuckle. "Randy will want a lot of it."

Curry looked over at him, "There's a couple places in the canyon it should only take a couple cases of dynamite at the most," he said, looking around the table.

"You don't know Randy," Gary said, chuckling and looking at everyone. "Randy likes BIG bangs and I do mean BIG BANGS." Gesturing with his hands, moving them from table level to over his head.

"Yeah hombre, sometimes he gets a little carried away," Luis said. "Just like he gets carried away when you piss him off. When something out of the ordinary happens they're not sure Randy's behind it, but they think he is."

"Except in the case of a fight," Sundance said. "You can tell it's him."

Larry leaned over and looked up the street; the people were coming in from all over. They had all heard about the bucking competition and they to wanted to see if it could be done. Also there were all kinds of men showing up with their teams of horses for the log pulling competition. Hoping they could make themselves a little extra money as well. But you could be sure they were really there for one reason, the bucking competition.

"Look at all those people up there around the corral checking out my horse, Larry said, bragging. "I bet there's fifty plus, if there's one."

241

"There's going to be one big party," Luis said cheering.

Looking over at Larry with a stern look on his face Gary started talking to him, "I don't care what happens later tonight, but right now we all have to keep our heads on straight. In other words LARRY… no drinking until it's over. Do you understand me?"

"Yeah, yeah I hear ya," Larry answers waving his hand at Gary. "You just don't worry about me, I'll be just fine."

"Don't you make me check your coat sleeves before you go outside," Gary said, "I know you too well." Looking over at Luis, "Luis you make sure too or I'll kick your ass as well."

"HEEEY hombre, just wait one minute," Luis said holding up his hands. "Don't even bring me into this battle between you two."

Just then the Doss brother's walked to the table, this time they had their other brother. Curry and Sundance looked at each other then back to the Doss's, they both started laughing. They couldn't believe it was possible, but that third one, he had to be the one they called Hosey…that man had by far, the biggest damn nose the had ever seen.

"When I met you two last night," Sundance said looking at Toad and Goof. "I honestly didn't think it was possible for anyone to have a bigger and longer nose," trying not to laugh too hard, he looked around the table. "But damned if that ain't the biggest nose I've ever seen." Then looking at the youngest one, "Goof, I can see where he gets his nickname." Then looking back over at Toad, "But how did you get the name, Toad?"

Toad looked down at both Sundance and Curry, touching the tip of his nose with his tongue; "Just ask the ladies…they'll tell ya." Toad answered, smiling.

"In your dreams," Randy said, as he and Butch came walking up, slapping Toad on the back, "In your dreams."

Looking around the table and then back to Randy, "Can you lick your eyebrows?" Hosey asked. "Cause I can."

Everyone started laughing; Randy looked over at Hosey, "Hosey, I'd like to introduce you here to our new friends Mr. Brigham Young," pointing at Butch, "Mr. Harry Jones," pointing at Sundance, "And

242

Chapter Eleven

Mr. Harvey Smith," pointing at Curry. "But I'm sure you know who they really are by now."

"If you guys are real serious about this job," Hosey said. "I'll stay sober until the job is done, except for a little peyote now and then. I hear you guys want to go out through Idaho, but we'd rather go to Seattle with our share," he said to the three outlaws. "By the way, just how much is our cut?"

"Your cut is what you can carry," Butch said with a serious look in his eyes and a small smile on his face. "Where you take it, I don't really care...you guys do plan on bringing along extra pack animals don't you?"

"Well hell yeah," Goof spoke up. "We're thinking at least two mules each."

"Where are you figuring on getting these extra pack animals?" Curry asked,

"I'd like a couple myself."

"Right over there in the log yard," Toad said. Taking a big bite of chewing tobacco and pointing in the direction of the log yard. "Right down there, they have maybe eighty to one hundred real strong mules over there. They used them to pull those logs around the log yard and load them on the trains with. They won't miss a half a dozen, least wise not right away."

"Well how about it then," Curry asked. "Could you get me a couple?"

"Don't see why not," Goof said shrugging his shoulders, "What's two more?"

Just then the waitress came up with a couple pots of coffee and a beer, pouring everyone a cup of coffee until she got to Larry, where she sat the mug of beer down.

"Can't have one just yet," Larry said, looking up at her and over at Gary.

"WHAT," the waitress hollered; "It's not beer thirty yet? It's after eleven o- clock."

"Nope, not today," Larry said. Pointing at Gary, "He won't let me because of the bucking competition."

243

Smiling, she looked down at Larry, then over to Gary. "That must be pure hell on you Larry," she said. Picking up the beer and filled his coffee cup.

"You know it," Larry answered smiling a little.

Just then a short chubby man came walking up to the table, in what Butch, Curry and Sundance all figured was a cheap three piece suit. They had all three been to big cities where you could get a good tailor to make you a nice suit. But then all they had to do was remember where they were, loggers and miners…who didn't wear three piece suits to work, so that was probably the best material he could get up here.

The man slapped Randy on the back, and then he put his hand on his shoulder. "I didn't think you were in town last night," the man said smiling. Looking around the three tables they had pulled together to accommodate everyone. "You didn't send me my usual customer?"

Sundance looked at Randy on the other side and end of the table, then back up to the man, "You must be Doc Bones?"

"Well that's what this here Young man started calling me a few years back," he said, pointing at Larry. "When all three of these boys started logging up here. You might say I know these young men real well, but especially this one here," he said looking back at Randy. "This one here usually always sends me a customer on the weekends. By the way Gary, Why the hell didn't you stop him Friday night from smashing that man's face so many times?"

"I did Doc," Gary answered with a small smile on his face. "He only hit him three, maybe four times in the face when he had him down."

"Incredible," Doc answered. "He not only broke that poor mans nose in three place's, but he broke both cheek Bones as well," looking back around the table, "He's still over there in my hospital rehabbing. I swear Randy, I'm half afraid you just might kill somebody one of these days. You really need to get control of that temper."

"W-W-W-well they shouldn't make F-F-F-fun of me," Randy answered smiling up at him.

244

Chapter Eleven

"So you still didn't answer my question about last night," Doc asked again. "Why didn't you send me a customer last night? I was waiting up."

"Well Doc," Sundance said smiling. "You might say this potential customer got up and left before it was too late, and that's why I'm on this end of the table this morning."

"Well I see there are some smart ones around," Doc said laughing. "And just who might you three young men be?"

Larry looked up at him, "Well Doc, these are our new friends Mr. Young, Mr. Smith, and Mr. Jones."

Reaching out his hand, Doc shook each one hand. "Ya know when I came through that Utah country by wagon train a few years back, they had a picture of a man who had a nickname Butch Cassidy, I think his real name was Parker...you sure look like him, Young man," he said looking at Butch.

"Well, I am from Utah," Butch said, "But I'm afraid I'm not this fella, Parker, did you say his name was, and to my knowledge we're not related?"

"How do you know you're not related?" Doc asked. "They all have so many wives down there. Hell, they all have to be related somehow... Why I remember when I came through there; they wanted me to convert to their religion. Hell, I was all for it," Doc said, looking around the table still smiling, "I kinda liked that idea of all those young ladies around to play with. But they said I'd have to give up my drinking and well, that just ain't happening. So I came up here," looking around the room. "To tell you the truth I like it even better up here. You see being the only Doctor around for twenty-five plus miles, why you could say me and some of these young ladies around here; we have a barter system, in exchange for my professional services. Fact, that's what I came in for...lunch and dessert."

"Lunch and dessert?" Gary asked, "What's your dessert?"

Looking around the room, Doc points over at a young blonde lady, "Her right there, she's my dessert today, after lunch anyway... hmmm...maybe dinner too."

"You dirty old man," Gary said.

245

"Well, Larry or Gary whichever one you are," the Doc said. "You only wish you could work out as nice a payment plan as I have."

"You're right old man," Larry couldn't help chuckle a little. "You better get it while you can today, cause later on you're going to be getting some customers from my horse down there."

"You boys really think he can go through ten men?" Doc asked, looking around the table.

"I have no doubt," Randy answered. "You should have been up at the logging camp Friday, when they came up to get me. When they fell that tree, and it came crashing to the ground. That horse came flat undone…That was one hell of a ride Larry made. Hell, I figured if he could ride him so could I." Looking around the table at everyone, "I tell you that was two of the longest jumps I remember being on…fact I think, no I know it would be easier to ride my stallion than it would be to ride that Roan."

"What makes you say that?" Butch asked.

"Because that horse likes to buck, you can just tell," Randy said. "It's in his spirit to be free, and he has a hell of a lot of power to send you flying…You'll see this afternoon Mr. Young. You get first shot at him today, Remember. Speaking of today, I need to get my team over to the log pull, I need some extra money."

"So why is that big Roan letting Larry ride him?" Butch asked.

"He must feel sorry for him, I mean just look at him," Gary said… "Wouldn't you feel sorry for him"? Looking at Larry, then over to Randy. They're all complaining about you down there, Randy," Gary said. "They said they wouldn't agree to let you enter a full set of four horses. You have to agree to use only three."

"Why is that?" Sundance asked.

"OHHH, I smoked them the last four competitions, so they don't want to play with me anymore…boo hoo, Randy said. "Hell, I only brought three anyhow. To tell you the truth I was looking forward to challenging Don Pierce's new team of Percheron's. I hear he's doing real good with them. Oh well, next time me and him will meet, and then it'll be four on four. Well, I need to get going if I'm going to get set up and ready," Randy said.

Chapter Eleven

"Before you leave Randy, I've got a question for you," Butch said, looking at him. "Just how the hell do you get up on those big monsters? I felt like a little kid last night, who was trying to get on a horse for his first time.

"You looked like one too," Randy said, chuckling. "It was fun watching you crawl threw the brush trying to climb up on that rock, to get aboard last night."

"So just how the hell do you get aboard?" Butch asked directly.

"I click my cheek, CK, CK twice, and they pick up their front left hooves, so I have a step." Randy said, still smiling.

"Why didn't you tell me about that in the smokehouse?" Butch asked.

"I was enjoying watching you," Randy answered, Then he stood up and both Sundance and Curry stood up at the same time, they looked at each other then back over at Randy. Sundance asked, "Mind if we tag along? We've never seen anything like this before."

"Sure," Randy said. Turning to the Doc patting him on the shoulder and smiling, "You take care you horny old man, I'll see ya later." He looked over at the two, "Come on, let's get going." Turning and heading towards the door. The three of them walked a total of maybe a hundred yards down the street. Before they could see the smokehouse setting out in the middle of an open area; they could see they had pulled four railroad cars up along the riverside of it. Just at a quick glance they could see it was going to be hard to get to without being seen by anyone. The three walked into the building, Sundance and Curry could see it was basically just an open area inside. Some flooring still remained, but most of it had either been used to build a fire or it had just rotted away. Randy's horses were tied on one side.

"There's where the tunnel comes out," Randy said pointing at a firebox in the center of the room.

Sundance walked over and looked at it; he even tried to move it. But it wouldn't budge. "Are you sure Randy?" Sundance asked. Continuing to looking around, "This hay and straw looks like it's been here a while."

"It unlocks from underneath, after they finish loading one guy stays up here and recovers it with straw. Fact it's usually the bank man, that way he thinks he's the only one who knows the tunnels exact location. Tell you the truth," Randy continued as he untied his horses. "They really haven't worried too much about being robbed, as you've noticed there really isn't any cover around here to hide yourself trying to get here to the shack. They usually have a couple deputies on guard looking out for anything or anyone who's not supposed to be around...so you'll have to take them out first." Then he started leading his horses out of the building with Curry and Sundance right behind him.

"You know Randy?" Sundance said. "I don't know a whole lot about pulling competitions but don't you need harnesses of some kind for those horses?"

"OH SHIT," Randy hollers. "I knew I forgot something yesterday. Damn that peyote anyway."

"What are you talking about?" Curry asked, as Randy turned around and headed back into the smokehouse.

"That peyote makes you forget shit if you take one hit too much," Randy snapped back. "I smoked a little on the way up to the logging camp. I had it on my mind harnesses and backpacks. That damn Cookie, he asked me to get some extra grub to bring back. I totally forgot about those damn harnesses. DAMMIT! Oh well, I really didn't want to work these fellows too hard today anyway with the weight you boys are going to put on them."

They both followed Randy back into the smokehouse laughing lightly; they didn't want to upset him. He was already getting mad they both thought, because he wouldn't be able to enter the log pulling competition. Neither one wanted to see just how good the Doc, old Doc Bones really was.

Re-entering the smokehouse Randy said, "Hold up." He walked over and grabbed the stallion's halter. "Here, tie these two over there," handing Curry and Sundance the reins. "That way you don't have to get around this stallion. Remember that, cause if you get too close to him he will kick you and send you flying across the room. Then he'll look back at you with a BIG SORRY look on his face, thinking to

Chapter Eleven

himself, I didn't mean to do that. Then it's off to Doc Bones. So don't even try to take him, cause he won't go with anyone but me." Randy walked over to the backpack, opening it up he took out a pair of clean socks, Then set down in an old chair and unlaced his boots and took his dirty socks off.

"Damn," Sundance said plugging his nose. He and Curry both backed away, "Those things stink to high heaven. Don't you ever change your socks?"

"Well of course I do," Randy answered. "I've just been wearing these longer because I wanted them good and ripe."

"What the hell for?" Curry asked.

"Cause this is my present to that fat ass Sheriff," Randy said. "You see that old fart uses that badge in the wrong way I feel. SEE, if he finds or catches one of these poor miners or loggers doing anything even slightly wrong, why he makes them let him have sex with their wives or worse their daughters. If they don't, he'll arrest them on some trumped up charge." Holding up one sock, he handed it to Sundance. Turning back to his backpack he pulled out a roll of tape, about two inch's wide and six-inch's in diameter. "Now this here is a new tape they came out with, they call it Purple Mule Tape, they claim it's as strong as a mule… I don't know about that, but it is strong. So what I want you to do is after you tie that fat ass up, I want you to gag that Sheriff with this sock, stuff his mouth full and run a couple of wraps of tape around his head so he can't spit it out."

"Alright," Sundance said. Grabbing the sock with just two fingers and plugging his nose with the other hand. Walking over to an empty can and dropped the sock in it, "You sure this won't kill him?" Sundance asked, knowing it wouldn't but it just might make him sick enough to throw up. Then he'd die in his own vomit and we'd get blamed for killing him.

"Don't worry about that," Randy said. Putting his new socks on and lacing his boots back up.

"I know you forgot your harnesses," Curry said to Randy. "But can't you just go over to the mill and borrow a sit from them?"

249

"You don't know a whole lot about big draft horses, do you?" Randy asked. "Those mules are so much smaller than these here are. Hell, I'd be lucky if I could get their harnesses over the heads of these three, let alone be able to work with them. No, no…I'm just out of this pull is all. You guys just remember DON'T ever get next to this big boy here." Randy said, slapping the stallion on the ass, "And make damn sure you're in here before they open that trap door, which is usually around nine thirty, ten o' clock at the latest."

"Oh, don't worry about that," Sundance said with a big smile on his face. "We'll damn sure be in here. You can count on that. So how about you take me and Curry down to the log yard and explain to us how everything works?"

"Sure," Randy said. "Come on lets get us some good seats and I'll explain it to you. DAMMIT, that really pisses me off; I know I still could have won with only three horses against their teams of four horses or mule's.

The three walked out of the smokehouse and over the bridge to the log yard. "You see they put the logs one hundred feet apart," Randy told the men. "The first teams pull them one way, then the next teams pull them back the other. You'll see all different kinds of teams; some will be matched sets like mine are. But then you will have your mixed sets…even sets of mules and then you'll have the ones who just have teams of saddle horses. Those guys are going to fall out first. Then of course your smaller mule teams will start to go." Just then they walked up to a young dark haired man, he wasn't much taller than Randy was. "Gentlemen, I'd like you to meet a real good friend of mine, his father and our father were killed the same way."

"How was that?" Sundance asked.

Don looked over at them, "Killed skidding logs." Then he stuck his hand out, "Don Pierce it's nice to meet you, whoever you are."

Randy looked over at Don, "Don, this is Sundance Kid and Kid Curry."

"Oh you're so full of shit Randy. What the hell would a couple of big name outlaws like them be doing up here…? Robbing the gold train?" Don asked.

Chapter Eleven

"I knew you weren't as dumb as you looked," Randy said.

"Alright, smart ass," Don said. Looking around, "Where's your team at? I think I've got a chance to beat you this time."

"Oh hell, I got to smoking that damn peyote and went off and forgot my harnesses," Randy answered.

"Haven't you learned yet to write shit down when you smoke that stuff, so you don't forget?" Don said.

"Yeah, yeah, I know," Randy said. "I'll get you during the Miner's Jubilee in August, Don."

"I'll be looking forward to it Randy," Don said. "Hey you wouldn't happen to have any peyote on you, would ya?"

"You guys really smoke that shit?" Sundance asked.

"HELL YEAH," Randy answered with a big smile on is face. "It beats getting drunk any day."

"I hear them Indians have visions when they smoke that stuff," Curry said with a serious look on his face. Looking back and forth between Randy and Don.

"OOHH HELL," Don said looking back at them. "That only happens if you smoke too much. All you need is just one or too small hits. That's all it takes to put you in a good mood for the rest of the night."

"If you smoke too much of it don't you don't get sick like you do on alcohol." Randy said.

"What happens to ya? I mean if you smoke too much of it?" Sundance asked.

"Well, just like the Indians say, 'you'll go to sleep and have some cool visions,' Randy said.

"I can't believe you guys really smoke that shit," Sundance said, again.

Randy looked over at them, "Hey, God made peyote and man made booze, WHO... do you trust?"

Starting to chuckle, Curry looked over at Sundance, "He does have a good point there."

"That's all fine and good," Sundance said. "But if you want to try it Curry..."

251

Looking him straight in the eyes. "You wait until this job is over with."

"Alright," Curry said. "If you have any of that stuff on you, Randy, how about giving me a little? When I get on that big steamer heading to San Francisco I'll smoke it then so I can party more."

"Don't worry, Curry," Randy said. "You're riding out with the Doss boys, they'll have plenty…trust me."

"How about me," Don asked. "Can I get some off you Randy? Chief Joseph caught me with a young squaw while back and now he won't let any of the brave's sale it to me anymore."

"Yeah sure," Randy said. Pulling out a bag from his pocket, opening it up he pulled out a little bit. "Here Don, but watch it, this stuff is real good. But you had better watch it with the Chief to, He'll have a castration wedding. "

"What's a castration wedding?" Curry asked

"Kinda like a shot gun wedding, only instead of a shot gun ole Chief Joseph will hang you up at fifty feet stark naked…then he throw's five knives at you seeing just how close he can get, if you get my meaning," Randy said. Turning back to the others.

"Come on, we can watch the competition from over here at the bleachers." The three worked their way back across the bridge over the river to the bleachers. The saloon owners already had some fine looking young ladies selling beer and whiskey at both competition areas. They each grabbed a beer and then headed up to get good seats so they could watch everything. "After this is over they'll turn these bleachers around so we can watch the bucking competitions from them."

"So how long does it usually take to find out who the winner is?" Sundance asked, looking over at Randy.

"Well, they usually start out with five teams going each way; the first two to cross the line move to the next round and the losers are done. Those logs all measure thirty-three feet in length. As you will soon see it only takes about five maybe six pulls to eliminate all the little guys, then maybe three or four more pulls to find the

Chapter Eleven

ultimate winner. They will add a log after each team has made the same pull."

"Boy those big black Percheron's of Don Pierces sure do look nice," Randy said. "But I still bet my Clydesdales could beat him four on four, ton for ton."

After they had watched three or four pulls, Randy said, "Come on lets go see how everything's going over at the Livery stables." Standing up, they started working his way back down the bleachers and through the crowd.

"Will you check out all these people?" Curry said. "Just where the hell did they all come from?"

"Where the hell you think?" Randy answered. "With the gold rush that hit this area up here, why, every gully and stream within fifty square miles of this place is chucked full of new people, hoping to find the next mother load."

"How long has the gold rush been going on?" Sundance asked.

"Just over a year now," Randy said. "Believe it or not, Sumpter used to be a nice little logging town, maybe one hundred people. Some lucky asshole found gold and all hell broke lose. Now you can hardly find a clean woman or a decent bed to sleep in."

"Tell me about it," Sundance said. "You're not the one who's been paying the bills all weekend." They continued fighting their way through the crowd. Just trying to get a half block to the Livery stable and the corral wasn't easy. It seemed like everyone in town had to get a look at that Roan before the competition.

"You boys are going to make a hell of a lot more money on this job, than you'll ever spend around here, and you know it" Randy said. "Hell, and that's just from the bucking competition."

"That's true," Curry said. "After this job, we're going to get to party a whole lot longer in the big city."

When they got to the corral, the Roan was running around like he knew he was on display and he was showing off. "Check him out," Randy said. Climbing up on the fence, "Come on, we can get there this way a hell of a lot faster."

253

The two followed Randy over the corral pole fence; the two looked at each other, smiling. Randy was right, the way the Roan was trotting around the arena looking at everyone looking at him…you could just tell he was feeling cocky. Some men were still building the bucking chute at the other end of the corral.

Sundance was thinking to himself about what Randy said earlier. About this horse having spirit. He was right, that big Roan knew something was up and he was the center of attention… and he liked it.

The three walked over and joined Larry, Gary and all the others. Sundance could see Larry was getting real fidgety. Looking down at his hands he could see Gary still wasn't allowing him to even have a beer yet. Even still Larry was talking that big Roan up. He had some money and was taking bets on all riders. Of course, Butch was right in on it himself. Randy made a side bet with Butch, betting just how long he was going to last.

"How much you want to put on it Randy, that I last at least a minimum of three jumps?" Butch challenged him

Randy reached into his pocket, pulled out his wallet and counted his money. "Well…I'll be easy on you" Randy said smiling. "I'll bet you one hundred dollars each jump…" Looking around at everyone. "If you make three jumps I'll pay you one hundred dollars for each, but for each one you don't make, you owe me one hundred dollar…do you get the picture?"

"Sure do," Butch said. "I'm not no greenhorn when it comes to riding some rough animals… I was a fair hand when it came to breaking horses back in Circleville growing up…so for every jump I stay over three you have to add one hundred dollars to the pot as well."

"Alright, I'll take that bet," Randy agreed. Turning in the direction of the bucking shoot and seeing them practicing pulling the gate open as fast as they could. "Well by the looks of things we're not too far from starting now."

Just then two young ladies walked up to them; each one had a pitcher of beer in one hand and glasses in the other. One of them

Chapter Eleven

looked over towards Larry, then back to Gary, they had all heard that Gary laid down the law earlier about Larry and drinking today. "So is it beer thirty yet?" the young lady asked looking at Larry, who was wiping his lips and licking them again at the same time.

"Go ahead," Gary said waving his hands at Larry. "Hell, pour me one too, but No Whiskey!" then he turned back to Larry. "You just as well go get that bronc saddle while you're at it."

"Thank you, your majesty," Larry said, grabbing a beer and heading to the Livery stable. "Come on Luis, you can help me."

"Well, what do you say we see if we can get anyone to place any bets?" Sundance asked. "Anyone want to bet that Mr. Young can ride this horse? I'll pay ten to one odds he can't."

Quickly everyone started murmuring, getting louder and louder. They talked between themselves; one man hollered back, "I'll take ten to one odds." Others started joining in on the bets. Some were figuring they would hold off a couple riders. By now the word had gotten around about that Roan and what had taken place up at the logging camp two days earlier. Just then a young lady came walking by with an empty beer tray. Sundance hollered over at her, "Young lady, would you please come here?"

The young lady had heard who he and his two friends really were. "Yes sweetie," she answered smiling, walking over to him. "Just what is it I can get for you beer, whiskey…me?" She said, moving her hips back and forth.

"Sure," Sundance said smiling. "I'd like to see you later, but right now we're kinda busy. Looks like we're going to be here for a while. For right now, if you could see to it that we never run out of beer it would be greatly appreciated. You will be greatly rewarded if you know what I mean."

"That will be no problem," the young lady said and she gave him a small kiss on the cheek. "You just let me know when you want something besides beer Mr. Jones."

"Oh I will," Sundance said with a big smile.

Just then Larry and Luis came walking back over to the corral, Larry holding the bronc saddle over his shoulder. "Well, boys it's time to make us some money." He opened the gate and walked out across the corral to the Roan. Laying the saddle down, Larry hooked the lead rope to the Roans halter. Reaching down and picked up the saddle. It only took just a couple minutes and he was climbing up in the saddle. "Easy big boy," he was saying, trying to calm the big Roan down. As soon he got sit in the saddle he could feel that big horse getting all tense. He'd never been in a crowd of people this big, and he wasn't sure he liked it. "Eeaassyy big boy," Larry said. "It's just me."

Slowly the Roan started walking. Larry slowly and nervously rode him up into the bucking Chute. They closed the gate behind them, Larry could tell the Roan didn't like it, fact he started fighting it just a little. Larry was quick to get off him; he had seen too many men get hurt inside the bucking chute when they had a fighter.

Calmly, Larry started talking to the Roan, still trying to calm him down. Just as Butch climbed up on the back of the bucking chute, he could see the men were already putting the flank strap on. Butch was actually happy to see the big Roan had started to settle down.

Leaning over, Butch pulled up the stirrup, looking back towards Larry, "Hope you don't mind if I reset this saddle?"

"Hell no," Larry said, smiling. "I know if it was me, I would."

"Where's the saddle horn?" Butch asked, looking up at Larry.

"It's a bronc saddle, they don't have a horn," Larry answered. "You'll also notice the stirrups are bigger too. That way you won't get your foot stuck in the stirrup and drug around the arena for a while."

Slowly Butch settled down in the saddle, he felt like he had a million butterflies in his stomach if he had one. Easily and carefully he measured out his reins, looking around, "Well boys, he ain't going to wait," Butch hollered. "LET'S GO!" Just then the men started to open the gate as another pulled on the flank strap. That was all it took, there was no reason to even open the gate any further, cause the Roan came flying straight up, out, and over the top of the gate and sending Butch flying a good six to eight feet higher into the air. Landing on his chest and face when he came crashing back to the ground, knocking the air out of him.

256

Chapter Eleven

"Thought we told you to reach for the ground Mr. Young," Larry hollered out. The Roan was still bucking around the arena jumping and snorting. Larry rode over on the pickup horse, reached over and unhooked the flank strap, reaching for the rein he lead him back to the chute for the next victim.

After all bet's were taken, the next young man reset the saddle, and then slowly climbed down on the back of the Roan. He was glad to see the Roan was settling down in the chute and not fighting as much, too. However he could still feel the Roan tense up. Reaching down and measuring his rein, he figured he'd give him a couple inches more, pushing his hat down over his head he hollered, "OUTSIDE!" Again just as they pulled on that flank strap that Roan went crazy. He went flying straight up from the ground on his first jump, driving his head down between his front legs with a mighty force, sending the young cowboy and his dreams straight into the ground, Head first.

Larry rode back over to the Roan and removed the flank strap, then taking up the Roan's rein again leading him back to the chute, where a young lady was waiting with a fresh beer. "Why, Thank you darling," he said while watched the next rider reset the saddle and get ready for his chance at fame.

The man slowly climbed down into the chute onto the Roan's back. The feeling in his stomach wasn't getting any less queasy. The man called the gate and the Roan came straight out with great power. After he came down on his front feet he spun his ass end around and doing a one eighty he send the man flying back into the chute that he had just came out of, before they even had time to close it. Everyone had seen a bull make that move, but never a horse.

Now Larry was getting a little cocky, riding back out to the Roan, reaching over and undid the flank strap and picked up the rein. He hollered out at everyone, "Who wants to bet me the next rider goes just as fast as everyone else so far?" He headed over towards Randy, Gary, Butch, Sundance, and the others. He could see the people were starting to pick up on the betting. Larry led the Roan back over to the chute, which was actually getting easier to do. He half figured the Roan was enjoying himself too.

257

Again the next cowboy reset the saddle and climbed onboard, this wasn't his first time in the chute and he was feeling real sure and cocky with himself. Fact, he was making a side bet with Larry. When he was saddled and ready, he called for the gate. Again when that flank strap was pulled that Roan went flying high. The Roan came down from his first jump and the man was feeling sure of himself. All of a sudden in the middle of the second jump the Roan sucked in his big shoulders and down with his back, bringing his ass up over his head, sending the man flying across the arena like he had been shot out of a cannon.

Again Larry retrieved the Roan, making sure he was slow enough so everybody could make more wagers on the next rider. This only meant more money for his and Gary's ranch. Starting to chuckle just a little. All of a sudden he remembered the last rider…that black man, C.R. Hall…Larry knew he could ride. They just don't give those big championship buckle's to just anyone…you have to earn them!

Looking back at the Roan, Larry knew he was enjoying himself as he watched the cowboys being carried out of the arena. Sometimes the Roan would jump into the man's direction as if to say, 'come on butt wheat, is that all you can handle?' Randy was right, this Roan had a wild spirit…a lot of it, and he didn't liked anyone on him.

Leading him back into the chute for the next rider, Larry was thinking to himself, would this be the last bucking competition him and this Roan would do? Would he settle down over the next year and let anyone ride him? It sure would be nice to do this for a couple more years like Grandpa Dude did with his big black mustang stallion. He knew they'd never be able to make this kind of money again, but he could maybe get twenty-five, thirty dollars a rider. Still it would bring in a little extra money at the Haine's Stampede, which was only a month and a half away; he would definitely try this again then.

Larry was so busy daydreaming about everything; the Roan had gone through the next four riders before he realized it. He was leading him back to the chute for the ninth rider when he heard one man ask another man, who had tried the Roan earlier, how much extra rein to give the horse. The man answered and said, "I'd give him at least four inches." Then he climbed down in the chute onto the back of the

Chapter Eleven

Roan. He couldn't get over how big this horse really was. He'd never remembered feeling so uncomfortable on a horse before, but for five thousand dollars, that would be real nice in his pocket. Taking a deep breath he called for the chute. When he came down from the first jump that Roan, again, with all his power he drove his head between his front two legs pulling the rein and driving the man headfirst into the ground. Rolling over he looked up at his friend, "That wasn't enough rein!"

The man turned towards everyone and then back to the man lying on the ground laughing, "It wasn't enough for me either," he answered. Everyone within earshot who heard the comment started laughing also.

Riding out Larry picked up the rein to the Roan and lead him back to the chute, looking up he could see C.R. standing there looking back at him from the back side of the chute.

"So Larry," C.R. asked. "You want to make a side bet here?

"Sure, why not?" Larry answered smiling. "Hell C.R., this horse hasn't even had a workout yet…nobody's lasted more than two jumps."

C.R. knew he was telling the truth, not one man had lasted even two jumps on this big Roan. "Well then, let's just leave it where we're at." Then he reset the saddle and climbed aboard. He had been on the back of a lot of horses in the last ten plus years of riding bucking horses, but he couldn't remember one quite this big, with the power he knew this one had. He had seen all those men before him go flying in every which direction. "Well hell," he thought to himself, "this horse wasn't going to wait forever."

"LETS GO BOYS," C.R. yelled out and when they threw the gate open C.R. came down from first jump in perfect position, he even had his spurs buried deep into the Roan's front shoulder's, they call it " marking him out. " By the third jump C.R. was feeling real good about himself and the situation. It was like he was sitting in a rocking chair just waiting for the whistle to blow. When all of a sudden that Roan came down and from out of nowhere he spun his ass around, doing a complete two seventy sending C.R. flying sideways off him, over the corral fence and into the crowd. "Holy Shit!" C.R. shouted out. Lying

259

on top of everybody, he started thinking to himself, that horse had more power and more moves than any horse he had ever seen before.

Larry started hollering, jumping up and down and ran across the arena to the Roan shouting, "I TOLD YA, I TOLD YA; I knew he could do it!" But then he remembered he still had to ride the Roan out of the corral or everyone got his money back. "Easy big boy," Larry was saying, walking up and picking up the rein. Then he reached up and unhooked the flank strap, still talking to the Roan. Actually he was apologizing to him. Then he picked up the stirrup. He slowly but firmly gave a big pull on the cinch. You be real nice and let me ride you out of here, I'll give you a big bucket of oats. Still calmly talking to the Roan the entire time. Then he put his foot into the stirrup and climbed aboard.

He could feel the Roan tense up underneath him. Still talking to him, "Easy big boy, it's just me." 'Boy I sure wish I had a second rein,' he thought to himself. When all of sudden the Roan came into a full rear, making Larry almost have to stand straight up and down in the stirrups, as if he was on the ground and standing straight up, making him have to grab a handful of mane to stay on. The Roan came down and took two giant crow hops. The bottoms of his hooves were still five plus feet off the ground with each crow hop; then, he took off running around the arena. Larry was waving his hat and shouting out telling everyone just how great his mighty Roan was, at the same time. After he and the Roan had gone around the arena a couple of times, he finally pulled up on the rein when he reached Gary, Butch, and the rest.

"I TOLD YA, I TOLD YA," he said, still hollering. "So how much money did we make Gary? And where's my bottle of whiskey?

"I don't know," Gary answered smiling and looking around at everyone with his hands full of money. "I don't know yet but I bet it's at least fifteen to twenty thousand."

Looking over at the young lady who had been keeping them in beer all afternoon, Larry hollered, "Throw me up that bottle." Looking over at Gary, "My jobs done for today, now it's party time." "You bet Larry," she hollered back, "Just what is it you need?"

Chapter Eleven

"Well, we can't go there just yet, but I need a bottle of whiskey and a beer. Hell, make that a pitcher of beer and bring it over to the Livery stable…I need to go brush down and grain my champion horse here." Turning back to Gary, Larry looked at him, taking his hat off, he scratched his head, "I thought C.R. was going to make it."

"The hell you say," Randy said. "I told you, that horse has HEART and A WILD SPIRIT; he was just setting him up is all." Turning towards Sundance, "Didn't I say when we were taking those last bets, that he'd only last four, maybe five jumps before that Roan threw him a curveball and would send him flying?"

"YEP, that you did, Randy," Sundance said. "In fact because of that bet with the Sheriff, why that old fart now owes us two hundred dollars."

"So how much did you figure you guys got back off him"" Larry asked. "I mean all three thousand?"

"Like I said, he still owes us two hundred over the three thousand," Sundance said. "Claims he has the money back in his office."

"Well, you just make sure he pays up," Randy said looking at Sundance, "And don't forget my gift to him tonight either."

"Well, hell boys," Gary shouted out. "Let's let Larry take care of his horse and we'll go play some cards."

"We playing with real money tonight?" Butch asked smiling.

"Hell no," Larry shouted. "That money is for our ranch, I don't want you even buying a round of drinks Gary, not until me and this young lady get back from the barn."

"Oh come on," Sundance said. "YOU, a WOMAN, and a BOTTLE OF WHISKEY… Hell that could be a couple hours."

Looking over at the young lady who already had everything Larry had requested, he stepped down out of the saddle, putting his arm around her, "You know Sundance, you just might be right. Little darling, why don't you just follow me and we'll go to the barn?" Turning back to everyone one last time, "SEE YA!"

CHAPTER TWELVE

Wapiti had been lying in his bed watching the sunlight come up over the mountaintops, thinking to himself what today would bring. Did Cathey really like him or was she just leading him on? She sure seemed to be a real nice lady. She had said she just turned seventeen, he was almost twenty. Most young men his age back at the settlement, and even hers age, heck they were already married. But more importantly right now was someone going to try and see just how far they could push him into another fight.

He was glad to be around the people and learn how to treat each different situation. But it sure would also be nice to get back out on the trail. He wondered about Sumpter and what it was going to be like. A real mining boomtown, he heard there were almost nine thousand people over there. John Day was big, at least two thousand people. Just how much bigger in size was it going to be and how did they all live?

Just then there was a knock on the door. "Wait just a minute," Wapiti hollered as he started crawling out of bed. He wasn't sure how long he'd been lying there daydreaming but it was daylight outside. The door opened up as he was halfway pulling his pants up. It was Cathey with a pot of coffee and washing water. Closing the door behind her she started walking over to the table. "CATHEY," Wapiti yelled out. "I'm not even dressed yet."

"Don't worry, Wapiti," Cathey said smiling. "I've seen my brother and dad and uncles in their pj's before."

Chapter Twelve

"Yeah, but if someone sees you here, they'll hang me!" Wapiti told her, pulling his pants on.

"Oh don't worry about it," Cathey said. "There's nobody downstairs yet. We don't open until seven on Sunday's."

"Well, what about all those people in the rooms up here?" Wapiti said with his eyes wide open. "They all know what room that Deputy Indian Marshal is in. SHIT…just one of them sees you in here with the door closed…I'm dead," he said in a serious but quiet voice.

"So why'd you want to be a lawman, Wapiti?" Cathey asked, pouring them two cups of coffee and handed one to him.

"Because I want everyone to be protected by the law, not just the white man," Wapiti answered. "Thanks for the coffee," taking the cup from her,

"Well, couldn't you do that just about anywhere?" Cathey asked. Sitting down on the edge of the bed, which made Wapiti feel even more uneasier.

"Not really," Wapiti answered. "Well, I guess I could, but it's the Marshal. He's the one making it possible. You think any white sheriff would ever hire me? Also, the Marshal can teach me a lot more. Like how to handle myself in a crowed room with people who don't want a damned Indian as a lawman to begin with. But most of all…teach me how and when to use my gun," he turned and pointed at it. "Right now with this big gun people think twice, but what if I'm wearing my pistol? I need to know how to shoot, fast and straight. Marshal says I'll get faster with practice."

"You are right about one thing," Cathey said. "No white Sheriff around here would hire an Indian for a deputy. Well, wash up and come down for breakfast," she said, standing up. Then she walked over and gave him another kiss on the cheek. With that she turned and walked towards the door. "Just how would you like your eggs this morning?" She asked, opening the door and looking back at Wapiti, with that big beautiful smile of hers.

"Hard, please," Wapiti answered. He wasn't sure just how long he'd been staring at her smile. She had a smile that was all her own, no other woman had that smile. Wapiti was thinking to himself as Cathey

263

turned and walked out the door. Wapiti walked over to the wash basin and filled it with water, smiling from ear to ear.

Maybe she really did like him; he sure did like her. But she lived here in John Day and the Marshal was based out of Prineville, which was one hundred and thirty miles away. Well, if the Great Spirit wanted it to happen, then it will happen. If not, then not…Splashing water on his face he stood up and looked in the mirror. Just what did the Great Spirit have planned for him in his life…? Would he be a good lawman or a short lived one? Turning around he picked up his shirt and started putting it on, the whole time thinking to himself about what might happen. One thing for sure, he wasn't going to find out until it did happen.

Strapping on his gun he walked over to the door, tying his hair behind his head. He walked out the door and down the hallway to the stairs. He could hear some voices from downstairs. Did anyone know that Cathey had been up to his room? He sure hoped not. Only one of the double doors between the saloon and the restaurant were open as Wapiti walked in. Just like every other time he walked into a room everyone stopped talking and all eyes were on him. Slowly he looked around the room; just then Sheriff Beyer walked in. They both acknowledged each other and sat down at the same table. This made Wapiti feel a little more at ease. The two had barely sit down when Cathey was pouring each a morning cup of coffee and putting Wapiti's breakfast down in front of him.

"Good morning, Sheriff," Cathey said, filling his coffee.

Wapiti could hear the men sitting just behind him talking. The things they were saying and making smart-ass remarks about him, they were talking loud enough for everyone to hear. "What makes him so special that he's the first one served?" one of them stated loud enough for everyone to hear. He was quite sure they didn't want Cathey being with him.

"Will you just look at that fellas?" one hollered. "Cathey is showing that filthy Red Skin more attention than anyone else."

"White girls have no right to be with no stinking Indian," another one said.

Chapter Twelve

"Don't listen to them Wapiti," Cathey said. Looking down at him with that big beautiful smile. "They're just a bunch of guys who are really NOBODIES trying to act big and mean, when they are really just being stupid," She said staring at them. "Sheriff, what is it I can get you for breakfast?"

"What Wapiti's having is fine with me," the Sheriff answered. "Only make my eggs over medium."

"Right away, Sheriff." Cathey leaned down and gave Wapiti another kiss, but this time it was on the lips. Standing up and looking around the restaurant which was already three-quarters full. "Just to let you all know, I will talk to, and be with, and kiss anyone I want to, when I want to, and if you don't like it then you had better just go eat someplace else." Then she turned and walked back towards the kitchen.

"Sounds like that young lady speaks her mind," Dennis said with a big smile on his face. "And she's not afraid to let everyone know it."

"You're right," Wapiti said to the Sheriff. Watching her walk away. "But I think she's going to get me into trouble with all these white eyes here."

"Don't let it worry you too much," Dennis said. "You'll find out most of them are all talk. Just as soon as you put your foot down they'll back off."

"I sure hope you're right," Wapiti said, looking around the room. "I just wonder how many more I'm going to have to fight before they leave me alone."

"Well, I'll tell ya Wapiti it's not going to be easy for a while," Dennis said. "But you stick with the Marshal and people will get to know your name real soon. They'll start to hear about just how good you are with your hands and feet; they'll slowly back off. But remember you will always have the one that won't. That's the one you're going to have to be able to tell who he is, so that you'll be ready for him ahead of time. It'll be easy to tell which ones will and which ones won't back down. In other words, soon you'll know which ones to worry about and which ones not to."

The two set there and ate their breakfast. The table of four young men behind Wapiti was still talking shit about him. Wapiti didn't want

265

people to think that he was easily provoked into a fight, so he just tried to ignore them. But after about forty five minutes of it Wapiti had heard all he wanted to hear because the rest of the people in the room were goading them on.

"ALRIGHT," Wapiti said. Standing up and turning around to the table. "Any time any or all of you want to start a fight you just let me know…I will be more than glad to extend the offer to anyone else as well." Looking directly down at the table of four men, "So, either put up or shut up. Do I make myself clear?"

When he had finished the entire room went quiet. Everyone was looking at this young buck Indian; he had already proved he could handle himself in a fistfight. Then they all looked at the table of four men then around the rest of the room. Was anyone going to take him up on his offer?

Then one of the men sitting at the table looked back up at Wapiti laughing, "Hell chief we're just funning with ya. You don't have to take everything so serious. Jeez," the man said. Turning back around to his buddies, "Just joking is all," talking loud enough for everyone to hear him.

Just then the Marshal came walking into the room. Looking around at everyone, he walked over to Wapiti and Dennis. "Sounds like I got here just in time to bust some heads…I like busting heads before breakfast," Shawn said. Sitting down at the table, and looking around the room. "But it really just sounds like a bunch of hot air," still looking around the room. "With no one willing to back it up." He turned back towards the young men at the table. Cathey was pouring him a cup of coffee, smiling at him. He had to admit it, her smile was like nothing he had ever seen before, and it sure lit that pretty face up as well.

"Well Marshal, What can I get you for breakfast?" Cathey asked him.

"Well young lady," Shawn said smiling at her. "I'll have steak and eggs, make my steak rare and my eggs over easy, please."

"Any way you want them Marshal," Cathey told him. Then she looked back over at Wapiti. "Can I get you anything else, Deputy?"

266

Chapter Twelve

"No thanks, Cathey," Wapiti said smiling at her. "I need to get all the chips out so the gamblers can get started."

Leaning back in his chair and pulling his pocket watch out Shawn looked at it, "Wapiti it's only...seven thirty. The games aren't supposed to start until nine o' clock. Why don't you sit back down for awhile?"

Standing up Wapiti looked down at the Marshal. "Well Marshal, I know that, but maybe some of them might show up early and want to get started."

"That's not a bad idea," Shawn answered. "But if I'm not in there you just remember my nine o' clock deadline, if they are one minute late, they're out. If they don't like it you just tell them to take it up with me."

"Yes sir, Marshal," Wapiti said. Turning and walking out of the restaurant and into the saloon. He could see the door to the office was open, which meant Cork was inside. Walking over he knocked on the door and stuck his head in, "Cork, you in here?"

"Yeah, come on in Wapiti," Cork answered.

Wapiti walked in the office, looking around the room real quick. He asked Cork where the bags of chips were.

"Right here Wapiti," Cork answered. Pulling open the bottom drawer of his desk. "Almost couldn't get them all in here. So what was all the commotion about in the restaurant?"

"Not much," Wapiti said, bending over and started picking up the bags of chips. "Just some guys talking out their ass's is all."

"I was thinking I was going to have to order even more tables and chairs," Cork said smiling at Wapiti. "That man down at the furniture store is glad to see me come in because that means I need to spend more money on furniture. You'd think he'd cut me a break, especially since I've already had to order at least a half dozen new chairs and three new tables since these games began. But I'll be damned if he will."

"Why should he? " Wapiti asked. "He has to make a living too. Do you give him money off your beer or whiskey or any of your ladies when he comes in here? Do ya?"

267

Marshal Shawn Felton and the Wild Bunch

"HELL NO," Cork snapped back. "That would be cutting my own throat; you have any idea how much money I would lose if I cut everyone a deal…Hell boy, what the hell you thinking of?"

Starting to chuckle, Wapiti looked over at Cork, "Don't you think he feels the same way about his merchandise?"

"Where did you learn so much about business?" Cork asked looking over at Wapiti with a smile on his face.

"Well Corky," looking him straight in the face. "My dad didn't raise no fool, and he taught me right from wrong. And a preacher lady at the settlement I lived in once told me, "God said to do onto others as you would have them do unto you."

"Didn't think you'd be able to quote the bible," Cork said with a serious look on his face.

"Pastor George and his wife Nancy not only taught us how to read, write, and speak English, they also taught us the ways and the laws of the white man. But mostly, the laws and the commandments of the Great Spirit, they called him God, and his son, the Lord Jesus Christ."

"WELL, don't you even try preaching to me," Cork answered. "If I wanted to be preached to I'd go to church," Cork said, starting to chuckle. "I think if I even got near the door to any church God would strike me down with a mighty bolt of lightning."

"Marshal says the same thing," Wapiti said. "Could you help me pack these bags of chips out? I don't want to have to make two trips. Someone just might try to steal a bag or two when I'm in between trips."

"Sure Wapiti," Cork answered. Reaching over, picking up an armload of bags. "Tell you the truth Wapiti; I'll be glad when this is all over with."

Walking towards the door, Wapiti turned towards Corky, "Why is that…? Shoot you're making a whole lot of money on this tournament. Not just in sales of alcohol and women, you started this tournament with over one hundred players. Each with a buy in of one thousand dollars, and you're only paying out fifty thousand to the ultimate winner. That makes you the biggest winner of all."

268

Chapter Twelve

"Well hell boy," Cork stated. "I may be mostly Polish but like you said my Dad didn't raise no fool, either. Why do you think I own my own bar?"

"I figured it was because you liked being a business man" Wapiti answered, as they walked to the bar.

"I do like the business, but as you also know, I also like to drink a lot of beer myself," Cork said.

"I have noticed that." Wapiti said, sitting his armload of bags on top of the bar. "You're the first man I've ever met that drinks beer with is breakfast."

"Now that's not true, I drink coffee with my breakfast, you're just not up yet, so you don't see me."

"Well, you weren't down here when I got down here this morning and I see you're already drinking a beer." Wapiti said smiling. A couple of players walked up and showed their tickets for their bags of chips.

"How many player do we have left?" Cork asked.

"Not real sure Cork," Wapiti answered. "Just a second and I'll tell ya." Then he started counting the bags. "With those three over there we have sixteen. It didn't take very long till everyone was coming up and getting his or her bag of chips.

There were two young ladies left in the game. One wore a fancy dress and the worst smelling perfume that Wapiti had ever smelled before. The other young lady who, from the beginning had always wore blue jeans and a long sleeve shirt, just like most of the men. But she definitely looked a whole lot better in those jeans than any man did. Cathey had told him that she was one of her Dad's sisters. He could see some family resemblance; they both had dark hair. But Denise's was a little darker. At least that's what Wapiti had thought Cathey told him, her name was. He really couldn't remember, fact was, he couldn't even remember most of what him and Cathey had talked about. He was just happy to be around her. She was the first lady he had ever met that he couldn't stop think-ing of, he didn't know why. He had just met her two days ago, but that really didn't matter to him. He had been handing out bags of chips but he didn't know for how long. He was still thinking of Cathey, all of a sudden he ran into the Marshal.

"You all right, son?" Shawn asked.

"Yeah, he's just fine Marshal," Cork said with a big smile on his face. "He's got Cathey on his mind... That's all he's been thinking of all morning."

Wapiti could feel his face starting to heat up. "I-I-I-I'm sorry Marshal," Wapiti said. Doing a quick count of the bags that were left. "We still have seven bags left, belonging to two different people."

Shawn pulled out his pocket watch; "Well it's only eight thirty... So they still have time. Now I know you like that young lady, and yes I know she likes you too son, but you have a job to do. You always have to pay attention to everything around you, because some of these men in here would take that daydreaming moment to deck you or shoot you." Putting his arm around Wapiti's shoulders Shawn couldn't help but smile. "I remember my first LUST...that's right I said lust, not love. That's all it is at first until you get to know each other better. I'll tell ya son...You say those two little words, and they totally change and want you to change too...Why that woman I was married to, hell she tried to tell me I couldn't have a beer all day or night with my friends anymore. She wanted me to work in a store all day and stay home all night. Well hell, I got to missing the open range and prairie,... and my beer. Let's just say she's back there with her store manager and I'm here with you fine people...And I might add, a whole lot happier."

"Oh Marshal, you get too carried away,' Wapiti said.

"You'll find out soon enough," Cork said chuckling. "I like my situation right here," Cork was pointing around the bar. "Because if it's her time of the month or she's in a bad mood, hell I'll just find me another lady. They don't seem to mind, so why should I?"

"What two little words you talking about Marshal?" Wapiti asked.

"I DO!" Both Cork and the Marshal answered at the same time," laughing, and then both started talking again at the same time. "You say those two little words and they think they own you from that point on.

"It can't be all that bad," Wapiti said. "If it is all that bad then why do so many people get married?"

270

Chapter Twelve

"Well son, I guess it just isn't for some of us lifetime bachelors," Cork said.

Just then a man who had the last bag of chips walked up to the bar, "Excuse me Marshal, can I please get my chips?"

Pulling out his watch and looking at it, "By golly it's five minutes before nine o' clock, and not one person was late." Then Shawn tossed him two bag's; "Good luck Young man."

"ALRIGHT," Shawn yelled out. "Now listen up, now that everyone is here the minimum bet is five hundred dollars. At noon it goes to a thousand. I want these games over early tonight."

"Marshal, that ain't fair, I only have twenty- one hundred and fifty dollars left," one man shouted out.

"Well sir," Shawn said, lighting up a cigar. "Looks like you're on your way out anyway. So why don't you just throw those chips in the pot and get out of the game? Hell you're not going to win anyway."

Knowing that the Marshal was right, the man stood up and picked up his chips, cursing a little bit as he threw his chips into the middle of the table and walked up to the bar, "Give me a bottle, please."

Then two more men stood up and threw their chips into the middle of the table; they too barely had enough for two maybe three bets if they were lucky.

"Well Wapiti, I think you can handle this for a while," Shawn said. "I need to go down to the Livery stable and make damn sure all our supplies were delivered yesterday...If not, I'm going looking for a store owner. You quit thinking about that young lady, and keep your mind on the job here at hand," Shawn said pointing. Then turning, he headed towards the door; he could hear some kind of commotion starting in the restaurant. But he didn't seem to pay it no never mind, he walked out of the saloon and onto the boardwalk.

He didn't like it; EVERYONE he walked by had to say good morning or hello. He couldn't remember ever being in a town so friendly. He could see most of the people out and about were on their way to church. He couldn't remember the last time he had been to church. He headed towards the Livery stable, still trying to remember the last time...Had to have been when he was still married. Boy that sure was

271

a long time ago, something like thirty or more years ago if a day. He knew one thing for sure; it was going to be nice to get the hell out of town and back on the trail. He still had a lot to teach Wapiti, before he knew it he was standing in front of the Livery stable. Opening the door he walked in and hollered out, "ANYONE HOME?"

"Back here, Marshal," Roy answered back. So Shawn just walked in the direction of the voice.

"So how's everything going over at the poker tournament?" Roy asked, shaking the Marshal's hand.

"Just fine, just fine," Shawn said. "Everything is going just fine Mr. Larkin."

"Roy, please Marshal, just call me Roy…So has my daughter been taking good care of you?" Roy asked.

"You mean Cathey?" Shawn asked smiling. "She's doing just fine, except she don't wake me up with a pot of coffee like she does my Deputy in the mornings."

"Speaking of young Wapiti," Roy said, "just what kind of man is he?"

"Well Roy, I'll tell ya," Shawn said, throwing his chest out. "He's got a good head on his shoulders; he's not one to jump to conclusions. Most importantly…He can handle himself real well with his hands and feet."

"I know that one is right," Roy answered with a small chuckle. "You just have to look at Jack and Sam for that, they'll be wearing those bruises for quite a while."

"Yes, they will," Shawn said, chuckling.

"So you think you could at least get young Wapiti to cut his hair?" Roy asked.

"Well Roy, his people believe that their hair is strong medicine, the longer and thicker it is, then the Great Spirit will give them more strength."

"Well, can't you tell him that's all nonsense?" Roy said. "Hell your hair has nothing to do with your strength.

"Well hell Roy, I know that," Shawn said. "But you know sometimes a man needs an edge out there, so I'll respect that and so will everyone else." Shawn answered in a very stern voice.

Chapter Twelve

"You're right Marshal", Roy said. "I can respect that. But to change the subject, what the hell you need with six more cases of pistol and four more cases of rifle ammo for? Are you planning to go to war with someone?"

"No, no," Shawn said. "That's for Wapiti. He needs his target practice…So while we're riding along I'll throw pine cone or a corn biscuit in the air and holler "PULL" at the same time…Then he has to pull his gun and shoot it out of the air. Well at least he tries to shoot them out of the air."

"That sounds like a fun way of teaching a young man how to shoot," Roy said. "But over at the mercantile, they sell a round piece of wood, about three inches in diameter, some are painted orange and some are white for night shooting. He calls them pigeons. You throw those in the air; you really never know just which direction it might take. Me and my brothers, nephews, son, and anyone else, who wants to join in on the fun, we'll get a couple bags for target practice. Then we find out just how good you really are from the draw."

"That sounds like fun," Shawn said with a big smile on his face. "You wouldn't know how to get a hold of the store owner would ya?"

"Lives right in the back of the store Marshal," Roy said. "I could get you a gunny sack of those to take with you. Heck, a whole bag doesn't weigh more than ten, maybe fifteen pounds at the most. I keep a bag at the house all the time. It gives us something to do and unwind, and it makes us just a little bit better shots at the same time, but practicing off the back of a horse, that's one I never thought of."

"I can't tell you how many times that I've had to shoot off my horse at a dead run," Shawn said. "Why I've had some battles where I put my reins between my teeth, my pistol in one hand and my rifle in the other."

"Now come on, Marshal. You sure you ain't stretching that just a little?" Roy asked.

"Well, a couple different groups of outlaws didn't think I could either. But I'm here, and well, they're not…!" Shawn answered proudly.

"If you'd like Marshal, I'll go over and pick you up a bag of pigeons," Roy said.

"Sure, why don't you do that Roy?" Shawn said. "That's if it's not too much trouble, or I could go over and get them myself."

"It's no trouble Marshal," Roy said. "I need to get a few things myself."

Shawn was leaning up against one of the stalls as they talked. Reaching in his pocket he pulled out his watch, "HOLY COW it's almost twelve o' clock. I hope Wapiti hasn't had any trouble. Either way I need to get back. You know Roy, why don't you come with me? I'll buy you lunch, that way you can meet Wapiti yourself."

Standing up, dropping the horse's foot that he had been reshoeing, he had a big smile on his face. "It might be nice to meet the lad, I like to surprise em', see just how they'll react the first time." Roy said, smiling.

"I think the word you're looking for, is squirm, isn't it?" Shawn asked.

"Now that you mention it…Yep…. See Marshal, I have four daughters. It's really fun meeting those boys for the first time, it's even better when you're cleaning your gun. Starting to chuckle, "Yeah, let's go to lunch." They walked towards the door; let me grab my out to lunch sign."

They started walking up the street. Roy looked back over at the Marshal, making a muscle with his right arm, which was at least twenty inches plus around in diameter. Hell Shawn thought to himself those arms are bigger than mine and rock solid, definitely not a set of arms you would want to let get a hold of you. They would probably crush every bone in your body. But now that Shawn took a second look at Roy, he could see that for a man that was at least in his late-forty's, he was bigger and stronger than most men half his age, he didn't look like he had any fat on him either.

"I like to arm wrestle the boys the first time I meet them," Roy said smiling.

"Do you ever lose?" Shawn asked, smiling. "Those are just about the biggest arms I've ever seen."

"Nope, not too often," Roy said. "But I have a nephew who logs over around Sumpter, you go over there, I'll guarantee you will see

Chapter Twelve

his work. He runs a team of six Clydesdales, skidding logs. He's just a short shit, but boy he flat hurts people. Damn good kid, don't get me wrong Marshal, he's a good man. Help anyone anytime and only ask for two little words in return…Thank you. But that young man has a temper, and he hurts people. The bigger they are the better he likes em'. He hangs out with his two younger brothers who are identical twins, and I do mean identical. I have no idea how even their mother tells them apart."

"So he likes to fight a little?" Shawn said. "What's wrong with that? Hell even I like to raise a little hell now and then."

"NOOO…He don't go looking for trouble, it always comes to him voluntarily. I'll tell you Marshal; his eyes turn fiery red. Like the gates of hell just opened up. Fact I don't even think he realizes just how bad he hurts people. The only ones that can get him to settle down are those two twins. If they're not around; you'd better make damn sure you have at least five or six BIG men to sit on him until he cools down. If you try it alone, well, he'll throw you off and send you flying into and through the wall, just like he was throwing a piece of fire wood. Then you also had better hope he's not finished with the first man he's working on, cause if he is, then he'll be coming after you, then you and everyone else involved will be going to the Doctor. Then you better hope he's a good Doctor." Roy said, sounding real serious.

"Well, when we get there I'll just have to look him up," Shawn said.

"They won't be hard to find Marshal," Roy said. "Just listen to which saloon all the commotion is coming from."

"So he likes to drink and cause trouble, huh?" Shawn asked.

"Nope, fact I don't think he even drink that much at all. But he stutters a little, and men make fun of him…that's all it takes." Roy answered.

They walked and talked all the way to the saloon. Shawn still had to say "HI" to everyone they passed. "Roy, what is it with people in this town? EVERYONE and I do mean everyone I walk by has to say hello." Looking around and leaning over so he didn't have to speak too loud, "What's up with that?"

275

"Hell Marshal, you're the great Marshal Shawn Felton. You're known for bringing them in lying over the saddle, not sitting up." Roy answered, "they're all afraid of you."

"Well now Roy, they all make that decision for me. The moment they pull out that gun." Shawn said. "If you pull it, you had damn sure be ready to use it."

"I hear ya Marshal," Roy said. "A gun is not a toy, you pull it you better know how to use it. And you better not hesitate."

As they got closer to the saloon; they could hear the crowd of people hollering. You could tell by the cheers that they were egging someone on. But Shawn wasn't too worried, because the noise was coming from the restaurant area. Yet as they got closer they could hear Cathey hollering for someone to leave her alone.

Walking through the front door, Shawn could see it was the same four young men from breakfast. Most everyone in the restaurant and saloon were all standing up and moving around so more people could get in and see what was going on. Just as Shawn started to speak up he saw Wapiti come in from the saloon. He went right up to the four men, reaching out he caught Cathey's arm, "Cathey, why don't you go in the back?"

"You want this to stop Chief, take that gun off…And we'll show you why white people and you red skins should keep to our own people and not mix." The man said angrily.

"No problem," Wapiti said. "You boys take your guns off and I'll do the same."

"No problem," all four said, unbuckling their holsters and laid them on the table. "You think you can take all four of us Chief? " One of the men shouted. "We're going to make you think twice about this," another one said. "First, for you wanting to be with a white woman, and second for thinking an Indian will ever be a law man. Now you take off that shotgun boy…And we'll be glad to teach you some manners."

Looking the four over, Wapiti walked over to them and laid his gun on the table. He quickly grabbed the closest man by the back of his head with both hands, smashing his face into one of those ten by

Chapter Twelve

ten woods beams that he had seen the Marshal use earlier. Smashing the man's nose and sending blood and teeth flying around the room, the man fell limp to the floor. Turning around just in time to duck under a flying fist, he brought his own fist up into the man's stomach, bringing him a couple feet up off the floor, taking all the air out of him. He grabbed him by the back of the head and brought his knee up and drove the man's face into it at the same time. Again sending more blood flying.

All of a sudden he felt a blow to the side of his head, turning to face the man, he stepped back a little, and the man threw his next blow into Wapiti's stomach. Not really doing much harm. Seeing the fourth man coming at him, Wapiti quickly stepped aside. Fully turned around to get as much speed as he could, he brought his leg up and his foot into the man's head. That sent him flying backwards over a chair and crashing down onto a table. Feeling yet another blow in his side, out of the corner of his eye, Wapiti saw the man behind him, real close. Throwing his right elbow back as hard as he could, he caught the man just under the chin, sending him back a couple of steps. Wapiti turned, then reached out and grabbed the man by the shirt, pulling him back to him with one arm and smashing his fist into the man's face with the other. Only this time he didn't let go of the man. He smashed his fist into his face four, maybe five times.

All of a sudden a pistol fired out and a man screamed. Dropping the man on the floor Wapiti turned as quickly as he could. Just behind him on the floor a man was holding his hand and screaming from the bullet hole in the middle of it.

"NOW, I DIDN'T MISS," Shawn said looking down at the young man. "I can't stand a back shooter." Shawn had sternness in his voice. The man and everyone else just listened to what he was saying. "I'll tell you son, I NEVER give a man a second chance. But in your case I made an exception...DON'T MAKE ME REGRET IT...Now the funs over with," waving his pistol around the room. "Now you boys just leave your guns here for now. You can pick them up tomorrow at the Sheriff's office. I don't want you boys getting drunk later, and thinking you're even bigger and badder than you really are from all the whiskey and beer you might drink. Let's just say, this way I won't have to kill one of you later. AND IF YOU DO come back…You damn sure better not bring a gun, understood gentlemen?" Shawn said, watching the four men climbed up off the floor to their feet. Each one hearing just what the Marshal had said, but they were looking at each other and back at Wapiti. Only one of them had gotten to hit him with a decent blow, it had been four to one, and the one kicked the fours asses.

A moment ago everyone in the restaurant and the saloon were cheering the four men. Now, the place was totally quiet. There were a few men talking, but they were talking in low voices Wapiti couldn't help but hear a couple of the guys close to him.

"Did you see that? Shit, it was four to one," the man said.

"Yeah," said another man. "Them men hardly laid a hand on that young buck."

Another man speaks up, "Counting these four, that makes eight scalps he could have taken this weekend."

Slowly everyone started walking away, going back to what they were doing beforehand. None of them wanted Wapiti to see their faces, because there was fear in some of them and rightly so. That young man had more than proved he could take care of himself.

Cathey came running up to Wapiti; she picked up a towel to wipe the blood out of the corner of his mouth. "Are you alright?"

"I'm fine," Wapiti answered. Looking around the room he could see that everyone was walking away.

"HOLD IT JUST ONE MINUTE," Wapiti yelled out. "Now maybe some of you think that me and Cathey shouldn't be together, Indian and white. Well, anymore of you want to do something about it, step up now or stay the hell out of my way. Because of that dip shit there," pointing at the man with the hole in his hand. "Because of him, this gun will never again leave my side. I'll still welcome any of you who think you can take me. But this gun will always be ready for back shooters. DO I MAKE MYSELF CLEAR?"

Everyone started agreeing with him as they backed away slowly. Some looking back at him, he didn't seem to be afraid of anything, at least when it came to fighting three or four men at a time. If he ever

Chapter Twelve

got half as fast with a pistol as he was with his fists and feet, there wouldn't be anyone, at least anyone in this town that could beat him and they all knew it.

After Wapiti had finished his speech Roy looked over at Shawn, "Never thought I'd see an Indian law man, but I think I'm about to meet my first."

Shawn stood back and looked at the situation, Roy and Gordy were both right, times were changing. By the grace of God there would be an Indian lawman...and God had seen to it that it would be up to him to bring Wapiti along and make a good lawman out of him. Shawn looked up and thought, 'He's a good man Lord, please just keep me around long enough to teach him as much as I can. He calls you the Great Spirit...I call you are Heavenly Father...you're both the same one. Looking up one more time, Shawn added one more thought, thanks for the opportunity, now just give me the time to teach and guide him, please Lord! Making the cross of trinity crossed his head and chest. Amen Dear Heavenly Father, Amen.'

Shawn walked over and patted Wapiti on the back. "Wapiti I'd like you to meet Roy Larkin, Cathey's dad."

Holding out his hand, they shook hands, "It's a pleasure to meet you, Sir," Wapiti said checking out the size of Roy's arms.

"Pleasure is all mine, Son," Roy said. "I was telling the Marshal on the way over here how I like to intimidate a young man, the first time I meet them, least ways the one's that might want to date one of my daughters. But I see I wouldn't intimidate you much."

"Dad, would you mind if Wapiti came over for dinner tonight?" Cathey asked, with a big smile on her face. "I mean, he's leaving in the morning, and..."

"Yes Cathey," Roy said holding up his hand. "The young man is more than welcome."

"You too, Marshal," Cathey said. "Dinner will be around six o clock."

"Well young lady," Shawn said. Tipping his hat to her, "I do appreciate the offer, but I'm afraid one of us has to be here until the games are over with."

279

"Well then Marshal," Cathey said still smiling. "If you don't make it, I will make sure to bring you a big helping of food."

"Much appreciated young lady, much appreciated," Shawn said. "Well now why don't you two go to lunch? I'll take over the games for now."

"Thanks Marshal," Wapiti said. Then he and Cathey walked over and sat down at a table.

"Marshal," Roy said. "I think I'll just get me something to go for lunch. I still have a lot of work to do yet," shaking the Marshal's hand, Roy turned and walked away. Shawn turned and walked back into the saloon.

"Alright everyone, listen up, the minimum bet just went to One Thousand dollars. So if you have less than a couple thousand dollars just throw it in the middle and get out."

Two men stood up, cursing a little as they literally did throw their chips into the middle of the table and turned and walked away. Their hopes of winning that fifty thousand dollars were gone.

"Now, it looks like we're down to nine people," Shawn said. "So let's get on with it. I have a dinner engagement I'd like to make." Looking back into the restaurant, he could see Wapiti and Cathey sitting at a table talking. Shawn turned and walked back up to the bar. "You know Cork," Shawn said, pointing his thumb back towards the two young lovebirds. "It's a good thing we're leaving town tomorrow or that boy would be married inside a week. Charlie, how about a beer?"

"I think you're right Marshal," Cork answers chuckling. "And you're right. IT'S LUST, but they don't know that yet."

"Well hell Cork," Shawn said, looking down the bar at all the patrons. "We all need that in ours lives at least once."

All of a sudden Shawn looked down the bar and saw a young man who quickly turned his head when he noticed the Marshal looking at him. "Just a minute Cork, I'll be right back." Reaching over he picked up his beer and started walking towards the young man. Walking up behind him, the man tried to hide his face. Reaching over Shawn put his hand on the young man's shoulder, turning him around. "Well now young fellow, just why are you trying to hide?" Then he got a second

Chapter Twelve

look at just who it was. "FLOYD?" Shawn said with excitement in his voice. "Floyd Larkin, Just what the hell are you doing...? You're supposed to be in jail."

Leaning back in his chair and taking a pull off his beer, Floyd held up a wooden key. With a shit-eating grin on his face he looked at the Marshal, "I told you I wasn't going to be in there much longer, didn't I?"

Taking a quick look around the room, Shawn looked back at Floyd. "What the hell are you doing here? What if the Sheriff was here? Better yet, THE JUDGE? Why your ass would be up in that county lockup for the rest of your time. Here give me that." Shawn said taking the wooden key out of Floyd's hand. Looking at it, "Damn, good job, I must say."

"Oh hell," Floyd said laughing, taking another pull off his beer. "I could have been out two weeks ago...but the first key I made broke on me."

"What the hell are you doing here?" Shawn asked again with excitement still in his voice, but in a low voice, so as not to be heard by anyone else. "Don't you think you better get your ass out of town?"

"Don't have any money," Floyd said holding up his beer. "Hell, Charlie bought this for me."

Reaching into his pants pocket, and then up into his vest pouch, Shawn pulled out his wallet. Opening it up, he pulled out a couple hundred dollars. "Here take this. Go over to the Livery, I'm sure your brother will have a cheap horse you can buy off him. Then you get the hell out of town. I'll talk with the Sheriff and the Judge for you. Now get the hell out of here."

"Just let me have one more beer first," Floyd said.

"You really do want to go back to jail don't you...? You'd better get that beer to go Mr.... Better yet, Charlie," Shawn hollered. "Give me a bottle please."

"Sure thing Marshal," Charlie handed him a bottle of whiskey and a shot glass.

"Don't need the glass, Charlie," Shawn told him. Then he handed Floyd the bottle.

"Take this and get the hell out of town,"

"Just let me finish my beer first," Floyd said, taking a drink.

"I don't believe you Young man," Shawn said. Helping Floyd up off his barstool, taking him towards the back office. "Now you get out of here, and get the hell out of town. Stay off the main streets and work your way to the Livery." Opening the back door Shawn tossed Floyd out. Kicking him in the ass at the same time. "I'll try and talk the judge out of putting any paper on you, NOW GET OUT OF HERE." Shawn closed and locked the door and returned to the bar.

Walking back in, he ordered himself another beer. Shawn looked over at Cork, "You believe that Young man? In jail on what I'd say are trumped up charges, but then he breaks out of jail…And comes to the bar instead of getting out of town."

"Some of those Larkin boys aren't too bright," Cork answered. "But I got to tell ya Marshal, I think I'd head for the nearest bar and beer myself. But, just like you said…I'd get that beer to go. Hell, I'm almost a full blood Pollock and I ain't that stupid. Also every Sunday the Judge and his wife have a big fight because he didn't go to church or if he did make it to church, but he fell asleep and started snoring again. Either way he should be getting here in just a little while, usually around three isn't it Charlie?"

Just then one of the players hollered out, standing up, he threw his cards on the table, "DAMMIT! Bet everything I had on damn aces and eight's, now I know why they call it a dead mans hand. SHIT…" He picked up his chips, counted them out, "A measly eight hundred left. I can't believe it. Lady, I don't know who taught you to play poker," looking at Denise. "Everyone has some kind of twitch or move to let you know if they're bluffing, but I swear your face never changes." Tossing his money into the middle of the table, "That goes into the next pot Denise, if you want it; you're going to have to win it." Then tipping his hat to her, he walked out the door.

CHAPTER THIRTEEN

Gary looked down at all the money in his hands. Then looking at everyone else's hands and pockets, Randy, Luis, the three Doss brothers and
all three of the Outlaws had money sticking out everywhere. That Roan
had made them more damn money than any of them could have ever
imagined. Gary looked over and saw Larry walking away, leading the
Roan and a little Betty under his arm. "The hell with Larry," Gary said.

"Will you check this out? Just look at all this damn money we just
made. Hell, this was more fun than robbing any bank, isn't it Butch"…?
Sundance asked

"Sure the hell was," said Butch. "A whole hell of a lot more fun!"
Looking over at Sundance…"Let's not let that fat ass Sheriff off with
that extra two hundred he owes us."

"Don't worry about him," Randy said looking over at the other
two outlaws. "Don't even worry about that fat ass Sheriff; you might
say I gave Sundance here a present for him. So you make damn sure
he doesn't forget it."

"What is it?" Butch asked…

"Oh no," said Randy. "That way you won't forget to ask him about
it later, cause you won't want to miss it…Will he Curry?"

"No you won't Butch," Curry said. "Randy, he gave…"

"Shut up, Curry," Randy said, with a glare in his eyes that sent a
shiver up Curry's spine. "He'll find out later. This way he won't forget
to ask about it before you all leave."

Holding up his hands and taking three big steps back, "Sorry Randy," Curry said. "It's really a rotten situation, if you know what I mean," he cracked a small smile hoping to calm Randy down.

Gary looked over at everyone again; "Did you hear Larry? He said I couldn't buy a round until he gets back. Well the hell with him, he just went into the hay loft with that little Betty, he's definitely going to be a while and I'm thirsty. It's time to party. He's right about one thing; this money is for our ranch. Sorry boys but I'm only playing with chips again…Let's go, first two rounds are on me and Larry. That's the least Larry can do, after all you put up the money to start with."

"Randy, here's that three hundred I owe you," Butch said, handing him the money.

"What's this for?" Randy asked looking at the money.

"We said one hundred dollars a jump. Remember?" Butch said rubbing his chest.

"Then here," Randy said, handing him back fifty. "I figure you were on him for at least a half a jump." Then slapping him on the back. "Why don't you men let me buy you at least one round before you leave our fair city? You're going to be even richer than you are now, then."

"LET'S GO," Gary said to all the rest and started walking across and up the street to the Elk Horn Saloon and Brothel. All nine of them walked into the saloon, moving the chairs and pulling three tables together, they all set down. Still laughing and cheering about the last two and a half hours, Butch pulled out his pocket watch, it was just about seven o clock, and everyone had to be in position well ahead of time.

"All you gentlemen coming with us tonight had better order something to eat," Butch suggested. "It's going to be a long night." Which he knew everyone else already knew, because they were all ordering rare steaks and coffee, not alcohol.

"So you boys going to be off to the big city after tonight?" Randy asked.

"Yeah…sure am Randy," Butch answered. "Ever been to a big city Randy?"

Chapter Thirteen

"Went down to Portland once," Randy answered. "Couldn't believe it, that city has over fifty thousand people, and all those tall buildings... No thanks, I'll stay here."

"Fifty thousand," Sundance busted up laughing. "Shit that's nothing. You should go to New York City. There are five main Burgh's, last time I was out there, they said there was over a million and a half people lived in and around that city."

"Oh bullshit," Gary spoke up. "Now, who's telling bullshit stories?"

"No, no," Butch said. "He's not telling no bullshit stories."

"There are five main Burgh's to the city," Sundance said. "Shit, at least two of those Burghs," looking around at the others to see who was listening. "If you're a white boy, YOU DO NOT WANT to go there alone. Hell, you'd think you're in Africa. Literally hundreds of thousands of black people and some of them don't want any white boy's around."

"Oh really?" Randy said. "I seen my first black man two...maybe three years ago. Him and his wife came in on one of the wagon trains, seemed like a real nice fellow." He was a black smith, dam good one to. They were low on money, said he'd shoe my team for half the normal price. But, when he finished, I paid him twice as much. He did that good of a job."

"Didn't say they weren't nice people," Sundance said. "But you go into a city of nothing but them blackies and you'll soon find out your white ass ain't welcome."

"I don't care," Randy said. "It still wasn't right for those people back there to own them like they were livestock, to sell and trade any time they wanted."

"Don't get me wrong," Sundance said smiling. "Growing up we had an old black family down the street. The grandfather told us them slave owners had sex with the young black girls all the time. When the baby was born they'd either kill it or sold it right out to another slave owner so no one knew. There are a lot of those young ladies now, they were re-bred by even more white men, heck, they look like they just have a good tan, you can't tell the difference."

"That just isn't right, "Gary said. "I don't care what anyone said, those people should be treated no different than you or me."

"Not to change the subject or anything," Randy said. "But how the hell would they build houses for a million people? There isn't enough land to build all those houses."

"Hell, they have buildings out there thirty, forty floors high," Sundance said.

"You're not joking are you?" Randy asked, finishing his dinner and taking a big bite of chewing tobacco.

"No I'm not Randy," Sundance said. "Why do you think I came out west? There were just too many people. Don't get me wrong, I like the things the big city has to offer. But I still like the smaller towns," starting to chuckle. "Fact if I ever get me enough money to retire, I wouldn't mind a town like Baker City."

"Hell, just how much money do you need?" Randy asked. Looking at all three outlaws, "I mean hell, you're going to make one hell of a haul out of here tonight."

Just then the sheriff walked up and sat down at the table between Butch and Sundance. "Sorry I don't have that two hundred I owe you boys, but I was thinking that since they didn't ship any gold last week… Well, let's just say there will be more gold than you boys will be able to haul. So, how about I slow things down even a little more than I planned? I can take longer just getting the posse to the train, wherever down river you boys stop it. How about you boys give me a few more thousand and I'll tell you what time she's pulling out in the morning," still looking back and forth between the two. "That way you won't have to get up real early and get to where you need to be. Like maybe the narrows, just a couple miles below the dredges? Or, looking back around the table at everyone else. "That is unless these men here told you a better spot."

"What the hell are you talking about Sheriff?" Gary asked. "Whatever these men are or are not up to, let's get one thing very clear; we have nothing to do with it. We just made a shit load of money on a bucking horse and as far as I know that's all these men are up to as well. Hell, They put up the money to begin with."

Chapter Thirteen

"Now look Mr. Parker or Cassidy, whichever you want to go by, I really don't care but we made a deal last night," the Sheriff said. "But..."

"That's right we did," Butch said. Lighting up his cigar. "If I remember, we paid you three thousand dollars for the very same thing you're asking us about again...I don't know Sheriff."

"Look Butch," the Sheriff said. "You know damn good and well you got all that money back from me today in the bucking competition."

"Alright," Sundance said smiling. "Guess you could still turn us over for the reward," winking his eye at everyone. "Here," reaching in his pocket and pulling out a wad of money, unrolling it. Sundance counted out fifteen hundred dollars, "Catch up with me a little later and I'll give you the other fifteen, alright Sheriff?"

"Sure thing Mr. Sundance," the Sheriff answered. "I have a quick job I have to go do in about an hour, so I'll look for you boys when I get back."

"What kind of job?" Randy asked smiling at him.

"Uhhh...I have to feed and check the prisoners over at the jail, is all," the Sheriff said to them. Then standing up, he turned and walked away.

Toad looked down at his watch, "Well, gentlemen it's time for me and Goof to get going." Looking down at Curry, then back at everyone else. "It's going to take some time getting eight mules packed up and ready to move with all that weight. They keep their empty grain bags over there, so we'll grab a couple bundles of those to hide everything in."

"Alright," Butch said. "You boys don't come in until I whistle twice. If I only whistle once, then something's wrong, you boys just hold back in the timber and out of sight."

"No problem, Butch," Toad answered. "I know where they keep two lookouts; one is on this side of the street, between the buildings. The other is in the loft over at the Livery. We'll leave him for you to get."

"Sounds good," Sundance said. "But you make sure you bring him with you, that way we can tie them all up together, then we'll know just exactly where everyone is."

"Sure thing," Toad said, looking down at the Larkin boys. "Well guys, if everything works out we'll see you in a couple weeks," Then the Doss brothers turned and walked out the door.

Two men walked up and stood in front of Randy. One look, and it was obvious he was the man from Friday night. His cheekbones still swollen up so bad, the man could hardly see. Randy couldn't help it he busted up laughing. "Are you having a hard time seeing anything? Maybe drinking or eating too?"

"You telling me this little man did that to you?" The big man said. The man from Friday night was big, but this character was even bigger. Not only taller by a good three, four inches but also twenty plus pounds heavier, all muscle.

Curry leaned over to Sundance, in a low voice; "Randy did that to that man...? Hell he's at least twice if not three times bigger than he is."

"Shut up," Sundance said whispering, and holding his hand up. "Just sit and watch."

The big man looked down at Randy, "Well little man, let's just see how tough you really are."

"Sure," Randy said, with a big smile on his face. "What did you have in mind?"

The big man took his coat off and handed it over to his friend, the one with the smashed face. Rolling up his sleeves, he sat down in Goof's old chair right beside Randy.

"Ooohhh," Randy said chuckling. "Look out boys, he's rolling up his sleeves, am I supposed to be scared."

"You sure have a big mouth for such a little man," the big man said. Putting his elbow on the table. "Why don't we arm-wrestle here and we'll just see how tough you really are?" He took his other hand and slapped Randy on the back of the head. Randy's eyes started to open up and turn hell fire red.

"Alright a-hole," Randy said, putting his arm on the table. "I don't know just what you think this is going to prove, but I'll play along." Randy looked at everyone sitting at the table, reaching over he grabbed the big man's hand and put his elbow on the table. Randy's hand almost disappeared inside the big mans hand. His arm was barely half as long

288

Chapter Thirteen

to. "You just say when, whenever you're ready that is," Randy said still holding his beer in his other hand.

"NOW," the man said, starting to pull with all his might, but Randy just sat there like nothing at all was going on. Fact he started to laugh, taking a drink off his beer. "OOOHHH, this guy is real strong. I guess maybe I should worry or something." Randy could see he was making the big man madder. But he really didn't give a shit; this guy came looking for him, not the other way around.

"Oh hell Randy," Gary said. "Why don't you just get this over with so we can get back to our party?"

"All right," Randy said. Slamming the man's hand into the table with a smashing thud. Still hanging on to the man's hand, Randy started laughing even louder. "Why don't you go and grow up? Come back later and I might let you try again."

Everyone in the saloon started laughing, and this did nothing but make the man even madder. Swinging his left arm with all he had, smashing it into the side of Randy's cheek. The only problem was, Randy's head didn't move. The big man couldn't believe it, why no man had ever with stood his punches before. They were always at least knocked back a couple feet.

Randy was still hanging onto the man's hand, smashing his fist into the man's face, sending blood flying from his nose. The big man came at Randy with another blow. Randy dropped the man's hand and blocked the punch. With all his power he drove his fist into the man's lower rib cage. That punch lifted him a good two and a half feet off the floor. Reaching over with his left, Randy picked the man up, holding him in place as he smashed his fist into the man's rib cage a couple more times. The big man started coughing up blood. Still holding him up again, Randy smashed his fist into the man's face sending even more blood, and a couple teeth flying around the room.

Just then Larry came back into the room, he hadn't seen every-thing, but he knew someone had to stop him. Fact he and Gary both reached Randy at the same time.

289

"Alright Bro," Larry said, trying to calm Randy down. "You've had enough fun, now let him go."

"Alright," Randy said. "I suppose you're right." He opened his fist from around the man's neck; the man fell almost lifeless to the floor.

"Holy shit," Curry said. "I-I-I-I never seen anyone of any size do as much hurt'en to a man in my life. I'm telling you Sundance, Butch… Tell me, just how many times did he hit that poor man? He was swinging so fast, I couldn't tell if he was throwing a punch or recocking… You know?"

"Yeah, we know," both Butch and Sundance said at the same time. They looked over at the man still laying on the floor and his buddy trying to get him up. Sundance looked back to Curry; "We got to see the first big man there Friday night…Now you know why I got the hell out of here last night," Sundance said, smiling. "He didn't even look mad," Curry said, still whispering. "I'll tell you one thing; Just the look he gave me outside sent a shiver up my spine. After what he did to this monster of a man. I mean hell…Just look at him lying there on the floor. Three men are having a hell of a time trying to pick him up… Man, next time he even begins to look at me like he might be getting mad, I'm gone like a big dog."

"I hear ya," Butch said. "I'll be knocking people over just to get out of his way…"

"Now that the fun is over, let's get back to the more serious things at hand. Curry, you and Hosey go over to the Livery stable and take out the man there. Then you two pack a bunch of hay bundle's to fill the rest of those gunnysacks with that Toad and Goof are getting. We'll be the last two out; we'll look around for anymore lookouts. It's eight thirty now, so you get going, we'll be right behind you. About thirty minutes behind you," Butch said to the others.

"Alright," Curry answered him. Curry and Hosey got up, took one last drink of beer and headed towards the door. Except Hosey, he reached over and grabbed a bottle of whiskey on his way out. "John Day is at least two days away and I know I'll get thirsty before I get there."

Chapter Thirteen

"CURRY," Gary hollered, "whatever you do, don't get separated from these guy's in that back county. Those lonely mountain men are plum crazy… They find a nice sweet young city boy like you all alone out there. Well, let's just say, your ass might not be a virgin when you come out of those mountains."

With that everyone busted up laughing, "That ain't no bull shit," Randy said, glaring into Curry's eyes.

Curry tried to crack a smile, while wondering if what Gary had told him was true or not. Then he turned and followed after Hosey. Remembering some of the stories he had heard about them mountain men. Some hadn't seen another living person in years.

"You know Butch, Sundance," Randy said. "I've been doing some thinking; I'll let you go up to Fifteen bag's. That's a total of six hundred pounds on each horse, but no more…Even if that means you have to leave some behind."

"You think there's really going to be that much gold?" Butch asked.

"I don't think, I know," Randy said. "Besides, gold is measured in troy pounds, twelve ounces to the pound, so each bag really only weight's about forty pounds real weight. Still, twelve ounces times six hundred pounds at forty dollars an ounce, hell, you're getting out of here with more money than you ever dreamed of."

"You're right," Sundance thought about it for a minute. "And most importantly they're your horses and trust me, neither one of us want to upset you. But you really think there's that much gold in that tunnel?"

"They usually load fifty plus bags every week at fifty pound a bags, every shipment. That good for nothing Sheriff said they didn't ship last week, remember. So yeah, I'll bet there's a hundred plus bags in that tunnel. Each mule, seven bags each, seven time eight, that's fifty six, plus thirty. Hell that's only eighty six bag's… you just might have to leave some behind."

"Wouldn't that be a shame, Butch?" Sundance said smiling. "At forty dollars an ounce we're going to make a damn good haul." Reaching in his pocket, Butch pulled out a roll of cash and tossed it to Randy, "There's just over ten grand in that roll, you guys have really been fun to be around." They all started laughing and shaking each other's hands. "Don't know if we'll ever get back this way, but we'll definitely look you boys up if we do."

The two turned and walked out the door, stopping on the wood sidewalk, they both looked up and down the street. The lights were still on up at the bank.

"Look Sundance," Butch said. "It looks like they still have a look-out on the hillside up behind the bank."

"No problem Butch, we can sneak around and get him last." The two started walking across the street to the Livery stable. Slowly looking all around as they walked. They could see that Curry and Hosey had already saddled their horses up, so they could get out fast. Both Butch and Sundance walked over to their horses and did the same, leaving the cinch strap just a little loose. So all they would have to do is spend thirty seconds tightening their saddles and they could get out of there.

Butch and Sundance went to the back door of the stable and down to the riverbank. There wasn't much cover for them to run down the riverbank, under the bridge, up the side of the smokehouse, and then inside. Looking around "Curry, Hosey where are you guys?" Butch asked in a loud whisper.

"Over here Butch," Curry said, walking toward them. "So where's this tunnel come up at?"

"Under the stove? Did you get your lookouts?" Sundance asked.

"You sure didn't see him in the loft did you?" Hosey answered. "Fact we have one other too. Toad and Goof had him in the Livery stable waiting for us. Fact they had them both tied up and blindfolded." Looking over at the two men tied up in the corner. Hosey started chuckling. "The one dumb shit tried to fight with us on the trip over. He fell in that cold river, now look at him...He's shivering like a little baby. Sure wish it was still winter, then the dumb shit would really be cold."

Just then they heard a whistle from the timber. "Wait here," Butch said. "We still have one more look-out to get." Turning to the door he ran outside and worked his way down the riverbank, until he came to the edge of the timber, calling out for Goof and Toad.

Chapter Thirteen

"Over here Butch," Toad said. "Figure this was the safest way into the smoke house."

"It is," Butch said. "Goof come with me, we still have one more lookout. Toad I'll fire my pistol twice. That means we have him and you can get those mules in the smokehouse. Then as soon as you secure that tunnel you can start loading them up.

"Let's go," Goof said, jumping off his horse. "Is he just in the bushes up on the hillside behind the bank?"

"Yeah he is," Butch said. The two ran as fast and yet as quietly through the timber and the darkness until they came to the back of the bank. They both stopped and started looking around.

"There," Goof pointed. "Just behind that big fir, up about fifty yards. See him? He's trying to cover up that cigarette he's smoking."

"Got him, let's go," Butch said. The two worked their way up and around the man, holding his hand up, Goof told Butch to hold up. He slowly walked up behind the man, taking out his pistol, Goof hit the man over the back of the head. Knocking him out cold.

Butch came running up behind Goof handing him a roll of that purple mule tape. Taping the man up, mouth, hands, and feet. Both men looked down in the back windows of the bank. They could still see people moving around. Standing up, Goof leaned back down and started picking the man up, "Come on Butch, and help me get him over my shoulder." It didn't take long and the man was loaded up and they were heading back through the timber. "Damn it," Butch said. "We're too close to the bank, I can't signal Toad."

"Signal him, hell," Goof said. "You can signal him when it's your turn to pack this fellow. I'm just glad he isn't one of those guys Randy likes to beat up on."

Butch couldn't help but start chuckling. "You and me both, if he was, we'd need us a pack mule." When they had gone a couple hundred yards, Butch stopped. "Alright, we should be behind the saloon, I'll pack him now." Then firing two shots in the air.

Looking around, Butch took the man from Goof and the two headed back towards the smokehouse. They could run out across the opening without too much worry of being seen. They had all the out-post men in hand, but they did stop one last time and look around just before they came out of the cover of the timber.

"Here, give him to me," Goof said. "It's time for a fresh set of legs to haul him."

"Alright," Butch said. The man began to stir during the handoff, "Look Mr., if you know what's good for you, you'll keep your mouth shut. So we won't have to hurt you anymore." Then the two took off across the open field. It didn't take them very long to get to the smoke-house, and inside and out of sight.

Everyone was still standing around; Goof took the man and laid him over in the corner where the other two were sitting. Goof took a piece of cloth and tied it around his eyes, just like the other two. "It'll be better if you don't see us, because if you did then we'd have to shoot you. Do I make myself clear?"

"Yes sir, Mr.," the men said. "They don't pay me enough money to die for them; you don't even worry about us. We all partied too much today, so I think we'll just lay here and take a nap, so good night," one man said. "I hope you boys really don't get caught. These a-holes just cut our pay in half, said they couldn't be robbed."

Goof started chuckling, then returned to the others; everyone was just standing around looking at each other. "Sundance, you don't suppose these guys were supposed to check in or something do ya?"

"Hell if I know," Butch said, pulling out his pocket watch. "Randy said they usually started loading between nine thirty and ten, and it's almost fifteen past ten now."

Just then they all heard the locks unlocking and the stove started to move. They could hear people talking and joking about the day. The Doss's all had their faces covered with handkerchiefs, the three big outlaws didn't. They wanted those rich a-holes to know who it was that robbed them. The stove moved and two men came up out, both Butch and Sundance put their guns into the men's back, "Reach," they both whispered.

"No problem Mr.," they both said. "You just tell us what you want us to do…You're the boss now," one man said. The two

Chapter Thirteen

removed their guns and dropped them on the floor, "We'll be glad to help you load if you let us have a bag or two, that'll more than make us happy."

"You know, Butch, that's not a bad idea," Sundance said. "That way we can get loaded faster."

"Alright," Butch said. "How many more guns are down there?"

"Just the Sheriff," one man said. "Those a-holes just laid everybody off except a couple of us. They said they weren't worried about being robbed anymore."

"They told us if we wanted to keep our jobs we'd have to take a fifty percent pay cut," the other man said. "Damn near everybody quit them. This is great," he said, starting to chuckle. "But really guy's just one bag…and we'll help load you guys up. Shit there's over a hundred bags down there."

Sniffing the air, Butch looked around the room. "What the hell is that smell?"

"I don't know," said one of the men. "It's never stunk like that in here before."

Starting to chuckle, "That's Randy's gift to the Sheriff," Sundance said looking over at Butch.

"What the hell is it?" Butch said, covering his nose.

"Show you later," Sundance said. "Let's get down there and get to work."

Grabbing one man on the shoulder, turning him around. "One gun? How many people?" Butch asked.

"Just the banker and the man from the mining company," the man answered.

"Good lets go," Butch said, pushing the man back down the stairs into the tunnel with Sundance following. The four of them walked down the tunnel. Butch and Sundance just about shit their pants when they saw the bags of gold. All nicely stacked along the wall. They could hear the others up the tunnel talking. Slowly they moved along the tunnel and rounded the corner, where they could see the others. "Reach," Sundance said, pointing his gun at them. "Sheriff, don't try to be no hero…Just throw that pistol over here with your left hand."

295

"Yes sir," he answered. Throwing his gun on the dirt floor then stuck both his hands in the air.

Walking up to them, "Alright, one at a time, put your hands behind your back." Sundance took that tape that Randy had given them, wrapping their wrists together. Laying them on the floor, he taped their feet. Hollering back down the tunnel, "CURRY BRING ME THE CAN," Sundance said. Everyone could smell it as it got closer; Sundance turned to the other two and put tape over their mouths. Then turning towards the Sheriff, "Oh yeah, here's that other fifteen hundred dollars we agreed on Sheriff," stuffing the money in his pocket.

"What the hell are you talking about a-hole?" The Sheriff shouted out.

"Well, how the hell else would we have known how, when, and where to rob all this gold?" Sundance asked, grabbing the sock.

"What the hell is that?" the Sheriff yelled. While the others were trying to move away from the smell.

"It's what me and Butch like to do for crooked lawmen you might say," Sundance said, smiling. Then he stuffed the sock in the Sheriff's mouth. He was fighting with all his will that he might get away from Sundance and whatever that was he had in his hand. With his hands tied behind his back and his feet tied together he couldn't get very far. Grabbing his head and holding it still, Sundance stuffed the sock in his mouth, then taking the tape he made two complete wraps around his head, just to make sure it didn't fall out. Then Sundance stood up, looked over at Butch. "So was it worth the wait to see what he had in mind for the Sheriff?"

"Sure was," Butch said, still covering his nose. Then the two walked back down the tunnel. "Lets get the hell out of here, that thing stinks to high heaven. You two get going," Butch said, pushing the other two in the back. "You have work to do…so get going."

The men started coming out of the tunnel with bags of gold, Toad and Goof started loading them in the gunnysacks, then filling them the rest of the way with hay.

Picking up a shovel, Toad handed it to Goof, "Go down by the creek and dig a big enough hole for at least five bags of gold." Looking

Chapter Thirteen

around at the others, he continued, "If something should go wrong, we're going to have a little backup money."

"You got it, Toad," Goof said. Grabbing one bag and a shovel then headed out the door.

"Where is he going?" Curry asked when he brought up two more bags of gold.

"Don't worry about it, "Toad said. "You're still getting more than your share of that gold. That's just a little backup plan of my own."

"No problem," Curry said. "I don't blame you one bit. How much you figure we can put on each mule anyhow?"

"Seven bags," Toad said. "Any more than that and it would be too much for them to haul twelve to fourteen hours a day."

"Sounds good to me," Curry said, slapping Toad on the back. "nearly six hundred pounds each, that's enough for me."

"I hope to shout," Toad said smiling. "Now get your ass back down there and bring more up. I don't want to be here all night". Goof returned and grabbed two more bags then he turned and ran back out the door.

Everyone was working as hard and as fast as they could to get loaded. The bags that were to be loaded on the Clydesdales were to be doubled up so each bag weighed two hundred pounds.

They were loading up the last two mules when Sundance grabbed one of the guards who was helping load, "Here," he handed him two bag's of gold. "You get out there as fast as you can and hide this, and then get your ass back here. Remember that if you're not tied up with the rest of them, they'll know that you made a deal with us. And they KNOW who you are, so you two men more than likely wouldn't get very far. If you're tied up with the rest of them, you can salt a little claim for a couple of years for yourselves."

"No problem," the man answered. "I'll be back before you know it."

"Hey, hold it," the other man said. "How about you let him take two more bags? There's still going to be at least fifteen, twenty bag's left that you men can't haul…So do you mind if we take a few extra bag's Mister?"

297

"Hell no," Sundance said. "But only he takes them out and hides them, so you'd better trust him."

"I have no problem with that," the man answered. "I do have one small request if you don't mind."

"What is it?" Sundance asked, as Toad picked one of the bags up and tied it on the Clydesdales.

"I know you said 'dirty lawmen' down there to the Sheriff when you stuffed that rag in his mouth, or whatever the hell it was. I only know it was the worst smelling thing I've ever smelt." The man was saying.

"Grab that bag right there," Sundance said. "Then hurry up and tell me what it is you're saying or asking."

"Well...what I'm saying is we're not real lawmen, we're just bank guards. So when you tie us up, please don't put whatever the hell that was in our mouths too." The man pleaded.

"Don't worry about it," Sundance said. "That was a special present for that fat ass, no good Sheriff."

"Thank you," the man answered, smiling. "I was worried for a little while, we did have to temporarily ungag him for a minute, because he started throwing up and we didn't want him to die in his own vomit. Then you guys would be wanted for murder."

"Thanks," Sundance said smiling. "Now let's get back to work."

"Yes sir...Whoever you are. I mean, I know one of you is supposed to be Butch Cassidy, one Sundance Kid, and one Kid Curry. I don't know just which one you are but I would really like to thank you for everything. Now, to tell you the truth, it's time to tie us up, cause I don't think you guys can haul anymore."

"He's right Sundance," Butch said. "Where's his partner at?"

"Right here sir," the man answered. Walking back into the room. "Let's get down there so you men can tie us up. Just please don't put us too close to that Sheriff. I can still smell whatever the hell that is you put in his mouth up here."

"Deal," Butch said. "Now let's go." Pulling his gun out he pointed it at the two men.

"WHOA"...they both said at the same time putting their hands in the air. "You don't need that...we're not going to do anything stupid."

Chapter Thirteen

"I know that?" Butch said. "But we have to make it look real, so let's go."

The three turned and walked back down the stairs. Butch took them up to the other end where the others were tied and gagged, and did the same to them.

"Well gentlemen," Butch said with a big grin on his face. "It's been a real pleasant stay in your little city here. Looking down at the Sheriff, who was almost as white as a ghost. "We'd really like to thank you Sheriff for all your help."

Just then the Sheriff started kicking and fighting and trying to talk through the gag.

"What's that Sheriff?" Butch said. "You trying to say thank you to me? NOOO, NOOO Sheriff, it's us who need to thank you, just like Sundance said earlier, we couldn't have done it without your help."

Again the Sheriff started kicking and fighting against the restraints.

Tipping his hat to everyone Butch put his pistol back in his holster and headed back out the tunnel. Just as soon as he came up, the others pushed the stove back into place, then covered the area with straw?

Looking around at everyone, Butch started shaking the Doss brother's hands. "It's been a pleasure to meet you men," Butch said. "I know I will never forget any of you. You can count on that."

"You sure the hell can," Sundance said. "You three will always have the biggest damn noses we've ever seen. Curry we'll catch up with you around Los Angeles in a month or two."

"Alright," Curry said, shaking their hands. "You boys take care. I still don't know why you want to go back out across that flat empty desert for, but I'll see ya when I see ya."

Butch reached into his holster and pulled out his pistol and fired three shots into the air.

"What the hell was that for?" Hosey asked.

"That's Randy's signal to know we're finished and are heading out of town. This is telling him to go light the back door." Looking down at his pocket watch, "Well boys," Butch said. "Let's get the hell out of here." They all grabbed their lead ropes and headed in the same direction, following the riverbed to the timberline.

299

Back in the saloon the four, Randy, the twins, and Luis were playing poker, with chips of course. Randy heard the gunshots; throwing his cards in the middle of the table, reaching in his pocket for his chewing tobacco. "Well now, it's time to go have some fun. Anybody want to come?"

"What kind of fun?" Larry asked.

"Those three shot were Butch's way of telling me they're loaded up and heading out. So...now...I head down to light the back door. I could use at least one of you, cause I'd like to add a little bit more nitro. Make a bigger bang you might say, we need everyone to hear it."

"Randy I'm quite sure what you guys took last night. Wasn't it something like six cases?" I'm sure that is enough," Gary asked with a smile on his face. Then throwing his cards into the middle of the table, "But I'll go with you."

"Yeah it was," Randy said. "But a few more won't hurt."

"Well hell Randy," Larry said with a grin from ear to ear. "I don't have to see it to appreciate it; I'll be able to hear it from here. Besides," kicking his feet up on the table and holding up his beer, "Ever since that beautiful Roan over there bucked all those men off...and I rode him out of the arena...Well, what I'm saying is these women around here aren't charging me for anything. Hell, they can't keep their hands off of me, so I'm staying here and getting it while the getting is good. IF YOU KNOW WHAT I MEAN?" Taking a long pull of his beer.

"Yeah Hombre, Larry's right," Luis said. "These women just can't wait to get in bed with us. Not Sharon of course, but pretty much all the others...so I think I'm going to stay here too Amigo, I hope you understand."

"Sure, no problem," Gary said. Standing up, "Looks like it's me and you Randy. But how about we go out the back door so maybe, just maybe, no one will see us and try to blame us for any of this. Since we did party with them boys all weekend." He reached over and took the bottle of whiskey out of Larry's hand. "You can get yourself another one; I'm taking this one with me."

300

Chapter Thirteen

Randy stood up and the two slowly worked their way to the back door and outside. "Come on Gary, lets go get a few more cases of TNT," then they ran down the alley between the buildings. The mining supply store was just two buildings down. Walking up to the side door, Randy looked over at Gary, "Check it out," Randy pointed to the glass in the window. "The dumb shit already replaced the glass. Oh well, guess he's going to have to fix it again," Starting to chuckle a little, as he smashed his elbow through the corner pane again. Then stuck his hand inside and opened the door, "Yep, he's just going to have to fix it again."

"Let's just get the shit and get out of here," Gary answered.

"Alright, alright," Randy said. "Just thought I'd point that out. Come over here, this is where he keeps it." Picking up a crowbar Randy walked over to the cage that the dynamite and nitro was in. Breaking the lock and hasp off, he opened it up. "Here Gary," Randy said, handing him three cases of nitro, then he turned and grabbed three more. Each one holding twenty four, twelve ounce bottles. "Now let's get the hell out of here. You go get your horse and borrow a mule if you can, we'll use him as the pack animal. Hell they ain't going to miss him; we'll be back by daylight. I'll go grab my stallion. I'll meet you on the road heading out of town."

"Alright," Gary said. He worked his way between the buildings and back to Main Street. Looking up and down the street as far as he could see it was almost dead quiet. He crossed the street packing his three cases of nitro into the Livery stable. Sitting everything down, he hurried and saddled his horse. Turning and looking around, it was just his luck there was a nice pack mule in the next stall over. As fast as he could Gary put the packsaddle on him loaded up the nitro and walked both animals to the door. Taking one more quick glance out the door to check out the street, he climbed aboard his horse, leading the mule he headed down the road to find Randy. Which didn't take very long, he was waiting just inside the timberline.

"What the hell took so long?" Randy asked, riding down off the hill to the road.

"Well, unlike you Randy," Gary answered. "I had to saddle up, you didn't."

"They just don't make a saddle big enough for this big boy," Randy said slapping the horse across the neck. Quickly they loaded Randy's nitro, then the two headed down the road.

"So why are we going down to light this Randy?" Gary asked. "Why don't they light it when they ride by it?"

"Because they're going out through Whitney to Unity. Then I think they changed their mind and are going out through Portland too." Randy answered.

"Why didn't they just go out with the others?" Gary asked.

"I told Butch I thought it would be better if they split up and went different directions. That way they wouldn't all get caught if any of them by chance did." Randy said.

"Sounds like a good move to me," Gary said. "I'm sure glad we know this road, its flat ass dark out here tonight. I thought Toad told us the moon was going to be full tonight. Shit, you can't even see the stars."

"I wonder how those big city boys are doing out here in the real wilderness. I bet Curry has never been out of the city much, and if he has, I bet he took a train or a stagecoach."

"The Doss's are going to have fun with him," Gary said.

"I'm sure we'll hear about it when they get back," Randy said.

"Don't you mean if they get back? Once this robbery gets out on the telegraph lines there won't be a lawman or bounty hunter within three hundred miles, not looking for them. That 15% reward that the mining company will have on the return of that gold will be really tempting."

"You're right, that's why we're cutting the wire this way, and Butch said they'd cut the line going to Whitney. Toad is right by going up to Seattle to sell his gold. Like he said, they'll think they came out of Alaska, and not pay them much attention when they try to sell it."

"They'll just have to watch out for every outlaw and bounty hunter in this part of the country getting there... Then," Gary said chuckling

Chapter Thirteen

a little. "They'll have to hide from every outlaw in the country. Packing all that cash back…they have a real exciting month ahead of them until they get back, if they get back."

"Oh they'll get back! You just wait and see." Just then Randy pulled up on his reins. "I'm going to cross the river here. When you get down to the cliffs; you know where the first level area is about eighty feet up? Where there's that big overhang?"

"I know where you're talking about;" Gary said. "I can ride most of the way up there from the back side."

"That's where Butch stockpiled his, just under the overhang. When you get everything in place, follow the fuse line down so you'll know just where it is. I'll throw my fuse across the river to you. Better yet, we'll both light at the same time and meet back up here."

"Sounds good to me," Gary said. "I'll see ya at the river when we light it up. Just so I know…how long of fuse time do we have?"

"Thirty minutes," Randy answered. Then turning his horse and headed across the river. "Thirty minutes," He hollered back, riding out of sight into the darkness.

Gary turned his horse and mule and headed down the river. He couldn't see because of the darkness from the clouds but he knew where Randy was talking about. He had thought of that spot in the past, if they had ever needed to get away fast that would be the perfect place to blow the canyon. Riding at a good trot it took him ten minutes to get as close with the horses as he could, picking up only one box of nitro he headed in the direction of the overhang. He knew it was going to take at least two trips, so he would pack light the first trip just in case he might slip. But for once luck was on his side; it only took a couple minutes to find Butch's pile. Sitting his box down with the three that were already there. He shook his head and looked across the river, in the general area he figured Randy might be. This sure was going to be big and loud, starting to chuckle, then he turned and headed back to get the other two cases.

Looking up at the sky, then back to the trail in front of him. It sure would be a lot easier if he had just a little light to see. Those clouds must be extra thick up there; it did look like a storm might be moving in earlier tonight after the bucking competition. He thought to himself

Reaching his horse and mule, Gary grabbed both cases and returned to the stockpile. Looking around he found where Butch had rolled up the fuse; it was all rolled up just like a rope. Picking it up, Gary threw it over the face of the cliff; he would light it from down there. He wasn't worried about it catching up on anything, because there wasn't anything but sheer straight up and down cliff on that side. Fact they had to drill to dynamite these cliffs when they put the road and railway through. They all knew it wouldn't be hard to ride around this canyon, it wasn't just a good back door, it was an illusion, to make everyone think they came this way.

Randy always could make a good back door, Gary was thinking, working his way back to his horse and mule, and then he turned them down the hill. He had to be real careful, he couldn't see the ground below his horse's chest, he was glad that Dude had picked this mustang for him. He sure knew how to pick a good horse, just like that Roan he picked for Larry. This mustang was just as good as the Roan, and just as sure footed. Thank God he wasn't as ornery as that Roan.

It was Dude who went with Randy to Portland to pick out those six Clydesdales, out of the fifty that were shipped in for logging over there. Dude helped Randy break and train them to. Still that stallion will only let Randy on his back. He wasn't sure if this big sorrel he rode would give anyone trouble, but if the person was just even a little bit unsure of himself he would know it. And give him a lot of hell to see who the boss really was, YOU OR HIM…Dude had given each one of them a horse that would only be true to them, fact just like Randy's stallion, this boy had taken him home drunk more than once.

Before he knew it they had made their way off the mountainside and back to the road. Gary rode over towards the fuse. Riding up to it, looking across the river he saw Randy light a branch on fire and held it up, letting him know where he was. Riding over to the edge of the river, they tried to talk, but the noise of the rapids made it hard to hear each other. After five minutes of hollering back and forth they worked

Chapter Thirteen

out that Randy would light another branch on fire that was the signal to light the fuses.

Gary rode back over to his fuse. Sitting up on his horse holding the fuse, he started chuckling; this was going to be one big explosion. All of a sudden he saw Randy lighting the branch on fire. It hadn't taken him as long as Gary thought it would. Lighting his match, Gary reached over and lit the fuse, which put a big smile on his face. The sparks from the fuse line frightened the mule and he wanted to fight. "Fine you ornery piece of shit," Gary said, tying the lead rope around his saddle horn. He knew his big sorrel would pull that mule to hell and back if need be. It didn't take long to catch back up with Randy.

"Come on Gary, I want to get up above black mountain overlook before it goes off." Randy said, turning his horse.

"Oh this damn mule don't want to play fair, so why don't you take him. Your horse can pull him easier and faster than mine can," Gary shouted.

"Hell just let him go, they'll think the robbers stole him to pack all that nitro," Randy said.

"You're right," Gary answered, untying the mule and letting him go.

Let's get up on that cliff across from Black Mountain."

"That's where I'm talking about;" Randy said, pointing. "It's a great viewpoint to watch from." Then they turned their horses, and headed up the mountain. Angling their way up to make the climb easier on the horses. This side of the canyon was steeper than the other side. Riding their horses at a slow gallop they reached the top in plenty of time. Randy reached into his gunnysack that he always carried with him, instead of saddlebags. Pulling out his pipe and bag of peyote he smiled, "You want a hit of this Gary?"

"HELL NO," Gary answered. "The last time I smoked that shit I lost two days. I couldn't tell you what happened, except all the strange shit I saw in my dreams."

Laughing, Randy started to load up a bowl in his pipe, looking over at Gary. "You smoked way too much if you went on a two day voyage into the future."

305

"What the hell you mean voyage?" Gary asked.

"You know the Indians say that after they smoke it, the Great Spirit shows them things that are going to come or happen to them in the near future." Randy told Gary. Tying their horse's up, they walked out on the point of the cliff where they could get a good view of the canyon below. It would be a great spot to view the explosion from, which should be happening in just a couple minutes. Even though they could barley see the canyon because of the darkness, from the heavy cloudbank that had rolled in late afternoon. Sitting down, Randy lit his pipe, taking a big pull. Then handing it to Gary, "You sure you don't want some? It'll make you feel better and happier."

"No thanks," Gary answered, taking a pull off his bottle of whisky. "I'm all ready happy, I'll just keep to this," taking another pull off the bottle. "Here, you want some of this?"

"HELL NO," Randy said. "You mix these two, then you will really be off in la la land for a couple of days. Tomorrow we have to go to Prineville to meet this Marshal Shawn Felton and find out why he did what he did to Brad. It will take both of us to keep Larry from getting too carried away and not listen to the Marshal's side of the story...you know that"

"I know your right Randy" Gary said..."But Hell Randy, they couldn't even have a funeral for him, for any of them... There was noting left, just Crow bait and a nice new swimming hole for the kid's."

Just then the nitro went off, KABOOOM...the entire sky lit up, it turned those heavy dark couldn't see through clouds as bright as if it were midday, and fiery red at the same time. It went from a deep red almost purple red color at the base to crystal clear at the edges. It looked like the sun was on fire and coming up. The sky was only lit up for maybe thirty seconds at the most, but because of the cloudbank, you could hear the echoing repeating it's self over and over. Why that boom would not only be heard in Sumpter fifteen plus miles back up the road, but also everywhere in the same radius in all directions, maybe even further.

"HOLY SHIT," Randy jumped to his feet. "Wasn't that just about the best fireworks you've ever seen Gary?"

"It's a damn good thing we hobbled those horses or they'd be headed for the barn," Gary said...Looking back over at Randy,

Chapter Thirteen

"Come on Bro, let's get back to town. I'm sure everyone is wide awake now."

Toad looked around at everyone once Butch and Sundance had cleared the open field to the Livery stable, without even being noticed. By now most everyone in town was home sleeping off the drinking of the day, and feeling real broke after losing all their hard earned money and gold dust on that Roan. It wouldn't hit most of them until tomorrow, after they woke up and looked in their pocket-books and wallets.

"Alright listen up," Toad said. "Curry...I want you right behind me, and I mean right behind me. Goof you bring up the rear, better yet. Hosey you bring up the rear, in case anyone is following us you can shoot them."

"Sure, make me be the one who gets hung if we get caught. Thanks little brother," Hosey answered.

"Alright, just wing them then," Toad said. "But we all keep this in a straight line going out. Straight down the riverbank until we hit the timber. The smokehouse should keep us out of sight from Main Street." Toad double-checked everyone's packs one more time for snugness, then climbing aboard his horse.

"Let's get going, and keep it tight." Turning his horse out the door, and down the river, it didn't take them long to get under the cover of the timber, it just seemed like it did. After they were a good hundred yards into the timber, Toad turned them in the direction of getting back across the river and back around town.

'Damn,' Curry said thinking to himself. "I thought Toad said we should have a full moon tonight. How the hell am I supposed to stay on his ass when I can't even see you?' He looked up into the sky and all he could see was pitch black, there wasn't a star anywhere. Those clouds had rolled in later in the day, it's already after midnight and those clouds were real thick, and the Lodge pole timber they were riding through was just as thick. Hell, he couldn't see twenty feet into that timber, yet alone see Toad's front mule he was leading. They would be lucky if the storm held off until morning. Curry was still thinking about

307

the country theses three were taking him into. Most of it was still total wilderness, not too many people. What people that were they were all mountain men, people who had come up into the mountains years ago to get away from everyone down below in the towns and cities. It wasn't like he hadn't ever camped out in the wild before, because he had, but at least them times he knew he would be fine because there would be a house or town within a day's ride.

He remembered coming out over the mountains on a train from back east; riding that train over the Rocky Mountain was one thing. You sure hoped that train wasn't going to jump the track. One simple mistake out here and a man could get killed if his horse lost his footing or you just got stupid and fell off your horse. They more than likely wouldn't get you to a doctor in time.

He noticed Toad had them at a real good pace going out around town. They had made a loop of at least two or three miles around town, which wasn't easy, because of all the lodge pole trees. They were small in diameter, but thick, hard to ride though and around them. The darkness made the ride seem longer than it really was. Still, Curry was happy when they came back to the main road leading to Granite. If you could call it a road, it was more like a trail cut through the thick lodge pole pinetrees. Looking down, not only could he not see the sky, but also he couldn't see the ground either, and it was only a few feet away.

Nobody had said a word since they left the smokehouse. He sure hoped he could, well actually, he knew he could trust the Doss's. He knew the kind of men these Doss men were. They were the kind of people who would help anyone, anytime without question. They would also stand behind their word, they wouldn't steal from ya, well at least not from a working man, this was a little different. This was from a big company that already had its share of wealth.

Finally it was Goof who broke the silence. "Toad I don't smell any fires. So does that mean we're far enough out of town that we can settle down and smoke a cigarette?"

Looking back at Goof, Toad could tell by the way Curry was hanging onto them reins that he was nervous. "Ya, go ahead. So Curry what the hell kind of horse is that you're riding?"

Chapter Thirteen

Straightening his back up, because he was proud of the gilding he was riding, "It's a registered Arabian. They come from overseas in the Arab countries. Isn't he about the prettiest horse you ever seen?"

"How the hell can you ride that high stepping thing?" Goof asked. "That has to be the most uncomfortable ride I've ever seen."

"Check out the way he holds his head and tail high in the air, acts just like some of those rich people. He has his head so far up in the air I bet he can't even see these mustangs we're riding," Hosey said.

"I'll have you know, I paid fifteen hundred dollars for this horse." Curry said trying to justify the way the horse carried itself.

"Fifteen hundred dollars?" Goof shouted out. "If we have to run fast through the brush, because a posse or the law catch's up with us, you don't have to worry about your horse taking your head off on a low branch; you have to worry about him knocking himself out on those low branches."

"I'll put him up in a foot race against any of those horses your riding on flat open ground anytime," Curry said.

"On flat open ground?" Toad stated. "Does it look like we're on flat open ground? You want a horse that's surefooted where we're going. I know these horses aren't half as pretty as yours, but I don't want a pretty horse."

"Me either," hollered Hosey. "Give me a mustang or at least a horse that's not afraid of the mountains and the wildlife in it. Hell, I bet if a deer or elk, either one, jumped out, why I bet that horse of yours would go plum ape shit."

"I'd like to see what he'll do when he smells a bear or lion," Goof joined in on the fun. "I bet he'd really go berserk."

Just then a rattlesnake made itself known that they where to close, rattling his rattle. No more had that snake started and that fancy horse went to bucking, throwing Curry off and down over the side of the hill a good fifteen feet.

Reaching out and grabbing the reins as the horse came running by, Toad quickly tied the rein off around his saddle horn, flipping

309

the Arabian half way around, along with the two mules at the same time.

Everyone busted up laughing. "Now I see why you backed out of your chance to ride that Roan today," Hosey said.

"Hell, he can't even stay on one that's been broke to ride," Goof said. "Least wise not around a little rattlesnake."

They all came to a stop as Curry worked his way back up the side of the hill and back over to his horse. Climbing back on he turned his face to the others, "Alright you bunch of smartasses, let's get going."

"Sure thing," Toad said. "But you better let me take the lead because you have no idea where you're going…Do ya?"

"No I don't," Curry said with just a little embarrassment in his voice. "So why don't you just get back up here and lead us through, Please"

"Alright, alright," Toad said. Riding up alongside Curry, then past him. "Well, come on city man, we got a lot of ground to cover. I figure they won't find out about the robbery until eight or nine in the morning, if we're lucky. With everyone being hung over it'll take them at least a couple hours to get a posse together. They'll probably be headed the wrong way because of Randy's back door."

"I don't know how that little shit does it," Goof said. "But that man can come up with more ways to throw someone off his trail. Send them in a totally different direction than he went."

"So do you think we'll know when he blows up the canyon?" Curry asked. Looking around at Goof and Hosey.

"Trust me, Randy told me they took six cases of nitro last night, and he's taking more tonight…Hell, everyone in the valley and halfway up the mountain will hear that go off with this heavy cloudbank above us."

"Getting back to the more important agenda here," Hosey said. "But if that high dollar horse of yours is afraid of one little rattlesnake…Just what the hell are you going to do when we come across a bear, or even worse, a lion?"

"There are no lions in this area," Curry said with skepticism in his voice.

Chapter Thirteen

"THE HELL THERE AINT," They all hollered. "Those things are as thick as flies between here and John Day." Toad said

"What about that big grizzly bear that's been killing everyone's livestock in the area?" Goof asked. First looking at Curry, and then back to his brothers. "Hell, I've heard them say he's at least eight feet tall."

"Bullshit Goof," Curry said with nervousness in his voice. "Those bears don't get that big."

"The hell they don't," Hosey said in a stern voice. "I've seen grizzlies in Montana stretched out in front of me dead. They had one that was at least ten, almost eleven feet tall, and weighed a good five hundred plus pounds...and that ain't no bullshit!"

They could all tell they were getting to Curry. "I heard that just a week ago, some mountain men were riding along thinking nothing was going to happen, and then all of a sudden his horse's perked his ears up. From out of nowhere, this big mountain lion flew out from a low branch of a large fir tree and attacked them. Digging his claws and teeth into the horse's neck, breaking it before they even hit the ground. The man said from the tip of nose, to the tip of his tail, that lion was all of ten, twelve feet in length. Said he couldn't back away fast enough, he didn't want to be next on that lion's dinner list."

"I-I-I-I thought you said there was going to be moonlight tonight?" Curry asked looking at Toad. "Why is it so damn dark out here?"

"First, there's this cloud bank that rolled in, so second, the moon light can't shine through." Toad answered.

"You make damn sure your eyes are on that horse's head," Hosey said. "He'll either smell them or hear them, long before we'll see them."

They could see Curry was looking all around, trying to see into the darkness of the timber. If he was lucky he could see maybe twenty feet. Their stories were starting to really making him feel uneasy in his saddle. It was as if he could hear every twig breaking, and every pinecone fall to the ground, making him look in that direction instantly.

"Who cares about the bears and the lions?" Goof said looking around. Trying to look serious cause he and Curry were riding side by

311

side. "I'm more afraid of running into one of those Sashquatch's up here."

"What the hell is a Sashquatch?" Curry asked.

"Don't really know," Goof said. "Some say they're half man and half bear. He walks upright like a man, except he's covered with hair from head to toe just like a bear. Believe it or not, the Indians in these areas say they've seen them up to twelve feet tall."

"Now I know you're feeding me a line of bullshit," Curry said. "You guys are just picking on me because I'm from the city."

"Can't say as I ever seen one," Toad said. "But about two years ago I came back this way from John Day, I camped out one night, I staked out and hobbled my horse. When in the middle of the night I heard a scream like I'd never heard before, it brought me up out of a deep sleep. I looked over and my horse was gone. I figured being hobbled he wouldn't get too far so I went back to sleep."

"The next morning I got up and went to go find him, it turned out that was the easiest track I ever followed. To start with, there was a huge blood spot where my horse was killed. Whatever it was, drug him a good half-mile or so before he started eating on him. We were down along the riverbed and meadows, so the ground was real soft; it left at least a dozen footprints in the mud. They looked human enough, but they were about fifteen inches in length. I started trying to track him further. His stride was two of mine. When I got to my horse the only thing that was left was his back and a front shoulders, the rest of him was gone…I grabbed my rifle and went looking for the Sashquatch, but when it got into some down fallen timber I lost all sign of him. I could see some places where he stepped from one tree to another. I had to climb in between them, while he was stepping over everything. And that ain't no bullshit story," Toad said, looking back at Curry, who was not comfortable at all, Toad thought to himself.

Curry was thinking to himself how much of what they were telling him was true. He had heard about lions attacking horses and other animals that they wanted for food. Butch had told him many stories about killing big mountain lions at his parent's house just outside of Circleville, Utah. He had also heard stories all the way over the Rockies

Chapter Thirteen

about them grizzly bears. They had been known to attack a man without cause or provocation. Kill him, eat half of him there, and then bury what was left for a later meal. This Sashquatch thing they were talking about…this was the first time he had heard of them. "What was that?" he jumped a little in his saddle and looked into the darkness that they were riding through.

Curry wasn't really sure just how much of this was true. He knew these three had grown up around here. One thing was sure; he didn't know what this country looked like, for sure, because of the darkness. He could still almost hear every little thing that was happening around them, every twig breaking as their horse's stepped on it, pinecones falling out of trees, he could even hear all the little squirrel that were running from tree to tree.

Just then it sounded like all hell broke loose, like a mighty bolt of lightning had burst right above their heads, Curry and his horse jumped ten feet straight up into the air, sending Curry flying through the air and crashing back to the ground. As everyone else got their horses under control, Goof turned around looking like it was no big deal, until he saw Curry flying through the air. Busting up laughing he spit out his chewing juice. Looking back they could all see the clouds light up. "Sounds like and looks like Randy lit it off." Goof said. Turning his head and looking towards everyone "check out how much of that sky he lit up." Seeing Curry on the ground they all started laughing, "What the hell you doing down there Curry…? You're not scared are you?"

"Piss off Goof," Curry said. Standing up, knocking the dust off, then he started walking toward his horse. It sure hurt like hell, but he wasn't about to let these three know. They would just harass him more. One more important thing he thought to himself, I will be glad when daylight finally comes, then he could see where they were going and maybe these guy's will run out of stories.

313

CHAPTER FOURTEEN

Wapiti walked into the restaurant side of the establishment, taking a quick look around the room. He could see it was at least half full maybe more, walking over and sitting down at a table by the wall. Cathey came over and sat down too.

"Why are you sitting all the way back here, Wapiti?" Cathey asked. "No one's going to do anything, you know that."

"It's not that Cathey, these white eyes don't scare me," Wapiti said with a big smile on his face, and loud enough for those near by to hear. "But from this table I can see everyone coming and going from the restaurant and saloon, and more importantly... no one can get behind me."

"You know Wapiti," Cathey said, with that big beautiful smile. "Now that the Sheriff knows you, and knows you can handle yourself...I bet he would take you on as a deputy."

"What? Here in John Day?" Wapiti asked.

"Why not? You said you wanted to be a lawman," Cathey said with excitement in her voice.

"It's not just being a lawman Cathey. It's knowing how to handle each situation." Wapiti said, looking in to her eyes.

"You can learn that here," Cathey said.

"It's like I told you earlier Cathey, it's the Marshall himself. There's so much more I could learn off him than anyone else could ever teach me. Not only how to handle each situation, but also to know how to...

314

Chapter Fourteen

And which ones to watch out for. Like which one will be more likely to make the first move, and which one might hesitate. More importantly, how to shoot straight and fast. Like he's been teaching me ever since we left Prineville, last week. Just like yesterday when that man came through that crowd of people, hell Cathey, there were at least seventy people or more between the Marshal and that man coming through the crowd to back shoot me. He pushed me aside, pulled and shot all at the same time. Hitting only his target…right where he aimed, right between the eys's. He didn't hesitate even a fraction of a second, if he had, I would be dead…I need to know I can make that same shot, not once in a while, but every time, without hesitation."

"Do you think you could talk him into maybe sticking around this area?" Cathey asked.

Wapiti could see the sadness in her eyes. "The Governor say's where he's supposed to be based out of," Wapiti answered.

"My dad's mom is from the Prineville area," Cathey said. "Maybe I could go live with some of my family over there for a while."

Wapiti looked at her with serious eyes. "Do you think for one minute your dad would let you follow an Indian ANYWHERE?"

"I told you the color of a man's skin doesn't matter to my father. My dad's mom's was more than half Indian." Cathey answered

"That don't matter Cathey. I mean maybe he said it don't, but if it came right down to it…Your pa would still rather see you with one of these white eyes than a filthy red skin." Wapiti said

"He's not like that I'm telling you Wapiti," Cathey answered. "Really he's not; you'll see when you come over for dinner tonight."

"You're the one who'll see Cathey. I just hope he don't tear me apart with those huge arms he has." Wapiti answered.

"So then you will come for dinner?" Cathey asked.

"Of course I will." Wapiti answered, standing up, "I need to get back inside, the Marshal hasn't eaten yet either."

"Alright Wapiti," Cathey said, standing up, leaning over and giving him another kiss on the cheek. When she did, Wapiti couldn't help but notice everyone in the restaurant was watching. But when they noticed he had seen them, they all turned their heads away.

Reluctantly, he bent over and gave Cathey a kiss on her cheek, "I need to get back now Cathey, I'll see you later…I promise."

Looking at him walking away, "Remember, dinner's at six o' clock. I'll be back then so I can show you the way, or my brother Mike will come and get you." Cathey called out.

"Okay," Wapiti answered. He couldn't stop looking at the big smile that was on her face. "I'll see you then." Walking back into the saloon, thinking to himself, 'Would her family really accept him and allow him and Cathey to have a life together.' Oh hell, what was he even thinking about it for? Cathey lived here and the Marshal was based out of Prineville. It was at least one hundred and twenty to one hundred and forty miles between the two, then he looked up towards the heavens. "Great Spirit…Am I a fool for wanting to have Cathey in my life? Is it just a fantasy? Only you know whether it will or won't happen…but it would be nice to have her to share my life with."

No other girl or lady had ever made his heart pound so hard, with just the hopes of seeing her again. Not to mention how his heart wanted to jump right out of his chest every time he's with her. Well, he had a job to do, and the Marshal had told him that if anyone was going to try something, it would be when they thought he was daydreaming, because then they had the edge on him.

Taking a quick look around the room Wapiti counted seven players left, and one was Cathey's aunt. She had thick black hair, if she had a good tan, you might think she was an Indian. He couldn't help but notice that she hadn't been wearing a dress the entire tournament. He could tell she wasn't afraid of work, fact he bet she could work right along side a man all day, then go home at night and do all the cooking and cleaning. She was closer to his age he thought, about twenty.

Looking over at the other table he could see one of the Seebart brothers who he had had the trouble with the first morning. He chuckled just a little because Jack was still carrying a big bruise that covered most of his under jaw. Cathey had said that Denise and Jack had been dating for a couple of years, said she won't marry him until they have enough money to buy a house. Smiling at them he hoped that maybe just one of them might win, so they could do just that. Both

Chapter Fourteen

of them seemed to be doing real good, at each table, they had most of the chips. Then Wapiti turned and walked over to Corky and the Marshal. "Well Marshal, why don't you go get yourself some food? I know you're hungry."

"Well, thank ya Wapiti," Shawn said. Leaning up against the bar, "But I'm saving room for a good home cooked meal tonight. Remember Cathey invited me too?"

"I know and I'm glad," Wapiti said. "I won't be all alone with her family; my stomach is all tied up in knots."

Both Cork and the Marshal busted up laughing. "That's lust if I ever seen it, Shawn," Cork said.

"You could be right Cork," Shawn answered, looking over at Wapiti. "It's only going to get worse son, it's only going to get worse, as the day goes on."

"Geeeee thanks," Wapiti said. Rubbing his stomach… "Thanks a lot.

Patting him on the back, he was still smiling. "Don't worry son that feeling will go away after you meet the family," Shawn said.

Then all of a sudden one of the players started shouting, "DAMN YOU woman I know you didn't get your card."

"Then why'd you fold your hand?" Denise said in a calm voice.

"You're trying to buy that damn pot," the man shouted out. "I don't know who taught you to play; I'll admit you're good, I've never seen anyone bluff as good as you can. Fact your face doesn't change whether you have a pat hand or you're bluffing."

"What's the trouble over here?" Shawn yelled out, working his way though the crowd of spectators over to the last two tables of players.

"She's trying to buy the pot by betting more money than I have, and she knows it Marshal," the man shouted.

"Now just calm down, Young man," Shawn said. "We'll get to the bottom of this."

"Young lady, are you…trying to buy the pot?" Shawn asked.

"I don't see where that matters," Denise answered. "Even if I was, that man sitting right there made the last three raises, not me." She said pointing.

317

"I knew he didn't make his hand, I know he is bluffing," the man said. "But her…Why…she thinks she can bluff her way through anything."

Looking down at the pile of chips in front of Denise, Shawn couldn't help but smile. "Looks to me like she's real good at it. Playing cards and bluffing. Hell, everyone who's ever played the game knows you have to be able to do both. So just what's the trouble?"

"They both knew I only had nine hundred dollars left, and rule number three is you can't buy anymore chips. You have to play with what you have."

"That's right," Shawn said, throwing his chest out. "So just how short are you from covering the bet as it stands right now?"

"Two hundred dollars," the man answered. His face was turning red from all his hollering.

"Well now, just calm down," Shawn said still smiling at him. "You knew the rules when you started, but I see no reason why, that is if no one else cares," looking around the table, "I'll let you take the money, one time out of your pocket, that's if nobody else minds."

They all shook their heads; it didn't matter to them. Hell there was at least twenty thousand dollars in that pot and whoever won it would have a few extra hundred dollars cash in his pocket. Even if they did ultimately loose.

"I know damn good and well she didn't get that spade flush, so does everyone here," the man said still hollering. "I don't think I should have to put anymore money in than I have in front of me on the table…I KNOW she's full of shit…I just know it."

"There's only one way you're going to find out what she's holding, either put up everything you have, plus the additional two hundred, or throw your cards down and get the hell out of the game," Shawn stated firmly, waving his fist towards the door.

"FINE," the man hollered back. Reaching in his pocket, trying to find the additional two hundred dollars. Then picking up his chips and the money he threw them in the middle of the table. "NOW I call… and no one had better try to raise it anymore." He turned his cards

Chapter Fourteen

over revealing three kings, "Now then… Young lady, let's just see you beat that."

Looking at him with a small grin on her face, she laid down the other two spades in her hand. Not only the other king, but also the Ace to go with it. "Royal flush," she said. Beginning to chuckle a little, and then looking over at the other man who was still holding his cards. "Can you beat that?"

"HELL NO," the man said smiling. "He's right…I was bluffing." Laying his cards face down on the table, so no one could see what he was holding.

"Well there you go Mr., she has it, and you don't," Shawn said smiling. "Now you're out of the game and even a few extra hundred dollars poorer. So take it like a man and get the hell out of here and away from the table."

"The hell I will," the man shouted back. "I'm not leaving from this chair, just look around. There ain't an empty seat anywhere except this one. I damn sure want to see who wins this damn game. So, if you don't mind Marshal, I'll just sit right here and keep my mouth shut."

"Sounds good to me Young man, but you better keep your mouth shut or I'll put my fist in it…Do I make myself clear?" Shawn reiterated.

"Crystal, Marshal," the man answered, pulling his chair away from the table a couple of feet and sat back down. "Is this okay Marshal?"

"It is," Shawn answered. Looking around the two tables. "Well now, we're down to six players, so how about everyone join together and sit at one table?"

Everyone started looking around; two tables meant that you still had a better chance of beating out a couple of the other players with less money more quickly. But the Marshal was in charge, and no one wanted to get on his bad side. They all looked around just a little longer, then at the other table; not the one Denise was sitting at, they all picked up their chips and moved over to her table.

Shawn turned and walked back over to the bar, pulling out his pocket watch and looking at it. "Well Wapiti, it's just after two o' clock, if everything goes well, I'll be able to join you for dinner."

319

"So what time do you think we'll be leaving in the morning Marshal?" Wapiti asked.

"When I was out earlier I noticed the clouds rolling in. Looks like it might rain tonight or tomorrow," Shawn said. "So we're likely to get a little wet, but I figure we'll get out of town by six at the latest. Roy don't know me as well as Gordy does, so I'll have to look everything over to make sure I know where everything is, so if we need it…I can get to it. Why…You in a hurry to leave already son? I kinda figured you'd want to stick around."

"I do," Wapiti answered quickly. "But it will be nice to get back on the trail. Do you think that when we come back from Sumpter we can come back through here?

"I thought that question might come up," Shawn said. Taking a pull off his beer. "I just didn't think it would come up before we left."

Charlie was replacing everyone's empty beers with fresh glasses. Starting to smile he looked back over at Wapiti, then back at both Cork and the Marshal. "Don't you remember the first girl you fell head over heels for? Hell you couldn't get back soon enough from anywhere. I still feel that way about my wife, she wishes I could make more money off my saddle making business, then I wouldn't have to come up here around all these young ladies. But like I keep telling her, from the first time I met her, no other woman even catches my eye anymore."

"Oh now come on Charlie," Shawn said. "You telling me you don't look at other woman and wonder?"

"Nope, I don't," Charlie answered. "Sure when I see a pretty lady I will look at her maybe or maybe not. Take Denise over there playing cards, she's a beautiful young lady and she knows what she wants. If Jack there can ever get her to marry him, he'll feel the same way in thirty years about her, as I do my wife."

"Now just how the hell would you know that?" Shawn asked chuckling. Looking over at the two of them sitting across the table from each other.

"Sometimes you can just tell these things Marshal," Charlie said smiling. "Sometimes you can just tell…Take you for instance; I'd say

Chapter Fourteen

you were married once…But it didn't work, because you like the open road."

"You sure hit that one on the head. I was married for a short time; she wanted me to be a store clerk. A more boring job I never had. I was glad when a herd of cattle came through town; the trail hands would talk about this or that that had happened to them on the drive…Just knew I couldn't stay there anymore. She told me it was either her or a ranch…There was no way she wanted anything to do with those stinking cattle and all the hard work them farm women had to do. Shawn, she told me, you were not meant to settle down in one spot very long. Then she handed me a duffel bag with my clothes in it, and told me if you leave, DON'T come back. Well you can see, I didn't go back, and I haven't looked back either."

Just then another man stood up and threw his cards down on the table. "Well shit," he said. Picking up his last few chips and counted them, three hundred and fifty dollars. "You sure can play poker young lady. I would like to say it's been a pleasure…But well," as he threw the rest of his chips into the middle of the table. "If I said that I'd be lying." He tipped his hat to her; "Maybe we'll meet again someday." Taking one more look around the room, he walked out the door.

"FIVE LEFT, it's getting closer to dinner time and I'm getting hungry," Shawn said.

"Marshal, I'm going to go up and get a bath before we go," Wapiti said. "That's if you don't mind."

"Not at all, Deputy," Shawn said with a big smile on his face.

"A bath," Cork hollered. "Hell, now we know you're getting serious. You just had a bath last night. Most people are lucky if they take two in a week and young Wapiti here is taking one every night. You just make sure you go over to the barber and get a shave, and have him put some of that stinky water he has on you afterwards, the ladies seem to like it."

"You guys just leave me alone," Wapiti said. "You know I'm nervous enough as it is." Looking back over to Cork. "What the hell do I have to shave for? Most Indians can't grow hair on their faces, least

321

not a full blooded Indian," Then he turned and started walking up the stairs towards the bathhouse.

"Hey, wait a minute Wapiti," Shawn said, chuckling a little. "You don't take all afternoon, because I'd like one too. I took one first night in, but not since."

"We know," Wapiti said. "I can smell you all the way over here."

"You know Marshal," Cork said. "Never thought I'd live to see an Indian law man. But there goes the first, and I don't think he cares what anybody thinks. Fact if they don't like it, he'll just put his fist in their mouth and make them accept it."

"I do believe you're right Cork," Shawn answered, proudly.

"What on earth ever gave you the idea to put a ten gauge on him?" Cork asked. "Hell a twelve gauge would have done the job."

"I thought I already told you...You can see he can handle his feet and fists...and he's never been around guns. So I got him a forty-four, but he needs time to learn how to use it. So I got Gordy to cut that one down, I knew no one would like taking orders from an Indian, but with that double barrel Ten Gauge... it would make every man think twice before they tried anything to serious."

"I know it made these boys around here sit up and think twice," Cork said. "I bet he doesn't ever take it off again, not since that man yesterday tried to back shoot him, and then the one this afternoon."

"I bet you're right Cork, I was younger than him the last time I took my gun off for a fistfight. You just never know when someone will pull a gun or knife out of their boot's if you start beating him to bad."

"You took it off yesterday," Corky said. "With those three in the restaurant."

"Hell I knew they were all talk. Besides Wapiti was right behind me with that big hog leg."

Just then another man stood up cursing, throwing his cards on the table, "That's what I get for thinking you were bluffing Denise. I've never known anyone as lucky as you and this boyfriend of yours here." He said, pointing at Jack. The man looked over at the Marshal, "I know I'm out of the game, but do you mind if I keep my seat here."

Chapter Fourteen

Looking around at the players, "I too would like to see just who does win this game."

"Noo...I don't mind," Shawn said. "But if I catch you passing any signals across the table to your buddy there, I'll break both your arms, then I'll throw you both out on your heads, CLEAR?"

"I don't know what you think you did or didn't see Marshal," the man answered. "But if it'll make you happy, I'll keep my hands in my pockets."

Just then the judge came walking up to the bar. "Whiskey, Charlie with a beer chaser."

"Shawn," Cork said. "I told you the Judge would be in around three."

"Just how are you doing today, your Honor," Shawn said. Patting him on the shoulder and sitting down beside him, with a big smile on his face.

"Just what are you smiling at Felton?" Judge English asked.

"Now your Honor, I thought we started off on the right foot," Shawn said.

"I hope you plan on teaching your Deputy to bring any and all wanted fugitives to a court of law, and not your way." Judge English said. "You might say your reputation precedes you. I don't think any Sheriff, or Deputy, and no Marshal should decide if a man lives or dies for his crime. That should be left up to the Judge and the jury to decide what should happen to him, either hanging or jail time."

Shawn leaned over to the Judge, "I've seen your type of justice over there in the town jail with that young man Floyd Larkin...And another thing...YOUR Honor, I've never shot anyone who wasn't shooting at me first."

"I got a wire from a Judge Monson over in Prineville. In the twenty plus years you've either been a Deputy U.S. Marshal or a U.S. Marshal. You've killed over one hundred men. Now don't you think that's taking the law into your own hands? It's up to the law and not to you whether a man lives or dies. Wasn't it just a little over a week ago you killed seven or eight more supposed outlaws."

Marshal Shawn Felton and the Wild Bunch

"NOW YOUR HONOR, That wasn't totally my fault. They had me out numbered...Like you said eight to one. My plan was to just wound the driver when they all got in the middle of the river," Shawn said apologetically.

"That's another thing, what kind of idiot would take an Indian boy on as a lawman?" The Judge growled back. "Why that's like pouring kerosene on a fire."

"Well now, Your Honor, if you'd been around here these last couple of days you would have seen just how well that Young man has handle himself," Shawn said with a whole lot of bragging in his voice. "Why these men have grown to respect that Young man."

"Oh by the way," Shawn reached into his pocket and pulled out the wooden key he had taken off of Floyd. Waving it around the Judge's face, and then leaning towards the Judge, "You see this little key?"

"So what?" the Judge answered.

"Well, it just happens to fit one of those jail cells over in the town jail." Shawn said. He could see the Judge's eyes getting bigger and his face redder. "That's right YOUR HONOR...I took this key off Floyd right here in this bar not two hours ago, and furthermore, I gave him enough money to get out of your county."

"YOU DID WHAT?" the judge shouted. "Why I have just a half a notion to throw you in jail for that. I'll put a poster out on him and have him back in county lockup inside a week."

"Just what are you going to put on that poster for the reason he's wanted, Your Honor," Shawn said started to chuckle. "You put the real reason on that poster and you'll get laughed clean out of the country... You say I make up my own laws...Just how the hell can you justify a poster on that young man. Hell, if you don't watch out he just might become your son in law...Then what are you going to do?"

"Give me that damn key," the Judge said reaching out for it. Shawn being a good head taller than the Judge held the key up in the air. "Charlie, what day of the month is it?"

"Hell I don't know, Marshal," Charlie answered looking around the counter, "Cork do you have a calendar anywhere?"

324

Chapter Fourteen

"I think there's one in the front drawer under the cash register," Cork answered walking over, opening the drawer and pushed some papers around. "Here's one…Let's see…It's the last day of the tournament, so that makes it the twenty fifth of May. Why's that Marshal?"

Still holding the key up, Shawn looked back at the judge. "Now if you promise to hang this above your jail cell entrance, on a plaque and say…hmmm…. Something like…On the twenty fifth of May, eighteen ninety-two Floyd Larkin carved this key and broke out of jail. That's why we no longer serve knives with your dinner;" starting to chuckle louder, "Charlie pour his Honor here a drink on me."

"The games ain't over yet," Cork hollered. "I'm still buying your drinks Marshal." Looking over at the Judge smiling… "Maybe I don't want to buy him a drink. After all he had the gull to fine me ten dollars for drunk and disorderly last month."

"You drunk and disorderly, Cork?" Shawn asked. "When aren't you…? At least drunk that is?"

"Seven o' clock, Marshal," Cork answered, still smiling.

"Which seven o' clock you talking about?" Shawn said.

"Every day at seven o' clock in the morning," Cork said.

"You're not sober then either," the Judge stated firmly. "If they ever come up with a way to measure how much alcohol a man has been drinking, it would still come back over the limit, just a little lower than usual…But you would STILL BE, legally drunk!"

With that comment everyone at the bar who could hear the conversation busted up laughing.

"You know, after the tournament was over I WAS going to buy the house a round," Cork said. "But you all just pissed me off."

Just then Wapiti came walking back into the room. "He also thinks he's fooling everyone in the morning with his coffee," Wapiti says, starting to chuckle. "It may have some coffee in it, but it's about half whiskey."

"Some people like their coffee with sugar…I like mine with whiskey," Cork said, smiling.

Just then another man stood up hollering, throwing his cards on the table. "Well it sure has been a fun last few days, but I guess it just

325

wasn't my time to hit it big." Looking around the room, then back at Denise. "If I were you guys I wouldn't let her play in any more games…She's good," tipping his hat to the last three players. "I know who I think is going to win this. And you two don't have a chance," he said to the men and turned and walked up to the bar, "Give me one for the road please."

Shawn turned and walked over to the table, Denise not only had a huge pile of chips in front of her, but she also had three large bags lying on the floor beside her. Jack had quite a pile himself. Then he looked over at the third man who was lucky if he even had a couple thousand left. "You know Young man," Shawn said pointing at all three players and their piles of chips. "I hate to say this, but it don't look like you have much of a chance in hell either and I've got a dinner engagement I'd like to get to."

Reaching in and pulling out his pocket watch and looking at it. "It's almost four o' clock now. The way I understand it, young lady, Jack…I hear you two are an item. Fifty thousand dollar's is real good for a young couple just starting out. So if you two plan on getting married we could end this game right now…Looking down at Denise…You do intend to marry this guy don't ya?"

"I don't know Marshal," Denise said. With a big grin on her face, looking back and forth between Jack and the Marshal. "He hasn't asked me."

"Well, why don't you ask her son? So we can all go home," Shawn suggested.

"WHAT? Right here in front of everyone? Don't you think that might be something I'd like to ask when it's just the two of us?" Jack said. "Besides I don't know if she would marry me even if I asked her."

"Well then, since both of you have almost every chip in the house between you. It would take the rest of the night and part of tomorrow before you two could finish the game. So, since more than likely you two just might end up together, how about you just split the fifty thousand and we call it a day?" Shawn asked.

Jack and Denise looked at each other then over at the third player; "Well what do you have to say about this Mr.?" Denise asked.

Chapter Fourteen

The man looked down at his little pile of chips then back over to Denise's pile and the bags on the floor. "I know one thing for sure, the Marshal is right...I don't have a chance in hell of winning this thing, and to tell you the truth I'm getting a little tired. None of us have gotten much rest these last few days...And well..." Looking around the room, and stopped when he saw one of the young ladies that work there. "Well I think I will just get that young lady right there." Pointing. "That's if she wants to join me, and I'm going to call it a day. Get me a bottle, and then maybe she will join me up in my room...Where I'll lick my wounds and wait for another game. That will be a game, that you are not a part of young lady. Just like quite a few others have said, you have one hell of a poker face...I've played in many big games, with a whole lot of different players... and everyone has some kind of tell-tell sign of what they're holding in their hands. Even if it's a bluff...But I'll be damned if I've ever seen any clue in your face, your eyes, and your actions, to give me the slightest idea as to what you were holding." Sticking out his hand, he shook Denise's hand first, then Jack's.

Looking over at Jack and standing up, "Mr. if you're lucky enough to get this young lady to marry you, then you're a very lucky man. Because not only is she a beautiful lady, but she also has a good head on her shoulders. You can just tell by looking at her that she knows what she wants. And I'll just bet you she gets exactly what she wants whenever she wants it. I want you both to know and you too Mr. Bukowiec...this has been a fun weekend, but sadly it must come to an end." He picked up the rest of his chips; he dropped them into Jack's pile. "I know you'll get those back from him someday, and maybe even more." Then turning and walking to the bar, grabbed him a bottle of whiskey and the young lady by the hand, and headed upstairs. "Good night everyone," he hollered out.

Shawn turned around and looked at Wapiti and then over to Cork. "Looks like I have just enough time to get a bath before dinner, so if you'll excuse me, I'm heading that way."

"I told them you'd be there in just a few minutes Marshal. So they should have all the hot water you need." Wapiti said.

"Well I thank ya Wapiti." Shawn said, turning to the crowd of people, "Now for the rest of you…me and Wapiti are going to get an early start in the morning. I know it has been an exciting weekend, but I need my rest. So after ten o' clock this evening I don't want to hear a peep. IF I DO, and I have to come downstairs to break up any ruckus, well let's just say somebody won't be walking out of here." Then he turned towards the bathing room.

Wapiti turned and walked over to the bar where Cork and Charlie were sitting. "Well Cork, it looks like I didn't cause too much trouble around here this weekend. Most of your establishment is still in its place."

"Yes sir Wapiti it is," Cork said with a big smile on his face, looking down from his thrown "I've got to tell ya, when you and the Marshal first came in, I didn't think you would hold up through the weekend before you had gotten a good beating. But I was wrong, fact is, it's been a lot of fun watching you make mincemeat out of these men." Sticking out his hand, "Fact I'd like to shake the hand of the first Indian Marshal and even buy you a drink."

"Thanks Cork, but I'll hold off on that drink for right now," Wapiti said. "If you don't mind. I'll have it when I get back from dinner, just before I go to bed."

"Sure son, anytime," Cork answered. "And I mean that. Anytime you pass through this way; there'll always be a free drink and room for you Wapiti. Even if you're no longer a Deputy Marshal."

Just then three drifters, cowboys came walking up to the bar, one accidentally bumped into the back of Wapiti. Wapiti turned to see what was going on, the man turned real quick to apologize to who ever he just fell into, "I'm sssss…What the hell is an Indian doing in a bar?" Looking around the room, "What the hell you doing in here boy?" Then the man noticed the badge on Wapiti's vest. He reached out and grabbed hold of it to get a better look. "Check this out boys, he has a toy badge that says he's a U.S. Deputy Marshal…What Judge would be fool enough to give a badge to an Injun." They all three started laughing back and forth. One of the other men looked down at what Wapiti was drinking; reaching over he picked up the glass and took

Chapter Fourteen

a smell. "Hell boys, this bucks drinking sarsaparilla...What's wrong Chief? Can't hold your liquor?" Patting the other two on their back.

Wapiti started looking the three over. He knew these men obviously hadn't been here for the weekend. The first man who started it was just a little taller and maybe not as heavy as Wapiti was, the second was standing on Wapiti's left was just about the same size as he was. The third, who was working his way to Wapiti's right side, was at least four maybe five inches taller and a good forty plus pounds bigger. None of them had much fat on them, he could tell that right off. The biggest of the three would be more likely than the others to make the first move. However, Wapiti felt the man might try to start a fight, preferably when he wasn't looking at him.

Then that very same man started laughing..."I can't believe you people would allow an InJun in here. What the hell kind of people are you? That you would allow this to happen!"

One man just a couple stools down from the commotion stood up and started walking away from the situation. "You boys don't know what you're getting yourselves into with that young buck there. Fact is he's already bested eight men this weekend."

The first man still looking around the room then back at Wapiti. "What the hell you talking about? This buck don't even have a mark on him. You telling me he's beat eight men?" Looking Wapiti's over he sees the ten gauge. "Damn boys, check that out. Is that supposed to scare us or something?" The man asked Wapiti. "Maybe he can scare you fools, but you just take that off boy and we'll teach you a lesson."

"That ain't even happening," Wapiti said. "I'll let you try me mister, but this stays on my side."

"What's wrong boy?" the third man asked. "In case we start kicking your ass, you can stop us by pulling that hog leg?"

"I don't need it," Wapiti said.

"We'll take ours off and lay them up here on the bar," the first man said laughing. As all three were doing just that, unbuckling their gun's and untying their holsters. "Now you just take that off and we'll have some fun. I hear you Injuns think you can take three or four white eyes on at the same time. So do you want to dance? Or are you afraid?"

329

"Not at all," Wapiti answered. "HOWEVER, let's get a few rules laid out right now. Anything and I do mean anything gets broke, it comes out of your pocket." He stated firmly, handing Cork his ten gauge. "Cork you keep that aimed right at these men, if one of them reaches for a pistol from someone in the crowd, Then you blow his hand off with one barrel, save the second barrel for the next one that reaches for a gun." Looking around the room, "Any of you standing up close here with a gun had better move back," Wapiti ordered. "Cause if one of these men reach's for your gun, that shotgun will get a piece of you too."

Just then everybody within fifteen feet of them got up and moved backwards. The first man started talking again, "You people are all a bunch of chicken shits aren't you?" Looking over at his two companions. "Will you just look at how fast these chicken shits turned and ran? No wonder he was able to beat one or two of them at a time."

The man on his left started talking; "BOY WE have no problem paying for any damage's, because we're going to take it out of your hide."

Out of the corner of his eye, Wapiti saw the man on his right start to throw a punch, turning and going down low Wapiti smashed his right fist into the big man's ribcage. The man knew he had just had a couple ribs broke. Grabbing him by the back of the head Wapiti smashed his face into the top of the bar. Sending the man's blood flying everywhere as he fell to the floor, knocking him out cold.

Wapiti felt a blow in his side, seeing that the man in front was getting ready to unload, Wapiti stood up and blocked the man's arm with his left and smashed his right into the man's mouth, sending him backwards a couple of steps. Following the man Wapiti reached out with his left and grabbed the man by the shirt. Pulling him back towards himself, he smashed his right into the man's stomach. This punch lifted him up off the floor, and knocked every once of air out of him. Holding the man up Wapiti threw his right one more time, coming up under the man's chin, sending him flying up and backwards. Crashing down on top of a table, then rolling off, and falling to the floor.

Chapter Fourteen

Turning towards the last man, he felt a smashing blow to the side of his face. Wapiti turned and ducked at the same time. Coming up under the man's next punch. Turning with all his speed and all his power in his legs he smashed his foot into the man's stomach, causing the man to bend over while moving back wards. Reaching out and grabbing the man by the hair, Wapiti picked him up and brought his knee up into the mans face as he drove the man's head down. Smashing the man's face down into his knee, sending blood and teeth everywhere. Just for good measure Wapiti smashed the man's face into his knee one more time.

Still holding the man's head, Wapiti looked around the room. Pulled his knife out of his belt and put it to the man's head. "The next one I am taking. " He stated, dropping the man lifeless to the floor.

Reaching over to Cork, Wapiti grabbed his shotgun. Then looking down at three men who were slowly picking themselves off the floor. "You tell all your friends and everyone you meet, that there's a new lawman in the country. You make damn sure you tell them he's an Indian and will take on anyone, anytime, anywhere, any day. You make damn sure and tell them my name is Wapiti." Then reaching over grabbing a hold of the man who bumped into him, he helped him to his feet. Cocking his right arm for one more blow if needed…"You got something you want to say to me for bumping into me? Or do I still need to teach you some manners?"

The man was looking through his bloody and blurry eyes, "No sir Deputy. I'm sorry…Next time I'll make sure and watch where I'm going." The man answered.

Both the other men, who were just starting to stand back up. "They to were telling him just how sorry they were. Can we buy you a drink?" they offered.

"That won't be necessary boys," Cork said smiling. "His drinks are on the house. But you do owe me twenty five dollars for that table."

"No problem Mr.," the leader said. "No problem at all. Barkeep, I sure could use a drink. So if you'll pour, I'll pay for everything at the same time." Reaching into his pocket and pulled out his money.

Looking over towards the washrooms, the biggest of the three men saw Marshal Felton still drying his hair off as he walked out. "Wapiti just what kind of fun am I missing out on?"

"Not much Marshal," the big man said. "Just a slight misunderstanding with your Deputy. But it's all straightened out now."

Shawn looked the three men over, he could see teeth missing, noses broke, and blood soaked shirts, and one man holding his ribs trying to breath, you could tell by the look on his face each and every breath he took hurt, he was having a hard time breathing. "Well now Mr.," Shawn said, starting to chuckle. "I can see there was a little trouble here…. Are we going to have anymore?"

"NO SIR," all three men said at the same time. "None at all Marshal." Then the biggest of them looked over at Shawn, "If we'd known he was with you Marshal we wouldn't have bothered him."

"By the looks of you three and the looks of Wapiti, I don't think you bothered him too much at all. But I think you might want to go find a doctor Young man. You're breathing like you got kicked in the ribs by a horse."

The man reached over and grabbed one of the shots of whiskey that Charlie had poured. "Yes sir Marshal," the man said looking over at Wapiti, and taking the shot. "I think you're right on both, I feel like I've been kicked by a horse and I was going to ask if anyone knew where the doctors office was."

"Three doors down," Cork said. "Fact for the entertainment, you boys pay for that table, and I'll pay for this round." Just then a man put his hand on Wapiti's shoulder and stuck his other hand out to shake Wapiti's hand. "Mike, Mike Larkin, Sir, it's a pleasure to meet you."

"Please don't call me Sir, Mike," Wapiti said, looking over at him. He could see Mike was a couple inches shorter than he was but he was built just like his dad, big arms and big chest. Looking down he could also tell by the way his pants were tight around his legs there was a lot of muscle in them too.

Pointing at the blood in the corner of Wapiti's mouth, Mike was smiling. "Now you make sure you tell Cathey I had nothing to do with that, or I'll get even worse. She already warned me." Mike turned

332

Chapter Fourteen

towards the Marshal. Extending out his hand, "Marshal Felton, Sir... Mike Larkin, I'm here to get both you and Wapiti for dinner. It's only a few blocks, but Cathey didn't want you getting lost."

Tossing the towel on the bar Shawn combed his hair, then put his hat on his head. With a real big smile on his face, "Well gentlemen, I can't tell ya how long it's been since I've had a good home cooked meal, so if you will excuse us, Mr. Larkin," waving his hand, "If you'll lead the way Sir, we'll follow you." Then the three walked towards the door and outside. Looking up the street they could see the three men from Wapiti's last fight helping each other up the stairs to the doctor's office. Shawn couldn't help but chuckle, pointing at them. "Always remember that boys, don't ask me why, but for some reason you always have to walk UP stairs to the doctor's office."

The three walked up the street, Mike turned to Wapiti, "I got to tell you Wapiti that was a lot of fun to watch. I don't think I've seen three men get their asses kicked that fast in a long time. Where did you learn to fight like that?"

"My dad," Wapiti answered. "He said you always put all your weight and power into every punch and kick. Said that way you won't need to hit them as many times, and to make sure that every punch you throw sets up a second to follow right behind the first."

"Well, all I know is you have a hell of a lot of power in your punches," Mike said. Looking back between the Marshal and Wapiti, "When you brought that uppercut into that man's stomach, shoot, you lifted him a good two and a half maybe three feet off the floor." Starting to chuckle a little, "Hell I bet he didn't get his breath back until he'd been laying on that floor for at least three or four minutes.

"What I'd like to know," Wapiti said smiling. "Is how the hell did you and your Dad get all those muscles?"

Pointing down the street in front of them as they walked Mike pointed out a wagon used for hauling logs out of the mountains to the mill. "Each one of those wheels are six feet tall, eight inches wide and weigh three hundred plus pounds. When they break, and they will break, we have to change them. If we're lucky, they can get down here to the Livery, but most of the time we have to go up into the mountains

333

Marshal Shawn Felton and the Wild Bunch

to fix them. Then you have all those draft horses they use for pulling those wagons." Starting to chuckle, "Some of those big boys don't like to be shod, so you better be able to hang on."

Mike stopped and opened the gate into the yard of their house. Just at a quick glance Wapiti could see it was a beautiful two-story house. Walking up the steps both Wapiti and Shawn could smell the food cooking, just the aroma alone made them even hungrier than they really were. Wapiti's stomach felt like it was all twisted up in knots inside, he could hear everyone talking, he could hardly wait to see Cathey again, but her family was inside this house. Would they really accept him, or were he and Cathey just wishful thinking. Mike opened the door and walked in, Wapiti took a quick look around the room, there were at least thirty people inside if there was one.

He could see Cathey walking towards him, and he knew Jack, Denise, Sam, and a couple others he recognized from to tournament. Cathey grabbed him by the arm, leaning up she gave him another kiss on the cheek, and he could feel his face heating up as everyone came up and introduced themselves to him. He was so nervous; he couldn't even remember their names. Then Cathey introduced him to her mom. "Wapiti this is my mom, Louise."

Holding out his hand to shake her hand trying to be polite, he could see right off where Cathey got that beautiful smile of hers.

Just then he felt a hand on his shoulder, turning around he could see it was Jack. "You know Deputy, I haven't had a chance to apologize for our stupidity Friday morning at the restaurant," Jack said. Rubbing his still bruised jaw and trying not to laugh. "But you sure let us know right away we were picking on the wrong Indian…you should have seen Lavern afterwards. HELL, he had to go home, he literally pissed his pants when you pulled that hog leg out. He said those were the biggest two barrels he had ever seen. Said he couldn't even see around them barrels, all he wanted to do is get the hell out of there before you let loose with just one barrel."

"I wasn't sure just how many more people were going to jump into the fight," Wapiti said. "I figured maybe it was my only chance to change their minds."

334

Chapter Fourteen

Shawn was working his way around the room meeting everyone. However he was heading for the kitchen and all that wonderful smelling food. He was almost there when out of the corner of his eye he saw Floyd sitting down in a chair, way back in the corner. Shawn looked at him in disgust and disbelief that he was still in town. Walking towards him Shawn started talking, "FLOYD, what the hell you still doing in town?"

"Well Marshal," Floyd said standing up, smiling and holding out his hand. "It's like this; Roy had three wheels he had to put on a couple of trailers for the loggers. Told me if I'd help, he'd give me twice the horse than the one I could afford. So if need be when I got over around Baker City and all I could find was work as a cowhand...then I'd have a good horse for the job."

"I'll have you know that Judge came in just shortly after I kicked your ass out," Shawn said, lighting a cigar. "If I were you, I think I'd get going while the going is good, just like I told you earlier."

"I was going to head out, but then Roy told me about Wapiti and the big dinner tonight... well...I couldn't turn down a spread of food like this, not after jail food for the last four months."

Looking over at Floyd smiling, "Now that I can understand," Shawn said. Looking back towards the table, the women were in the process of putting all that good smelling food out. "Now son that is one thing I can agree with you on. I really don't remember just how long it's been for me since I had a good home cooked meal. Heck back home I get a whole lot of Mexican food. It's good mind ya, hotter than Haiti's... But there's nothing like a good old fashion home cooked meal..." Wiping his mouth with his hand. "I can hardly wait to get in there. So just when do you intend on leaving? Like I said, I talked to the judge and he still wants a piece of your ass, if you know what I'm saying son."

"Yes sir, I do Marshal, I intend to leave right after dinner. Besides Prairie City is only fifteen miles down the road. They have that big fancy Brothel over there. I can't afford them. But, they have a nice saloon there as well. Not all the young ladies there are as nice looking as the ones down at the Silver Dollar...But they'll do just fine. If you know what I mean Marshal?" Floyd said, with a big smile on his face.

Starting to chuckle Shawn looked at Floyd, "Yes I do. I was young and dumb once myself, course then the women were a lot tougher, and they didn't have all that paint to put on their face like they do now. Back then you knew what she was going to look like in the morning... Now day's you don't."

Floyd looked up at the Marshal laughing; "You're damn straight on that."

"Alright you men, you can talk later," Louise said. "Right now let's sit down to dinner." Everyone headed towards the table. Wapiti walked over to the table; he couldn't help but notice all the food. There were mashed potatoes, fried chicken, steaks, ribs, and biscuits as big as his hand. Pulling out a chair for him, Cathey said, "Here Wapiti you sit here and I'll sit beside you."

The Marshal was sitting on the other end of the table, where he and Roy were talking. Wapiti could see that Roy was keeping one eye on him, which made him feel just a little uncomfortable, which Cathey could see. Leaning over to him, Cathey whispered in his ear. "Don't worry about dad Wapiti, he just likes to make all us girl's boyfriends feel nervous."

"He's real good it," Wapiti answered.

Denise and Louise started pouring a big glass of milk for everyone. Wapiti looked around the table; he could see the Marshal was checking it out as well. Wapiti figured it had been years since the Marshal had had milk for dinner. That thought put a real big smile on his face. Reaching over the Marshals shoulder, Louise put a mug of beer down in front of him, "Figured you might enjoy this with your dinner Marshal."

"Thank you, Ma-am," Shawn answered. "You're right."

Looking around the table and then around the rest of the room where all the kids were sitting and eating, Wapiti couldn't remember ever sitting down to eat with so many white eyes before. When he first walked in the door, he was thinking he hoped it would get over with fast, so they could get out of there. But everyone was being real nice to him, fact they were talking to him like he was one of them and not an Indian. Looking around the room at everyone at the table and all

Chapter Fourteen

those kids, in no time at all, all those knots in his stomach were gone, and the food was filling it up.

It was by far the best meal he had ever had. Everyone was talking about all the dumb or just plain stupid things they had done in their lives. Even the Marshal had stories of dumb and stupid things he had done. One time he was to bring in two bad desperados, he called them. They got to bullshitting and drinking and got him flat ass drunk. He passed out…when he woke up the next morning they were gone. Took him another four days to track them back down again. Had to do the same job twice he said, but he only got paid for it once. He had been a young lawman at that time…He's never done it again. Get drunk that is, while he had prisoners in his custody.

But Wapiti couldn't help but keep looking at the arms on Roy and Mike. Someone like that, in a fight, if they ever got a hold of you, they would flat squeeze a man in half. Dinner lasted maybe a total of forty-five minutes, but to Wapiti it only felt like ten or fifteen. That didn't matter, cause he couldn't remember ever eating that much food in one sitting before. Everything tasted so good that when he finished he felt like he had made a pig out of himself.

"Well now then," Roy said, standing up. "Marshal, you remember me telling you about those three inch wood pigeons?"

"Sure do," Shawn answered. "Did you manage to get us some for the trip?"

"Yes sir I did," Roy said smiling. Looking around at all the men sitting at the table. "Fact, you might say I went a little overboard. I picked up a couple extra bags and also some more ammo…Figured we could do some target practice ourselves tonight." Looking back at the Marshal, Roy chuckled, "I hope you don't mind, I put them all on your Marshal's charge account that you have state wide."

"Hell no, I don't mind at all," Shawn said. "That sounds like a lot of fun. We only have maybe an hour and a half of daylight left so we better get at it."

"That's not a problem Marshal," Roy said. "They paint them orange and white, the orange ones you shoot during the day. At night you build a bon fire, then you can see the white ones. So what do you say Marshal...? You want to teach us Larkin boys or those who married in or about to marry into the Larkin family, how to shoot?"

"Now that sounds like fun. However," pointing over to Wapiti. "The only gun Wapiti has is that ten gauge, and I don't have my rifle."

"No problem Marshal," Cathey said. "I'd be more than glad to run over to the saloon and get them for you. Denise would you like to go with me?"

"Sure Cathey," Denise answered. The two turned and walked towards the door. "We'll be back before you guys even get started."

Walking over to the cupboard Roy pulled out a gallon jug of whiskey. "It just wouldn't be a proper shootout without a bottle of Kentucky bourbon."

"You're right," Shawn said, licking his lips and reaching for the bottle. "What do you say we men go outside for the games? I'll show you boys just how this is done."

Jack and Sam were both standing nearby, "Well Marshal, you want to put a wager on whether or not you'll hit the flying target? Also every round, we put a dollar in a can to see who hits the most in a row without missing. The pot starts back up after it's won." Sam said.

Looking around the room Shawn could see Floyd talking to Louise, "Floyd, you going to come and join us outside for a while?"

"No Marshal, I want to get to Prairie City," Floyd said. "So I'll know what she's going to look like in the morning."

With that comment both Floyd and Shawn started chuckling. Roy looked over at Shawn as they walked towards the door, "What's that all about Marshal?"

"Nothing Roy," Shawn said. "It's just a little joke between us. I'll tell ya later. Now lets go make some money." All the men walked out the back door, leaving the women with the job of not only cooking that big wonderful meal, but then the job of cleaning it all up.

CHAPTER FIFTEEN

Butch and Sundance were each holding the reins to a horse, look-ing out from behind the building and up the street. There still were a few people walking down Main Street. Luckily most of them were drunk and couldn't see ten feet in front of themselves. They started out across the large open field between them and the Livery stable. At least it backed up to the river, so they could follow it and maybe not be noticed, but with these two big horses, there was no chance in hell of hiding them.

As quickly as they could they crossed the opening to the back door of the Livery stable. Tying the two horses up to the door, they hur-ried in, synched up their saddles, and were back out in just a couple minutes. Reaching over and each took a lead rope then climbed into their saddles.

Looking back over at the packs on the horses, Toad had picks, shovels, and on one he even put a small slues box. Toad had those packs looking like they really were wanta be gold miners, hoping on hit-ting the mother load, which they really had just done, Hit The Mother Load!. The two turned their horses back across the river into the log yard, but trying to stay in the shadows which was easy to do because of the cloud cover. They could barely see thirty feet in front of them, in no time they were on the main road and in the timber and better cover.

Butch was thinking to himself, they had gotten the town drunk and stole all their money while they were passed out. In no time they had reached the turnoff to Whitney. Which Randy had shown and told him how to go. Stopping at a telegraph pole, Butch climbed up on the back of his horse and cut the line. We'll cut it again further down. But they will think it's only cut here. Randy's going to cut line further down too. That way they will have to send out a second search team to repair it. That should give us a little more time.

It wasn't a real heavily traveled road. In fact Butch almost missed it. Looking up at the sky then over at Sundance, "I thought Toad said we'd have moonlight tonight. Hell there isn't even a star in the sky."

"He did," Sundance said. "But it's that cloud bank that rolled in. It's blocking the moon, so we will just have to pay real close attention, and not accidentally get off the main road."

"Hell I don't care about that," Butch said. "Randy told me how to go; I'm not going to get lost. I just hope those clouds don't open up and start raining on us."

"Butch you know better than to say something like that," Sundance said. "Hell, usually you no sooner say something like that, and it will start raining…So don't say it again."

"You know Sundance, this job was almost too easy," Butch said, as the two rode along at a good gallop. "I mean check this out, we're riding out of town just after stealing over twelve hundred pounds of gold, not to mention all the gold the other's have…And there's no one chasing us."

"It damn sure wouldn't have been even half this easy if we hadn't come across those Larkin boys," Sundance said.

"It wouldn't have been as much fun either," Butch said. "Hell, I bet we made close to forty thousand on that big Roan of Larry's alone."

"Speaking of which," Sundance said. "What went through your mind when you were on top of that Roan?"

"On top of him? What the hell you talking about, being on top of him?" Butch said. "Hell the only time I was on top of him was in the chute, after I called that gate, the next thing I knew I was flying through the sky. Fact I had to pay Randy an additional two hundred and fifty dollars."

"Why's that?" Sundance said.

340

Chapter Fifteen

"We had a hundred dollar bet on each jump, side bet," Butch said. "For three jumps… I thought I owed him the full three hundred, but he gave me the benefit of the doubt, said I was on him for at least a half a jump…Said that Roan flung me off his hind quarter's and launched me towards Mar's."

"That was real nice of him," Sundance said chuckling. "Because that is exactly what it looked like to me to, he came down and you didn't. Fact he was thru his second buck before you came back to earth."

"I'll tell you Sundance, I've been on a few bucking horses in my time," Butch said. "I didn't want them boys to know it, but I have. Fact I've been on a lot of horses that where supposed to be broke, and weren't. Randy was right, not only does he not want anyone on him, but also that damn Roan has more power than any horse I've ever been on. I honestly thought I could stay on for at least three jumps."

"I'll tell you one thing Butch; I don't remember when I've had so much fun. Those Larkin boys sure know how to party. I still don't see how anyone can tell Larry and Gary apart. Most twins there's something a little different between them, but those two are identical, like looking into a mirror."

""I figured out how to tell them apart," Butch said.

"Oh really? So why don't you tell me how to do it?" Sundance asked

"Larry is the one who always has a beer in his hand. Unless Gary won't let him, calls them his Barley Pop's." Butch said, chuckling.

"You're right," Sundance said shaking his head and starting to chuckle. "Larry does like his "barley pops."

"I know one thing that we're for damn sure going to do when get down to Portland. Before we catch the steamer to Los Angles, we are going to find someone we can trust enough to bring these horses back to Randy…I don't even want to think of him coming after me," Butch said.

"I know you're right about that," Sundance answered. "Randy said they have the Miner's Jubilee rodeo, and different logging competitions the last week of August. I thought maybe we'd come back for another job."

"WHAT!" Butch shouted out. "Are you out of your mind?"

"Why not?" Sundance said. Getting a big smile on his face. "They won't remember us."

"How the hell you figure that?" Butch said. "Sure the Doss's covered their faces…but we didn't…remember?"

"Do you think that banker, and that mining man will still have a job after eight o' clock in the morning? Just as soon as this is discovered, I bet they're all be out of a job within a week. And that Sheriff… Hell, he'll be lucky if they don't hang him." Sundance said, starting to chuckle. "Who do you think they're going to believe US OR HIM? If not for him, how else could we have known where that tunnel came up and when they loaded the gold?"

Starting to laugh along with Sundance, Butch looked over at him, "You're right about that. Then you put that extra fifteen hundred dollars in his pocket, that won't weigh much in his favor."

"So how long you think until Randy blows that canyon?" Sundance asked.

"Not real sure, it's a good hour, maybe an hour and fifteen minute ride down there at a good gallop. Don't ask me why, but he said he wanted to add more nitro. Hell, we took six large cases already. So if he's going alone it'll take longer than if someone goes with him," Butch answered

"Oh, I bet Gary will go with him," Sundance said. "If anyone."

"Yeah, by now Larry's got some little Betty under his arm and only one thing on his mind," Butch said still chuckling. "We never did get that five thousand back, that first little Betty took off us, did we?" Butch said.

"Hell, she was on her way somewhere, anywhere five second after she got that money….and you know it" Sundance said. "But how do you figure we didn't get our money back…Not to mention the forty thousand plus in cash, but these two horses loaded down with gold and no one on our tail just yet…How can you say we didn't get our money back? I'd say that was a real good five thousand dollar investment."

"For once you're right," Butch said.

Chapter Fifteen

All of a sudden it sounded like this entire side of the world was blowing up. Both their horses reared up from fear of the noise, and the continuing echo's. Looking back over in the direction of the blast, it made the clouds in the area light up as if it were mid-day, then turning bright red from all the dust and burning embers.

"HOLY SHIT," they both shouted. Trying to get their horse's under control and looking up at the sky at the same time.

"Whoa big boy," Butch hollered at his horse, looking back at the explosion and the back at Sundance, "DID YOU SEE THAT?"

"Hell yeah," hollered Sundance. "A blind man could see that. Hell I bet it woke everyone in Sumpter up."

Butch looked both at the sky, as it was still lit up and then back at Sundance. "Gary did say Randy liked to make big bangs with his back doors."

"I'll tell you Butch," Sundance said. "That's the biggest back door I've ever seen…And it's not even real, it's a fake back door."

"I don't think Randy does anything little," Butch said. "I know he don't when you make him mad. He likes them bigger and he hurts them with what I'd consider was cruel and unnecessary punishment. Hell, he don't have to hurt them half as bad as he does to get their attention…But he likes to finish the job…And I'd say he was finishing this job just fine."

"You know Butch? When we come back in August we can use the same diversion tactics," Sundance said. "But next time really go that way. They'll be thinking it's another diversion to fool them again. They'll think they're smart and head out through John Day and down to Portland. When we're really going to go out through Idaho and down through Utah."

"You just might be on to something there Sundance," Butch said. "So just how well do you think Curry's holding up?"

"Ooh, I think them Doss boys are having fun with him," Sundance said. "Especially since they know he's a city boy, and that fancy Arabian gilding he bought. I tried to talk him out of that horse, but he liked the way he held his head and tail up high and walked with those high fancy steps. I tried for hours to try and talk him in to what I thought was a

343

good trail horse. But you know Curry, once he gets his mind set…Well, there's just no changing it."

"I bet he wishes he would have listened to you now," Butch said. "I mean sure, we're riding through wilderness too. But by the way I hear it, that country they're going through there's nobody, maybe a couple crazy mountain men here or there. Gary told me there's a lot of steep country back in that area."

"I still bet they're coming up with all kinds of different stories about people being eaten up by all kinds of different wild animals in the area," Sundance said.

"You're right, and with this cloud bank making it even darker than usual, I bet he's squirming in his saddle," Butch said. Both men started laughing, before they knew it they came to Whitney valley. Randy told them it would be the first little town they'd come to. He had told them to stay in the timber if possible and ride around the small town until they got to the river. Then follow it through the mountains. There was a semblance of a road but with it being dark they might not be able to keep on it, it was more of a trail than a road. So they decided to stick to the river, they both came out just about the same area around Unity. From Whitney to Unity was just over twenty-five miles; if everything went as expected they should arrive in Unity early afternoon.

Now that's how you close a back door. Not that it'll stop anyone; I mean hell, all they have to do is go back up river a few hundred yards and cross over. Hell that posse might just figure on heading over the mountains here and come out at Hereford. "Let's get out of here," Randy said. "I'm tired."

"I hear ya on being tired," Gary said. Looking back at the fake back door and shaking his head. He could still smell the TNT in the air, putting his foot in the stirrup he climbed aboard. "Let's head for town."

"Well it sounds like everybody got away safely," Randy said.

"How you know that Randy," Gary asked.

"Are you crazy?" Randy said. "If anyone would have seen them, that church bell would be ringing, to wake everyone up."

Chapter Fifteen

"Hell you just woke everyone up," Gary said chuckling. "Hell you might have woke everybody up in Baker City too."

"Ya think?" Randy said, taking a bite off his chewing tobacco and chuckling. "Well let's kick these horses in the ass and get going." Doing just that and that big Clydesdale took off at a full run, with Gary right behind. The two rode hard and fast, fact it barely took them over forty five minutes to get back to Sumpter. As they approached town, they could see some people were still out in the streets looking around and talking about the explosion. Randy and Gary stopped at the timberline and looked everything over. There was still a good two plus hours of night left Gary could easily just ride into town and go to the Livery stable; no one would give him a second look. But that big Clydesdale would for sure catch their attention.

Gary looked over at Randy; "I'll stay on the road. Give me at least three minutes. That way they'll be looking at me, and you should be able to ride up the river bed staying out of sight behind the smoke-house so no one sees you coming in. Just make sure you use the back door to the saloon. That way we can sneak up to our rooms and to bed. I want to get an early start, old man Boyer said he'd hold our jobs for two weeks, after that he'd find someone else to help Dude with the horses."

Daylight was just coming up over the mountains when Larry awoke. He knew they wanted to get an early start. Getting dressed he walked two doors down and woke Luis. "Come on, let's get down to the restaurant, and get some grub to go. Then we'll wake Randy and Gary."

Wiping the sleep out of his eyes, Luis looked up at Larry, "The hell WE will, YOU! Wake Randy...I'll wake Gary."

"Yeah, yeah, whatever, just come on. I'll go down and order a dozen fried egg sandwiches to go. I'll meet you in Gary's room in five minutes with a pot of coffee." Then he turned and walked out the door.

Larry was feeling real happy and sure of himself, and maybe a little cocky. On his way down the stairs, he couldn't keep from thinking about yesterday. Dude had told them there would never be another

345

horse like his black stallion, that could go through ten men. It's too bad the old man wasn't there to see it; he would have enjoyed it too. Fact if he had been there, the town would have been a lot drier, because he could hold enough for three men if need be. But that only happened around the rodeos and after all the bull riders were done. He said that was one time you had better be stone sober. When you're trying to dodge a bull and get a cowboy out of the way safely.

Walking back to the kitchen, he could see the cook was just starting to get the oven hot for cooking. But that sweet smell of coffee was already brewing, reaching over Larry poured himself a cup, then looked back into the kitchen. "Hey cookie," he hollered. "Could I place a quick order and come back and pick it up say…twenty minutes?"

"You sure can Mr. Larkin… I played that horse of yours all the way until the end. You could say I made me a whole lot of money. See I was down at the Calvary fort when that Colonel tried to have a dozen different men try to break him. That man was mad as hell that no one could break him. I seen a sergeant tell him and I quote, 'you're the one who wants him broke so bad…break him your damn self.' That Colonel made that Sergeant a buck private right now. When I seen you boys coming into town, I couldn't believe it was the same horse, until I saw that big 55 brand on his hip. I got to tell ya, I couldn't believe it. But then I also seen you try to get on him the next morning and right off I knew it was the same horse. You just tell me what you boys need for the road and I'll give it to ya on the house…Call it a payback for all the money you made me yesterday.'

"Well thank ya," Larry said. "We need a dozen fried egg sandwiches." Reaching over he grabbed a pot of coffee and three more cups. Put this on it too.

Turning and heading back upstairs to the others. If he had to be the one to wake Randy, at least he had a cup of coffee. Hopefully that would calm him down a little bit; he would think someone was waking him up for work. He was glad to see Gary's door open, he walked in and was hoping to see Randy…But he wasn't there.

"Here" he said, sitting the coffee and the cups down. Then refilling his and one more he walked across the hall to Randy's room. Calling

Chapter Fifteen

out before he walked in, "It's only me Randy," Larry said looking around the room, first to the bed, which was empty, then over to the washbasin. He sure was glad to see Randy up. "Here," he said, handing him his coffee. "I ordered some fried egg sandwiches for breakfast; they should be done by the time we get down there."

"I don't know what everyone's in such a big hurry for," Randy said in a gruff voice. "We can't leave until they discover the robbery, and I can report my horses missing." He pulled out his pocket watch and looked at it. "Hell it's not even seven o' clock yet. Those guys probably won't be found for at least another two hours."

"Damned if you're not right," Gary said, as he and Luis were standing at the door. "DAMMIT," he shouted. "I was wanting to at least make it to the cabin on the John Day River today. Just look outside, those clouds aren't going to hold off much longer before it starts raining on us."

"Well aren't you just full of good news?" Randy said. "First you get us up too damned early, and now you're telling me we're all going to get wet.

Just then there was a lot of commotion going on outside. Some man came running down the street hollering, "We've been robbed, we've been robbed." The church bell started ringing; they were trying to wake everyone up. Looking out the window and in the direction of the bank they could see men coming outside. They were all hollering at the Sheriff, who was trying to defend himself. "It wasn't me" they could hear him hollering. The Sheriff reached in his pocket and pulled out the money, handing it over to the other two men. "Here take it," throwing the money at them. Which really ended up flying all around. "I don't care what they said. I had nothing to do with this I tell ya."

"Then just how the hell did they know how we loaded the gold?" the banker hollered back at him.

"How the hell am I supposed to know?" the Sheriff answered. He was pointing over at the mining man. "He's the one that fired everyone. Hell there's at least a dozen men who know how, where, and when that gold is transferred. Just think of it, those boys had their faces covered. It could have been any one of the men you fired last week helping out.

Marshal Shawn Felton and the Wild Bunch

Now if you'll get the hell out of my way, I have a posse to get together so we can head down river."

"What makes you think they went down river?" the banker asked, sternly.

"You heard that blast last night just as well as I did. Those boys think that if they blow up the canyon they could slow us down. You men forget I grew up around here, they're going out over Duley Mountain and through Idaho." The Sheriff answered

"Just how do you know they're going that way Sheriff?" the mining man asked.

"You mind telling me why they would go half way down the canyon, blow it up, then go another way? You forget those men don't know this country that well. They were playing poker all weekend with them Larkin boys. We need to talk to them," the Sheriff hollered. "I'll bet they were the men wearing the handkerchiefs…I'll just bet you they're not even in town."

The four of them had been leaning out the window in Randy's room listening to all that was going on below, watching the streets fill up with people as the news got out. "What the hell you talking about?" Randy hollered down at them. "What the hell did us Larkin boys supposedly do this time?"

Everyone looked up at them. "You know damn good and well what I'm talking about. Those men you were playing all your bullshit poker games with just happened to be Butch Cassidy and Sundance Kid and you knew it." Sheriff Hendricksen blurted out.

"They were who?" Gary hollered back down at them.

"You know damn good and well who they were. Don't try playing stupid with me!" the Sheriff hollered back.

"Who? Harvey Smith, Harry Jones, and Brigham Young?" Gary asked the Sheriff. "Who did you say they really are?"

"You boys know damn good and well who they are." The Sheriff yelled out again.

Just then a man came running out of the smokehouse. "Sheriff, I don't think they had anything to do with it."

"Just what makes you say that?" the Sheriff asked.

348

Chapter Fifteen

The man looked up at Randy, "Randy they took two of your horses." He said, looking back at the Sheriff and the others.

"WHAT? Randy hollered back down. "Who took my horses? I'll be right down and someone had better be joking or THERE WILL BE HELL TO PAY!"

Randy turned around and looked at the others, "Do you think I sounded mad enough or do I need to get madder?"

"No, No, that sounds real good," Gary said. "Lets all go down, acting like we don't know anything."

All four headed down the stairs, just as the Sheriff and the two men in them cheap suits were walking in.

Reaching out and grabbing the Sheriff by the shirt, "What the hell is this? Someone took my horses? You crooked piece of shit. Who the hell were those guys really? Randy said, shoving the Sheriff up against the wall. Hell we all saw you and them talking back and forth all weekend."

"BULLSHIT," the Sheriff hollered back. "The only time I talked to them was over at the bucking competition yesterday."

"Bullshit," Gary yelled back. "I know of at least three times you came over to our table, and then you and them went outside to talk."

"So they were right then," hollered the mining company man. "Just like I heard the one who called himself Sundance say, 'Thank you for all your help,' as he stuffed that money in your pocket."

By now there were at least a couple hundred people who had gathered around. There was the usual fifteen percent reward offered on all bank robberies and that gold was being held in the bank, and the mining company was offering another ten percent on top of that. Nobody had any idea of just how much gold had been stolen, but one thing was for sure, whoever was a part of that posse was going to have tens of thousands of dollars to divide up amongst them. And that was free money.

"Those horses are my livelihood," Randy said. Starting to wave his fist a little. "You had better get your fat ass out there and find them AND my horses. If you come back without them I'll take their value out of your hide. DO I MAKE MYSELF CLEAR SHERIFF...Now

349

we have to go to Prineville to take care of family business. We'll be back in two weeks. My animals had better be here when I get back or you had better not be, you worthless piece of shit." Randy said, smashing him back against the wall, then turning and walking towards the restaurant, not saying a word.

The others followed behind, trying as hard as they could not to laugh. They all had to get the hell out of there before they did bust up laughing. The four walked into the restaurant and the cook handed them their sandwiches

I put a nice ham steak on each sandwich as well, he said.

Thanks, Randy said, grabbing the bag, keeping his face covered. He was trying so hard to act mad, but at the same time everything had worked out just the way it was supposed to. Turning back to the others, "Alright, now we need to get the hell out of here ourselves. You guys get the horses and your gear. I'll meet you in front of the Livery in five minutes."

The four men walked out onto the boardwalk, they could see the crowd was growing by the minute and that fat ass Sheriff was giving orders, trying to act like a big shot. They could tell he was literally pissed off, he had hoped on having a trap in place down river, you could tell he wanted that reward. In no time at all, there was at least two hundred men saddled up and ready to go. So just as soon as the deputy brought his horse up and he drug his fat ass up into the saddle, the posse headed out of town just as fast as their horses could go.

Randy was leading his horse across the street as they rode by and he started laughing, his back door had worked. Those idiots had no clue as to just where them outlaws had gone. With them going in two different directions and in two small groups, they had no chance of finding their tracks. It wasn't long and the other three came leading their horses out of the stable, laughing their heads off.

"So how long after they get back from this wild goose chase do you think that Sheriff will be able to keep his job?" Larry said, looking down the road at the cloud of dust.

"I'll bet he's no where around when we get back," Luis said. "Fact I bet he don't even come back with the posse."

Chapter Fifteen

"You think they'll stay out a couple of days?" Larry said, climbing aboard the Roan, still chuckling. But no sooner had he gotten into the saddle and the Roan went sky high, just like every other time. Larry dug his spurs into his front shoulders, making the Roan even madder. Everyone was cheering and running in every which direction, but they couldn't get out of that Roans way. The two of them went up the street; the Roan kept it up for a good ten to twelve hard jumps. Then another three or four half-hearted crow hops and finally came to a stand still. Everyone was still shouting and hollering, cause they had just seen something done that ten men couldn't do yesterday. That was to see someone actually ride that big powerful Roan. "That makes one more time I've had to show him who the boss really is," Larry shouted out. He still couldn't help but wonder if that Roan would ever settle down or would this be his standard morning ritual, only time would tell. Larry looked back at the others he could see they were all still laughing. "Alright you smartasses," he yelled out. "Why don't one of you just climb in this saddle?"

All at once they all started answering, "No thanks, he's your horse hombre." Randy hollered, "You forget I already tried him." Clicking his cheek he climbed upon the big Clydesdale stallion. "Tell you what Larry," Randy said. "I tried yours, now you try this big boy right here."

"That's alright," Larry said, starting to chuckle. "You're all still a bunch of pussies, every one of you. Ten men tried and ten men died or flew away with the greatest of ease...Now let's get out of here," Turning the Roan, he headed in the direction of Granite.

The four hadn't even been on the trail for maybe fifteen minutes when it started sprinkling a little rain. "Damn it Larry. Why'd you have to say it was going to rain?" Gary said, pulling his rain slicker out and putting it on. "At least we can stay under the trees for some protection."

"You think we'll still make the north fork of the John Day today?" Luis asked.

"Don't worry about getting a little wet Luis, you aren't made of sugar, you won't melt," Gary said

"Shit does deteriorate when it gets wet though," Randy said.

"Piss off, both of you," Luis said putting on his rain slicker. "I just don't like riding and getting soaked at the same time. In weather like this, this time of the year, the country we're heading into, hell if this turns into a snowstorm and we don't have no shelter we might be in trouble."

"Don't worry about it Luis," Gary shouted back at him. "You know Larry's got at least two bottles if not more on him. So when it starts to get real cold we can start drinking it and warm ourselves up from the inside out.

It had been the longest night of Curry's life, he couldn't remember feeling so uncomfortable. He wouldn't want to admit it, but he was sure glad to see the sun coming up. He knew the Doss's were goading with him with all their stories. He had no idea just how far they had come or how far they still had to go. For the first time he could finally see the rugged country they were going threw. The trail they were taking was actually easy riding, especially because they were riding down in the bottom of the mountain valley. He could hear the river running off in the distance as they rode. But until it got lighter, he couldn't tell just how big or where the river was.

Slowly the sky began to light everything up around him; Curry was in awe of everything. Some of these trees were at least twelve to fifteen feet straight through at the bottom. He had heard that the redwood trees in California were even bigger than these. The way the clouds laid in on the mountaintops made him feel like those mountains reached all the way to heaven. Looking around at everyone, Curry could tell they were just as tired as he was. They had been up all day yesterday and all night to. "Toad," Curry asked, "Just when do you think we'll get to Granite?"

"We went around Granite a couple hours ago," Toad answered.

"Really," Curry said. Looking back and forth between everyone. "I don't ever remember going by any houses or anything else that had any lights on to let you know it was there."

"Hell the only thing that Granite had was a saloon and stable's, but now there's at least ten, twelve other house's going up. But there's only

Chapter Fifteen

one lady in town to cure your itch, if you know what I mean. Let's just say there's enough of her to squash a little man." Starting to chuckle, "I bet if she rolled over on a man, she would flatten him flatter than a pancake." Hosey said

"I thought we might stop and get some supplies." Curry said.

"Oh hell yeah," Goof said with a serious chuckle. "We'll just ride up to the nearest town leading eight mules, all of which are loaded heavy and all that gold that was stolen last night, you think they wouldn't notice us? That's why Randy made us a back door. Make everyone think we went that way, you dumb shit. If we pull into any town with this mule train this side of Seattle everyone is going to know EXACTLY where it came from."

"So how long until we get to the cabin?" Curry asked.

"We're only a few miles away from it now; we should be there in a couple hours at the most." Toad answered

Just then Toad's horse popped up his ears and he stuck his nose in the air. Then he started getting a little jumpy at the same time. Looking back he could see Goof and Hosey's horses doing the same thing. Curry's horse on the other hand was really jumping and whining a lot.

"Shut that damn animal up and get him under control," Toad yelled. "By the way these horses are acting, we have some company, and it isn't human."

"I'd say it's either a bear or mountain lion," Goof said. Pulling on his reins and looking in the direction that the horses were paying attention to...Do you guys smell anything?" he asked, continuing to look around.

"No I don't," Hosey said. He was looking in the same general area. "The wind is blowing in the wrong direction for me."

"What do you mean? Can you smell anything?" Curry asked.

"You'd be able to smell a bear," Toad said. They were still putting their big long nose in the air just like animals were. "Hold on tight to your mules boys, cause whatever it is, we're getting closer and closer."

"You don't suppose it could be one of those Sasquatch's, do ya Toad?" Hosey said, taking another turn with his lead rope around the saddle horn, just incase they tried to get away.

353

Just then a mountain lion let out a mighty scream. He had been laying in wait for them on the lower branches of the big ponderosa pine tree. Sending that big fancy horse of Curry's sky high and wanting to get the hell out of there. That horse started bucking as high and as fast as he could, and with all the power he had in him, he looked a little like the Roan. In any case it didn't take long before Curry was flying through the air, and not with the greatest of ease.

Toad managed to catch the loose reins as that Arabian came flying by. As quickly as he could he tied the reins around his saddle horn, actually giving himself rope burn on his hand.

The lion came flying out of the trees, hoping to have a horse for an early breakfast. He hadn't even gotten all four paws on the ground before Goof fired his rifle. Curry was lucky these boys had all been taught to shoot and not waste any bullets. Goof's shot was true, hitting the big lion just behind the ear on the side of his head. Killing him before he even hit the ground.

As all the excitement was coming to an end, Curry slowly started standing up. Trying to catch his breath, while most of his body hurt like hell. That horse had thrown him right on top of a downfall tree, making it feel like he had at least a couple broken ribs. He couldn't help but notice how those horses the Doss brothers were riding hardly moved when that lion attacked. Yet that good for nothing high priced piece of shit horse he had went absolutely berserk. Holding on to his ribs Curry walked over to Toad to get his horse. It was still fidgety, and upset about everything. He sure wished he had listened to Sundance and bought himself a good trail horse. He knew one thing for damn sure, if he got out of this country alive, first thing he was going to do was sell that damned horse, and get himself a mustang, or at least a horse that was brought up in this country. One that wasn't afraid of a lion's or bear's should anything like this ever happen again.

Toad handed him his reins, "I told you these lions will attack a man on a horse when they're hungry, you going to be alright?"

"Yeah," Curry said still holding his ribs and breathing real lightly. He grabbed his reins, then tightening his cinch strap, then slowly he

Chapter Fifteen

climbed back up into the saddle. "Come on," he said. "Let's get down to that cabin so I can rest up a little bit."

"Goof, I want to thank you," Curry said. "If you hadn't made that shot I would be lion food."

"Hell Curry, you're welcome," Goof said. "I don't miss often. Dad used to send us out to get meat with only one shell, if we came back empty handed, we did without dinner that night."

"That's why we would take our bows and arrows along," Toad said. "So if we missed the long rifle shot, we could maybe work our way up close enough to get him with an arrow."

"I miss shooting at the chickens," Hosey said.

"Chickens?" Curry asked with a skeptical tone in his voice. "What the hell does a chicken have to do with what we're talking about?"

"That was the best practice we got," Hosey said. "Dad would give us a twenty two caliber pistol, tell us only to shoot him in the head, cause if you hit him anywhere else you'd tear him up too much."

"A twenty two caliber pistol," Curry said. "Hell that won't tear nothing up. I mean hell…That's just a tiny bullet."

"Maybe so," Goof answered. "Believe it or not if you hit that chicken in the chest it will cause you to lose much needed meat."

"Speaking of meat," Curry said. "It's been a long time since we had anything to eat."

"Don't worry about it, Curry," Toad said. "When we get down to the cabin we can catch some fish, or we might get lucky and come across a couple of grouse, or even better, a deer. Either way we will still have something to eat in just a little while…I promise."

Just then five grouse flew up in front of them; all at once the Doss's pulled their pistols and shot. Curry heard only three shots, and damned if every shot didn't count, but four birds fell out of the sky. "Dinner is served," hollered Goof. "And I got two of them in one shot."

"The hell you did," Toad said. "It was me that got two with one shot."

"What the hell does it matter just who got two in one shot," Hosey said, climbing off his horse and walking around picking up the four birds. "The only thing that matters is now not only do we have

355

breakfast, but with four birds we have dinner. Check it out Curry," Hosey said holding up the birds. "These three are all head shots only." Then he took a second look at the fourth bird. "Now it really don't matter which one of you got the second bird cause whichever one of you did get him. You shot him through the ass and out the head…and blew the rest of him apart." Shaking his head he dropped the bird back on the ground. "Hell there's not enough of him left to even bother with."

"Don't worry about it, Hosey," Toad said. "I brought my fishing line and some flies, we won't starve."

"Hell I know that," Hosey said. Climbing back aboard his horse. "But I'd rather have grouse over trout any day." Riding up alongside Curry, he tried to tie the birds down to his saddle. When that big fancy Arabian smelled the blood from the birds, he jumped straight sideways just as fast as he could. Almost sending Curry back to the ground, because he wasn't paying attention. "Would you look at that, guys, Curry's horse is afraid of the smell of blood."

"Quit your complaining, Hosey," Goof said. "We can easily get another grouse, these mountains are full of them and you know it." Looking up into the sky he pulled out his rain slicker. "I'm glad we're only a few miles from the cabin, because this rain is going to be with us all day. At least there we'll have a dry warm place to spend the rest of today and tonight out of this rain."

"You think the twins and Randy will catch up with us tonight?" Toad asked, pulling out his peyote pipe.

"Who the hell gives a shit," Hosey said. "Just fill that thing up I need a couple tokes off that."

"You know it," Goof spook up. 'You ever try any of this peyote Curry?" He asked, pulling out his bag of peyote.

"Hell no, I hear that stuff makes you see visions, and mess's with your mind." Curry answered

"Oh hell no," Hosey chuckled. "You want to see visions…? Come with me when we get to Portland or Seattle, I'll take you over to the China side of town and get you some of that opium. Now that will make you see visions. Here Toad hand me that pipe."

Chapter Fifteen

"Just hold on Bogart," Toad said. "Let me fill it first." He stopped his horse and took out a match, lighting it on his pant leg then lighting the pipe. By now both Hosey and Goof were sitting beside him waiting for their hit of peyote.

"So what exactly does that shit make you feel like?" Curry asked. Watching all three passing the pipe between them.

"Kind of like being drunk I guess," Toad said. "If you don't smoke too much of it, it makes you relaxed and lazy ...But if you do smoke too much of it, it gives you the munchies, and then all you want to do is sit around and eat."

"Why are you three all so skinny if that shit makes you want to eat?" Curry asked them. He was really contemplating whether or not to try it.

"You get on the other end of a ten foot cross cut saws all day and you'll see why we're skinny," Toad said, taking another pull off the pipe then handing it to Curry. "You fall ten, twelve trees a day, you'll find out how we burn it all off."

"That's no shit," Goof said. Reaching for the pipe. "Hell Toad, this city boy don't want any of that, so just give it to me."

"Alright, alright," Curry said. "Just hold your horses, I'll try it once, laying his reins over his saddle horn, he took a hold of the pipe. Leaning over to a match that Toad already had lit; Curry put the pipe up to his mouth and took a big deep puff off the pipe. Instantly he started coughing his head off and got real light headed feeling. He thought he was going to fall off his horse. "HOLY SHIT, he shouted, grabbing his saddle horn, I feel like I just had a dozen shots of whiskey all at one time."

"Alright" Toad said, taking his pipe back, and dumping out the ashes. "It's dead, so let's get going." Then looking back up at Curry, who was slumped over in his saddle and swaying from side to side. Toad started to chuckle, "Check out the city boy, one hit and he's already in la la land."

"What are you talking about? Curry say's, trying to right himself back up in his saddle.

"Here," Goof said laughing. "Give me your reins and you just hold onto the saddle. Hell, we're only a mile from the cabin at the most."

357

Turning his horse, he headed the mule train down river again. "Hell, he only took one hit…He looks like he's been smoking all day, don't it?"

"Hey guys…It's raining," Curry say's, wiping the water out of his eyes.

"Yes it is Curry," Toad answered. "Now be a good boy and put your rain slicker on."

Instantly Curry grabbed hold of the saddle horn again, trying not to fall off his horse, his head rolled back and his face skyward, as the rain lightly fall upon his face. He felt as if he was floating through the air, and not even sitting on a horse at all. He couldn't see the tops of the mountains because of the clouds. He felt like he was flying over the area when all of a sudden he seen a bald eagle soaring high up there in the sky. That must be nice to see all the country like he can, he thought to himself. Then Curry looked down into Granite creek, them salmon running up that river to spawn had to be at least half as long as one of his legs. Then looking down river a few hundred yards he could see a couple bear's catching those salmon for breakfast. Something moved in the brush to his right. Quickly he turned to get a better look, when out of the brush came the biggest buck he had ever seen, four points on each side.

He was from back east, where all's they have are white tail deer. The rack on this mule deer buck was so big. Why, you could put two white tail racks inside and still have room left over. Then all of a sudden Curry sees the image of a large man, with a U.S. Marshal's badge pinned to his chest. Curry gave the big man a quick glance over. Right off he noticed the lever on his riffle. The lever had been modified much larger than the standard lever, to accommodate his large hand. Taking a closer look, he could see smoke` coming out of the barrel. Suddenly Curry felt a deep burning sensation in the middle of his chest. Starting to shiver a little, he tried to regain control and come awake. The Doss's were helping him off his horse at the cabin; they were all laughing and talking about him. But he couldn't make out just what it was they were saying as they laid him on the cabin floor. One of them turned towards the door to go back out side. When he opened the door, Curry could see the image of the big man, the Marshal's badge pinned to his chest,

Chapter Fifteen

holding the smoking rifle in one hand, the deep burning sensation was returning to his chest, as Curry fall's fast asleep.

The four had been riding in the cold rain for a good two and a half-hours. It wasn't spring in the high country yet, the farmers and ranchers down in Baker Valley would be loving this rain, but up here it was barely thirty-five degrees, just warm enough that it was still rain and not snow. This was a cold rain; they all knew it was only about five plus miles more to Granite, so if they kept their horses moving at a good pace, they could make it in just over an hour. The road up to Granite really wasn't much of a road; it was more like a trail cut through all the lodge pole trees. They were so thick out across the mountain valleys that it made it hard for you to see very deep into the timber. In some areas the road wasn't even wide enough for two wagons to pass.

The only thing any of them could think about was getting to Granite. They may not have much to offer up there but they did have a small bar and restaurant where they could get out of the cold for a while.

"How much longer to Granite Randy?" Gary shouted over to him.

"Really couldn't tell for sure," Randy answered. "With all this fog and rain a person really can't get his bearings right. I mean, I know where we are. Just by guessing I'd say we're within five, maybe six miles most."

"SHIT," hollered Larry. "I was hoping to get down to the North Fork today at least. You know Toad and them are there sleeping off last night right now and staying nice and warm in that old cabin."

"I don't care," Randy said. "I don't know just how much gold they have on them from the robbery, but I do know... I don't want to be with them, if and when they get caught. I don't want anyone thinking we had anything to do with that robbery in any way, shape, or form. Right now everyone thinks they stole my horses, and that's the way I want to keep it."

"I don't know what you're worried about, Amigo," Luis said. "They cut the telegraph lines."

"I don't care. You know as well as I do, once they find where it's been cut, it only takes a few minute's to repair. By now they have repaired them, and everyone in the county and state knows about the robbery. And everyone and I DO mean EVERYONE is out looking for them right now. They know the bank has a standing fifteen percent reward on any and all robberies. Not to mention the mining company, they will be adding ten percent more reward money on top of the banks."

"He's right Larry, and you know it," Gary said. "I personally don't want to see them until they get back. Even then everyone is going to wonder how all of a sudden they came into all that money."

"I know you're right, but it sure would be nice to see all that gold." Larry said, smiling

"They should be there by now," Randy said. "Unless something came up, and you know they're not going to go any further in this cold rain. They'll probably wait until morning to pull out. I know they don't have a motel in Granite, so we'll have to sleep in the Livery stable with the animals. But at least we will be dry tonight."

"So you're saying this is as far as you want to go today?" Larry asked. "We only have two weeks. Hell, we just spent three and a half day's of that in Sumpter."

"Randy's right, Larry," Gary shouted over the rain and thunder. "It's too damn cold to go on any further today. Hell one of us just might catch pneumonia if we keep going."

Just then they could smell smoke coming from some of the houses fireplaces. Through the heavy mist and rain they could make out some buildings as they rode into town. They were all glad to finally be here, cause that meant they would be out of this freezing rain."

It was cold as hell outside as they rode into the Livery stable but just getting out of the rain and wind made it feel at least twenty degrees warmer. Riding in side the blacksmith was there to meet them.

"What can I do for you men today?" the man asked.

Shaking the rain off their slickers, they began to dismount their horses. "How much for the night?" Gary asked.

Chapter Fifteen

The man looked at each of them, one at a time. The word had already reached town about the robbery. Randy had told the Doss brothers very sternly NOT to cut the telegraph lines this way. Because there would be absolutely no way or reason to cut it if nobody came this way. "Dollar and a half each for the animals, but that includes grain and hay both for your horses."

"Sounds fair enough," Randy said, removing his rain slicker. "We all know there's no sleeping quarters in town. So how much more for each of us to bed down in your hay loft tonight?"

"Well," the man said. "Make it two buck a piece and we'll call it good."

Reaching in his pocket, Gary pulled out a hand full of money. Handing the man a twenty-dollar bill, "Will this cover everything?"

"YES SIR," the man answered with a big smile on his face. "That and then some." Just then he got a good look at the Roan as Larry pulled his saddle off. He could see the big fifty-five brand on his hip. "Hey, that isn't the horse I heard about; bucking off ten men down in Sumpter yesterday is it?" the man said with excitement in his voice.

Larry looked over at him with a big smile on his face. "Sure the hell is," he answered.

"Boy I sure wish I could have gotten down there to see that, I heard it was a sight to see," the man said.

"Don't worry about it," Randy said. "You'll see it again in the morning."

"How's that?" the man asked, with a funny look on his face.

"Cause," Larry shouted. "He still don't like it when anyone gets on him. Least not right off," starting to chuckle, looking around at everyone. "I sure will be glad when the day comes that he knows it's me, and he stops trying to buck me off.

They all laughed at that, then thanked the man for letting them sleep in the loft for the night. All four men ran across the street to the bar, which was also the dry goods store, the restaurant, Saloon and the hardware store all in one. Walking in the door, they all stopped and looked around.

361

"This way," Larry said. Turning and walking back to the bar counter which was along the back wall. Walking up to the bar, Larry ordered four hot cups of coffee for everyone. Which none of them could believe, it was well after twelve o' clock in the afternoon and Larry was ordering coffee.

"You feeling alright, Larry," Luis asked.

Picking up the coffee, handing everyone a cup, "Yep, I'm fine… Why?" Larry asked.

The four all started sitting down at one of the tables. Looking back over to Larry Gary asked, "You ordered coffee in the middle of the day?"

"What the hell did you expect?" Reaching into his pocket and pulled out a fifth of whiskey, "I'm just about half frozen through," Larry said.

"I knew he had some alcohol somewhere," Randy said.

"Hell yeah," Larry said. Pouring a good healthy shot worth of whiskey into his coffee, 'This and this together, will have me ready for a cold beer in about…hmmm…ten, fifteen minutes. He said, holding them both up. Anyone else want some?" Passing the bottle around the table.

"Give me that," Randy said. Grabbing the bottle and pouring only about a shot at the most. Randy really wasn't much of a drinker, but Larry was right. A hot cup of java, topped off with a little whiskey will warm you up from the inside out, faster. Fact everyone knew it, and joined in themselves.

Just then a young Indian Squaw, who was almost as big around, as she was tall, walked up to the table. Walking up behind Larry she put her hands on his shoulders and looked around the table. "Is there anything else I can get any of you gentleman?"

Larry turned and looked up smiling at the young ladies voice. Then seeing who she was, he jumped sideways and out of his chair. Hollering, "HELL NO, get away from me you fat cow."

Everyone else couldn't help but chuckle. "Come on, Hombre," Luis said. "That squaw will keep you warm all over."

Chapter Fifteen

Slowly sitting back down, the young lady walked over to another table of men who had just walked in. Shivering his shoulders, Larry looked around at everyone, "Damn that's scary. Luis, don't you ever let me get that drunk."

"You don't have to worry about me getting in your way, Luis," Randy said chuckling. "I know I couldn't drink that much, and if by chance I happen to smoke too much peyote...Hell, I'll just fall asleep."

"Did anyone bring any cards?" Gary asked.

"Of course, Hombre," Luis said. Pulling out his saddlebags and opened them up, then pulled out a box of cards and chips.

"I wonder just how Curry's holding up with the Doss's?" Randy asked. "I bet they had that city boy shitting in his pants last night."

"I wonder if Toad told him his Sashquatch story?" Larry said. Counting out chips for everyone.

"You know he did," Randy said. "I could just see his eyes when they told him there was still a lot of lonely mountain men running around up here, and what they would do to a city boy if they caught him alone?"

"He did kind of squirm around in his chair a little bit didn't he?" Gary said, picking up his cards.

363

CHAPTER SIXTEEN

Everyone quickly picked up their pistols and rifles, and followed the Marshal and Roy out the back door. This was going to be fun. Not only because of the shooting competition, but because they were going to get to see the great Marshal Shawn Felton shoot. Sam, Jack and Wapiti had seen the shot he made yesterday in the saloon. Mike and Roy and everyone else had only heard about it. There had to be at least seventy plus people between the Marshal and the man trying to back shoot Wapiti, and the Marshal hit him right between the eyes.

Walking over to the gunny sacks, Shawn picked up one of the pigeons, looking back at Roy, "Shoot this whole bag couldn't weigh more than ten pounds, he says, picking up the bag. How many of these pigeons are in each bag?"

"Two hundred," Roy said. Picking one up and throwing it into the air and started to pull his pistol. But before he could get it out of the holster, Shawn pulled his, and blew it out of the sky. Roy could not believe it, his hand was already on his pistol before he threw it up, and the Marshal's wasn't. He still pulled and shot before him. He started looking around at everyone else, who were just as impressed by the shot, because they had all seen what had just happened too.

None of them had ever seen anyone pull and shoot as if by pure instinct and hit his target true before.

"HOLY SHIT," Sam shouted. "Remind me not to try and draw against you Marshal...Not that I would mind ya!"

364

Chapter Sixteen

"I don't think anyone here would, Sam," Jack said. "None of us here, and I do mean NONE of us are even half that fast. So we'll just see who can hit the most pigeons in a row without missing."

"Wapiti pull out that hog leg, let's just see what it will do," Shawn said.

"Alright Marshal," Wapiti answered, pulling it out, and then holding it at waist height with his left hand on top of both barrels "Let it go Marshal."

Shawn threw one in the air; Wapiti followed it, and pulled the trigger. Blowing it into at least a thousand pieces, if not more. The power of the recoil from the blast of the shotgun caused both of Wapiti's hands to come up over his head.

"Now just wait one minute," Mike said pointing over at Wapiti. "He doesn't get to use that does he? Hell, he'll never miss, not even if he gets drunk."

"Oh no," Shawn said, pointing at Lavern at the same time. "I just wanted everyone to see what would happen if he ever did have to use it on someone."

"Marshal, I already had a good idea," Lavern said, tying his holster to his leg.

"Why don't you throw one for me Marshal?" Lavern asked. Being just a little nervous, asking the Marshal to throw one up for him.

Shawn threw one in the air; Lavern drew and shot, missing the target. Putting his pistol back in his holster, he turned a little red. "Heck," he said holding his hands up and starting to chuckle a little. "I never said I was a gunfighter, and I don't ever intend to be one."

"Nothing wrong with that son," Shawn said. "You're smarter than most, if you know it. But just remember one thing..." He looked around at everyone. "Don't take a gun to town and let somebody goad you into drawing against them. It's better to be a live coward, than a dead hero...Now let's have some fun."

"So Roy, just how do we have to pay for this shooting game of yours?" Shawn asked taking a pull off the gallon jug of whiskey.

"Everyone puts a dollar in the hat," Roy said, dropping in his dollar. "Everyone gets their chance. First we all shoot just one pigeon,

365

and then we throw up two and so on until someone doesn't hit all the targets. You still get to shoot after you miss, you just don't get to win the money."

"So let me get this straight," Shawn said. "Whoever hits the most in a row without missing wins the money…Correct?"

"Sure can't pull any wool over your eyes can we Marshal?" Jack said smiling. "Roy throw one for me." pulling his pistol and fired, shooting the pigeon in half.

Just then Cathey and Denise returned with Wapiti's pistol and rifle and the Marshal's rifle. Denise handed the Marshal his rifle, "Marshal, why do you have that big lever on your rifle?"

"Well, young lady I'll tell ya," holding up his hand. "My hands are too big to get into your standard lever action, so I had Gordy, the blacksmith back home make this lever for me. That way if need be I can use my pistol with one hand and my rifle in the other."

"Oh bullshit," Roy said chuckling. "You expect us to believe you can use both your rifle and pistol at the same time?"

"Bullshit you say…I'll show you Young man just how come I've been around so long. Wapiti throw two of those in the air then follow it with two more."

"Yes sir, Marshal," Wapiti said, grabbing four pigeons, two in each hand. "Just let me know when."

Standing full up and throwing his chest out, just like a cocky banter rooster in the chicken yard, still showing who's the biggest and the baddest of them all. "Why if I couldn't do this, I would have been dead a long time ago. Why, there's been time's when I've had to put my reins between my teeth, put my pistol in my left hand, my rifle in my right, and ride straight into those out laws firing both weapon's at the same time."

Turning around quickly, "Now Wapiti." Shawn shouted, as Wapiti threw all four wood disk's into the air at the same time, two in one direction and two in the other. The first two were still on their way up when Shawn blew them out of the sky. Shooting the third with his pistol then flipping and recocking his rifle with his right. He blew the fourth pigeon out of the sky just as it made its turn to come back down.

Chapter Sixteen

Everyone started laughing and cheering, even the women had seen what he done. Louise looked over at Roy, "I'll wager against anyone who thinks he can top that."

Everyone was agreeing with her, they looked back and forth at each other, and then back to the Marshal. They all had seen some trick shooters at the fairs, but never pistol and rifle at the same time. He didn't throw that rifle around when he was cocking it. He cocked it with one hand by holding it straight out away from the body and flipping his wrist. Some of them started seeing if they could even cock their rifle that way. Soon everyone took their chance shooting at the pigeons; Shawn showed them how he cocked his rifle. He told them that's why it also helps to have the bigger lever.

It wasn't long before everyone had shot the first round. They threw up just one more pigeon, starting the second round with. Shawn shooting it out of the sky, and looked around. "I thought we went up a pigeon after each round."

"Well Marshal, we usually do three rounds each at each target," Jack said. "So after we shoot three rounds at one then we move up to two for three rounds then three and so on and on, makes the game last a little longer."

"Well hell, we know we can all hit one," Shawn said, picking up his beer. "So let's get on with it already." Still holding his beer and putting his pistol back, Mike threw two up. Acting like he wasn't paying Mike any attention, but as Mike threw them up in the air, as if by pure instinct, Shawn turned, fired, and blew both out of the sky. "NEXT," he hollered, "Let's hurry up so I can win this big pot of money. Wapiti and I have to get up early and get going. Speaking of which, Roy how about I give you an extra fifty dollars to have me and Wapiti loaded up and ready to leave by sun up?"

"You don't have to do that Marshal, that comes with my job," Roy said. Stepping up to take his turn, shooting both out of the sky.

"Don't worry about it, Roy," Shawn said. "I'll just put it on my expense account. Just like all these pigeons and ammo here tonight." He said starting to chuckle.

By the end of the third round Wapiti and Sam were out of the competition. But they were still allowed to shoot at each set, just not eligible to win the money. A whole eight dollars. But that really didn't matter. It was just a chance to unwind and have fun anyway. And a chance for Wapiti to get better and faster with his pistol. After the next round of four pigeons only Roy and Shawn remained still in the competition. Wapiti reached down in the bag and pulled out five pigeons. Roy was up first and, with a quick sixth shot he hit the fifth pigeon.

"You're slipping Roy," Shawn said, hollering pull, then hit all five of his pigeons with just five shots. Wapiti threw six more up into the air and Roy missed the last one, Shawn hadn't missed anything in a long time, picking up his rifle, "Throw 'em Wapiti." He yelled out. Using both pistol and rifle at the same time he blew all six out of the sky. The men had been shooting for a good hour and a half, and the sun had set enough that they needed to light a fire for the night shoot. Pulling out his pocket watch, and checking the time. "Well men it's almost eight thirty and me and Wapiti need to get an early start. Those clouds up there look like they just might want to open up and rain on us. Roy, if you have any of those left after you men finish tonight, how about you throw some on my mule? That way Wapiti will have something to shoot at besides my corn biscuits."

"Already did Marshal," Roy said. "Fact I got you a half bag of both already," he said. "And don't worry about any extra money. I have other work I need to get done, so I will be up anyway."

Shawn looked around for Wapiti, after a few minutes he could see that him and Cathey were over by the back door talking. They were talking about how long it might be before they would see each other again. Cathey was telling Wapiti that her Grandma Larkin was from Prineville, the Demaris's. Mom mentioned that I could go stay with one of them."

Shawn walked over to them cause it was time for them to leave. "Don't worry Young Lady," Shawn said with a big smile on his face. "If it's possible we'll come back through this way, but I can't make any promises…But I will try…Come on Wapiti let's get going."

Chapter Sixteen

Saying goodbye to everyone one more time the two turned and headed down the street back to the Silver Dollar Saloon. Shawn was right they needed to get back; Wapiti was tired and needed some sleep, especially since the Marshal wanted to leave by sun up. The two talked about how nice the Larkin family had been, and just how good that meal was too. Shawn reminded Wapiti it would be quite a while before they would have anything like that to eat again, not for a long time. Before Wapiti knew it they were walking through the front door of the saloon. The crowd was a little rowdy, but not too bad. Walking in everyone looked at them, and the room went quiet.

"Well since it seems that I already have everyone's attention," Shawn said. "I only want to say this once. Now we're fixing to go up and get some sleep so we can leave your fair city in the morning. So I would appreciate it, if you would keep it down one last night."

"No problem Marshal," everyone started saying at the same time. "You won't even know we're down here."

"Charlie, why don't you throw me a bottle of the good stuff? It looks like rain, and up in those mountains it's going to get cold. This way I can warm myself from the inside out, if you know what I mean." Shawn asked walking towards the bar.

"Sure do, Marshal," Charlie answered. Reaching under the counter and pulling out a full bottle of whiskey and tossing it to the Marshal.

"Thanks Charlie," Shawn said, Heading up the stairs. "Cork it's been a pleasure to meet you and to do business with you Sir. If I get back this way I'll be sure to stop in."

"You better old man," Cork said. "You know I'll always have room here for you, and you too Wapiti. I mean it and I don't want either one of you to forget it."

"Trust me," Shawn said, looking at Wapiti and then back to Cork. "We won't forget it." Then the two turned and walked upstairs to their rooms and sleep.

That night was the hardest night Wapiti had ever had when it came to falling asleep. He was dead tired, but couldn't seem to sleep; all he could think of was Cathey. He sure was going to miss her; he sure hoped they would come back this way. He didn't remember how or

369

just when he did fall asleep, the next thing he knew was the Marshal was waking him up.

"Come on son, it's time to get going…" Shawn said, looking down at Wapiti who was trying to wake up. He knew exactly what was on his mind, and it wasn't what lay ahead of them. He knew it was Cathey and how long until they would see each other again. "Come on Romeo," he said. "Let's get going…and get your head back on business."

Wapiti rolled over out of bed, and was just reaching for his pants as Shawn turned and walked out the door. "Wait Marshal, give a man a chance to get dressed first," Wapiti hollered.

"I said an hour before sun up, and we're about three minutes away from that," Shawn said. Stopping and looking back at Wapiti, "I'll meet you downstairs, the cook is supposed to have breakfast to go for us."

"Why you always in such a hurry?" Wapiti asked the Marshal. "Haven't you ever heard of stopping and smelling the roses?" he said, pulling his pants up. Then pulling on his boots, he ran out of the room still putting his shirt on and packing everything else.

Walking as fast as he could to catch the Marshal, Wapiti finished getting dressed.

He was glad to see the cook was handing him a cup of coffee. "Thanks MA'AM, and thank you for everything else this last weekend. I know you had a whole lot of people to feed, but you always gave me more than I could eat."

"You're welcome son," She said. "You just take care of the Marshal here…And listen to him. He can teach you a lot, but keep that bottle away from him if you can." She said.

"Are you joking ma-am, he's twice as big as me and a whole lot faster with that gun than I am," Wapiti said.

"I have to agree with young Wapiti there," Shawn said smiling. "You always made sure I had more than my fill too…I'll be remembering that apple pie all the way to Sumpter and back."

"Well now Marshal, you won't have to think about it too long," She said. "I wrapped a couple of pieces for you."

"Well, we need to get going ma-am," Shawn said, tipping his hat.

Chapter Sixteen

Then Shawn and Wapiti turned and walked out the door. It was still dark outside, but Wapiti knew it wouldn't be for long. He caught a cold chill all of a sudden when he looked up at the sky. Those clouds were so thick and black, just full of rain waiting to come down. It was so dark out side, if it hadn't been for the light that Roy had on at the Livery stable just two block's away; they wouldn't have been able to see it.

When they walked through the door Wapiti could smell the fire burning, and the coffee cooking. Which he was glad for, cause he only had a half a cup back at the restaurant. Walking in, Roy looked at them and he filled two more cups.

"Good morning Marshal, Wapiti," Roy said, handing each of them a cup of coffee. "Almost ready, just have to tie those two bags of pigeons to put on and you'll be good to go."

"You wouldn't have a smaller bag of some sort so I could keep some with me on my horse would you Roy?" Shawn asked.

"I should have something right over here Marshal," Roy said. Looking through a box of rags, and pulling out a half gunny sack. "Here Marshal," he said, tossing it to him. "That should do just fine."

"Thanks Roy," Shawn said. Filling it with orange pigeons. "Wapiti you better get our rain gear out. "We're going to get wet before mornings over. I can smell it in the air."

"So how long have you been a Marshal, Marshal?" Roy asked.

Standing up and walking to his horse, Shawn looked at him, "Been a Lawman of sort's for near thirty five plus year's…But A Deputy U.S. Marshal for the last twenty plus.

Roy, it's came to my knowledge, that one of those young men I accidentally blew up last week was one of your nephew's, Shawn said, Looking straight into Roy's eye's. Which one was he?

"Brad, The leader of the bunch" Roy said.

" Why haven't you said anything? Shawn asked

"Well Marshal, I grew up in that area, Roy answered. I was in the courtroom when you told Judge Monson how it happened… Like I said, I grew up in that area, and I know of at least three times I've

371

missed a big buck deer in the river gorge because that shall rock sliding out under my feet just as I pulled the trigger.

"Mind if I ask you what kind of man he was, outlaw aside," Shawn asked.

Good man, Roy said, proudly. He liked to party, but he didn't like to work…So he robbed banks… Told me he did his hold ups early in the morning. Said, most bank managers would go into work at least a couple hour's before they opened up. Said there was very few people up and around that time in the morning. Which meant less chance of any gunplay.

They sure are quick to put Dead on those wanted poster', Shawn said. Hell, even I borrowed a few dollars from a trading post or two when I was younger. But I needed a road stake.

I've killed a chicken or two, but I've never stole any money, from anyone." Roy said. But Brad on the other hand…I believe he was responsible for twenty or more bank jobs.

I would like to apologize to the Young man's mother, Shawn said.

I'll see to it she knows, Roy said. …Just so's you know Marshal I don't hold nothing against you for what you had to do. Neither does anyone else in the family. But when you get over to Sumpter and the Baker City area, you're going to run into those three nephews of mine I told you about, the Twins and Randy…You'll have to explain it to them, they were close. Tell you the truth I half expected them to come and find you and find out why you did what you did. Like I did when I went over to Prineville last week."

"Now these three nephews of yours, I'm not going to have to kill them too am I?" Shawn asked.

"No, no…least I hope not," Roy said. They're good boys; they get a little hot under the collar now and then. But they like to settle things with their hands. Not guns."

"Now I'm glad to hear that," Shawn said smiling. "I'm still pretty good with my hands." Making a fist and looking at it. "I do like me a good fistfight."

Chapter Sixteen

"You just remember the one called Randy...Marshal," Roy said smiling. "That little man likes to fight to. To him, the bigger the better...That little man runs a team of six Clydesdales skidding logs. He has A LOT of power in those arms. Nine point nine times out of ten, whoever the man is on the receiving end of his punishment will, and I repeat WILL be needing a doctor. The twin they call Gary, now he's got a level head on his shoulders. I guess you could say he has the brains of the bunch, Randy has the muscle and Larry's the joker." Starting to chuckle, they all have a knack of getting into and getting out of trouble, or being somewhere else long before anyone else finds out anything is aria.

Grabbing the lead rope, Shawn climbed aboard his horse. "I'll remember that when I come across them," Shawn said, with a big smile on his face. "Well Roy, it's time to get on the trail, but I'm sure we'll be back some day." Turning his horse and mule, he headed towards the door. "Wapiti let's get out of here."

"Right behind ya Marshal," Wapiti answered. "Mr. Larkin will you tell Cathey bye for me?"

"No son I won't," Roy said. "I'll tell her you said you'll see her when you get back, I never say goodbye...because that means it just might be the last time I see ya. So you just take care of yourself Young man and get back here safe." Holding out his hand, he shook Wapiti's hand. "You're a good man son, if I didn't mean it, I wouldn't say it. Now get the hell out of here, Cathey will be here when you get back."

Wapiti turned his head, "Thanks Roy." Then kicking his horse so he could catch up to the Marshal. He noticed pulling up beside the Marshal, that the daylight was just starting to come up over the mountain tops, it was still dark down in the valley however. "So Marshal, when do you think we'll make the cabin?"

"Well Wapiti," Shawn said, lighting a cigar. "We'll have to push hard, but we should make it before nightfall if all goes well."

CHAPTER SEVENTEEN

It was almost noon when Butch and Sundance came riding into Unity; there really wasn't a whole lot there. The Livery stable was at the edge of town as you came in; next to it was the Mercantile Store. The bar and restaurant were across the street, maybe one hundred houses at the most, a log yard to load the logs on the Baker City- Sumpter railroad. But other than that there wasn't much. Fact there wasn't even anyone walking around town.

They pulled up to the Livery stable and hollered out to see if anyone was around. Out walked a short man, maybe five feet five inches tall. But he definitely had huge arms on him, wiping the grease off his hands; he walked up to them holding out his hand. "Terry Larkin gentlemen, just what can I do for you?" Looking them over.

"Well, we were hoping on finding a place to sleep and eat," Butch said smiling and looking around. "I can see where we can get some grub, but where can a man get a room to rest for a while?"

Walking around the two Clydesdales, Terry looked back up at the two men. "So you're the famous Butch Cassidy and Sundance Kid, are ya?"

"What are you talking about?" Sundance asked. "We're just a couple of hopeful gold miners."

"YA RIGHT, it came over the wire a couple hours ago about the robbery and the missing of these two Clydesdales. Some mules were also stolen from the log yard to haul all that gold away with.

Chapter Seventeen

What are you taking about sir, Butch answered. We're just a couple of hopeful miners ourselves.

If you were just a couple hopeful miners'... then what are you doing with my little brother's draft horses?" Terry asked.

Looking down at Terry as they both began to dismount, "You telling me you're related to Randy and those twins, Larry and Gary?"

"Yep," Terry said with a big smile on his face. "You just have to promise me you won't tell anyone... You know everyone in the country's looking for these two Clydesdales. Like I said, it came over the wire that you men stole these horses and robbed all the gold before they could load it on the train."

"Now, just wait one minute Mr. Larkin. First thing, we rented these animals from Randy; we're paying him real good money for their use."

"Oh hell, I know that," Terry said chuckling. "If Randy didn't want you to have these horses, you wouldn't have them... I just don't believe it... Randy said he knew how to pull it off, the gold robbery that is. Said it would be like taking candy from a baby. But like I said, everyone in the country is looking for these two horses. My house," Terry said pointing "Is the second house down. Take your animals down there and put them in my barn, hide your load under the hay. There's two empty rooms upstairs, take your bedroll up there and catch yourselves a nap. No one will even know you're in town; the watering hole across the street has decent food. There's even a real nice young lady over there who's the waitress, she's about five feet two inches tall and weighs about one hundred pounds, long blonde hair...Her name's Julie... Now that's my girl. There's plenty of other young ladies over there... Do I make myself clear?"

"You mind if we go down to you're place first and wash a little trail dust off," Butch asked.

"Hell no, but let's get these horse off the street first." Turning and walking back into the Livery stable.

"I have a nice setup at the house. I have a hundred gallon drum full of water, you light a fire under it, take your nap and when you get up you'll have some nice hot water. Then all you have to do is add cold right from the pump. After you empty the water, you turn the valve and fill the tank back up so you can keep hot water…So Randy helped you boys pull this job off?" Terry said. "He said we should do it and get rich ourselves when he found out how and when they loaded it. Randy, being Randy, no one ever paid him no never mind when they seen that stallion in there. He'd been stabling him in that old smoke house long before the gold strike…Damn, I can't tell you how many times I fished that river, and I was walking on all of that gold and didn't even know it."

"Your brother Randy's quite different," Butch said with a smirk on his face.

"Don't piss him off and he can be a lot of fun to party with," Sundance said. "But that Larry, he sure can put the alcohol away, can't he?"

"Hell he drinks it like its water," Terry answered. "He doesn't realize until it till it's too late sometimes just how much he has had to drink, the next thing you know he's stupid drunk."

"You said you knew Randy let us borrow these horses and we didn't steal them," Butch said. "How did you know that?"

"Easy, if Randy takes more than his stallion, he ties that big stallion in the middle," starting to chuckle, "You get within five feet of him and he don't know you, then you're going to fly through the air. Kind of like those guys you see in the circus…Just not with the greatest of ease, and neither one of you are hurt'en… Nope, these horses were tied to the other side of the smokehouse," he said. "And I'm another one of Randy's back doors that he didn't tell you or anyone else about. Now then like I said out there, these animals are hot and real easy to see." Pointing to the back of the stables where at least a dozen blue gray dapple Percherons' stood in their stalls. "You take those two down to my barn, hide the gold. When you leave, we'll switch horses. I'll use these to pull my logging wagons with, I have three sets of six. But as you can see I have to repair a wheel here. Anyway, back to MY HORSES. I'm sure you had an agreement with Randy over the use of these two, and I know you already paid him. So I won't ask much more for mine in exchange, and I'll get these back over to him next week."

Chapter Seventeen

"We had a fifteen thousand dollar return bonus with Randy," Butch said. "To make sure they got back in good condition. How much are you going to charge us?"

"I'll just transfer it here," Terry said. "Now, I know Randy told you how he felt about his horses…Well, I feel the same about mine. I DON'T know where you're going, but he doe's. If my animals don't look this good when they come back to me, I will come find you…" Turning and looking them both in the eyes, "I'll bring Randy with me, and I KNOW you have seen some of his work by now."

"Oh yeah," both Butch and Sundance said at the same time. "Fact Sundance ran and hid."

"Smart man," Terry said. "So why the hell you want to be outlaws for? I see you're smart enough to run from danger. Why go looking for it?"

"The excitement," Sundance said smiling. "You get to party on someone else's money."

"Someone else's hard earned money," Terry said. "Why don't you guys get a real job like the rest of us? I'll finish up here come home take a bath, then I'll show you guys the big city. I'll see ya later." Turning and walking back to the logging wagon he was putting a wheel on.

Butch and Sundance lead their horse's down the small hill and around the barn, they were talking along the way. "Did you see the guns on him, Butch," Sundance said. He put his hand around his upper arm. "Him and Randy are just about the same height, and both look like someone you would not want to piss off."

"We and everyone else knows you DON'T want to piss Randy off," Butch said. "I'll bet Terry would hurt you too, if he ever got a hold of ya."

"I don't know about you Butch, but I'm tired and ready for a long nap," Sundance said.

"I hear ya, Sundance," Butch answered. "It'll be nice when we wake up, we'll be able to have a hot bath."

The two walked in the back door of the barn, Sundance pointed down at the creek running through town. "I hear ya on the hot bath Butch," Sundance said. "I thought we were going to have to climb into the creek down there." The two didn't talk much more, they were too tired. They just hurried and unloaded everything, then took Terry's advice and put all the heavy bags of gold under the haystack, which was harder than it sounded. There wasn't enough hay down below, so one had to climb up into the loft and pitch more down while the other had to pitch it over and cover the bags of gold. twelve big beautiful heavy bags of gold, each one weighing one hundred and fifty pounds each, troy weight that is. They picked up their bedrolls and headed for the house. While they were walking up to the house they could see one of Terry's neighbor ladies out back hanging up laundry. Just by looking at her they knew she had been watching their every move. She hadn't been there when they went in the barn, but they knew she had seen them. They both tipped their hats and said good afternoon to her as they walked into the house. Butch walked over and lit the firebox under the water barrel. It was actually an easy setup. A potbelly stove with a tank of water sitting on its own stand, but still sitting on the stove.

Butch and Sundance had not been gone for thirty minute's when at least twenty plus men come riding into town, their horses covered in sweat. They stopped to water their horses and fill their canteens. Terry couldn't help but overhear that they were all looking to claim that big reward. Some of them even asked Terry why he didn't join in. They figured that Cassidy and Sundance would be heading for Ontario, They were coming from Prairie City, hoped they could cut them off before they got too far into Idaho.

"That's quite alright, my three log drivers are already out looking and so is the rest of the town. I'll just stick around here and get caught up on some extra work I need to get done."

"You're the one going to miss out on all that reward," the men were saying. They tightened up their cinches, climbed aboard their horses and headed out across the desert towards Ontario.

Terry finished up with the work he had to do then went home and took a nice hot bath. By the time those two woke up the water would be re-heated enough for both of them. One thing was for sure; he wouldn't have much work for the next couple of days. What with everyone out chasing all that gold. Laying there in the tub he couldn't

Chapter Seventeen

help but think about going down to the barn and borrowing just half of one of those bags of gold. Then him and his brothers could buy a couple of the ranches up Beaver Creek. Hell, they could buy the whole damn valley with that much money. Aw hell, he'd get caught somehow and he knew it.

Terry hurried and took his bath, then went upstairs and woke Sundance up first. "Sorry Sundance but I flipped a coin on which one of you to wake first, YOU LOST. I made you a pot of coffee downstairs. By the time you and Butch wash that dust off it'll be dinnertime, and I'm hungry. I haven't eaten since breakfast." Looking over at Sundance with a smile on his face, "I thought about going down to the barn while you men slept and take a little of that gold."

"Why didn't ya?" Sundance asked.

"I'm not a thief," Terry answered in a stern voice.

"I didn't mean it like that Terry," Sundance said. "Please don't take it wrong.

"I know," Terry answered. Shacking Sundance's hand, which was extended to him with the apology.

Sundance had seen the power in Randy's arms, Terry and Randy were both the same height, Randy weighed a little more, but Terry's muscles were much more defined. He didn't want to see if Terry got even half as mad as Randy did. "Well, if you will excuse me, I'm going to the bath." then turning he walked towards the bathroom.

Terry looked over at Butch as he walked into the room, "So just what did you guys blow up last night?"

Butch started chuckling, "That wasn't us…That was your brother Randy."

"Another one of his back doors, huh?" Terry said, starting to smile.

"You heard that clear over here? " Butch asked.

"What? Are you kidding, with that cloudbank holding everything in, we heard the echoes for minutes. It was loud enough to wake a heavy sleeper," Terry said. "You know…Those three get in and out of more trouble than anyone I know…Don't ask me how, but Randy started figuring out back doors, when those three were only five maybe six years old."

"Really," Butch asked. "What kind of trouble did they get into when they were kids? At that age, couldn't have been too bad."

"They liked to play with fire…Literally…Hell they burnt fences, barns, chicken coops, and even a brand new bridge over the powder river in Baker City one time. I'm here to tell you the law wanted to put those three away for life." Terry said, seriously

"What about Randy's temper?" Butch asked. "I've never seen so much power in any man before, not even in men twice his size."

"I hear ya Butch," Terry said. "Fact I think if he could harness that power when he wanted to, I think he'd just be able to out pull your average saddle horse at one of these timber carnivals we have every year. But to answer your question, when he was younger he stuttered a lot and people would make fun of him. I could tell you stories of him taking on three and four kids or men at one time… He's the only one that walks away, acting just like nothing even happened."

"I wouldn't bet against him," Butch said, with a big smile on his face. "We saw him hit one man, just once in the face. He not only crushed the man's nose but he also broke his cheekbones. Then, two days later, I still don't think that man could see through all the swelling. When he did come out of the Doc's place two days later and his big brother came in with him, laughing at him and at Randy. The first guy, mind ya, six foot plus, maybe two fifty, but his brother was even bigger…Randy made him look like a fool. The other man, the second man, who was a good three, four inches taller, and at least fifty pounds heavier, he challenged Randy to an arm wrestling match. Randy just laughed at the man for a good thirty to forty seconds, then he smashed the big mans hand into the table. Pissing the big man off, so he hit Randy with everything he had. Randy hardly moved at all, then still holding onto the man's hand, Randy pulled on the huge man like he was a twig. Then he flat started to beat the shit out of him. Hell by the time the twins got him off the man and settled down, the man was coughing up blood all over the place."

"Yep," Terry said. "That's us Polish/Irishmen or Irish/Polish men; we have a habit of doing that. Either we get mad and do something

Chapter Seventeen

stupid, or we do something stupid and get mad. Either way there's going to be a fight before the night's over with."

The two had been talking for about twenty minutes when Sundance came out of the bathroom, wiping his hair with a towel. "Thanks a lot Terry, that's better than most bath houses I've been in. I refilled the water tank, and relit the fire for you Butch."

"Thanks," Butch said. Standing up and walking towards the washroom.

"Hurry up," Terry said. "I'm hungry."

"Don't worry we are too," Butch said. "I promise I'll be quick." Then he turned and walked into the room.

Terry and Sundance sat and talked for about fifteen minutes when Butch came out. "I filled the tank back up for you Terry, but I didn't relight the fire."

"Thanks," Terry said. "Now let's go get some dinner." The three walked out the door and headed across the street to the Water Hole saloon and restaurant.

"Where's everyone at?" Sundance asked as they crossed the street. "By the looks of things, there are at least a hundred homes in town."

Terry stopped at the door, looked up and down the street. "There are one hundred and twenty houses, maybe a total of three hundred people. But when it came across the wire about nine o' clock this morning about the gold robbery, and you guys were said to be headed towards Ontario... Everyone in town saddled up and took off. Hell the bank has a standard fifteen percent reward around here and the mining company threw in another ten percents, whoever finds you two are going to get rich real quick. But the wire said there was at least six of you." Walking into the restaurant, "So where's that rest of your gang?"

They sat down at a table, Sundance looked over at Terry, "The Doss's and Kid Curry, went out through Granite."

"The DOSS'S?" Terry said. "Those boys are always looking for a fast way to get rich." Just then Julie came up and sat down on Terry's lap. She had a pot of coffee and was pouring everyone a cup; she gave Terry a kiss on the cheek.

"Hi sweetheart," Julie said. "Who are your new friends?"

381

Extending his hand towards the two men, "Gentlemen, I'd like you to meet Julie, Julie this is Mr. Jones and Mr. Smith."

"No way," Julie said quietly, but with excitement in her voice. "You telling me these are the men who robbed the train."

"Now what would give you that idea Julie?" Butch asked, looking around the table.

"Terry only uses Smith and Jones when he's introducing me to one of his outlaw friends. So just how did you happen to meet them Terry?"

"Figured out who they were the second they came into the Livery stable," Terry said smiling.

"Just how'd you do that," Julie said. Then it hit her, "Ooh yeah, that's right the wire said they stole two of Randy's Clydesdales. No wonder you knew right off who they were. But what makes you think they really didn't steal Randy's horses?"

"Easy," Terry said starting to chuckle. "You know that big stallion of Randy's? You get anywhere around him at night and you're going flying…And neither one of these two don't have a mark on them, so I knew Randy had to have tied the three horses apart from each other, allowing them to get these two. Also, I could see Toad's work when it came to covering up and disguising the load."

Julie took their orders and went back into the kitchen. Butch and Sundance started looking around the rooms, which only the support beams, separated the restaurant from the bar side. There were maybe eight people in the place, a couple old men and five or six young ladies, who were obviously very upset that all the men were out of town. It meant they weren't going to make very much money tonight. There were a few of them that were actually nice looking young ladies, and at least they did have enough manners to leave them alone while they ate dinner.

"So you said we could switch those two Clydesdales with a couple of your horses Terry?" Sundance asked.

"No problem, but I think you just might have loaded them a little heavy, so I'll let you have one more, to lighten the load on each animal." Terry answered

382

Chapter Seventeen

"How much are you going to charge us for their use?" Butch asked. As Julie sat their food down in front of them, Sundance and Butch couldn't help but look at her. She was a beautiful young lady, just over five feet tall, couldn't be much more than a hundred pounds, long blonde hair, big beautiful blue eye's, and that short, tight skirt...it showed off every curve in her sexy body. Terry was definitely a lucky man. However neither one tried to make it obvious that they were checking her out. Sundance had almost had to go meet Doc. Bones up close and personal when he made a comment about Sharon in front of Randy. At the same time they both looked at each other then back over to Terry. Those were some of the biggest and cut arms and chest they had ever seen on any man. They had seen what happened when you made Randy mad...and could only imagine what might happen if you pissed Terry off? Neither one wanted to find out. But one thing was for sure, them Larkin boys sure were lucky when it came to finding beautiful women.

"So you men going out through Idaho?" Terry asked while they ate.

"Not anymore," Butch said. "Randy's back door was just meant to make everyone think we went that way, fact, he called it a fake back-door. Cause really we're going down to the Columbia, catch a barge on to Portland, then down to Los Angles. So just how much money you going to charge us for the use of your horse's.

"I'm sure you already paid Randy enough," Terry said. "So I'll just get him to split some of it with me."

"We only met him once," Sundance said with a big smile on his face, "But I don't think Randy's the sharing type. Besides, this is the biggest haul we've ever made. Not to mention the money we made off that big Roan of Larry's."

"So it's true, then?" Terry asked. "That Roan really did best ten men?"

"DID HE, did he ever," Butch said. Looking up into Julie's big blue eyes as she refilled his coffee. "Nobody but the last rider even stayed on him for more than two jumps," starting to chuckle. "Hell, I didn't even make it a half of jump and that horse sent me to the moon and back. And I'm here to tell ya, it hurt when I came back to earth."

383

Terry looked up a Julie, "So Hugh still closing the restaurant at eight o' clock tonight? Like all week nights?"

"No, Hugh figured with everyone out looking for these two, that we weren't going to be busy, so he said we're closing at six." Looking up at the clock on the wall, "Which is only fifteen minutes away. So why don't you let me get cleaned up back there and I'll be right back. Then we can party a little." She turned and looked back and forth between Butch and Sundance. "We can all unwind a little, with some FAMOUS outlaws," Julie said, standing up, giving Terry another kiss and went in the back room, stopping just about half way. "Would any of you want a piece of apple pie...? It was just made today."

All three men spoke up and answered at the same time, "Yes please." The three were just finishing up dinner when Julie returned with the apple pie with a big scoop of ice cream and boy did it smell good.

"Well, how about we take our pie, go over to the bar side, get us a box of chips and play a little poker?" Terry said, standing up.

Butch and Sundance looked at each other as they stood up to follow. "So we take it you don't gamble with real money either?" Sundance said with a big smile on his face.

"HELL NO," Terry said. Looking at the two men, "I work too damn hard for my money to throw it away on some dumb card game."

The three sit down at their new table, a young lady brought over each one a beer and Terry's box of chips.

Then Butch looked back over at Terry. "I know you said we don't owe you anything for the use of your animals, but you're going to be without a full team for at least three weeks, maybe longer We made more money on that Roan than we've ever made on any bank robbery. Put the gold on top of that..." Reaching in his pocket Butch pulled out a handful of money. Quickly he counted out ten thousand dollars and handed the pile to Terry. "This should cover it, I think."

Terry glanced at the money; he didn't know just how much was there offhand. He wasn't going to count it in front of them, he didn't want them thinking he didn't trust them. Besides that was the biggest stack of "C" notes he had ever seen. Just then Julie walked up and sits

Chapter Seventeen

down on Terry's lap. Both Butch and Sundance still tried to make it not obvious that they were checking her out, because they both remembered how Randy was over Sharon. Terry started shuffling the cards; Julie started counting out chips. "You men don't mind if a lady plays to, do ya?" Julie asked

"No ma-am," they both said. "Fact it would be a pleasure to have your company," Butch answered.

"So you were up in Sumpter, and seen the bucking competition? Those three brothers are something else," Julie said trying not to laugh too loud..."They're plum crazy you might say. But true to the end...If they give you their word on something, they stand behind it."

Sundance looked at all three of them and started laughing, "CRAZY...I'd have to say that's the best way to describe Larry. PLUM CRAZY"

"So just which one of you is playing Smith and which one is Jones?" Julie asked. Looking at them with those big beautiful blue eyes.

Sundance held up his hand, "I'm A.K.A., Jones, or Sundance Kid, My real name Harry Longbough ma-am. And this is A.K.A. Mr. Brigham Young, Butch Cassidy, or Robert LeRoy Parker. Mr. Smith went out the other way with the Doss brothers."

WHAT, who got the Doss's in on this, Julie said in a loud whisper.

Who else, but The Master Mind of The Entire Job, Randy. Butch said, leaning back in his chair with a big shit eat'en grin on his face.

"So just how much did my future in-law have to do with your little robbery?" Julie asked, looking back and forth between the two.

Couldn't have done it without them, Butch answered, smiling. Well, I guess we could have. But it would have taken us at least two more weeks to figure out, if we were lucky... Randy already had it planned down to the last little detail.

"So was that one of his back doors that woke us up last night?" Julie asked smiling.

Just then two more young ladies walked up to the table and looked down at Butch and Sundance.

"Would you men like some company for a while?" the taller of the two asked. She was a real pretty brunette, a little over five and a half feet tall, long thick black hair that went half way down her back. The other was just as nice looking, with long dishwater blonde hair. They were both very pretty ladies. But they both wished either one of them were the young lady sitting across the table. But they would be good company for the night, the brunette was smiling, "I'm T…"

Butch held up his hand. "Darling to tell you the truth I won't remember either of your names this time next week and neither will my friend here. But if you'd like to party a little tonight," looking over at Sundance and smiling. "We'd enjoy the company. Just then the door came open and men started piling in. All talking about the ride, and wouldn't it be nice if their posse would be the lucky ones and catch the outlaws. Butch could see the men had posters in their hands. All hollering at the bartender to line up a round, they had fifty miles of dust to wash down.

Terry looked over at Butch and Sundance, "Ladies, why don't you take these gentlemen out the back door and over to my house?" He heard one of the men ask where the blacksmith lived; they had thrown a few shoes, and needed to get them fixed so they could ride come first light.

"Mr. Smith, I'll go up and get a couple bottles of whiskey. I made a couple three-gallon barrels to hold beer in. I'll grab one of those as well." Looking back over to the bar area, "I'll charge them my late night overtime rate's," Terry said. "And if they want to sleep in my stable's to get out of the rain…they'll pay for that too."

"Sure do thank you Terry, for all your hospitality," Sundance said as they all stood up. "I don't care what anyone says about you Larkin brothers, you're on a short list of people we KNOW we can trust."

"Don't worry about anyone else in here either, even if they do think you are who you are they won't say anything," Terry said looking around the room. "Fact just look around at those other ladies, first you took all the men out of town, making them mad as hell, more than likely. But now you just brought in a whole new crowd of new men. Granted those boys are going to have to go down in the cold creek and wash up before any of these ladies will have them. I'm sure they'll raise

Chapter Seventeen

their rates and make some extra money tonight…I'll bring my horses down when I finish up tonight."

"Well here then," Sundance said. Reaching in his pocket and pulled out another wad of cash. "Since you're helping us out by getting them all ready tonight, so they can leave at sun up. Let us pay you a little extra for your work tonight."

Holding his hands up, "You men already paid me for this and more," Terry said. "Trust me…Besides like I said, I'm charging them my overtime wage's, and like I also said, if they want to sleep in my Livery stable out of the rain, that's going to cost them more."

Then Butch, Sundance, and the two young ladies walked out the back door. Terry walked up to the bar, "Hugh give me two bottles and one of those small barrels I made you full of beer, please." Then turning and looking at the crowd, "I'm the local blacksmith…The day is done for me…So if you want me to take care of those animals out there it's going to cost you a little more."

"WHAT DO YOU MEAN by charging us more than normal?" One man yelled out. "We're riding for the law. We should get it free just like any other law posse."

"I'll bet there isn't one badge amongst you. You all are just hoping you might get lucky. The state won't pay me for my work because there isn't one real lawman amongst you. You're nothing more than a bunch of bounty hunters, and they have to pay their own bill and so will you or I'm going home to party and then sleep. I'll get around to you in the morning, the whole time those big train robbers are getting further and further away from you."

"Alright, alright, we'll pay your overtime wages," another man said.

"Let's get our horses over their men, then maybe this man here will open the kitchen back up," another shouted.

Hugh looked over at Julie; "You want to stick around and waitress for a few more hours?"

"No thanks Hugh," Julie said. "I'm going to help Terry, then go home, take a hot bath and go to bed for some real excitement."

387

Marshal Shawn Felton and the Wild Bunch

With that comment everyone shut up and looked over at her, they knew she was right. Because spending the night with her would definitely be exciting.

"You bring your horses down to the Livery," Terry said. "I need to go to my house for a couple minutes. Put them in the middle corral. That way when I'm done checking them over, I'll put them in the front corral. That way we know which ones are done. Each man will attach ten dollars to the halters…If there's no money…I won't check that horse out. However, if I get to your horse, moneys there, but nothing had to be done to your horse, your money will still be on your halter. I won't rip you off. Now one more thing, any of you want to sleep out of the rain and be dry tonight? It's going to cost you two dollars to sleep in my stable. I'll take all the horses that are inside and put them outside to make more room for you. But you have to clean the stalls out yourselves; I do have fresh straw out back"

"TWO DOLLARS?" one man yelled out "Livery stables usually only charge four bits."

"I don't care," Terry say's, wearing a shit eating grin. "When you pay for your spot, I'll give you a string to tie around your toes. If you don't have one, and I catch you, first I'll take about fifty dollars out of you in pain… The nearest real doctor is back in John Day or Ontario. If I catch you not paying, YOU WILL need that doctor, I promise."

Terry picked up the pony keg as he called it, grabbed the two bottles of whiskey. "Just so you all know…I DO NOT MAKE THREATS," continuing to look around the room. He walked toward the door, "I ONLY MAKE PROMISES. Do I make myself clear?"

They all agreed real quickly as they watched Terry walk by them and out the door. One man made the comment, "His arms are bigger than my legs." Reaching out his hand he handed Terry twelve dollars. "Sir I'd just like to pay in advance.'

Terry stopped, looked down at the money, "Now do I look like I have that string on me now?" Shaking his head, Terry headed towards the door, 'I'll see ya down at the Livery in fifteen minutes." Then Terry and Julie walked out the door and crossed the street to his house.

Chapter Seventeen

Julie looked at Terry, "How much money and which one was it who gave you all that money?"

"Butch Cassidy," Terry said. "And I have no clue on how much money. But it's the biggest bundle I've ever held in my hands at one time. Fact it will help us out a lot… Now if you want, we could start that family we've been putting off because of lack of money."

Julie smiled at Terry, putting her arms around him she gave him a big hug, "We'll just have to see about that Terry."

Walking into the house they could see both Butch and Sundance dancing with the young ladies. They didn't have any music playing and Butch was trying to sing, and that's all it was…. Trying. "Damn Butch what the hell you call that?" Terry said. "You know I do have a pho-nograph over there," he said pointing. "You keep singing, and you're going to break out my windows."

"You think I sing bad?" Butch said smiling. "You should hear Mr. Jones's sing."

"Oh come on Butch," the brunette said. "You don't have to use those phony names around us. We won't tell anyone…Not until after you're long gone."

"Then we can charge more," the little blonde said. "Because then we can say you chose us over every ALL the other girl's in the house tonight."

"Well, I have to go to work now," Terry said. "But if you guys think of it, how about you light the fire under that hot water tank in about two hours? Me and Julie here," putting his arm around her. "We're both going to need a bath after we finish over there."

"You sure that's going to be enough water for two baths?" Butch asked. Pouring everyone a beer and started to hand Terry one.

"No thanks," Terry said. "I'll get one later. But to answer your question about that being enough water, hell we only need to fill the tub full once." Leaning over and giving Julie a kiss on the cheek. "I'm not sure just how long we'll be, so maybe I'll see ya before you leave and maybe not, so you guys take care of yourselves." Terry said shack-ing their hands, and then he and Julie walked out the door.

389

CHAPTER EIGHTEEN

It was mid afternoon when Curry woke up, slowly sitting up; he started looking around the one room cabin. Right off he could see the fire burning but most of the wood had burnt down. Getting up he started walking across the room to put a few more pieces of wood on. Curry could see the Doss's all had their bedrolls out and were sleeping. Looking over on the table, he saw at least two thirds of one of the grouse still sitting on the table for him. Picking it up, he started thinking about what did or did not really happen.

That Lion had to have jumped out of that tree at him, because it was after that they shot the grouse. Then they got him to smoke that peyote. It really hadn't been that bad, just one puff of that shit made him feel like he drank a whole bottle of whiskey by himself…Only it didn't make him sick, and he don't have a hang over. Going over to the door, Curry walked outside, closing the door behind him.

It was still raining. It was a cold slow drizzling rain. Slowly he walked over to the river edge, looking in it he realized he didn't imagine the salmon swimming upstream. They were big and red in color. Still trying to remember all that happened, he remembered the image of the big law man with the special rifle, and that burning sensation he had in his chest, as if he was shot. Which slowing started returning, just thinking of the big lawman and that smoking rifle. Who was he? What did it mean…? The Indians said they smoke peyote and the Great Spirit will show them what's to come in their life. Who was that

Chapter Eighteen

big law man anyways? Curry didn't know. Whoever it was, if he ever came across him he was defiantly going to make a wide path around him.

Continuing to walk around outside, Curry looked up towards the mountaintops, which he still couldn't see them because of all the clouds. Walking up river he looked around out back of the cabin and seen all four saddle horses. Where were the mules and all that gold? The Doss's weren't stupid, he thought to himself. They must have staked them out someplace safe and out of sight, just in case someone came along.

Looking up and down the river, as far as he could see there were no mules. Curry had no clue as to where they were, but it really didn't matter. He knew they would not be going anywhere tonight, because of the rain.

He had been walking and eating the grouse. He had had sage hen and other prairie chickens, least that's what they called them, but this bird was one of the best he had ever eaten. Curry got to wonder just what kind of story's the Doss's would come up with tonight to get him worried and a little scared.

The rain was cold, but at the same time it was so peaceful here, he thought to himself. Walking over to the horses, he could see they still had grain and some grass hay for food. He walked back in the cabin, trying to be quiet. Goof rolled over and woke up as Curry came in with an armload of firewood.

"Still raining outside?" Goof asked, whispering so as not to wake the others.

"Yeah," Curry answered in the same low voice. "Looks like its going to last all day and maybe all night as well."

"That's alright," Goof said, rolling a cigarette. "It will give that posse that much more time to get to Idaho and we can get further away this way. Hell if we're lucky we'll be in Seattle and no one will be the wiser. They'll think we all got away through Idaho and are hiding out somewhere in Utah." Starting to chuckle a little, Goof looked over at Curry, "So how did you like your first high on peyote?"

391

"First off, it made me feel like I drank a whole fifth of whiskey, at once. Made me feel real light headed, thought I was going to fall off my horse." Curry answered

"You almost did," Goof said. "Fact I had to lead your horse the rest of the way here. What were you mumbling about? Don't shoot, don't shoot?"

"I don't remember," Curry said. "I saw the image of a big man, some kinda Lawman; I think he was shooting me…dead."

"They say that stuff will make you see things that are to come in your future. Just like yesterday with that lion. Last week Toad and me smoked some and I had me one of those visions. I saw all of us riding down the canyon and that lion jumping out at us. Only in my dream, no one got a shot off. That lion killed a stranger that was riding with us. So when everything came together, I KNEW something was going to happen. Wasn't quite sure just what or when, but I knew it would be soon, so I was ready with my rifle… Damn good thing I did to, or you would have been the stranger in my vision that got killed."

"The last time I smoked that shit," Hosey spoke up. "I had me a vision of leading a mule train full of gold. Tell you the truth I figured it was just wishful thinking…but look at what we're doing right now… Leading a mule train full of gold."

"Did that vision tell you if we get caught or not?" Curry asked chuckling.

"Don't really remember," Hosey said. "But I remember seeing a young buck Indian, wanna be lawman, with a big U.S. Deputy Marshal. Don't know if we got away or not, because Goof here woke me up for work before the vision finished."

"You're so full of shit about that Marshal," Curry said. "You just made that up because you heard me tell Goof about my vision with the Marshal shooting me."

No I'm not, Hosey answered. I only remember it because the Marshal you're talking about, in my vision had an Indian Law Man with him.

Now we all know your full of shit Hosey, Toad said shacking his head. An Indian lawman…you sure that one wasn't from smoking that opium shit.

392

Chapter Eighteen

NO IT WASN'T, Hosey answered. I find myself on a ship out in the middle of the ocean when I smoke that.

"I don't know what the hell you're talking about," Toad said. Standing up and walking over to the fire for a cup of coffee. "I've been smoking that shit for years, and I've never had any visions of anything."

"So what are we going to get for dinner tonight?" Hosey asked.

"Hell the river's full of HUGE fish," Curry said.

"It's the spring steelhead run," Toad said. "When they get this far up river they're no good to eat."

"Why's that?" Curry asked, looking confused.

"These waters are their spawning grounds," Toad said. "They won't eat anything now, then after they lay their eggs, they die. There's still plenty of other fish in that river that are good eating though. Goof, why don't you go grab some fish line out of my gear and let's go catch some dinner?"

"We ate so damn many fish growing up," Hosey said. "I can't stand them anymore. I'm going to take a hike and see if I can't find a deer or some more grouse."

"Now Hosey, you don't need to go and kill any deer," Goof said. "We don't need that much food. We'll be in John Day late tomorrow night at the latest."

Picking up his rifle, he headed towards the door. Hosey looked back at the others, "I don't care…You want fish for dinner and breakfast that's fine, but as for me, I DON'T. Curry you want to come with me or go with them fishing?"

"I sure would like to try and catch just one of the steelhead out there in that river," Curry said, rubbing his hands together with excitement.

"Didn't you just hear Goof?" Hosey said. "Those fish won't eat anymore. They will all lay their eggs, and be dead in just a couple of weeks. I'll tell you another thing, you go down to that river; you better have one eye on lookout for bears."

"Why is that?" Curry asked. Looking first at Hosey and then back at the other two.

Toad started chuckle; "Those bear's will be down at that river by the hundreds hoping for a fish dinner as well as us."

393

"Well then," Curry said, with a small smile on his face. "I'm going with Hosey." Then the two walked out the door.

"You know Toad," Goof said. "Deer steak does sound better, so how about we just go take care of the mules, make sure the gold is still covered, and get some wood for the night?"

Walking outside, they buttoned up their coats. It was getting on late afternoon, the sun was nowhere in sight because of the thick rain clouds, and it had been a steady rain all day. "I tell ya Toad, the man who built that cabin knew what he was doing. Not only has it stood the test of time, but it also doesn't take much fire to keep it warm."

"Yeah, yeah," Toad said. "Let's just go take care of the animals." Looking towards Hosey, "You just make sure you get something good to eat." Then the two groups each went their separate ways.

Hosey and Curry had only gone a short ways when Hosey pulled out his pipe and bag of peyote. Loading the pipe as they walked, Hosey looked over at Curry, "You want another pull off this?"

Holding up both hands, "No thanks," Curry said smiling. "Trust me I did enjoy it, it made the trip peaceful and at the same time I saw everything around me for the first time. I know I would have rode right by all those deer and elk before and probably wouldn't have seen them. I think I'll wait until this jobs over before I smoke any more."

"What deer and elk you talking about?" Hosey asked with a strange look on his face.

"I bet I saw at least twenty bucks and ten to twelve huge bull elk," Curry said. "Fact there was one buck; he had the biggest rack of horns I've ever seen in my life."

"The hell you say," Hosey said. "If we'd seen any deer or elk on the trip down here, we wouldn't be out here right now hunting for food."

"Bullshit Hosey," Curry said. He just felt like Hosey had called him a liar. "You standing here, telling me we didn't ride by, or see any deer or elk after you boys shot those grouse?"

"That's what I'm saying," Hosey said. Taking a pull off the pipe, then he handed it to Curry as a gesture.

"No thanks Hosey," Curry said. "I can't believe you're telling me I imagined all that."

Chapter Eighteen

"Oh hell, Curry," Hosey said. Trying not to laugh too loud because he didn't want to scare any wildlife off if they should stumble onto something. Looking down at Curry's peril handled, shiny silver forty four hanging in his holster, "So you any good with that thing or do you just wear it for show?"

"I can hit what I'm shooting at, if that's what you mean," Curry said. "Don't think I could shoot the head off a bird at fifty feet, flying away like you and your brothers…But I do hit what I'm shooting at."

"Ever kill anyone?" Hosey asked.

"Can't say I know for sure," Curry answered. "I've had to shoot my way out of more than a few robberies. I know I've hit a few men… Don't know for sure if any died though. The papers have said, after we pulled off a job that so and so had been shot and killed in the shootout. I couldn't say it was my bullet that done the job…Butch and Sundance, they like to plan a job out so you don't have to use your gun for anything more than an attention getter. They say they've never fired a shot at anyone on any job. Said they've had to shoot over a few heads or light a stick of dynamite now and then. They're proud of the fact that they've never killed anyone in a robbery. Which is just fine with me…You ever kill anyone Hosey?"

"Yeah…two," Hosey said. Stopping and looking right into Curry's eyes. "It was either them or me, I don't like gunplay, but if you pull it, you damn sure better be willing to use it. They're not toys. If you pull one on me you had better not hesitate, because I promise you I won't. If you make me pull it, I WILL use it."

"I hear ya," Curry said. "A gun is no toy. So don't treat it like one." Just then a couple doe's walked out in front of them, stopping Curry pointed them out to Hosey. "Take one of those and let's get out of the rain."

"No, those two will be having babies any time now," Hosey said. "We'll wait and see if we can't get a small buck instead. It really shouldn't be much longer." He say's, offering Curry the pipe again, "You sure you don't want a hit before I put this away?"

Holding both hands back up again and smiling, "NO THANKS," Curry said assuredly.

"Don't know why not," Hosey was chuckling. "Nobody brought any whiskey, and this will make the night go by faster."

"Speak for yourself Hosey," Curry said. "I brought two bottles with me and I know Toad brought at least one."

"Why those assholes told me they didn't have time to get anything," Hosey said. "Shoot I wanted a couple of shots on our way down to keep me warm inside."

Just then a little forked horn buck jumped up and started to run. He didn't get even ten feet before Hosey drilled him. Dead center in the back of the head, sending him tumbling to the ground, dead before he hit it. "Come on," Hosey said. "Let's get the back strap and one hind quarter just in case someone else happens to come by and needs to keep warm for the night."

"Alright," Curry said. The two walked over to the little buck, "That's a nice four point."

Hosey looked at Curry, kneeling down to cut out the meat, "Four point? What the hell you talking about? This is only a forket horn, or two point."

"No it's not," Curry said. Counting the points on both sides.

"WHAT?" shouted Hosey, busting up laughing. "You don't count both sides, you only count one side."

"What the hell you talking about Hosey?" Curry snapped. "Back home we hunt whitetail deer, we always count both sides."

Cutting into the back, Hosey started skinning the deer. "Well I don't care how you count them back east, out here we only count one side. Cut that hind quarter off there real quick, will you Curry? So we can get back to the cabin. I don't know about you, but I feel like this rain slicker still lets a lot of water through and I'm cold and hungry. Besides Toad and Goof should be done feeding the animals and finished finding enough wood for the night. We might have to pick up some more before we leave in the morning."

"What do you mean? Pack more in the morning before we leave?" Curry asked as he finished cutting the hindquarter off and stood up. We won't need any more wood.

396

Chapter Eighteen

"Yes We Do," Hosey said, seriously "not for us, but that way the next man that comes along at least has dry wood to start a fire with." Just like when we got here. Oh yeah, you weren't quite all here when we got here, were you, you was doing a lot of mumbling, but we couldn't understand who you were talking to?"

"I don't really remember," Curry said chuckling a little. "By the way, where did you guys put the mules and the gold?"

"Don't worry about it," Hosey said. "Just to ease your mind so you don't think we're ripping you off or anything. There's a small draw about a half mile up the main canyon there," pointing his rifle in the general direction. "It's kind of hidden out of sight, fact, if you didn't know it was there you would just ride right on by it and not realize it."

The two walked back to the cabin. Hosey was packing all the meat, while he was having Curry pickup and drag some decent pieces of wood that were lying on the ground.

"We can break these up when we get back to the cabin, just in case Goof and Toad didn't get enough."

When the two came back out at the river edge, Hosey made it a point to tell Curry it was Granite Creek, and that it poured into the North fork of the John Day River just down from the cabin a hundred feet or so. Then they turned and followed it downstream towards the cabin. Curry figured they'd been gone for right about an hour, maybe a little longer. They came across Goof who was fishing. He was pulling them fish out just as fast as he could throw his line in. Granted most of them were only six to eight inches long. But he did have a half dozen that were twelve plus inches each. Curry could tell he was having fun with his makeshift fishing pole. It was just a stick that he had tied a fifteen foot piece of line to with a man made fly on it. Just watching Goof, Curry could tell that it would be a whole lot of fun.

"You wouldn't happen to have any more line, and those fly's you're using would you Goof?" Curry asked.

"Sure do, right here in my pouch." Goof answered

"Do you mind if I join ya," Curry asked.

397

"Heck no, but whatever you catch you have to throw back. There's no way we'll be able to eat them all." Goof said, tossing him his pouch. You'll find everything you need in there.

"No problem." Curry drug his woodpile up to the cabin, he would break it later. He went in the cabin, grabbed a bottle of whiskey out of his saddle bag, and ran back to the river. Looking around he found a nice willow and cut it off for a pole. He had done this when he was a kid back home, but they had always used worms as bait. He had never seen them use a fly tied to a hook before.

The rain was letting up a bit, but it was still raining. It was mostly dew from the clouds sitting so low. But with his rain slicker's on and his bottle of whiskey to warm him, Curry was having the time of his life. Most of the fish he caught were only six to eight inches in length, but once in a while he would hook one about twelve to fifteen inches long. He also found out that Toad was right, them big steelhead salmon would not take the hook, but it sure was fun watching them dance in the water. Some still swimming upstream and some were obviously laying their eggs. He forgot the rest of the world was even around.

Catching all these fish was so relaxing, until he walked around the bend and out in the middle of the river he saw a mother bear catching fish while her two cubs played both in and out of the water. He knew it was real this time, because he hadn't smoked any of that peyote. After watching them for a few minutes, Curry turned around and started fishing back towards the cabin. To his amazement the cabin was nowhere in sight

Oh well, he thought to himself. I'll get back, when I get there. Turning back down stream, he started fishing again.

CHAPTER NINETEEN

It had started raining about mid-morning Wapiti figured. It was getting colder the higher up the mountain they rode; he only hoped it didn't turn to snow before they got to the cabin. Wapiti wasn't one to complain, but he was getting chilly, he stopped once to grab an extra warm wool shirt, but even then the Marshal made a big deal out of it. Hollering at him to hurry up. They had a long way to go to get to the cabin. Wapiti really didn't care if they made the cabin or not, a good lean to and a warm fire would do just fine and be dry enough for him right now. Every now and then the Marshal would holler "PULL" and throw one of them wooden pigeons up in the air. Even that was getting hard to do, not only because of the rain slicker and the extra shirt. But that cold rain was making his muscles tighten up. Heck, Wapiti thought to himself, they hadn't even stopped to eat any lunch. The only time they did stop the Marshal grabbed a piece of that apple pie the cook made, but he ate that riding. All the food was on the pack mule, well not everything; the Marshal was nice enough to give him a couple corn biscuits to eat. He looked at them, and ate them half heartedly.

Even though it was a cold rainy day, the country they were riding through Wapiti thought was very beautiful country. Watching the salmon swim up river to spawn was quite a sight. This far up the fish were turning red in color. In some places they were actually riding through the river, he could see some of them were laying their eggs. Even with all the cold rain, he couldn't believe how many deer and elk

399

were out feeding. You'd think they would be somewhere lying down to keep warm. Wapiti hoped they'd get to the cabin soon, the way he figured it, they only had maybe an hour of daylight left, and it would be hard to find the wood in the dark. Not to mention trying to get it to burn, with it all being wet. That wasn't going to be easy. Just then Wapiti could see the Marshal slowing up, putting his nose in the air, at the same time Wapiti could smell smoke too.

The Marshal was waving him to come up, so he did. "Wapiti, the way I figure it, we're about a half mile from the cabin now. You smell that smoke?" Shawn asked.

"Yes sir Marshal," that meant they wouldn't have to worry about starting a fire, Wapiti thought to himself.

"Son, now listen," the Marshal said. Pointing around as he was talking. "I've had the opportunity to catch me some cattle rustlers in this cabin before. Granite Creek pours into the John Day just about a half-mile up above those heavy rapids. If you go up Granite Creek just about the same distance, there's a small stream, maybe only two feet wide, follow that creek a few hundred yards up into the timber, it drops into a nice bowl. It's big enough to hide thirty or forty head of cattle for the night. They'll stay in there because of the food and water, I'll wait here, and you high tail it across that river and go and see if we'll get lucky twice. Now make sure you don't get caught should they have a man out checking on the cows."

"No problem Marshal." Wapiti answered, turning his horse down the hill, across the river and up the other side. All of a sudden things had gotten exciting, fact he totally forgot all about the cold. His adrenaline was flowing and with all the excitement he was all of a sudden warmed all through. Quickly he worked his way through the timber, staying away from the river. The Marshal had given Wapiti a pretty good description of just how the two rivers came together. So he just went cross-country. It wasn't long before he came to the stream the Marshal had told him about. Quickly and quietly he climbed off his horse and tied him up. Then he took his rain slicker and the extra shirt off. He knew the rain slicker would make too much noise and the shirt was too bright a color, it could be seen from a long distance off.

400

Chapter Nineteen

Staying low and running as fast as he could Wapiti worked his way along the stream. It didn't take long for him to come to the area the Marshal had told him about, he could see eight mules grazing; they were all hobbled, so they would not run off. It was just like the Marshal had said a good place to hide animals. Slowly looking around to make sure there was no one else in the area, Wapiti worked his way closer to the mules for a better look.

Lying on the ground all stacked upright were eight backpacks, one for each mule. Continuing to look around a little, Wapiti couldn't see if there was anything to go with those packs, the rain had washed out any tracks that their owners might have made, which didn't make much sense. Why hide them out of sight like this if they weren't trying to hide anything? He would let the Marshal know he'd be able to figure something out. He quickly worked his way back to his horse and then back to the Marshal, which didn't take all that long. Riding up to the Marshal, who was taking a pull off his whiskey bottle. "Well Marshal, there's eight pack mules and a backpack for each one. But I could find anything that they would be packing."

"Alright Wapiti," Shawn said. "Now it maybe there's nothing here, or maybe there is. You just act like nothing's up. We'll just act thankful to share the cabin with them if they don't mind."

"No problem," Wapiti said, turning his horse and following the Marshal up the trail. Soon Wapiti could see the spot that Roy said there used to be a waterfall until a rockslide came down and just turned it into steep heavy rapids. Just as they got to the top of the slide area, Wapiti could see the cabin on the other side of the two rivers, and smoke coming out of the chimney. All of a sudden it donned on him, he hadn't put his rain slicker back on. Reaching for both the shirt and the slicker he quickly put them back on. He could see the bridge that crossed over the river. Riding up to it Wapiti could see how simple it was built. Just two big logs laying flat across the river and a bunch of lodge pole tree's all about the same diameter and length nailed down to the bigger logs. It was a nice wide bridge, at least six, seven feet wide. You couldn't get a wagon across it, but then you couldn't get a wagon up this canyon either.

401

As they rode up to the cabin the Marshal yelled out, "HELLO you in the cabin, this is U.S. Marshal Shawn Felton, and we sure would like to be able to come in out of the cold and rain."

"Holy shit," Hosey said. Standing up and walking towards the door. "The one Marshal YOU don't want around, why he can smell a skunk a mile off. In other words, you all watch what you say, and how you act. If you even act like we're up to no good, he'll smell it. We have to let them in for the night, or HE WILL know something's up. But we'll let them leave first in the morning. We'll give them at least a two hour head start," he demanded quietly, opening the door. "Marshal, put your horses around back in the lean two, then come on in where it's nice and warm."

"Thank you Young man," Shawn answered, turning his horse towards the back. Looking back at Wapiti, "Yep, something's up alright, he's just a little too eager to let us in."

"You know Marshal," Wapiti said with a small grin on his face. "Not everyone is an outlaw."

Shawn climbed down off his horse and he pointed to his nose, "I can smell it son. You just wait and see…you just wait and see"

The two started unsaddling and putting their gear away, Shawn looked back over at Wapiti, "We'll make like we need to get an early start. We'll leave just after sun up, ride up river about an hour then circle back around and catch them with whatever it is they're hiding along with them mules."

Wapiti didn't say anything; he just kept nodding his head. The two walked back around to the door, Shawn knocked, opening the door, they both walked in. Taking off their rain gear and shaking it outside, so as not to get anyone wet.

"Now that's just about the coldest rain I've been in, in quite a while," Shawn said. Looking around the room at everyone then back over to the fire. He threw his rain gear over a wood stump and leaned his rifle up against the end of the table. Walking over to the fire and knelt down to warm his hands, "I'm Marshal Shawn Felton and this is my deputy Wapiti."

"WHAT," Hosey yelled out. "An Indian lawman, have you lost your mind Marshal?"

Chapter Nineteen

Looking around at them again, to get a better look, Shawn could tell only one of them was not related. He didn't have a nose on him like the other three did. The fourth man was almost as white as a ghost, almost like he had just seen a ghost himself.

Wapiti walked around the room introducing himself to each of the men. He shook their hands and of course they all used their nicknames.

Shawn stood up laughing with his back to the fire, "You tellen me that not only did God curse you with those noses, big enough to smell a man ten miles away but then your parents went and named you Hosey, you Toad, and you Goof? He said pointing. You boys had some real cruel parents."

"Noo," Toad said chuckling. "I'm Scott, that's Terry and Randy. We've just had these nicknames since we were kids. They've stuck with us…very few people even know our real names."

"Well hell," Shawn said, pulling out his bottle. "I figure anyone with that big a nose and those off the wall names, I do believe you're right about one thing and that's that no one would ever forget you once they met ya." Then looking over at Hosey, "I can see why they call you Hosey, hell your nose is almost twice as long as these two together, and you…Goof is it? You're definitely the goofiest looking all right. But where the hell did Toad come from?"

Starting to chuckle, Toad looked over at the Marshal and handed him a cup for his whiskey and coffee. "Dad said when I was a kid; I'd always stick my tongue out like a frog trying to catch flies. He told me, starting to chuckle louder…Said one day all the women would love me for it. Didn't know what he meant until I got older," then looking around the room at everyone…"Come to find out he was right." With that everyone busted up laughing.

"You're dreaming," hollered Hosey.

"Well Mr. Smith, just how'd you get tied up with these boys here," Shawn asked. Standing full up, and puffing his chest out for effect.

"I-I-I-I am new to the area, I'm a gambler, and these men said they could get me through to John Day faster this way. Figured I'd go check

403

it out. I'm glad I took them up on the offer, because this is the prettiest country I've ever seen." Curry answered, glaring at the fire flickering off the over sized lever on the Marshal's rifle, leaning up against the table, not three feet from him His heart stopped beating. Thinking to himself…The man in the vision. Just thinking of it he could feel the deep burning sensation returning to his chest. Then looking over at Wapiti, it was just like Hosey's vision he said the big Marshal had an Indian Deputy. Rubbing his chest with his hand, what did it all mean. Slowly he tried to stand up. Feeling fuzzy and light headed, if he didn't get out of there he might pass out from fear. He extended his hand to the Marshal, "I've heard about you Sir. I'm glad you're not chasing after me."

"Well Young man you just stay out of trouble and I won't have any reason to come looking for ya," Shawn said…"As far as the rest of you, are concerned about Wapiti, here being a Deputy U.S. Marshall. Well I'll have you know we spent the weekend in John Day. You just ask those boys there what he did to them and how he changed their minds about him being a lawman."

"Marshal, Wapiti," Goof said. "There's still a half of back strap of deer here already cooked, that's if you men are hungry. If that's not enough, we have a hind quarter out in the lean to."

"Well thank ya Young man," Shawn said. Reaching out and cutting himself off a big piece.

"What about you, Wapiti?" Goof asked.

"Thank you very much," Wapiti answered. "The Marshal's been wanting to get here all day, and to tell you the truth, Goof is it…? I'm hungry, tired, and cold. Can't tell ya just how thankful we are to you men for letting us share the cabin and your food."

"Wapiti, your tribe smoke peyote?" Hosey said smiling.

"Sometimes," Wapiti said. "We smoke it to seek guidance or to see what the Great Spirit might show us, of what's to come."

"Well here," Hosey said smiling, taking out his pipe and peyote.

"That's what's wrong with you white eyes," Wapiti said, reaching for the pipe. He looked at it and then sat it on the table. "You take the sacred smoke of the Indian, and you treat it like it's whiskey…You

404

Chapter Nineteen

smoke too much of it. I'll bet none of you here have ever seen or had the Great Spirit take you on a trip...Showing you what lay ahead for you. Tell you which direction in life you should go."

"I've had more than one vision," Hosey said. "Why just last week I smoked some," he raised his hands above his head, "The Great Spirit took me on a trip across a large body of water where all them China men live." Looking around at everyone and started to chuckle. "So tell me what that's supposed to mean."

"Says you like China men's opium and women over white women," Wapiti said.

Just then both Goof and Toad started laughing, "Will you get a load of that Hosey?" Toad said. "This young deputy, Wapiti here, just figured you out real quick, didn't he?"

"It was easy," Wapiti said. "I can smell the opium on him. Maybe two, three days since he last smoked any, but I can still smell it." Then he looked over at Curry, "I can see in your eyes these white eyes got you to smoke some peyote...You seen something that scared you. I don't know what, but I could see it in your eyes just as soon as we came in the door. Almost like you'd seen us somewhere before but you don't know how or when."

Curry didn't say a word; he just looked around the room at everyone, then back over at the Marshal who was standing in front of the fireplace. It was just like the vision he had seen earlier, a big law man with the modified rifle. Only he wasn't holding his rifle. Curry's eyes went down to the Marshal's pistol, then back up to the Marshal and that rifle leaning up against the table..

"Now that you mention it Wapiti," Shawn said. "He does look like he's seen a ghost."

"Naw, it ain't that," Curry said. "I got me some bad eats back in Sumpter. Made me sick to my stomach." Standing up he walked toward the door. "Fact, I think I'll go outside for a little while." Looking back over at the Marshal, Curry could feel the sweat starting to run down his face. Unbuckling his gun belt, he laid it on the table. "I just want everyone here to know I'm not looking for any trouble." Then he turned and walked out the door.

Shawn took the last pull off his bottle, "Any of you have some whiskey?"

"Sure do Marshal," Toad said, handing him his bottle.

"Marshal," Wapiti said. "I think I'm going to join Mr. Smith outside." Walking over, he poured two cups of coffee and walked out the door.

Just after Wapiti walked out the door and closed it behind him, Shawn looked over at the Doss's, "Now you boys seem like nice smart young men to me..." Leaning over the table, he looked at each and every one of them. "So you mind telling me just what the hell you're doing running with Kid Curry?"

"WHOOO?" they all hollered. Tying to act surprised.

"You heard me...That's Harvey Logan, A.K.A. Kid Curry," Shawn said in a stern but quiet voice.

"NO WAY," Toad answered. "When we met him and his two buddies in Sumpter he told us his last name was Smith."

"Two others you say?" Shawn asked, with excitement in his voice, yet a fierce look on his face. "So what did the other two call themselves?"

"Jone's and Young," Goof said. "Why? Who do you think they really are?"

"OOHH, I think I know who they were, and I know you know exactly who they were too." Shawn said standing full up and taking another pull off the whiskey bottle. "I'll just bet they were A.K.A. Butch Cassidy and the Sundance Kid."

"Oh bullshit," Toad yelled back. "What the hell would those guys be doing in this part of the country?"

"They were known to have robbed a bank in Portland two and a half weeks ago, then last week they robbed a small bank in Haines... Now I don't know if they were up there planning a job, or just spending the loot they got from Portland." Then looking back and forth at all of them, "You wouldn't know where those other two went, would ya?" Shawn asked

"The one that called himself Mr. Young," Goof said, looking at everyone. "Said he was from Utah, and was going back to visit his family."

Chapter Nineteen

"I sure would like to catch those boys before I retire," Shawn said. "That'd be a nice feather in my hat."

"So what are you going to do about him?" Toad said, pointing outside.

"Aw hell, he ain't worth too much," Shawn said. "And he's not a real bad Hombre. That wild bunch that Butch Cassidy runs with, they've never killed or shot anyone in a holdup."

"Wapiti and I are heading to Sumpter, thought I'd show the lad a boomtown. Let him get his feet wet as far as being a lawman is concerned. Shawn said, smiling. But he's already gotten more experience than I thought he'd get. We would have been in Sumpter last weekend, but they had a poker tournament in John Day and the Sheriff asked if we'd help keep the peace. If ya get my meaning," Shawn said with a big smile and a stern look on his face.

"So you're really not joking with us, Marshal?" Goof asked. "That man out there is really Kid Curry?" Still trying to play dumb.

Wapiti followed behind Curry to the edge of the John Day River, where Granite Creek flowed in. Walking up beside him, he handed him a cup of coffee then knelt down closer to the water. "I see in your eyes that you have smoked the peyote. But not like these other white eyes do."

"That's true," Curry said. "Those guys all took two or three puffs off the pipe...Hell, I only took one."

"Tell me, what did the Great Spirit show you...? I know he showed you us, the Marshal or me I mean, but what else did you see?" Wapiti asked

"At first it was beautiful and peaceful; I saw a great bald eagle as he flew high above the valley floor, yet below the clouds and the rain. Then I saw the fish swimming up river, and we weren't anywhere near the river. It was as if I could reach out and touch them. I saw bears, deer, and elk. I couldn't believe how big their horns were...Then I saw mountain lions running and playing like kitten's, you know...Like kittens around the barnyard, Curry answered

"What did he show you about the Marshal?" Wapiti asked.

"Who said he showed me anything about the Marshal? " Curry snapped back.

"Your eyes told me," Wapiti said. Throwing a stone across the river, making it skip. "When we came in tonight, you looked at the Marshal like you had seen him before…Even though you did a good job of trying to hide it. You have great fear in your Spirit for him…" Looking back into Curry's eyes, "I can see it. Tell me, what did the Great Spirit show you?"

"I really don't remember," Curry said, skipping a rock across the river. "I do remember seeing a big law man with the lever on his rifle modified to fit his big hands," pointing back to the cabin. "He was holding his rifle and smoke was coming out of the barrel…Then I got a deep burning sensation in my chest, like I'd been shot, then I fell asleep."

"You know the one they call Hosey?" Wapiti asked.

"Yeah," Curry said nodding his head.

"Remember he said the Great Spirit took him to China? And I told him it was because of his love for their opium," Wapiti said.

"Yeah," Curry said.

"Sometimes he shows us great and wonderful things, and sometimes he shows us of what is to come…He does it so that maybe if we're wise we can change what happens, before it happens." Wapiti said

"What do you mean?" Curry asked looking over at Wapiti.

"Well sir," Wapiti said. "Mr. Smith…I think maybe the Great Spirit is showing you what will happen. If and when you come across this law man…I'm not saying it's the Marshal in there, but it could be. What the Great Spirit may be showing you is if you draw your gun against this man, you will lose… And Mr. Smith, he doesn't give second chances, nor does he miss. If you think you need to pull your pistol on him… You'd better not hesitate…?" Looking Curry straight in the eyes, "HE WON'T. That I promise you."

"Do you think he would make me draw against him?" Curry asked.

"NOPE," Wapiti answered. "The Marshal said he has not shot or killed any man who did not go for his gun first…He made a shot in

Chapter Nineteen

John Day. The man tried to back shoot me after I kicked him out of the poker tournament. The man already had his gun out of his holster and was making his way through the crowd to shoot me. There were at least seventy people between that man and us, the Marshal threw me aside, drew and fired. Don't ask me how, through all those people… But he hit only that man, and right between the eyes." Even though it was night and dark outside Wapiti could see Curry's face turning whiter.

"What should I do?" Curry asked. "Should I…Hmmm… Maybe sleep in the lean two with the animals?"

"He ain't gonna shoot you," Wapiti said. "Just because you go back in. Hell, he'll offer you a shot of whiskey off his bottle and ask you if you're alright…" starting to smile, "And I think you could use a shot of whiskey right now…You took your gun off… Leave it off. I promise you, he won't shoot you. Even if you're not Mr. Smith and you're someone else, and you're wanted by the law…I've seen it in his eyes… He don't like to kill…So what do ya say, shall we go back in Mr. Smith?"

"Yeah…Alright," Curry said, taking the last swallow of coffee from his cup. "Wapiti," he said, looking him straight in the eye. "Thanks for the talk…It really helped. I don't think I'm going to be smoking any more of that peyote."

"Why not?" Wapiti asked. "Didn't the Great Spirit take you on a grand voyage around the mountains? Show you something that might come true if you don't stop it? Just don't smoke it like those white eyes in there. Only smoke it when you need help, knowledge or guidance from the Great Spirit." Wapiti turned and walked into the cabin.

"Everything alright with that young lad, Wapiti?" Shawn asked. Taking the bottle back out of Hosey's hands. "You Doss boys drink too much whiskey…" Taking a big pull off the bottle. "Hell there's barely enough here for me."

"It's our whiskey Marshal," Toad said, taking the bottle back.

"So did that Mr. Smith see a ghost Wapiti or what?" Shawn asked again.

"Something like that Marshal," Wapiti said. The door opened up and Curry walked back in.

409

Reaching over to Toad, Shawn took the bottle of whiskey and handed it to Curry. Looking back at everyone else Shawn smiled. "I think Mr. Smith here needs a shot more than any of the rest of us right now."

Picking up the bottle, Curry took two real big gulps. "Thanks Marshal." Then turning back towards the Marshal and Toad, "So who do I give this to?"

Both men stretched out their hands for the bottle. Toad was first to grab it. "Don't worry old man," he said, starting to chuckle. "I still have one more bottle…" Looking around the room. "We're not going to run out anytime soon, besides I want to get some sleep tonight so we can get an early start."

"I hear ya," Shawn said. "Me and Wapiti need to get over to Sumpter and see if we can find us some real outlaws. While we were in John Day, rumor was that Butch Cassidy and Sundance Kid had been seen over there…Boy I sure would like to get myself just one more big named outlaw before I retire and young Wapiti here, takes my place."

"Marshal," Hosey hollered. "You really think they're going to let an Indian be a lawman…He'll have to fight his way through hell and back before any white man will not only listen to an Indian lawman, but show him any respect, you're dreaming!"

"Well son," Shawn said. "They felt that way in John Day too, until they tried to take a hold of that Young man…How many scalps could you have taken Wapiti?" He asked, throwing his chest out. "Wasn't it something like eleven or twelve…Some three and four at a time."

"Oh now, come on Marshal," Hosey said. With a small little smile on his face as he looked over at Wapiti. "You sure you aren't stretching it just a little."

"Well you boys are heading that way," Shawn said. Smiling and picking up his bed roll. "When you get there, just look around town at everyone who's sporting some healthy bruises. Now, it looks like it's put your bed roll wherever you can." Kicking Goof in the leg, "Move over a little bit Young man, let this old man through."

Toad loaded up the fireplace, laid out his bedroll, and they all went to sleep.

CHAPTER TWENTY

The four had been playing cards all afternoon; the rain just kept coming down. Larry had managed to have at least three cups of coffee before he started in on beer. However, each one of those cups had at least two shots of whiskey in them, and Randy, why he just pulled out his peyote pipe and took a big pull off it. He never was one who drank too often. Even though most of the people in the place couldn't stand the smell of peyote, it smelled like a skunk had just farted inside the place. Most people didn't like it when someone lit up inside, but with Randy being Randy; nobody paid him any attention.

All day long more cold, wet hopeful miners came into the store. After all it was the only place in town. Larry couldn't help but laugh at them poor love starved men. Why no sooner would that fat squaw come out from behind the curtain with one customer then she would head right back in with another. There weren't any logger's up in this country yet. There would be some day, and they all knew it. Some of those miners looked like they'd spent all their time digging in tunnels, still covered in dirt from head to toe. More than half looked like they hadn't seen water in a week's, but that didn't seem to bother that squaw much. All four men shivered at the idea of being that hard up for a woman.

Looking around the room Gary picked up his next hand of cards, "I didn't think there was that many people up in this area, but damn, I bet there's twenty five to thirty people in here tonight."

411

"No there's not," Larry said with a chuckle. "There's twenty four to twenty nine and one fat squaw. Remember? And she's real busy."

"Just look at them fools," Randy said. "Digging in that ground for that lost treasure...The mother load...isn't that's what they call it."

"Well Hombres," Luis said. With all the deer and elk up here at least they won't starve to death."

Just then a half-drunk kid, one of those hopeful miners, tripped and fell over onto Randy's lap. Even though this kid had no idea who Randy was, eighty percent of the others did, and they all started to step back. Randy grabbed the young seventeen-maybe eighteen-year-old man by the back of his collar and helped him stand back up. Reaching into his pocket Randy pulled out a fifty dollar bill and put it in the Young man's pocket and pushed him away, saying, "You go have a good night...and you make sure you stay away from that buffalo woman, there's other ways." Then he sat back down.

No one could believe their eyes to what had just happened. Randy didn't lay a hand on the Young man. "What was up with that?" One man looked over at another. "He had just smoked some of that peyote, what, five minutes ago?"

"So what?" another man said.

"Well," the first man said smiling. "They say that shit mellows the spirit...maybe he needs to smoke more of it."

With that comment everyone who heard it, including all four of them all started to laugh.

"What?" Randy said, waving his hand. "He's just a kid...Hell he isn't even wet behind the ears yet. I bet it's probably his first time getting drunk..." Looking around the table, then back in the direction of the Young man. "Besides, he's too small right now...Just like fishing, throw the small ones back, let him grow up...They'll be back!" Then he took a pull off his beer, smiling from ear to ear.

"I wonder just how much gold those guys got away with? " Gary said. "I hear they get fifty plus bags a week between all three dredges out in that valley."

Chapter Twenty

"Shoot Amigo," Luis said. "If that's the case, remember that Sheriff said they didn't ship last week. Said they had twice as much gold down in that tunnel."

"Sounds like they'll have a full load," Larry said. "I sure would like to see just how big a pile all that gold would make."

"Well now that's one thing we won't ever have a chance to see," Gary said. "I figure they stayed the day at the cabin and tonight as well. If we get up early we could make the cabin in just a couple hours in the morning then John Day by nightfall."

"What are you going to do if we catch up with them?" Randy asked. "I don't know about you, but I don't want to be anywhere around those guys if the law comes around…" Looking around the table at everyone. "I don't want them thinking we had anything to do with that."

"I hear ya," Larry said. "I don't want to go to jail for something I had nothing to do with…Well not totally with, we didn't do the actual robbery itself."

"Hell," hollered Gary, starting to chuckle. "You can't say we didn't have anything to do with it. We weren't in on the actual robbery, but we sure as hell did make a lot of money off the pre-robbery festivities." Patting his pocket, where his wallet was and it was full of money, not to mention the money they all had in their saddlebags.

"I just hope we don't come across any other outlaws, that might want to rob us," Larry said.

"Well guys like I was trying to say earlier," Gary said. "I want to get an early start, so I'm heading over to the Livery, and catch up on some much needed rest."

"I think I'll join ya," Randy said, standing up.

"It's not even dark outside yet," Larry said.

"I don't care Larry," Gary said. "When I wake up in the morning, I'm saddling up your horse too. So you and Luis can stay up as long as you want. But come sun-up we're out of here."

"Alright, alright," Larry said. "Come on Luis let's get some sleep too."

Then the four of them walked out the door and over to the Livery. Grabbing their bed rolls they all climbed the ladder to the loft and the soft haystack to sleep on.

CHAPTER TWENTY ONE

Everyone in the house was awakened when the posse took off out of town. The sound of their horses hoofs pounding heavily on the ground, as they rode by. Terry looked out the window; he could hardly believe it was already daylight outside. He's usually awake at least thirty or forty minutes before the sun comes up. But he and Julie had been up late re-shoeing all those horses. He knew they were up well past midnight, looking over in bed he could see Julie sleeping. He sure would be happy when she slept there every night. Fact Terry knew Dewayne would be in to talk to him later. When Julie tells Dewayne she helped him out last night, he'll understand. Only he'll think she slept in one of the other rooms. That's if she don't tell him that Butch Cassidy and Sundance Kid were here. Right off he'll tell her that someone was just trying to make her think that's who they were. But then when she shows him Randy's two Clydesdales and Terry's missing three horses, then he'll know it is true.

Rolling over and sitting up, Julie saw Terry just sitting there staring at her. "What's up?" she asked. Pulling that long beautiful blonde hair out of her face, with a big smile.

"Nothing," Terry said. "Just waiting for the day when you're there every morning."

"Sure, you will be," Julie answered. I'll go start the coffee while you get the others up." She leaned over and jumped out of bed, walking to the door; stopped, turned around and looked at Terry…"ME TOO" … blowing him a kiss and went downstairs.

Terry got out of bed, slipped his jeans and boots on. Hollering out, "All those hopeful bounty hunters just rode out of town. So let's get you loaded up and out of here too."

Last night before he went to bed, he did count the money that Butch gave him. TEN THOUSAND DOLLARS, damn that is a whole lot of money. They had also told him that the twins and Randy made another thirty, maybe closer to forty thousand dollars. Hell now they could just about buy the entire Beaver Creek valley. From the main road in the middle at the bottom end of the valley, all the way to the top of Dooley Mountain. Well at least close to all of that. But I'd have to move my teams and logging trailers over there. Hell Randy already had the skidding covered with his Clydesdales. They could start they're own logging company too. Well enough daydreaming, you've got to get them men fed, loaded up and out of here. He sure wished he could have partied more with them last night. I sure would like to hear more about that Roan. Granted those three were decent bronc riders, BUT I'M BETTER, he smiled, picked up his shirt and walked out the door. Stopping at the other two doors and knocking, "Butch, Sundance… Let's go…I'll see ya downstairs."

Butch and Sundance weren't all that far behind Terry. "You sound like you want us out," Butch said in a joking voice.

"Oh hell, I'm not too worried about that. No one knows those Clydesdales are anywhere around here. They did have pictures of both of you…But everyone's looking for those two big Clydesdales. They'll be able to see them miles off with a set of binoculars."

"Sure would hate to be someone who thought he was lucky to have two big horses like that and that posse catches up with them," Sundance said. "Hell they'll make them unload everything."

"That's if they don't stat shooting first before they search the pack's. Some of those men in those posse's are trigger happy." Butch said, I mean hell…its just money."

"YEAH, THEIR'S" Terry yelled. "I wonder why they want it back." Starting to chuckle. "Now those gold miners over there, they can afford to share. Believe me they're making plenty enough to share. Shit, the way they are mining that valley with those big dredges… I bet

Chapter Twenty One

it won't take them two years, three at the most before they have that whole valley mined up.

"Well I'll tell ya," Sundance said. "We've robbed maybe…hmmm… twenty maybe twenty five trains now…This is the first time we ever got the money before they even got it loaded. I thought we would have to blow the canyon to stop the train, but the way Randy had everything figured out, hell this way was a lot more fun for some reason."

"I wonder how that big fat good for nothing Sheriff made out," Butch said. "I'll tell ya, you should have seen the faces on that mine owner and banker when you stuffed that fifteen hundred dollars into that Sheriff's pocket Butch," Sundance said. "It was priceless."

"So how much longer on that coffee?" Sundance asked.

Just then Julie came walking in through the back door. "Just hold your horses; it'll be done when it gets done. Now if you men want me to make breakfast you're going to have to get out of the kitchen or sit at the table. But just get out of my way."

"DAMN," Butch said. "We know who runs this house."

"I thought you said you weren't married yet," Sundance said.

"We're not," Terry answered, leaning over and giving Julie a kiss on the cheek. Just as the coffee started to boil. "I just like to let her think she's the boss."

Both Butch and Sundance answered at the same time; "There's no thinking about it. That young lady IS the boss already. But if you don't mind Julie we'll take that cup of coffee to go, we really need to get loaded up and get down the road."

"Well here then," Julie said. Pouring herself a cup, "You men take this pot of coffee down to the barn, and I'll make another. I'll make some fried egg and ham steak sandwiches and bring them all down to you." Julie handed them each a cup and Sundance took the coffeepot. Then she kicked them out of the house. They all three laughed as they walked out the back door.

The three filled their cups up and headed down to the barn. It was all new timber inside and out. The beams were made out of twelve by twelve-solid wood. Three stories tall, the main floor came off even from the hillside and the hay loft above that, with the third floor underneath. That's where all the horses and gold were hiding. When it came to packing the bags of gold Terry would put one over each shoulder, Butch and Sundance couldn't believe it, hell it was all they could do to pack just one. Which of course Terry made a point of letting them know how weak they were.

"Well just how the hell did you get all those muscles you have, Terry?" Sundance asked.

"You replace all those logging trailer wheels," Terry said smiling. "Those wheels are six feet high and ten inches wide. And weigh close to four hundred pounds each, I double them up on my wagons. So I can carry more logs, but also so I can limp a load in on one wheel if I need to. Stops me from having to go all the way back out to replace one."

"What, not everyone doubles up theirs like you do?" Butch asks.

"NOPE...and I charge them by the mile to go out and replace one of them," Terry said. "Fact, I make good money doing just that. I have two trailers out there right now, I was supposed to go fix them, but their owners are off chasing you. So until they get back, and I know I will get paid, they'll just sit where they are."

"Well we sure are glad we came across you here," Butch said. "With everyone looking for these two Clydesdales we wouldn't have made it much past John Day if we were lucky." Turning to Sundance with a big smile on his face, "Hell, with these new horses, no one will even give us a second look."

"You didn't just happen to run into me," Terry answered, seriously. "I told you...I was another one of Randy's back doors." "He just didn't tell you about me, is all...But I'm sure he told you about them fat squaw's in Austin Junction, knowing you would choose to come thru here instead".

"We will make sure your horses are returned in just as good of shape as they are now, I promise," Sundance said. "We'll find a good person, one we think we can trust to return them."

They were only about half loaded when Julie walked in. "Your two girlfriends just left, but I told them we woke you up when we finished with the posse's horses. So as far as they know you guys have been gone for hours. They couldn't believe that you really were who you

Chapter Twenty One

said you were…Shoot; they acted like it was their first time… all jittery and giggly. Hell, they didn't even want to stick around for coffee. They just wanted to get back to the boarding house and tell all the other girls."

"We do have that effect on women," Butch said. "When they find out who we are…They get all giggly and squirmy. Sometimes it makes it even more fun."

"Yeah, yeah," Julie said smiling. "Every outlaw I ever had the pleasure or displeasure of meeting all say the same thing… That the women go crazy around them when they find out they're with a wanted man. I guess it's that, they all try to use it and make you feel sorry for them, like they won't be alive tomorrow so…ppplllleeeaass-seee. You believe that shit Terry. Worse yet, IT WORKS." Still shaking her head as she handed everyone a thick toasted egg and ham steak sandwich.

They all thanked her, and then they refilled their coffee cups, took a couple bites and a couple swallows of coffee and went over to get more bags of gold. Putting four hundred pounds on each horse. Trying to camouflage it so it looked like they were still wannabe gold prospectors. "Only problem," Terry said. "You'll be heading in the wrong direction, but there's gold over there too. Also, they had a big poker tournament in John Day last weekend and Marshal Shawn Felton was they're keeping the game safe. Said he was heading to Sumpter by way of Granite, he could change course so watch it around Prairie City. If he does go the Granite way, it's said Felton can smell out just about anything. He'll play like he could care less who you are…then circle back around and get ya. There's only one place that would have been dry through that storm; there's only one cabin up there. It's at the mouth of the Granite Creek, so chances are the rest of your group spent the night with old Marshal Felton and a young buck Indian he's teaching to be a law man." Terry said, shaking his head. "Some of those guys in the posse said that buck bested at least a dozen men or more by himself, all with just his hands and feet."

"An Indian lawman?" Sundance yelled out. "Just what the hell is this world coming to?"

419

Marshal Shawn Felton and the Wild Bunch

"Forget about the Indian," Butch said. "Let's hear more about this MARSHAL FELTON. He's known for bringing them in over the saddle, not sitting up. I can shoot mind ya…I just don't like to."

"Well now all I can tell ya about him, is drop your guns or run. If you hesitate YOU'RE DEAD," Terry said.

"Shit Butch, Curry and the Doss brother's went that way," Sundance said.

"You got Goof and Toad in on this?" Julie said chuckling. "This job was doomed from the start. Hell nothing ever goes those guy's way."

"Hold up in Prairie for the night," Terry said. "If they do get caught, Randy and the twins are going to go talk with the Marshal themselves. If something goes wrong one of them might try and catch you between Prairie and John Day so just hold up a little while at the Gutridge Brothel. If they did get caught, Randy will send Gary to try and catch up with you. They will know I would hold you up if I thought something might go wrong.

Why this Gutridge Brothel, Sundance asked.

Trust me; you won't want to pass it up, Terry said, with a big smile on his face, and Julie poking him in the side. It sounds like your friends and our friend might need some help. If so, Randy will have it all figured out by the time he gets there."

Starting to chuckle, Butch looked over at Sundance. "I wonder just what kind of back door he'll have this time?"

"Don't know," Terry said "But he'll have it figured out. Somehow he'll manage to get the Doss's free, and you guys a few extra hours of a head start. But DON'T go through Dayville. If anyone there sees ya they might get a little suspicious, especially if they hear about a jailbreak too."

Leaning over and giving Julie a kiss on the cheek and holding out his hand to Terry, Butch grabbed the reins of his horse and they all started walking out of the barn. "It's been a real pleasure running into you Sir and your whole damn crazy family." Climbing aboard his horse and looking back down at Julie. That long blonde curly hair, those big beautiful blue eyes, "Young lady, what I told them two last night…I

420

Chapter Twenty One

didn't want to know their names, because I wouldn't remember their names past next week. Hell, I can't remember them now. But you Julie are one lady I think I will remember for quite a while..."

"You know that's true," Sundance says, shacking Terry's hand... "I just don't know how you and your brothers do it, but I won't forget Sharon either. You're lucky men." Butch and Sundance turned their horses and headed out of town.

CHAPTER TWENTY TWO

The fire had died out a few hours earlier and the cabin was getting chilly inside. The cold was causing everyone to stir a little as they tried to stay warm. No one wanted to get out of his bedroll to restart the fire.

"Well now, just which one of you pansy asses are going to drag your ass out from under your bedroll and get that fire started?" Shawn snarled out.

"Well I don't see you dragging your old fat ass out," Hosey said. "Hell I'm sure you could tell us all stories about how warm it is right now compared to what you've seen."

"Now that you mention it, I have, Mr. Hose Nose," Shawn said chuckling. "I will say one thing though; I've seen something on this hunt'en trip I've never seen before."

"What's that?" Goof asked.

"You three Doss boys...You by far have the biggest damn noses I've ever seen on any man's face," Shawn said, chuckling

"FINE," Wapiti shouts out. "I'll get up and start the fire, but one of you has to go get the water to make the coffee, cause my people don't drink it. I don't know how to make it, and I want a cup! So one of you drag his ass down to the river and get that water."

"Alright," Goof said. Climbing out from under his bedroll and put his boots on, wrapped himself up in a coat he grabbed the coffeepot and headed out the door.

422

Chapter Twenty Two

"I guess I'll get my fishing gear out and go catch me and Wapiti some breakfast," Shawn said. Rolling over, beginning to roll up his bedroll.

"There's no need for that Marshal," Toad said. "We have at least fifteen to twenty real nice size fish on a stringer down in the river already. We caught them yesterday afternoon when we was trying to kill time and have some fun."

"Well alright then," Shawn said. "I've got lard and potatoes in my bags. I'll get it out and then we can have a nice breakfast before we part ways."

Wapiti had the fire burning good and Toad was lighting the lamp, when Goof came back in with his pants wet up past his knees. "Damn," he hollered, walking back in the cabin. "It's so damn dark out there you can't see two feet in front of yourself."

"Looks like you tried to take a bath," Shawn said. "Where are all those fish we heard about for breakfast?"

"Hell if I know," Goof answered. "Give me that lamp Toad and I'll go back out and find'em. This time without falling in that damn Cold River."

Everyone started laughing at him as he grabbed the lamp and headed back outside. "Well, at least he brought water for coffee," Toad said still chuckling. "Here Hosey, toss me that bag of coffee and I'll get it started."

Tossing a bag of food and a frying pan on the table, Shawn looked around at everyone. "Well, there's some spuds and one frying pan. I'm sure you boys have another pan that we can cook the fish in."

Pulling out their pan, Toad started cutting up the spuds. Putting a big scoop of lard in each pan so as not to burn the food. Goof came walking back in the door, fish in one hand, and an unlit lamp in the other. He was totally soaked from head to toe.

"What the hell happened to you?" Hosey said to Goof who threw the fish on the table.

"Awww piss on all of you. I got out there looking for them damn fish, and no sooner did I find them and a bear came out of the brush after me and the fish. Before I knew it, I fell over backwards into the river. The splash scared the bear away...But damn if that river ain't cold." He walked over to the fireplace to try to warm up. Then taking his clothes off, he hung them by the fire to dry while everyone was still laughing at him.

Toad went through his saddlebags and found a bag of flour. Dumping some on the plate, he rolled the fish in it before he placed them in the frying pan.

"You know Young man," Shawn said, watching Goof undress. "If you'd taken a bar of soap with you, you wouldn't need to take a bath later."

"The next time we need something from outside one of you can go. You'll see...It's too damn dark out there. Hell, you wouldn't even know where the cabin was if it weren't for the light from the fire. Besides that, it must have rained all night. All those rocks out there are slippery when wet. That alone makes it hard enough to walk, but then you bring a bear into it...Hell, I didn't know which way to go."

"So just where you boys all off to anyway?" Shawn asked. "The gold rush is back behind you."

"We're loggers," Toad answered. "Hell since they discovered gold in Sumpter...A man can't even afford a decent lady or a decent place to stay. The prices over there have gone sky high. We fall timber for a living, figure we might do better in John Day until that gold runs out in Sumpter."

"So you boys think that gold will run out soon, do ya?" Shawn asked.

"Shoot, with those newfangled dredges they're using now..." Hosey looked around the room. "Hell, I'll bet they will have that whole damn valley picked clean in just a couple years. Then there won't be anything left but a bunch of empty buildings and a few loggers again."

"Just like it was a year ago," Toad said. Pouring everyone a cup of coffee.

"I heard they were pulling a lot of gold out of that ground over there," Shawn said. Still wondering to himself, had these young men pulled off a train robbery with Butch and Sundance? After all, that's what Butch and Sundance were known for, robbing trains and holding

Chapter Twenty Two

up banks. He hadn't heard about anything, but then him and Wapiti did get out of John Day pretty early yesterday morning. Could be it hadn't gone out over the wire yet. Maybe, just maybe that's what all those pack mules were for. It would be smart not to keep all that gold around those mules. That would be too easy to find, if that was the case, just how much gold did they get away with if they needed eight mules to haul it? Just how much did the others get away with? "Well if you boys fall timber," Shawn said looking around the room. "Where's your saws at?"

"Out in the lean two with the animals," Toad answered quickly. Even though those saws were just part of his camouflage. "Hell, it don't matter if they get wet. I have five, ten footers out there; two are sharp and ready for work. But I need to sharpen the other three."

"So just how long something like that take you Toad," Shawn asked. Filling a plate up with food, which he handed to Wapiti and then filled a plate for himself.

Toad wasn't stupid; he wanted to feed them first, because the sooner they got out of there the better. "Well sir, takes about an hour and a half to file each saw, each one will last you two days if you file it right."

"How you get that big tree to go where you want it to?" Shawn asked.

"The tree tells you where it's going to fall, each one is different," Toad said seriously. "The way they lean, or which side has more branches. But then you also have to think about the limbers and skidding teams, you don't want it rolling down hill on them and get someone killed." Toad said. "You cut about one third of the way through in the direction you want it to fall, then you use your broad axe to cut that piece out in a " V shape", that's called the under cut. Then you go to the back side and start cutting again."

"Then hope no one is in the way of that big tree," Goof added.

"That's why you're supposed to holler T-I-M-B-E-R, as it's falling" Toad said.

"So how many people you killed Marshal?" Goof asked looking at him.

"Too damn many sons," Shawn said. Then turning and looking at everyone, with a serious, but sorrowful look in his face "Too damn many...But I always gave each and every one of them a chance not to draw. Hell, I'd rather be in a good old fistfight any day."

"I hear ya don't leave many standing that way either Marshal." Hosey said.

Setting his plate on the table, Shawn started smiling, "Don't do the crime, if you can't do the time. But it's better to do the time, least then when you get out, you can start over again. But you pull that gun...You just might not get to start over." Looking out the window Shawn could see daylight was starting to come up over the mountains. "Wapiti, when you finish eating, go and wash these plates and our pan out. Then we'll get out of these young men's hair.

"You don't need to run off on our account Marshal," Toad said. "We still have plenty of food here."

"Thanks son, but no thanks." He looked down at Curry who was just sitting back in the corner, eating his food, and not saying anything, keeping his eyes on every move the Marshal made. His pistol and holster were still lying on the table. Shawn reached over and picked it up, looked at it, then tossed it to him. "Here son, you better put this back on. Never know when or how you'll need it out here," smiling at him a little. "Hell you might have to kill a rattlesnake right out the front door, you never can tell."

"Thanks Marshal," Curry said. Laying the holster beside him on the ground. "I'll put it on later, when we're ready to leave."

Wapiti walked out the door with the dishes, looking back at Goof who was refilling his plate. "This is just one of the things a deputy gets to do, THE DISHES."

Shawn reached around to each of them and shook their hands, "Well boys, we thank you for sharing your warm cabin with us last night, but now we need to get going." Then turning, he walked towards the door.

Everyone was saying goodbye, and looking at each other. They didn't think Shawn had suspected anything, they were all feeling like they had just fooled that old man.

Chapter Twenty Two

If he only knew what they had, they wouldn't get out of the cabin. Goof picked up the rest of the dishes and walked out the door. Looking back at the lean to he could see the Marshal was saddling up. He kept walking towards the river, passed Wapiti going the other way. "Being the youngest brother, I get to wash all the dishes."

Wapiti stuck out his hand; "It was nice to meet all of you. Make sure you tell everyone I said thanks for everything. Who knows, maybe we'll run into each other again. But as for right now, if I don't get my ass up there and get loaded, I won't hear the end of it all day." The two shook hands and each went his own way.

Goof was just finishing up with the dishes and heading back to the cabin as the two rode out. Goof walked back in the door, everyone was celebrating, only quietly.

Hosey looked over at Goof, "Give them a couple minutes then you go out the window and follow them up river a couple miles. When you're sure they're not turning back, you high tail it back here. We'll wait about twenty minutes, and then we'll go and start loading everything up. But should they turn back this way, you get your ass back here. Oh…one more thing…make sure they don't see you. If they do, that Marshal just might want to come back for a second look."

"No shit, Sherlock," Goof said, climbing out the back window and into the brush. They still weren't out of sight; they were riding side by side and talking. Goof worked his way through the timber, then he saw Wapiti take off up the trail.

The two rode up the trail leaving the four behind, Shawn looked over at Wapiti, "You high tail it up the trail, stay off the main trail so no one can see you or your track's. If you see anyone coming get back here and let me know. I just as soon no one knew we're out here." Glancing over his shoulder Shawn saw Goof running through the brush. "I told them boys about our wood pigeons for target practicing. So when I shoot four rounds from my rifle, that means Goof over there has turned back. That's your sign to get back here so we can get back to them, and catch them loading up, whatever it is they need eight pack mules for."

"Sure thing Marshal," Wapiti answered. Turning his horse up the trail he took off.

Shawn just sat back and enjoyed the scenery. He still kept one eye on Goof, without him knowing it, or at least he hoped Goof didn't notice him looking at him. He'd been doing this for too many years, so he'd gotten pretty good at it. Watching everything and seeing everything around him but still acting like he didn't care. He was glad to see Goof only followed them for a couple miles. Maybe thirty, forty minutes at the most. He was just about to fire his warning shots when Wapiti came riding down the side of the hill.

"Marshal, we have four riders coming down the trail about two miles up." Wapiti said, pointing.

"Good," Shawn said. "We just lost Goof. So let's cut off this main trail and fall back on the other ridge over there."

CHAPTER TWENTY THREE

Gary was up and awake at least an hour before daylight. Going down from of the loft, he saddled everyone's horses. The Roan was a little fidgety; you could tell he knew he was Gary and not Larry. He was sure the Roan knew something was different but he didn't know what it was. Then he went back upstairs and woke everyone up; Larry wanted to know where the coffee was.

"What the hell you talking about Larry," Gary said. "We're in a Livery stable, if we build a fire; we'd probably burn it down." Larry was still complaining as they all climbed aboard their horses. Each and every one of them was wishing they did have at least one cup of coffee. There was just something about it that made you wake up.

The clouds were still thick and heavy overhead; there still weren't any stars visible, they were lucky if they could see fifteen feet in front of them. It was a good trail to follow; it followed the river most of the way, once in a while it did pull away from the river, but you could still hear it flowing.

Gary was in front leading the way, Randy right behind him. Everyone could hear every step that big Clydesdale made. They were happy they didn't need to be quiet. They could all hear Larry back there cursing that they not only didn't have any morning coffee, but they didn't have anything to eat either. Gary was in too big of a hurry as far as he was concerned. Heck, they had heard that Marshal Felton was in John Day anyway. As far as he was concerned they should have gone

429

through Whitney to Austin Junction to John Day, it would have been faster he thought to himself. But Gary figured all the posses would be that way and Felton would more than likely come this way. But as far as Larry was thinking it was just wishful thinking. When he probably took the same direction of the others.

All the horses were keeping their heads down low so they could see the trail, all except the Roan. His head was up and he wanted to go, this slow pace they were riding at wasn't only getting on Larry's nerves, but also the Roan's. Hell if they had waited until daylight, they'd be able to ride faster. Larry figured they'd been riding for a good thirty minutes when he looked up at the mountaintops and all the clouds; they were just starting to light up a little. It was still pitch dark in the bottom of the valleys, because the light hadn't reached there yet. But it would soon.

All of a sudden they could smell smoke from a fire, somewhere in front of them. Larry quickly started looking around for the fire, kicking the Roan he quickly took over the lead. In just a short while he could see the fire. Riding up he could see two men with a big coffeepot on their fire. Boy did that smell good, reaching in his saddlebags Larry pulled out his cup and jumped off the Roan.

"Can you guys spare a cup of that coffee?" Larry asked.

The two men looked at each other and then back to Larry as the other three pulled up.

"How about you kiss our asses?" One of the men said.

"Come on Larry, these boys aren't in a sharing mood." Gary told him.

"I don't know who you think you are Mister," the other man said. "But we barely have enough for ourselves."

"Gary, just hold up a minute," Larry hollered. Reaching in his pocked and pulled out a fifty-dollar bill. "I'll pay you this for a cup, this is a hell of a lot more then it's worth. But this is the smallest bill I have on me."

At first both men argued and said "No way," to Larry, thinking it was a one or maybe five-dollar bill. But when they saw it was a fifty dollar bill, shit they could go up to Granite and get themselves a beer, a

Chapter Twenty Three

few other supply's and even have money for that squaw. She was better than Rosy and her five sisters any day. But you still had to have a few beers in you first for her. They both changed their minds real quick. "Well hell, here boys. Get your cups out and we'll fill ya up." Larry was already holding on the man's hand and filling his cup up.

"Alright," Gary said, pulling up on his reins. "Everyone fill up and we'll get out of here." Which didn't take that long at all, because both Randy and Luis had been digging for their cups already.

Randy already had it in his mind; he wasn't going on without a cup of that coffee. Whether those two men wanted to share or not. Larry just happened to offer to pay them first.

Quickly the man with the coffee went to the other three and filled their cups while Larry climbed back aboard the Roan. But that Roan just had to be ornery, jumping forward making Larry spill his coffee all over himself, and damned if it wasn't hot. After he cursed the Roan out and got him settled back down he asked the man for a refill. Which he was more than glad to oblige him with.

The four headed on down the trail, with Gary in the lead. Larry was bringing up the rear. That had to be just about the best cup of coffee any of them had had in a long time. It even managed to warm them up inside just a little.

Randy hollered back at Larry, as he finished his cup, "You should have taken the whole pot for what you paid them boys. Then we all could have had a second cup."

"If it would have been up to Mr. Boss man up front there, we wouldn't have even had this one, Larry shouted out. Making sure Gary heard him.

"Don't worry Larry," Gary said. "I'm sure there will still be enough coals left in the fire pit at the cabin to make us a pot in case the Doss's and Curry aren't far enough in front of us." Just then, it was starting to get daylight enough for everyone to see their surroundings. Gary pulled up on his reins looking down at the ground. "Randy come up here and check this out," pointing to the ground. "Looks like someone was coming up the trail this way leading a pack mule, but then another person come down the hill here and joined up with him right here."

431

"Sure does," Randy said. "Then they crossed back over the river right over there. See?" he said pointing. Taking a bite of his chewing tobacco, "If I didn't know better I'd say someone is backtracking."

"Could be somebody looking to get back to the Doss's," Larry said reaching for Randy's chewing tobacco, "I don't know who it could be, looks like only two. I know they can handle them, but not if they get surprised and shot in the back while they're loading up."

"These tracks are only about fifteen minutes old at the most," Randy said, kneeling down for a closer look at them.

"You know they don't have that gold with them while they were in the cabin," Gary said I'll bet they stashed the gold and put the mules in that little hollow up Lost creek.

"Come on," Larry said, kicking the Roan. "They're only maybe two miles away from us at the most. Let's get to them before it's too late." The others put their spurs in the sides of their horses and they raced to catch Larry.

The four of them were riding as fast and as hard as they could through the timber. In and out of the river from time to time. As soon as they hit Lost Creek, they turned their horses off the main trail and started working their way up the ridge through the timber. They hadn't even gone a couple hundred yards when they heard an eagle call out. "That has to be Goof," Randy said. "The others can only do wolves or coyotes." Stopping their horses and looking around they saw Goof up in a tree. Who appeared to be trying to hide from them the best he could, until he saw who they were. He gave out another big screech to let everyone know it was all right. The four rode over to where Hosey, Toad, and Curry were loading up.

"You guys sure do know how to give a man a heart attack," Toad said. Putting one more bag on top of a mule. "Hell it was bad enough last night."

"Why? What happened last night?" Randy asked.

"Oh not much," Toad said. "Until about an hour before sundown and Marshal Shawn Felton and his new deputy showed up...So why did you guys come riding in so fast? Hell, we thought that Marshal was backtracking on us."

Chapter Twenty Three

"I don't know if that's who it is or not," Gary said. "Whoever was coming up the canyon, all of a sudden crossed over the river and their tracks were heading this way."

"OH SHIT," hollered Hosey. "I knew that old man wasn't fooled for one minute. Didn't I tell you guys he could smell out trouble, if there was any?"

"Well, let's don't just sit here," Toad said, looking at the others. "Let's hurry up and get this loaded and get the hell out of here before he has a chance to find us." They all turned and started walking towards the stash. Then looking up on the hillside a couple hundred yards or so, there stood the Marshal with his rifle in one hand and his pistol in the other. He had a real big smile on his face.

"You're right Hose nose, I can smell a rat when I see one," Shawn said.

Slowly they all started looking around for Wapiti, and there he was only maybe twenty yards at the most with that double barrel ten gauge pointed right at them. They had no idea where it came from, cause he wasn't wearing it last night.

"Now I'm not quite sure just what is or is not going on here," Shawn said. "But one thing is for sure," waving his rifle at them. "I know I sure would be a whole lot happier if you boys would untie them holsters and drop them gun's on the ground."

"No problem," the Doss's and Curry answered. As all four dropped their gun belts to the ground.

Then the Marshal looked over at the other four still sitting on their horses, "Now you four…Drop em', or I'll drop you."

"Now just wait one minute Marshal," Gary shouted back up to him. "We've been chasing these outlaws since yesterday morning after they robbed the gold train in Sumpter."

"I don't care what you claim, Young man," Shawn stated firmly. "You boys drop your guns and we'll figure this all out in a minute or two."

"No problem Marshal," Luis answered, throwing both his rifles and his pistol on the ground, looking back at Wapiti and that ten gauge. "You just tell him not to get trigger happy," Everyone else followed after him saying the same thing.

433

Shawn and Wapiti both started walking closer towards everybody, "So just what's this about a gold robbery?" Shawn asked.

"Well just like my brother was trying to say Marshal, these boys were in on a robbery in Sumpter yesterday." Randy said, with a big smile on his face. "There's a big reward out for these four."

"If that's the case, then why didn't you come up with your guns drawn and ready for a shootout?" Shawn asked.

"Well hell, Marshal," Gary said smiling. "We don't want to shoot anyone if we don't have to."

"Well now, it sounded more to me like you boys all knew each other," Shawn stated, waving his pistol around a little. "Why don't you boys just finish loading up those mules, while I figure out who's full of shit and who's not. So just who are you young men anyway?"

"I'm Gary, and these are my brothers Larry and Randy Larkin." Pointing back to Luis, "And this is Luis Nevares."

"You boys wouldn't happen to be related to Roy Larkin over in John Day would you?" Shawn asked.

"Sure would Marshal, he's our dad's oldest brother," Gary answered. "Why?"

"He told me I might run into you boys if I came this way," Shawn answered.

"Now you just wait one minute there old man," Larry shouted. "There's a twenty five percent reward for whoever finds these boys and brings that gold back. You're not going to cheat us out of all that money."

"We'll just see about that," Shawn said, throwing his chest out. "No one is going to take any reward that is not rightfully theirs. Wapiti pick up those guns, and I'll figure out who is who here in just a minute…You sure you boys don't know each other?"

"Of course we know who they are," Randy said. "Hell we grew up with them. Sure they're all older than we are, but we know who they are. Fact Toad and Goof there fall timber for one of the outfits I skid logs for. Sure we know who they are…But that doesn't mean we hang out together."

434

Chapter Twenty Three

"I understand that," Shawn said, with a small smile on his face. "It just seems to me you boys were awful chummy with each other when you rode up."

"That don't mean we have to like'em," Gary said. "Just means we know them."

"That could be true," Shawn said. "That could be true. Fact I know quite a few people myself that I've worked with, but that didn't necessarily make them my friends. I know you boys weren't part of this mess," Pointing to the four as they were bringing out even more bags of gold. "Because Wapiti and I had the pleasure of these men's company last night...It was fun too, I must admit. That Toad is a good cook as well."

"Then why don't you give us our guns back?" Larry hollered. "Hell, we knew they would stay in the cabin during that rain storm. Why the hell else you think we left Granite so early this morning for?"

"That may be," Shawn said. "But if you don't mind, we'll just go back to John Day, then we'll get this mess all straightened out there."

Reaching into his saddlebags Luis pulled out a roll of purple mule tape. "Here Marshal, why don't you tie them boys up with this so they don't get away?"

"Oh trust me young man," Shawn said with a big smile on his face. "I have something better than that...I have chains and irons...They won't be getting away."

"Marshal, I was hoping to go see my girl in Prairie City," Gary said, "After we caught these guys, and claimed the reward. But since you're here...Well there's really no reason for me to stick around, so how about you give me my guns back and I'll get the hell out of here and meet back up with you tomorrow sometime in John Day."

"Now, how do I know I can trust you young man?" Shawn asked in a stern voice.

"Just who in the hell am I gonna tell, Marshal?" Gary exclaimed with a smile on his face. "My uncles? Or my cousins? Because I damn sure don't know anyone else over here, except my girlfriend. Who just happened to move over here with her family two months ago..."

435

Marshal Shawn Felton and the Wild Bunch

"Hell we knew these guys came this way, just as soon as we got to the smoke house. We went down to get Randy's Clydesdales, two were missing. Their tracks followed the riverbank till they got into the timber, then down the road towards Dooley Mountain and out towards Idaho. But what that dumb ass Sheriff and everyone else DIDN'T see was the mule train tracks heading off into the woods and circling back around town and heading this way. Hell we knew they had a good head start on us, but at the same time we figured whoever it was, that robbed all that gold would hold up in the cabin down here during the storm. So we waited it out on Granite, knowing we could catch up with them in the morning.

"Just the same, Son, I don't want anyone getting in ahead of me," Shawn said looking over at Gary. "I don't want anyone tipped off that we're bringing these boys and all that gold in."

"WELL NO SHIT," Gary said. Neither do we. There's the banks standard fifteen percent reward…The mining companies have added another ten percent…So twenty five percent of ALL THAT GOLD," Gary shouts out again, pointing to the mules and all the gunny sacks. "IS OURS! Do you think for one minute WE want anyone, and I do mean anyone knowing you're bringing them in? I THINK NOT… Besides Marshal, IF, and I do mean IF, we were in on this, you would already be dead."

Rearing back and standing full up, Shawn glared at Gary. "Would you just tell me how the hell you think you could pull that off…Since you don't have a firearm, amongst ya." Pointing to the pile of guns at Wapiti's feet.

"Well sir, it's like this….. You didn't see Larry drop a gun did ya… That's because he don't carry one. BUT HE DOES carry four knives on him… SOMEWHERE. …And he's just as fast or faster with them than most men are with guns. Not to mention he's only standing fifteen feet away from you," Gary said.

"So what are you telling me?" Shawn asked pointing towards Larry but still looking at Gary. "You telling me that boy can throw a knife faster than I can draw my pistol?"

No sooner had he finished than three knives came flying past his head. The first one took his hat off his head, and the next two came within just inches of his nose. All three stuck in a large tamarack tree just behind the Marshal's head. As everyone started laughing.

"That was fun and easy, Marshal," Larry said. "And I still have one more...Where should I put it?"

Shawn just stood there in amazement, staring at those knives in the tree. "Well I'll be damned," Shawn said in amazement, scratching his head, feeling like he had just eaten some crow. He crowed and they answered, he thought to himself, and real quick too.

Turning and looking at Larry, Shawn smiled, "I'll let you keep that fourth knife...You are good." He stuck his hand out towards Larry's as Larry came walking up to get his knives out of the tree. Chuckling and looking at everyone, he shook the Marshal's hand. Then pointing at the knives sticking in the tree, "I'm slipping, that sure isn't a very tight grouping at all...You have a big head Marshal. I can usually put them all in a four to six inch group." Still chuckling, and pulling them out of the tree.

"Now then Marshal," Gary said. "Why don't you have that deputy of yours follow those boys back up to that stash? Make sure they don't leave a bag or two behind for the future... Say for like when they get out of prison."

That's not a bad idea young man," Shawn said, pointing at Wapiti. "Why don't you go check on those men and make sure that they're not doing just that?"

"NOW MARSHAL," Gary said in a stern fearless voice. "YOU, me, Larry, and Randy need to have us a little talk."

"You're awful cocky young man," Shawn said, setting down on a dead tree, still holding his pistol in one hand and his rifle in the other. "So say what it is you want to say and make your peace with it."

Then all three Larkin boys walked up and basically surrounded the Marshal, which made him feel just a little uncomfortable. He remembered what Roy had told him about these three. Said two you couldn't tell apart, one from the other. And he was right. The other one Randy had the bad temper and liked to hurt people. Just one look into his eyes and Shawn could see what Roy was talking about. Looking into those eyes even sent a small chill up his spine, and nobody at done that in a very long time. He shuddered just a little bit.

"Just over a week ago, on the Rouge River... You killed a cousin of ours...Brad..." looking around at his two brothers, then back to the Marshal. "We all knew Brad was an outlaw...Sure, we know he's killed a few men. But as far as we knew it's always in self defense, even when he was running to get away from a posse," Gary starting to smile a little. "But hell, those posse's were shooting at him too. So why don't you just tell us why you did? What you did? And why you had to do it that way...? Hell Marshal, our Aunt didn't even get to bury him, cause there was nothing left!"

To start with, those boy's stole a wagonload of nitro; twenty four bottle's a case nitro, and it was eight to one. So I figured I wait till I had them all together, it took me three day's till the moment was right. I waited till they all got into the middle of the river before I made my play, Shawn was explaining, firmly. HONESTLY MEN, it was my intention to just wound the driver of that wagon...But that loose shall rock slid under my feet just as I stood up and pulled the trigger, hitting into the load of nitro. That wagon was stacked at least five cases' high under that canvas tarp.

You said you met our uncle Roy, Randy asked.

Yes I did, Shawn answered.

Did you ever discuss this with him, Randy asked.

Yes I did, Shawn stated. Fact he told me he was in the courtroom when I gave my testimony to the Judge!

We all know you like to bring them in over the saddle, Larry shouted out.

Settle down Larry, Randy ordered. If you and Uncle Roy discussed this, and he can find no fault in you...Then how can we, he said, looking back and forth between the twins. You both know as well as I do, that shale rock can be like walking on a sheet of ice. Take your feet right out from under you.

" I'm satisfied that the Marshal did all he could to bring him in alive. Brad and his men chose to come in over the saddle, when they robbed their first bank." talking seriously. "In a manner of speaking

Chapter Twenty Three

they came in over the saddle. Just in smaller piece's over the saddle." Randy stated firmly.

"Yeah, but those saddles and horses were all in a million pieces," Larry said.

"We just had to know Marshal," Gary said. Holding out his hand, "I, we just had to know the truth." The other two followed suit and shook the Marshal's hand.

Gary looked over at Wapiti, then back up to the Marshal, "You really think any white man is going to let an Indian lawman tell them want he can, or cannot do?"

Shawn looked over at Wapiti, "Yes I do...Fact is, you're looking at the first one right there."

"That ain't ever happ'en," Randy said with a big smile. "Why he's going to have to fight someone just about every day."

"You're right, Randy," Shawn said, nodding his head in agreement. "The whole town of John Day felt that very same way when we pulled in Thursday afternoon," starting to chuckle. "But by the time we departed town yesterday morning...Pretty much the entire town changed their heart. At least eleven or twelve, I lost count; they won't be forgetting him any time soon. You might say, he changed their minds...They'll be wearing that changed mind for a while."

"So how about it Marshal?" Gary asked again. "You going to let me go see my girl? It's been to long if you get my meaning. Hell, if you need extra guns, those Doss boys are all crack shots. I'd bet on them in a shoot out...They don't miss. I'll catch back up with you tomorrow in John Day to get our reward."

"I'll tell ya young man, I mean men," Shawn said. "Only because I know your Uncle and I do believe you boys are telling me the truth about just how you came to be here...I'll let you go, but.... I would like the other three to stick around incase WE do need their gun experience. But can this one shoot as well as he throws his knives?"

"Hell yeah," Larry hollered. "I just don't carry one, cause...Well, you just might say my mouth gets me into a whole lot of trouble."

"SOMETIMES," Randy said with a chuckle. "More like ALL the time."

"Well marshal, if you think we're letting that gold out of our sight your crazy. But if you want us to ride along for extra guns, if need be," Luis said. "Then you had better give us our guns back. I don't want to wait until someone is already shootin' at us before you give them back."

"Alright then," Shawn said. Starting to hand everyone's rifles and pistols back. "But I'll be bringing up the rear, just in case you decide you want all this gold for yourselves." He opened one of the bags, digging through the straw till he found the bag of gold inside. Pulling it out and opening it up, "This is the stuff dreams are made of," He said, retying the bag and replacing it.

Randy leaned over to Gary as they were all picking up their guns, "I sent Butch and Sundance to Terry in Unity...So look for his Blue dapple Percheron's, not my Clydesdales. They'll know Marshal Felton came this way, get your ass down to that Gutridge whore house and find them..." Still looking around to make sure no-one could hear. "I know Terry will tell them to wait there, that if something went wrong, we'd get them a message some how. So I'm hoping they will hold up there and wait just to be on the safe side. Just in case the Doss's did run into the Marshal and get caught. I might be able to figure out yet another back door. Meet me around mid-night at the river just outside of John Day, I'll have something figured out by then...I hope."

Gary quickly tied his pistol down to his leg, "We'll be waiting for you," Gary said. Climbing aboard his horse and with one big wave of his hat; he hit his horse in the ass and was gone. "I'll see you guys tomorrow" he hollered back.

"Wapiti," Shawn shouted out. "We get all that gold loaded?"

"Yes sir, Marshal," Wapiti answered. "We're just tying everything down now."

"Good, now let's get some handcuffs on those men, get everyone and everything tied together and let's get the hell out of here. If you're lucky Wapiti you just might get to see Cathey tonight, that's if we get there in time."

That put a big smile on Wapiti's face, then he started shouting out orders. "Come on boys, we have some traveling to do today," Wapiti said.

440

Chapter Twenty Three

Seeing the excitement in Wapiti's attitude and the smile on his face made Randy chuckle. "So just who is this Cathey he's so all fired up about getting back to?"

Climbing up in his saddle Shawn looked over at Randy, "Why your cousin, Cathey."

"Oh bullshit," Larry said, climbing up into the saddle.

"No sir young man," Shawn said. This put a big smile on his face. "Just how do you think we met most of your Uncles and Aunts over there…? How else would we have known who you boys were? Get em' loaded up Wapiti. I'd like to get back in time for a piece of apple pie."

"Yes sir, Marshal," Wapiti answered. "I just need to tie a couple more of these mules together and I'll be finished."

"You just make sure you tie them mules together extra tight…We don't want to lose any of our reward money." Randy told Wapiti.

The Doss boys didn't know just what was up, but they knew the Larkin boys too well. Fact they all considered themselves to be basically more like brothers than friends, and no way would they let them go to jail if they could keep them out. Gary had gone on ahead for something…But what…? What kind of back door is Randy going to come up with this time? Because they sure as hell needed one now!

Gary was riding hard and fast, he had a lot of ground to cover and not enough time to cover it. He knew that Larry and Randy would sort out some kind of plan by the time he got back with Butch and Sundance and they all met up at the river. He wasn't too worried about running his big sorrel hard like this.

He only had to make it to Prairie City. Gary had a thousand different things going through his mind as he rode. Would Butch and Sundance even know? Hell if he didn't hurry they could easily make it to John Day ahead of him, their ride was a hell of a lot easier to travel. Fact, they had a road. Hell this was barely a trail he was on.

He would make a quick check around Prairie City for them. If they went through Unity, they would definitely run into Terry. Shit he owns the only Livery stable in town. But what if he was out in the mountains changing a wheel on a logging trailer and got stuck in the rainstorm? Hell, there would be posses coming out of John Day as well. A wild

441

bunch of men, with no one really in charge, all hoping to get lucky and find the robbers for themselves…

Once they fixed the telegraph line there would be posses coming from Idaho this way too. But if Terry wasn't in they would sleep in the Livery stable out of the rain… Terry would definitely find them then. He'd know right off that Randy was ok with it because neither one of them would be limping or just flat out not walking, he started to chuckle. You don't want to be anywhere around that stallion in the middle of the night. He kicks first, then looks to see what was behind him, as your sailing across the room. And he's thinking to himself, the stallion that is, thinking to himself OOOOPPPPSSS… guess I shouldn't have done that.

NO Terry would know those gildings were tied up somewhere else to make it easy for them to get to. Terry would also know that everyone would be looking for those two Clydesdales. Smiling, bet he works out some sort of deal for himself when he switches horses with them for those big blue dapple Percheron's of his.

So I'll be looking for sets of horses, Terry's big blue dapple's and not Randy's Clydesdales, when I get to Prairie City. Terry would also know that Marshal Felton went this way. Hell even we had heard about the big poker game over in John Day and that Felton was there before we pulled out of Sumpter.

No one believed it, when they heard that he had an Indian deputy…Everyone thought it was just a bullshit story. So nobody really gave it a second thought. But, they had guessed wrong. Because not only was that old Marshal there, but that old man even smelled out the robbers.

Shawn would have Wapiti riding point, just out of sight from anyone coming up the canyon. No one would know he was there, and he'd be able to backtrack just like he did before…Boy if they didn't bullshit their way into a hell of a lot of reward money, starting to chuckle.

He couldn't remember that much bullshit flying around in one conversation before. How the hell did it work out that they would get the reward? What was it that they had done for God to give them so much money all at once? Shoot, the money they made off that Roan

Chapter Twenty Three

was just over forty thousand dollars. The money Randy got for renting out his horses…Now the gold reward…. Who knows how much that will be. Shoot every one of those pack mules had seven bags of gold on them…Smiling and laughing at the same time. He could tell by the way those guys packed them bags that they defiantly weighed more than fifty pounds. Which was just what one bag of gold was supposed to weigh…"THANK YOU GOD…" he hollered. Kicking his horse in the side with his spurs.

"Lets go big boy, daddy has to go collect a bunch of money, and get some friends out of trouble…" Somehow…Randy will figure it out, and somehow he and the others would know. He hoped that Randy and him could find each other at the river. He couldn't just walk up into the jail in the middle of the night, ask Randy to come outside, then five minutes later break everyone all out of jail…Then look at the Marshal with a straight face and say, "No Marshal, we didn't have anything to do with this." Like hell he'd fall for that one twice. He knew Felton wouldn't bring them into Prairie City; he'd swing wide of town. Which would give me a little extra time…

He just hoped he could find Butch and Sundance in time. He'd been doing so much daydreaming that he was on the hill overlooking Prairie City before he knew it. One thing that was in his favor was the fact that Prairie City wasn't a very big town. Four, maybe five hundred people at the most. Only one Livery stable, two saloons, and the famous Gutridge Brothel.

He came riding into town; slowly looking around to see if by chance they had tied their horses up out front of one of the saloons. He knew they wouldn't be that stupid and leave those horses fully loaded, tied up just anywhere. Pulling up in front of the first saloon, he climbed off his horse. Wiping some of the sweat off his head, Gary led his horse over to the water trough. Everyone could tell he had been running that horse hard. He had made real good time considering everything, hell it was only mid afternoon. Then, looking around the streets, he could see just about everyone was staring at him.

Hell, by now everyone knew about that robbery. Why were they all checking him out? Did they think he was part of it? Just then two little old ladies came by, staring at both him and his horse. He tipped his hat to say good afternoon ladies; but they just laughed and hurried on down the street. After his horse had drunk his fill, Gary tied him to the hitching post. Then walking into the first saloon, he quickly looked around. Not seeing either of them inside he turned to the door and walked back out, then across the street to the Livery stable. Walking in and taking yet another quick look, he could see that neither Randy's nor Terry's horses were being stabled there. "SHIT," he hollered as he started to turn and walk out the door, when a short chubby man came out of one of the stalls

"You one of them Larkin boys?" the man asked.

"Yeah," Gary said. Stopping and turning around looking at the man, "Yes I am...Why?

"Well, a very nice young man came in about two hours ago, gave me fifty bucks. Said to tell you their out at the Gutridge Brothel."

"Thanks," Gary said, turning to walk out.

"Wait just one minute," the man said. "He also told me that if I told only you and no one else...Then you'd give me another fifty bucks."

"No problem," Gary said. Pulling some money out of his pocket, counting out fifty dollars, he handed it to the man. Just as the man reached out to take it, Gary held on to the other end, "You still haven't seen me or that other man who came in here...CLEAR?"

"Yes sir, young man," the man said with a big smile on his face. "I haven't made this much money in one day since I left Alaska."

"Why the hell did ya leave for then?" Gary asked.

"It's the winter up there," the man said. "It's dark damn near all winter long. Then in the summer, it's daylight all day long. You just try sleeping, when it's supposed to be night time and it's just like the middle of the day...No sir, after one winter and one summer I had to get out of there, ...So, I loaded up came back here."

"Well lucky you," Gary said. Walking out the door chuckling and shaking his head. "Hell, if I could make a hundred dollars a day shoeing horses and fixing wagon wheels, I'd stay there and get used to them funky hours."

Chapter Twenty Three

Walking back across the street, he untied his horse; he could still feel everyone's eye's in town on him. Slowly he climbed up into the saddle, turned his horse and headed out of town towards John Day.

The Gutridge Brothel was just on the edge of town. Looking down at all the dirt he was wearing with his clothes. "Hell they may not let me in," he thought to himself. That brothel was one high class and priced place. They wouldn't let just any cowhand in. Riding up to the barn to put his horse away; he was met by a BIG man. And damn was he ever big.

"What the hell you want drifter?" the man asked Gary as he dismounted his horse.

Gary looked inside the barn and could see all three of Terry's blue dapple Percheron's. He could tell it right off because they all still used dad's brand. It was an R with a backward L on the hip. That was except Larry's Roan, he still just had that big 55 on his hip. "I'm looking for the two men that rode in leading those Percheron's."

"Who the hell you think you are, asking me to remember everyone who comes in here leading a team of draft horses?" The man yelled back at him.

Walking towards the man Gary cut loose on him, "LOOK ASSHOLE, I've had a very long day, I'm dirty, thirsty, and hungry." Slowly the big man was walking backwards as the little man, whose eyes had turned into a fiery red glare and staring him down. "Now you have two choices. Tell me what I want to know...Or get the hell out of my way before I move you myself...UNDERSTAND?" Gary said. Putting his hand in the middle of the big man's chest, pushing him backwards a good six, eight feet, and causing him to stumble over his own two feet at the same time.

"Sorry Mr. Larkin, and yes...Mr. Jone's and Mr. Young are inside. Here, please let me take care of your horse sir, you just go on ahead and go in." Slowly standing up and reaching over, the man took the reins out of Gary's hands. Standing up and looking down at Gary, the man could see he was at least a foot taller and a hundred pounds heavier. However, he had heard plenty about these Larkin boys. They were all half-crazy and NOT afraid of anything or anyone, and this one

445

was just showing him that now. He figured if it came down to it, he might be able to take him. But one thing would be for sure, he would be hurting in the morning too…And this little man wasn't backing down. "I didn't know who you were, I'm sorry, it won't happen again."

"Thanks," Gary said, grabbing his saddlebags, turning and walking out of the barn, towards the big house. Stopping at the barn door, he looked back at the big man. "I want my horse, those three Percheron's and their two horses ready to leave town around eleven, understand?"

Then without waiting for an answer Gary headed across the yard and up the steps and through the doors. Walking in he slowly looked around, there was Butch playing poker, only this time it was with real money and not with chips.

No sooner had he walked up to the table and a pretty young lady was handing him a beer. "Sir if you'd like, for five dollars we have a nice hot bath."

Butch looked up and saw Gary, then looking back over at the young lady. "Darling, why don't you get two of those ready." He asked, picking up his money, "Sorry boys, but there comes a time when you just have to walk away."

"You asshole," one man hollers out. "Just when you have everyone's money."

"Now I told you boys when I sat down, I was waiting for someone and when he got here I was going to have to leave. You were all more than glad to let me in…But then you thought you were going to get my money, not the other way around." Then he started chuckling. He and Gary headed towards the bathing rooms and yet another nice hot bath for Butch in two days. Just looking at Gary you could tell it had been a whole lot longer, probably not since Sumpter, Butch was thinking.

"Terry told us to wait for you here for a while just in case something went wrong. So Sundance went and took the first bath, then was supposed to come and relieve me. That way one of us would be here when one of you boys got here. But that was over three hours ago. So I'm assuming he got sidetracked by one of these beautiful ladies."

"It's not hard to do here," Gary said, looking around the room.

Chapter Twenty Three

"Well, Terry told us about Marshal Felton being in John Day for some poker tournament. Rumor has it he's on his way to Sumpter, by way of Granite. He wanted to show that new Indian deputy he has the country up through there. Terry figured if that old Marshal was to run into those boys, it would be at the cabin."

"I know where he's talking about," Gary said. "And he did."

"Terry figured that if they did get caught," Butch said. "That somehow one of you guys would meet us here. Since you men were coming the same way and all. Said Randy would make sure it would be you. Because, well let's just say it, Larry is the life of any party, and can out drink most men. That would give Randy a chance to assess the situation, and try to figure out yet another back door."

"That's the plan," Gary said. "Fact we're supposed to meet him at the river just outside John Day around mid-night."

The two walked into the bathing room, they could see each tub had a curtain to go around it for privacy. "What's the purpose for the curtain?" Butch said smiling. "People afraid to let themselves be seen naked?"

"Nope," Gary said. They walked by a couple that had the curtains drawn, and you could hear both men and women's voices coming from behind each one. "There for privacy, all right, while your taking your bath and playing with one of these beautiful ladies Mr. Bill Gutridge has here."

"He does have some beauties," Butch said. Looking at four young ladies standing between his and Gary's tubs of steaming water. "Where does he get them all from? Shoot, they're all drop dead gorgeous, everyone of them."

"They say Bill Gutridge can charm the pants off any lady within two hours of meeting her. So when he goes to Portland or Seattle, hell he will even go over to Idaho looking for them."

"I wonder if he ever enjoys the fruits of his labor trying to find them?" Butch asks.

"They wouldn't be here if he didn't," Gary said chuckling. "Hell he gets to try them all out first. They say any women who has just spend one night with that man, will not only follow him anywhere, but will

447

do just about anything he wants of her just to get themselves another night or two in the pleasure of his company."

"That's one lucky man," Butch said, grabbing the hand of one of the four ladies.

"Just so you know," Gary said. "I know you don't care about the money, but you just spent an extra hundred dollars for her, and that is only for one hour."

"Hundred dollars an hour," Butch shouted out. "Are you joking, hell anywhere else for a hundred bucks you get her and all your drinks for the night."

"NOT HERE," Gary chuckled, grabbing one of the young ladies hands. "I ain't married yet…" he said, starting to close his curtain. "Oh yeah, one minute past one hour, and you pay for the second hour. More importantly, if you don't pay for that second hour…You think Randy hurts peoples? Well, Mr. Bill Gutridge is five feet, maybe nine, ten inches tall, one hundred and eighty pounds and he hurts people even worse in just about as much time. Fact I think if him and Randy ever went at it. They would both end up visiting Doc. Bones or any other doctor for a long stay."

"So how do you know so much about this place?" Butch asked smiling.

"Are you kidding…? Hell every young man for hundreds of miles in all directions can hardly wait for their eighteenth birthday. Bill won't let anyone younger in here, but on your eighteenth birthday Bill let's you have a lady for one and a half hours for only twenty bucks."

"Why the hell don't he move this place to a bigger city?" Butch asked. "Hell I bet he'd make more money."

"Hell no," Gary said. "Hell, men come from all over country just to come here. It gets them away from their wives for a while or if they're on their way to Portland or Seattle they turn off at Ontario and come this way. Just about the same miles…This is supposed to be the best whore house this side of the Mississippi."

"You know, their wives will find out," Butch said. "They always do."

Chapter Twenty Three

"That's why it's over here in the middle of nowhere," Gary said. "If they ask, the men always say, awww honey, you know you're the only one for me…Promise," he started chuckling again.

"So what time did you say we needed to leave by?" Butch asked again, looking at his watch.

"By ten thirty, eleven at the latest," Gary answered. "Why?"

"Because it's only four-thirty," Butch said. "I'll see you in a couple of hours." Then pulling his curtain shut and only Butch and that young lady knows for sure what happened after that.

The number one rule of the house was what happened here, stayed here. And rule two, no names are ever used.

Gary had been in the dining room for at least an hour before Sundance finally came in. Walking up to the table, with just about as big a smile on his face as one of those eighteen year old boys coming here for the first time. He pulled out a chair and sat down, looking over at Gary. "Well, now that I've had the main course, what's for dessert?" Starting to chuckle as another young lady brought him a menu and a cup of coffee.

"Thanks," Sundance said. This one was yet another foxy, knock out young lady. How does one man find all these beautiful ladies, and then get them to move to the middle of nowhere with him?

Just then Mr. Gutridge himself walked up to the table, "So you men enjoying yourselves?"

"Yes sir," they both said at the same time. "My compliments on a very fine establishment you have here, Sir," Sundance said, extending his hand. "I've been in some real nice brothels Mr. Gutridge, in a lot of big cities, and I have to say, this place outdoes them all."

"Well, I'm glad to see you approve," Bill answered.

Just then Butch came walking up to the table and sat down, Gary introduced him to Bill Gutridge. Butch also commented him on his fine establishment he had out here in the middle of nowhere.

"Well gentlemen, I do like it when I have the privilege of having…How would you say, interesting people in my place." Turning and pointing to the wall that was covered with pictures…"I have eight governors up there, from four different states, a dozen U.S. senators and even a couple U.S. congressmen. But you know the picture I need for right there in the center?

"No sir, I haven't got a clue…Who?" asked Butch.

Leaning over, putting both hands firmly on the table, then in a low voice "Me…With Butch Cassidy and Sundance Kid…Then right next to it, in the next week maybe two, when old Marshall Shawn Felton comes back empty handed, I'll get him to come and see your picture, then I'll take one with him holding your picture…And put them side by side… What do ya say boys? No one will even know for at least two weeks."

Butch and Sundance looked at each other and then back at Mr. Gutridge, "That sure would ruffle that old man's feathers wouldn't it Butch?" Sundance said chuckling and trying to drink his coffee at the same time. "Sure! Why not…? Gary, pull your chair around here too." Sundance said

"Only if I get a copy," Gary answered.

Bill looked down at him, "That's no problem at all young man," Bill said. He raised his hand to let the photographer know it was all right.

Butch looked Bill over; he wasn't the fancy dresser like you would think the man who owned this place would be. Just a new pair of jeans, and a nice dress shirt.

"So why aren't you boys drinking and partying it up?" Bill asked. "Hell all the posses went the other way yesterday and most won't start giving up until tomorrow at the earliest. Now I know you boys have already been having fun in here tonight, but I'll throw in the rest of the night on the house."

Pulling out his pocket watch and looking at it Bill, Butch answered, "Well Mr. Gutridge, I sure wish we could stay and take you up on that offer, we truly do. But you see we have somewhere we have to be in a couple hours. Then we have a boat to catch, if you get my meaning. Hell it's almost ten o' clock, that's just enough time for us to eat before we hit the trail for another long night." Looking back up to Bill, "There is one thing you could do for us."

"Anything men, just name it," Bill answered.

"We could use eight big hamburger sandwiches to go," Butch said.

Chapter Twenty Three

"No problem at all," Bill answered. "Would you like them delivered to you out at the barn? So you don't have to wait much longer."

"That would be nice, if it's not a problem," Sundance said. The three men stood up. "Sure do appreciate your hospitality, Mr. Gutridge." They all shook hands which felt like they just put their hands into a vise clamp, they all knew that Bill probably didn't realize it, but he had crushed each of their hands.

The three rubbing their hands walked out the door and over to the barn. As they walked into the barn, the big man Gary had a talk with earlier was starting to saddle their horses. He had one ready, but was having a hell of a time trying to get close enough to Gary's big sorrel.

"Don't worry about that big fella," Gary said with a smile on his face. Looking at everyone, "That horse doesn't like anyone else near him. The only thing that's going to happen to you if you keep trying to saddle him is you're going to get hurt. So why don't you just get the lead rope on those three Percheron's there." Gary grabbed his saddle, walked up to the big sorrel, "Easy boy," he said, beginning to saddle up. The stable man looked over at Butch and Sundance. "So why do you have these big draft horses for if they're not packing anything?"

Butch looked back at him, while he was tightening his cinch strap up. "We're taking them to the coast for skidding logs."

"You boys don't look like any loggers I've ever been around," The big man said looking them both over one more time.

"They're not for us," Butch said, reaching for their lead ropes. "We're not. Not that it's any of your business. But a man in Portland paid us to come over and buy them off a man in Unity. So now if you'll get the hell out of the way we'll get on down the road."

Just then the big man started talking to them some more...Gary looked over at him, "DON'T YOU EVER SHUT UP?" Then he walked past the man, accidentally on purpose pushing the man backwards causing him to trip over a wooden stool.

Everyone started laughing, climbing aboard their horses. Looking back at him, even though it was dark, they could see his face was as red as a beat. Reaching in his pocket, Gary pulled out a twenty dollar gold piece and threw it at him. "That's for brushing down and graining these animals."

451

The three turned their horses and headed down the hill, "That Bill Gutridge has the best brothel this side of Denver, if not further. Hell those women didn't even have to wear any makeup to be a total knockout." Looking back at the big three story house, with two big fifteen foot wide wrap around deck. It sits on top of the hill overlooking the entire town below.

"So where did you guys unload at?" Gary asked.

"About a mile outside of town this way. We came in a wide turn around town so nobody would see us, hiding everything. Then we made another wide turn back around town and came in from the other end. That way, when we left, we could pick everything up on our way out, and no one would ever see the load."

It didn't take them all that long to ride down the hill, and be on the main road heading out of town. Keeping an eye both ahead and behind them at the same time, they made their way to the stash. They could see the road just in case someone else happened to come by. "You going to help us load all this, Gary?" Butch asked, looking up at him still sitting atop his horse.

"Hell no," Gary said. "If the law or someone else just happens to come by, I want to be able to get the hell out of here fast. I'm not going to jail for something I had nothing to do with."

"Well now," Butch said. Starting to load up one of the horses. "What are you talking about? You had nothing to do with this?" Looking over at Sundance. "Hell Gary, we couldn't have pulled this off without you Larkin men."

"We may have helped with the pre-robbery festivities," Gary said still looking around them, to make sure no one was coming. The night was a lot clearer out and even though the moon was almost full and behind a few clouds, it sure did light up the night sky. "I wouldn't mind doing it again…It was fun. But just in case someone from town did decide to follow us…I want to be able to get the hell out of here."

"That's the second time you said you want to get the hell out of here Gary," Sundance said chuckling. "You know Butch; I think we've got ourselves a first time outlaw here."

Chapter Twenty Three

"Up yours Sundance," Gary said. "This isn't my first time...I just don't want it to be my last, I can tell you of quite of a few times Larry, Randy and me outsmarted the law...I just don't want to get caught with you guys, and all that gold."

"These sure are some nice horses Terry has," Butch said. "Sure was good we ran into him."

"You didn't JUST happen to run into Terry," Gary said. "Randy had that all figured out as well. Hell, he knew everyone would be looking for his horses, so he sent you this way so you could switch horses with Terry...You could call it another back door he had planned out ahead of time for you. He knew you would only have his animals for two, maybe three days most before he got them back to work."

"You mean we paid him all that money, thinking we were going to keep them for a month or two, and the entire time he knew we'd only have them two, three days most?" Butch hollered out in a low voice and he threw another bag of gold on a horse.

"That money was for planning out your heist," Gary said chuckling..."Two back doors on one job, costs ya...But just look at your haul...I'd say he earned that money for the use of his brain to pull this off...You guys still came out of there smell'en like a rose."

"Not just yet," Butch said. "We still have to get this stuff to Los Angeles and sold...But first we have to get our friend and your friends out of jail."

"You think Randy will have a plan worked out, in such a short time?" Sundance asked. "I mean he's only had a couple hours to figure this one out."

"Hell yes," Gary said. "His mind is always thinking...He'll have it figured out long before they even get to John Day. He even knew you would pay Terry something for the use of his horses." You did pay Terry something to, didn't you?

With that comment both Butch and Sundance stopped and stared at each other, shaking their heads. "Yes we did, they both said at the same time. He doe's plan ahead," Butch said.

453

As the two went back to work loading up, Sundance looked at the other two. "Hell, we could always use a man with his ability, be able to get us out of trouble in a hurry."

With that they all started laughing. "Only one problem," Gary said. "He won't leave this area and I think they'd figure out how to get you if you kept pulling the same job over and over."

"We wouldn't have to keep pulling the same job too many more times," Butch said. "Two maybe three more loads like this, and we'll be set for life."

"It's too bad we lost all that other gold," Sundance said. "Now we'll have to share some of this with them other boys…That's if we can get them out."

"There's no IF," Gary said. "It's WHEN…Promise…Randy will know how, trust me, and if I know Toad he's already stashed a couple extra bags if there was any left over."

Butch and Sundance looked back and forth at each other, then back to Gary, "I knew those two men that worked for the bank, the ones that helped us load, I know they each hid a couple bag's somewhere. There were so damn many bags; hell I didn't even count just how many was there when we started. And I don't remember seeing any left over when we left."

Still looking around the area, Gary looked back over to the two outlaws, "I sure wish you two would hurry up and get that shit loaded, so we can get out of here."

"We're doing the best we can," Butch said. "It would go faster if you'd get down here and help us."

"Forget you," Gary answered. "I told you I'm not getting off my horse." Looking around Gary knew that no one could see them from the road, because of all the cotton wood trees and high brush along the river. But still, he didn't feel comfortable at all.

"What's Randy going to do if we're late?" asked Butch.

"Wait," Gary said. "What do you think he will do? He's not in no hurry; he knows we'll be along shortly."

CHAPTER TWENTY FOUR

It didn't take much longer to finish loading everything and every-one up and ready to head down the trail. Shawn was shouting out orders to be done by who and how he wanted them done. "Wapiti, I want you out front with that hog leg out, you're pistol and rifle across your saddle. You two Larkin boys and you Mex," Shawn said. "This is your reward, so each of you lead the eight pack mules." Walking up to the four desperados that were standing by their hors-es and waiting to mount up, Shawn had the handcuffs in his hands. "Alright now one at a time mount up, then put your hands behind you so I can handcuff you…One of you three, tie their reins to the tail of these mules.

Curry was first one up, looking back at the Marshal, with his hands cuffed behind his back. "Now just what the hell are we supposed to hold on to?"

"You're seat, sonny," Shawn spouted out. "You hang on to the seat of that saddle." Then looking at the other three, "I'm cuffing you up this way, so it will detour any thoughts you might have of trying to run off. You try to take off in this country, hell I bet you wouldn't make it two hundred yards before you fell off your horse…I'm doing it this way, because I'll be bringing up the rear, I don't like shooting any man, but especially in their backs…Cause then the judge will start hollering again. Saying you did it again Felton, you brought them back in over the saddle yet again, instead of setting up."

455

Toad climbed aboard his horse and Shawn started cuffing him. "Marshal, this is some ruff country. I sure would like to be able to hold onto my saddle horn."

"I just bet you would young fella," Shawn said, smiling at them all again. "But like I said, being cuffed like this, none of you will get any ideas of trying to make a run for it...I don't want to have to shoot any of you boys. I kinda enjoyed your company last night. Maybe we'll do it again, after you get out of jail, say in a couple of years."

It didn't take much longer and they were all heading down the trail with Wapiti leading to way...The trail here was actually pretty wide, wide enough for the outlaws to ride side by side. They all were complaining about not being able to hold on very well, but Shawn just kept laughing. "Hold on tighter "

Curry was having the hardest time and Shawn couldn't help but bust his chops over it. "I've seen them rich men in big cities ride those fancy horses and acting like they were just something special. I always wondered if they would be any good up in the mountains, and now I see, and I think everyone here will agree, if that horse don't keep his head down, he's going to give himself a headache on a low branch. Bet right now he's give'en you a hell of an ass ack with all that fancy high stepping, isn't it A.K.A. Kid Curry," as everyone started laughing. "Bet next time you come out in God's country you bring yourself a horse that's trail wise, not a fancy high stepping dancing horse."

Randy pulled his mules up alongside Larry after they had been on the trail for a couple hours. "You got a bottle on ya?"

"Well yeah," Larry answered, hitting his saddlebags. "You know me, I'm never without."

"Well then," Randy said smiling. "Why don't you hang back with the Marshal and start sharing that bottle with him. Like you...it probably takes a lot to get him drunk. So let's get started."

Speaking of which, Toad calls out. "Randy, how about you get my pipe out, and we can all enjoy a bowl or two."

"Alright, alright," Shawn hollered. "What is it you boys talking about?"

Chapter Twenty Four

Toad hollers back, "I want Randy here to get my peyote pipe and my peyote out so we can smoke a bowl, old man." Starting to chuckle. "It sure will help this long slow trip go by faster."

"Why don't you pass that pipe this way?" Curry hollered over.

"Now we'll have none of that shit in my presence," Shawn hollered up at them.

"Just why the hell not Marshal?" Randy asked. Already loading up a pipe full. "It's no different than your whiskey really. When you stop and think about it…They both make you feel good, just peyote sometimes lets you see something that might be coming for you in the near future."

"I'll tell you what I see in their near future," Shawn said. "If they do smoke that shit, I see one of those boys falling off and cracking his head open after he smokes that shit. Then the judge will say I used cruel and abusive treatment to my prisoners."

"Don't worry about it," Toad said as Randy held the pipe in place so he could take a big toke.

"Wapiti," Randy hollered. "You want some of this peyote?"

Looking back with a big smile on his face, "Not right now." Wapiti answered. "But when we get back to town…Yeah. I'll smoke some with ya then."

As directed Larry fell back to Shawn, "Here Marshal," Larry said, pulling out his bottle. "Let's let them smoke all that shit they want."

"Thank you young man," Shawn said, taking the bottle. Opening it up, he took a good size pull off it. "So just what are you and your brother's going to do with all this reward money?"

Larry took the bottle back and took a pull off it himself, "Well Marshal, we've always wanted a place of our own. This money will enable us to buy a nice size ranch and still have plenty of money left over until the ranch starts paying for itself."

"Hell you boys could buy half the valley and still have money left over," Shawn said. "Where'd you put that bottle at?"

"I put it away," Larry answered. "So we'd have enough to last until John Day."

"Don't you worry about that," Shawn said. "You let me worry about that. You just bring that bottle back out." Just as Larry started pulling it out, Shawn grabbed it from him. "Besides, what's a little man like you doing with such a big bottle?" Taking another big pull off the bottle. "Shoot, you can't weight much more than a hundred and forty pounds if you're lucky."

Reaching over and taking the bottle back, Larry looked at the Marshal, "You just don't worry about how big I am. I'm big enough and that's all that matters...OLD MAN."

"I know you're one of the twins," Shawn said with a smile. "But that brother of yours there, Randy...Is he as bad as I've heard?"

"RANDY," Larry yelled out... "He's nothing Marshal...You and Wapiti have those badges on...So you don't have to worry. Sometimes people like to make fun of him because he stutters a little. Just the other night, this man, bigger than you Marshal, no shit," Larry said with excitement in his voice. "This guy challenged him to an arm wrestling match. You see Randy skids logs with a team of SIX Clydesdales. You might say he has powerful arms on him. That big guy couldn't even budge him. Randy started laughing, and then he slammed the man's arm down onto the table. I mean pissing him off, right now...! Well then he hauls back with everything he has and he hits Randy... To make a long story short let's just say Old Doc. Bones had to fix a whole lot of BONES on that man. His nose...Cheekbones...Ribs and a few other things...It only took maybe six or seven punches from Randy and that poor man was bleeding all over the floor, and praying for Randy to let him go."

"You expect me to believe that young man, up there," Shawn said pointing at Randy. "You tellin' me he threw a man my size around like he was throwing a rag doll around?"

"I tell ya Marshal, his eyes turn totally red sometimes...They look like the gates of Hell just opened up for business. Then only Gary, sometimes me, but usually only Gary can stop him." Larry said

"Your uncle Roy warned me about him," Shawn said. "Now that man and his son both have muscles on top of muscles...Roy

Chapter Twenty Four

tells me the last three times him and Randy arm wrestled, said he thought Randy let him win out of respect, not because he couldn't beat him."

"Those Livery stable owners around here have to replace those logging wheels. I don't know how much they weigh but I know it's a whole hell of a lot. We have another brother Terry over in Unity; him and Mike are built just about the same size. Mike's a couple inches taller, but Terry's ornerier then most people. Him and Randy are both five feet five and one half inches tall. Watch out for that extra half inch," Larry said. "Terry sometimes gets bored and goes looking for someone to play with...That's what he calls it. But it comes to Randy from all directions, Terry don't hurt them half as bad as Randy does. Fact he claims he's never won a fight or lost...Because they both hurt the next day, but it's a lot of fun...Is that crazy or what? He goes looking for a fight to have fun and unwind."

"Well now actually, yeah," Shawn answered with a big smile on his face "I know exactly what he's talking about. I like busting me a few heads now and then...Over shoot'en 'em."

"Well hell, Marshal, even I would rather get into a fistfight over a gunfight any day," Larry said. Handing the Marshal the bottle of whiskey. That's why I don't carry a gun usually, it's not that I can't use one mind ya...I just like to drink...And my mouth has a tendency to say shit without thinking...Pisses some people off real quick," he said, starting to chuckle.

"Just looking at you, I can see that very thing happening with you," Shawn said taking another pull off the bottle.

Larry wasn't sure just how long they had been riding; he was enjoying the Marshal's company. By the look Randy had given him earlier, it was his job to get the Marshal drunk. He didn't know if he could out drink him, but what the hell he had nothing better to do.

Just then Goof hollered out that he needed to go to the bathroom, then the others started hollering about the same thing.

"Alright, alright," Shawn said. "I'll let you down one at a time. Wapiti...Put that hog leg on these men, if they try anything, and I do mean anything; blow them away...NO QUESTIONS ASKED."

"Yes sir, Marshal," Wapiti answered. Turning his horse back towards everyone. Then the Marshal one at a time unlocked their handcuffs and let them down. Each one of them seemed to be more interested in walking around and stretching out, just a little bit if Shawn would have let them. "Hurry up you guys," Goof hollered. "I'm about ready to piss my pants."

"Just hold your horse's young man," Shawn said. "I'll be right with ya."

"What about something to eat?" Toad asked. Which again all the others joined in complaining about being hungry. Heck, they had been on the trail for at least five, six hours without a break, and they wanted just a short break to grab a quick bite to eat and stretch their legs a little.

"Alright," Shawn said. "Wapiti, no better yet Randy…You high tail it down trail and see if there's anyone coming up…Remember, you don't want anyone else getting any part of this reward, do ya?… So stay off the main trail, because right now we are the only tracks coming out…And in all this mud, we'll play hell trying to cover our trail…Besides, I don't care what you Larkin boys are saying, I know you do know these men, and they're your friends…You wouldn't want to get them shot or killed would ya? Not to mention you or your brother…Because if anyone does come up that trail," as Shawn stared straight at Randy. "Whoever they are, they'll take one look at us and know it's the gold…How do you say it? Just a quick look around, four men in handcuffs and eight pack mules loaded down… A lawman bringing them in. it wouldn't take them long to put two and two together, if you get my understanding. They just might want this gold for themselves…" looking around at everyone, "And I don't want any unnecessary killing."

Randy jumped off his stallion, "I understand Marshal. Goof, give me your horse for this job." Walking over and started helping Goof off his horse, with his hands still handcuffed behind his back. "My horse is too big for this job," Starting to chuckle. "You can hear him coming long before you can see this big boy."

"That is true Randy," Shawn said. "Hell you've been riding front door on this outlaw train we're running here, and I can feel the earth move with every step he takes."

460

Chapter Twenty Four

Randy climbed up in the saddle, looking back at the Marshal. "If you take off before I get back, I'll find ya, so don't worry about me."

"Wait just one minute," Goof yelled after Randy. "That stallion won't let anyone else near him, just how the hell am I supposed to ride him?"

Removing his handcuffs from behind him and cuffing him to one of the others, Shawn started chuckling. "Well, if we need to get out in a hurry...We'll find out just what kind of cowboy you are."

"I'm not any kind of cowboy, Marshal," Goof shouted. "I'm a logger."

Randy had only been gone maybe thirty minutes when he returned, "Two mountain men coming up the trail Marshal. We shouldn't have to worry about them."

"Good. Everyone load up, and let's get out of here. You boys promise not to try and run, if I let you keep your hands in front of you...? Cause the second just one of you tries to make a break for it, I'll shoot ya...Then the rest of you will be cuffed from the back again, UNDERSTOOD?"

"No problem Marshal," they all answered. They walked back over to their horses. Everyone rechecked their cinches and climbed aboard. Besides, none of them had any plans to make a run for it; they didn't want to get shot.

Larry got out another bottle of whiskey from Toad and fell back in line with the Marshal. Larry was only acting like he was taking as big a gulp's as Shawn was. He wasn't sure just how much this old fart could drink, but it was plain to see it was more than he could. Just then Randy pulled back to join them, "Larry you move up front, I want to talk to the Marshal for a minute."

"Alright," Larry said

"Wait just one minute young man," Shawn called out stopping Larry. Then he reached over and took the bottle out of Larry's hand. "Now you can carry on. Now then, Randy what's on your mind?"

"When we get these gold robbers to John Day, I want to stay with them in that little two room jail house until morning. They won't open the county jail till nine and I don't want these guys getting away, and we lose our reward money."

"You don't have to worry about that young man," Shawn said smiling. "I haven't lost a prisoner in many years. Hell, the last time I lost a prisoner, you were still in diapers. Besides once we get to town, all this gold will be with me till that bank opens up, then I'll put this gold in that new safe they have."

"I think it would be better to take it to the town jail instead," Randy said. "I mean hell, just look at those bags. I don't know just how much gold there is…You think that safe is big enough to hold it all?"

"You just let me worry about that Randy," Shawn said. Taking a long pull off the bottle.

"I'm just letting you know up front," Randy said. "I don't trust anyone, and I do mean anyone. I just as soon NO one even knows we're coming to town."

"Well I sure as hell ain't going to let anyone know," Shawn said. "And that won't happen anyhow cause we're all riding in together. Well with the exception of that brother of yours that went to see his girlfriend. But I don't think he's going to tell anyone."

"His girlfriend my ass," Randy started chuckling. "He went to the Gutridge Brothel over there…Hell his real girlfriend lives in Baker City."

"That's right that brothel is in Prairie City," Shawn said. "I forgot all about that."

"Gary damn sure didn't forget," Randy said. "He's been planning on going there ever since we started this trip."

"So you ever been there Randy?" Shawn asked.

"HELL YES," Randy answered. "Especially on my eighteenth birthday. Old man Gutridge gives you a woman at half the price for twice as long. Hell, every young man within hundreds of miles in all directions somehow will find a way to get over there on his eighteenth birthday. Just about every man going to Portland or Seattle on business, as soon as they get to Ontario they take the road that goes through Unity and go over there for the night. Then they go over to Mount Vernon and take the main road up to

Chapter Twenty Four

Pendleton, or they follow the John Day River down to Arlington on the Columbia. You gotta go over there Marshal, after all this is over with, of course."

"Now I don't know about that young man," Shawn said with a big smile on his face. "Any of those young ladies would give an old man like me a heart attack and kill me."

"Hell Marshal, we all have to go sometime," Randy said. "And I sure can't think of a better way to go."

"You do have a good point Randy," Shawn said still smiling. "But back to more serious business, just how long do you figure until we catch up with those two men you saw coming up the trail?"

"I figure they were just about a mile and a half out. So we should be coming up on them just about any time now, why?" Randy asked

"I like to know where I am in conjunction with any possible trouble," Shawn said. "You think if I took hold of those two pack mules, you and that big horse of yours could sneak through the brush and down the canyon and see if anyone else is coming, or would you rather change horses again?"

""No trouble at all Marshal," Randy answered. "But I had better keep riding this big boy, cause just like Goof said earlier, he won't let anyone but me even around him and I do mean anyone except me. It's the same with that big sorrel of Gary's and that big roan that Larry's riding. Last Sunday in Sumpter ten different men tried to ride that Roan. They all wished they had wings and knew how to fly, cause that Roan sent every one of them into outer space. Fact is, he still don't even like Larry being on him yet. I guess you might say our horses only want us on or around them."

"That's what makes a good horse if you ask me," Shawn said. "Then you don't have to worry about anyone stealing him."

"I'll get going Marshal," Randy said. "I should be back in about thirty minutes or so. But should I run into trouble or I need to warn you…I'll fire three shots from my pistol, wait ten seconds and fire three more."

"Just fire three Randy," Shawn said. "You fire all six and your gun will be empty."

463

"Only one of them," Randy said. "I still have three more in my saddle bags plus my rifle. So I won't run out of bullets. But to tell you the truth, I really don't expect to see anyone. Hell they all took out towards Idaho yesterday looking for these robbers. Not a single one noticed that pack trail leading out of the riverbank and back around town except us. Shoot Marshal, I'm not a very good tracker, but that trail was as plain as the nose on my face… Well Marshal, I need to get going, so I'll catch back up to you in about thirty minutes." Then he handed him his lead rope to the two mules and headed off through the timber and down the canyon.

Shawn could hear that big horse thundering off, shaking his head. He couldn't help but notice just how small Randy looked on that big Clydesdale. He rode him without a saddle; he had a rope with stur-ups braided into it. But then he didn't think they even made a saddle with a long enough cinch strap to fit around him. Yet he still wasn't quite sure how Randy stayed aboard that big thing, but he damn sure did. He also knew Randy was right about the fact that, that horse didn't like anyone else near him. Hell when they were loading every-thing up, he had walked behind that big horse, and he almost took my head off. Fact he would have, had I not been paying attention. He thought to himself.

He also couldn't help but notice that Randy didn't seem to be afraid of anything or anyone, you could just tell by his demeanor. He held his head high; it wasn't easy to get him to laugh. But there was something about him that made Shawn feel just a little uncomfortable. He knew Randy was not one to be pushed or told what to do. He couldn't spend much more time thinking about Randy, he needed to worry more about the job at hand.

Randy hadn't been gone five minutes when the two men came walking up the trail leading a pack mule. Right off the two men knew who the outlaws were. Well not really WHO they were, but what they had done, and just why they were under arrest. As the two climbed up on the hillside off the main trail to let the mule train through, along with everyone else to pass, they noticed right off they were all well armed.

Chapter Twenty Four

Wapiti was holding that ten gauge in his hand in front of himself; they had heard what that young buck Indian Deputy U.S. Marshal had done in John Day over the last weekend. But they couldn't help but drool as those eight pack mules loaded down with all that gold walked by. They both made comments about how they wished it was them that had gotten lucky enough to catch those outlaws. They also wondered out loud if the Marshal would let loose of just ONE of those bags of gold.

"I can't do that," Shawn answered them. "Hell if I could, I'd keep it for myself." Shawn still didn't feel totally comfortable with them behind them, so every now and then he would look back. Even though the two didn't seem to be paying them any attention, that could very well all just be part of their plan, he wasn't taking any chances on them NOT shooting him and all of them in the back.

Shawn had met mountain men like them before. They came down out of the mountains every spring to sell their hides and gold if they had been lucky and found any while they ran their trap lines. Usually, they would take a nice hot bath when they got into town. But the aroma coming off of those two even made Shawn turn his nose in the other direction. After they had passed them two, everyone had to comment on it. "We know they didn't get into the Gutridge Brothel," Shawn said.

"Those two would have to go to Granite to even get a chance at laying with any lady," Larry said. "But even then, that fat old squaw would raise her price. OOOHHH, that's right Marshal, you and Wapiti haven't got to meet her yet. She's just about as wide as she is tall… But then she only charge's five dollar's.

Still, Shawn knew that some of them mountain men were half-crazy; you could never tell just what they might try.

The mule train and prisoners had been riding for a good twenty minutes; they were all still laughing and joking about the two mountain men when Randy came riding up, hard and fast.

"Marshal, we have a group of twenty to twenty five men coming up the trail. With my binoculars I could tell right off it's a wanna be posse. They're packing enough firepower to stop an Indian raid. My

465

guess is since the posses going to and from Idaho haven't turned up anything yet, that someone got to thinking about the back way, this way."

"SHIT," Shawn yelled out. "We're going to be so easy to track. Just look at how heavy those mules are loaded, and how deep our tracks are in this mud. Hell, even a blind man would be able to follow us."

"That's how we found your trail so easy when we came down the canyon. That's also the reason we came in riding hard and fast like we did, we didn't want anyone beating us to all that reward money." Larry said.

"I'm not losing my catch to no wild mob," Shawn said, looking down the canyon, and both sides of the river. "Anyone have any ideas?"

"Yeah," Randy said. "You're carrying more ammo than you need Marshal. Let's say we fire fifty or sixty shots into the air and the ground...Say we fire about a hundred yards up into those trees, some of us shoot this way," pointing his finger. "And some of us shoot that way. Then you turn those mules around and get them in the river. Start heading upstream for...Only maybe fifty yards at most. Just long enough for that posse to think you turned around, then cross over in those deep rapids. Stay in deep enough and rough enough water coming back down river to wash your tracks away. I'm leaving Larry with you to keep track of our reward. Me and Luis will wait here till that posse gets up here. Which shouldn't take too long. After they hear the gunfire they'll come runn'en. I figure at a full run they should be here in about an hour and a half maybe two at the most. Luis and I'll act like a couple of dumb trackers; we'll ride up and down over these tracks enough so that they won't be able to make out who's who. The whole time you're working your way down the other side of the canyon, staying in the timber, stay out of Prairie City. We'll tell them some bullshit lie and catch back up with you in a couple hours."

"Alright boys," Shawn hollered. "Lets make some noise." Pulling his pistol, he started shooting. Then all of those who still had guns joined in, and after a good fire show that lasted about four to five minutes, they stopped. Shawn stuck out his big hand to Randy; "You

Chapter Twenty Four

got a good head on your shoulders when it comes to finding a way out of trouble young man...you should become a law man."

Starting to chuckle, "How do you figure I got so good at it?" Randy said.

"He's the reason we've never been caught Marshal," Larry said, starting to chuckle. "Randy can usually always find a back door or at least find a way to give us a couple extra hours ahead of a posse. Well, let's get out of here, Marshal if you don't mind, I'll take the lead, I know this country, and you and Wapiti don't."

"AGREED," Shawn said. "Now all you goofy look'en people and Mr. Curry, the last thing you want is that posse finding us," throwing his big chest out. "Cause if they do it will be with guns firing, and a lot of them. You just might get shot in the crossfire...So you ride HARD and SMART."

Larry turned his horse and mules into the river, pointing down as he went. "Everyone stay close enough right here so the water WON'T wash our tracks out, then at the base of those rapids we'll cross over, then head back downstream."

The others did as Larry suggested, "Marshal," Randy said. "It would be better and faster to mix up these tracks if we had one more horse."

"You're right," Shawn said. "Goof, go with them...But you keep the cuffs on. Randy, you had better bring him back with you or I'll put you in jail in his place understood Mr.?"

"Yes sir Marshal," Randy answered. "But just as soon as one of them sees those cuffs on him, they're going to figure something is up."

"As usual, you're right again Randy," Shawn said. "Goof get over here," taking the key out of his pocket. Still looking at Randy, "Remember he don't come back, you go to jail in his place. Now we've wasted a good three minutes, so lets get everyone out of here."

The three turned their horses and started back up the trail, even getting their horses to do a little sidestepping, running and stopping fast enough to slide their hoof prints. Of course that big Clydesdale of Randy's did the most damage to the ground. Randy figured they needed to mess up at least a half a mile of their trail, try to make it look

467

like they scuffled for a little ways before they turned back. He even had the other two pick up a couple hand full's of empty rifle cartridge's and spread them out over a larger area.

Now Larry is making it look like they crossed down there, so let's make it look like they crossed back up here. Pointing to an easy crossing area. The waters were calm and their tracks wouldn't wash out. Then they would work their way upstream, leaving them easy tracks to follow back up, as if we were giving chase.

About a third of a mile up in the rapids they all crossed back over the river and up the other side of the mountain. They turned and headed back in the direction they had started in the beginning. They stayed high enough off the trail that they would not only be seen but that they wouldn't be heard ether. But still be able to see the main trail below them.

They had just worked their way back to where it looked like all the commotion had taken place, at the same time the posse of men did. Randy was right it was a posse of gun carrying, greedy mob, and they rode hard to get up here. Those horses were breathing heavily, out of air and covered in sweat. As they had expected that posse began to fan out looking to see just what might have happened.

Back just a short distance some of them could see where the pack train of mules had gone back up river, as some followed their tracks, everyone else was hollering out orders at the same time. They went this way, one yelled out. No, they went this way, another yelled out. Randy couldn't help it, covering his mouth, he started chuckle'en. "Hell those guys have no idea just which one of them is in charge." They were all riding in different direction all at the same time up and down the trail. Adding even more horse track's to cover up the outlaw's tracks. "Alright," Randy said. "Let's get out of here and back to that reward money."

Turning their horses and heading back down the canyon, Goof looked over at Randy, "I know this is stupid to ask…But you are working on a way to get us out of this mess…Aren't you?"

"Why do you think I've had Larry back there with the Marshal the whole trip for?" Randy said. "This is one time his ability to

Chapter Twenty Four

drink is going to come in handy. Him and the Marshal have been nursing a couple of fifths of whiskey since we started out this morning."

"Well, that's all good and well," Goof said. "So where the hell did Gary go...? Not the brothel?"

"In a manner of speaking yes...He did," Randy said. "He went to get Sundance and Butch; I talked them into going out through Unity. That way they could change horses with Terry, and Terry might know if any posses came this way. So if he thought anything was to go wrong, that somehow we would get word to them there."

"And now, when we get back to John Day, you boys join in on the drinking too. Let the Marshal know it will be the last chance you'll have to get drunk for a few years. Hell he'll fall for that." The three rode the rest of the way back pretty much in silence. It didn't take them much more than an hour to catch back up with everyone.

Everyone fell back into line, taking back over their mules, Randy rode up to the Marshal, you should have seen them idiots Marshal. Not a one of them knows who's in charge. They were all hollering this way, no this way, those idiots didn't know which way was up or down. Shit when they left there, they went in ninety different directions, and there was only twenty five of them."

Shawn couldn't help but start chuckling himself, "Either way you bought us a couple extra hours, so now we can get these boys in in one piece."

"I hear ya Marshal," Randy answered. "Not just them...Us too! I'm not afraid of gunplay if I have to, it's just I'd rather not get in a shootout or have to shoot someone when I don't have to."

"I don't either, Son," Shawn said. "But a lot of them leave me no choice in the matter."

"Trust me, I understand Marshal," Randy said. "Don't pull it if you're not willing to use it. That's why I usually don't wear one. But if I have to pull it...I'm using it...With no hesitations. He stated, glaring straight into the Marshal's face. Which made Shawn draw back away from him a little. Well Marshal, why don't you give me those cuffs and I'll go put them back on Goof?"

469

"Alright son," Shawn said, handing them over to him. "Just one more thing…Where the hell did those boys pick up those nicknames?"

"You got me," Randy said with a smile on his face. "It's all we've ever known them by. In fact I didn't even know their real names until just a couple of years ago." Then he kicked his horse and caught up to Goof, "Give me your hands so I can put these back on you."

"Aww come on, Randy," Goof said.

"Sooorrry Goof, but we have to make this look real," Randy said. "Besides, now I'll take back over the lead and let Larry get back there to do the job he's good at. DRINKING!" He quickly cuffed Goof's hands, kicked his horse and caught up to Larry. "Alright, I'll take the lead. You still have any whiskey left?"

"Well yeah," Larry said, reaching into his saddle bags. "I still have two more bottles."

"Alright then, get back there and do your job. For once your ability to drink is going to help us out of this. But now don't you get too drunk just yet…We'll need you to ride into town and order dinner for everyone, to be brought to the jail as secretly as possible. We don't want anyone, and Larry I mean no one except Cathey, our cousin, to know."

"Is she still working at the Silver Dollar?" Larry asked.

"That's where Wapiti told me she worked, said that's where he met her," Randy said with a smile on his face. "Looks like we might become related to him someday."

"Well hell," Larry said. "Guess I better get to know him better. So how much longer you figure till we get to John Day?"

"I figure we still have at least forty five minutes till we clear Prairie City," Randy said. "Then, what maybe two hours from there. So we should be in just after dark. Which will help us not to be seen. After you order dinner, you just go over to the jail and wait for us there."

"Alright," Larry said, pulling on his reins so everyone could ride past him, till the Marshal pulled up alongside. Then Larry started bullshitting with him again. Who knew what Larry would come up with to talk about, but he would come up with something. You know he'll be telling the Marshal about his mighty bucking Roan he was

Chapter Twenty Four

riding; he would definitely ask the Marshal if he wanted to try him out for size.

"If I was your age, young man, I would be more than glad to take you up on your offer." Shawn answered. "But now I leave the bronc busting to all you young bucks."

"Speaking of bucks," Larry said. "You think young Wapiti there could ride him?"

"Couldn't tell ya Larry," Shawn said. "He seems to handle that big Medicine Hat real good, and those are high spirited horses."

"That's true," Larry said, handing the Marshal a bottle out of his saddlebags. "Our grandpa, Dude Larkin trains horses for a living. You've noticed, I'm sure that Randy clicks his cheeks, CK, CK, and that big stallion lifts his front foot for Randy to use as a step, so he can get aboard that big horse"

"Now that you mention it, yeah, I did notice that," Shawn said.

"Dude can teach a horse to do anything, and I do mean anything he wants it to. Heck we were always hanging out with him while he was breaking them when we were kids. You might say we grew up on half broke horses. Cause as soon as he was finished with one, that horse was sold…Fact if Dude said he was broke, you could put a newborn baby on that horse all by himself, that horse wouldn't do anything but walk in circles. But for us three when we got bucked off, he'd say, don't worry son…I'll bring him right back to ya."

"Oh you make it sound like you boys had it rough," Shawn said. The sun was just starting to go down behind the mountains, as Shawn pulled out his pocket watch, looking at it. "You know Larry; it's going to be dark in about twenty minutes. I figure we should be in John Day about an hour after dark. Why don't you ride on ahead and go to the Silver Dollar? Have the cook fry us up a bunch of chicken and anything else she has left over. I don't know about you, but I'm get'en hungry."

"Have her fix something else besides fried chicken," Hosey hollered back. "We just had grouse yesterday for breakfast AND lunch. Not to mention I had pheasant the night before, so I'm tired of bird if you get my meaning."

"You'll eat that chicken and be damn glad to get it young man," Shawn shouted out. "You keep complaining and I'll have her fix you a couple chicken shit sandwich's and maybe, just maybe, I'll let her give you some ketchup and mustard to go with it," Shawn said with a big smile on his face.

"Here Larry give me that bottle and your pack mules. After you order our dinner, go over to the bar, ask Cork to get that little five-gallon jug he has and fill it with beer, then take it over to the town jail. But for heavens sakes don't let anyone see ya. Tell Cork to let ya use the back door. Now get out of here."

"See you boys in John Day," Larry hollered, kicking the Roan, who instantly jumped straight up in the air, then took off at a dead run down the trail, jumping in and out of all the other horses like a jack rabbit running through the sage brush. "YEE HAA," Larry shouted, taking off across the valley. He wasn't about to waste any time; he really hadn't eaten much since last night up at Granite. Gary was in such a hurry to get out of there this morning, all he had to eat today was beef jerky. He didn't care what it was the Marshal wanted for dinner...he just wanted and needed some food in his stomack.

The Marshal said fried chicken, fried chicken it will be. But definitely not that chicken shit sandwich he said to ask her to make for Hosey. That didn't even sound good, that big ole supposed to be badass Marshal, really wasn't all that bad a man. Actually Larry thought him to be an Honorable Man. Fact he also knew that he didn't shoot first or in the back. He still was sorry for Brad, Said him and Uncle Roy talked about it to. Fact even said Roy made it over to Prineville for the court hearing. If Uncle Roy accepted accident's happen, then they could to.

Besides, he did try to get them all in one place with no way out. One man up against eight. That took balls, he thought to himself. If he'd tried to stop them any other way, there would have been a big shoot out. Were he, the Marshal could have been shot. If you stop and think about it, from his side, the law side. It was the safest way...

Chapter Twenty Four

That's why I don't pack a gun, Larry thought to himself. But no one knows about my knives, so if I ever have to protect myself against a gun happy person...I can.

Starting to chuckle a little, the look on the Marshal's face when he threw those three knives, that was priceless. He wouldn't do it again, because that old man did have his hands on his pistol before I threw the first one. But somehow he knew I was just funn'en with him.

Larry wondered how Gary had spent the last few hours up there at the Gutridge brothel, while the rest of them were out here trying to get everyone in safe; he's been playing with beautiful woman. Would Terry know to tell Butch and Sundance it was more than likely that the Marshal went this way? And more than likely smelled them out just like he did? Boy if we hadn't come along just in time to get the reward money... twenty five percent of all that gold we're bringing in is ours. Boy if we didn't hit the mother load...Without even try'en.

He slowed the big Roan down as he came into town, he didn't want to draw any attention to himself. He couldn't remember when it ever took this long to get down the street. But finally he made it to the Silver Dollar, dismounting and tying up the Roan he looked up and down the street, he could see the light was still on over at the Livery, turning back around he walked into the café side of the Brothel.

Walking in, he could see Cathey in the back. Walking up to her, he leaned over her and whispered in her ear, "So I hear my beautiful little cousin has an Indian lawman for a boyfriend."

Turning around, half-surprised, she gave him a hug, "It's good to see you again...Which one are you anyway?" Cathey asked.

"It's me Larry, the livelier one," Larry said smiling at her.

"So where are those other two maniacs at?" Cathey asked, looking around the room. "And just how did you hear about Wapiti?"

"Hell darlin," leaning over and still whispering in her ear. "Him, Marshal Felton, Randy, and them are bringing in those men who robbed the gold train in Sumpter. They should only be about thirty to forty-five minutes behind me. The Marshal wondered if you could have the cook, cook up enough food for ten men and keep it under

473

cover. The last thing we want is anyone in town knowing all that gold is here. Hell we'll have to fight everyone in town for it to keep our reward."

Slapping him on the shoulder, "You're so full of shit Larry, it ain't even funny" Cathey said, chuckling

"If I'm so full of it...Then how did I know about Wapiti?" Larry said smiling at her.

"You're not joking?" Cathey asked as her eyes lit up... "Sure Larry...Right away. Are they going to the city jail or county jail?"

"City," Larry answered.

"Alright, I'll get that pony keg Dad made just for such an occasion, and I'll get the cook to help me bring it all over...Tell Wapiti I'll be there as fast as we can get it cooked."

"Oh yeah, one more thing," Larry said. "Tell the cook to make a couple sandwich's that looks like chicken shit...The Marshal promised them to one of the outlaws," starting to chuckle. "I'll see ya in a few Cathey," then he turned and walked back out the door. Untied the Roan and walked back up the street to the Livery.

He could see Roy was wrestling with one of those logging trailer wheels, "Hey Uncle Roy, how ya do'en?" Larry said, walking in, leading the roan.

"Well howdy, lad," Roy said, standing up and extended his hand. "So now which one are you?"

"I'm the good look'en one, Larry," he said. "You're not going to believe what happened."

"I know about the train robbery, if that's what you're talking about," Roy said.

"Yeah, but what ya don't know is Randy and us caught them out-laws," Larry said. "We're gett'en that big reward. The Marshal will be in with them in about thirty minutes, then we'll need to sneak a pack train of mules and all their horses over here."

"You're so full of shit, Larry," Roy said. "Hell I figured you boys might have had something to do with it." Reaching over and taking the reins of the Roan. "So this is the famous bucking horse that bested ten riders last weekend?"

Chapter Twenty Four

"Sure the hell is!" Larry shouted out. "You should have seen it Uncle Roy, it was a lot of fun. Thought we were going to lose when a black man named Charley Hall, or C.R's what he went by and was the last rider, but that big Roan made a move I've only seen bulls do. He swung that ass totally around do'en a two-eighty while his front legs stood in one place. He sent him flying over the fence and into the grandstands."

"So are you telling me the truth about the Marshal bring'en them boys in?" Roy asked.

"WELL YEAH," Larry said smiling from ear to ear. "We're rich now Uncle Roy. Us three and Luis are going to go in together and buy up Beaver Creek, right outside of Baker City. We'll raise our own horses and get some cattle, no more working for someone else."

"That's great Son, your Dad would be proud of you boys," Roy said. "Maybe you can get Randy out of that logging before something happens to him too."

"He'll join in on buying the land, but he'll always run that team of draft horses and you know that," Larry said. "Once you get that logging in your blood, you can't get it out."

"Your Dad was the same way," Roy said. "You tell the Marshal I'll be over there as soon as I finish up here."

"Don't worry about it Uncle Roy, just leave the back door open and we'll put everything away," Larry said, starting to take the saddle off the Roan.

"Don't worry about this one son," Roy said, putting his hand on Larry's shoulder. "You just get back to where it is you need to be… Now you boys make sure you stop in tomorrow and tell your Aunt Louise hello or she'll be upset."

"No problem," Larry said. Walking back outside and down the street, over to the jail. Walking in he could see the Sheriff sitting at his desk, holding out his hand, he introduced himself and looked around the room. Larry could see the building wasn't built very strong. "What kind of jail is this? Most jails these days are made out of brick, or at least the cells areas are bricked in."

475

"We have county lockup just up the road," the Sheriff answered. "But why do you care how my jail is built anyway?"

"Well Sheriff," Larry said with a big smile on his face. He looked up at the clock on the wall. "Me and my brothers caught them men who robbed that train in Sumpter. Fact Marshal Felton and them outlaws should be arriving just any time now."

"HERE?" Dennis said. "He's bringing them here…Why didn't he take them back to Sumpter?"

"Didn't think they had a strong enough jail," Larry said. Starting to chuckle a little bit. "But this place isn't much better."

"It'll be alright for one night," Dennis said.

"I suppose you're right, Sheriff," Larry said. "At least they will have the cover of the night when they come into town. This jail backing up to the timber will help. Marshal said to have you open the back door." Looking around at the size of the office and the jail cell's together. Heck this place was lucky if it was twenty feet wide and thirty feet long at the most. Randy would have no trouble in figuring out a way to get everyone out of here. Hell, even he could see just how easy it would be to pull any of these walls down.

CHAPTER TWENTY FIVE

Just then there was a knock at the back door, both Larry and Dennis walked back, and opened the door. Shawn had everyone in line.

"Evening Sheriff," Shawn said. "I brought some customers for you." Looking back at everyone else, "You men that were involved in this robbery start unloading those bags and get them in here...FAST."

The four did as they were told, and started packing in those bags of gold. Shawn was having them put them in only one of the two cells. Said they all could share the other one till morning, then he'd transfer them and the gold to the county jail in the morning.

They had just about half the gold unloaded when Cathey and the cook came in the front door with their food, and man did it ever smell good. Of course Shawn was first to dig in, while he made the others continue to work unloading everything.

The cook walked over to the Marshal, "Marshal here's those two chicken shit sandwiches you asked for Who are they for?" Hosey couldn't help but overhear, he instantly started wondering what kind of sandwiches they really were, and was the Marshal really gunna make him eat them if they were?

"Marshal, where's Wapiti at?" Cathey asked.

"Well now young lady, he's out back making sure none of those men decide to try and make a break for it," Shawn said, still filling his plate with food. He had to fight around the Larkin brother's and Luis, who were filling their plates like they hadn't eaten for days or

477

even weeks. "Shouldn't you boys be helping Wapiti watch over those outlaws out there?"

"What the hell for?" Randy said. "He has that double barrel ten gauge. Those men aren't so stupid to try anything as long as he's holding that...Hell I'm half Polish, and I damn sure ain't that dumb."

"Me either," Larry shouted. "Besides we haven't eaten since last night. So if you don't mind OLD MAN, and even if you do...We don't?" With his plate full of food now, Larry smiled at the Marshal. Then walking over to a chair, sat down and started eating.

"That's the last of it," Wapiti said, walking in and locking the door behind him and the four outlaws'.

"Good," Shawn said holding a plate with two sandwiches on it. "Here you go Hose Nose. Just as I promised, two chicken shit sandwiches." Handing him the plate.

Hosey reluctantly took it, then slowly started looking around the room at everyone. Slowly he raised one of the slices of bread, lowering his nose down to smell it. "SSSHHHEEEWWW...." he said. "It's only a deviled egg sandwich." Everyone busted up laughing. Just then Charlie walked in the front door with a keg of beer and a couple more bottles of whiskey.

"THANK YOU," Larry said, jumping up, ran over and poured himself a beer. "Now everything's better," he yelled out.

Shawn was right behind him in line for a beer, "I have to agree with you Larry, there's nothing like a good cold beer with your dinner."

"Do you mind if we enjoy a couple of beers too, Marshal?" Toad asked, wiping his mouth.

"Not at all," Shawn said, started to chuckle. "Fact, you four had better get your fill in tonight, cause tomorrow morning you're off to the county lockup, then a good stretch behind bars....This will be your last chance for quite a while."

"Thanks, Marshal," they all answered. They all filled themselves a glass and a plate of food and sat down.

"OOOHHHH NO," Shawn said. "You four men just make yourselves comfortable inside that back cell right there." We'll be glad to get you anything more you might need.

478

Chapter Twenty Five

The four turned with their food and beer and walked into the cell as the Marshal slammed the door and locked it behind them, causing them to jump. "You just as well get used to looking at these bars, cause you're going to be staring at them for quite a while."

The Marshal turned and walked back over to his chair. Looking around the room he could see everyone was busy eating except Wapiti. He and Cathey were talking as he ate, which put a big smile on his face. He could remember how that felt when he was their age, but that was a long time ago. Then he looked over at the other three, "So you boys gunna party it up tonight?"

"Hell no," Larry shouted. "I'm staying right here all night...With all that gold."

"Hell son, I'll be here," Shawn said. "There's no sense in you boy's stick'en around."

"The hell there isn't," Larry said. "If someone comes through that door for the gold, they'll make you all drop your weapons. We don't get our reward till that gold is returned to Sumpter. They'll see I'm not armed, and won't give me a second glance..." Starting to chuckle. "They don't know about my four sisters...! No sir Marshal, I'm staying right here." Pulling another bottle out of his saddlebags, "I'm going to party right here tonight, Luis, do you have the cards and chips for poker?"

"Always do, Amigo," Luis answered. Pulling the chips and cards out of his saddlebags.

"Now just wait one moment boys," Shawn said with a smile on his face. "I'd like to play too...But they don't pay us Lawmen that much money."

"Don't worry about it, Marshal," Randy said. "Why do you think we play with chips for...? We don't play with real money, just those red, white, and blue chips."

Randy reached into his saddlebag and pulled out his peyote pipe. "Wapiti, you want in on this game?" he asked, loading his pipe up.

Cathey looked over at Wapiti, then leaning over she gave him a small kiss, "You have fun with the others tonight, we'll talk more later." Then she said goodnight to everyone and walked towards the door.

479

Stopping, she turned back and looked at everyone, "I'll stop off at the Silver Dollar and have Charlie bring over another barrel of beer."

"Well thank you, Young lady," Shawn said, holding up his beer. "That's real sweet of you Cathey. Now back to you men and this poker game. I believe me and Wapiti can afford your game, but someone needs to take these animals out there to the Livery stable."

"I'll do that," Randy said, standing up, lighting his pipe, and then handing it to Wapiti.

"HEY! Hand that back here," Hosey hollered. "This is gunna be the last night for any of us in here to party for a very long time."

"Just hold your horses Hosey," Randy said. "We'll get to you. Wapiti, after you have a couple tokes off this, here," he threw the bag of peyote on the table. "Give them the pipe and this; I'll go take care of the horses and mules."

"Randy," Larry said, "Uncle Roy said he'd leave the back door open, said he'd clear out the stables so we could hide those mules inside tonight, that way no one sees them, and gets any ideas. But just put the horses in the corral...no one will give them a second glance."

"Good idea," Randy said. "Luis, you want to give me a quick hand getting all of them over there?"

"Hell no," Luis answered, shuffling the cards. "Just tie their reins to their tails and lead them that way." Starting to smile, "I'm thirsty and still hungry."

"AND LAZY," Randy said, walking towards the back door. "You're all lazy, just a bunch of lazy bums." He said, closing the door behind himself.

He lit one of the lamps, still muttering under his breath, as he went to work tying all the animals together. How do you even lead a horse train of, let's see, starting to count. Eight mules and nine horses. He couldn't even stay on the back streets, leading that many animals. He would have to go out and around town, there's no chance in hell of going through town. Hell it's only nine thirty, maybe ten o' clock at the latest, and there were still all kinds of people in the saloons. Sure tomorrow was a workday and some of them would be hate'en it. But if he went through town he would surely be seen.

480

Chapter Twenty Five

It really didn't take him that long to tie all the horses and mules together, then he climbed aboard his big stallion and headed down the alleyway and out into the timber. Sure the jail was in the middle of town, but at least it sat up against the mountain. It was easy to disappear into the brush. With the moon light, it made it easy to see just where he was going. One thing was for sure, at least to him, it sounded like a herd of elk going through the timber, and some of those houses weren't that far away.

It was all right that Luis had stayed behind; he can get Larry going sometimes. Larry did a good job of getting and keeping the party going. Goof and Toad would get Wapiti to smoke just a little bit too much peyote and Larry was still working on getting the Marshal drunk. Was that even possible? Hell, Larry had been at it all day. Shit, they had already gone through three bottles of whiskey or more. Larry had made sure the Marshal had drunk most of that. Still, he seemed to be just fine when they got in tonight.

Now they were drinking beer and whiskey together, and playing poker. Larry will do his job, Randy was sure of that. He would have to excuse himself sometime around eleven thirty. Where would he say he was going at that hour? TO BED, he thought to himself, he was already tired; it had been a long day. He wasn't sure just how long it took him to get to the Livery stable with all his daydreaming, but he could see there was still a light on inside. Slowly he dismounted and walked up to the door. Cracking it open, he peered inside. He could see Roy was still shoeing a horse, opening the door; Randy slowly started leading all the animals in.

"I was wondering when you would finally get here," Roy said, standing up. "So tell me Randy, what did you boys have to do with this robbery?"

"NOTHIN," Randy said chuckling. "Well...We didn't do the robbery anyway. I just knew how and when they loaded the gold. So, I simply told them what I knew," still chuckling. "Besides, no one got hurt. Just some rich greedy men lost a little gold."

"You boys can't be tied to this can you," Roy asked again.

"Hell no," Randy answered. "Not even. The most anyone can say about us, is we made a lot of money on that big Roan right there," he say's pointing to the horse.

Marshal Shawn Felton and the Wild Bunch

"What's this about them stealing your horses to carry the gold off with?" Roy asked. "And speaking of which, where are your horses?"

"Well if everything went according to my plan, they should be in Unity with Terry, and they should have traded for a couple of his Percherons." The entire time they're talking Randy's taking care of all the horses. Removing their saddles and packs from the mules. "These four…leave saddled. They will have to be ready to leave in a hurry."

"Now just what the HELL are you up to Randy?" Roy asked.

"Nothing much Uncle Roy," Randy said still smiling. "Three of those men are good friends of ours. Fact, they wouldn't be in this fix, if we hadn't talked them into the robbery. So…I have a plan to get them all out."

"What are you going to do when that ole Marshal Felton finds out you boys were behind the breakout?" Roy said with a serious look on his face.

"HE WON'T be able to," Randy said. "Besides, by the time it goes down, Larry's going to have him so drunk…He won't even be able to stand. Let alone be able to ride a horse."

"You boys get caught, DON'T you even come to me for help," Roy said.

"Don't worry about it Uncle Roy, you keep forgetin," Randy said with a big smile on his face. "I plan shit out…And I've been working on this plan all day…But if you could finish up for me here I do need to get back to the jail. Need to make sure no one, and I mean no one gets any of that gold. That reward money is the ranch we've always wanted. Then with Terry's logging trailers and teams, my skidding team, we'll start our own logging company."

"Yeah, yeah," Roy said with a semi-smile. "You boys just make sure they can't tie you in on any of this."

"No problem, Uncle Roy," Randy said, walking towards the door. "Like I said, I've been working on this back door all day," then he turned and walked out.

"I can't believe one of you boys wouldn't go help him with all those animals," Shawn said.

482

Chapter Twenty Five

"Piss on him," Larry said. "Hell I bet he will probably call it a night well before midnight if not sooner." Holding up his chips, "Now, Marshal, Wapiti, the white chips are low, the red chips are medium, and the blue chips are the highest. He explained. I need another beer, how about you Marshal?"

"Don't mind if I do," Shawn said. "Now that those desperados are behind bars. We can let loose just a little till morning. Then we'll have to really start worrying about all that gold. Cause by then just about everyone will KNOW we have it and them."

Larry went around filling everyone's beers, looking back at the Marshal. "So have you ever been in a situation when you thought your goose was cooked for good.

Once, Shawn answered. I was a Texas Ranger then, and I arrested a fancy Monsignor from Spain I think. Anyway, I arrested him on one of those fancy steam ship's that run up the Mississippi River's…I arrested him, and on our way back to Texas, we came a crossed some men selling guns to the Indian's. To make a long story short. They caught us and hung us up in a tree. But the Monsignor met a young lady on that boat. Well sir, it just so happened those two had a little fling on that trip…She new I was a Lawman, but she talked her husband into letting us go, and go we did…There was at least one hundred of them, not to count the hundreds of Indians. I let the U.S. Calvary take care of them then turning towards Wapiti, so just what were you and Cathey talking about Wapiti?"

"Her Dad's Mom is from Prineville, she said that her Dad would let her move over there for a while. That's if she rode back with us Marshal."

"I don't think that would be a good idea for her to ride with us Wapiti," Shawn answered, picking up his cards. "You never know where or when we're going to run into some outlaws, and she just might end up in the middle of a gun battle. I don't want to have to be worried about her, when our thoughts should be on those shooting at us."

"Hey Hombre, we could go with you," Luis said. "Act kinda like an escort."

483

"Randy won't go for that," Larry said. Throwing in two red chips. "Now that we had our talk with the Marshal here, he'll be wanting to get back to work, and Gary as well…That's all those two ever think about."

Just then the Doss's started hollerin that they were out of beer and whiskey.

"I'll get it Marshal," Wapiti said, trying to stand up. A little peyote alone was fine, the same as a couple of beers, he was thinking to himself, reaching for the wall. But you put the two together…And well, that's a different story.

Slowly he walked over to the cell. Maybe I had better only take two at a time, he said, reaching out. Everyone started laughing at him. He didn't mind, after all this was his first time he'd ever gotten drunk. He figured it would be best if he didn't try to keep up with the others. They'd been do-en this drinking thing a whole lot longer than he had. He was trying to walk back with the glasses full of beer, trying not to spill any. Still thinking to himself, maybe it would be best if he slowed down a little.

It seemed to take him forever to walk back and forth, getting everyone more beer. He sure was glad when he finally got back to his chair… but there was Larry laughing and handing him the bottle of whiskey. "No thanks," he answered. But Larry just kept goading him on. "Oh hell," he said. "It's only one night, live a little." So reluctantly he took the bottle and another drink. Which made the room start turning, and turning, and turning, till he fell off his chair and passed out on the floor. Just then Randy walked back in the door. Looking down and seeing Wapiti on the floor, he couldn't help but smile. Thinking to himself, one down, and one to go. "So is there room for one more in this game?"

"Sure," Shawn said. "Here Randy have some of my chips." Pushing a small pile to him…Hell the only time I can win at this game is tonight, and that's because we aren't playing for real money." Taking another big pull off the whiskey bottle and handed it to Randy.

Sitting down at the table and seeing the Marshal handing him the bottle, Randy held his hand up. "No thanks, Marshal, I don't mind a beer now and then, but that stuff will kill ya."

Chapter Twenty Five

"Now I don't know that it will kill ya. But I know it will kill what ails ya," Shawn said with a big smile on his face. Pointing over at Larry, "Now there's a man that can drink almost as much as me...Fact give him a couple more years, and I bet he just might be able to out drink me."

"Only because you'll be dead by then," Larry said picking up his cards. "So you stick'en around tonight Randy?"

"No...Not unless the Marshal tells me I have to, then ya...I was hoping on going back to Prairie City and the Gutridge Brothel," Randy answered.

"Heck no young man," Shawn said. "If I was even just half my age I'd leave young Wapiti and Larry here to watch over these bad ass outlaws and I'd join ya. So what time does that place close anyway?"

"I don't know if they ever do," Larry said. "I've gone in there sometimes two, three o' clock in the morning, and they were still open. I got to tell ya Marshal, you really should go over there for a visit...I know you would enjoy yourself."

"Like I told you yesterday, or earlier today," Shawn said, throwing in one blue chip. "Just one of those young ladies would do me in."

Just then everyone in the room, including those all in the jail cells started laughing and saying just how terrible it would be to go out that way.

"Marshal, where have you found the phoniest lawman?" Randy asked.

"Well young man," Shawn said taking another pull off the bottle and handing it to Larry. "I'd have to say Texas...I tell ya, everyone of those boys have drunk water out of their horses hoof prints, and claimed to be dammed glad to get it. Not one or two of them mind ya...every single one of them." Waving his finger around at everyone. Hell, even when I was a Texas Ranger I never had to drink no water out of my horses hoof print.

"You know Marshal," Dennis said, enjoying all the festivities along with everyone else, except he didn't drink alcohol. But was enjoying the food and poker game, and listening in on how they were the ones who getting the reward. "So Marshal, I heard you ran with Quantrill's Raiders during the war...Is that true?"

485

"Yes sir," Shawn answered proudly.

"Quantrill's Raiders?" Randy hollered. "Weren't those guys just a bunch of outlaws, robbing and killing whoever got in their way?"

"Well young man, those Yankees thought they could go just anywhere they wanted and take our land and everything we owned," Shawn said.

"Where did Wapiti put my pipe?" Randy asked, looking around the room.

"It's over on the Sheriff's desk," Shawn said. "But if you're going to smoke that shit, would you mind taking it outside? It has an awful smell to it."

"No problem Marshal," Randy said with a big smile on his face. "Fact, if you don't mind Marshal. I'll take a pull off my pipe…Then, I'll take me a ride over to Prairie City…And have a little midnight fun," looking back and forth at everyone. "I mean hell, Larry has those knives of his, and should anyone break down the front door. Which I don't think is likely, but if it should, you have more than enough gun's to fight off a small army So I think my reward is in good hands."

Reaching down Randy picked up the bottle of whiskey, "Marshal I will have one shot with ya…I've had a lot of fun listening to all your stories today. Fact you can almost keep up with our brother Terry and Larry…they always have a story to tell." Picking up the bottle and making it look like he was taking a big pull off it, when he really wasn't, he handed the bottle back to the Marshal. "So let's see just how big a pull you can take Marshal."

"Well now Randy, when you get to be my age, you'll find there's no reason to hurry and drink everything you have right off, you need to make it last."

"Oh hell Marshal," Larry hollered, reaching for his saddlebags. "When I came into town and ordered dinner I picked up a couple extra bottles. So drink all you want…Cause I have more."

Extending his hand to the Marshal, Randy looked at him, "It's been fun riding with you old man." Starting to chuckle, "I'll see ya tomorrow. One of you want to grab this back door behind me?"

Chapter Twenty Five

"Sure thing, Hombre," Luis said. Standing up, and staggering a little on his feet, then followed Randy out back.

Quickly Randy climbed aboard, and headed back down behind the buildings till he came to the main road. Kicking the stallion he headed for the river. He'd start at the bridge and work his way back down the river. He had told Gary where to meet him just outside of town, on the Dayville side. That way after they destroyed this stick jailhouse, they could get out of town faster. He thought to himself smiling. This was going to be the easiest jailhouse he ever broke into or out of.

He couldn't believe just how piss poor that jail had been put up. But then he also knew that if the Marshal had wanted to, he wouldn't have had any trouble getting them to open the county jail up. So Randy was glad when the Marshal had agreed on the little jail house tonight, instead of the additional two-mile ride up the road to the county jail. What made it so easy to talk him into the little jail was the fact he wanted off that horses as bad as everyone else did…besides, what could go wrong? All of a sudden he heard a whistle. Calling out to Gary in a low voice, he waited for the three men to come to him.

"We tied the horses up just about a quarter mile down river," Gary said pointing…. "You figure out how to get them out of there yet?"

"I had it figured out first thirty seconds inside," Randy answered with a big smile. "We're going to go over to the Livery, and borrow us a couple of nice draft horses. Get a couple logging chains and pull that back wall out. Those steel bars may go from the floor to the ceiling in length, but there's nothing holding the rest of the wall up…Except a few two-by-four's and nails."

They were far enough out of town, that the four of them just rode straight up the riverbank to the main road leading into town. The four didn't talk much as they rode; they were busy looking up and down every street and alley that they rode by. Making sure that no one had heard of all that gold being in town, and planning somehow to take it. There were very few people walking the streets, it was just after midnight Randy figured as they rode up to the Livery stable. Still looking around, they dismounted.

487

"I told Uncle Roy to leave the horses saddled and ready to go in short order. Butch, you cinch those saddles up. Sundance you help me put these collars on these four draft horses right here. Gary, you look in the back room for some chains, or log wrappers either one."

"You really think we need four of these big fellas," Sundance asked. Leading two of them out of their stalls.

"Probably not," Randy said. "But I'd rather have them and not need them, than need them and not have them…We only have one chance at this."

"So just how's Larry doing at getting Marshal Felton drunk?" Gary asked looking at everyone.

"Like I told you earlier Gary," Randy answered. "For once his ability to drink like a fish out of water was going to help us out. When I left, Wapiti was passed out on the floor, and the Marshal along with Larry, hell I don't think either one of them could even stand up, yet alone walk anywhere."

"What do we do with these horses here when we're finished with them?" Butch asked, leading the horses out of their stalls and headed towards the door.

"Let them go," Randy said. "Hell, they're all gunna be tied together with the chains and part of the wall still be attached to them. They won't be go'en anywhere fast. Hell I bet they don't go very far before they're all tangled up around tree's or brush's. So whoever they belong to…Can't say we stole them."

"So is there any way to get some of that gold back while we're at this?" Sundance asked.

"Damn you're greedy," Gary said jokingly.

"Hell no," Randy said. "Don't even try to go there…Just be happy with what you have, and get the hell out of here."

They all mounted up and headed back out around town through the timber and keeping out of sight. Just in case someone was still up and moving around the streets. Riding up behind the jail, Randy pulled his handkerchief up over his face, Gary did the same thing. Quietly and quickly they tied the chains around the cell bars. Looking inside, they could see everyone. They could hear Larry and the Marshal talking as

Chapter Twenty Five

they rode down the hill. Hell if anyone was with in forty yards of this place they could hear those two. Who knew what they were talking about…And that didn't matter. Just listening to them, you couldn't hardly understand either of them; they were each slurring their words from drinking too much alcohol.

Everyone in the cells moved away from the window, as Gary quickly ran the chain around all four bars. "You boys ready to get the hell out of here!" he told them with a big smile on his face. They could see it in his eyes, but not on his face, cause it was covered up so no one could tell who he was. Just to play it safe. Then he turned and walked back towards the others, where Randy was in the process of hooking his chains to the back window and bar's, then hooked the chain's to the four big horses. Grabbing Gary's chain's he started laughing his head off.

"What's so damn funny Randy?" Sundance asked.

"Well ya see," pointing down at the window…"That window isn't two feet from the corner, starting to laugh harder. That whole damn corner of the building is coming out…Can you just imagine the look on the Marshal's face, when that happens…? That's going to be price-less. Alright, let's get serious here," Randy said. "Butch, Sundance, you two get those horses down there close where those boys can get on… Then you follow me till I say different…CLEAR?"

"Yes sir, Randy," they both said at the same time. "So where are you and Gary going after this?" Butch asked, extended his hand.

"Well, we both are supposed to be at the Gutridge Brothel for the night…" Taking his mask off, since they were at least fifty feet from the building and no one could see him. "So I guess we have to keep up our alibi…It's going to be a real tough alibi to keep, and we'll be enjoying every minute of it. I would like ya to know that I haven't had this much fun and made this damn much money…Speaking of which, how much did you have to pay Terry? I'll give you back what money I have on me, it's not all I owe you, but it's a fair trade."

Sundance extended his hand between the two. "Randy, do you think a couple thousand dollars is going to bother us right now? We have three draft horses loaded with gold just waiting for us and beside's…I can't remember ever robbing a bank and getting even half as much

489

cash as we made on that Roan alone, and never had near as much fun stealing it. Actually, you deserve a bigger cut than what you're making on this job than just a few thousand dollars for the use of your horses. Hell...You planned the whole damn robbery, EVEN the final escape."

"In that other jail cell is fifty six bags of gold, divided buy four, that's sixteen bags of gold," Randy said pointing back at the jail. "Twenty five percent of that gold is ours...I think I got paid real good for my planning of this job

"Damned if you didn't," Butch said chuckling. "Damned if you didn't. Even better, not only did you plan the job, pull it off... You even get the reward. Hell you stole a whole lot of gold and the law will be chasing us and patting you on the back."

Everyone started climbing aboard their horses, looking at each other with a grin from ear to ear on every one of them. "Remember," Randy said, looking at everyone, "YOU follow me...On three..." he hollered in a low loud voice. "ONE, TWO, THREE..." Then he kicked his stallion in the side and leading the other four with all their power, he took off. And Half the wall came flying out in one big piece. Allowing the Doss's and Curry the biggest escape hole they had ever seen. The four came running out and grabbed the nearest horse to them, climbing up in the saddle they followed the leader just as fast as they could go.

The moon was over three-quarter full, and put out more light than they needed. Fact, it almost seemed like daylight outside. They could easily see the logs and trees in front of them. Randy led them back around town, across the main road and back to the river. Which didn't take much time at all, and no one had even fired a shot. Being in the middle of the business section of town, and no houses close by, nobody had heard anything either. Pulling up on the reins of the stallion just inside the timber, next to the river. Turning and looking back at everyone as they came to a stop.

"Butch, Sundance, it's been a lot of fun..." Then the stallion, who was excited too, came up into a full rare. He was wanting to go. "Goof, Toad, and Hosey sorry you can't come to the Brothel in Prairie. But you can make Unity by morning." Which means you'll have to wait

Chapter Twenty Five

until tomorrow night to celebrate. But that should be all right, you can more than likely stay at Terry's...Luckily, he lives right across the street from the bar.

"Wait," Sundance said. "You Doss boys come with us; we'll give you a couple bags of gold.

"Don't worry about it," Toad said. "I had Goof bury ten bags."

"I hid two more bags where they caught up to us," Hosey said. "We're going to be able to pepper a mine for a very long time."

They all shook hands one last time, and wished each other good luck. Then they all headed out in two different directions. The Doss's would ride with Randy and Gary to Prairie City since it was on the way to Unity, and the other three outlaws, were off to happier and richer times that lay ahead of them.

"Piss on him and Gary both," Larry said as Randy walked out the door. "Maybe I won't make it down there tonight, but I damn sure will make it tomorrow, eh Luis?"

"You know it, Amigo," Luis answered. "Hell Marshal, you're not that old, you should come along...We'll even pay. Since we came into all this money, Sheriff, you come too." Luis offered waving the whiskey bottle back and forth.

Larry reached up and grabbed the bottle, "Don't you be spilling any of that now...Hell, that would be alcohol abuse."

"Now what was I saying, before I was interrupted. Luis said, oh, ya...Sheriff you come along with us, we'll pay for you a couple hours as well."

"And just what the hell am I supposed to tell my wife I'm going over there for?" Dennis asked.

"I don't know," Luis said, reaching for his beer. "I'm sure we can think of something before then."

Larry started to stand up; he gave Luis a funny look. "I need another beer...Anyone else?"

"Sure," Shawn answered. "While you're at it, why don't you see how our mighty outlaws are doin? They're not going to get anything for quite some time." Even Shawn noticed that he was starting to slur his words. Fact he couldn't remember when he had drank this much, and gotten this drunk. Then looking down on the floor, he glanced at Wapiti, he couldn't help but chuckle. "Hey Larry," he hollered. "Check out the Indian, can't hold his liquor."

Larry started chuckling with the Marshal, walking over to the cell, and taking everyone's empty glasses.

Toad looked over at Larry, speaking in a low voice. "We don't need anymore...We need to be ready when Randy and the others get here. We don't want to get too wasted and not be able to ride."

"Then wait till the Marshal ain't look'en, and slowly dump it out the window. You have to act like this is your last night. We don't want that old fart catching on that anything is up...Understand?"

"Is there anymore whiskey out there?" Hosey hollered out..."Hell, you let Randy out of here before we could smoke one last bowl of peyote."

"I don't have any peyote boys," Shawn said. "But here's another bottle." Tossing it towards them.

"Thanks," Hosey and Goof said at the same time.

"Does anyone have any chewing tobacco?" Toad asked.

Reaching into his pocket, Shawn pulled out a package of plug chewing tobacco; he threw it towards the cells, "here you go young man. Just keep it; I'll get me some more later."

"Thanks Marshal," Toad said. "Do you think if we gave you some money, we could stop at the store on the way to the county lockup tomorrow? So we could at least get some cigarettes and chewing tobacco before we go to jail."

"Sure thing son," Shawn said, smiling. "That's the least I can do for you. After all, none of you boys gave me any trouble at all bringing you in."

As Larry handed everyone back a full beer, Goof looked over at him. "How long you figure till Randy gets back with the others?"

"How the hell am I supposed to know," Larry answered whispering. "They'll get here when they get here." Turning, he walked back to the table, sitting down, he picked up his new hand of cards, " So what do I have in my hand?" he asked everyone.

492

Chapter Twenty Five

"How would we know that?" Dennis asked. "We didn't look at them."

"Ya right," Larry said. "Like I believe that. So you head'en back to Prineville tomorrow Marshal?"

"Nooo...Set out on this trip heading for Sumpter?" Shawn said, discarding two cards. "Besides, someone has to take all this gold back over to Sumpter. I suppose that job will fall on my shoulders being the only U.S. Deputy Marshal in the territory...Might hire you and your brothers to help get it and us back there safe. Cause just as soon as we leave town, every outlaw or want to be outlaw will be coming for us, and trying to take it away from us. I know that with that big reward they're offering is a hell of a lot of money... So let's say I pay each of you a hundred dollars a day. But you have to remember, that bank and those gold companies ain't paying any reward till this gold is back in their hands. So it would be in all your best interests to help me and young Wapiti out." He points to Wapiti, who is still sleeping on the floor.

"I guess we don't have much choice," Larry said. "But before we leave here, I want Randy and Gary with us. I don't want to wait and hope they catch up to us...I'll go over to Prairie in the morning and get them. Besides, it would be best if we hold off till night to get going, in fact the later the better. If it's dark when we leave then no one will see us. Just like when we came in tonight, no one seen us. Or if they did see us, they didn't think twice about it. But in the morning when the word gets out about us and the gold...You ain't going to move it one inch without everyone in the county watching."

"You're right about that," Shawn said. Taking the bottle of whiskey from Larry, and taking another drink.

Just then it sounded like the whole building was coming apart. The back corner and half the side wall was being pulled out, part of the roof came crashing down. Shawn tried to jump up, but he had had too much to drink and fell over his own two feet to the floor. "HOLY SHIT," he yelled out. Rolling over just in time to watch the prisoner's run out the hole where half the wall used to be. "I think the prisoners have just escaped on us, he said looking around the room at everyone...

493

Then setting up, he reached across the floor and picked up the bottle of whiskey. I lost some outlaws once when I was younger and they got me drunk out on the trail ..., then taking a big pull off the bottle. But this is the first time I ever had them in jail, got drunk, and lost my prisoners."

Everyone started hollering and wondering just what was going on and laughing at the Marshal lying on the floor at the same time.

Looking over at Dennis, "I told you a good saddle horse could pull this place apart," Shawn said, starting to smile. "But by the sounds of thing's who ever is out their, they borrowed a few draft horses from the Livery stable." Looking over at Larry, "I think I've just been bushwhacked."

"Bushwhacked?" Larry hollered. "By who?"

"By you Larkin boys! I don't know just how you did it, but something inside of me tells me you boys were in on this...Like it was yet another one of Randy's so called back doors."

"BULLSHIT," Larry hollered. "You know we've been right here the entire time."

Shawn looked over at the Sheriff, "Don't release them Doss boy's names... As far as I'm concerned, we got the gold back, and no one was hurt during the robbery, except for a crooked Sheriff losing his job... As far as I'm concerned, no harm, no foul... Those boys just tried to get lucky and didn't," Shawn said, starting to chuckle. "Fact I myself in my younger days did a few things that was against the law...But hell, I needed a road stake. So if anyone asks, we had Butch Cassidy's Wild Bunch as our prisoners. The only one we knew for sure of who he was Harvey Logan, A.K.A Kid Curry. The other's real names...God only knows for sure who they were. They were all short, fat, ugly, and stinky."

"Yes sir, Marshal," Dennis answered. "But I'm gunna get me some sleep before I go chasing any outlaws."

"I hear ya Sheriff," Shawn answered. "Besides, they won't get too far. Wapiti has already been passed out for a couple hours, so he will be good and rested. He can track them in the morning, leave us a sign as to which way they went and we can catch up to him later."

Chapter Twenty Five

Standing up and stumbling around, he picked up his rifle. Then slowly Shawn worked his way into the jail cell with all the gold, closing the door behind him.... "We'll discuss this in the morning." He said, laying down on the bunk, pulling a blanket up over himself, and fell fast asleep.

THE END

In Loving Memory to

Robert Dude Larkin Sr. August 12, 1939 – Feb. 8, 1973
Front picture from Paint Your Wagon movie set.

A Lover, A Fighter,
And A Wild Bull Rider
Also
Willy Blue
Rodeo Clown and Bull Fighter

Floyd Larkin – August 19, 1934 – August 24, 2004
Story about Floyd is true. It happened
May 25, 1956 at the Clark County
Courthouse in Prineville Oregon.

Shawn Felton-April 6, 1962 – February 1979
A Son, A Brother, A Friend
Who died too young

ABOUT THE AUTHOR

Born in Condon Oregon, I was raised in and around Dayville area till the age of five, then we moved to Baker City, Oregon were I Graduated high school in 1981, so some of you might think you know me.

Then in July 1982 I joined Uncle Sam's Canoe Club (U.S. Navy) and served both pre-com and then aboard the U.S.S. Shenandoah Ad-44, from February 1983- July 1987, so some of you might think you know me.

After leaving the Navy I briefly lived in Marshal Town Iowa. But couldn't handle the flat land, so in October of 1987 I moved to Pinecliff Colorado, were I drove truck, and was on High Country Volunteer Fire Dept. Then in January 1992, I was in the sleeper when heavy winds and black ice Jack-knifed the tractor on I-80, severing my spinal cord twice. Because of where my break was, the doctor's recommended I move to a area of low humidity. So I moved to Brookside, Utah. (just North of St. George, Utah). So some of you might think you know me.

In the fall of 2001 I wanted to sell my house, but the man who wanted to buy it, couldn't afford it, but he had a 1912 Block house in Circleville, Utah. That if I took the house as part of the sale then he could afford it. The old house had a lot of character, so I took the offer. So some of you might think you know me.

But in reality, very few of you do know me. Where am I now... God only knows!

But should we run into each other out there on the highway, remember look low, I'm a paraplegic so I will be in a wheel chair. Second clue as it might be me...Just ask anyone who knows me. My mouth will be running, telling jokes and story's, and everyone laughing, it just might be me.

Made in the USA
Charleston, SC
29 July 2015